THE WALKING DEAD

BOOK NINE

a continuing story of survival horror.

created by Robert Kirkman

image comics presents

The Walking Dead
book nine

ROBERT KIRKMAN
creator, writer

CHARLIE ADLARD
penciler, inker, cover

CLIFF RATHBURN
gray tones

RUS WOOTON
letterer

SEAN MACKIEWICZ
editor

Original series covers by
CHARLIE ADLARD & CLIFF RATHBURN

THE WALKING DEAD, BOOK NINE. First Printing. Published by Image Comics, Inc., Office of publication: 2001 Center Street, 6th Floor, Berkeley, California 94704. Copyright © 2013 Robert Kirkman, LLC. Originally published in single magazine form as THE WALKING DEAD #97-108. All rights reserved. THE WALKING DEAD™ (including all prominent characters featured herein), its logo and all character likenesses are trademarks of Robert Kirkman, unless otherwise noted. Image Comics® and its logos are registered trademarks of Image Comics, Inc. Skybound Entertainment and its logos are © and ™ of Skybound Entertainment, LLC. No part of this publication may be reproduced or transmitted, in any form or by any means (except for short excerpts for review purposes) without the express written permission of Image Comics, Inc. All names, characters, events and locales in this publication are entirely fictional. Any resemblance to actual persons (living or dead), events or places, without satiric intent, is coincidental. PRINTED IN CANADA. ISBN: 978-1-60706-798-6

For international rights inquiries, please contact foreign@skybound.com.

Chapter Seventeen:
Something to Fear

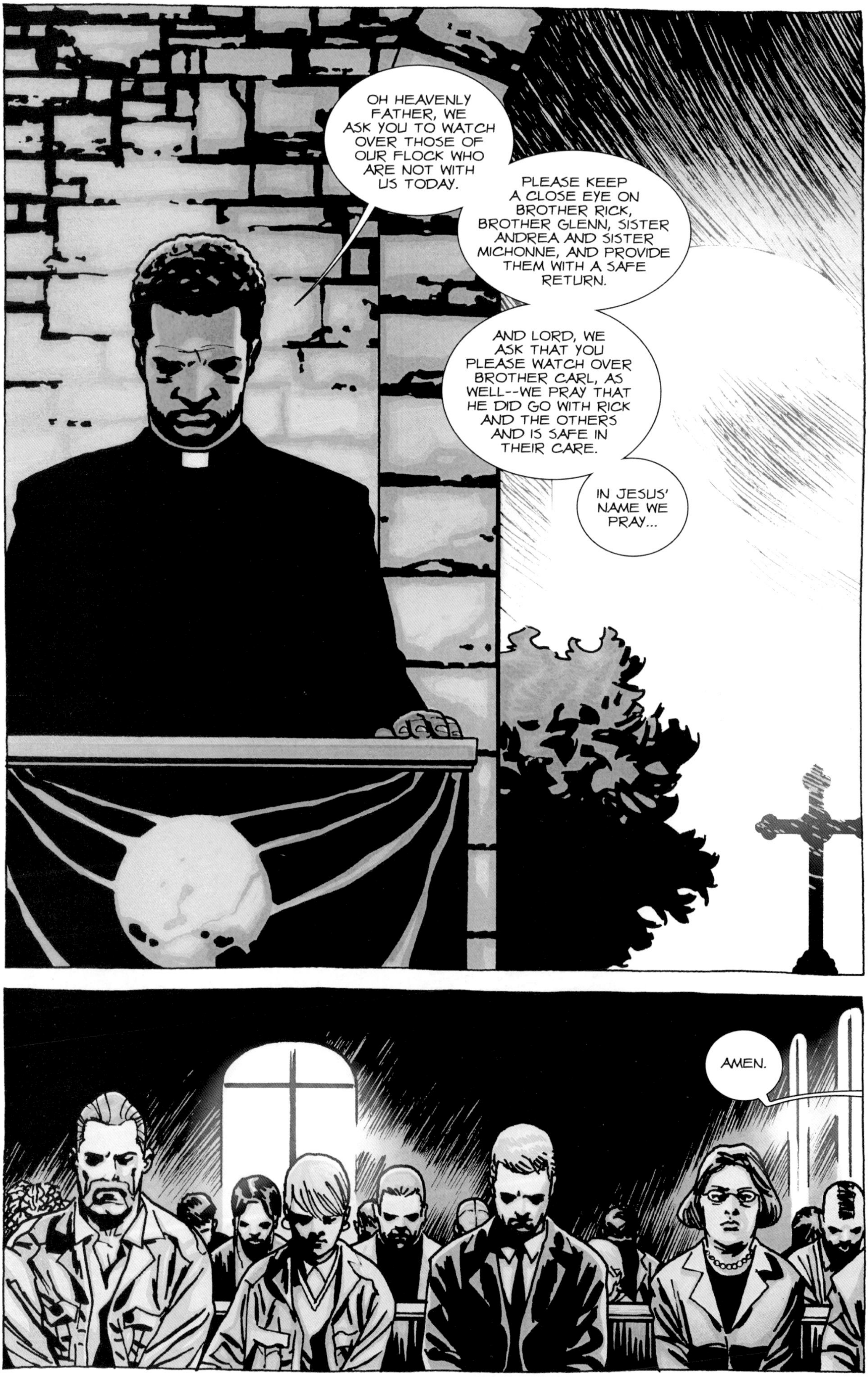
OH HEAVENLY FATHER, WE ASK YOU TO WATCH OVER THOSE OF OUR FLOCK WHO ARE NOT WITH US TODAY.
PLEASE KEEP A CLOSE EYE ON BROTHER RICK, BROTHER GLENN, SISTER ANDREA AND SISTER MICHONNE, AND PROVIDE THEM WITH A SAFE RETURN.
AND LORD, WE ASK THAT YOU PLEASE WATCH OVER BROTHER CARL, AS WELL--WE PRAY THAT HE DID GO WITH RICK AND THE OTHERS AND IS SAFE IN THEIR CARE.
IN JESUS' NAME WE PRAY...
AMEN.

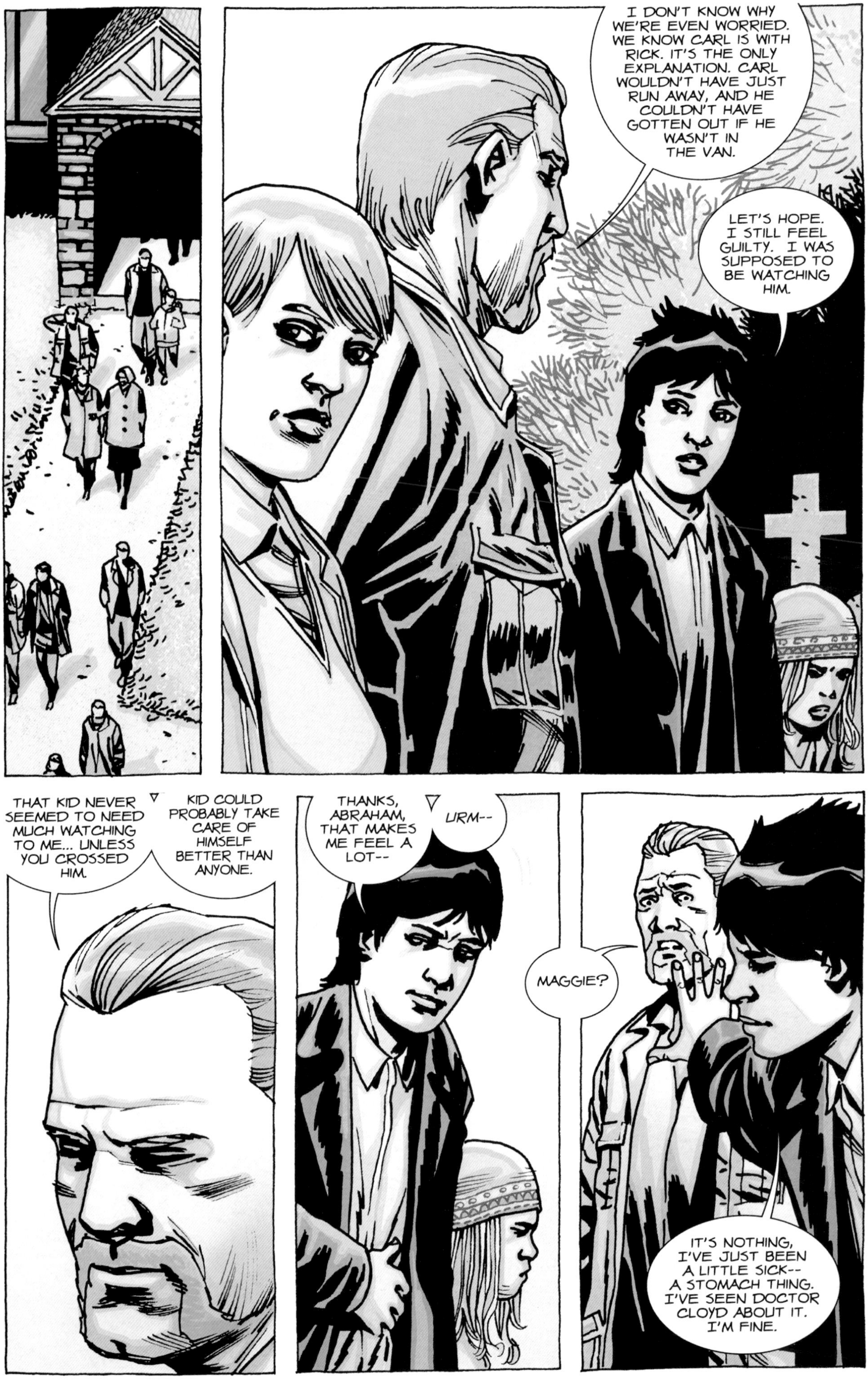
I DON'T KNOW WHY WE'RE EVEN WORRIED. WE KNOW CARL IS WITH RICK. IT'S THE ONLY EXPLANATION. CARL WOULDN'T HAVE JUST RUN AWAY, AND HE COULDN'T HAVE GOTTEN OUT IF HE WASN'T IN THE VAN.
LET'S HOPE. I STILL FEEL GUILTY. I WAS SUPPOSED TO BE WATCHING HIM.
THAT KID NEVER SEEMED TO NEED MUCH WATCHING TO ME... UNLESS YOU CROSSED HIM.
KID COULD PROBABLY TAKE CARE OF HIMSELF BETTER THAN ANYONE.
THANKS, ABRAHAM, THAT MAKES ME FEEL A LOT--
URM--
MAGGIE?
IT'S NOTHING, I'VE JUST BEEN A LITTLE SICK-- A STOMACH THING. I'VE SEEN DOCTOR CLOYD ABOUT IT. I'M FINE.

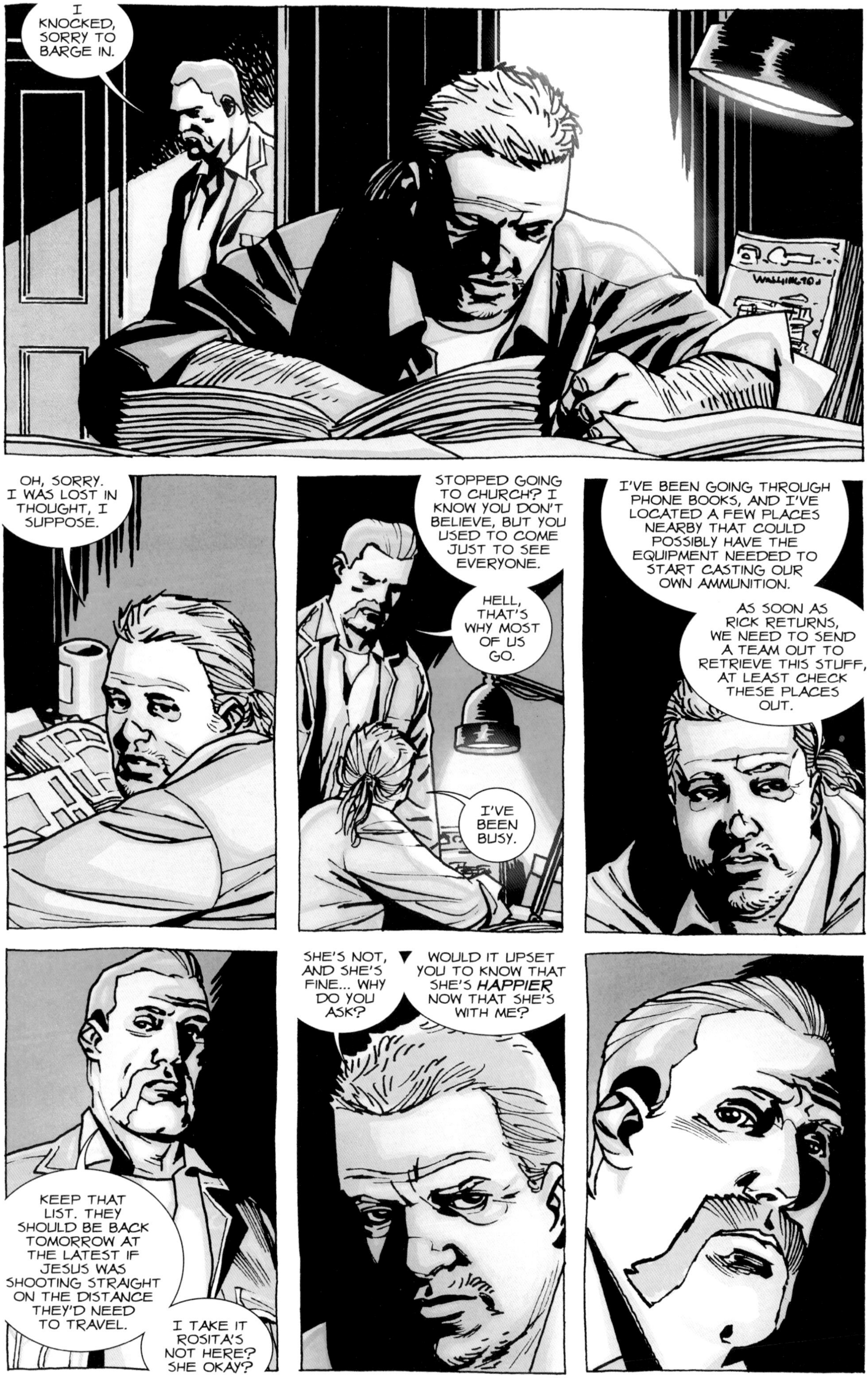
I KNOCKED, SORRY TO BARGE IN.
OH, SORRY. I WAS LOST IN THOUGHT, I SUPPOSE.
STOPPED GOING TO CHURCH? I KNOW YOU DON'T BELIEVE, BUT YOU USED TO COME JUST TO SEE EVERYONE.
HELL, THAT'S WHY MOST OF US GO.
I'VE BEEN BUSY.
I'VE BEEN GOING THROUGH PHONE BOOKS, AND I'VE LOCATED A FEW PLACES NEARBY THAT COULD POSSIBLY HAVE THE EQUIPMENT NEEDED TO START CASTING OUR OWN AMMUNITION.
AS SOON AS RICK RETURNS, WE NEED TO SEND A TEAM OUT TO RETRIEVE THIS STUFF, AT LEAST CHECK THESE PLACES OUT.
KEEP THAT LIST. THEY SHOULD BE BACK TOMORROW AT THE LATEST IF JESUS WAS SHOOTING STRAIGHT ON THE DISTANCE THEY'D NEED TO TRAVEL.
I TAKE IT ROSITA'S NOT HERE? SHE OKAY?
SHE'S NOT, AND SHE'S FINE... WHY DO YOU ASK?
WOULD IT UPSET YOU TO KNOW THAT SHE'S *HAPPIER* NOW THAT SHE'S WITH ME?

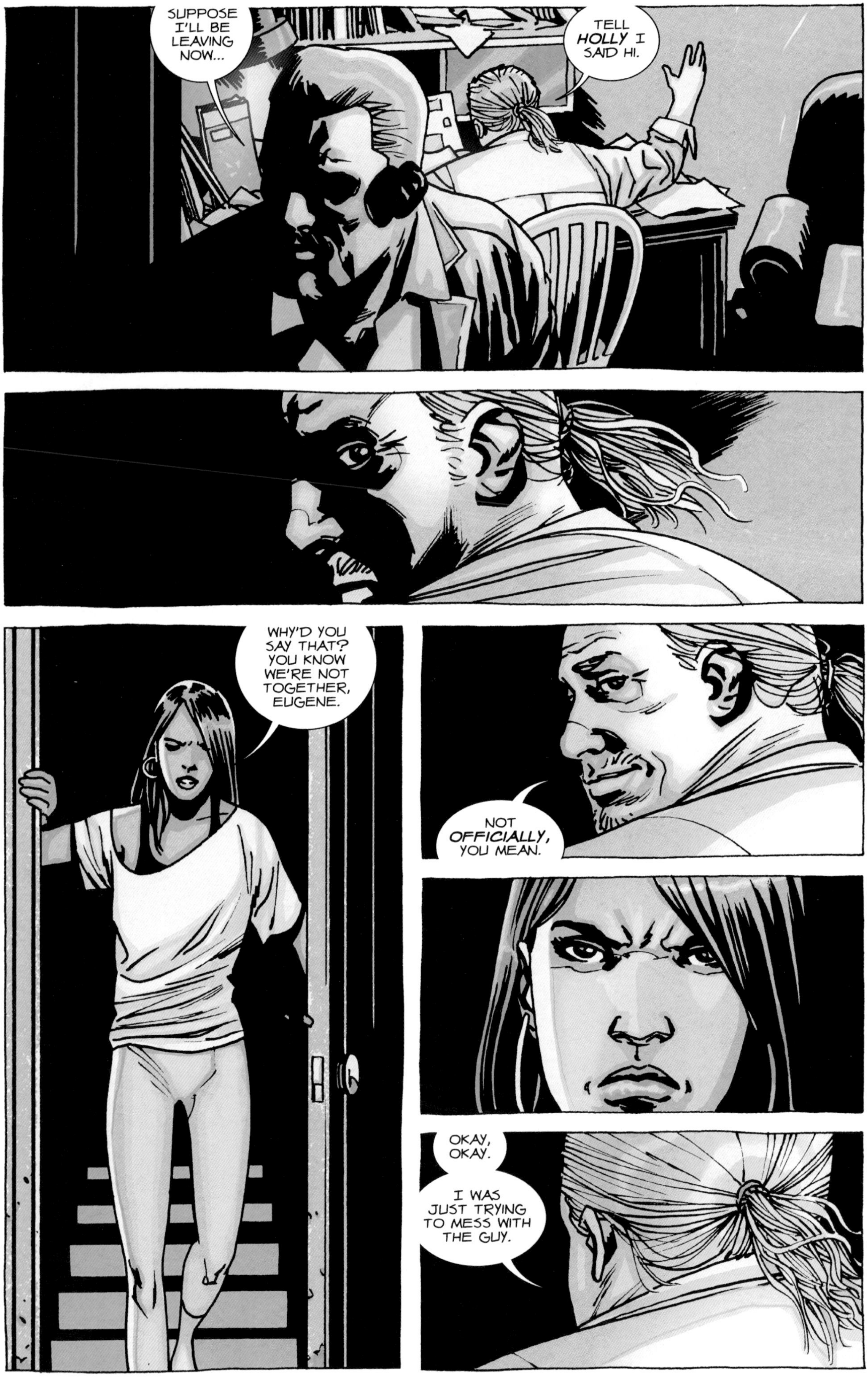
SUPPOSE I'LL BE LEAVING NOW...
TELL HOLLY I SAID HI.
WHY'D YOU SAY THAT? YOU KNOW WE'RE NOT TOGETHER, EUGENE.
NOT OFFICIALLY, YOU MEAN.
OKAY, OKAY.
I WAS JUST TRYING TO MESS WITH THE GUY.

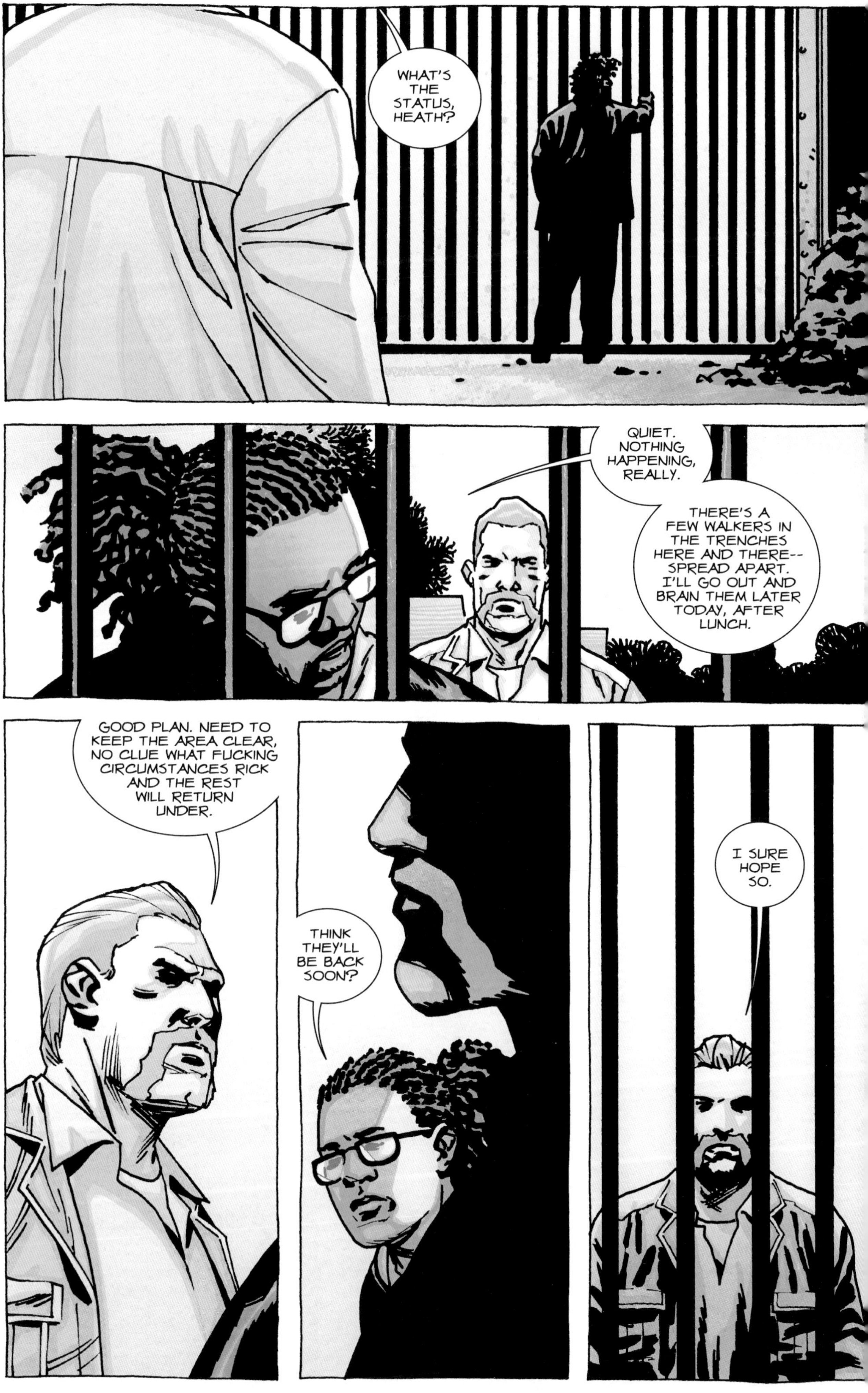
WHAT'S THE STATUS, HEATH?
QUIET. NOTHING HAPPENING, REALLY.
THERE'S A FEW WALKERS IN THE TRENCHES HERE AND THERE-- SPREAD APART. I'LL GO OUT AND BRAIN THEM LATER TODAY, AFTER LUNCH.
GOOD PLAN. NEED TO KEEP THE AREA CLEAR, NO CLUE WHAT FUCKING CIRCUMSTANCES RICK AND THE REST WILL RETURN UNDER.
THINK THEY'LL BE BACK SOON?
I SURE HOPE SO.

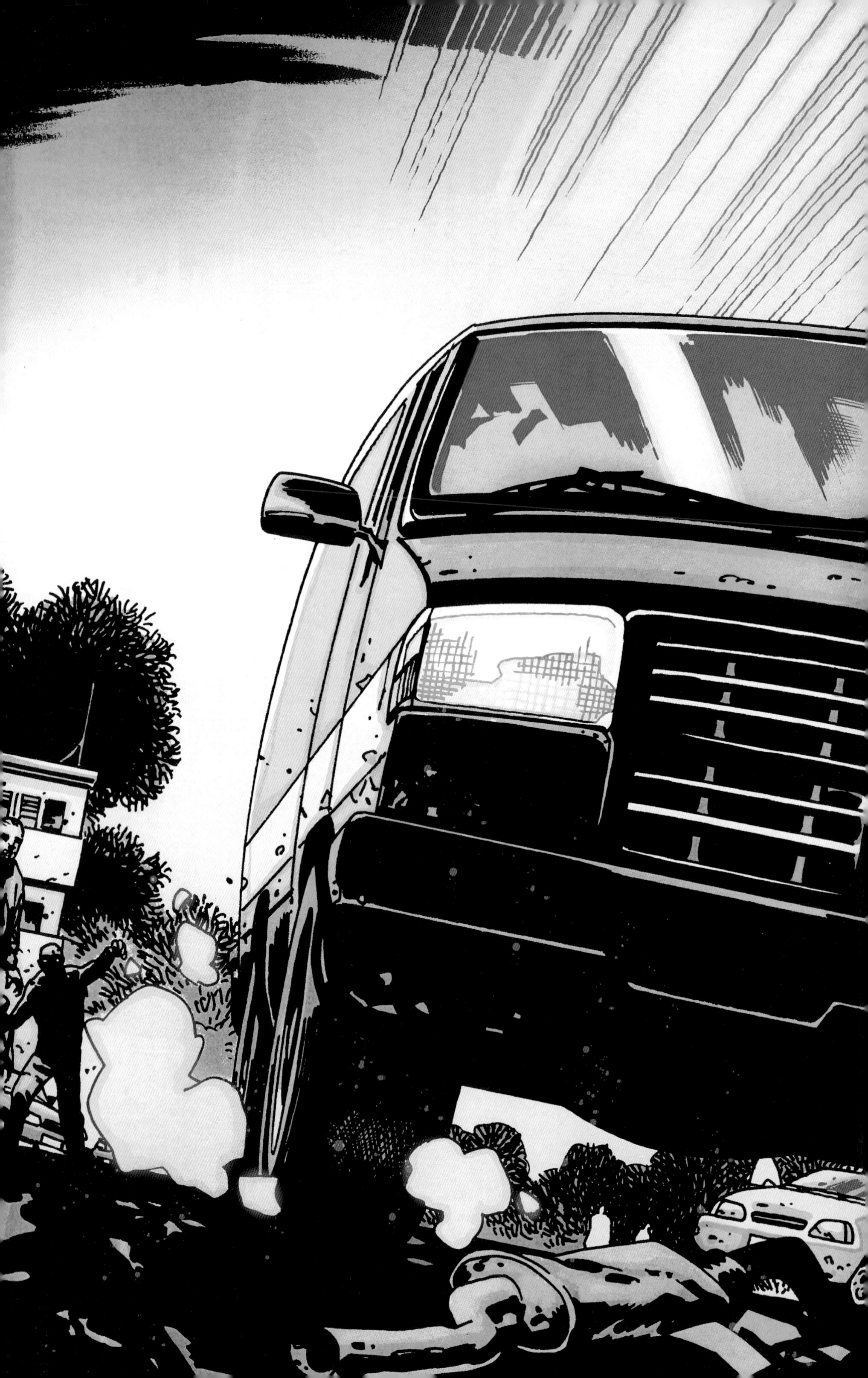

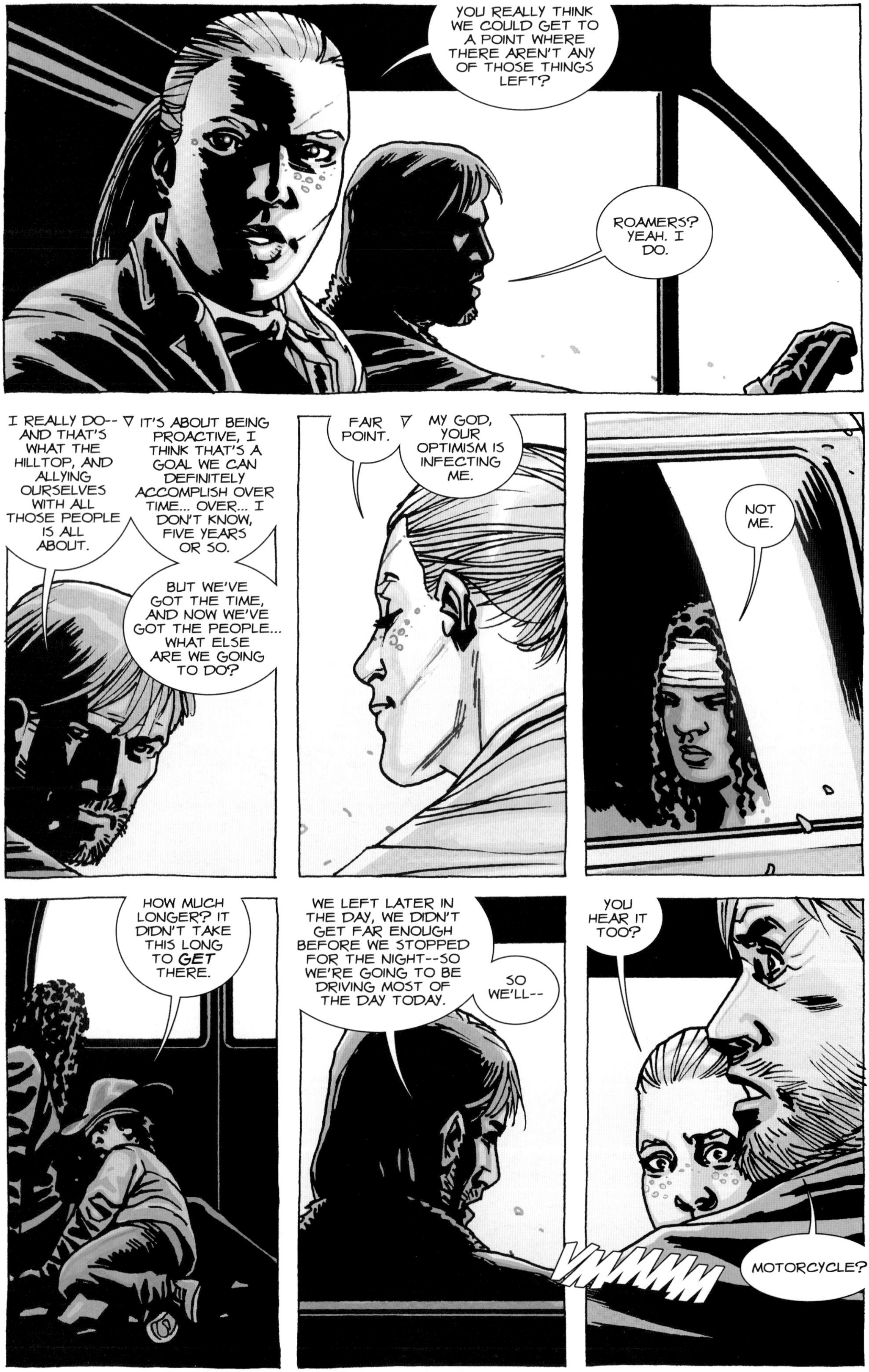
YOU REALLY THINK WE COULD GET TO A POINT WHERE THERE AREN'T ANY OF THOSE THINGS LEFT?
ROAMERS? YEAH. I DO.
I REALLY DO-- AND THAT'S WHAT THE HILLTOP, AND ALLYING OURSELVES WITH ALL THOSE PEOPLE IS ALL ABOUT.
IT'S ABOUT BEING PROACTIVE, I THINK THAT'S A GOAL WE CAN DEFINITELY ACCOMPLISH OVER TIME... OVER... I DON'T KNOW, FIVE YEARS OR SO.
BUT WE'VE GOT THE TIME, AND NOW WE'VE GOT THE PEOPLE... WHAT ELSE ARE WE GOING TO DO?
FAIR POINT.
MY GOD, YOUR OPTIMISM IS INFECTING ME.
NOT ME.
HOW MUCH LONGER? IT DIDN'T TAKE THIS LONG TO **GET** THERE.
WE LEFT LATER IN THE DAY, WE DIDN'T GET FAR ENOUGH BEFORE WE STOPPED FOR THE NIGHT--SO WE'RE GOING TO BE DRIVING MOST OF THE DAY TODAY.
SO WE'LL--
VMMMMM
YOU HEAR IT TOO?
MOTORCYCLE?

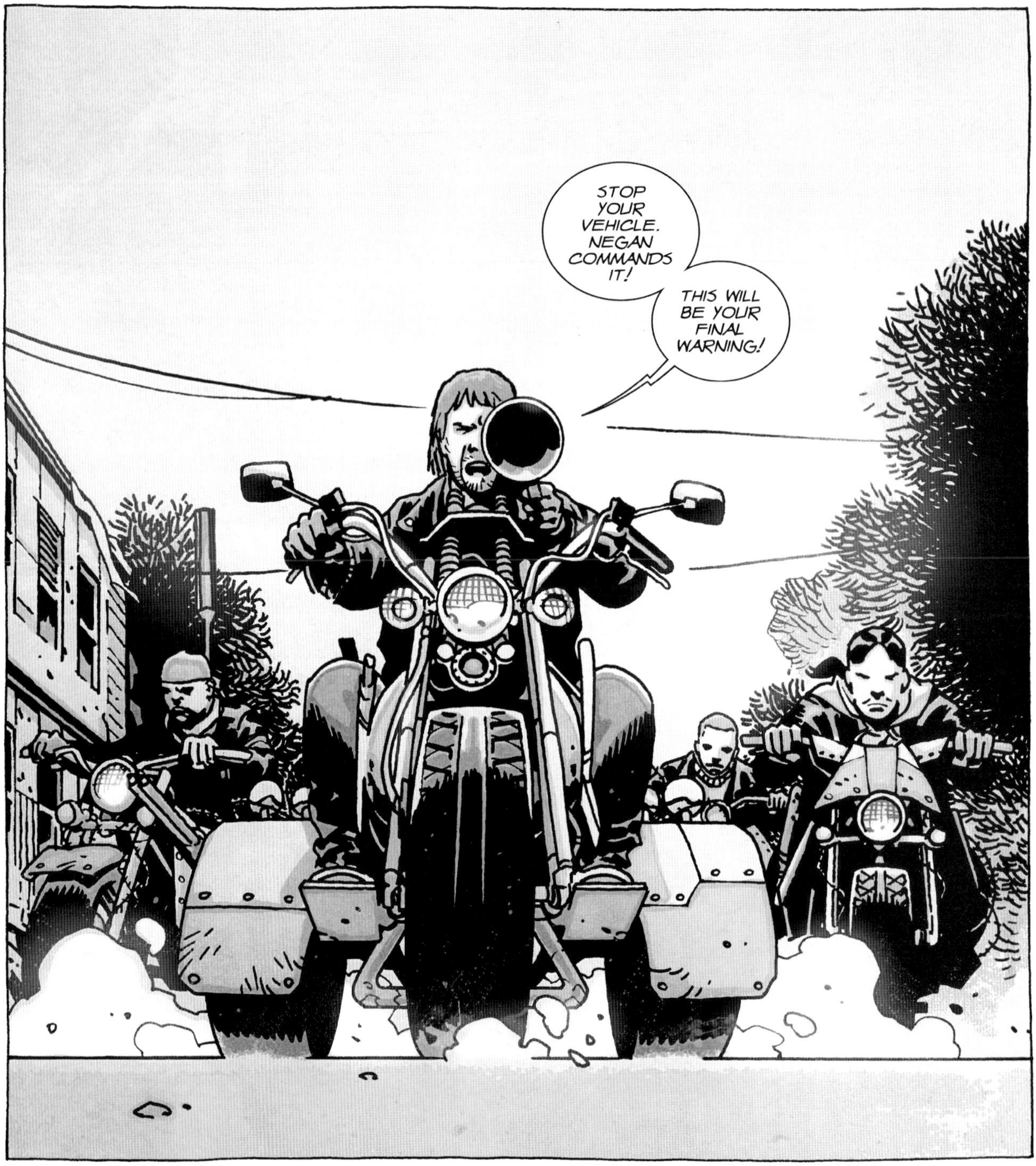
STOP YOUR VEHICLE. NEGAN COMMANDS IT!
THIS WILL BE YOUR FINAL WARNING!

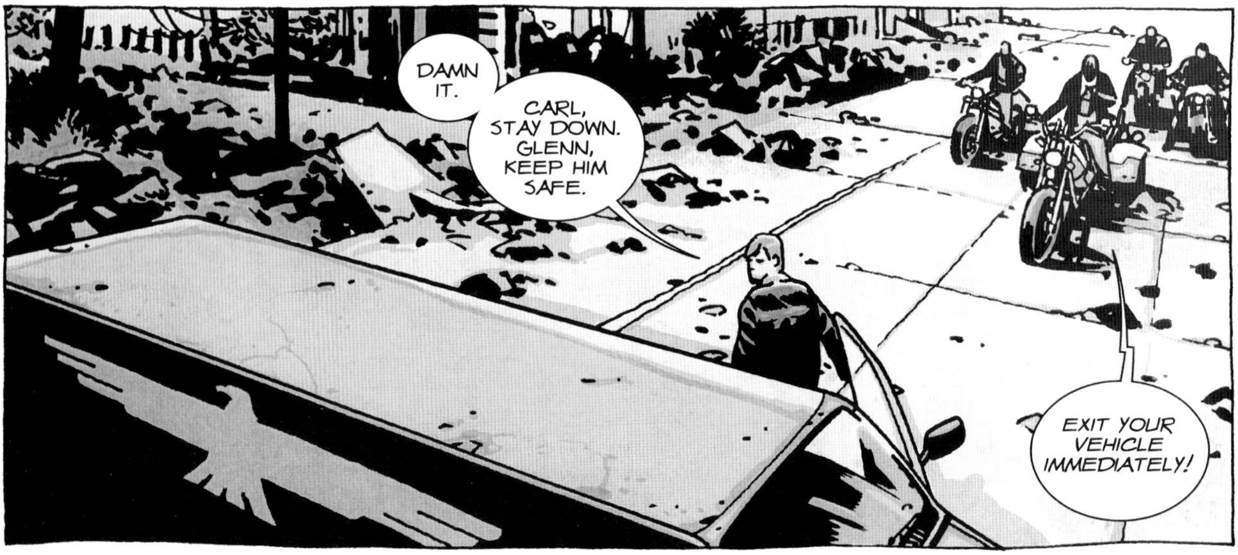
DAMN IT.
CARL, STAY DOWN. GLENN, KEEP HIM SAFE.
EXIT YOUR VEHICLE IMMEDIATELY!

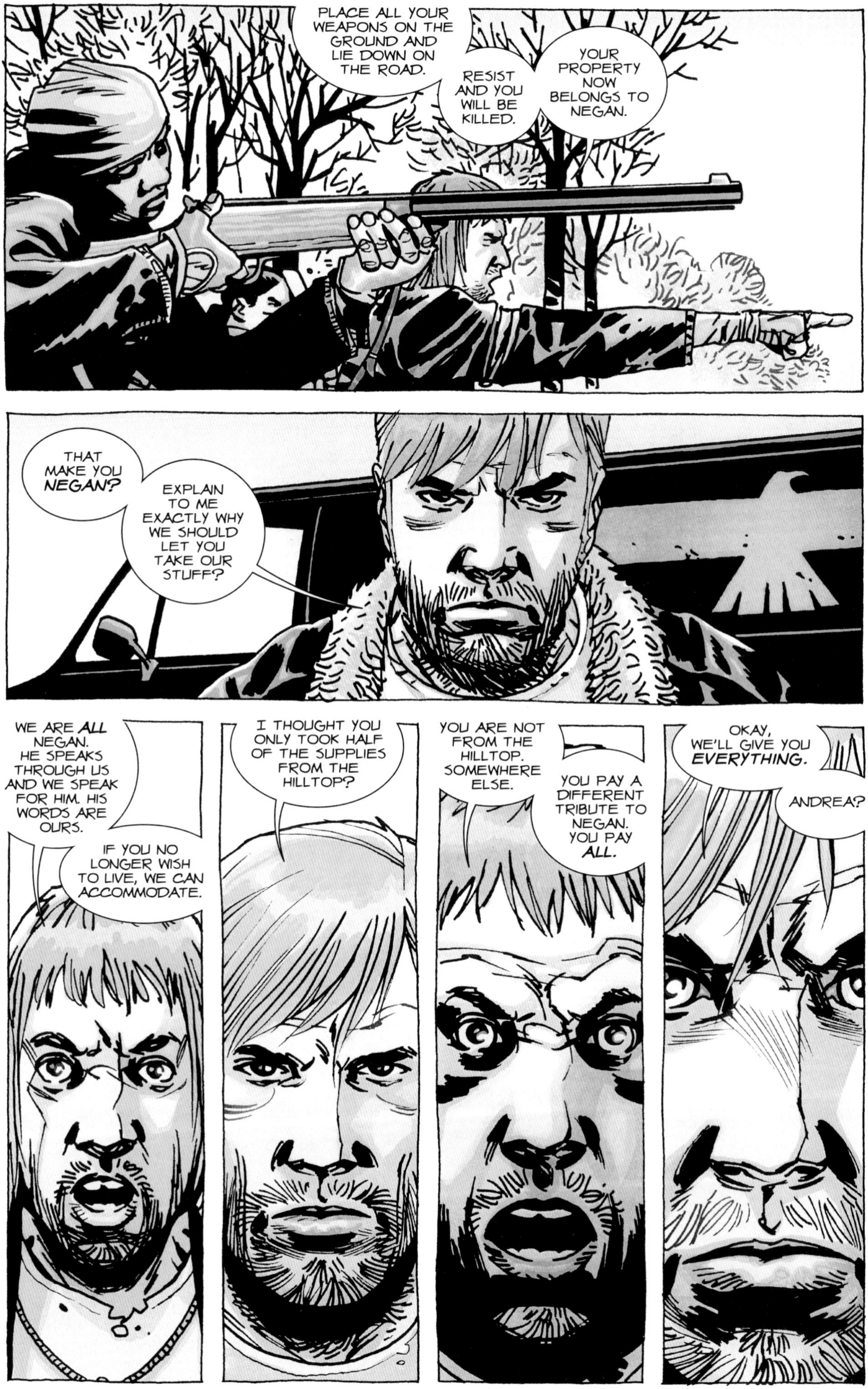
PLACE ALL YOUR WEAPONS ON THE GROUND AND LIE DOWN ON THE ROAD.
RESIST AND YOU WILL BE KILLED.
YOUR PROPERTY NOW BELONGS TO NEGAN.
THAT MAKE YOU NEGAN?
EXPLAIN TO ME EXACTLY WHY WE SHOULD LET YOU TAKE OUR STUFF?
WE ARE ALL NEGAN. HE SPEAKS THROUGH US AND WE SPEAK FOR HIM. HIS WORDS ARE OURS.
IF YOU NO LONGER WISH TO LIVE, WE CAN ACCOMMODATE.
I THOUGHT YOU ONLY TOOK HALF OF THE SUPPLIES FROM THE HILLTOP?
YOU ARE NOT FROM THE HILLTOP. SOMEWHERE ELSE.
YOU PAY A DIFFERENT TRIBUTE TO NEGAN. YOU PAY ALL.
OKAY, WE'LL GIVE YOU EVERYTHING.
ANDREA?

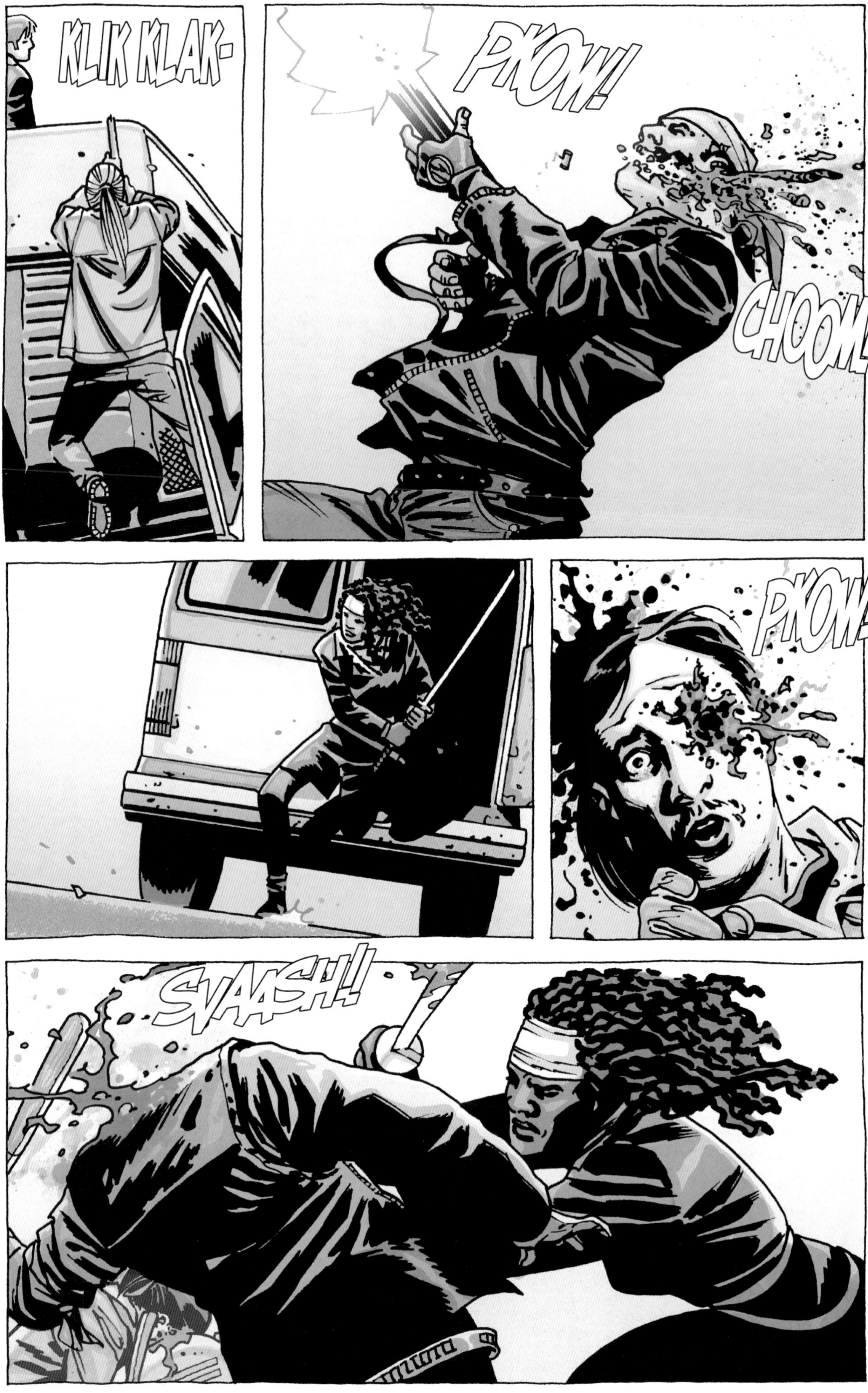
KLIK KLAK-
PKOW!
CHOOM!
PKOW!
SVAASH!!

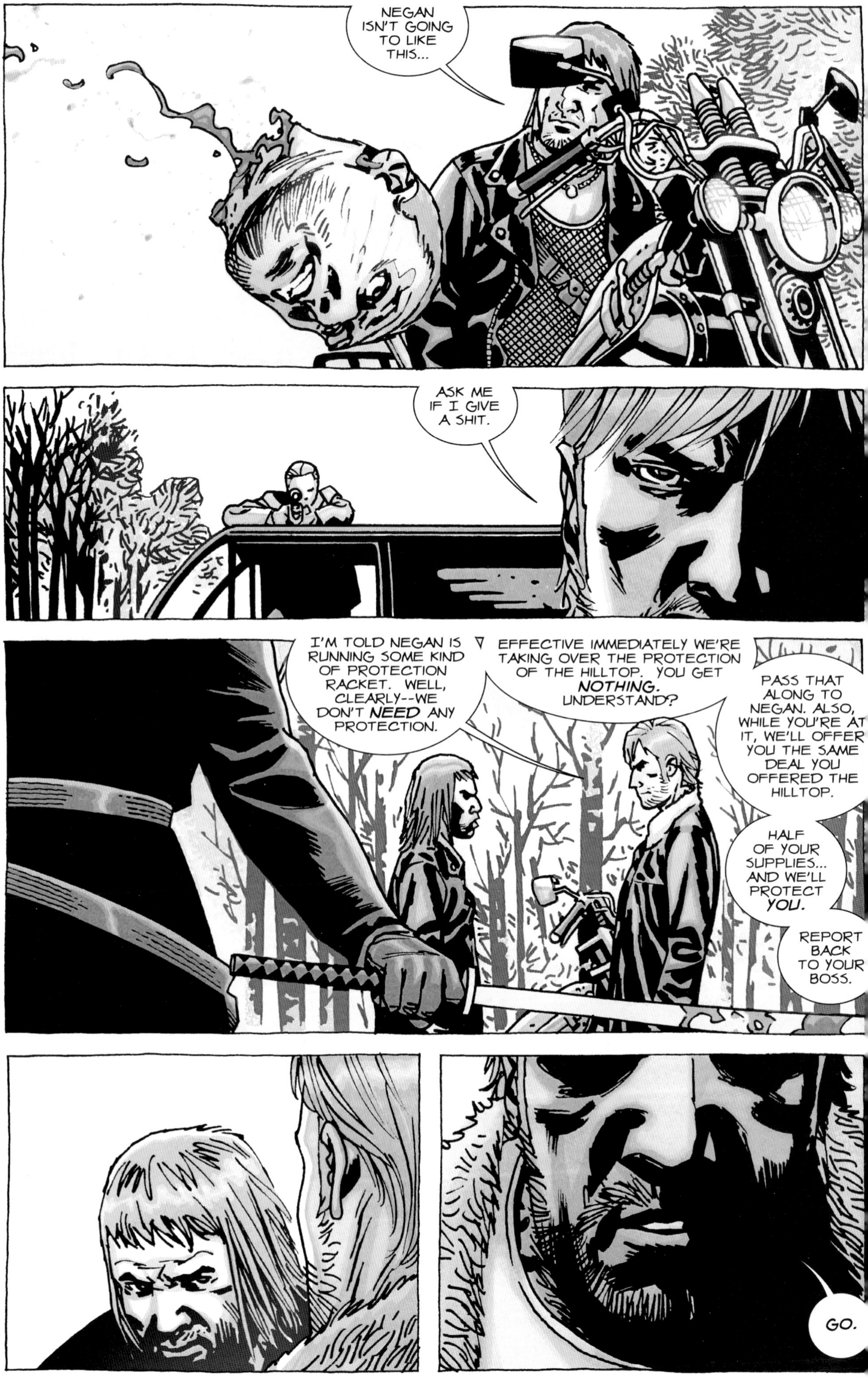
NEGAN ISN'T GOING TO LIKE THIS...
ASK ME IF I GIVE A SHIT.
I'M TOLD NEGAN IS RUNNING SOME KIND OF PROTECTION RACKET. WELL, CLEARLY--WE DON'T NEED ANY PROTECTION.
EFFECTIVE IMMEDIATELY WE'RE TAKING OVER THE PROTECTION OF THE HILLTOP. YOU GET NOTHING. UNDERSTAND?
PASS THAT ALONG TO NEGAN. ALSO, WHILE YOU'RE AT IT, WE'LL OFFER YOU THE SAME DEAL YOU OFFERED THE HILLTOP.
HALF OF YOUR SUPPLIES... AND WE'LL PROTECT YOU.
REPORT BACK TO YOUR BOSS.
GO.

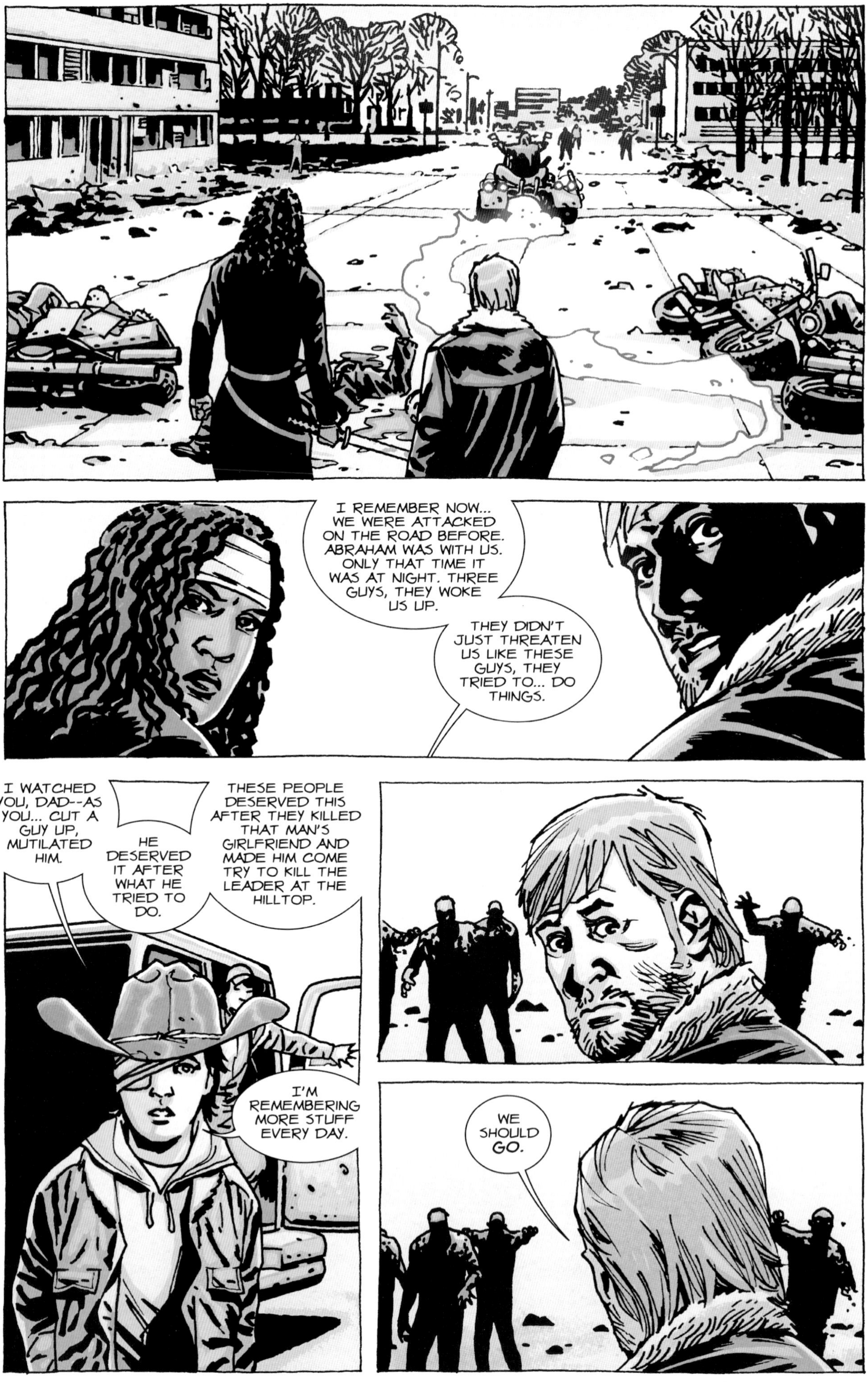
I REMEMBER NOW... WE WERE ATTACKED ON THE ROAD BEFORE. ABRAHAM WAS WITH US. ONLY THAT TIME IT WAS AT NIGHT. THREE GUYS, THEY WOKE US UP.
THEY DIDN'T JUST THREATEN US LIKE THESE GUYS, THEY TRIED TO... DO THINGS.
I WATCHED YOU, DAD--AS YOU... CUT A GUY UP, MUTILATED HIM.
HE DESERVED IT AFTER WHAT HE TRIED TO DO.
THESE PEOPLE DESERVED THIS AFTER THEY KILLED THAT MAN'S GIRLFRIEND AND MADE HIM COME TRY TO KILL THE LEADER AT THE HILLTOP.
I'M REMEMBERING MORE STUFF EVERY DAY.
WE SHOULD GO.

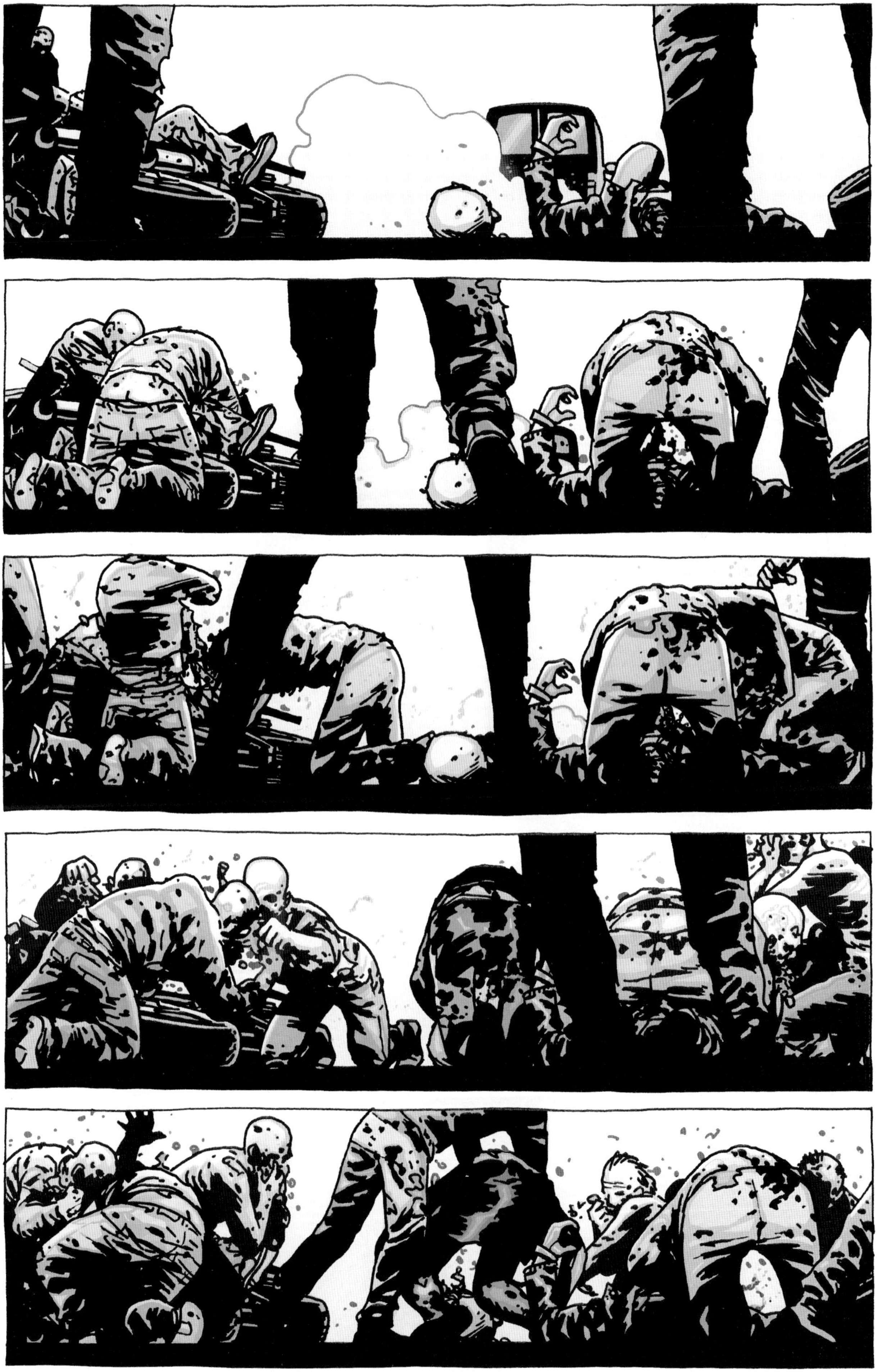

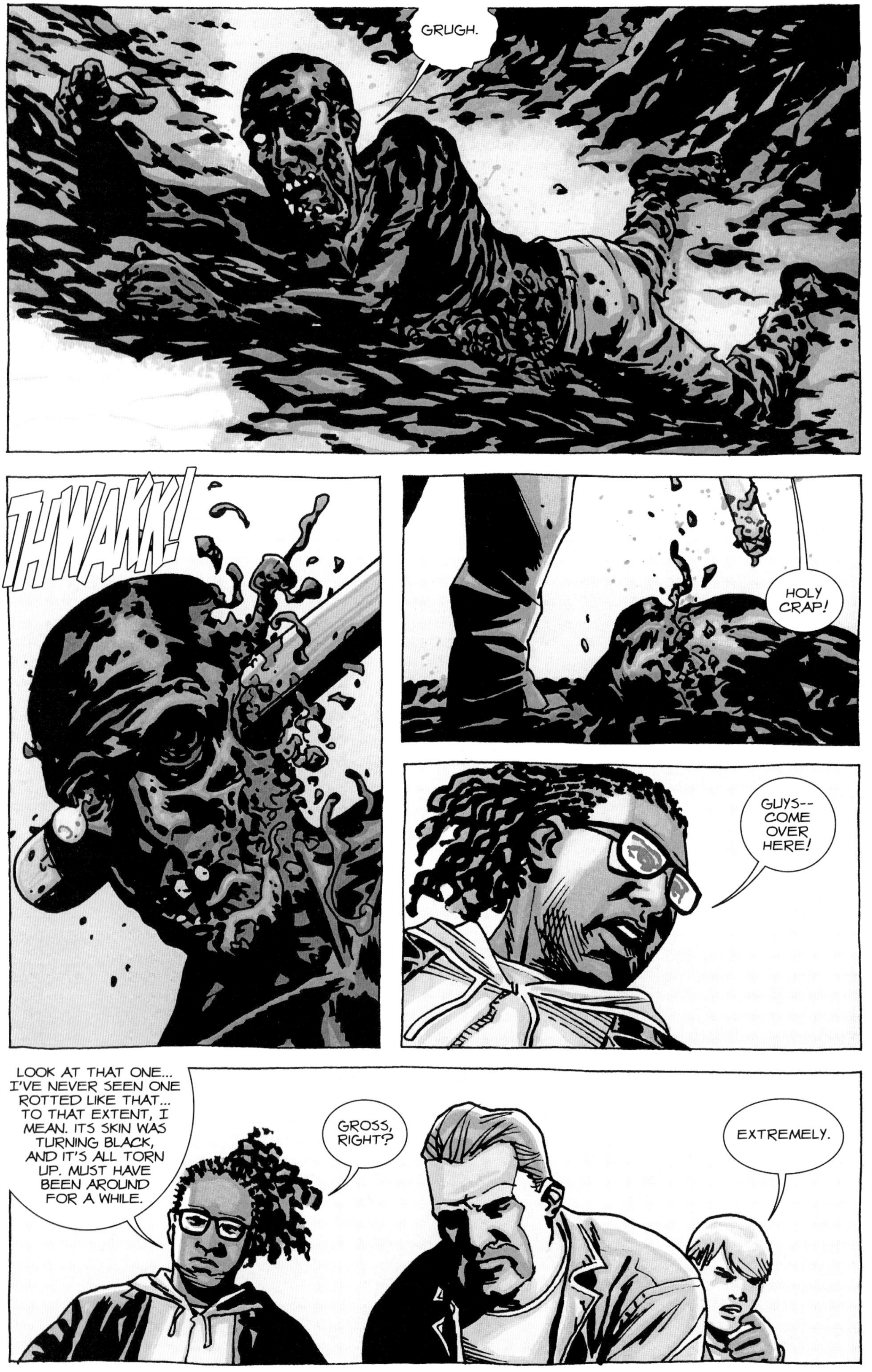
GRUGH.
THWAKK!
HOLY CRAP!
GUYS-- COME OVER HERE!
LOOK AT THAT ONE... I'VE NEVER SEEN ONE ROTTED LIKE THAT... TO THAT EXTENT, I MEAN. ITS SKIN WAS TURNING BLACK, AND IT'S ALL TORN UP. MUST HAVE BEEN AROUND FOR A WHILE.
GROSS, RIGHT?
EXTREMELY.

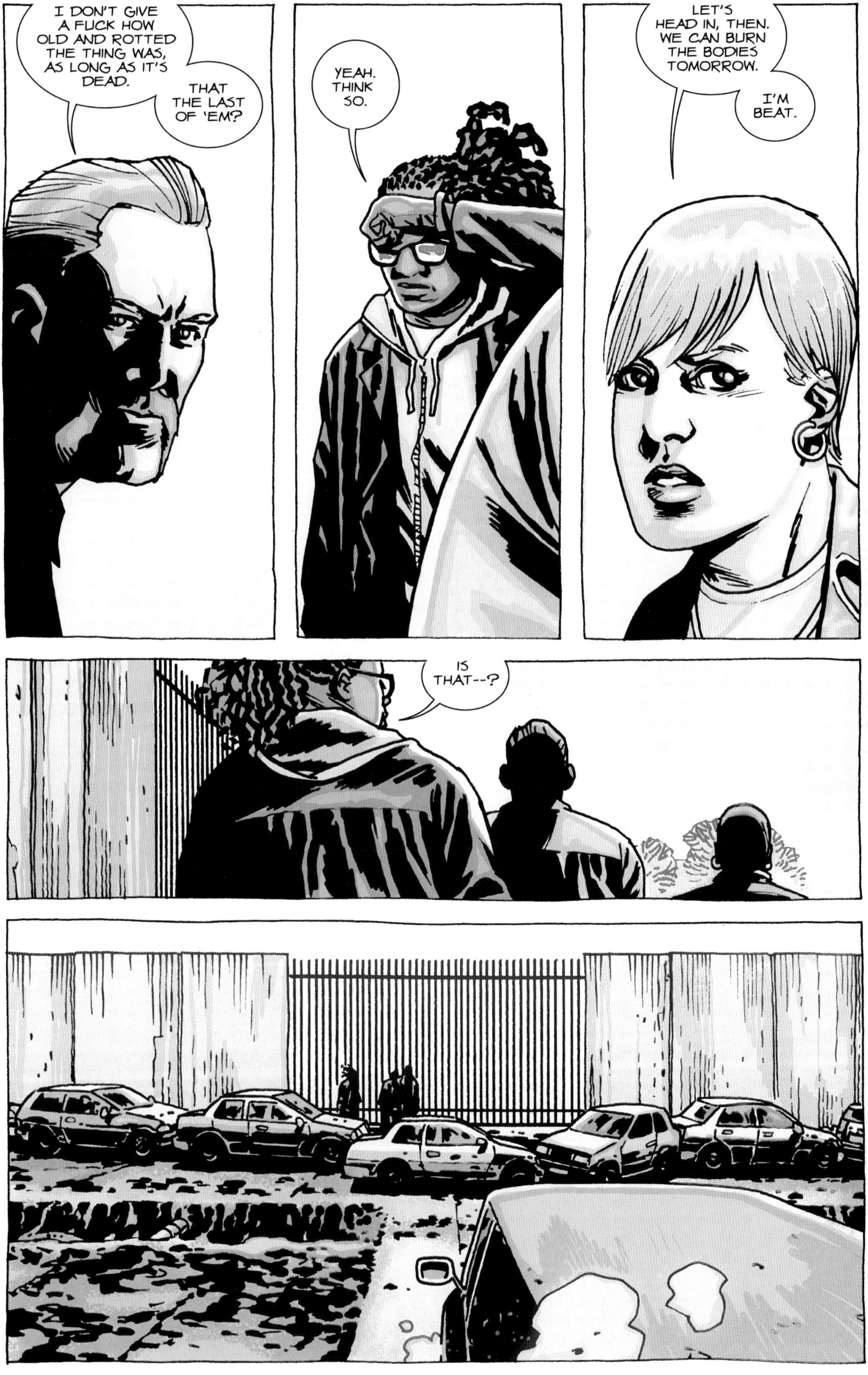
I DON'T GIVE A FUCK HOW OLD AND ROTTED THE THING WAS, AS LONG AS IT'S DEAD.
THAT THE LAST OF 'EM?
YEAH. THINK SO.
LET'S HEAD IN, THEN. WE CAN BURN THE BODIES TOMORROW.
I'M BEAT.
IS THAT--?

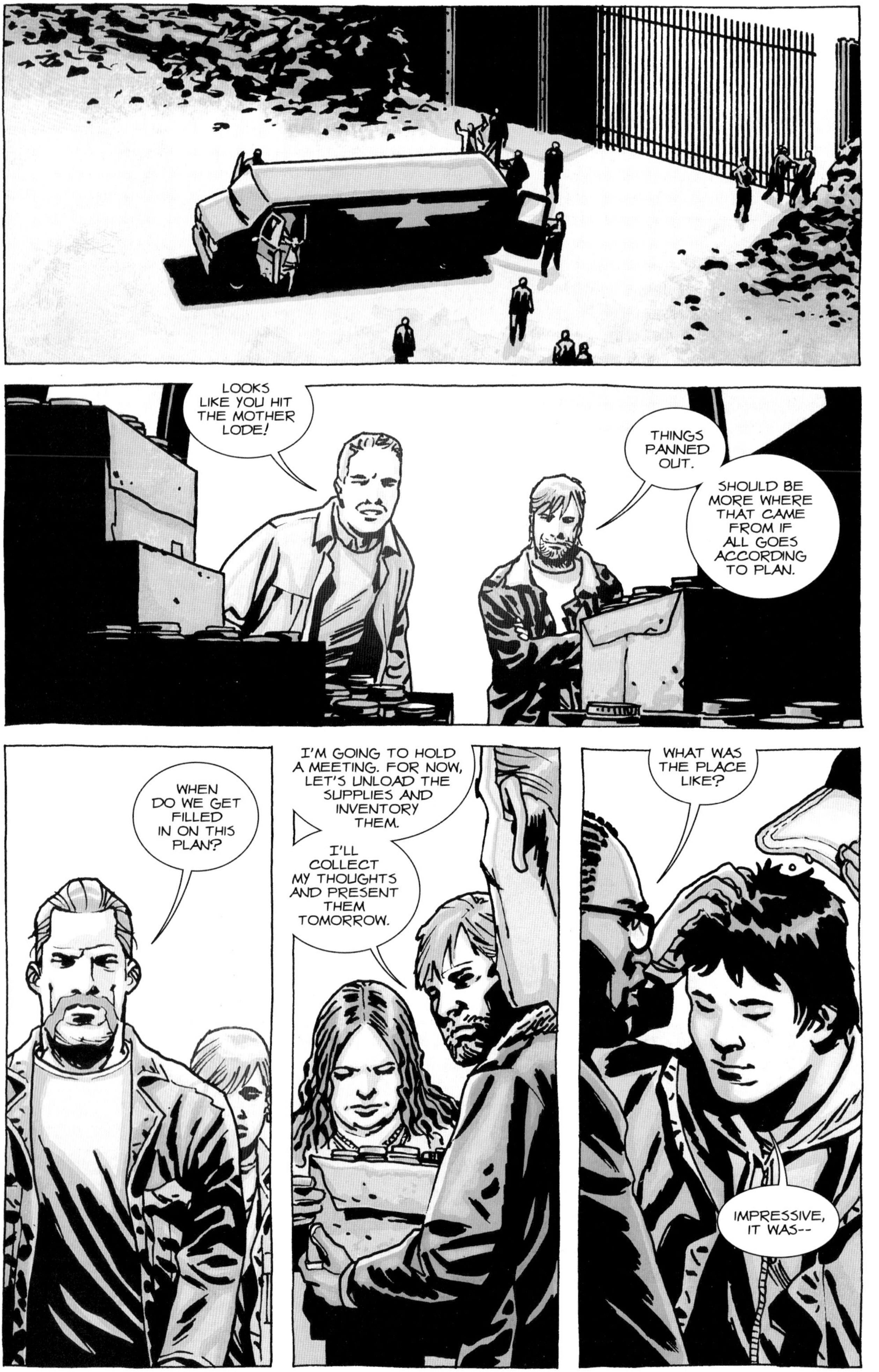
LOOKS LIKE YOU HIT THE MOTHER LODE!
THINGS PANNED OUT.
SHOULD BE MORE WHERE THAT CAME FROM IF ALL GOES ACCORDING TO PLAN.
WHEN DO WE GET FILLED IN ON THIS PLAN?
I'M GOING TO HOLD A MEETING. FOR NOW, LET'S UNLOAD THE SUPPLIES AND INVENTORY THEM.
I'LL COLLECT MY THOUGHTS AND PRESENT THEM TOMORROW.
WHAT WAS THE PLACE LIKE?
IMPRESSIVE, IT WAS--

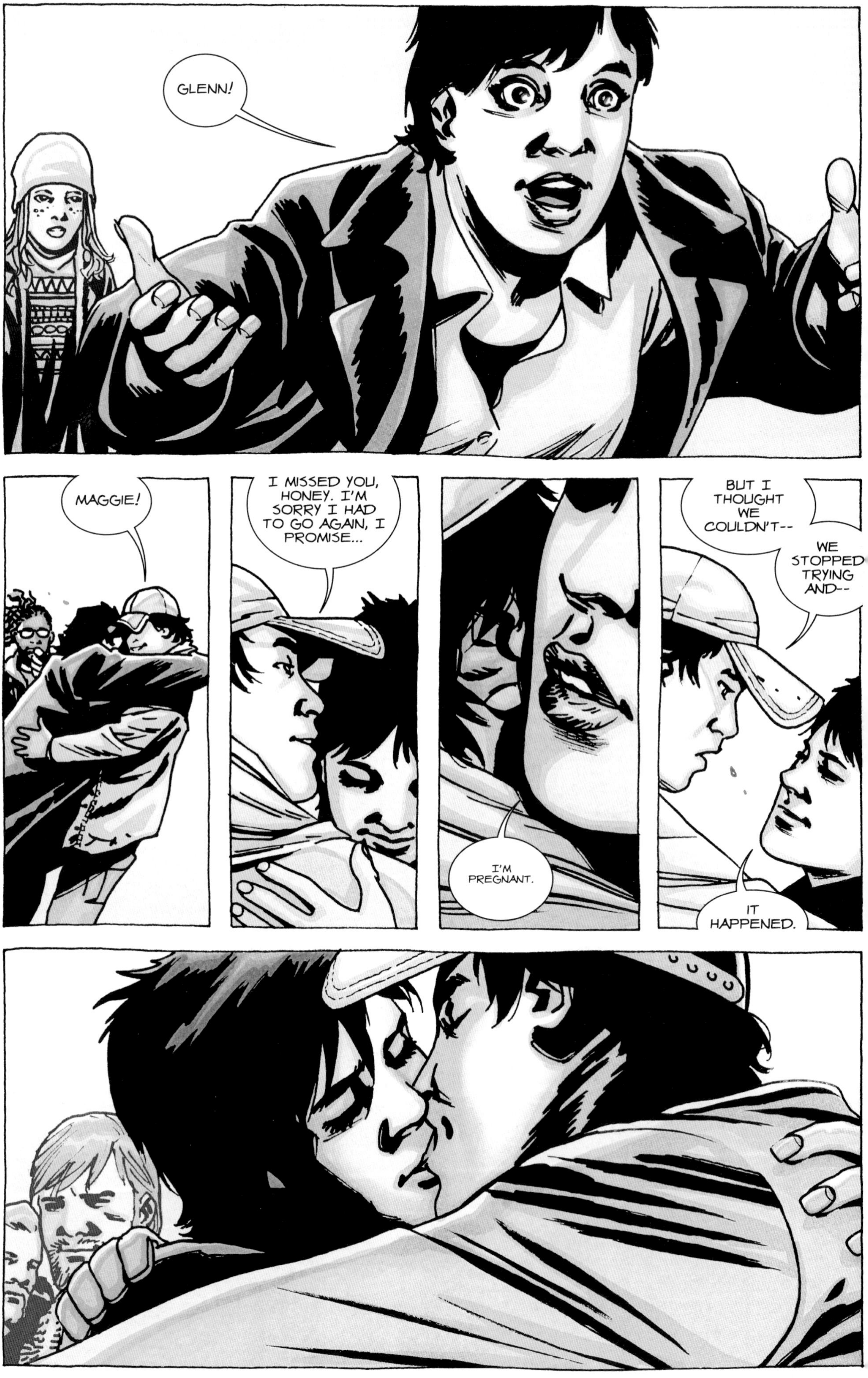
GLENN!
MAGGIE!
I MISSED YOU, HONEY. I'M SORRY I HAD TO GO AGAIN, I PROMISE...
I'M PREGNANT.
BUT I THOUGHT WE COULDN'T--
WE STOPPED TRYING AND--
IT HAPPENED.

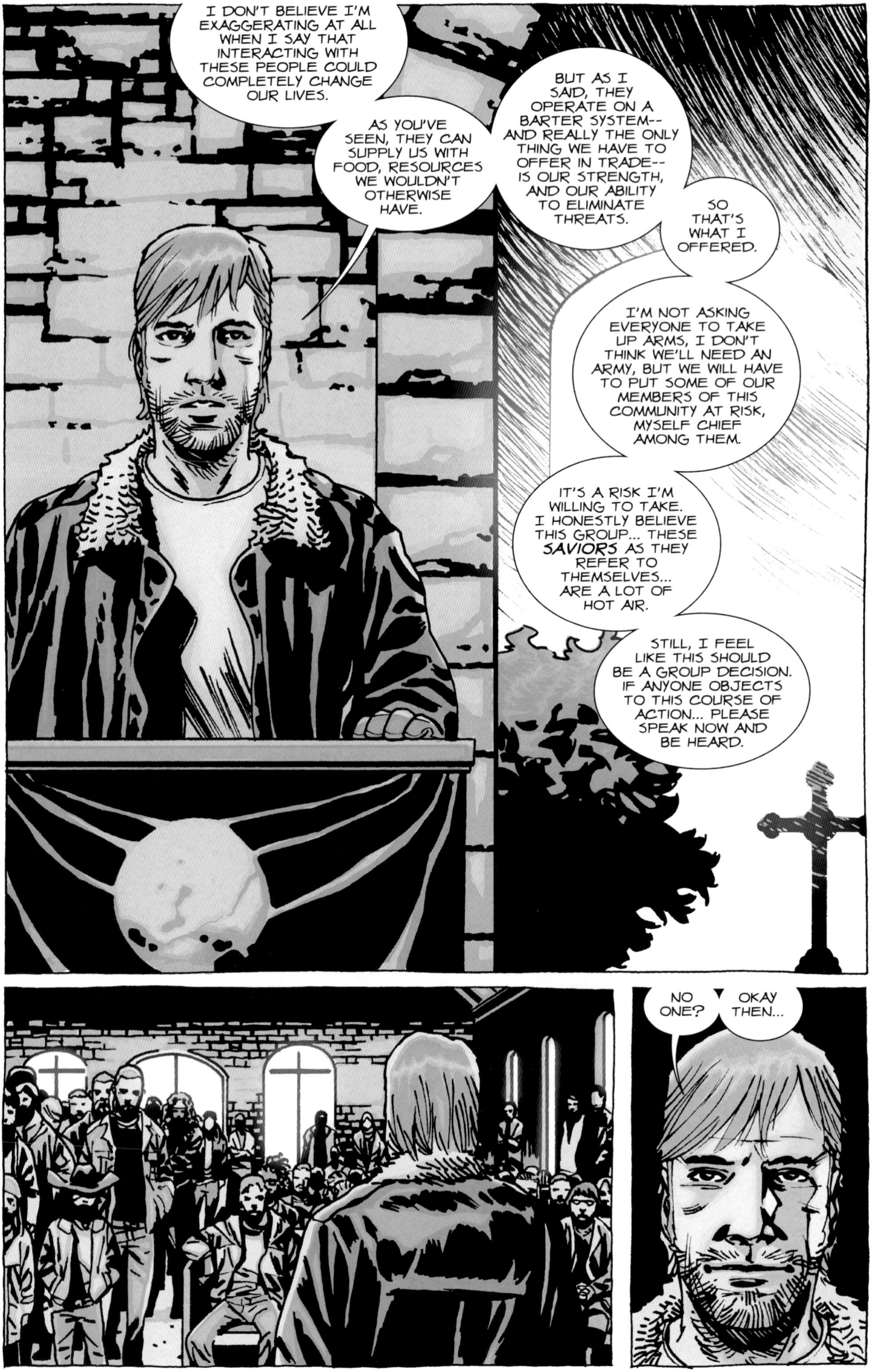
I DON'T BELIEVE I'M EXAGGERATING AT ALL WHEN I SAY THAT INTERACTING WITH THESE PEOPLE COULD COMPLETELY CHANGE OUR LIVES.
AS YOU'VE SEEN, THEY CAN SUPPLY US WITH FOOD, RESOURCES WE WOULDN'T OTHERWISE HAVE.
BUT AS I SAID, THEY OPERATE ON A BARTER SYSTEM-- AND REALLY THE ONLY THING WE HAVE TO OFFER IN TRADE-- IS OUR STRENGTH, AND OUR ABILITY TO ELIMINATE THREATS.
SO THAT'S WHAT I OFFERED.
I'M NOT ASKING EVERYONE TO TAKE UP ARMS, I DON'T THINK WE'LL NEED AN ARMY, BUT WE WILL HAVE TO PUT SOME OF OUR MEMBERS OF THIS COMMUNITY AT RISK, MYSELF CHIEF AMONG THEM.
IT'S A RISK I'M WILLING TO TAKE. I HONESTLY BELIEVE THIS GROUP... THESE *SAVIORS* AS THEY REFER TO THEMSELVES... ARE A LOT OF HOT AIR.
STILL, I FEEL LIKE THIS SHOULD BE A GROUP DECISION. IF ANYONE OBJECTS TO THIS COURSE OF ACTION... PLEASE SPEAK NOW AND BE HEARD.
NO ONE?
OKAY THEN...

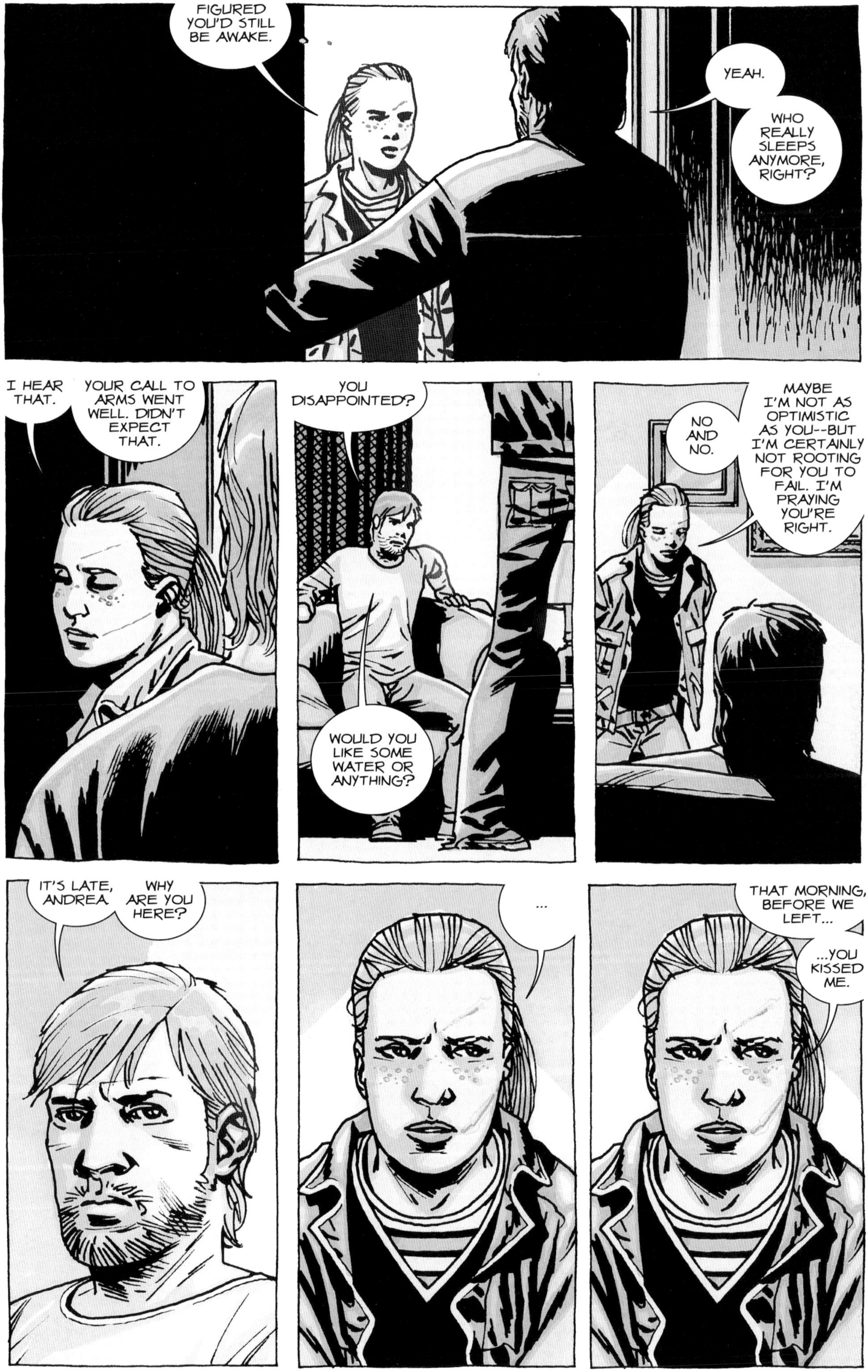
FIGURED YOU'D STILL BE AWAKE.
YEAH.
WHO REALLY SLEEPS ANYMORE, RIGHT?
I HEAR THAT.
YOUR CALL TO ARMS WENT WELL. DIDN'T EXPECT THAT.
YOU DISAPPOINTED?
WOULD YOU LIKE SOME WATER OR ANYTHING?
NO AND NO.
MAYBE I'M NOT AS OPTIMISTIC AS YOU--BUT I'M CERTAINLY NOT ROOTING FOR YOU TO FAIL. I'M PRAYING YOU'RE RIGHT.
IT'S LATE, ANDREA.
WHY ARE YOU HERE?
...
THAT MORNING, BEFORE WE LEFT...
...YOU KISSED ME.

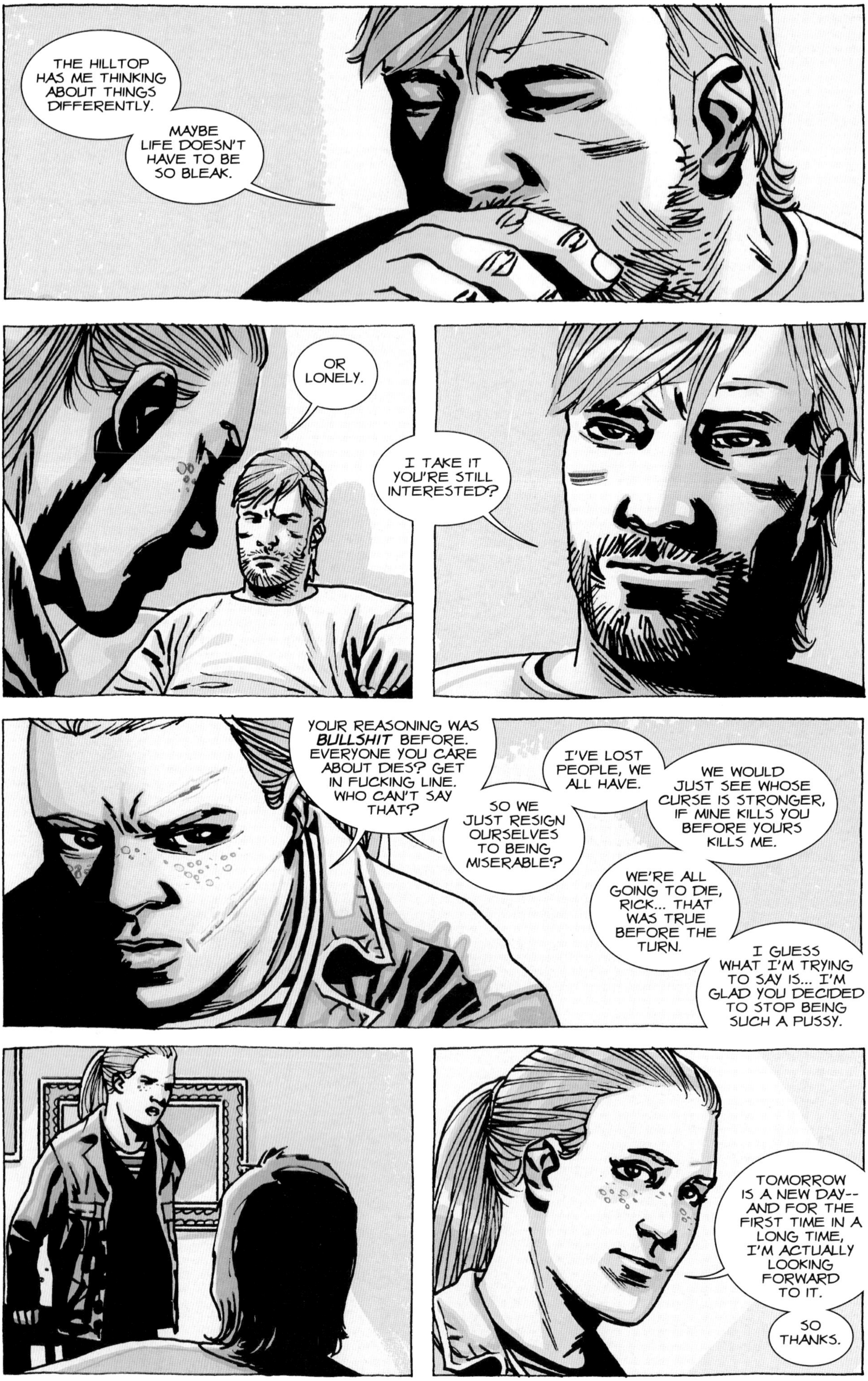
THE HILLTOP HAS ME THINKING ABOUT THINGS DIFFERENTLY.
MAYBE LIFE DOESN'T HAVE TO BE SO BLEAK.
OR LONELY.
I TAKE IT YOU'RE STILL INTERESTED?
YOUR REASONING WAS *BULLSHIT* BEFORE. EVERYONE YOU CARE ABOUT DIES? GET IN FUCKING LINE. WHO CAN'T SAY THAT?
SO WE JUST RESIGN OURSELVES TO BEING MISERABLE?
I'VE LOST PEOPLE, WE ALL HAVE.
WE WOULD JUST SEE WHOSE CURSE IS STRONGER, IF MINE KILLS YOU BEFORE YOURS KILLS ME.
WE'RE ALL GOING TO DIE, RICK... THAT WAS TRUE BEFORE THE TURN.
I GUESS WHAT I'M TRYING TO SAY IS... I'M GLAD YOU DECIDED TO STOP BEING SUCH A PUSSY.
TOMORROW IS A NEW DAY-- AND FOR THE FIRST TIME IN A LONG TIME, I'M ACTUALLY LOOKING FORWARD TO IT.
SO THANKS.

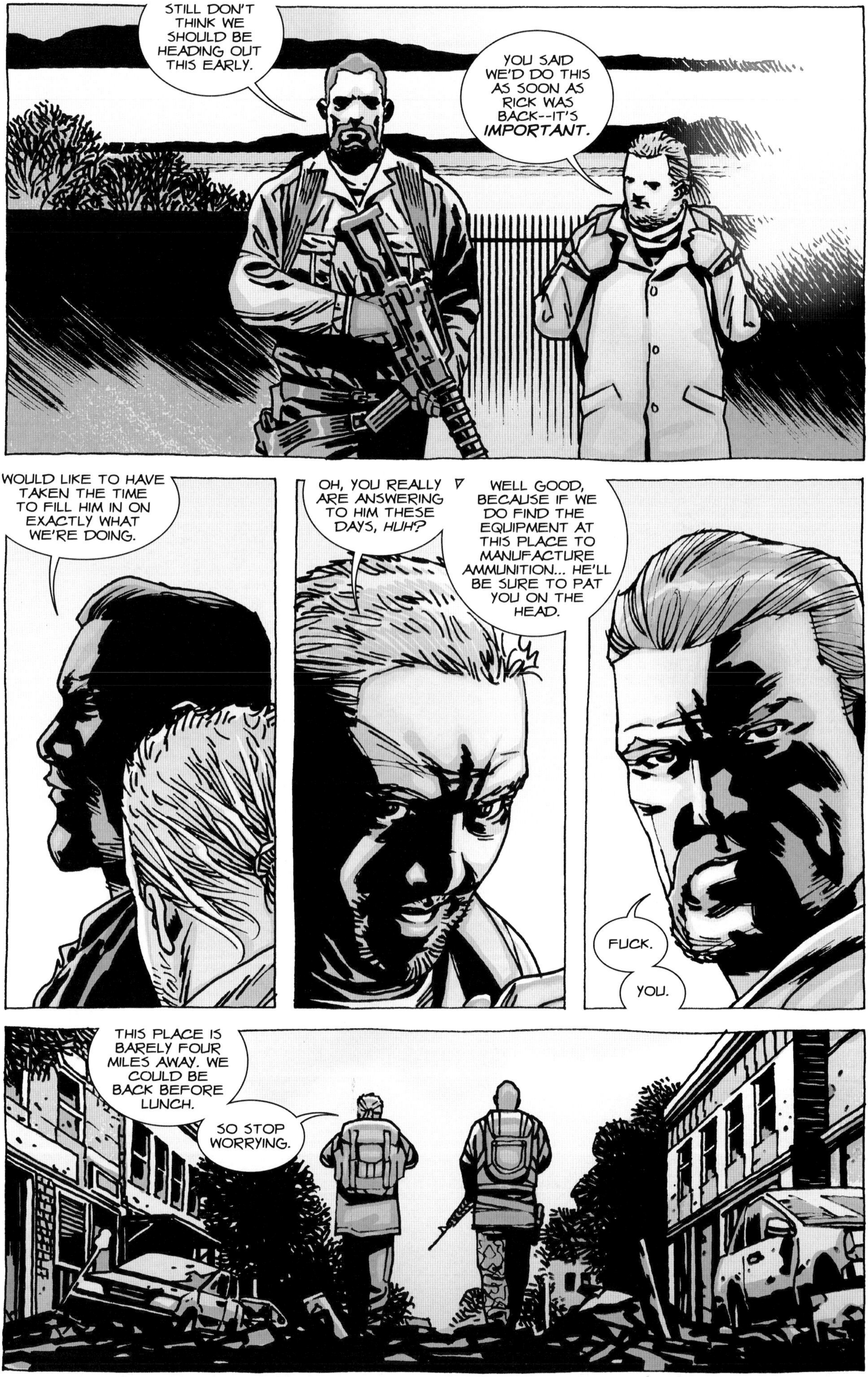
STILL DON'T THINK WE SHOULD BE HEADING OUT THIS EARLY.
YOU SAID WE'D DO THIS AS SOON AS RICK WAS BACK--IT'S IMPORTANT.
WOULD LIKE TO HAVE TAKEN THE TIME TO FILL HIM IN ON EXACTLY WHAT WE'RE DOING.
OH, YOU REALLY ARE ANSWERING TO HIM THESE DAYS, HUH?
WELL GOOD, BECAUSE IF WE DO FIND THE EQUIPMENT AT THIS PLACE TO MANUFACTURE AMMUNITION... HE'LL BE SURE TO PAT YOU ON THE HEAD.
FUCK.
YOU.
THIS PLACE IS BARELY FOUR MILES AWAY. WE COULD BE BACK BEFORE LUNCH.
SO STOP WORRYING.

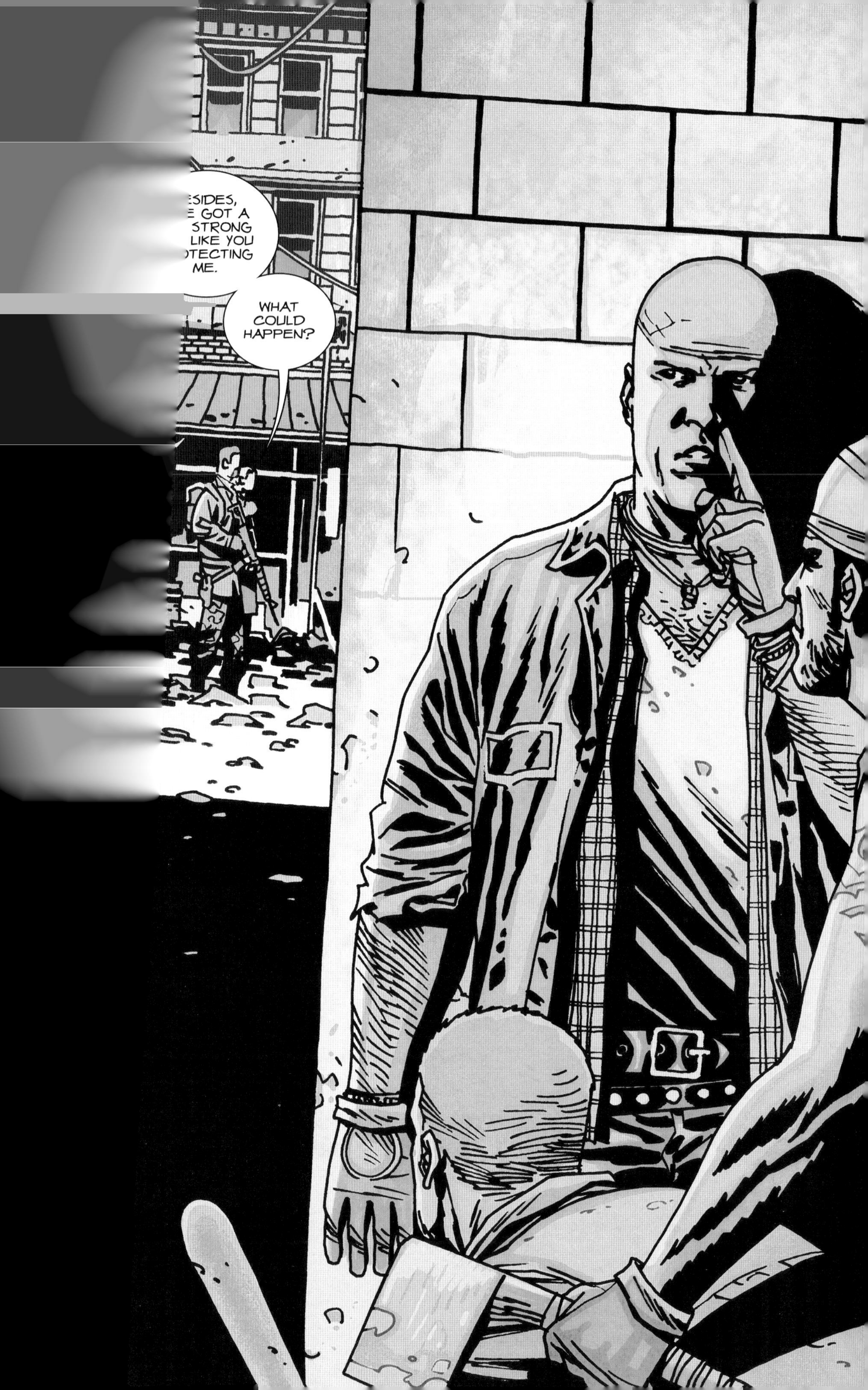
ESIDES,
E GOT A
STRONG
LIKE YOU
OTECTING
ME.
WHAT
COULD
HAPPEN?

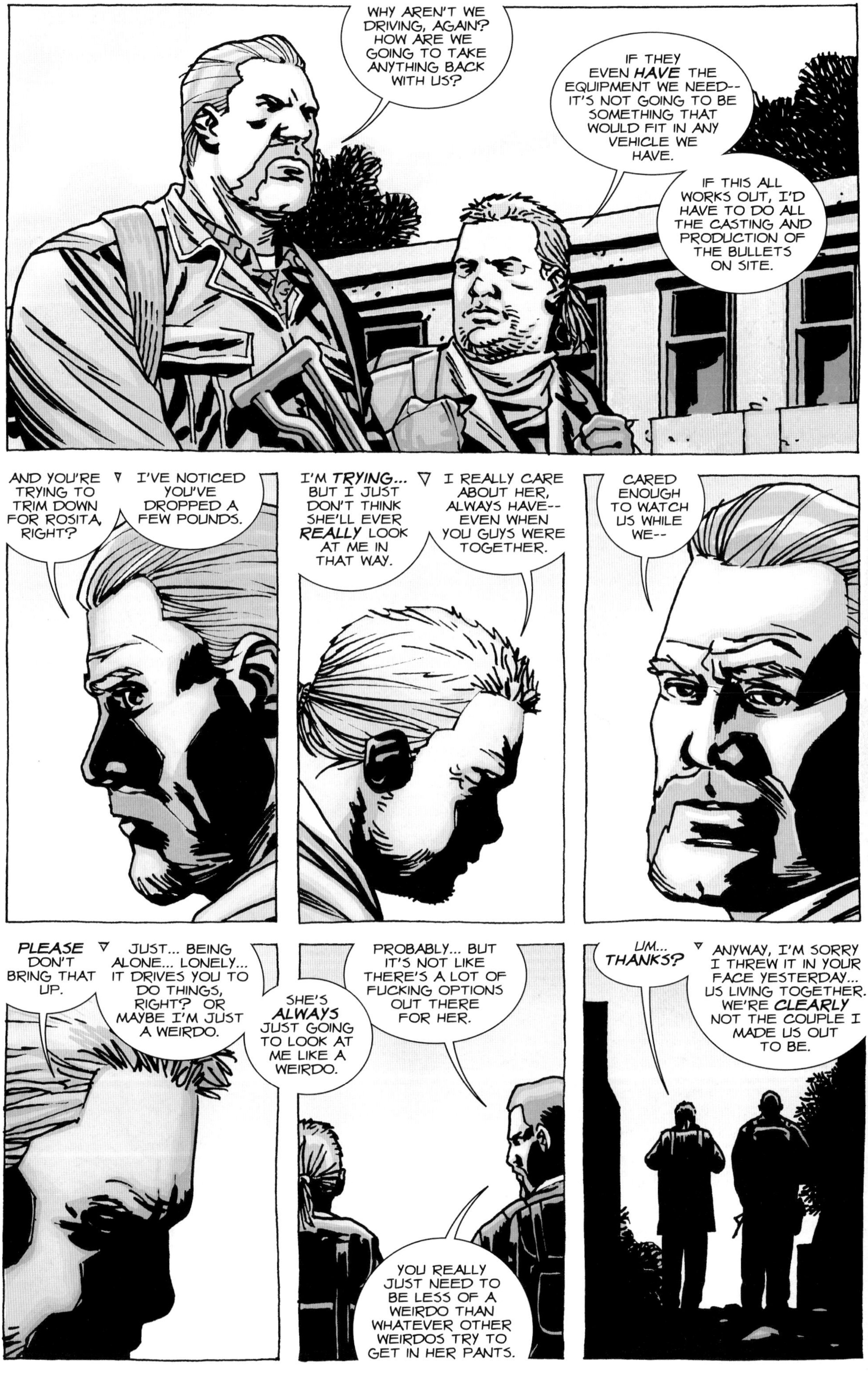
WHY AREN'T WE DRIVING, AGAIN? HOW ARE WE GOING TO TAKE ANYTHING BACK WITH US?
IF THEY EVEN HAVE THE EQUIPMENT WE NEED-- IT'S NOT GOING TO BE SOMETHING THAT WOULD FIT IN ANY VEHICLE WE HAVE.
IF THIS ALL WORKS OUT, I'D HAVE TO DO ALL THE CASTING AND PRODUCTION OF THE BULLETS ON SITE.
AND YOU'RE TRYING TO TRIM DOWN FOR ROSITA, RIGHT?
I'VE NOTICED YOU'VE DROPPED A FEW POUNDS.
I'M TRYING... BUT I JUST DON'T THINK SHE'LL EVER REALLY LOOK AT ME IN THAT WAY.
I REALLY CARE ABOUT HER, ALWAYS HAVE-- EVEN WHEN YOU GUYS WERE TOGETHER.
CARED ENOUGH TO WATCH US WHILE WE--
PLEASE DON'T BRING THAT UP.
JUST... BEING ALONE... LONELY... IT DRIVES YOU TO DO THINGS, RIGHT? OR MAYBE I'M JUST A WEIRDO.
SHE'S ALWAYS JUST GOING TO LOOK AT ME LIKE A WEIRDO.
PROBABLY... BUT IT'S NOT LIKE THERE'S A LOT OF FUCKING OPTIONS OUT THERE FOR HER.
YOU REALLY JUST NEED TO BE LESS OF A WEIRDO THAN WHATEVER OTHER WEIRDOS TRY TO GET IN HER PANTS.
UM... THANKS?
ANYWAY, I'M SORRY I THREW IT IN YOUR FACE YESTERDAY... US LIVING TOGETHER. WE'RE CLEARLY NOT THE COUPLE I MADE US OUT TO BE.

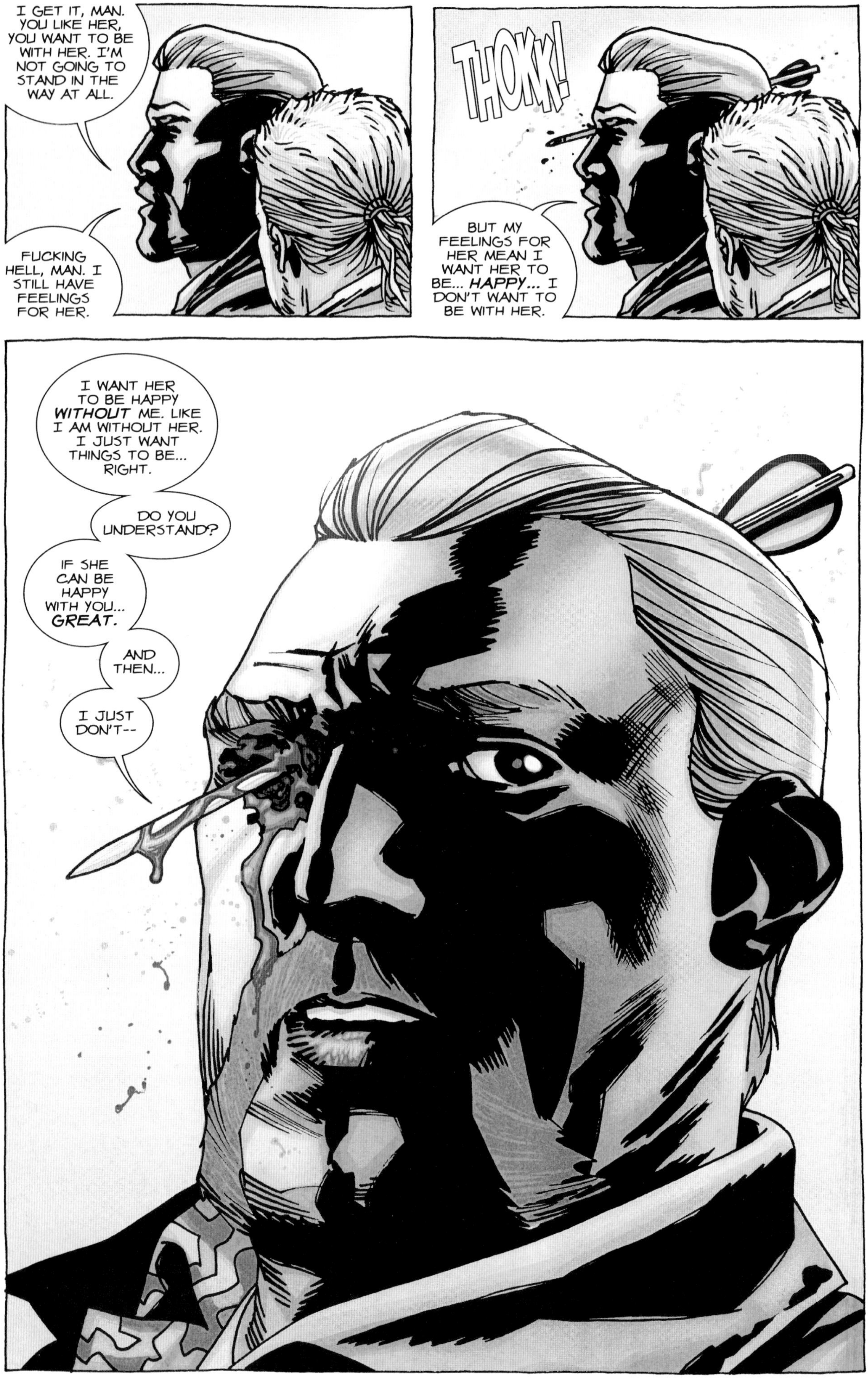
I GET IT, MAN. YOU LIKE HER, YOU WANT TO BE WITH HER. I'M NOT GOING TO STAND IN THE WAY AT ALL.
FUCKING HELL, MAN. I STILL HAVE FEELINGS FOR HER.
THOKK!
BUT MY FEELINGS FOR HER MEAN I WANT HER TO BE... HAPPY... I DON'T WANT TO BE WITH HER.
I WANT HER TO BE HAPPY WITHOUT ME. LIKE I AM WITHOUT HER. I JUST WANT THINGS TO BE... RIGHT.
DO YOU UNDERSTAND?
IF SHE CAN BE HAPPY WITH YOU... GREAT.
AND THEN...
I JUST DON'T--

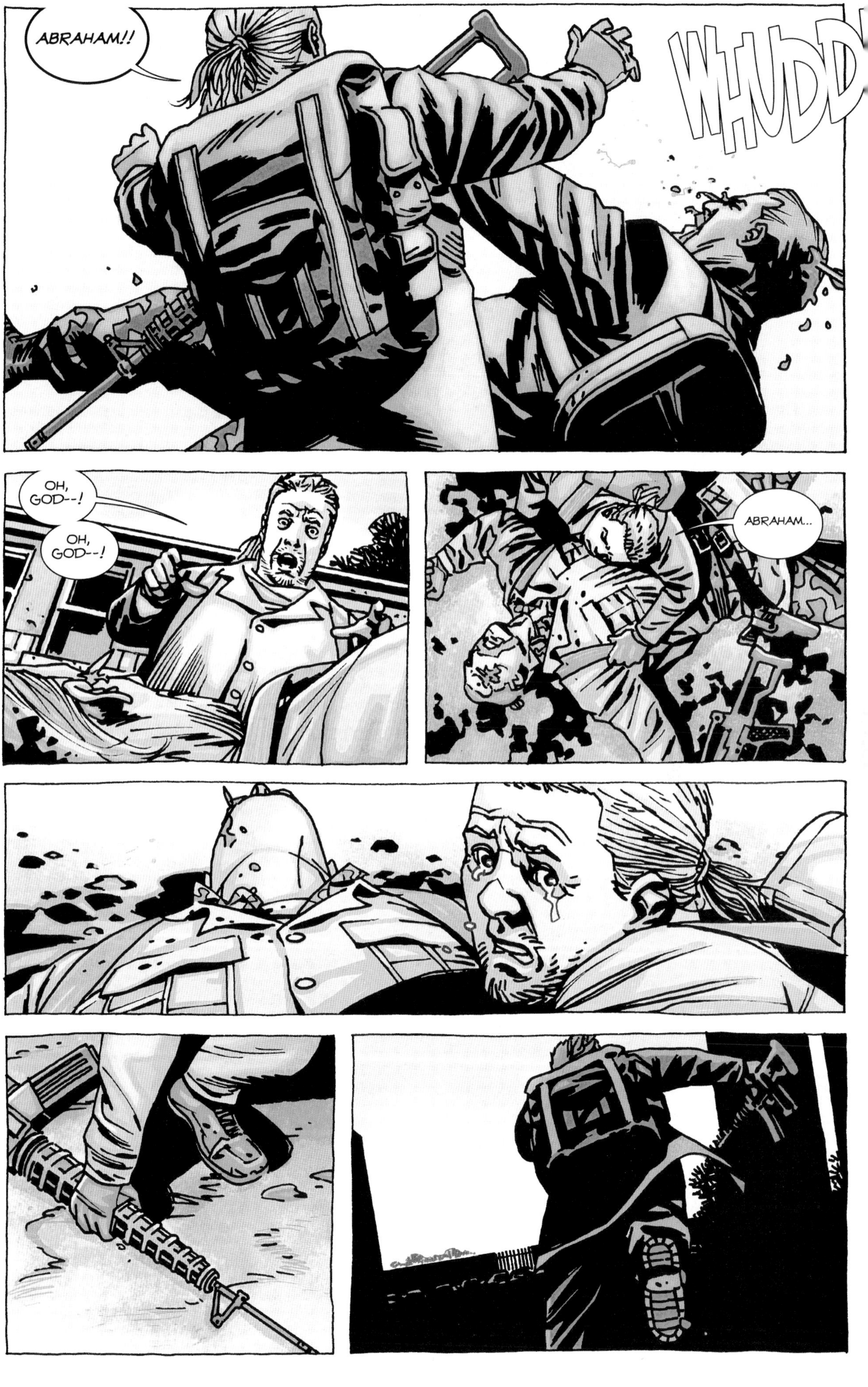
ABRAHAM!!
WHUDD
OH, GOD--!
OH, GOD--!
ABRAHAM...

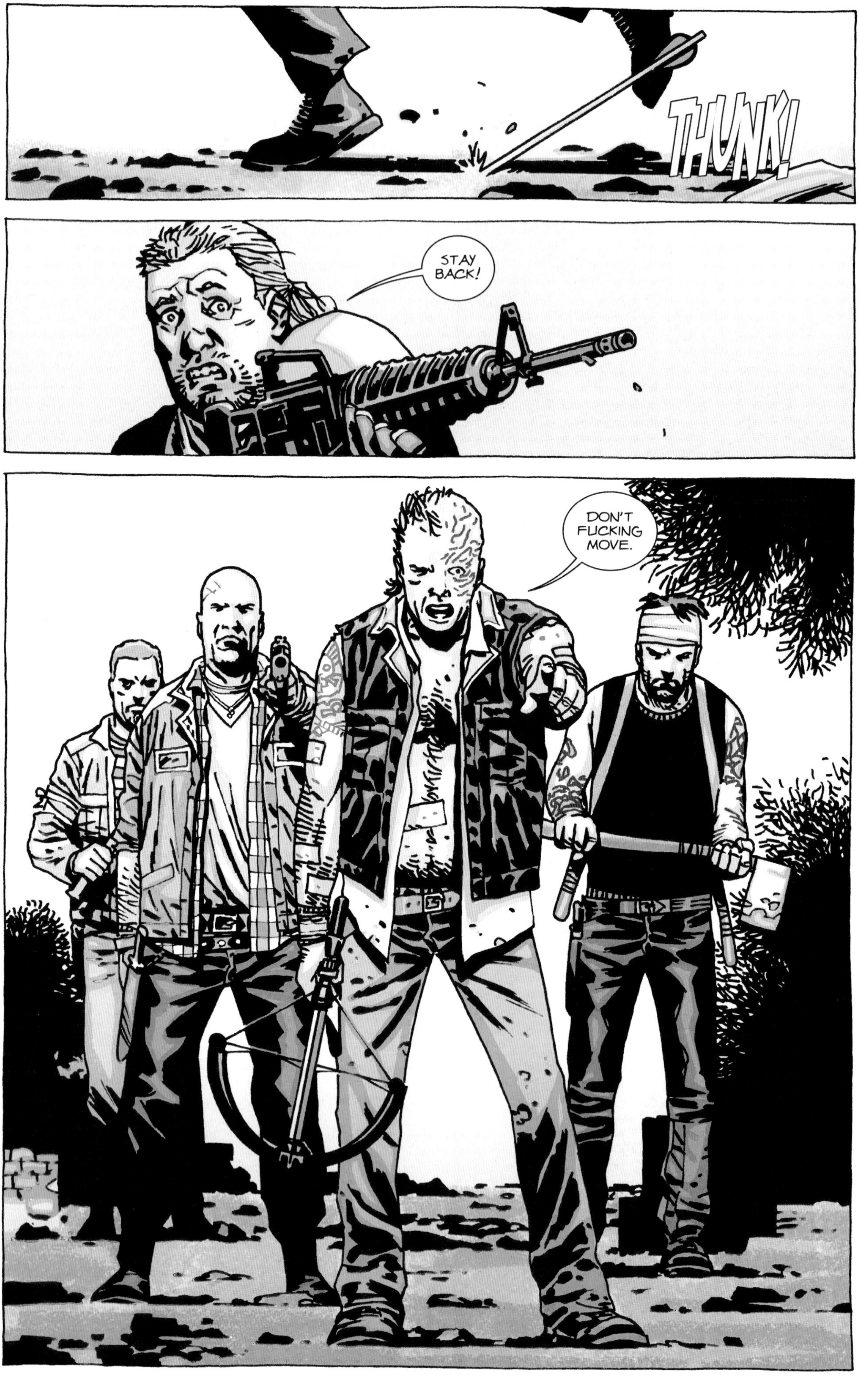
THUNK!
STAY BACK!
DON'T FUCKING MOVE.

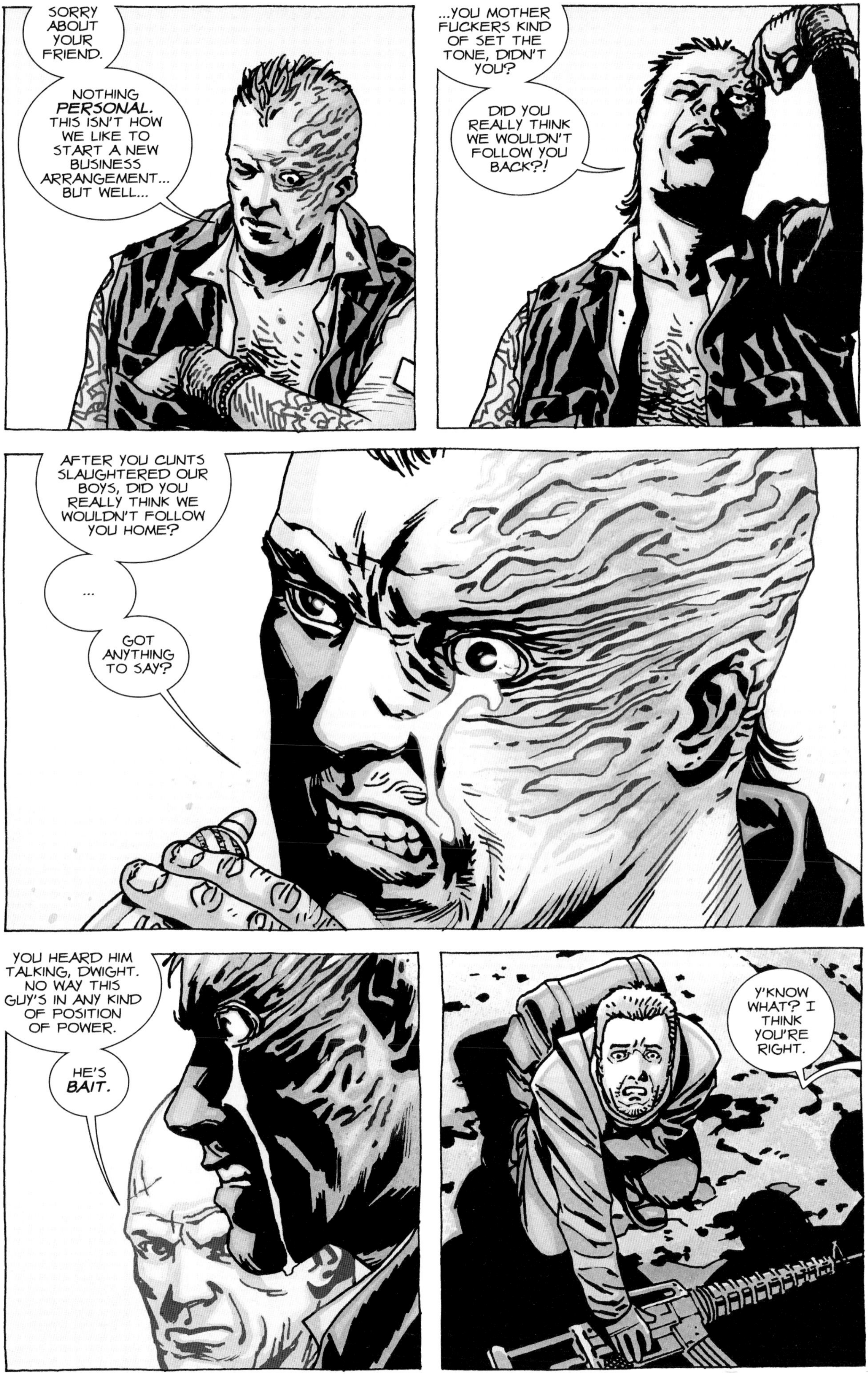
SORRY ABOUT YOUR FRIEND.
NOTHING PERSONAL. THIS ISN'T HOW WE LIKE TO START A NEW BUSINESS ARRANGEMENT... BUT WELL...
...YOU MOTHER FUCKERS KIND OF SET THE TONE, DIDN'T YOU?
DID YOU REALLY THINK WE WOULDN'T FOLLOW YOU BACK?!
AFTER YOU CUNTS SLAUGHTERED OUR BOYS, DID YOU REALLY THINK WE WOULDN'T FOLLOW YOU HOME?
...
GOT ANYTHING TO SAY?
YOU HEARD HIM TALKING, DWIGHT. NO WAY THIS GUY'S IN ANY KIND OF POSITION OF POWER.
HE'S BAIT.
Y'KNOW WHAT? I THINK YOU'RE RIGHT.

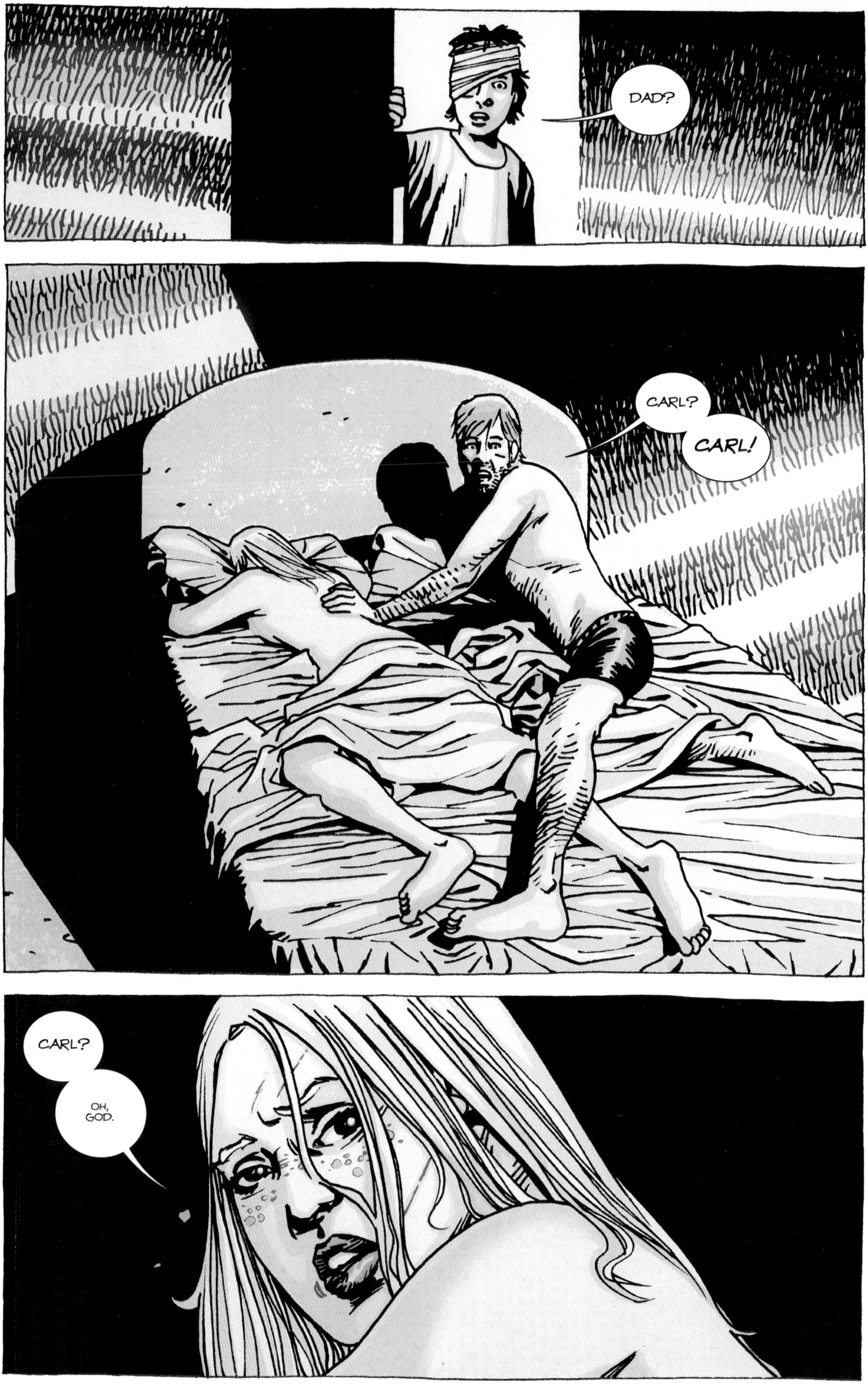
DAD?
CARL?
CARL!
CARL?
OH, GOD.

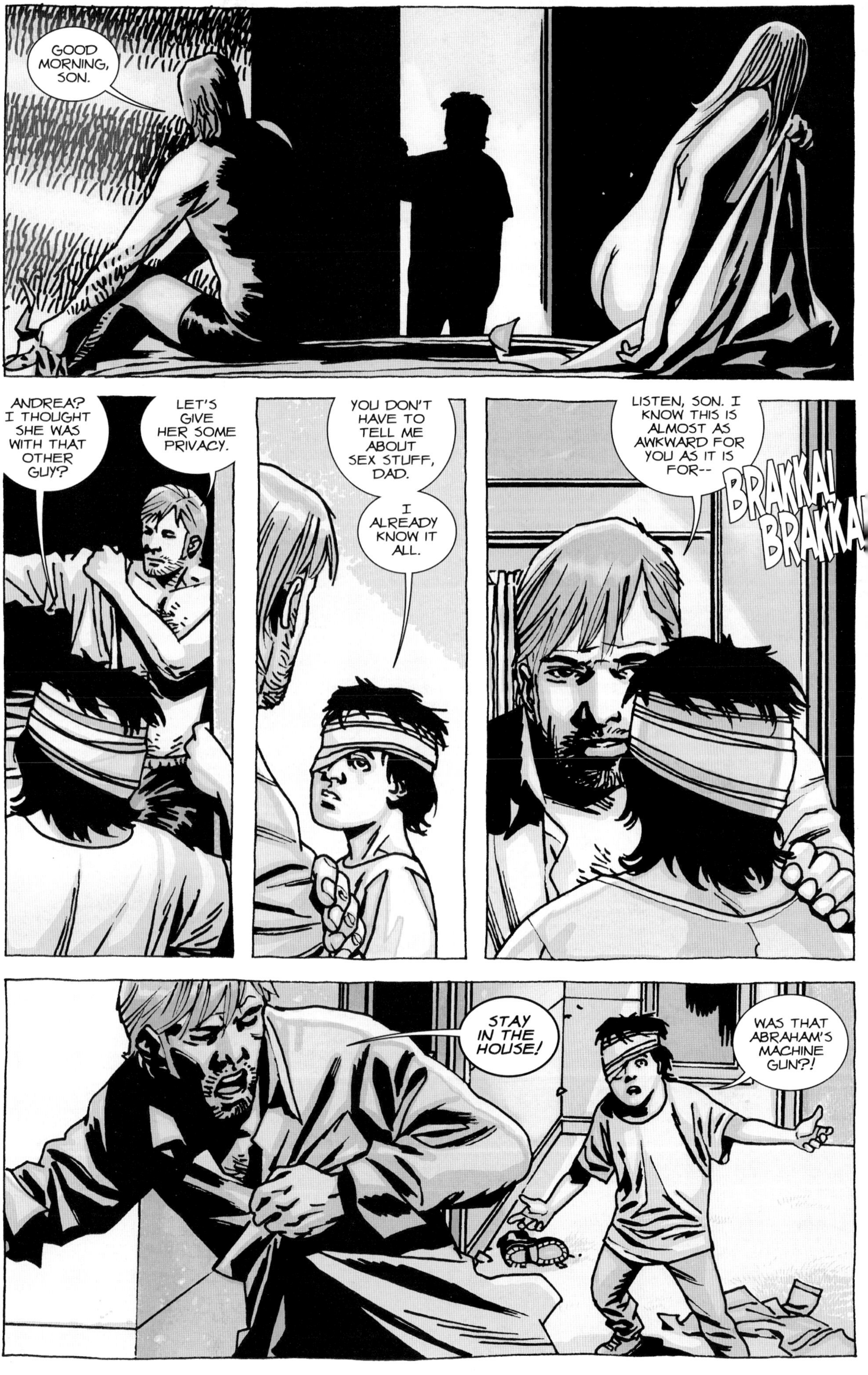
GOOD MORNING, SON.
ANDREA? I THOUGHT SHE WAS WITH THAT OTHER GUY?
LET'S GIVE HER SOME PRIVACY.
YOU DON'T HAVE TO TELL ME ABOUT SEX STUFF, DAD.
I ALREADY KNOW IT ALL.
LISTEN, SON. I KNOW THIS IS ALMOST AS AWKWARD FOR YOU AS IT IS FOR--
BRAKKA! BRAKKA!
STAY IN THE HOUSE!
WAS THAT ABRAHAM'S MACHINE GUN?!

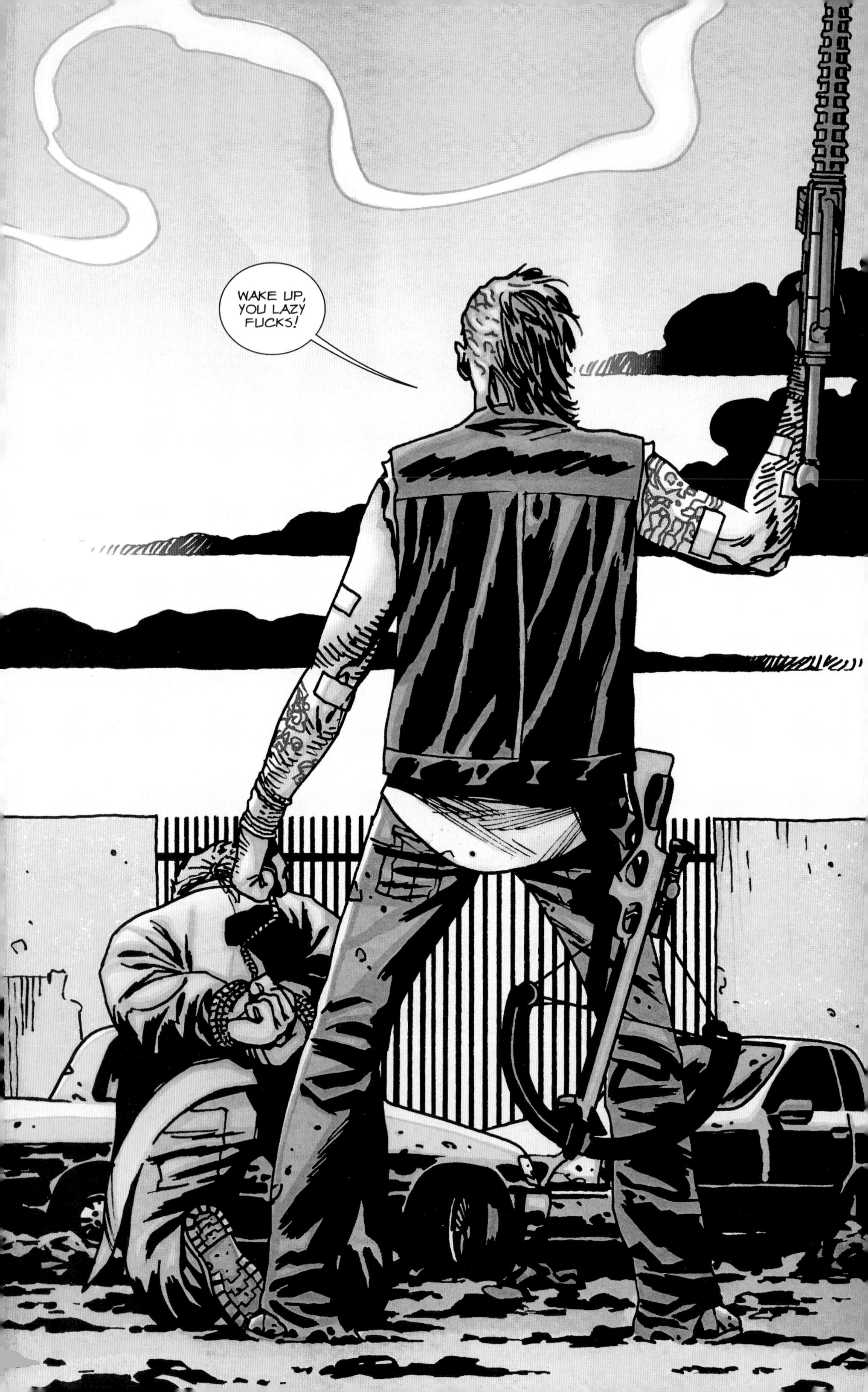
WAKE UP, YOU LAZY FUCKS!

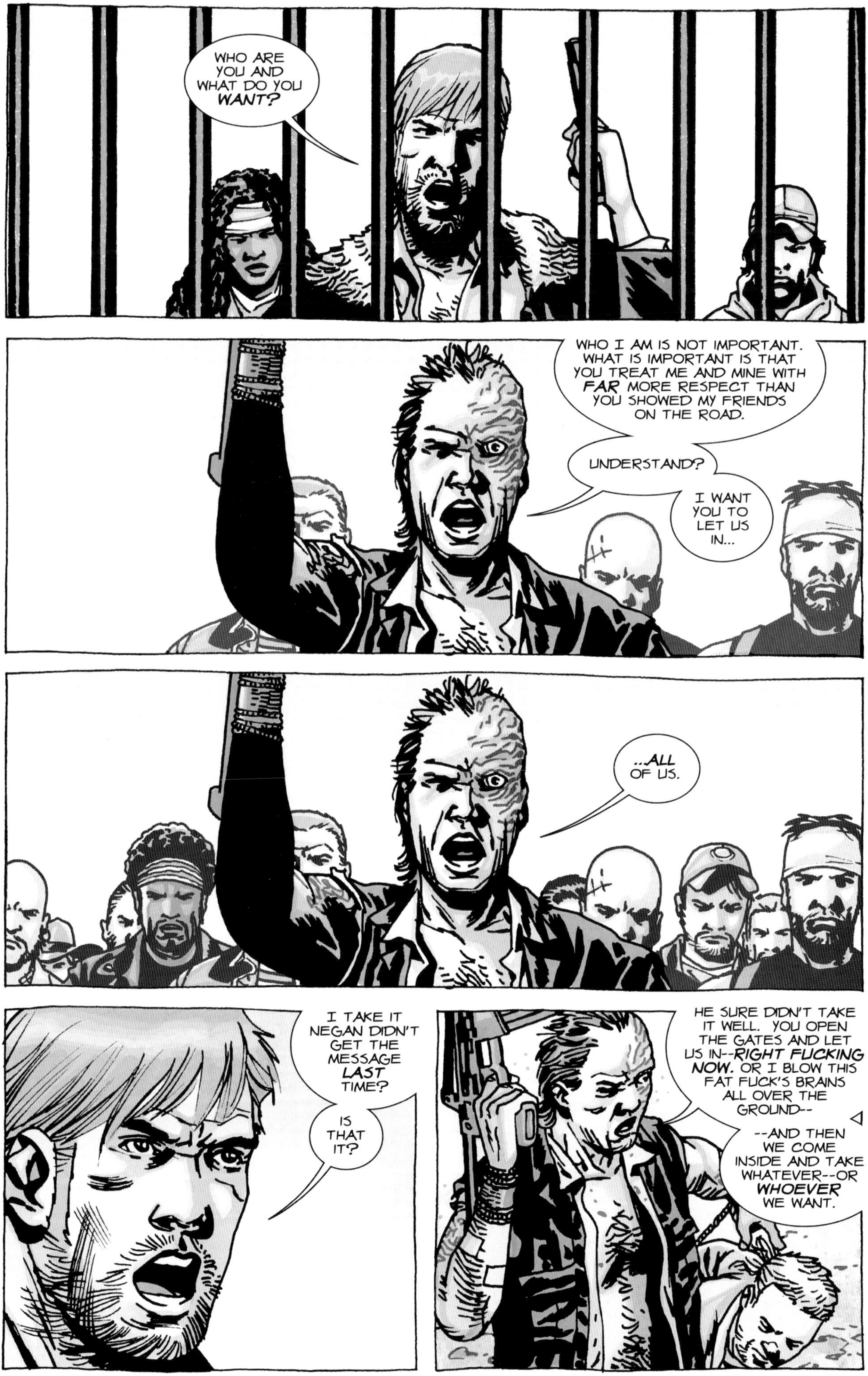
WHO ARE YOU AND WHAT DO YOU *WANT?*
WHO I AM IS NOT IMPORTANT. WHAT IS IMPORTANT IS THAT YOU TREAT ME AND MINE WITH *FAR* MORE RESPECT THAN YOU SHOWED MY FRIENDS ON THE ROAD.
UNDERSTAND?
I WANT YOU TO LET US IN...
...*ALL* OF US.
I TAKE IT NEGAN DIDN'T GET THE MESSAGE *LAST* TIME?
IS THAT IT?
HE SURE DIDN'T TAKE IT WELL. YOU OPEN THE GATES AND LET US IN--*RIGHT FUCKING NOW.* OR I BLOW THIS FAT FUCK'S BRAINS ALL OVER THE GROUND--
--AND THEN WE COME INSIDE AND TAKE WHATEVER--OR *WHOEVER* WE WANT.

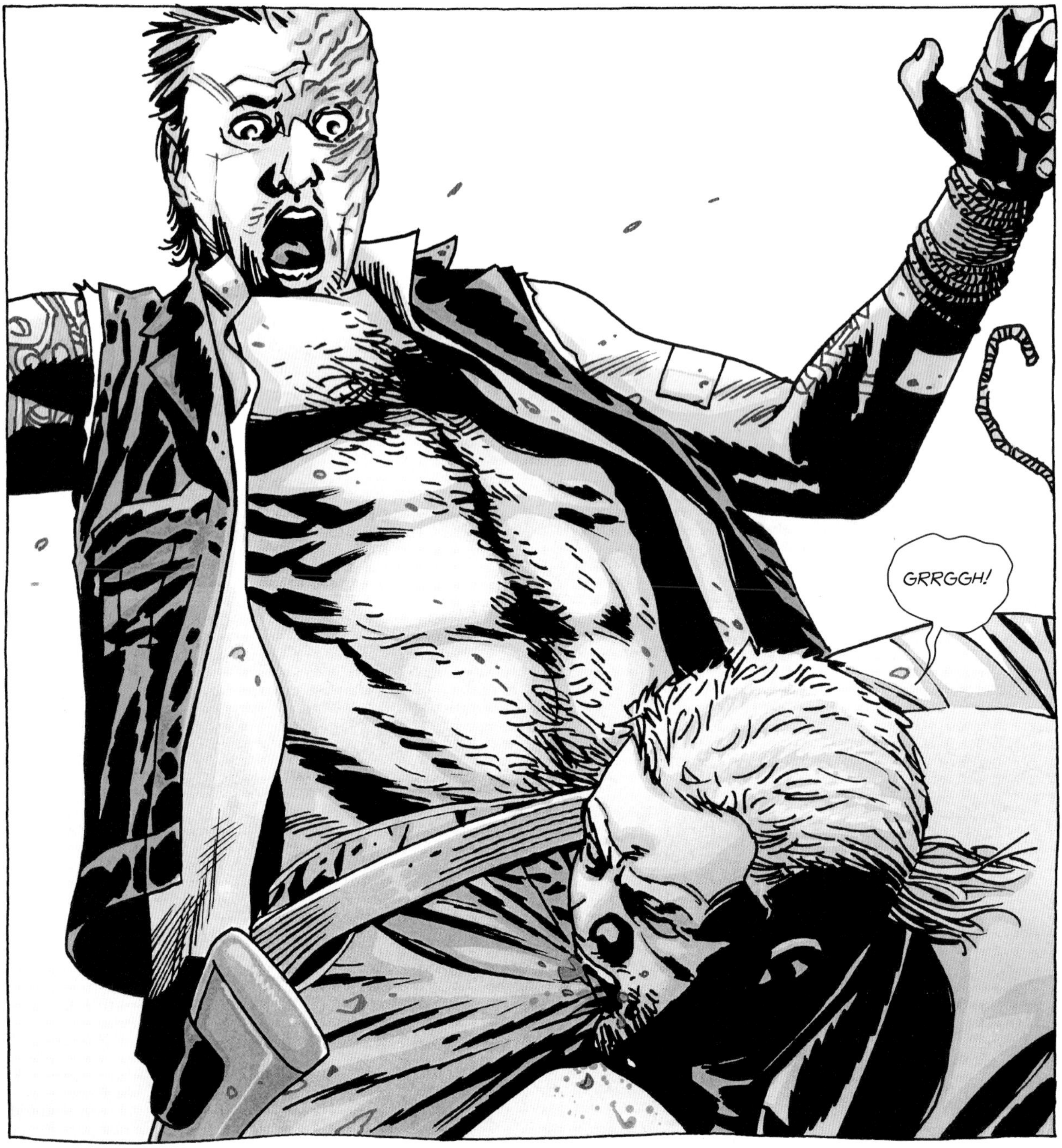
GRRGGH!

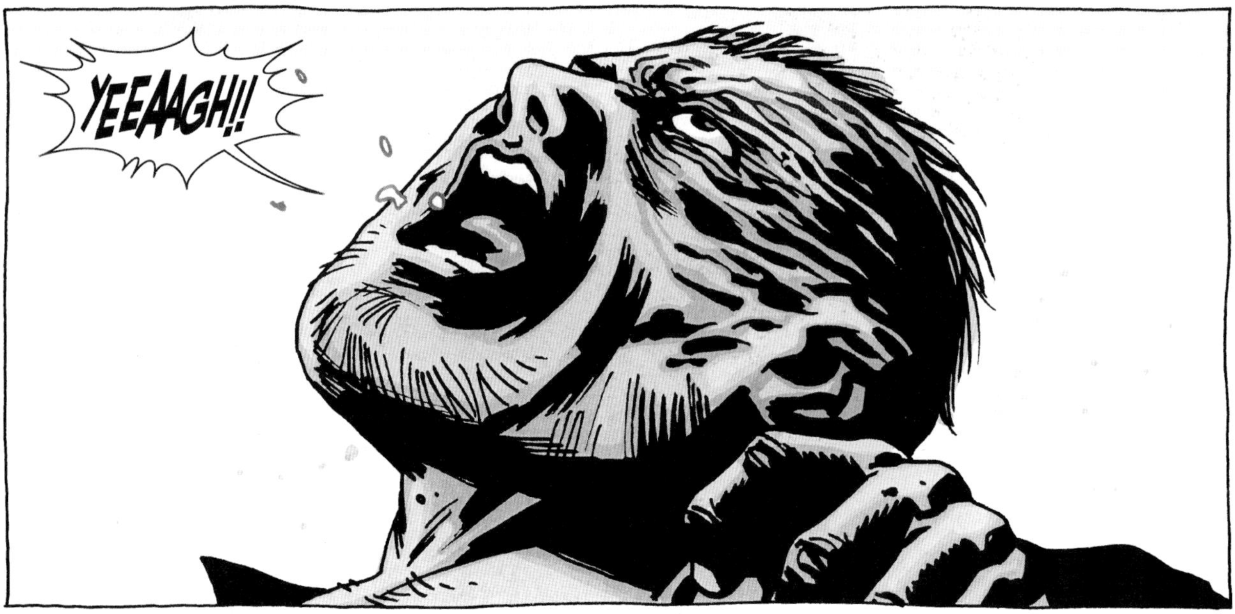
YEEAAGH!!

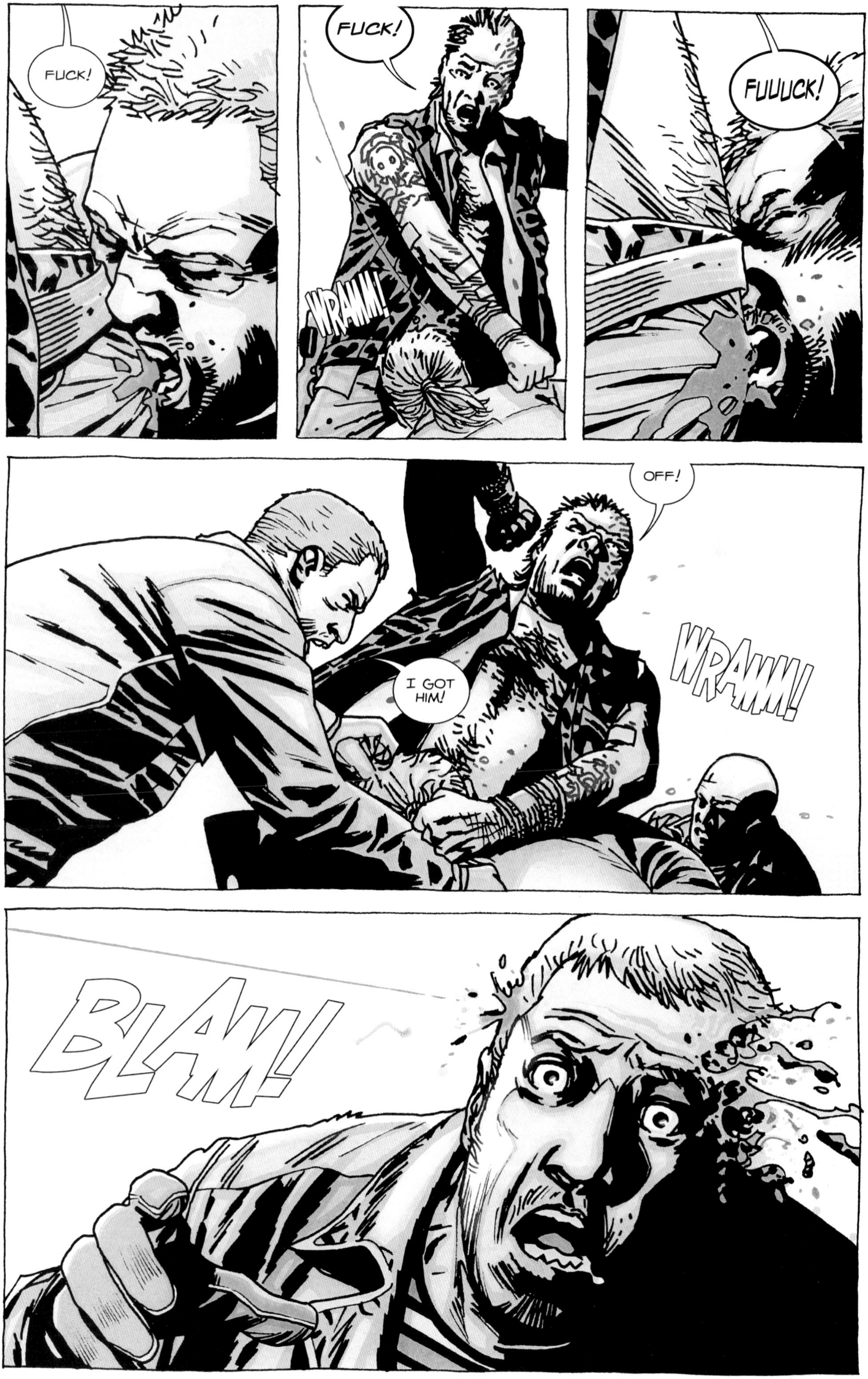

FUCK!
FUCK!
WRAMM!
FUUUCK!
OFF!
I GOT HIM!
WRAMM!
BLAM!

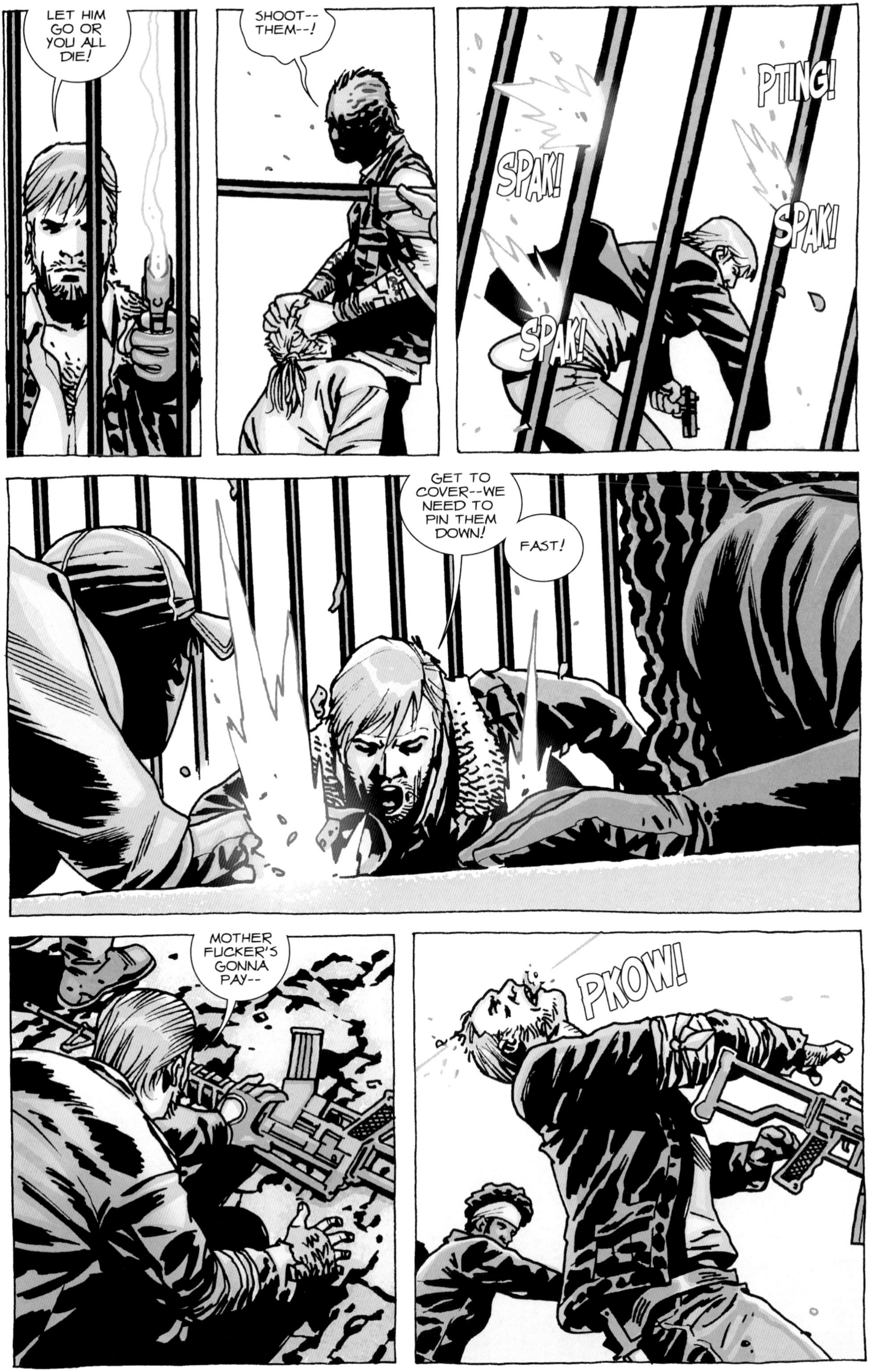
LET HIM GO OR YOU ALL DIE!
SHOOT-- THEM--!
PTING!
SPAK!
SPAK!
SPAK!
GET TO COVER--WE NEED TO PIN THEM DOWN!
FAST!
MOTHER FUCKER'S GONNA PAY--
PKOW!

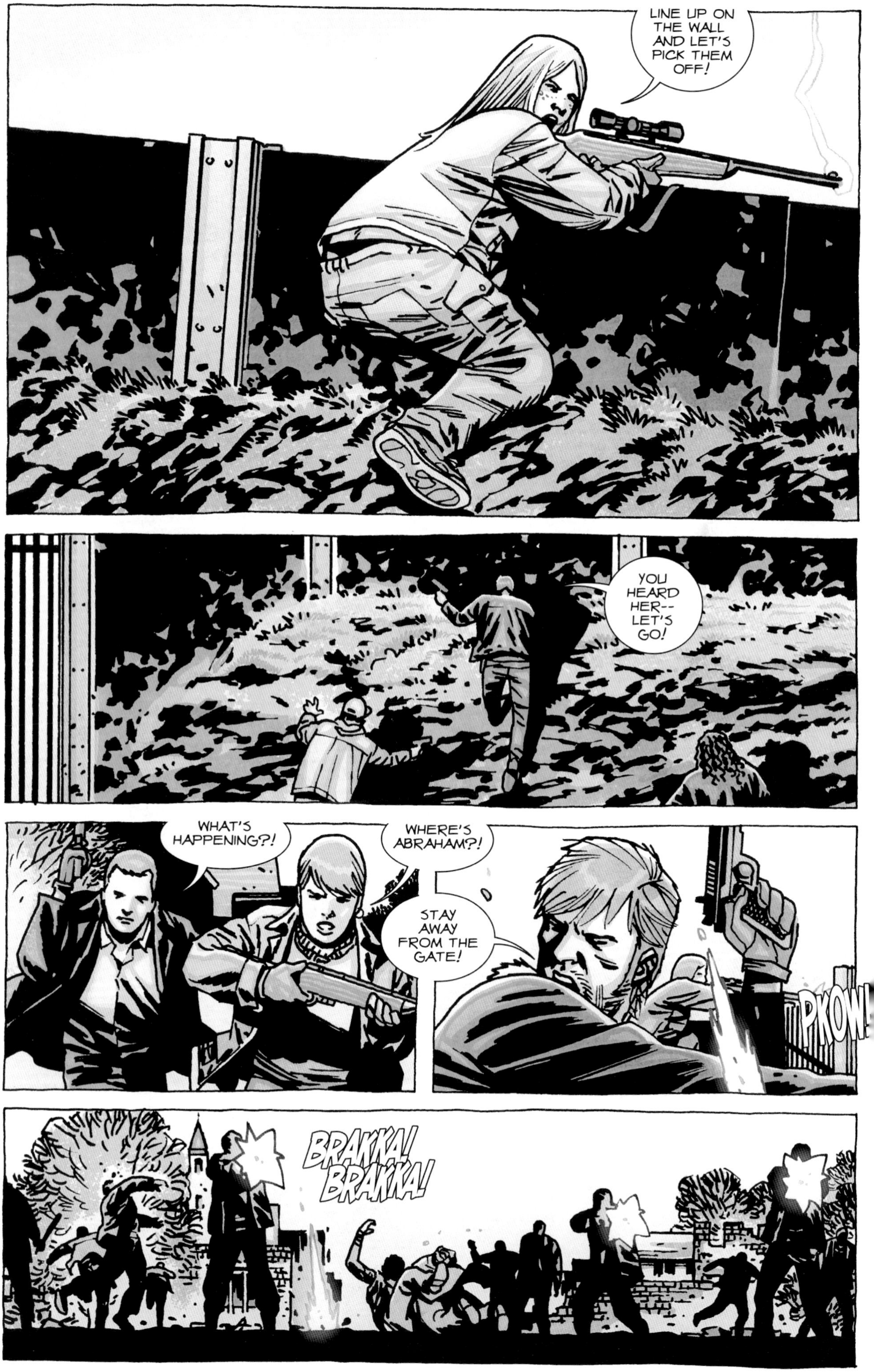
LINE UP ON THE WALL AND LET'S PICK THEM OFF!
YOU HEARD HER-- LET'S GO!
WHAT'S HAPPENING?!
WHERE'S ABRAHAM?!
STAY AWAY FROM THE GATE!
PKOW!
BRAKKA! BRAKKA!

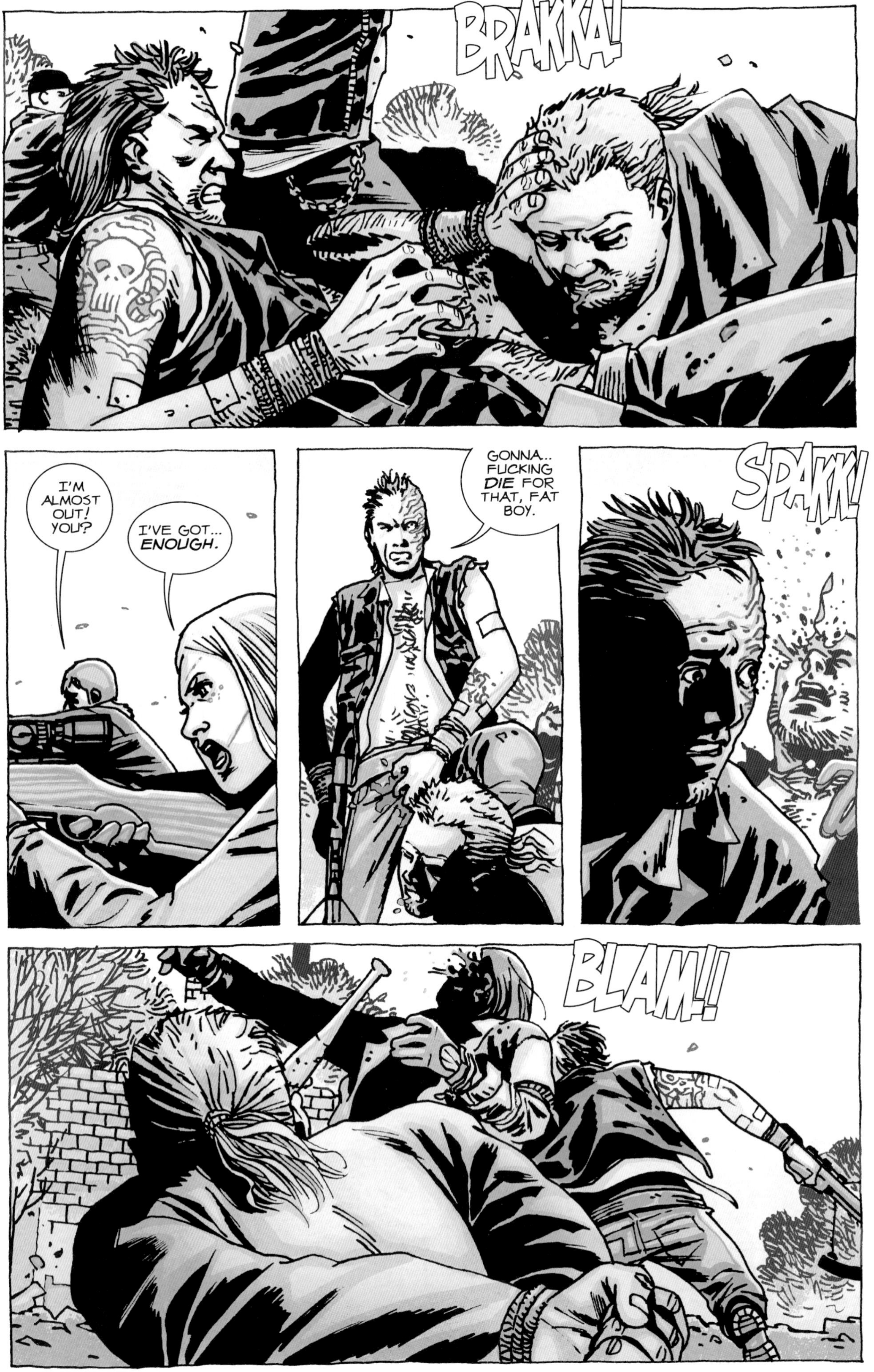
BRAKKA!
I'M ALMOST OUT! YOU?
I'VE GOT... ENOUGH.
GONNA.. FUCKING DIE FOR THAT, FAT BOY.
SPAKK!
BLAM!!

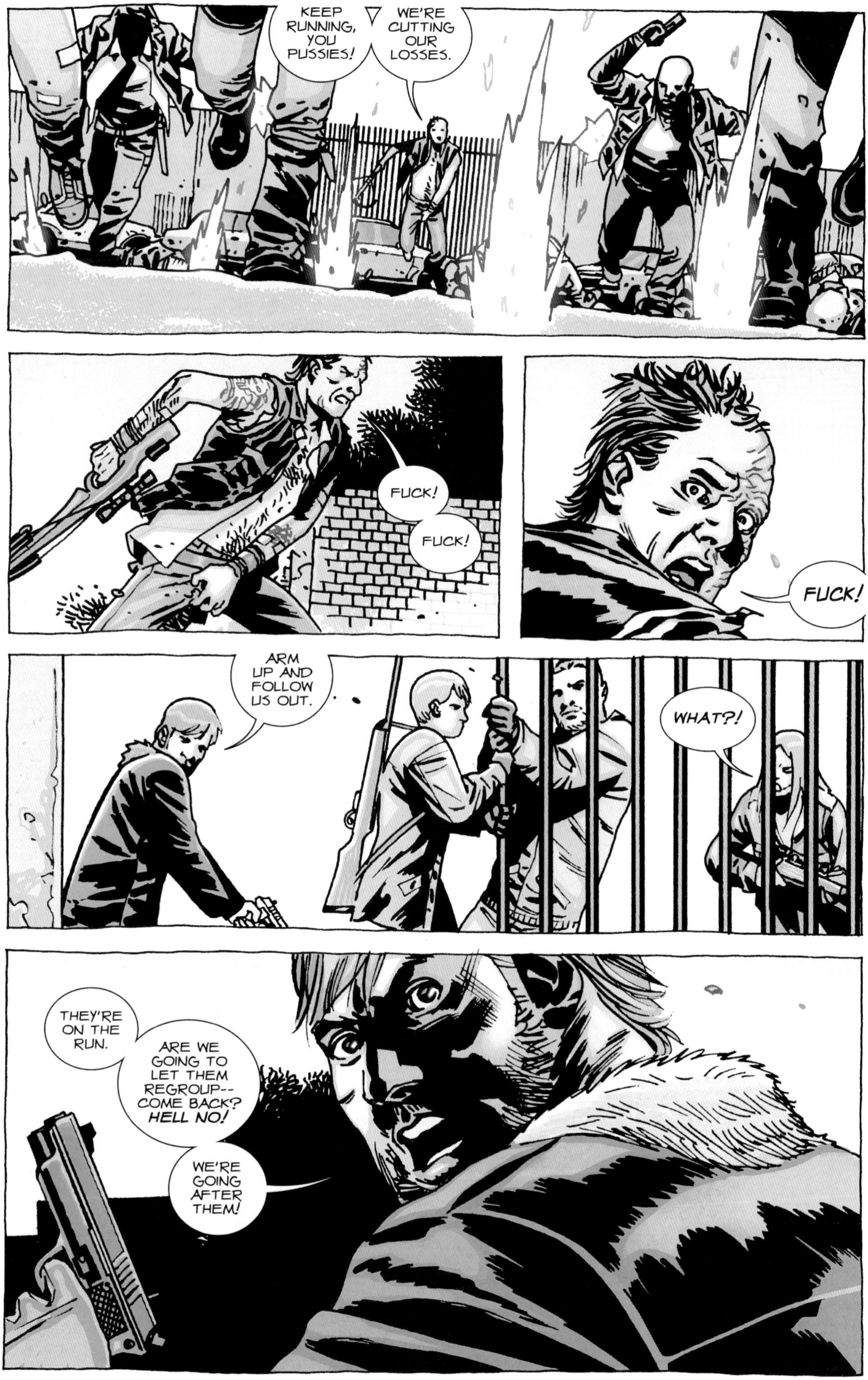
KEEP RUNNING, YOU PUSSIES!
WE'RE CUTTING OUR LOSSES.
FUCK!
FUCK!
FUCK!
ARM UP AND FOLLOW US OUT.
WHAT?!
THEY'RE ON THE RUN.
ARE WE GOING TO LET THEM REGROUP-- COME BACK? HELL NO!
WE'RE GOING AFTER THEM!

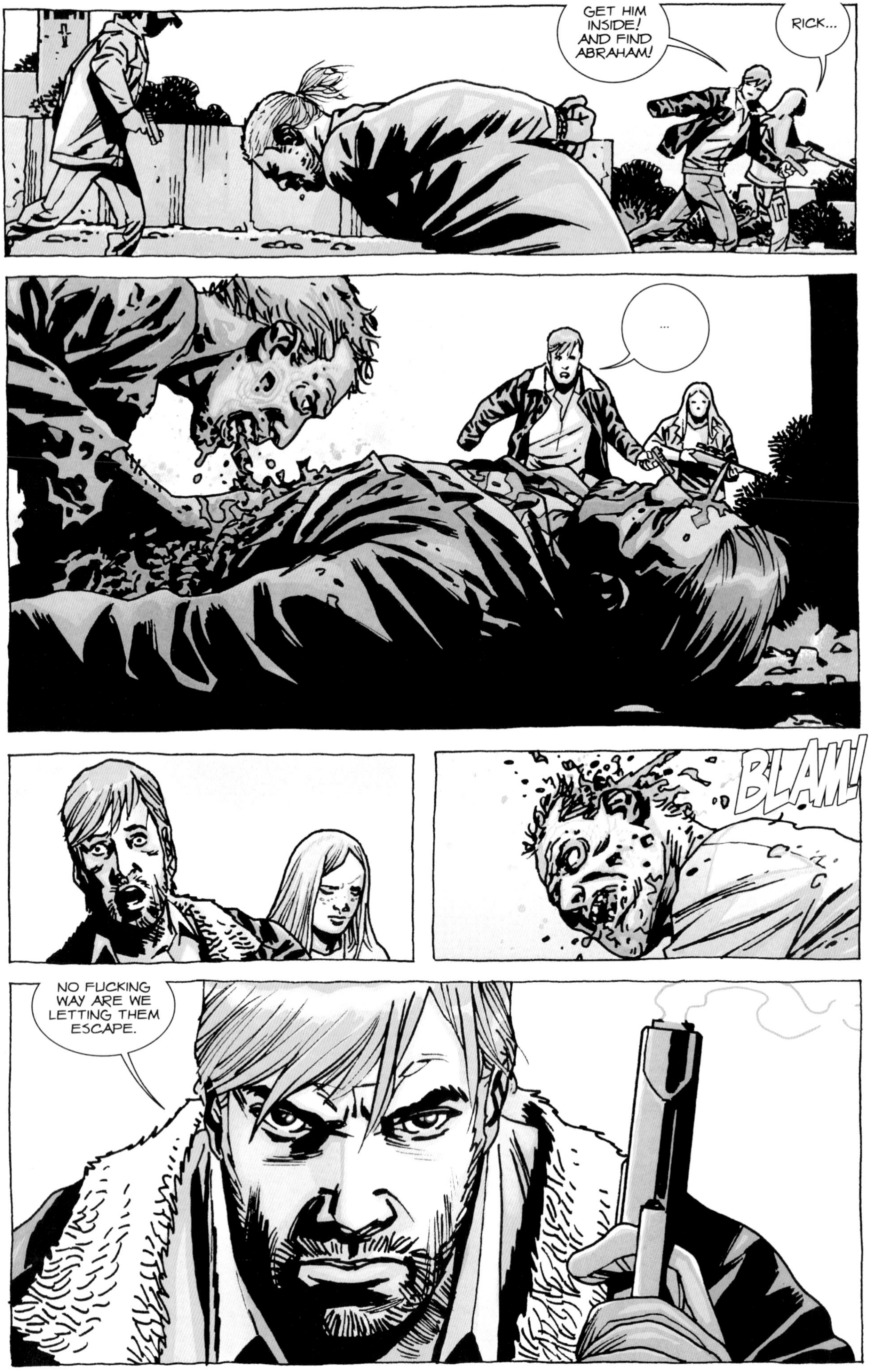
GET HIM INSIDE! AND FIND ABRAHAM!
RICK...
...
BLAM!
NO FUCKING WAY ARE WE LETTING THEM ESCAPE.

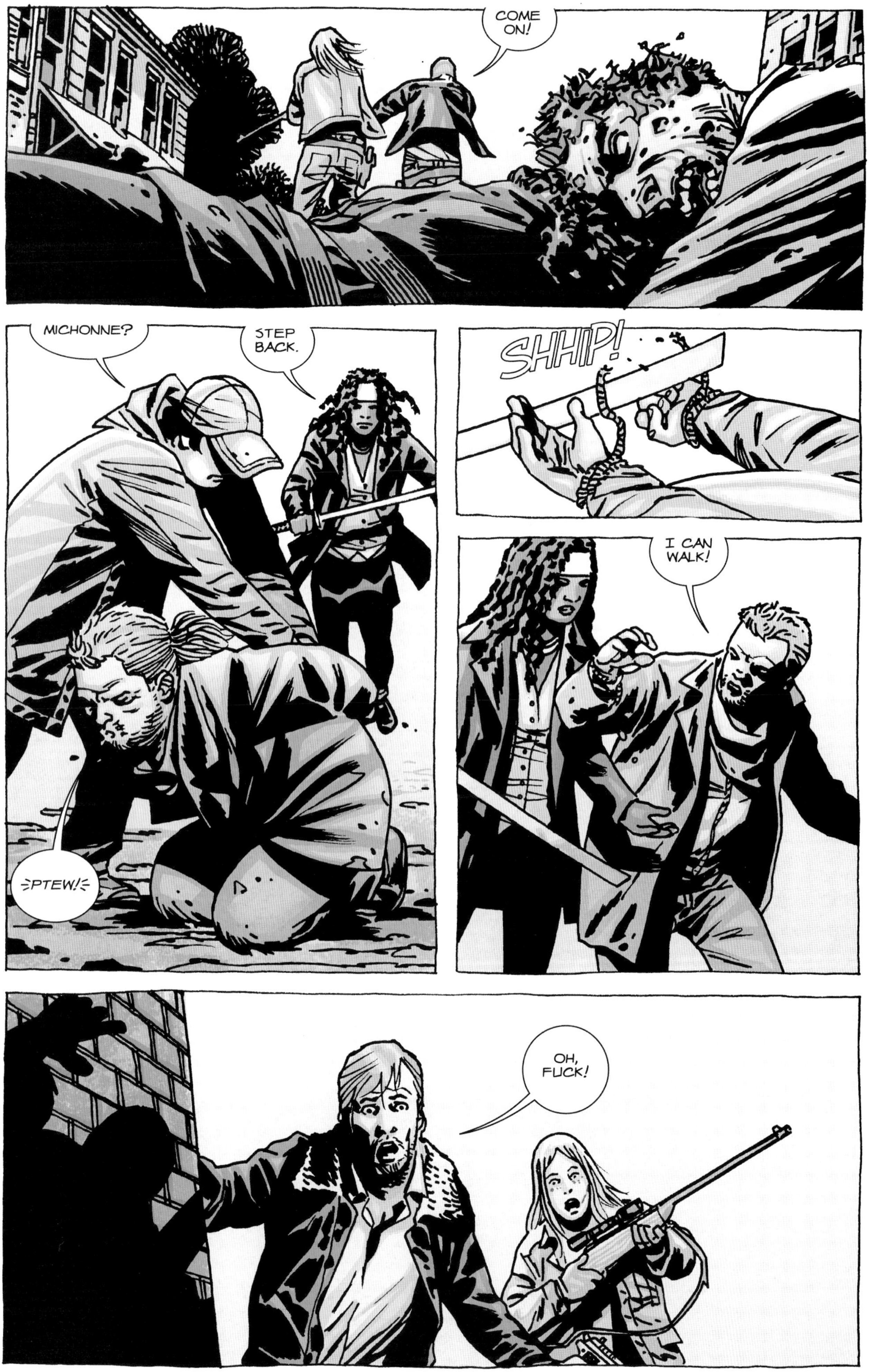
COME ON!
MICHONNE?
STEP BACK.
PTEW!
SHHIP!
I CAN WALK!
OH, FUCK!

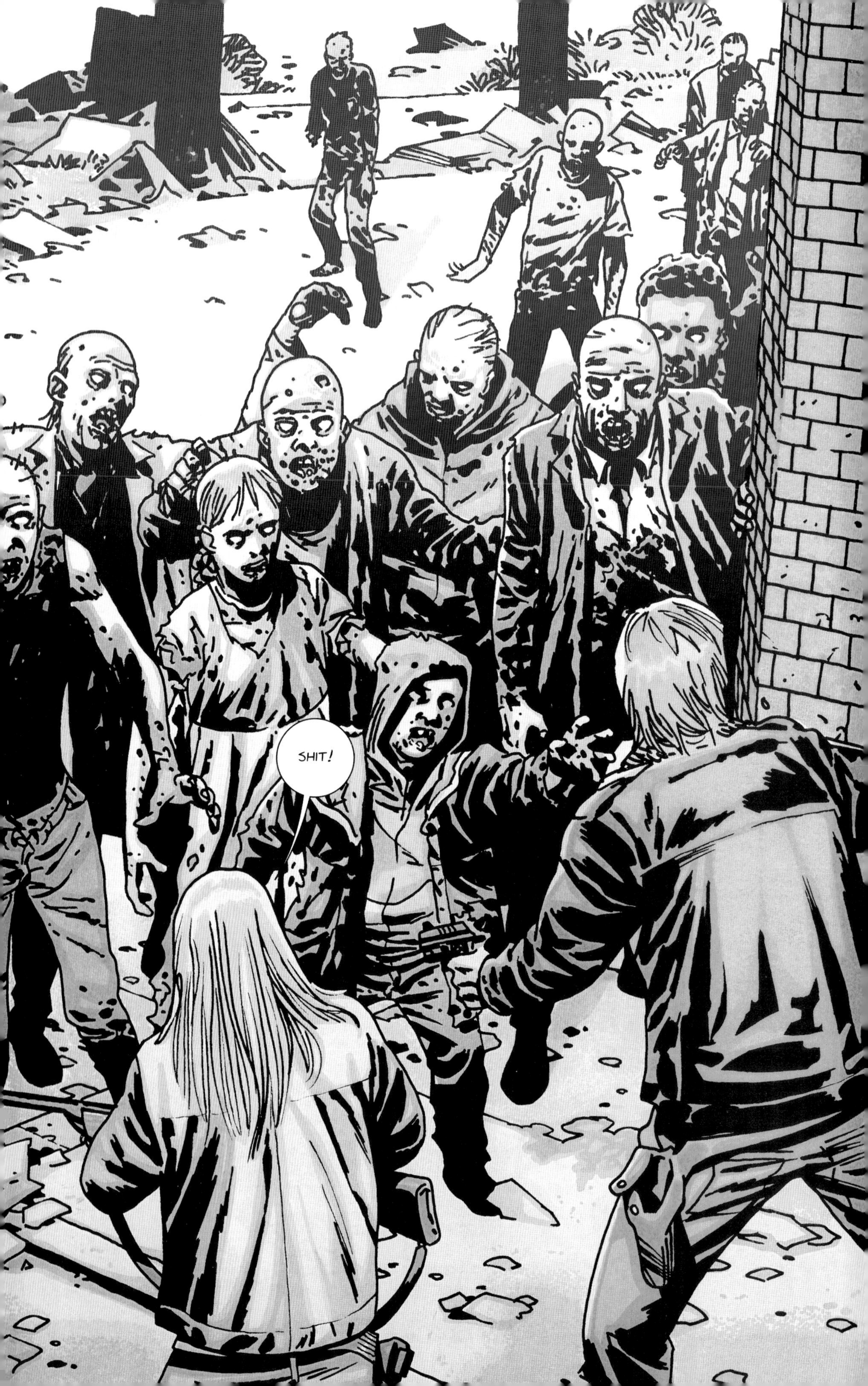
SHIT!

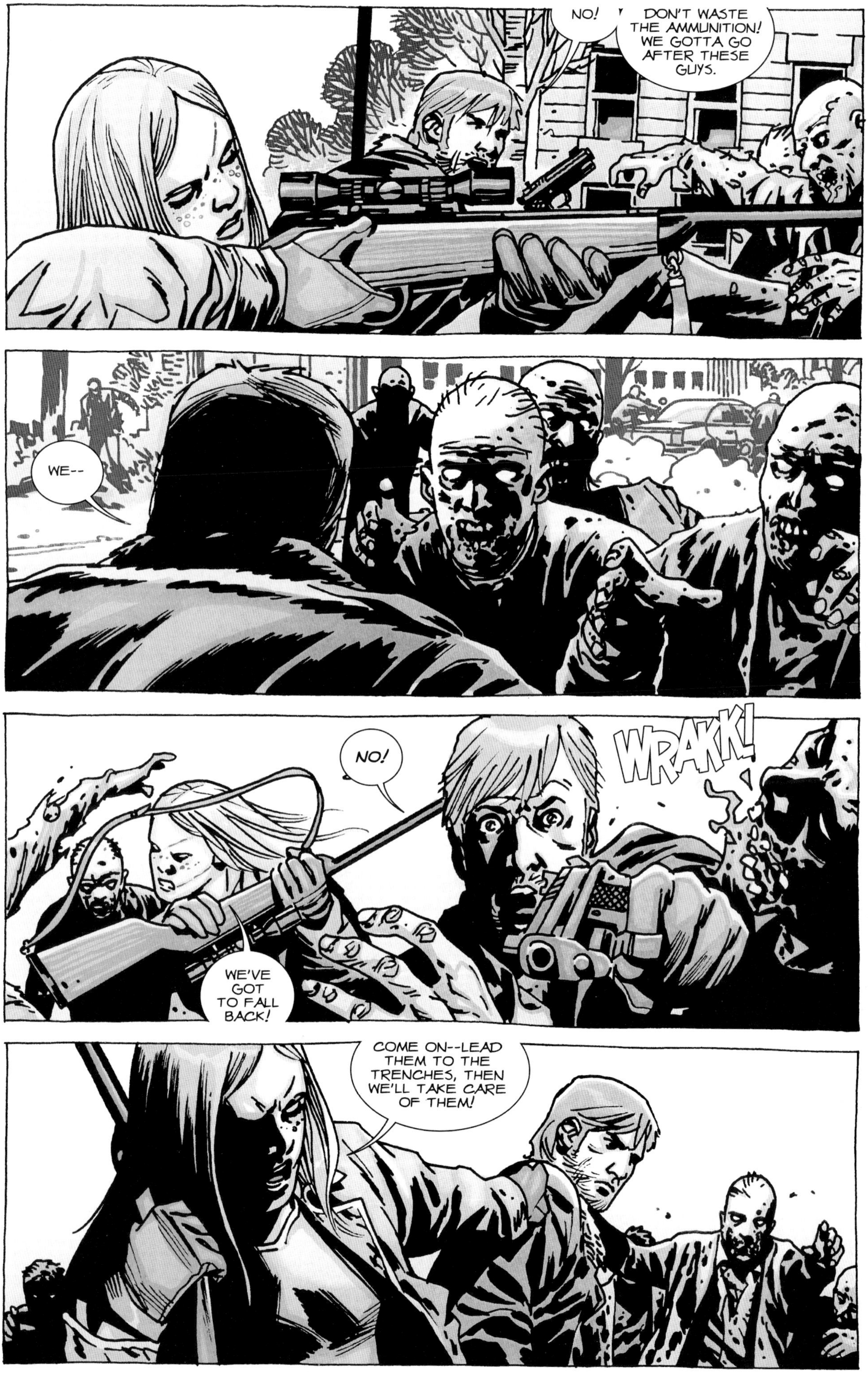
NO!
DON'T WASTE THE AMMUNITION! WE GOTTA GO AFTER THESE GUYS.
WE--
NO!
WRAKK!
WE'VE GOT TO FALL BACK!
COME ON--LEAD THEM TO THE TRENCHES, THEN WE'LL TAKE CARE OF THEM!

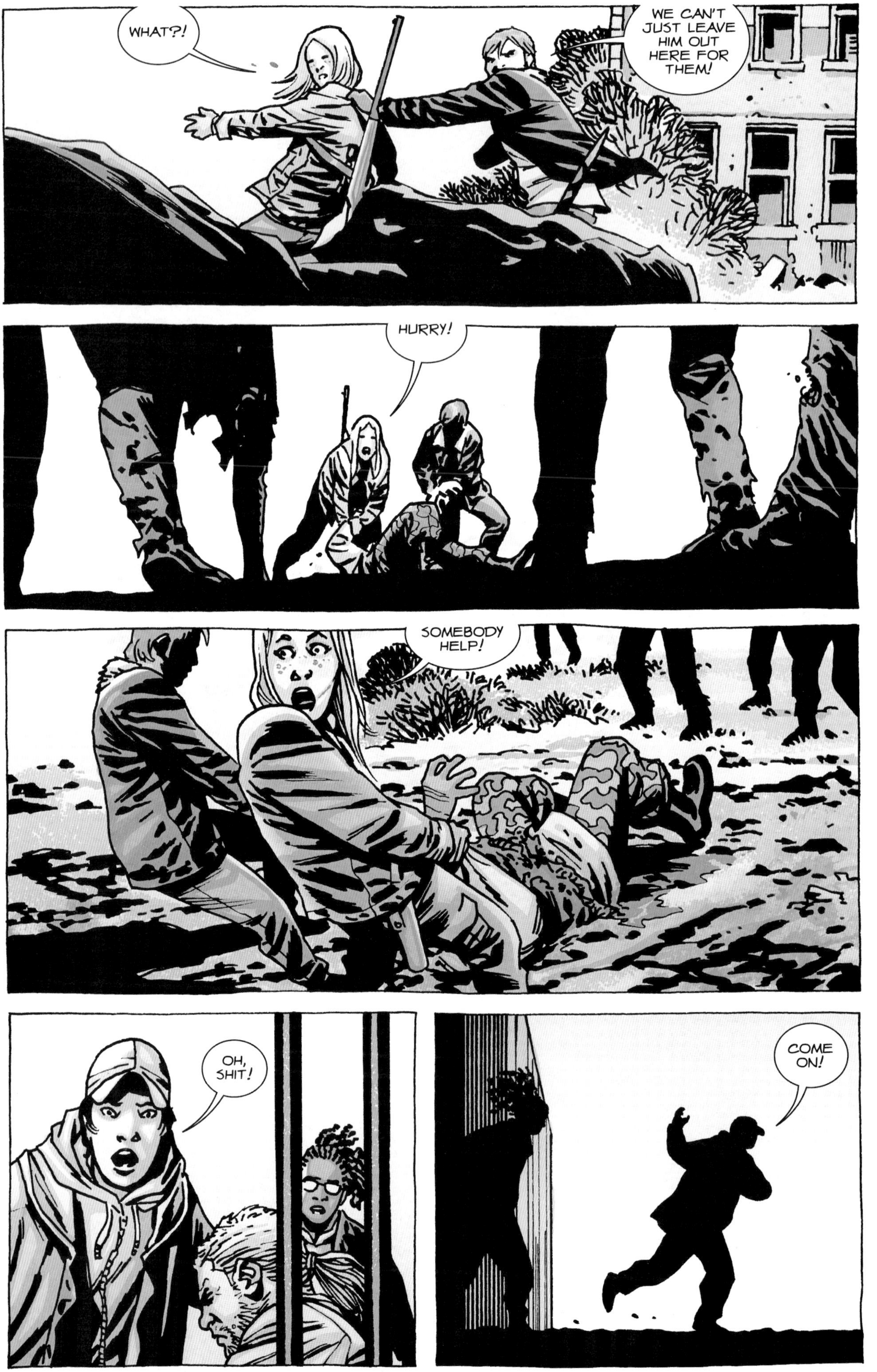
WHAT?!
WE CAN'T JUST LEAVE HIM OUT HERE FOR THEM!
HURRY!
SOMEBODY HELP!
OH, SHIT!
COME ON!

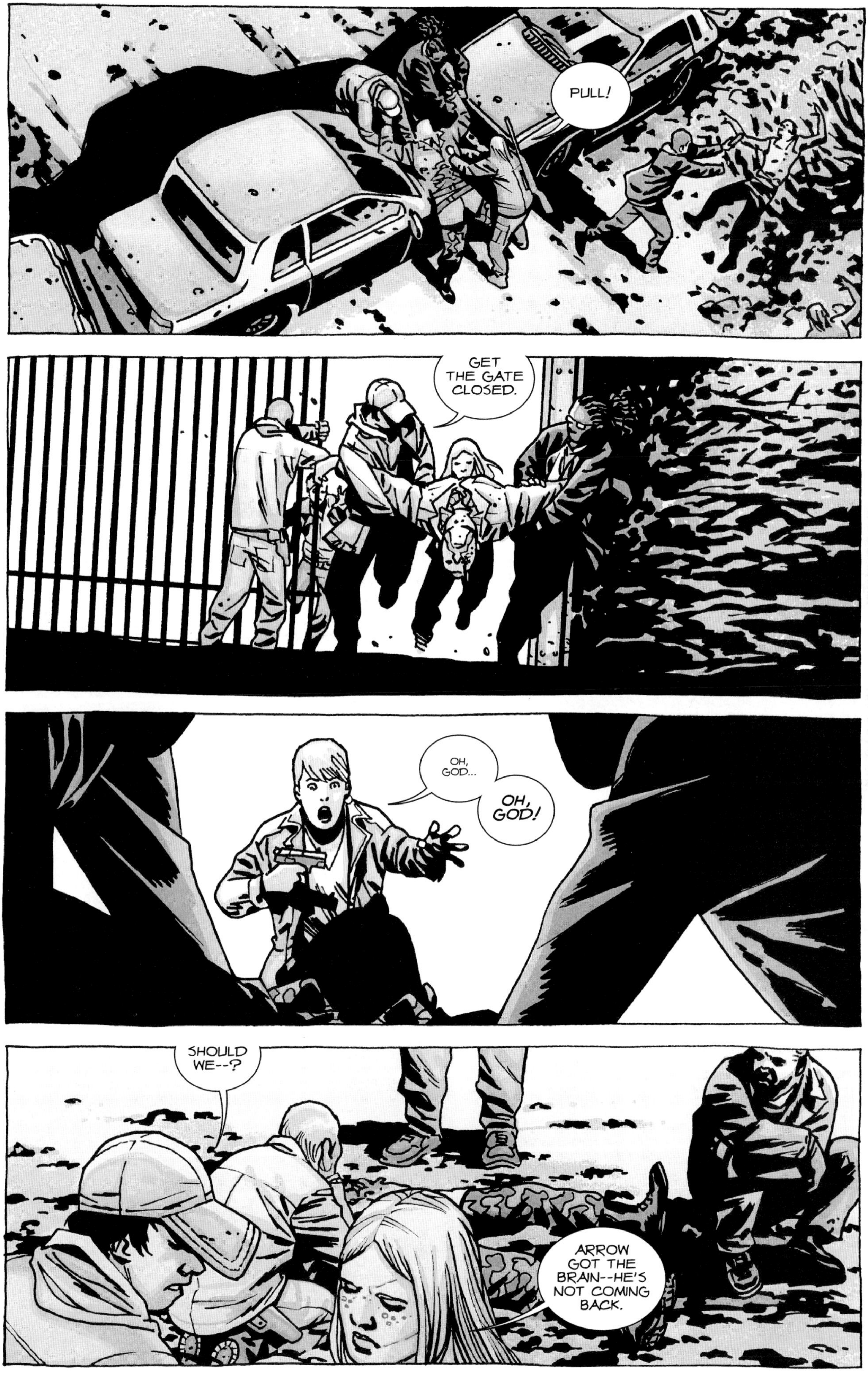
PULL!
GET THE GATE CLOSED.
OH, GOD...
OH, GOD!
SHOULD WE--?
ARROW GOT THE BRAIN--HE'S NOT COMING BACK.

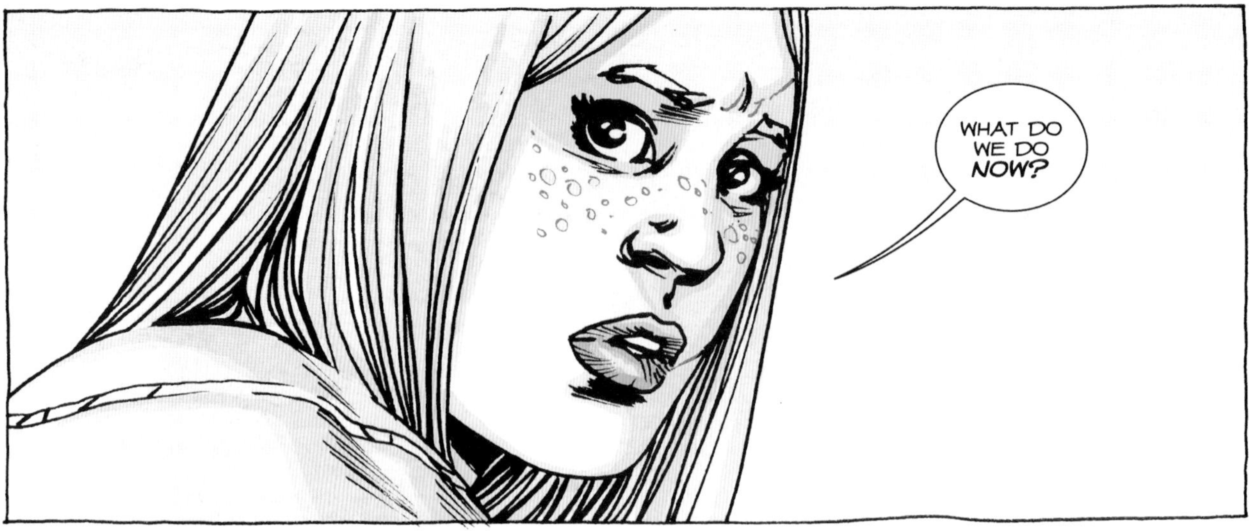
WHAT DO WE DO NOW?

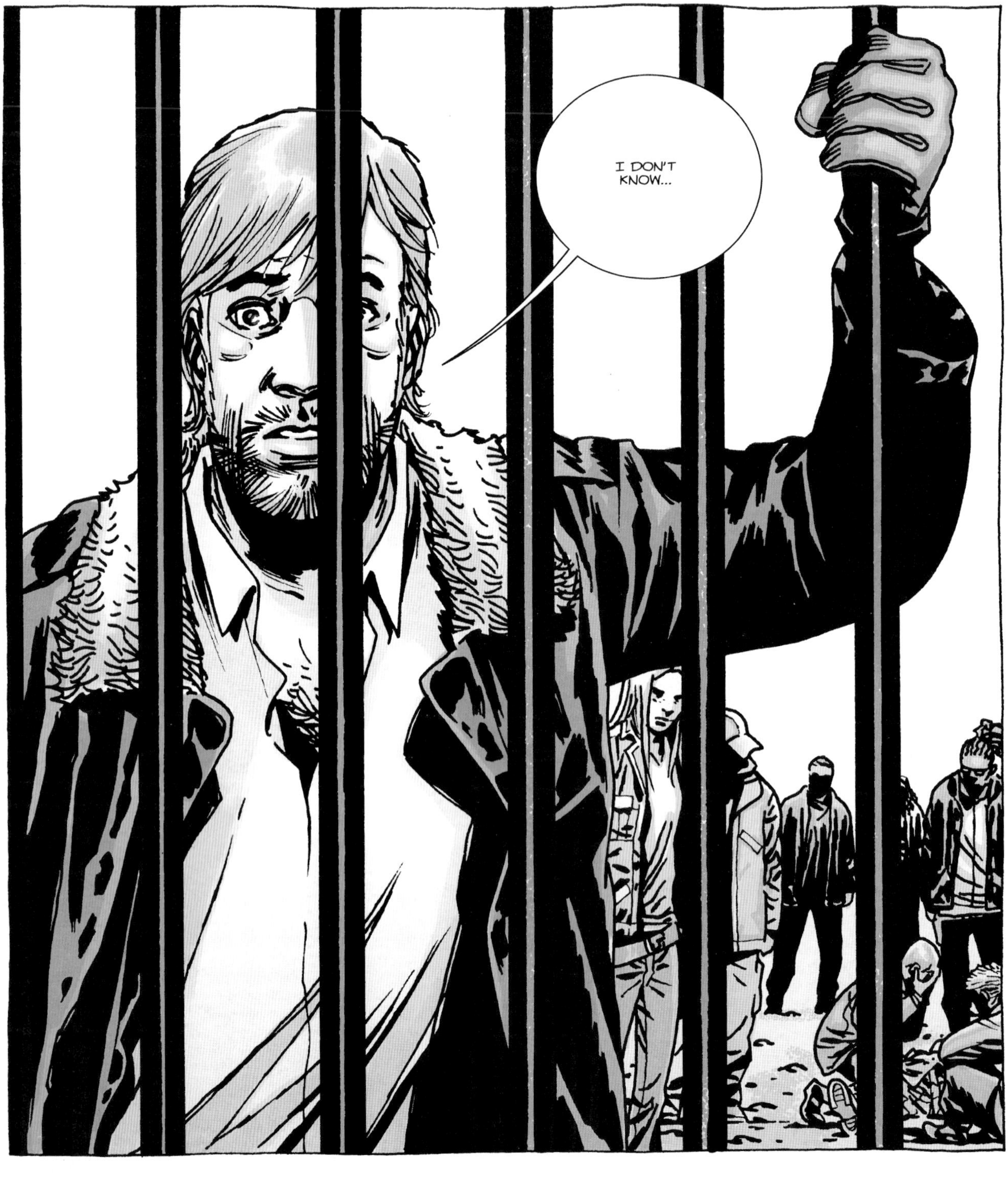
I DON'T KNOW...

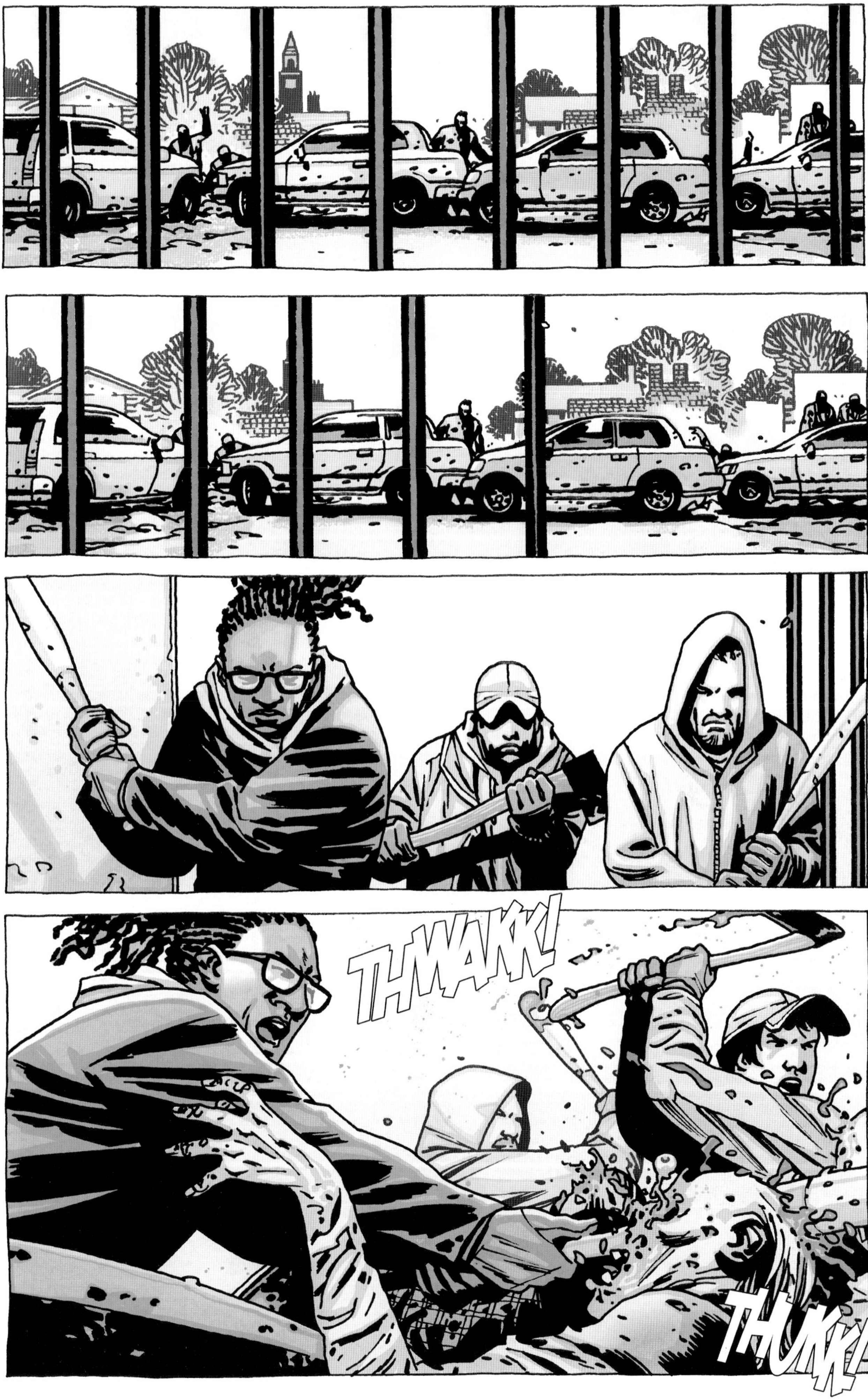
THWAKK!
THUNK!

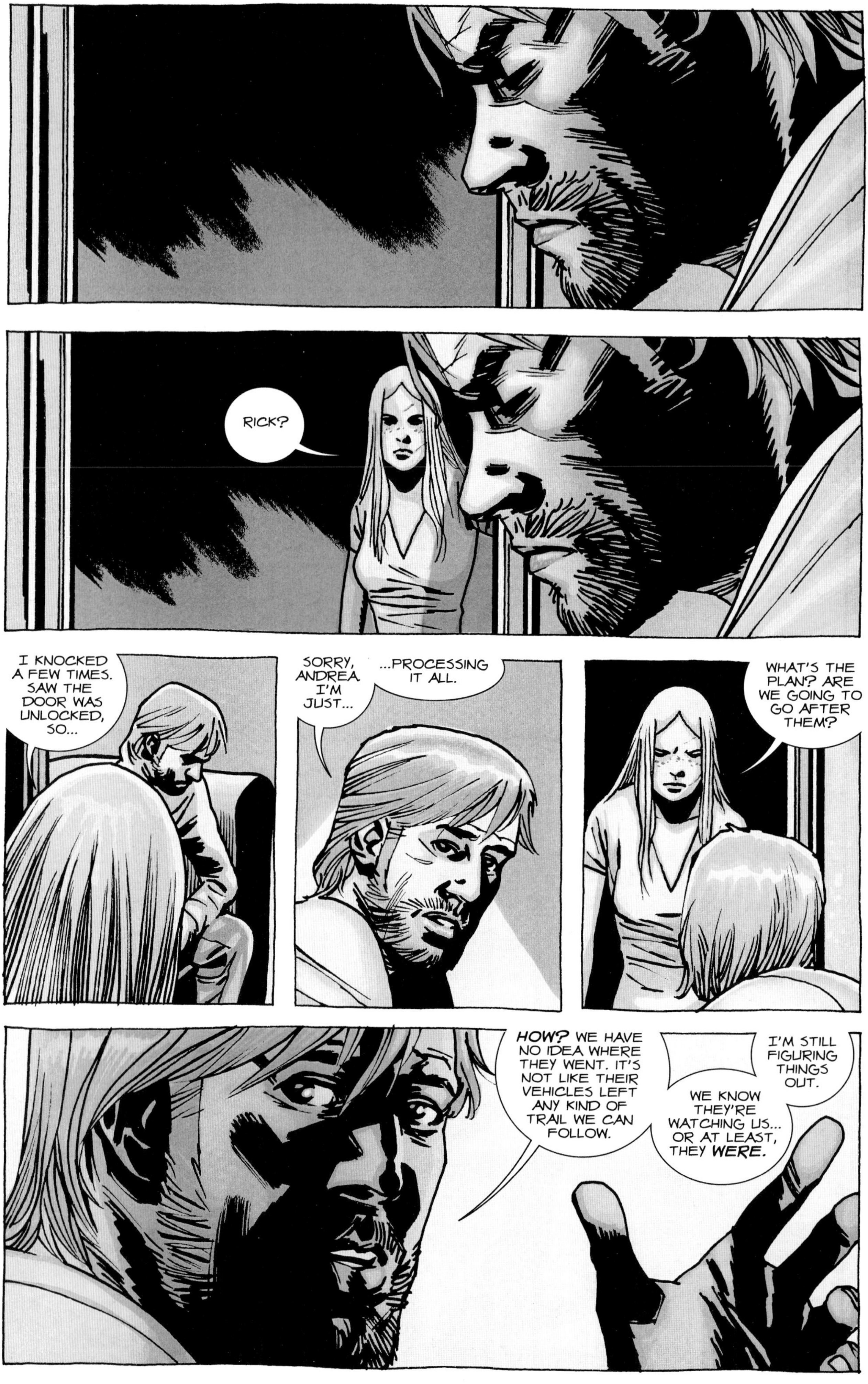
RICK?
I KNOCKED A FEW TIMES. SAW THE DOOR WAS UNLOCKED, SO...
SORRY, ANDREA I'M JUST...
...PROCESSING IT ALL.
WHAT'S THE PLAN? ARE WE GOING TO GO AFTER THEM?
HOW? WE HAVE NO IDEA WHERE THEY WENT. IT'S NOT LIKE THEIR VEHICLES LEFT ANY KIND OF TRAIL WE CAN FOLLOW.
I'M STILL FIGURING THINGS OUT.
WE KNOW THEY'RE WATCHING US... OR AT LEAST, THEY WERE.

I KNOW WE'RE SUPPOSED TO BE USED TO THIS BY NOW, BUT I'M NOT...

...CAN I SLEEP HERE TONIGHT?

YOU CAN SLEEP HERE *EVERY* NIGHT.

...CAN I SLEEP HERE TONIGHT?

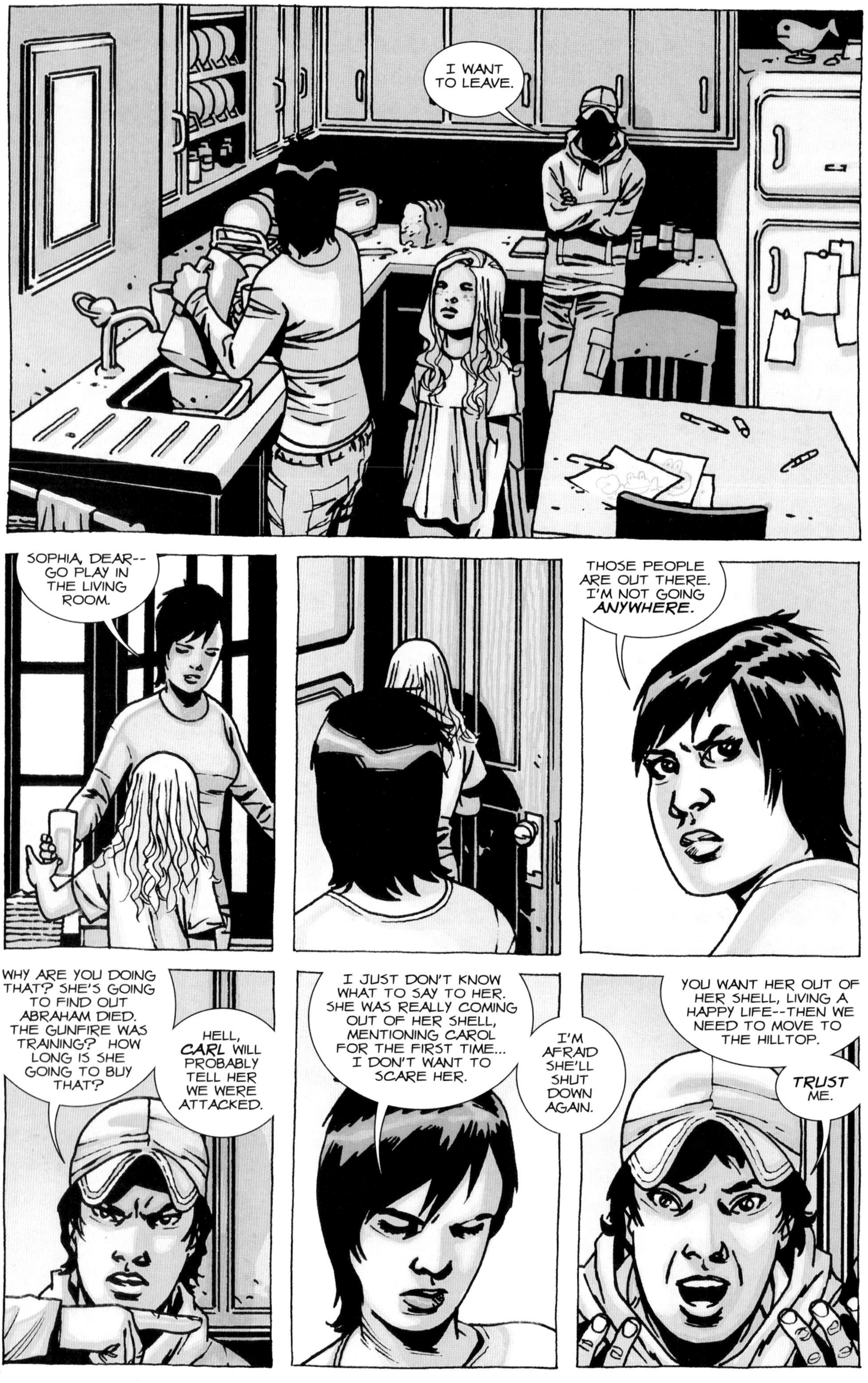

I WANT TO LEAVE.
SOPHIA, DEAR-- GO PLAY IN THE LIVING ROOM.
THOSE PEOPLE ARE OUT THERE. I'M NOT GOING ANYWHERE.
WHY ARE YOU DOING THAT? SHE'S GOING TO FIND OUT ABRAHAM DIED. THE GUNFIRE WAS TRAINING? HOW LONG IS SHE GOING TO BUY THAT?
HELL, CARL WILL PROBABLY TELL HER WE WERE ATTACKED.
I JUST DON'T KNOW WHAT TO SAY TO HER. SHE WAS REALLY COMING OUT OF HER SHELL, MENTIONING CAROL FOR THE FIRST TIME... I DON'T WANT TO SCARE HER.
I'M AFRAID SHE'LL SHUT DOWN AGAIN.
YOU WANT HER OUT OF HER SHELL, LIVING A HAPPY LIFE--THEN WE NEED TO MOVE TO THE HILLTOP.
TRUST ME.

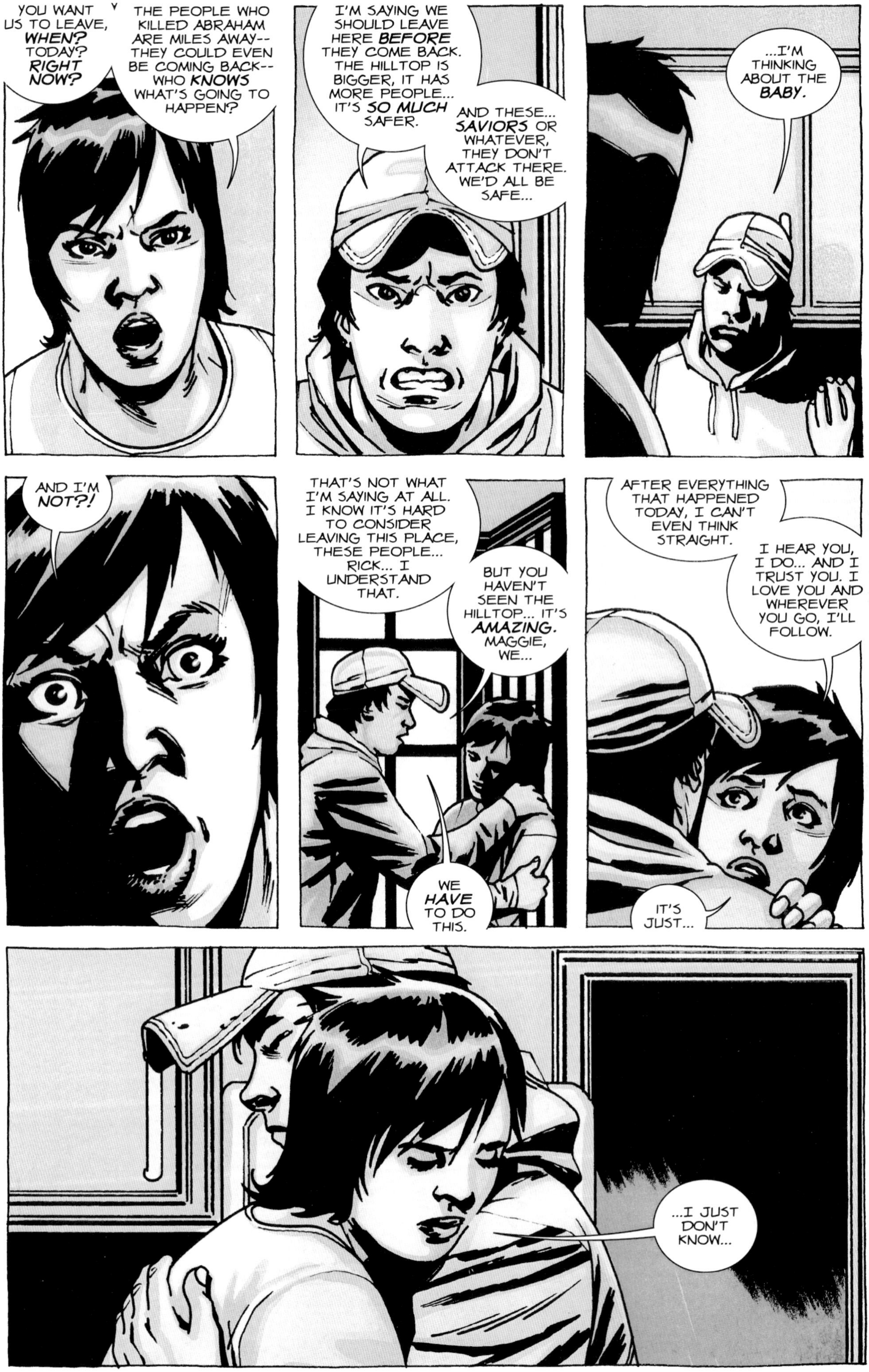
YOU WANT US TO LEAVE, WHEN? TODAY? RIGHT NOW?
THE PEOPLE WHO KILLED ABRAHAM ARE MILES AWAY-- THEY COULD EVEN BE COMING BACK-- WHO KNOWS WHAT'S GOING TO HAPPEN?
I'M SAYING WE SHOULD LEAVE HERE BEFORE THEY COME BACK. THE HILLTOP IS BIGGER, IT HAS MORE PEOPLE... IT'S SO MUCH SAFER.
AND THESE... SAVIORS OR WHATEVER, THEY DON'T ATTACK THERE. WE'D ALL BE SAFE...
...I'M THINKING ABOUT THE BABY.
AND I'M NOT?!
THAT'S NOT WHAT I'M SAYING AT ALL. I KNOW IT'S HARD TO CONSIDER LEAVING THIS PLACE, THESE PEOPLE... RICK... I UNDERSTAND THAT.
BUT YOU HAVEN'T SEEN THE HILLTOP... IT'S AMAZING. MAGGIE, WE...
WE HAVE TO DO THIS.
AFTER EVERYTHING THAT HAPPENED TODAY, I CAN'T EVEN THINK STRAIGHT.
I HEAR YOU, I DO... AND I TRUST YOU. I LOVE YOU AND WHEREVER YOU GO, I'LL FOLLOW.
IT'S JUST...
...I JUST DON'T KNOW...

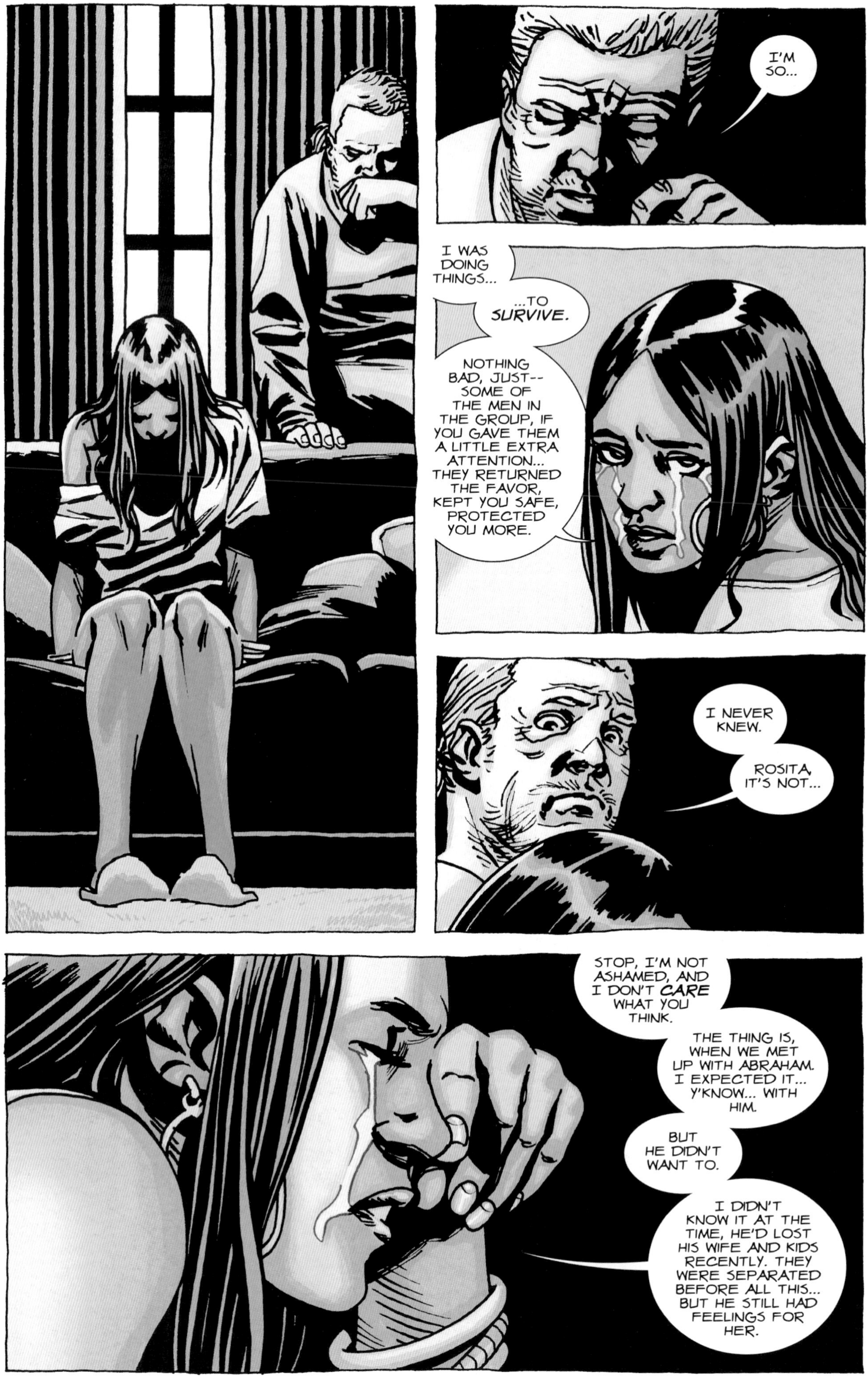
I'M SO...
I WAS DOING THINGS...
...TO SURVIVE.
NOTHING BAD, JUST-- SOME OF THE MEN IN THE GROUP, IF YOU GAVE THEM A LITTLE EXTRA ATTENTION... THEY RETURNED THE FAVOR, KEPT YOU SAFE, PROTECTED YOU MORE.
I NEVER KNEW.
ROSITA, IT'S NOT...
STOP, I'M NOT ASHAMED, AND I DON'T CARE WHAT YOU THINK.
THE THING IS, WHEN WE MET UP WITH ABRAHAM. I EXPECTED IT... Y'KNOW... WITH HIM.
BUT HE DIDN'T WANT TO.
I DIDN'T KNOW IT AT THE TIME, HE'D LOST HIS WIFE AND KIDS RECENTLY. THEY WERE SEPARATED BEFORE ALL THIS... BUT HE STILL HAD FEELINGS FOR HER.

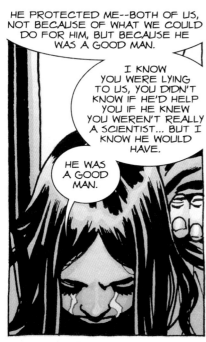

HE PROTECTED ME--BOTH OF US, NOT BECAUSE OF WHAT WE COULD DO FOR HIM, BUT BECAUSE HE WAS A GOOD MAN.

I KNOW YOU WERE LYING TO US, YOU DIDN'T KNOW IF HE'D HELP YOU IF HE KNEW YOU WEREN'T REALLY A SCIENTIST... BUT I KNOW HE WOULD HAVE.

HE WAS A GOOD MAN.

YES... HE WAS.

SO WHEN THINGS STARTED HAPPENING, AND WE WERE TOGETHER. I THOUGHT...

...I THOUGHT HE *REALLY* LOVED ME.

I THOUGHT WHAT WE HAD WAS...

...

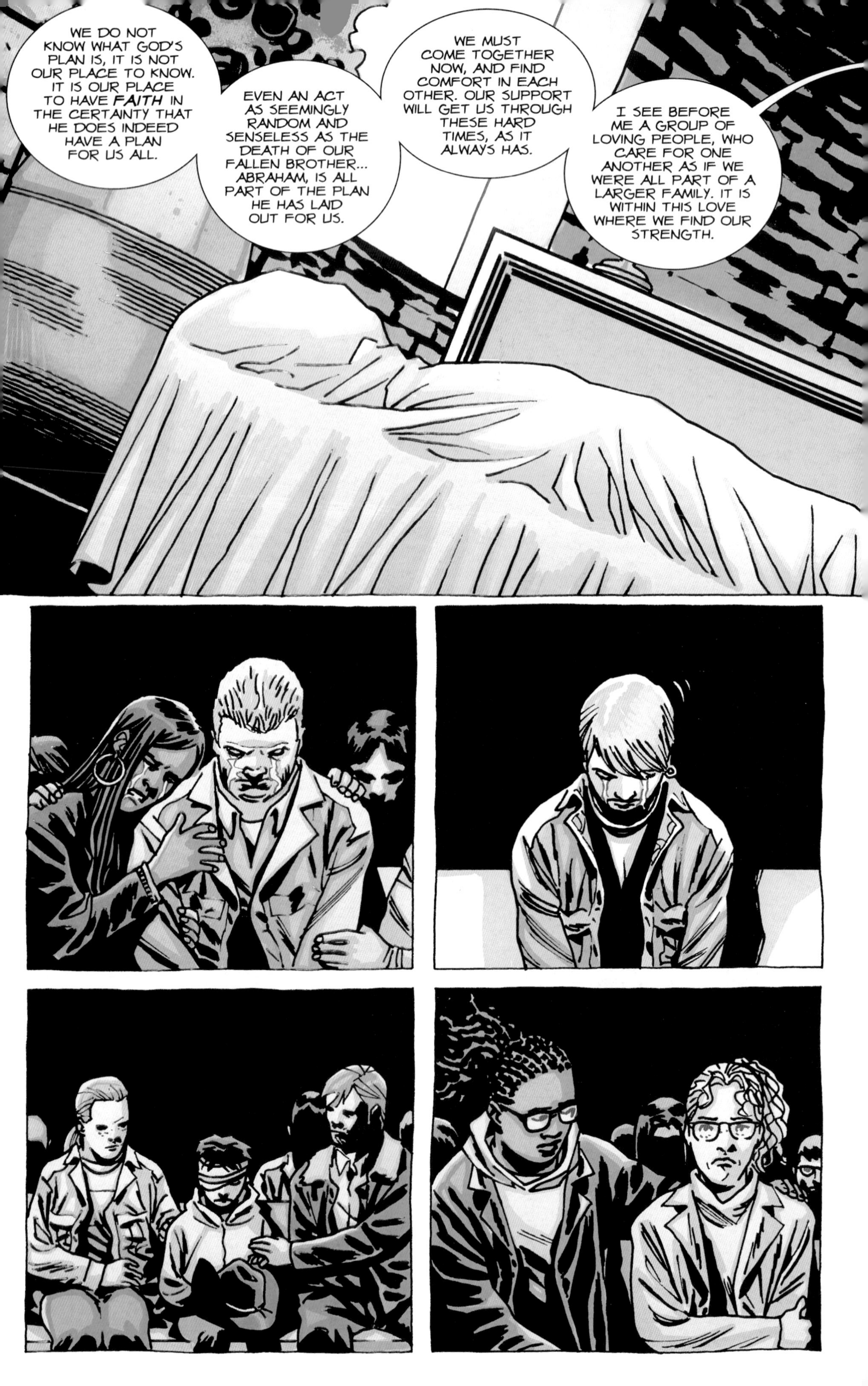
WE DO NOT KNOW WHAT GOD'S PLAN IS, IT IS NOT OUR PLACE TO KNOW. IT IS OUR PLACE TO HAVE FAITH IN THE CERTAINTY THAT HE DOES INDEED HAVE A PLAN FOR US ALL.
EVEN AN ACT AS SEEMINGLY RANDOM AND SENSELESS AS THE DEATH OF OUR FALLEN BROTHER... ABRAHAM, IS ALL PART OF THE PLAN HE HAS LAID OUT FOR US.
WE MUST COME TOGETHER NOW, AND FIND COMFORT IN EACH OTHER. OUR SUPPORT WILL GET US THROUGH THESE HARD TIMES, AS IT ALWAYS HAS.
I SEE BEFORE ME A GROUP OF LOVING PEOPLE, WHO CARE FOR ONE ANOTHER AS IF WE WERE ALL PART OF A LARGER FAMILY. IT IS WITHIN THIS LOVE WHERE WE FIND OUR STRENGTH.

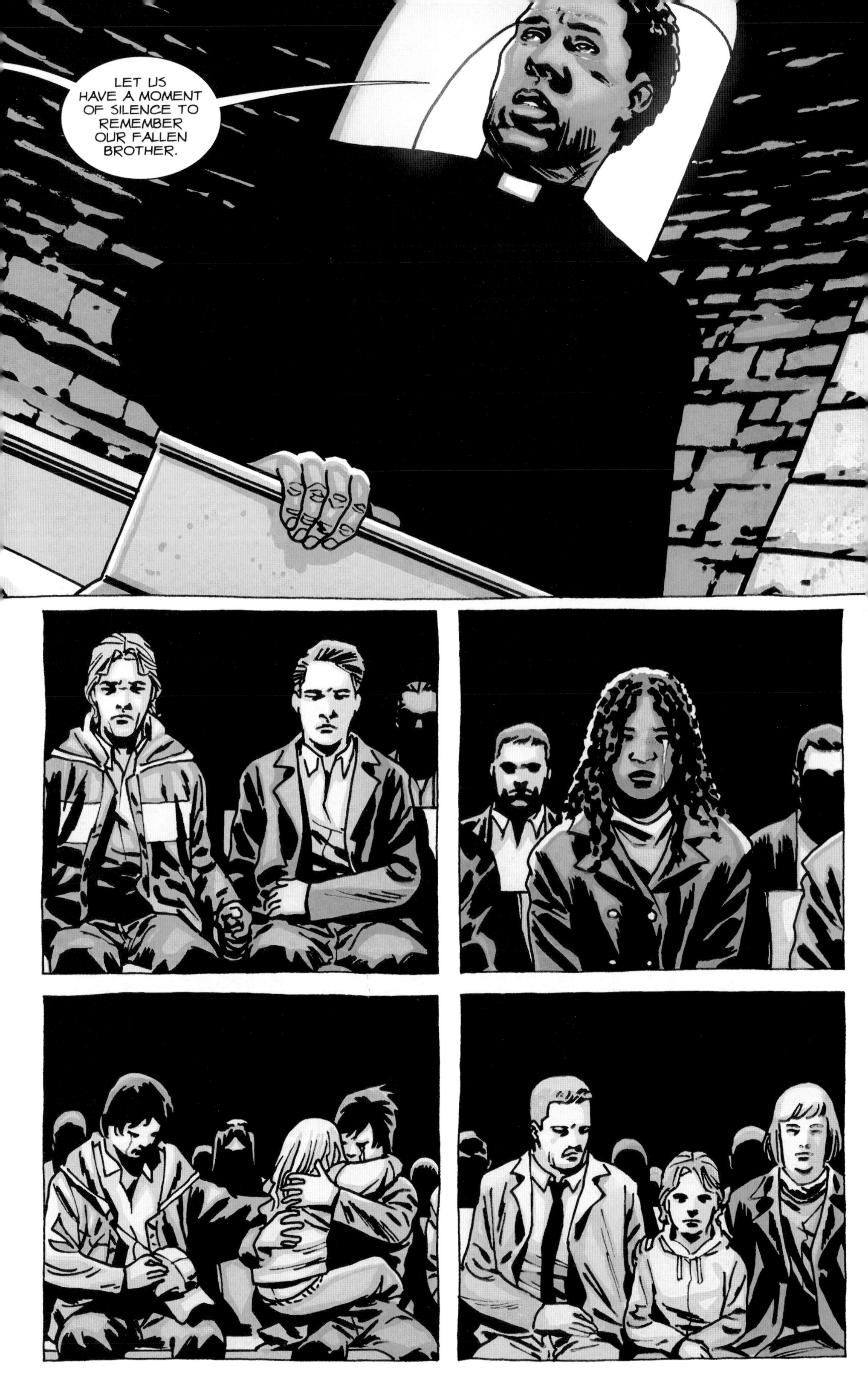
LET US HAVE A MOMENT OF SILENCE TO REMEMBER OUR FALLEN BROTHER.

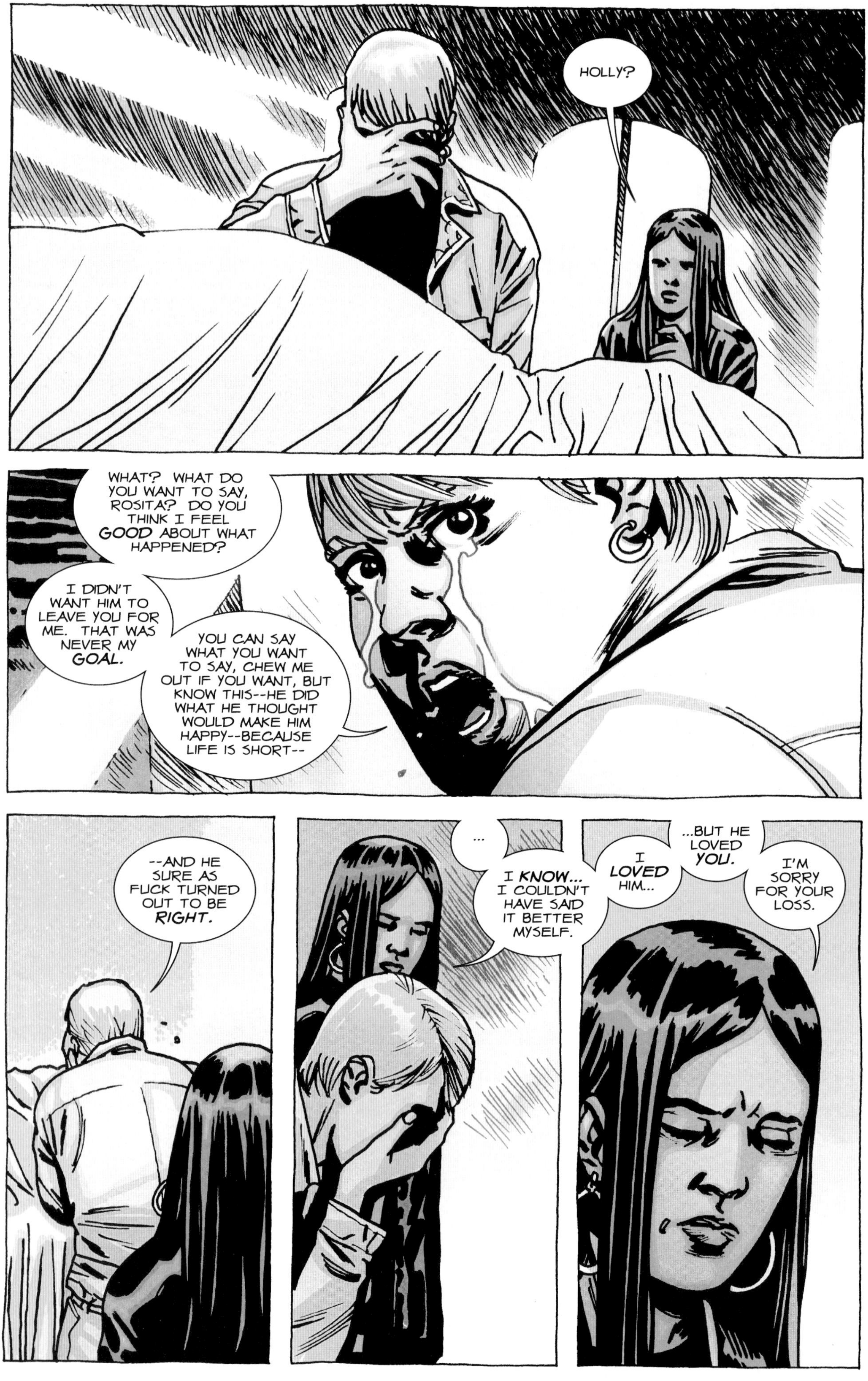
HOLLY?
WHAT? WHAT DO YOU WANT TO SAY, ROSITA? DO YOU THINK I FEEL **GOOD** ABOUT WHAT HAPPENED?
I DIDN'T WANT HIM TO LEAVE YOU FOR ME. THAT WAS NEVER MY **GOAL.**
YOU CAN SAY WHAT YOU WANT TO SAY, CHEW ME OUT IF YOU WANT, BUT KNOW THIS--HE DID WHAT HE THOUGHT WOULD MAKE HIM HAPPY--BECAUSE LIFE IS SHORT--
--AND HE SURE AS FUCK TURNED OUT TO BE **RIGHT.**
...
I **KNOW...** I COULDN'T HAVE SAID IT BETTER MYSELF.
I **LOVED** HIM...
...BUT HE LOVED **YOU.**
I'M SORRY FOR YOUR LOSS.

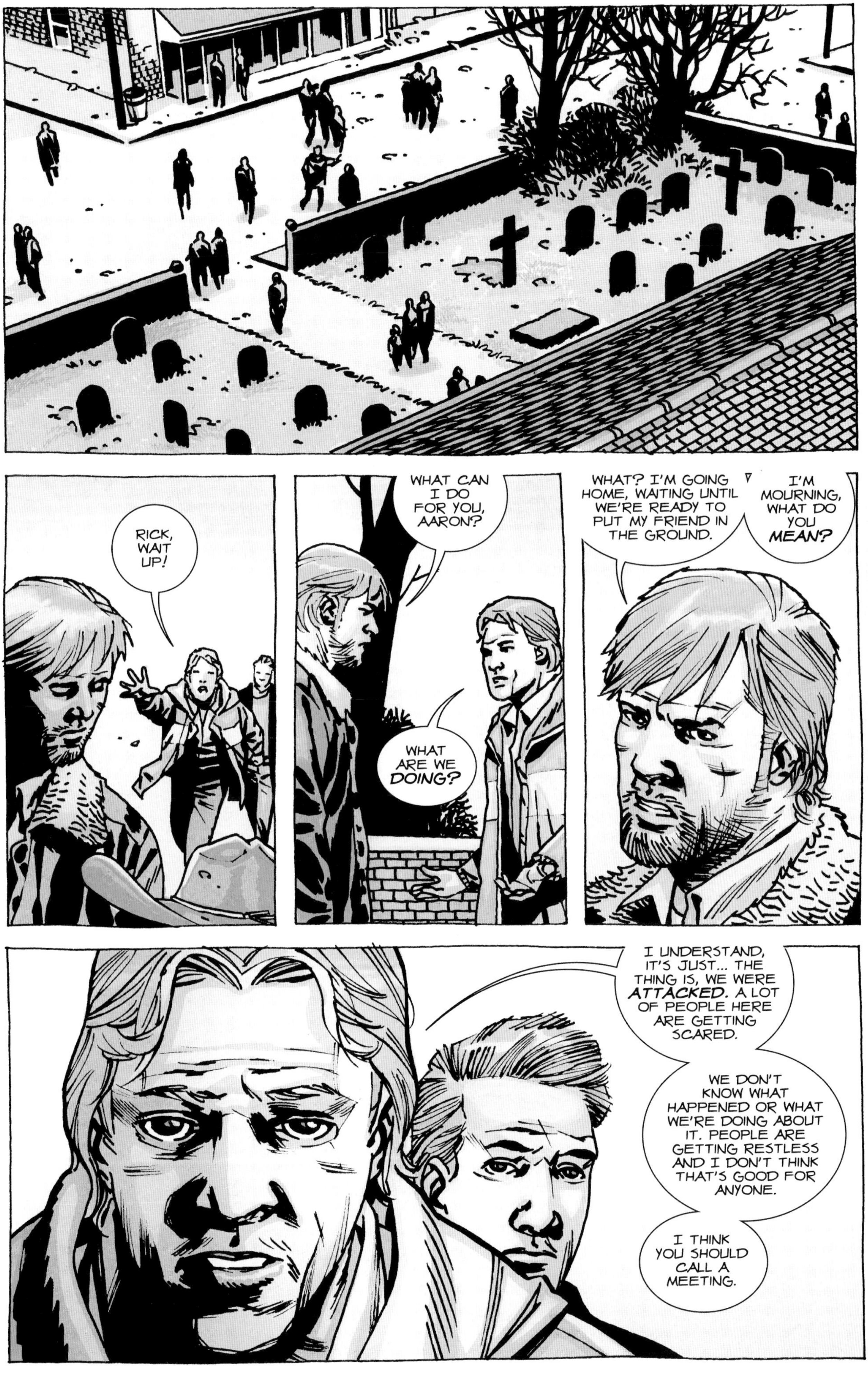
RICK, WAIT UP!
WHAT CAN I DO FOR YOU, AARON?
WHAT ARE WE DOING?
WHAT? I'M GOING HOME, WAITING UNTIL WE'RE READY TO PUT MY FRIEND IN THE GROUND.
I'M MOURNING, WHAT DO YOU MEAN?
I UNDERSTAND, IT'S JUST... THE THING IS, WE WERE ATTACKED. A LOT OF PEOPLE HERE ARE GETTING SCARED.
WE DON'T KNOW WHAT HAPPENED OR WHAT WE'RE DOING ABOUT IT. PEOPLE ARE GETTING RESTLESS AND I DON'T THINK THAT'S GOOD FOR ANYONE.
I THINK YOU SHOULD CALL A MEETING.

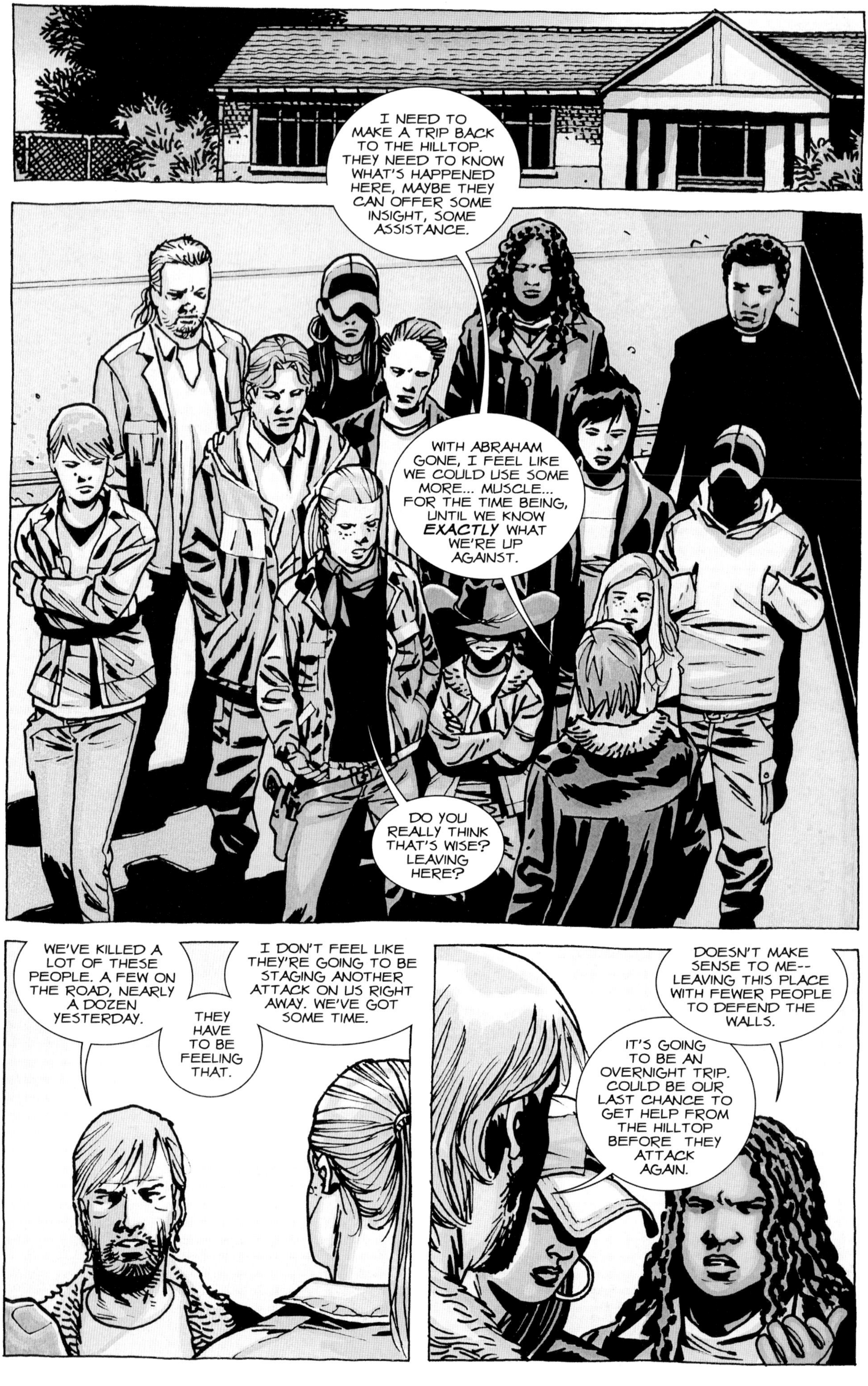
I NEED TO MAKE A TRIP BACK TO THE HILLTOP. THEY NEED TO KNOW WHAT'S HAPPENED HERE, MAYBE THEY CAN OFFER SOME INSIGHT, SOME ASSISTANCE.
WITH ABRAHAM GONE, I FEEL LIKE WE COULD USE SOME MORE... MUSCLE... FOR THE TIME BEING, UNTIL WE KNOW *EXACTLY* WHAT WE'RE UP AGAINST.
DO YOU REALLY THINK THAT'S WISE? LEAVING HERE?
WE'VE KILLED A LOT OF THESE PEOPLE. A FEW ON THE ROAD, NEARLY A DOZEN YESTERDAY.
THEY HAVE TO BE FEELING THAT.
I DON'T FEEL LIKE THEY'RE GOING TO BE STAGING ANOTHER ATTACK ON US RIGHT AWAY. WE'VE GOT SOME TIME.
DOESN'T MAKE SENSE TO ME-- LEAVING THIS PLACE WITH FEWER PEOPLE TO DEFEND THE WALLS.
IT'S GOING TO BE AN OVERNIGHT TRIP. COULD BE OUR LAST CHANCE TO GET HELP FROM THE HILLTOP BEFORE THEY ATTACK AGAIN.

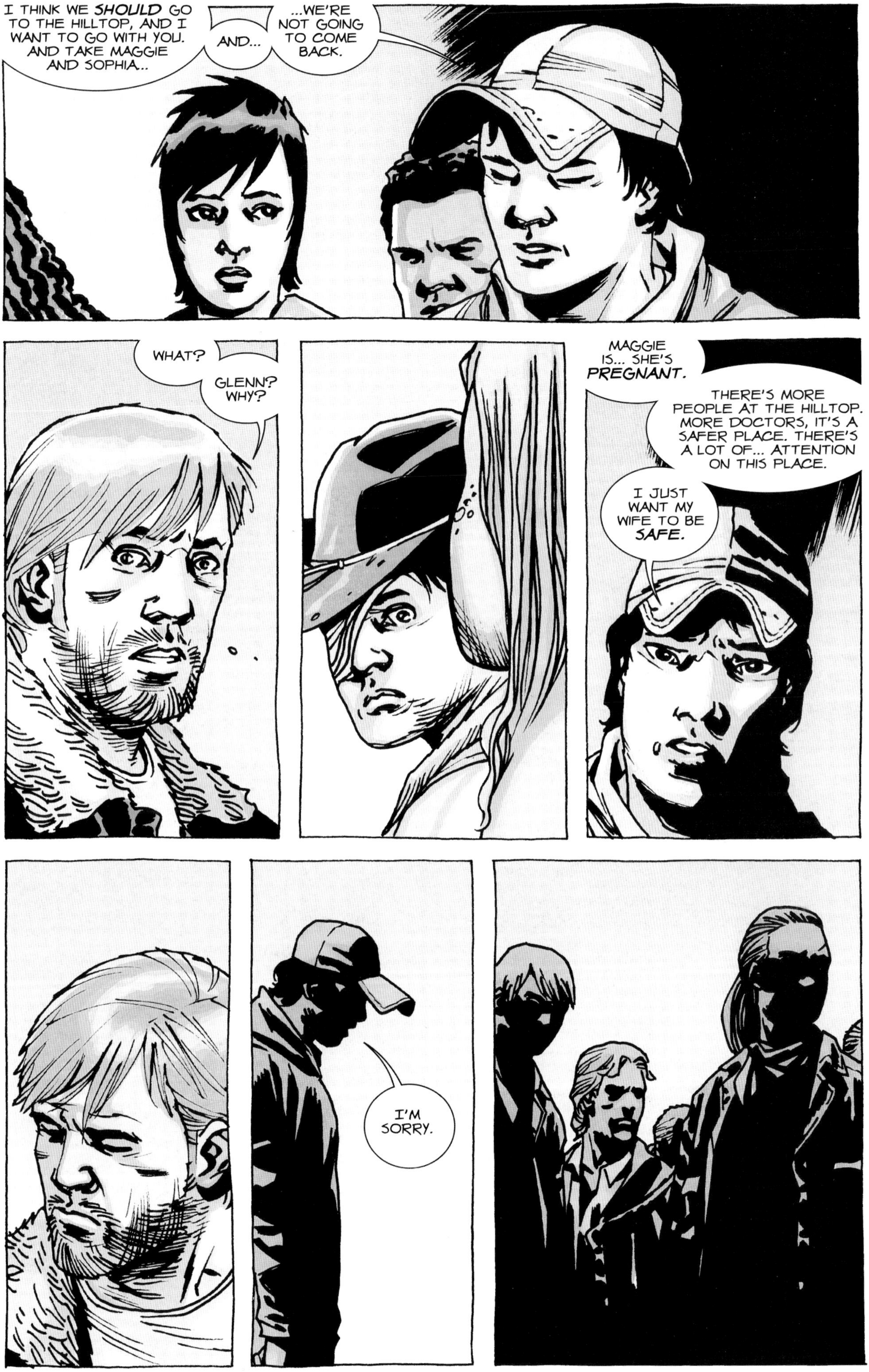

I THINK WE SHOULD GO TO THE HILLTOP, AND I WANT TO GO WITH YOU. AND TAKE MAGGIE AND SOPHIA...
AND...
...WE'RE NOT GOING TO COME BACK.
WHAT?
GLENN? WHY?
MAGGIE IS... SHE'S PREGNANT.
THERE'S MORE PEOPLE AT THE HILLTOP. MORE DOCTORS, IT'S A SAFER PLACE. THERE'S A LOT OF... ATTENTION ON THIS PLACE.
I JUST WANT MY WIFE TO BE SAFE.
I'M SORRY.

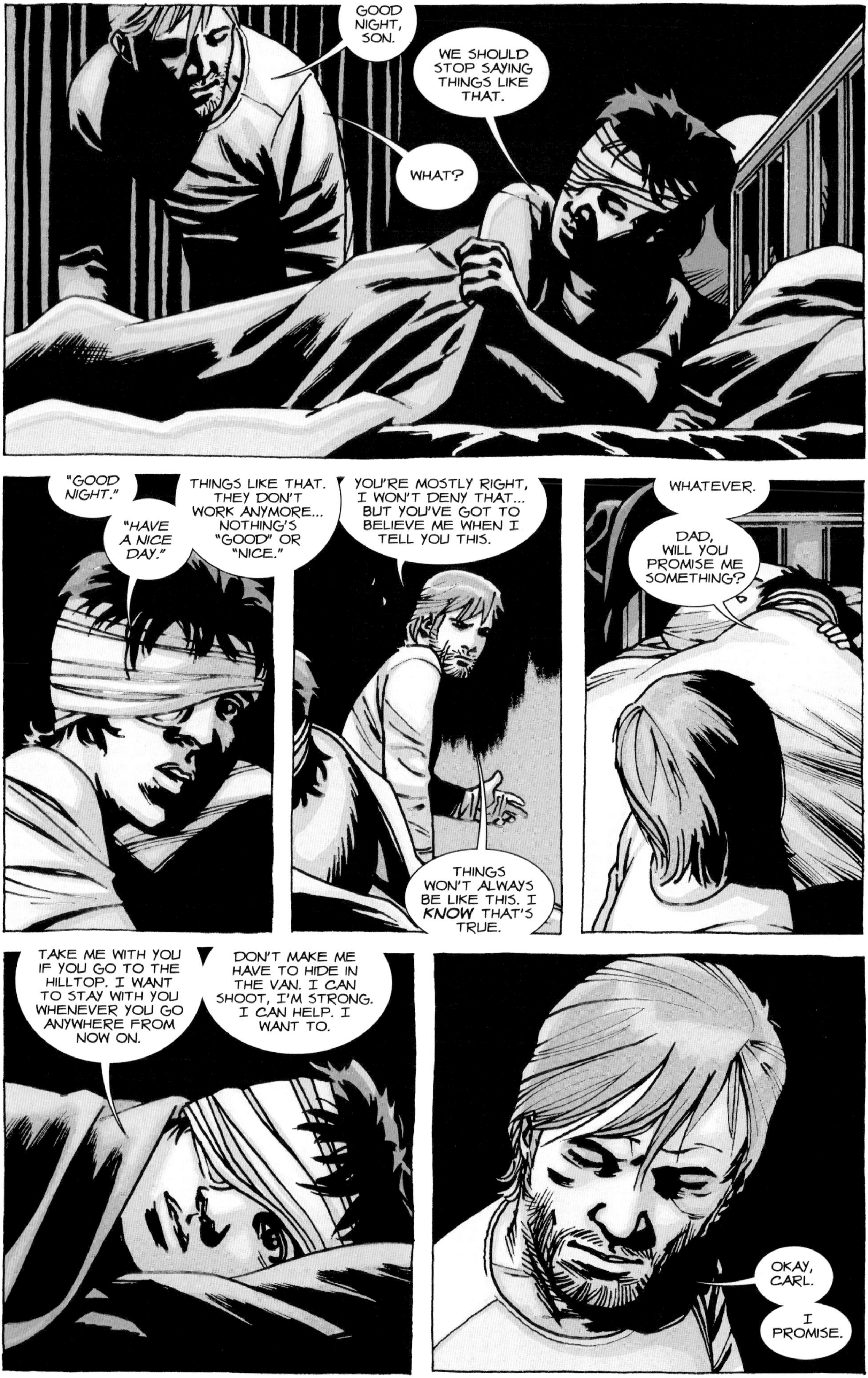
GOOD NIGHT, SON.
WE SHOULD STOP SAYING THINGS LIKE THAT.
WHAT?
"GOOD NIGHT."
"HAVE A NICE DAY."
THINGS LIKE THAT. THEY DON'T WORK ANYMORE... NOTHING'S "GOOD" OR "NICE."
YOU'RE MOSTLY RIGHT, I WON'T DENY THAT... BUT YOU'VE GOT TO BELIEVE ME WHEN I TELL YOU THIS.
THINGS WON'T ALWAYS BE LIKE THIS. I *KNOW* THAT'S TRUE.
WHATEVER.
DAD, WILL YOU PROMISE ME SOMETHING?
TAKE ME WITH YOU IF YOU GO TO THE HILLTOP. I WANT TO STAY WITH YOU WHENEVER YOU GO ANYWHERE FROM NOW ON.
DON'T MAKE ME HAVE TO HIDE IN THE VAN. I CAN SHOOT, I'M STRONG. I CAN HELP. I WANT TO.
OKAY, CARL.
I PROMISE.

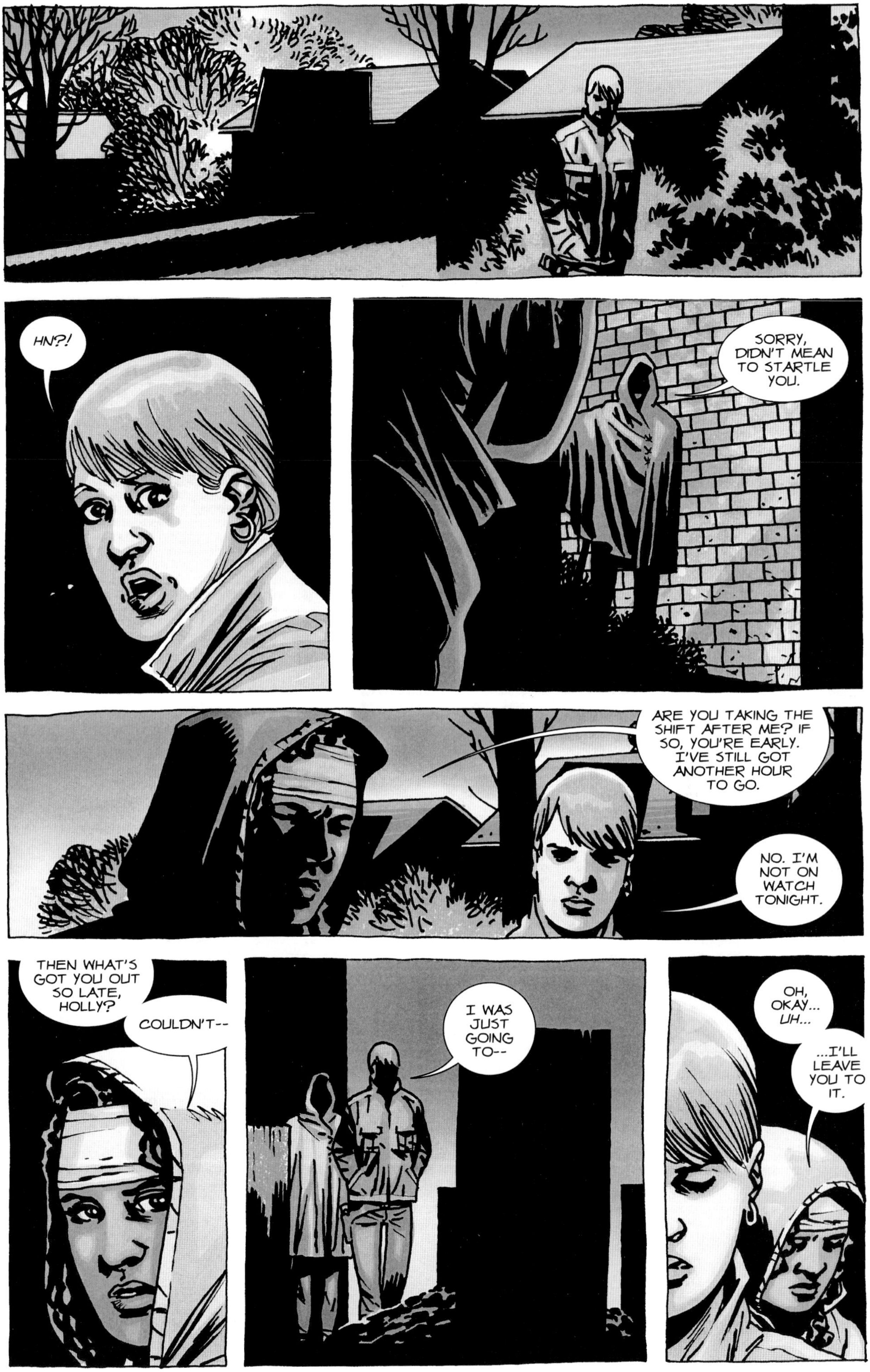

HN?!
SORRY, DIDN'T MEAN TO STARTLE YOU.
ARE YOU TAKING THE SHIFT AFTER ME? IF SO, YOU'RE EARLY. I'VE STILL GOT ANOTHER HOUR TO GO.
NO. I'M NOT ON WATCH TONIGHT.
THEN WHAT'S GOT YOU OUT SO LATE, HOLLY?
COULDN'T--
I WAS JUST GOING TO--
OH, OKAY... UH...
...I'LL LEAVE YOU TO IT.

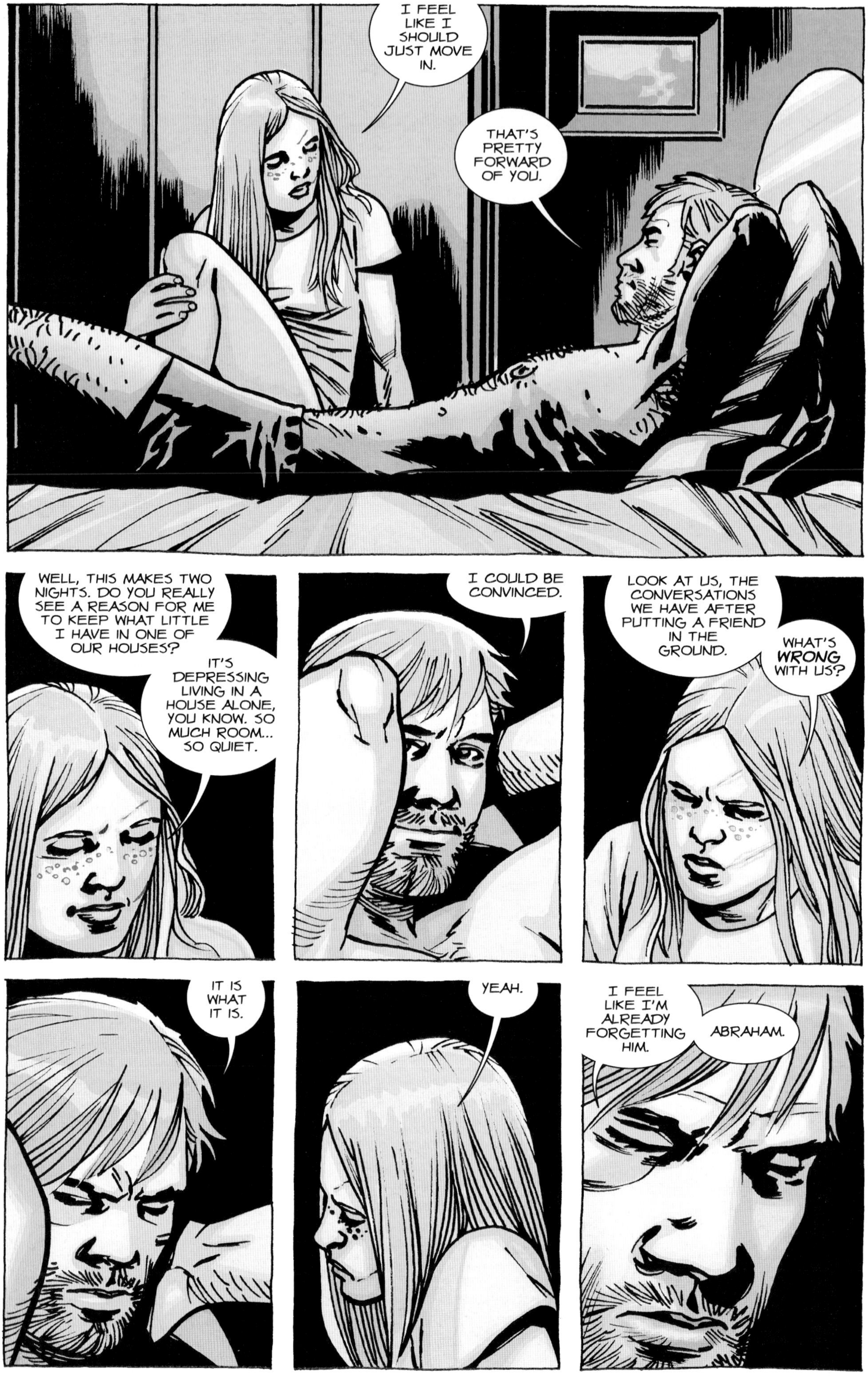
I FEEL LIKE I SHOULD JUST MOVE IN.
THAT'S PRETTY FORWARD OF YOU.
WELL, THIS MAKES TWO NIGHTS. DO YOU REALLY SEE A REASON FOR ME TO KEEP WHAT LITTLE I HAVE IN ONE OF OUR HOUSES?
IT'S DEPRESSING LIVING IN A HOUSE ALONE, YOU KNOW. SO MUCH ROOM... SO QUIET.
I COULD BE CONVINCED.
LOOK AT US, THE CONVERSATIONS WE HAVE AFTER PUTTING A FRIEND IN THE GROUND.
WHAT'S **WRONG** WITH US?
IT IS WHAT IT IS.
YEAH.
I FEEL LIKE I'M ALREADY FORGETTING HIM.
ABRAHAM.

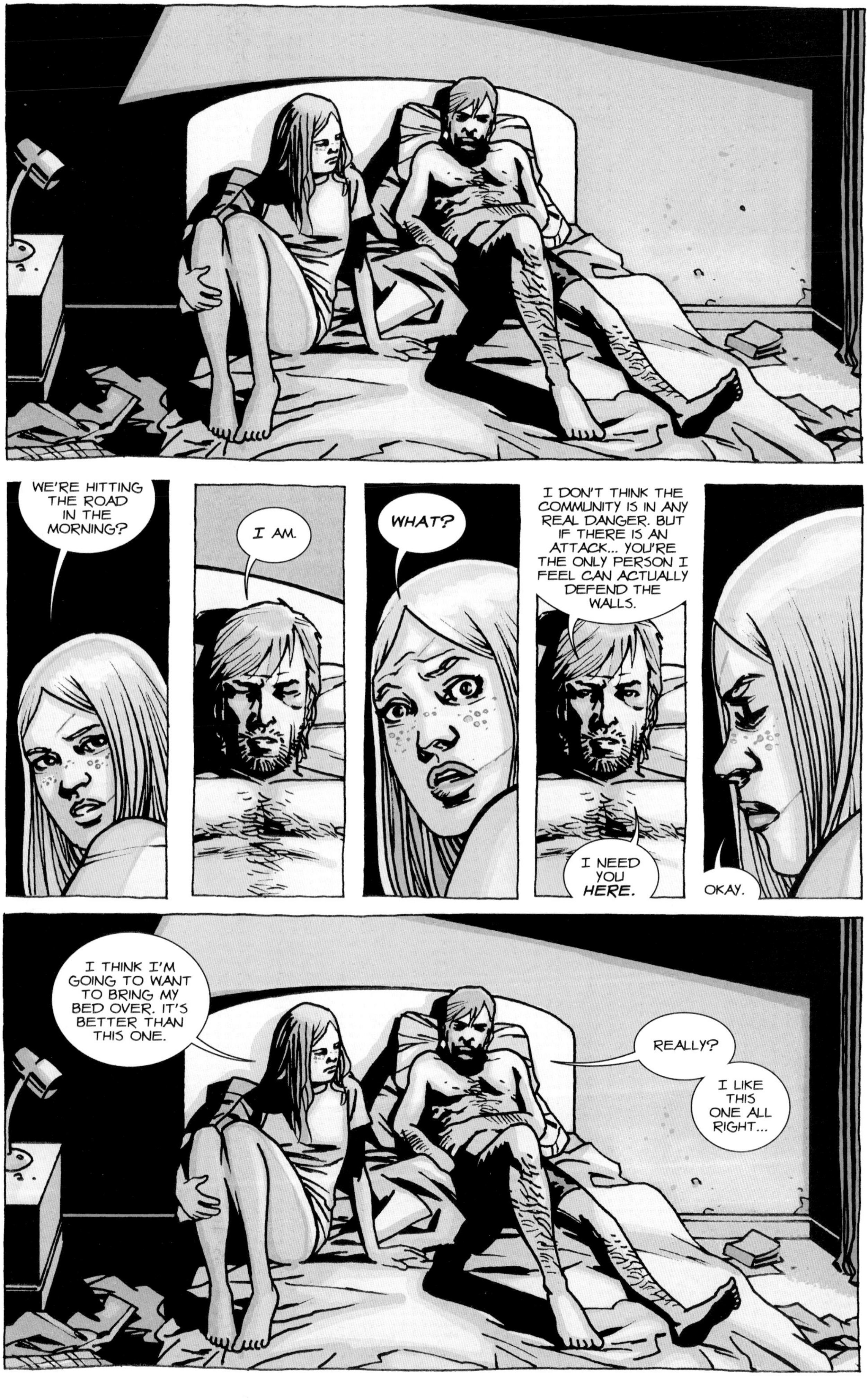
WE'RE HITTING THE ROAD IN THE MORNING?
I AM.
WHAT?
I DON'T THINK THE COMMUNITY IS IN ANY REAL DANGER. BUT IF THERE IS AN ATTACK... YOU'RE THE ONLY PERSON I FEEL CAN ACTUALLY DEFEND THE WALLS.
I NEED YOU HERE.
OKAY.
I THINK I'M GOING TO WANT TO BRING MY BED OVER. IT'S BETTER THAN THIS ONE.
REALLY?
I LIKE THIS ONE ALL RIGHT...

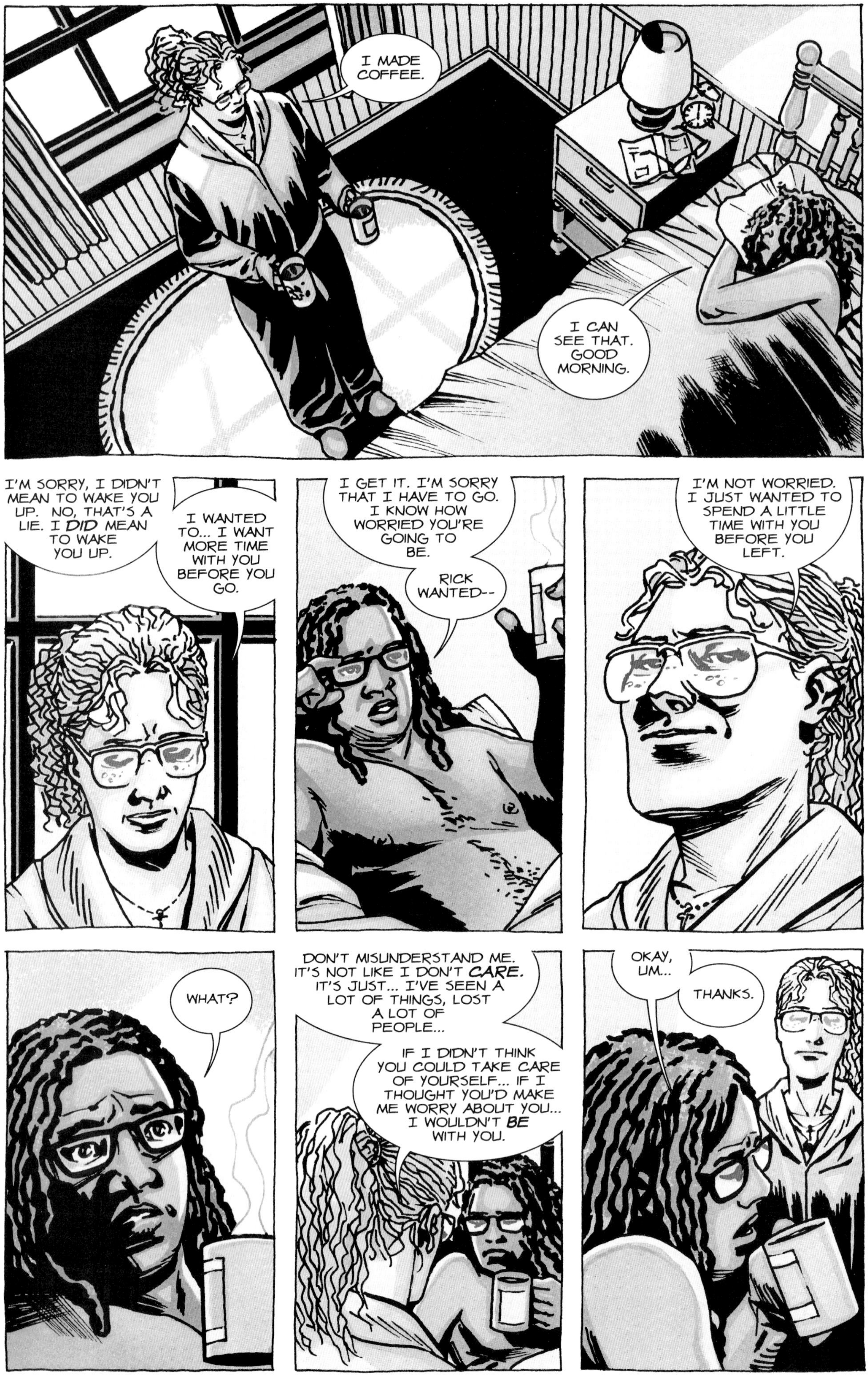
I MADE COFFEE.
I CAN SEE THAT. GOOD MORNING.
I'M SORRY, I DIDN'T MEAN TO WAKE YOU UP. NO, THAT'S A LIE. I *DID* MEAN TO WAKE YOU UP.
I WANTED TO... I WANT MORE TIME WITH YOU BEFORE YOU GO.
I GET IT. I'M SORRY THAT I HAVE TO GO. I KNOW HOW WORRIED YOU'RE GOING TO BE.
RICK WANTED--
I'M NOT WORRIED. I JUST WANTED TO SPEND A LITTLE TIME WITH YOU BEFORE YOU LEFT.
WHAT?
DON'T MISUNDERSTAND ME. IT'S NOT LIKE I DON'T *CARE.* IT'S JUST... I'VE SEEN A LOT OF THINGS, LOST A LOT OF PEOPLE...
IF I DIDN'T THINK YOU COULD TAKE CARE OF YOURSELF... IF I THOUGHT YOU'D MAKE ME WORRY ABOUT YOU... I WOULDN'T *BE* WITH YOU.
OKAY, UM...
THANKS.

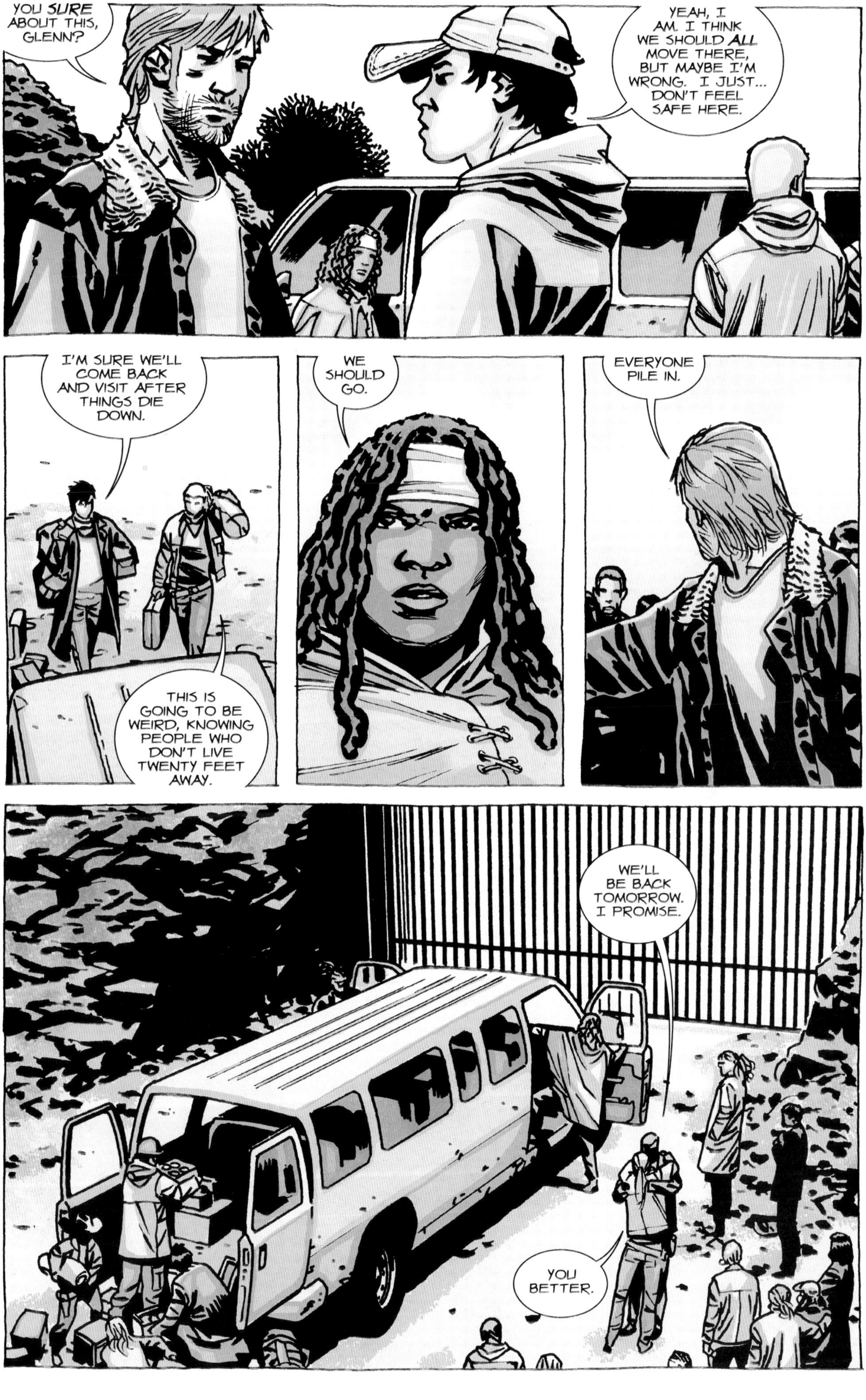
YOU SURE ABOUT THIS, GLENN?
YEAH, I AM. I THINK WE SHOULD ALL MOVE THERE, BUT MAYBE I'M WRONG. I JUST... DON'T FEEL SAFE HERE.
I'M SURE WE'LL COME BACK AND VISIT AFTER THINGS DIE DOWN.
THIS IS GOING TO BE WEIRD, KNOWING PEOPLE WHO DON'T LIVE TWENTY FEET AWAY.
WE SHOULD GO.
EVERYONE PILE IN.
WE'LL BE BACK TOMORROW. I PROMISE.
YOU BETTER.

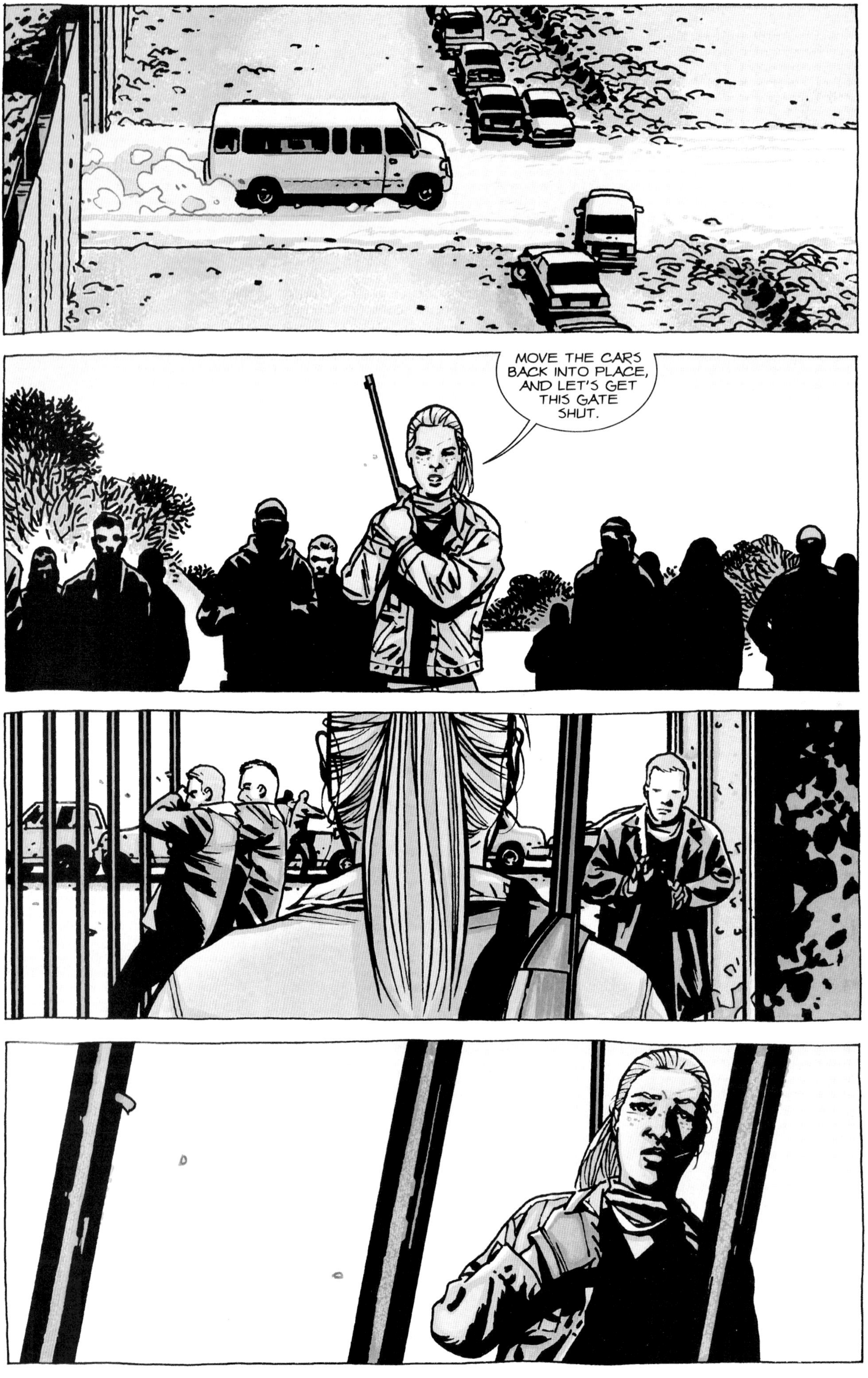
MOVE THE CARS BACK INTO PLACE, AND LET'S GET THIS GATE SHUT.

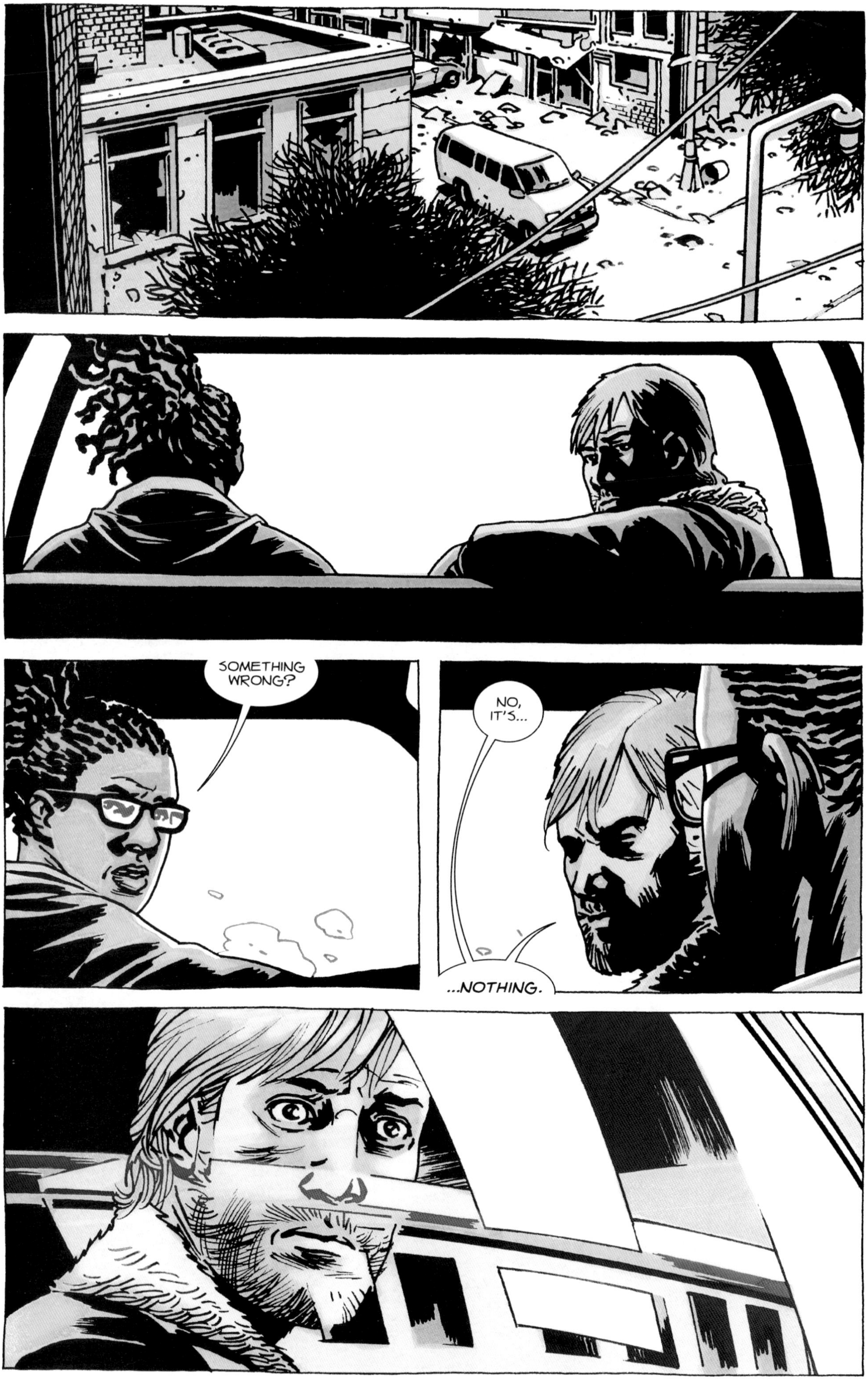
SOMETHING WRONG?
NO, IT'S...
...NOTHING.

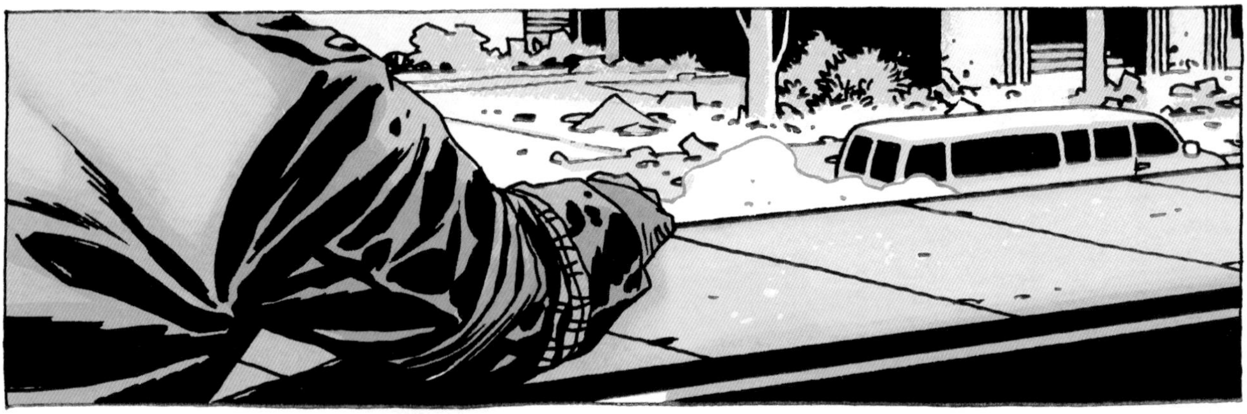

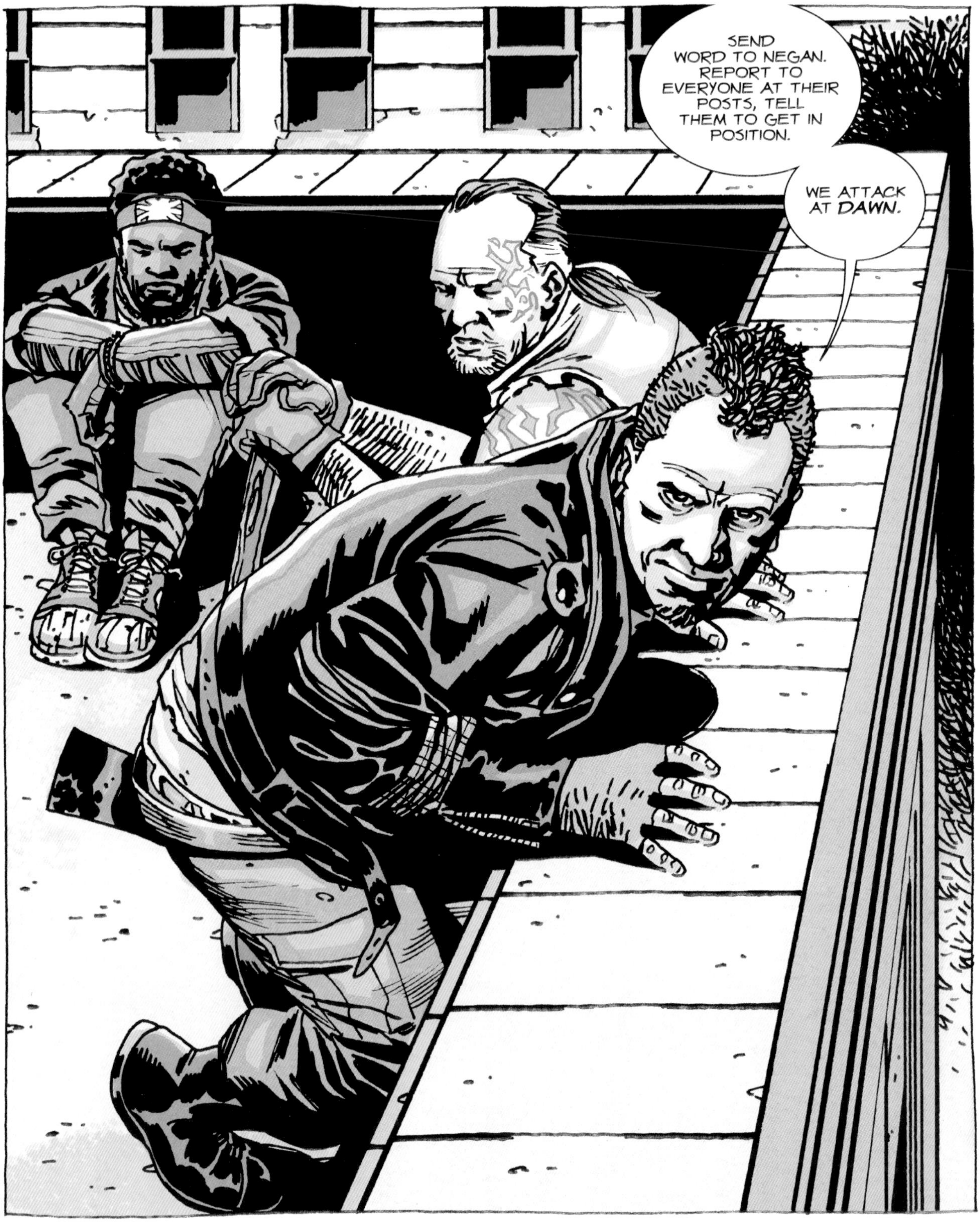
SEND WORD TO NEGAN. REPORT TO EVERYONE AT THEIR POSTS, TELL THEM TO GET IN POSITION.
WE ATTACK AT *DAWN.*

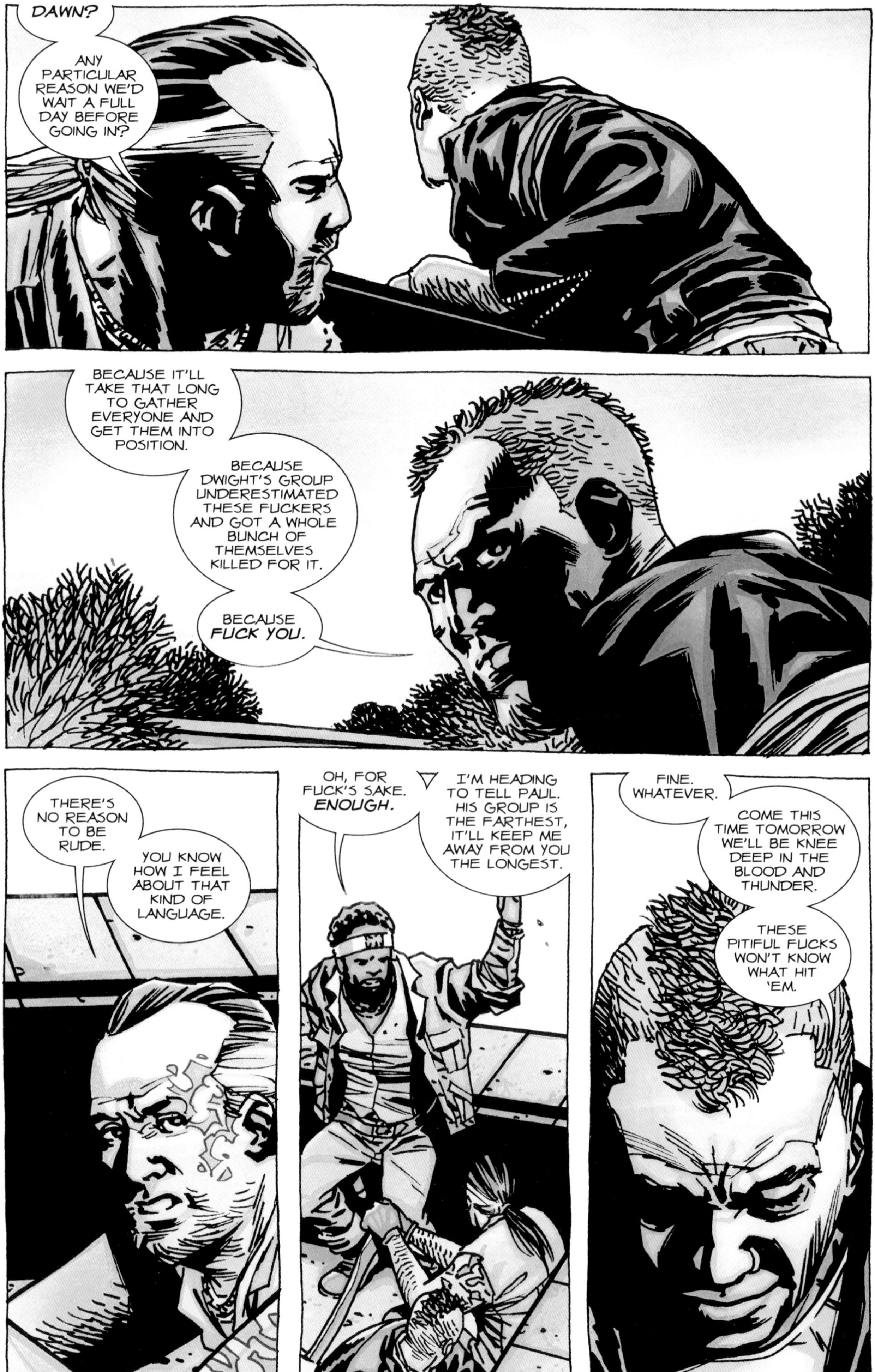
DAWN?
ANY PARTICULAR REASON WE'D WAIT A FULL DAY BEFORE GOING IN?
BECAUSE IT'LL TAKE THAT LONG TO GATHER EVERYONE AND GET THEM INTO POSITION.
BECAUSE DWIGHT'S GROUP UNDERESTIMATED THESE FUCKERS AND GOT A WHOLE BUNCH OF THEMSELVES KILLED FOR IT.
BECAUSE *FUCK YOU.*
THERE'S NO REASON TO BE RUDE.
YOU KNOW HOW I FEEL ABOUT THAT KIND OF LANGUAGE.
OH, FOR FUCK'S SAKE. *ENOUGH.*
I'M HEADING TO TELL PAUL. HIS GROUP IS THE FARTHEST, IT'LL KEEP ME AWAY FROM YOU THE LONGEST.
FINE. WHATEVER.
COME THIS TIME TOMORROW WE'LL BE KNEE DEEP IN THE BLOOD AND THUNDER.
THESE PITIFUL FUCKS WON'T KNOW WHAT HIT 'EM.

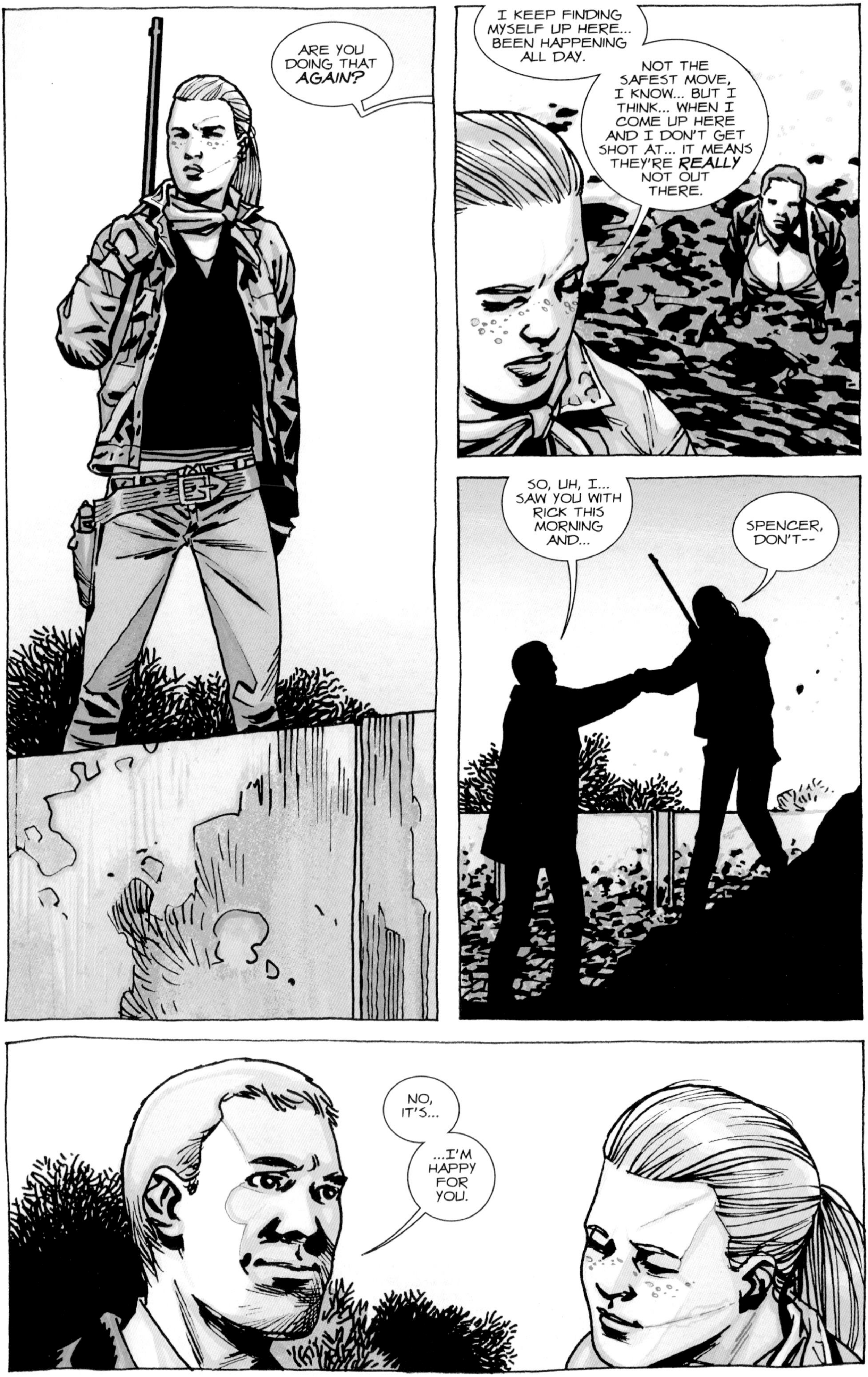
ARE YOU DOING THAT AGAIN?
I KEEP FINDING MYSELF UP HERE... BEEN HAPPENING ALL DAY.
NOT THE SAFEST MOVE, I KNOW... BUT I THINK... WHEN I COME UP HERE AND I DON'T GET SHOT AT... IT MEANS THEY'RE REALLY NOT OUT THERE.
SO, UH, I... SAW YOU WITH RICK THIS MORNING AND...
SPENCER, DON'T--
NO, IT'S...
...I'M HAPPY FOR YOU.

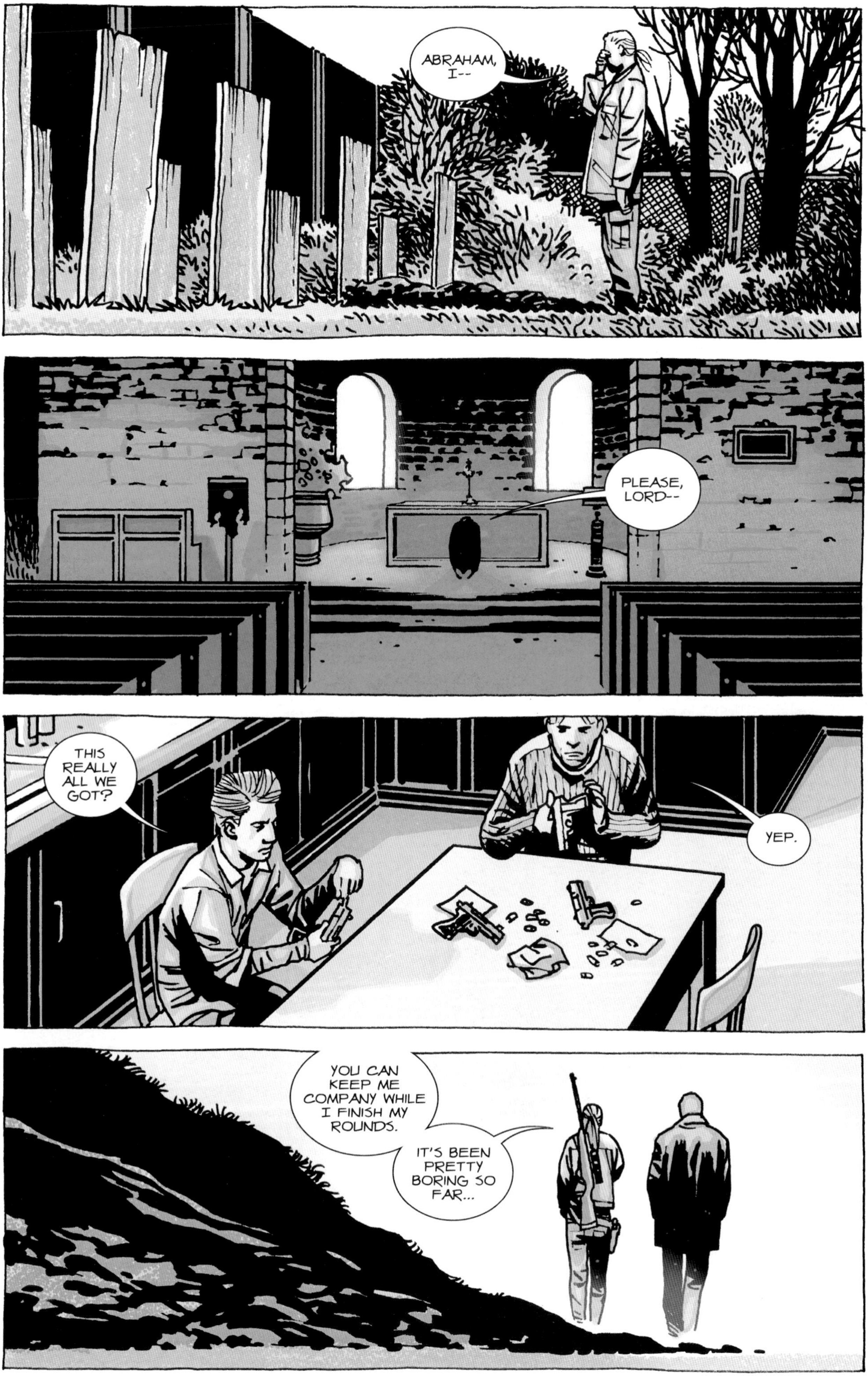
ABRAHAM, I--
PLEASE, LORD--
THIS REALLY ALL WE GOT?
YEP.
YOU CAN KEEP ME COMPANY WHILE I FINISH MY ROUNDS.
IT'S BEEN PRETTY BORING SO FAR...

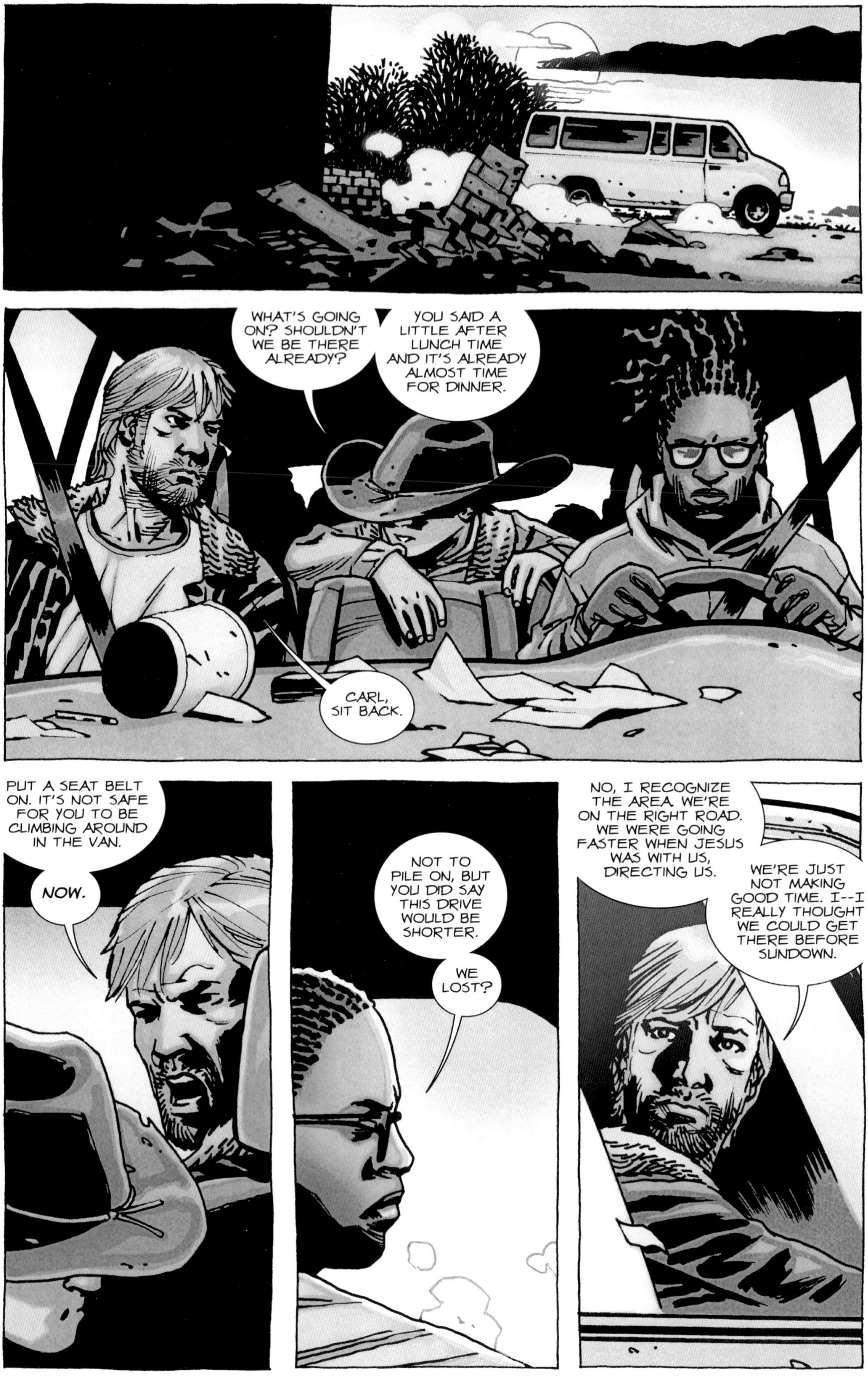
WHAT'S GOING ON? SHOULDN'T WE BE THERE ALREADY?
YOU SAID A LITTLE AFTER LUNCH TIME AND IT'S ALREADY ALMOST TIME FOR DINNER.
CARL, SIT BACK.
PUT A SEAT BELT ON. IT'S NOT SAFE FOR YOU TO BE CLIMBING AROUND IN THE VAN.
NOW.
NOT TO PILE ON, BUT YOU DID SAY THIS DRIVE WOULD BE SHORTER.
WE LOST?
NO, I RECOGNIZE THE AREA WE'RE ON THE RIGHT ROAD. WE WERE GOING FASTER WHEN JESUS WAS WITH US, DIRECTING US.
WE'RE JUST NOT MAKING GOOD TIME. I--I REALLY THOUGHT WE COULD GET THERE BEFORE SUNDOWN.

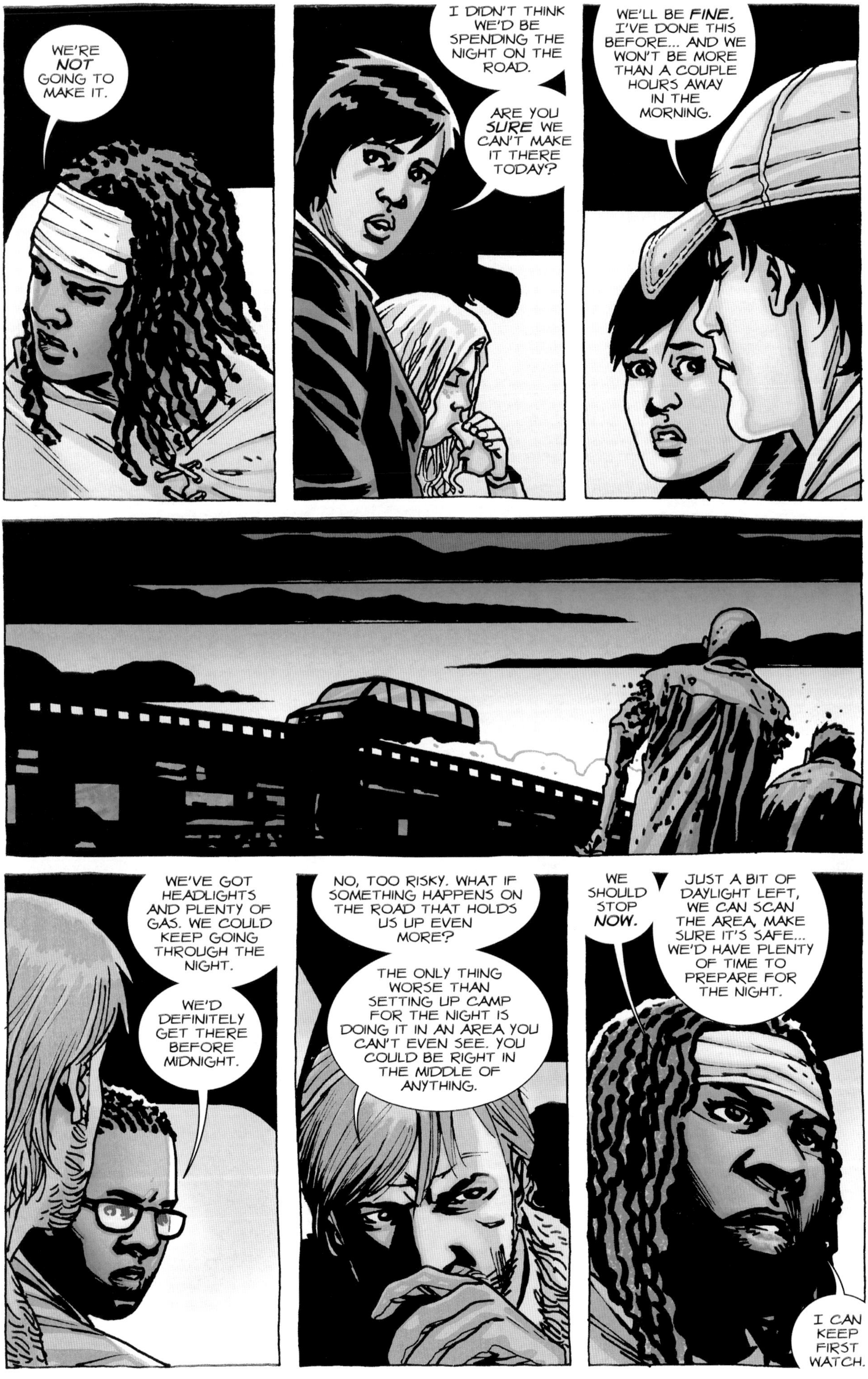
WE'RE NOT GOING TO MAKE IT.
I DIDN'T THINK WE'D BE SPENDING THE NIGHT ON THE ROAD.
ARE YOU SURE WE CAN'T MAKE IT THERE TODAY?
WE'LL BE FINE. I'VE DONE THIS BEFORE... AND WE WON'T BE MORE THAN A COUPLE HOURS AWAY IN THE MORNING.
WE'VE GOT HEADLIGHTS AND PLENTY OF GAS. WE COULD KEEP GOING THROUGH THE NIGHT.
WE'D DEFINITELY GET THERE BEFORE MIDNIGHT.
NO, TOO RISKY. WHAT IF SOMETHING HAPPENS ON THE ROAD THAT HOLDS US UP EVEN MORE?
THE ONLY THING WORSE THAN SETTING UP CAMP FOR THE NIGHT IS DOING IT IN AN AREA YOU CAN'T EVEN SEE. YOU COULD BE RIGHT IN THE MIDDLE OF ANYTHING.
WE SHOULD STOP NOW.
JUST A BIT OF DAYLIGHT LEFT, WE CAN SCAN THE AREA, MAKE SURE IT'S SAFE... WE'D HAVE PLENTY OF TIME TO PREPARE FOR THE NIGHT.
I CAN KEEP FIRST WATCH.

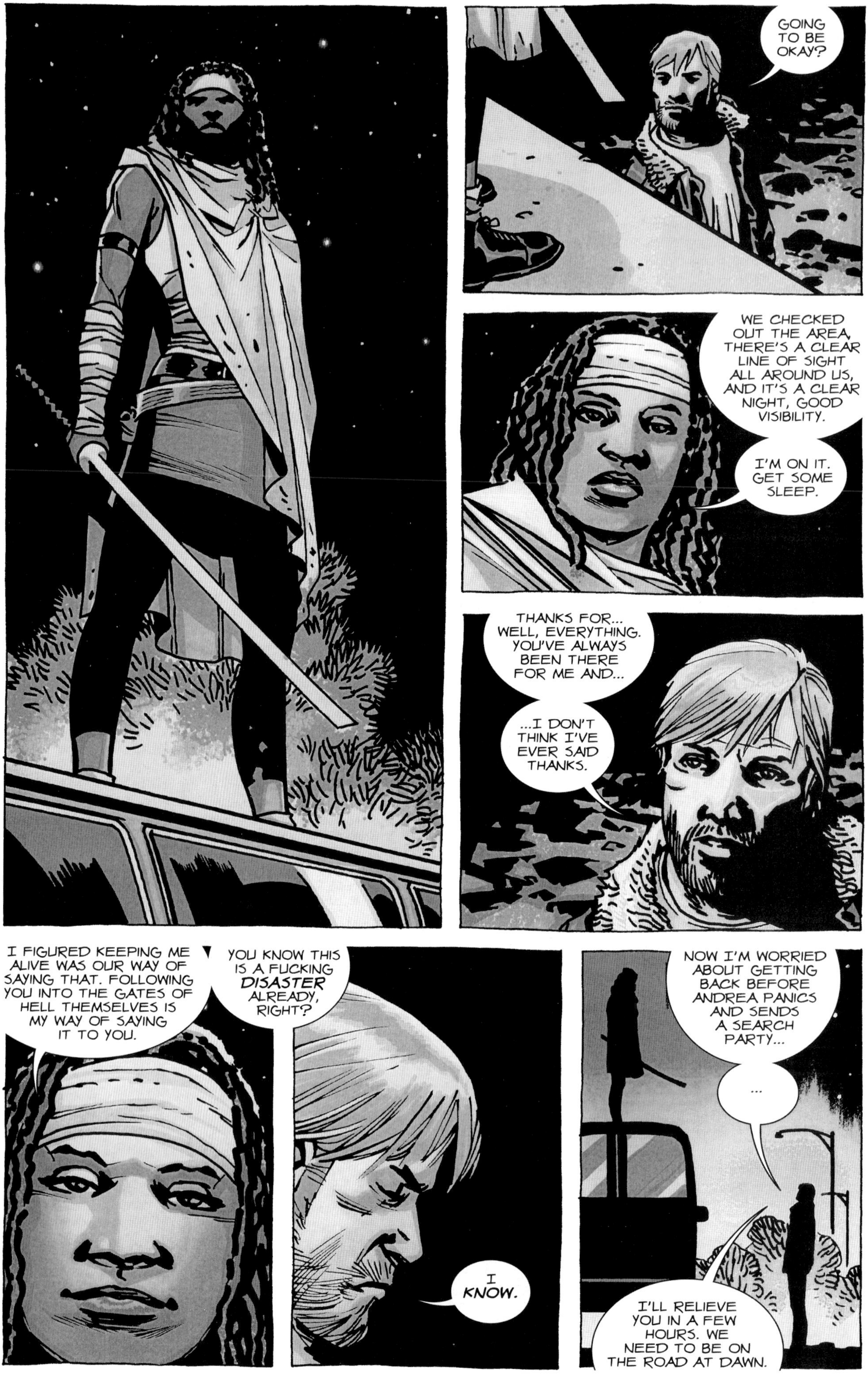
GOING TO BE OKAY?
WE CHECKED OUT THE AREA, THERE'S A CLEAR LINE OF SIGHT ALL AROUND US, AND IT'S A CLEAR NIGHT, GOOD VISIBILITY.
I'M ON IT. GET SOME SLEEP.
THANKS FOR... WELL, EVERYTHING. YOU'VE ALWAYS BEEN THERE FOR ME AND...
...I DON'T THINK I'VE EVER SAID THANKS.
I FIGURED KEEPING ME ALIVE WAS OUR WAY OF SAYING THAT. FOLLOWING YOU INTO THE GATES OF HELL THEMSELVES IS MY WAY OF SAYING IT TO YOU.
YOU KNOW THIS IS A FUCKING *DISASTER* ALREADY, RIGHT?
I *KNOW.*
NOW I'M WORRIED ABOUT GETTING BACK BEFORE ANDREA PANICS AND SENDS A SEARCH PARTY...
...
I'LL RELIEVE YOU IN A FEW HOURS. WE NEED TO BE ON THE ROAD AT DAWN.

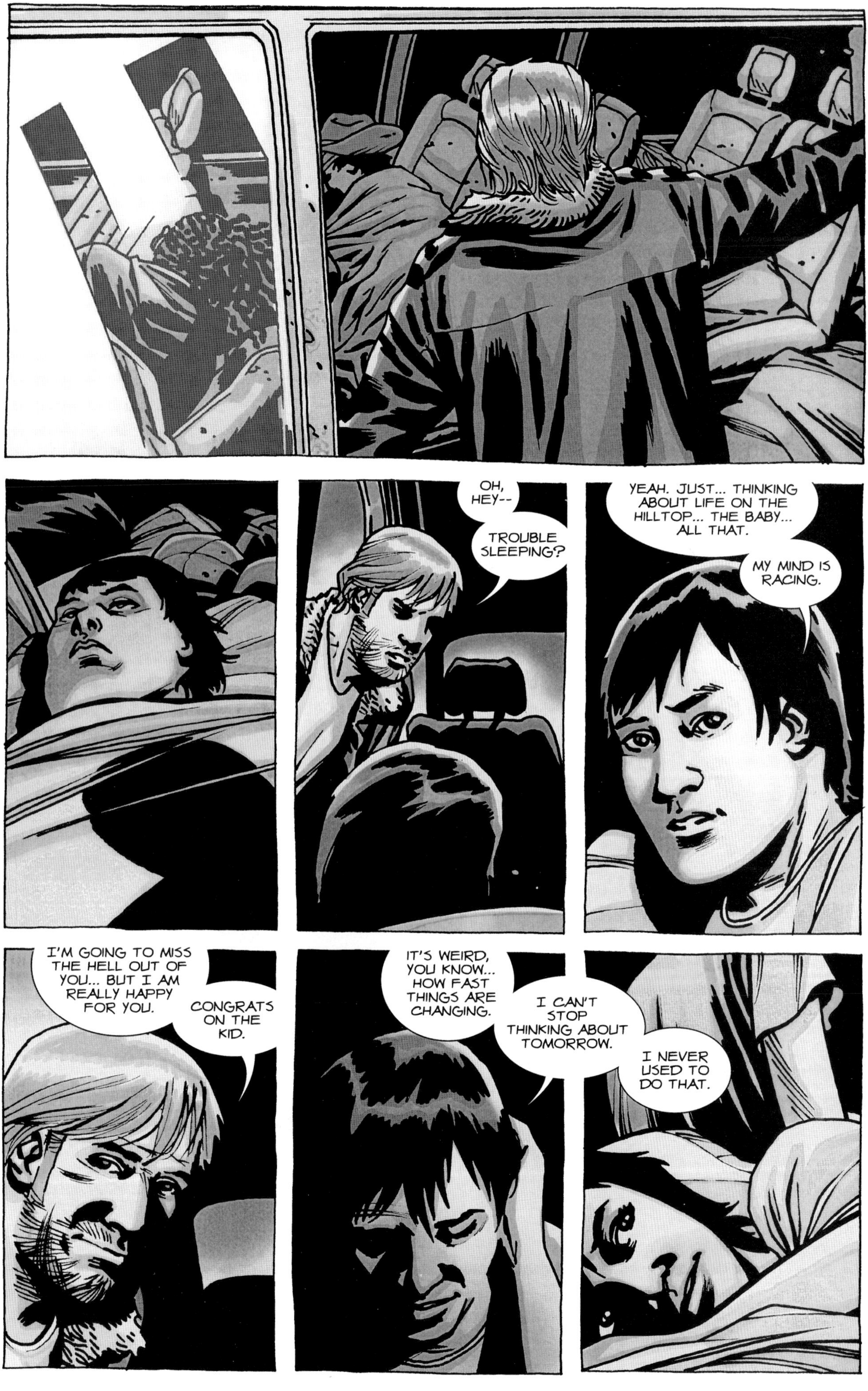
OH, HEY--
TROUBLE SLEEPING?
YEAH. JUST... THINKING ABOUT LIFE ON THE HILLTOP... THE BABY... ALL THAT.
MY MIND IS RACING.
I'M GOING TO MISS THE HELL OUT OF YOU... BUT I AM REALLY HAPPY FOR YOU.
CONGRATS ON THE KID.
IT'S WEIRD, YOU KNOW... HOW FAST THINGS ARE CHANGING.
I CAN'T STOP THINKING ABOUT TOMORROW.
I NEVER USED TO DO THAT.

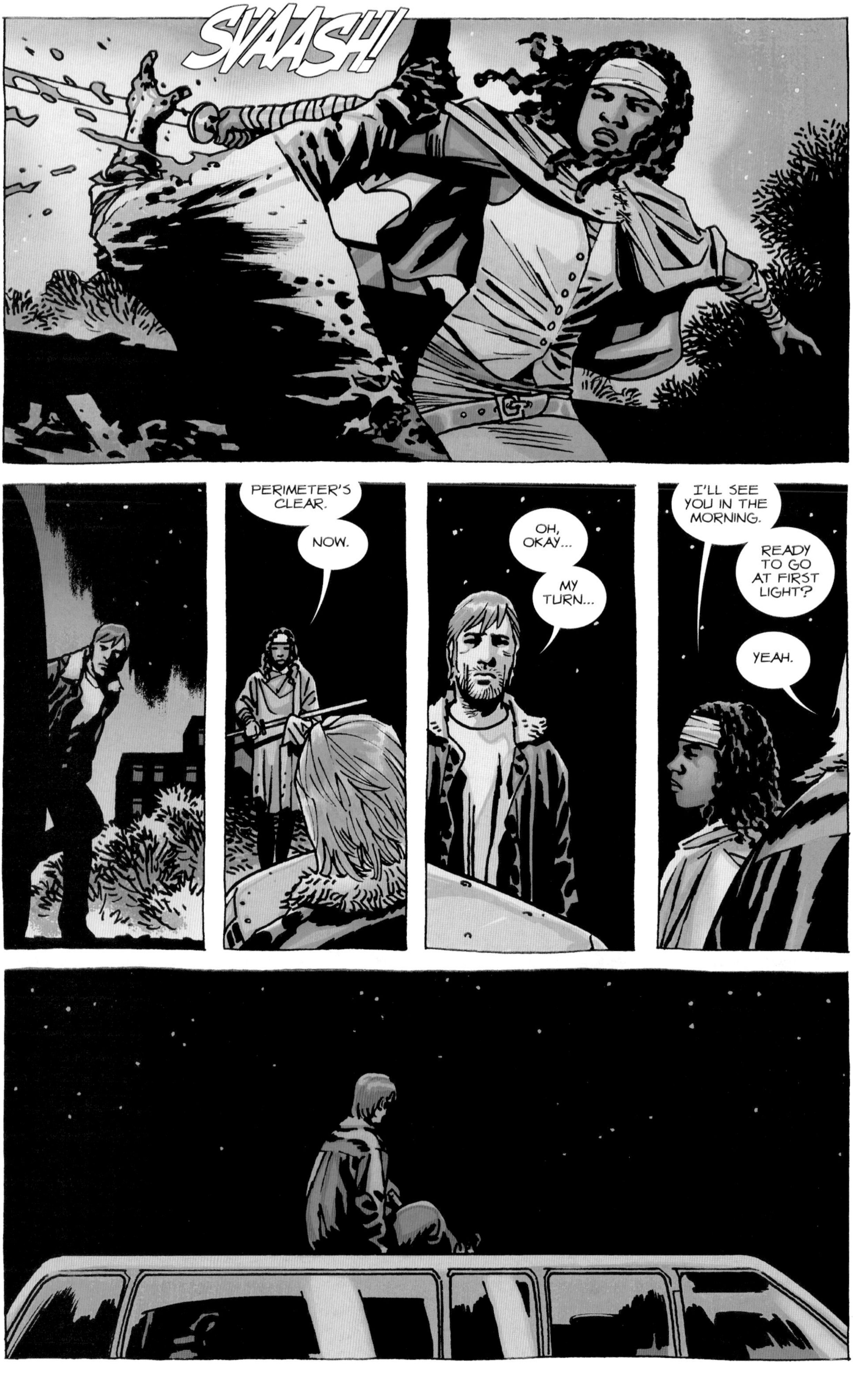
SVAASH!
PERIMETER'S CLEAR.
NOW.
OH, OKAY...
MY TURN...
I'LL SEE YOU IN THE MORNING.
READY TO GO AT FIRST LIGHT?
YEAH.

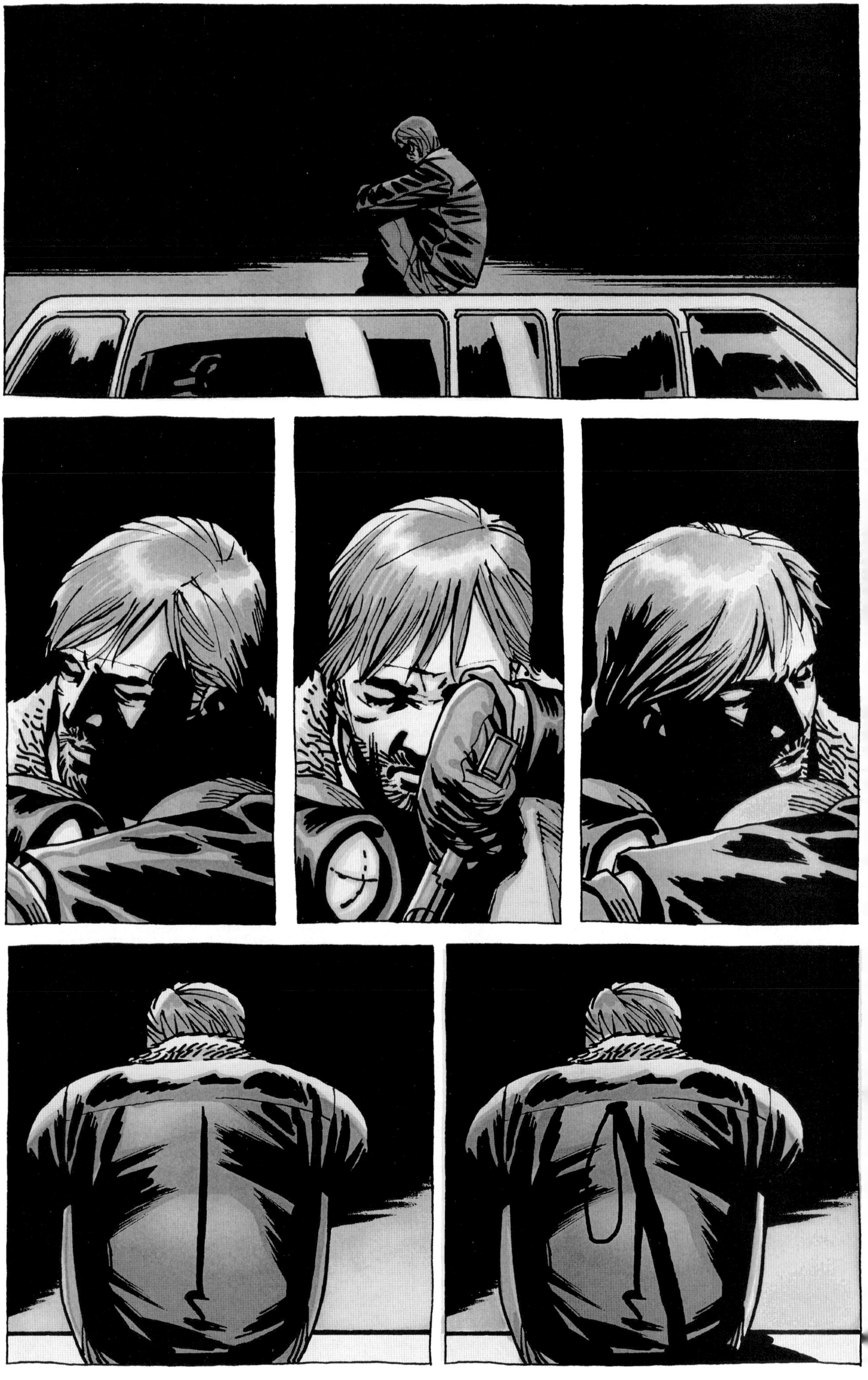

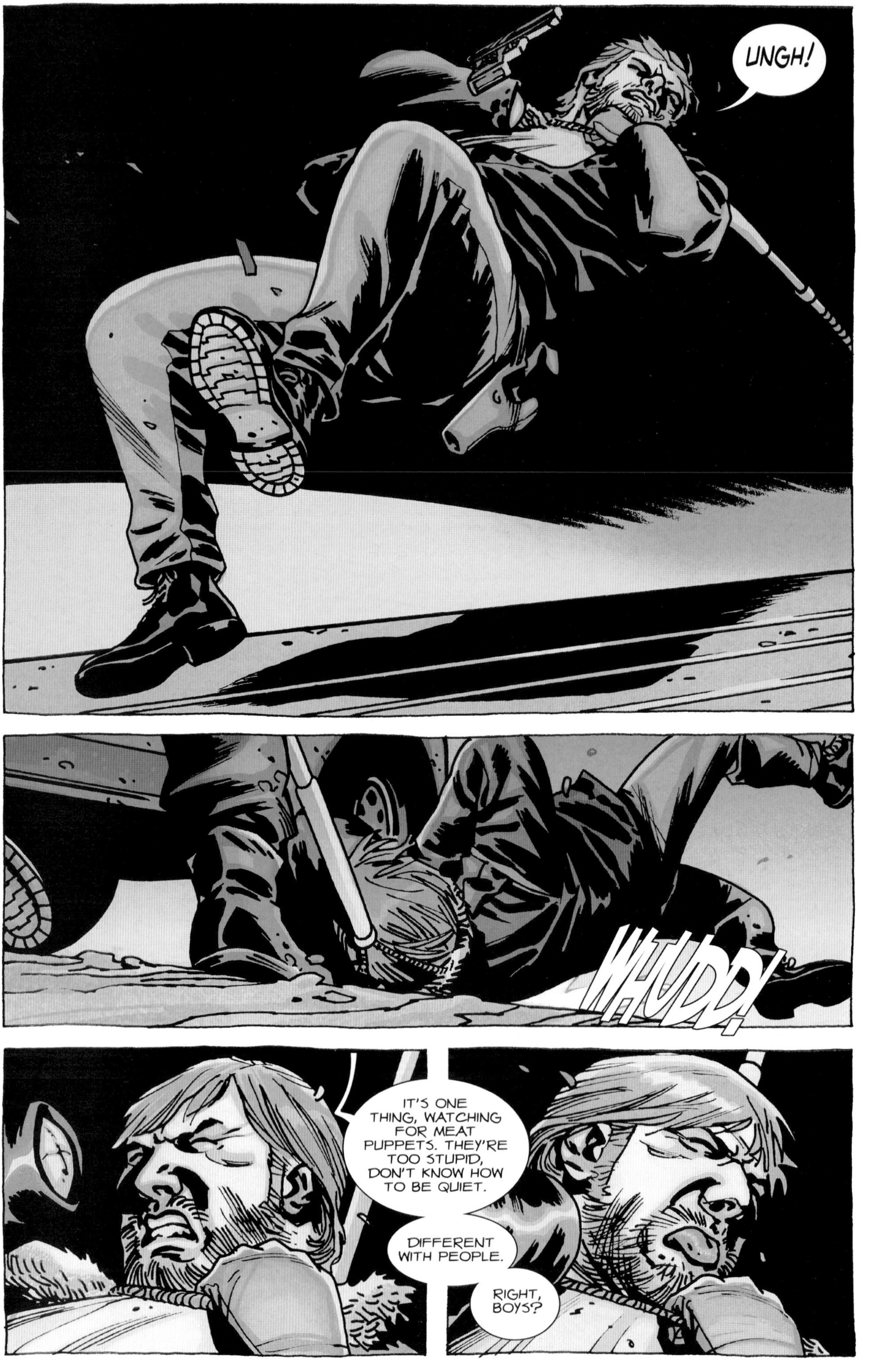
UNGH!
WHUDD!
IT'S ONE THING, WATCHING FOR MEAT PUPPETS. THEY'RE TOO STUPID, DON'T KNOW HOW TO BE QUIET.
DIFFERENT WITH PEOPLE.
RIGHT, BOYS?

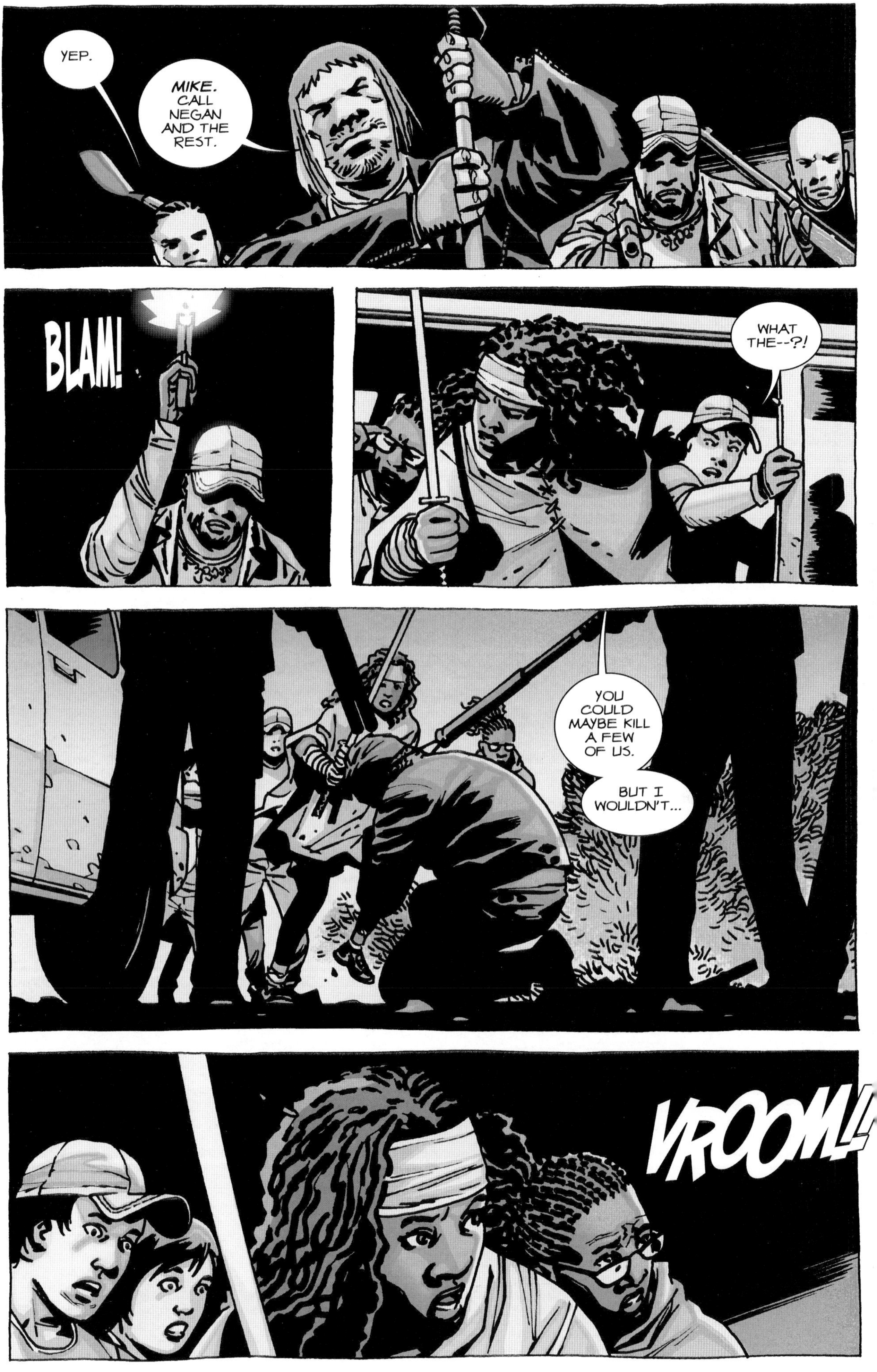
YEP.
MIKE. CALL NEGAN AND THE REST.
BLAM!
WHAT THE--?!
YOU COULD MAYBE KILL A FEW OF US.
BUT I WOULDN'T...
VROOM!!

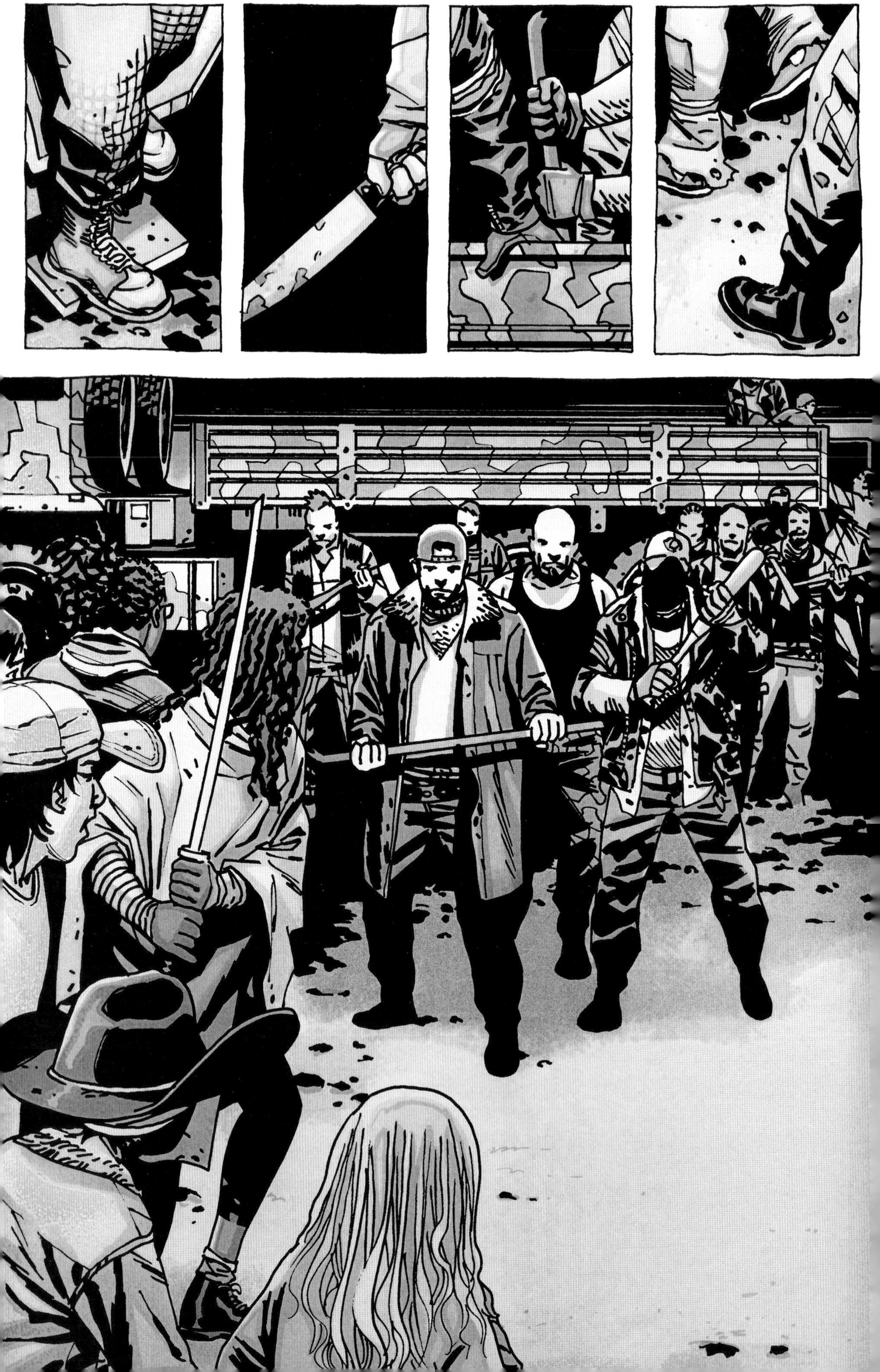

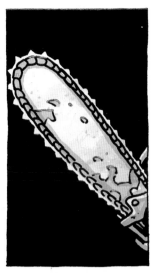

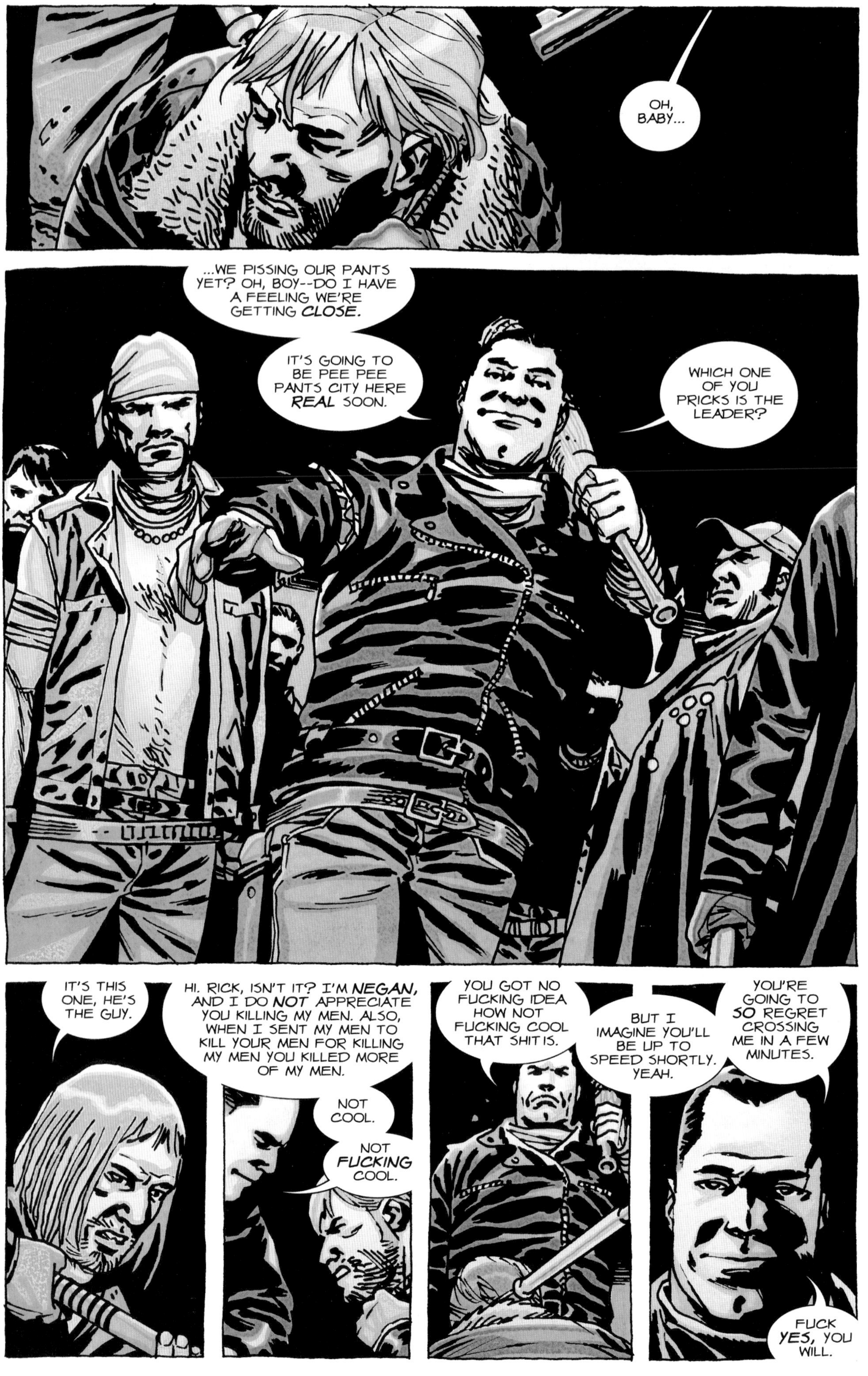
OH, BABY...
...WE PISSING OUR PANTS YET? OH, BOY--DO I HAVE A FEELING WE'RE GETTING CLOSE.
IT'S GOING TO BE PEE PEE PANTS CITY HERE REAL SOON.
WHICH ONE OF YOU PRICKS IS THE LEADER?
IT'S THIS ONE, HE'S THE GUY.
HI. RICK, ISN'T IT? I'M NEGAN, AND I DO NOT APPRECIATE YOU KILLING MY MEN. ALSO, WHEN I SENT MY MEN TO KILL YOUR MEN FOR KILLING MY MEN YOU KILLED MORE OF MY MEN.
NOT COOL.
NOT FUCKING COOL.
YOU GOT NO FUCKING IDEA HOW NOT FUCKING COOL THAT SHIT IS.
BUT I IMAGINE YOU'LL BE UP TO SPEED SHORTLY. YEAH.
YOU'RE GOING TO SO REGRET CROSSING ME IN A FEW MINUTES.
FUCK YES, YOU WILL.

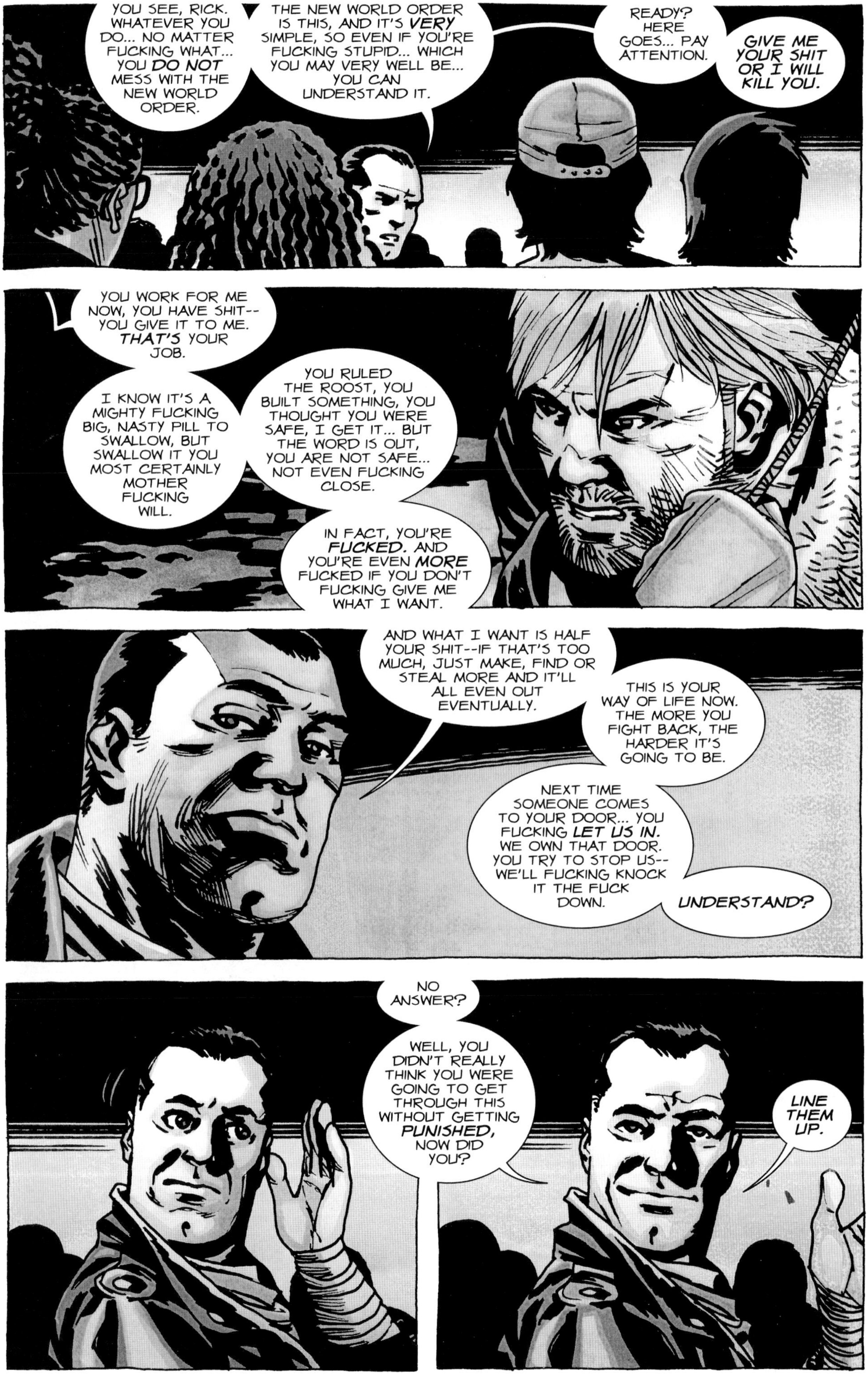
YOU SEE, RICK. WHATEVER YOU DO... NO MATTER FUCKING WHAT... YOU DO NOT MESS WITH THE NEW WORLD ORDER.
THE NEW WORLD ORDER IS THIS, AND IT'S VERY SIMPLE, SO EVEN IF YOU'RE FUCKING STUPID... WHICH YOU MAY VERY WELL BE... YOU CAN UNDERSTAND IT.
READY? HERE GOES... PAY ATTENTION.
GIVE ME YOUR SHIT OR I WILL KILL YOU.
YOU WORK FOR ME NOW, YOU HAVE SHIT-- YOU GIVE IT TO ME. THAT'S YOUR JOB.
I KNOW IT'S A MIGHTY FUCKING BIG, NASTY PILL TO SWALLOW, BUT SWALLOW IT YOU MOST CERTAINLY MOTHER FUCKING WILL.
YOU RULED THE ROOST, YOU BUILT SOMETHING, YOU THOUGHT YOU WERE SAFE, I GET IT... BUT THE WORD IS OUT, YOU ARE NOT SAFE... NOT EVEN FUCKING CLOSE.
IN FACT, YOU'RE FUCKED. AND YOU'RE EVEN MORE FUCKED IF YOU DON'T FUCKING GIVE ME WHAT I WANT.
AND WHAT I WANT IS HALF YOUR SHIT--IF THAT'S TOO MUCH, JUST MAKE, FIND OR STEAL MORE AND IT'LL ALL EVEN OUT EVENTUALLY.
THIS IS YOUR WAY OF LIFE NOW. THE MORE YOU FIGHT BACK, THE HARDER IT'S GOING TO BE.
NEXT TIME SOMEONE COMES TO YOUR DOOR... YOU FUCKING LET US IN. WE OWN THAT DOOR. YOU TRY TO STOP US-- WE'LL FUCKING KNOCK IT THE FUCK DOWN.
UNDERSTAND?
NO ANSWER?
WELL, YOU DIDN'T REALLY THINK YOU WERE GOING TO GET THROUGH THIS WITHOUT GETTING PUNISHED, NOW DID YOU?
LINE THEM UP.

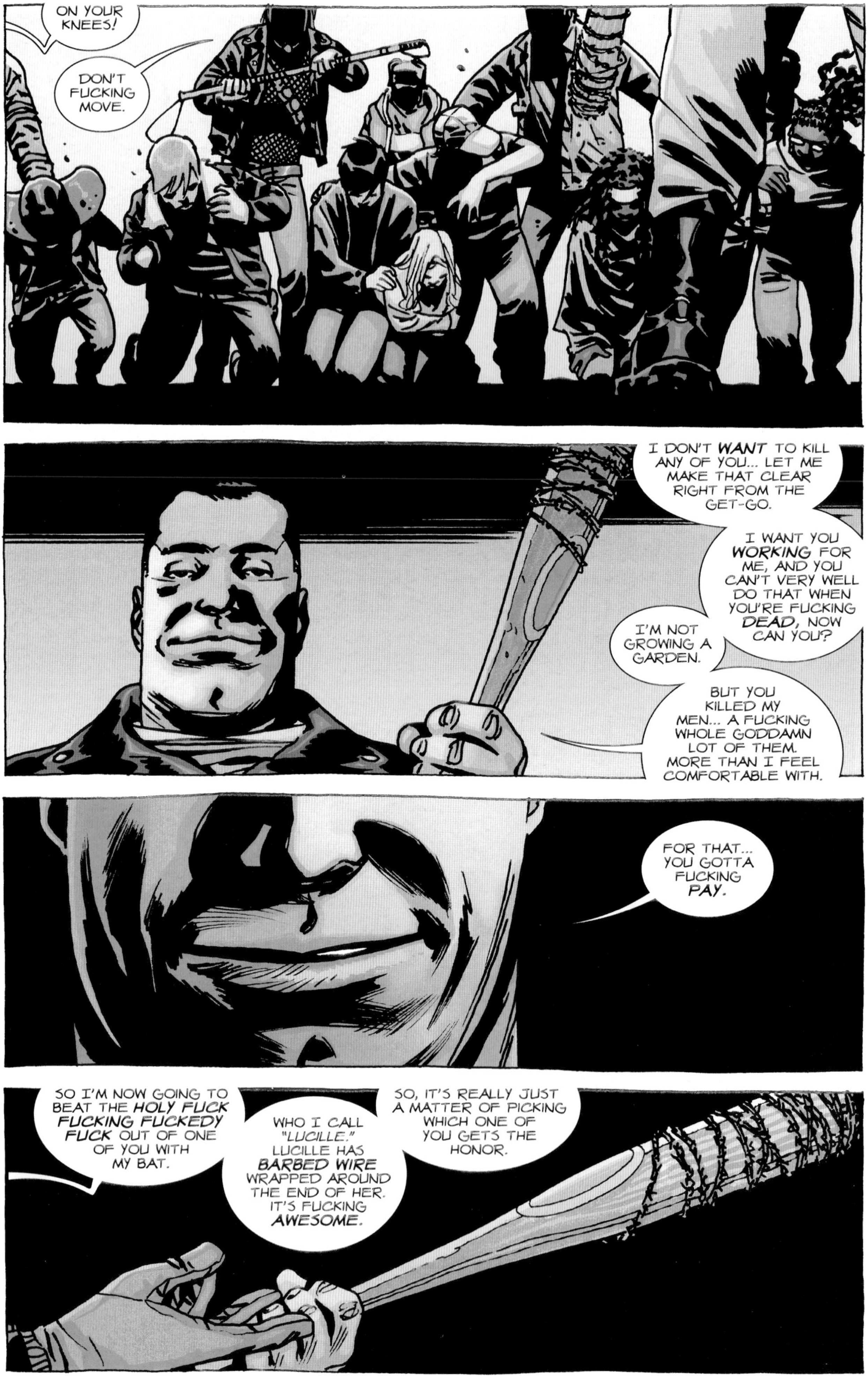

ON YOUR KNEES!
DON'T FUCKING MOVE.
I DON'T WANT TO KILL ANY OF YOU... LET ME MAKE THAT CLEAR RIGHT FROM THE GET-GO.
I WANT YOU WORKING FOR ME, AND YOU CAN'T VERY WELL DO THAT WHEN YOU'RE FUCKING DEAD, NOW CAN YOU?
I'M NOT GROWING A GARDEN.
BUT YOU KILLED MY MEN... A FUCKING WHOLE GODDAMN LOT OF THEM. MORE THAN I FEEL COMFORTABLE WITH.
FOR THAT... YOU GOTTA FUCKING PAY.
SO I'M NOW GOING TO BEAT THE HOLY FUCK FUCKING FUCKEDY FUCK OUT OF ONE OF YOU WITH MY BAT.
WHO I CALL "LUCILLE." LUCILLE HAS BARBED WIRE WRAPPED AROUND THE END OF HER. IT'S FUCKING AWESOME.
SO, IT'S REALLY JUST A MATTER OF PICKING WHICH ONE OF YOU GETS THE HONOR.

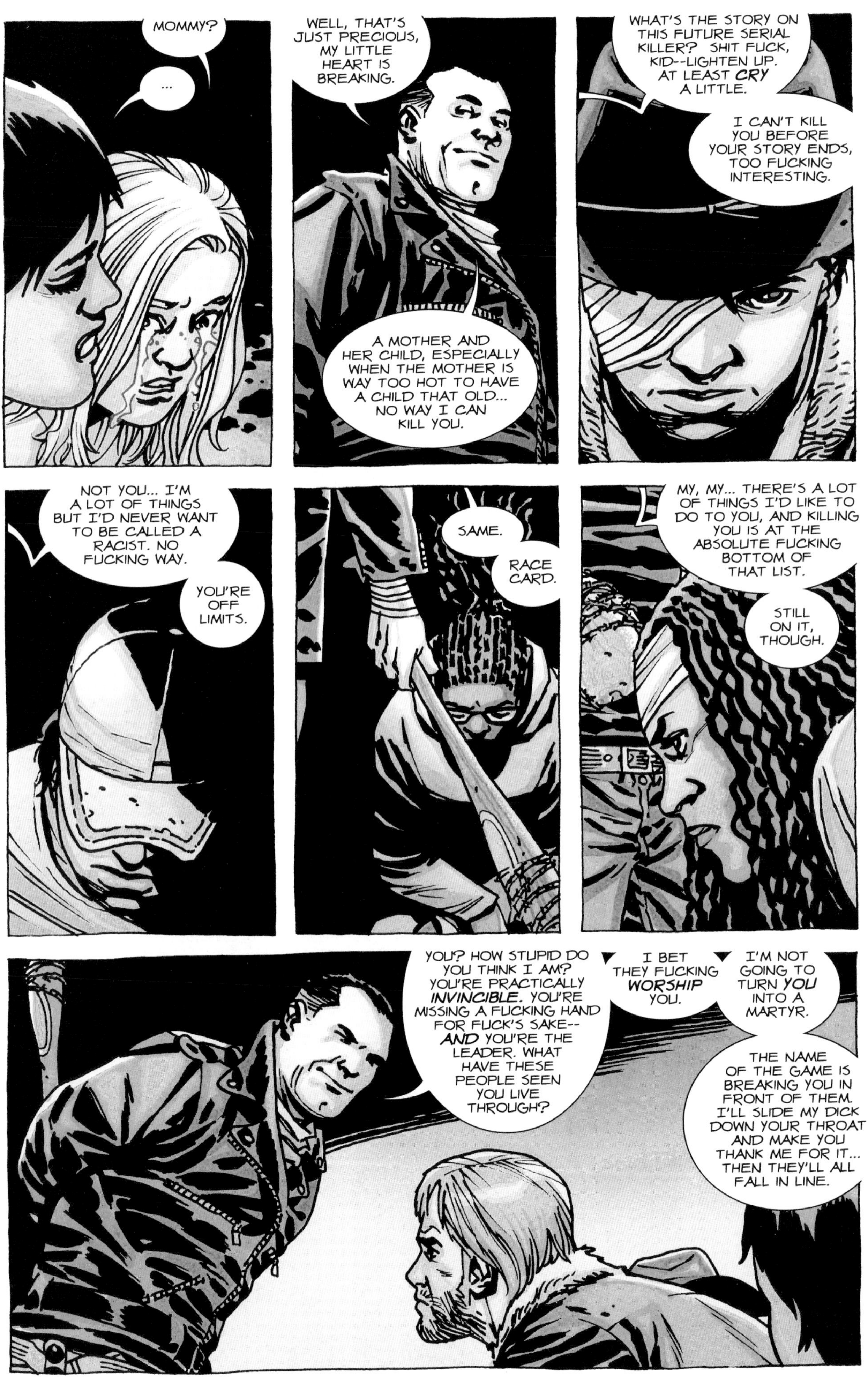
MOMMY?
...
WELL, THAT'S JUST PRECIOUS, MY LITTLE HEART IS BREAKING.
A MOTHER AND HER CHILD, ESPECIALLY WHEN THE MOTHER IS WAY TOO HOT TO HAVE A CHILD THAT OLD... NO WAY I CAN KILL YOU.
WHAT'S THE STORY ON THIS FUTURE SERIAL KILLER? SHIT FUCK, KID--LIGHTEN UP. AT LEAST CRY A LITTLE.
I CAN'T KILL YOU BEFORE YOUR STORY ENDS, TOO FUCKING INTERESTING.
NOT YOU... I'M A LOT OF THINGS BUT I'D NEVER WANT TO BE CALLED A RACIST. NO FUCKING WAY.
YOU'RE OFF LIMITS.
SAME.
RACE CARD.
MY, MY... THERE'S A LOT OF THINGS I'D LIKE TO DO TO YOU, AND KILLING YOU IS AT THE ABSOLUTE FUCKING BOTTOM OF THAT LIST.
STILL ON IT, THOUGH.
YOU? HOW STUPID DO YOU THINK I AM? YOU'RE PRACTICALLY INVINCIBLE. YOU'RE MISSING A FUCKING HAND FOR FUCK'S SAKE-- AND YOU'RE THE LEADER. WHAT HAVE THESE PEOPLE SEEN YOU LIVE THROUGH?
I BET THEY FUCKING WORSHIP YOU.
I'M NOT GOING TO TURN YOU INTO A MARTYR.
THE NAME OF THE GAME IS BREAKING YOU IN FRONT OF THEM. I'LL SLIDE MY DICK DOWN YOUR THROAT AND MAKE YOU THANK ME FOR IT... THEN THEY'LL ALL FALL IN LINE.

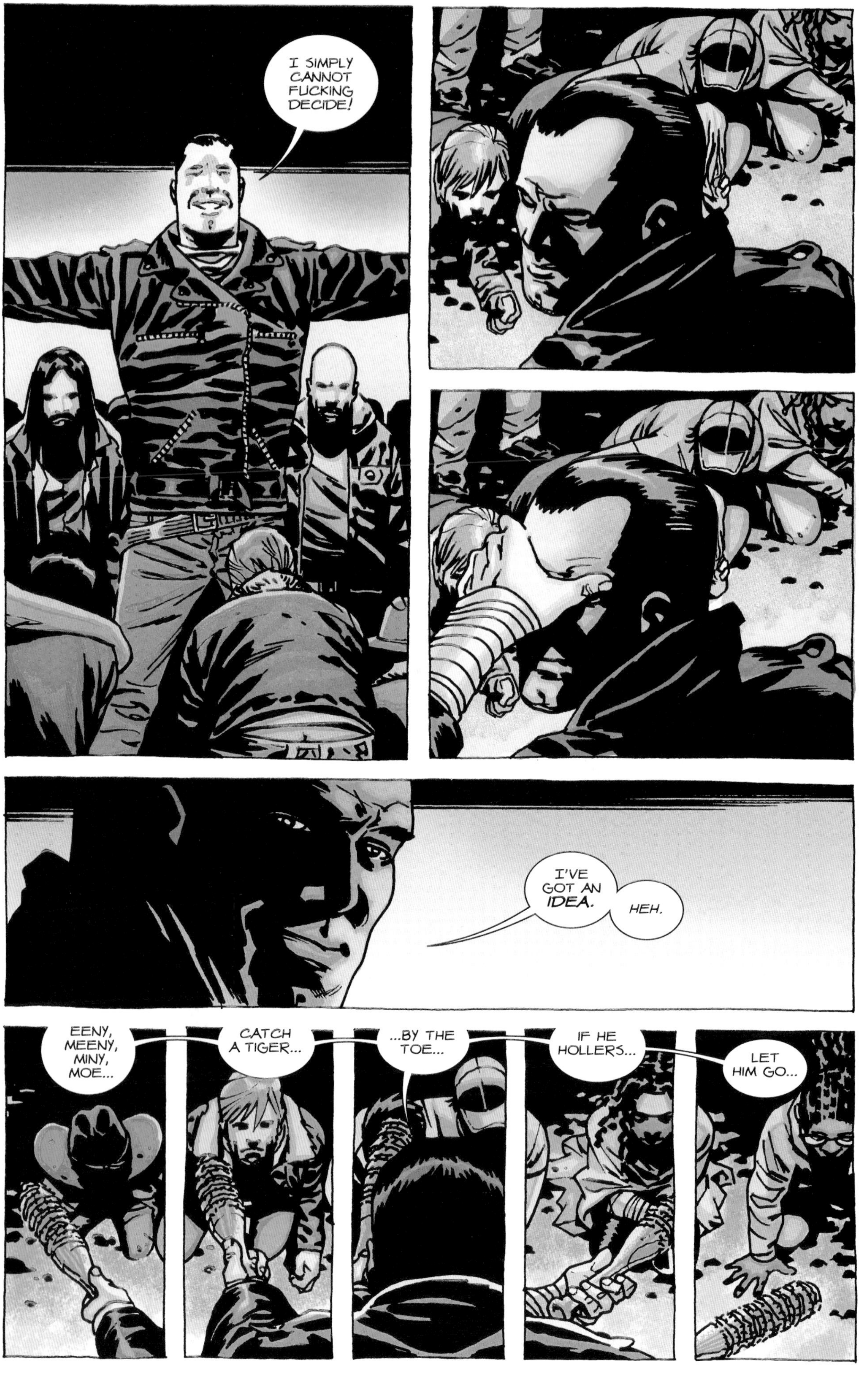
I SIMPLY CANNOT FUCKING DECIDE!
I'VE GOT AN IDEA.
HEH.
EENY, MEENY, MINY, MOE...
CATCH A TIGER...
...BY THE TOE...
IF HE HOLLERS...
LET HIM GO...

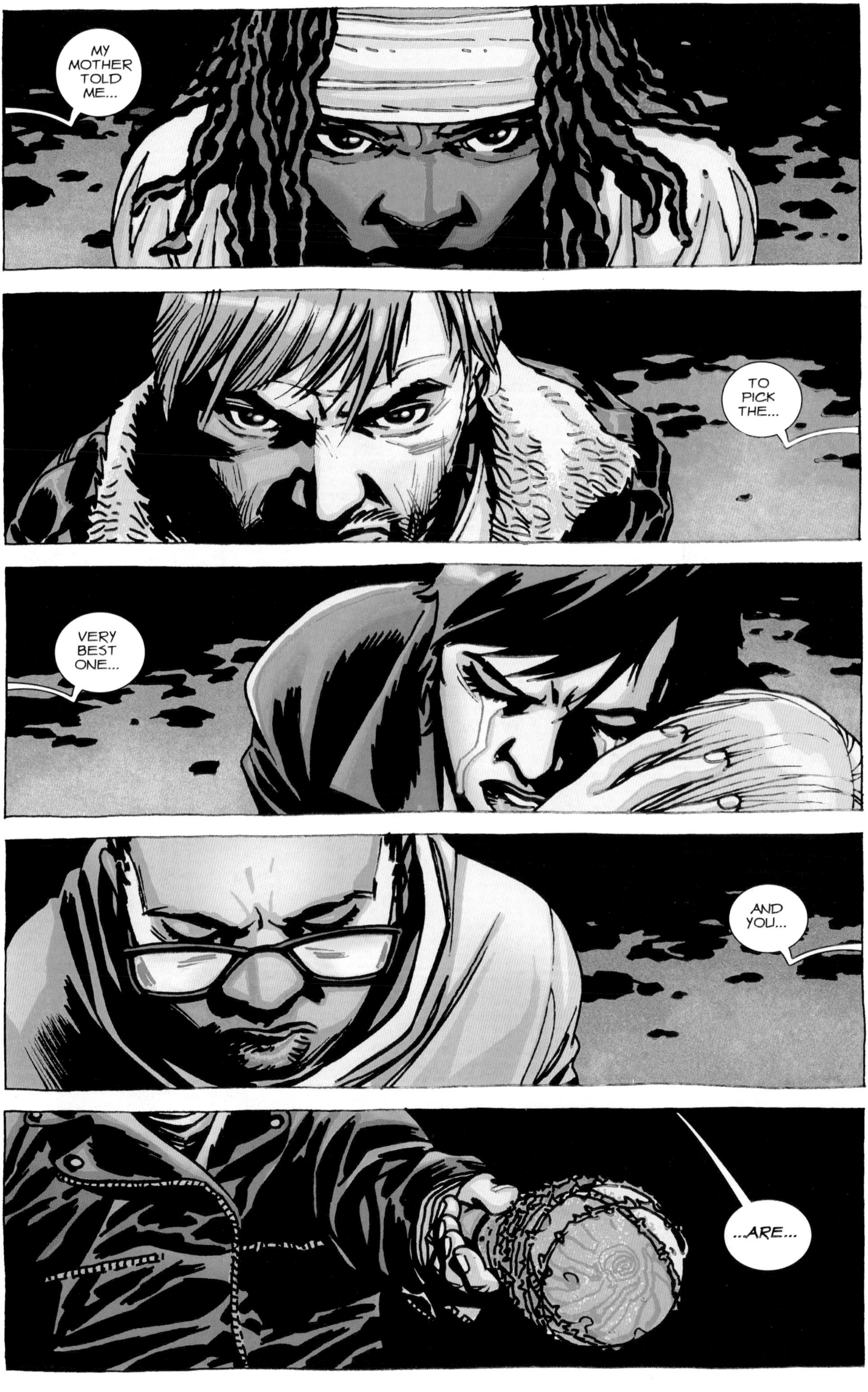
MY MOTHER TOLD ME...
TO PICK THE...
VERY BEST ONE...
AND YOU...
...ARE...

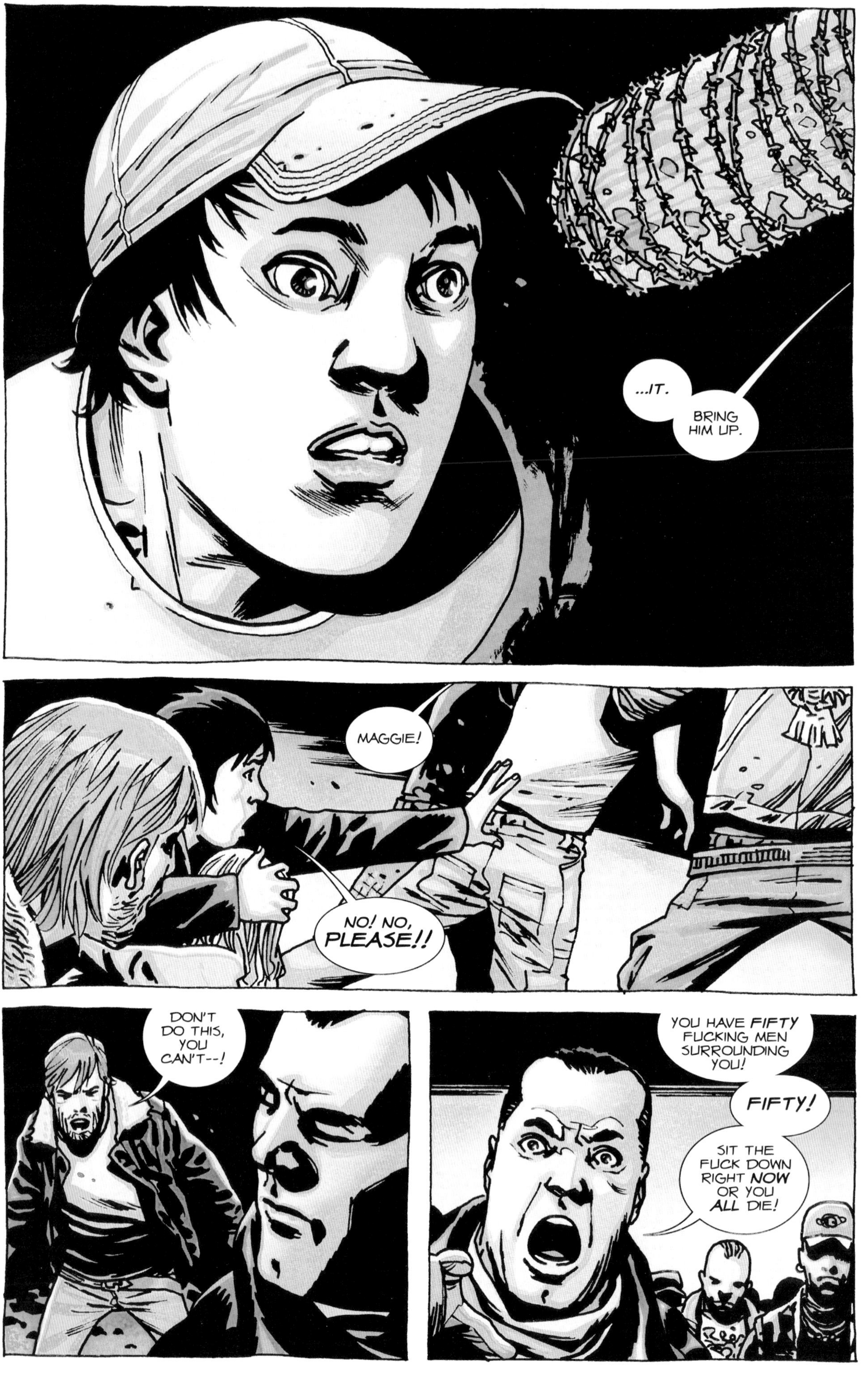
...IT.
BRING HIM UP.
MAGGIE!
NO! NO, PLEASE!!
DON'T DO THIS, YOU CAN'T--!
YOU HAVE FIFTY FUCKING MEN SURROUNDING YOU!
FIFTY!
SIT THE FUCK DOWN RIGHT NOW OR YOU ALL DIE!

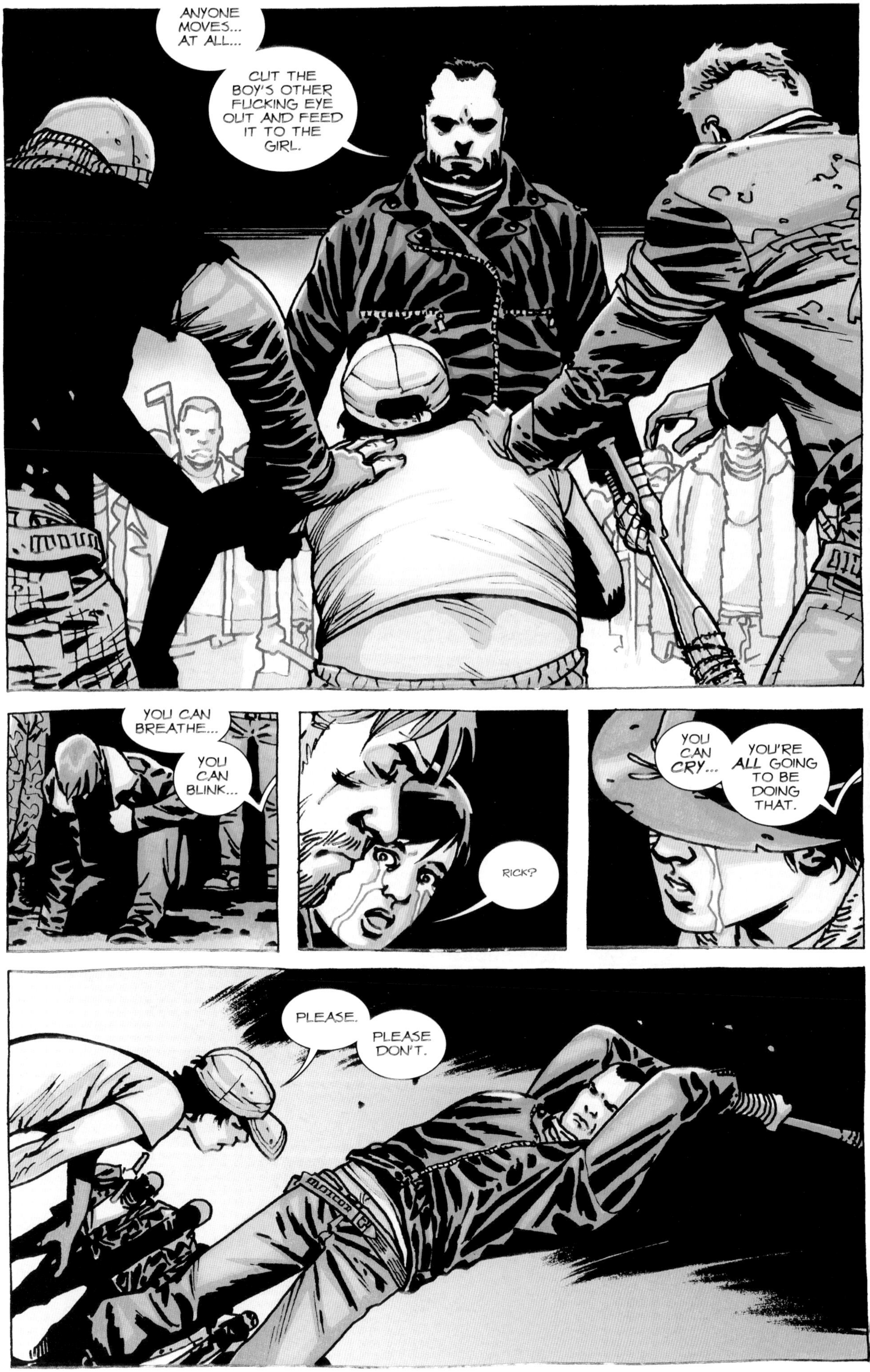
ANYONE MOVES... AT ALL...
CUT THE BOY'S OTHER FUCKING EYE OUT AND FEED IT TO THE GIRL.
YOU CAN BREATHE...
YOU CAN BLINK...
RICK?
YOU CAN CRY...
YOU'RE ALL GOING TO BE DOING THAT.
PLEASE.
PLEASE DON'T.

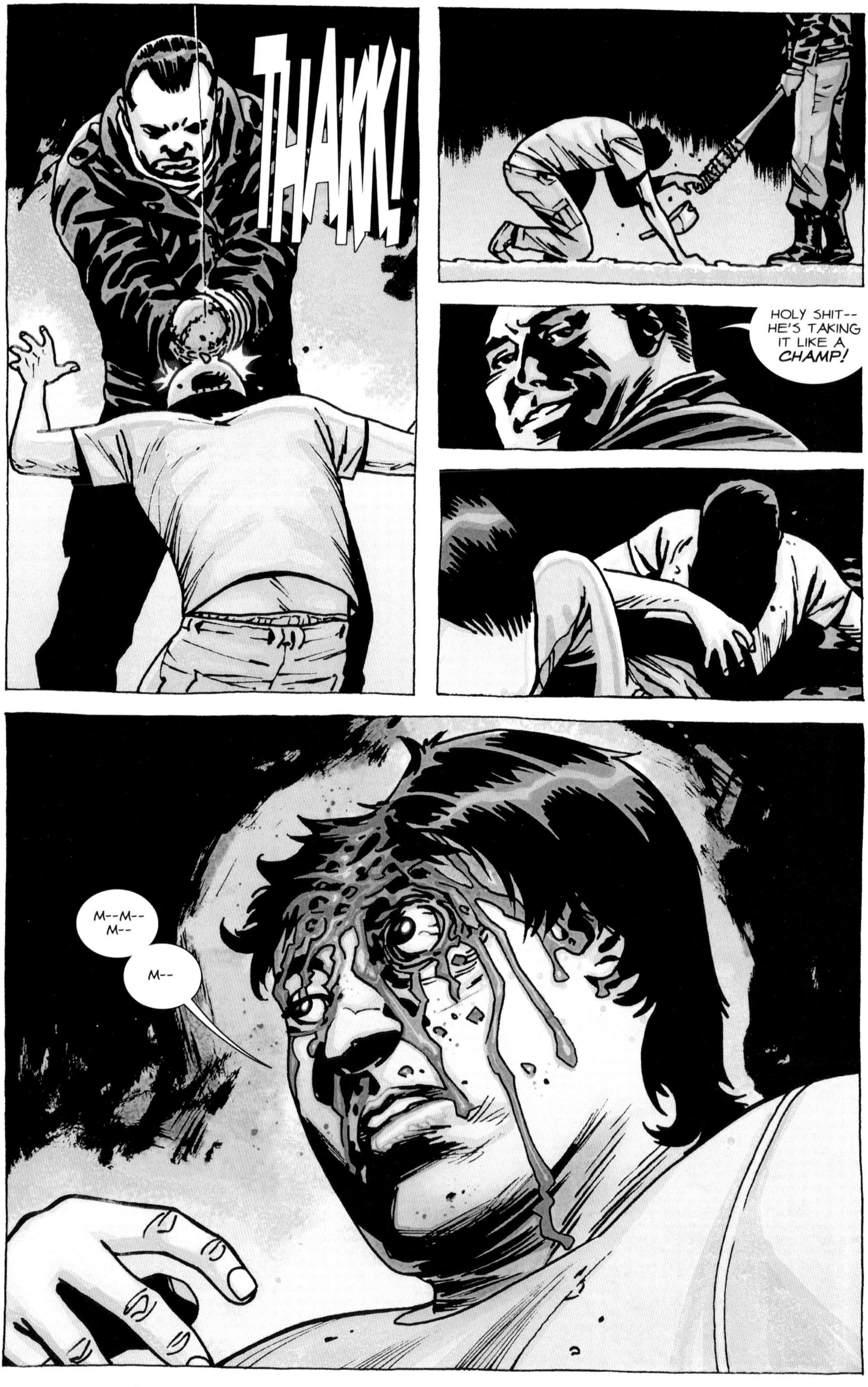
THAKK!
HOLY SHIT-- HE'S TAKING IT LIKE A CHAMP!
M--M-- M--
M--

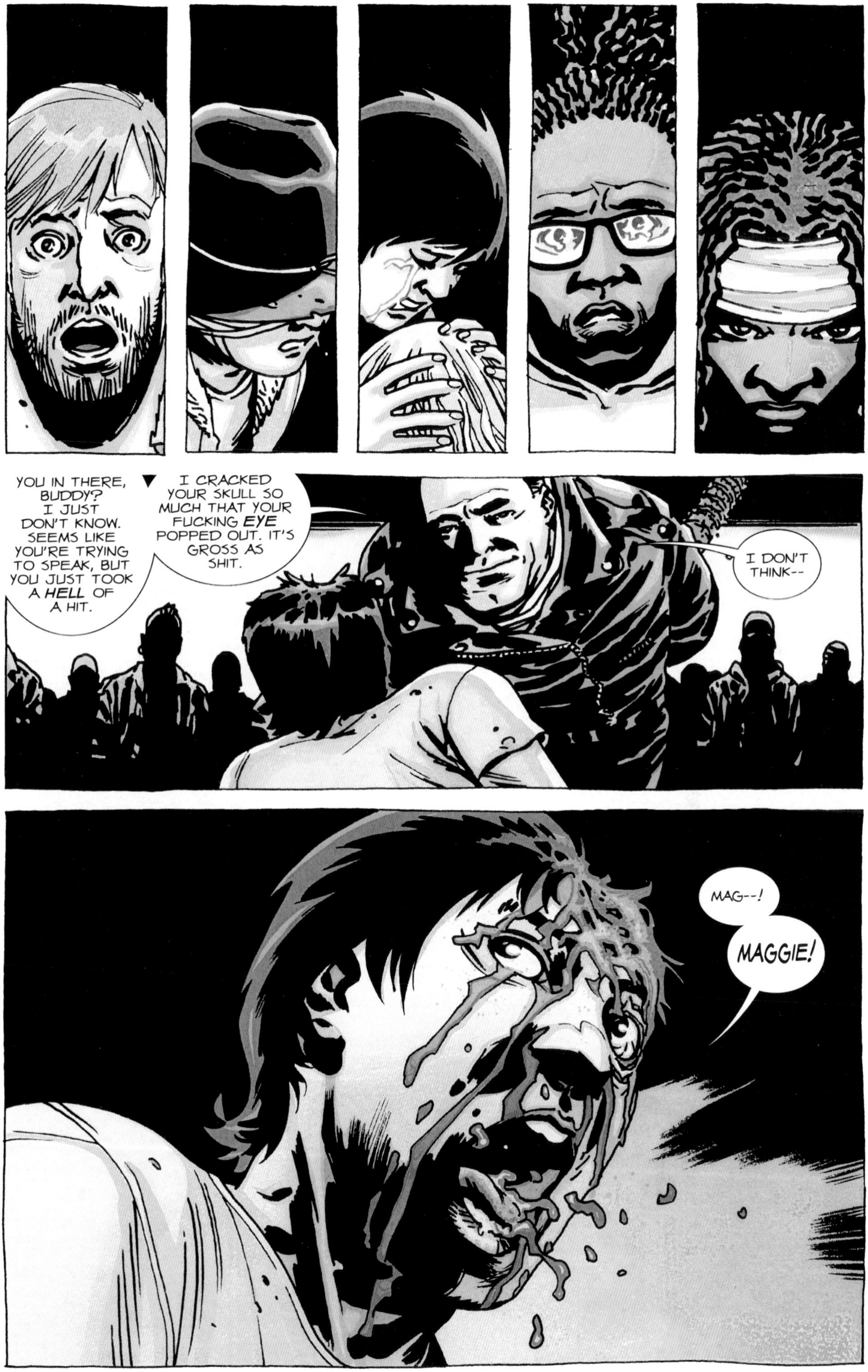

YOU IN THERE, BUDDY? I JUST DON'T KNOW. SEEMS LIKE YOU'RE TRYING TO SPEAK, BUT YOU JUST TOOK A HELL OF A HIT.
I CRACKED YOUR SKULL SO MUCH THAT YOUR FUCKING EYE POPPED OUT. IT'S GROSS AS SHIT.
I DON'T THINK--
MAG--!
MAGGIE!

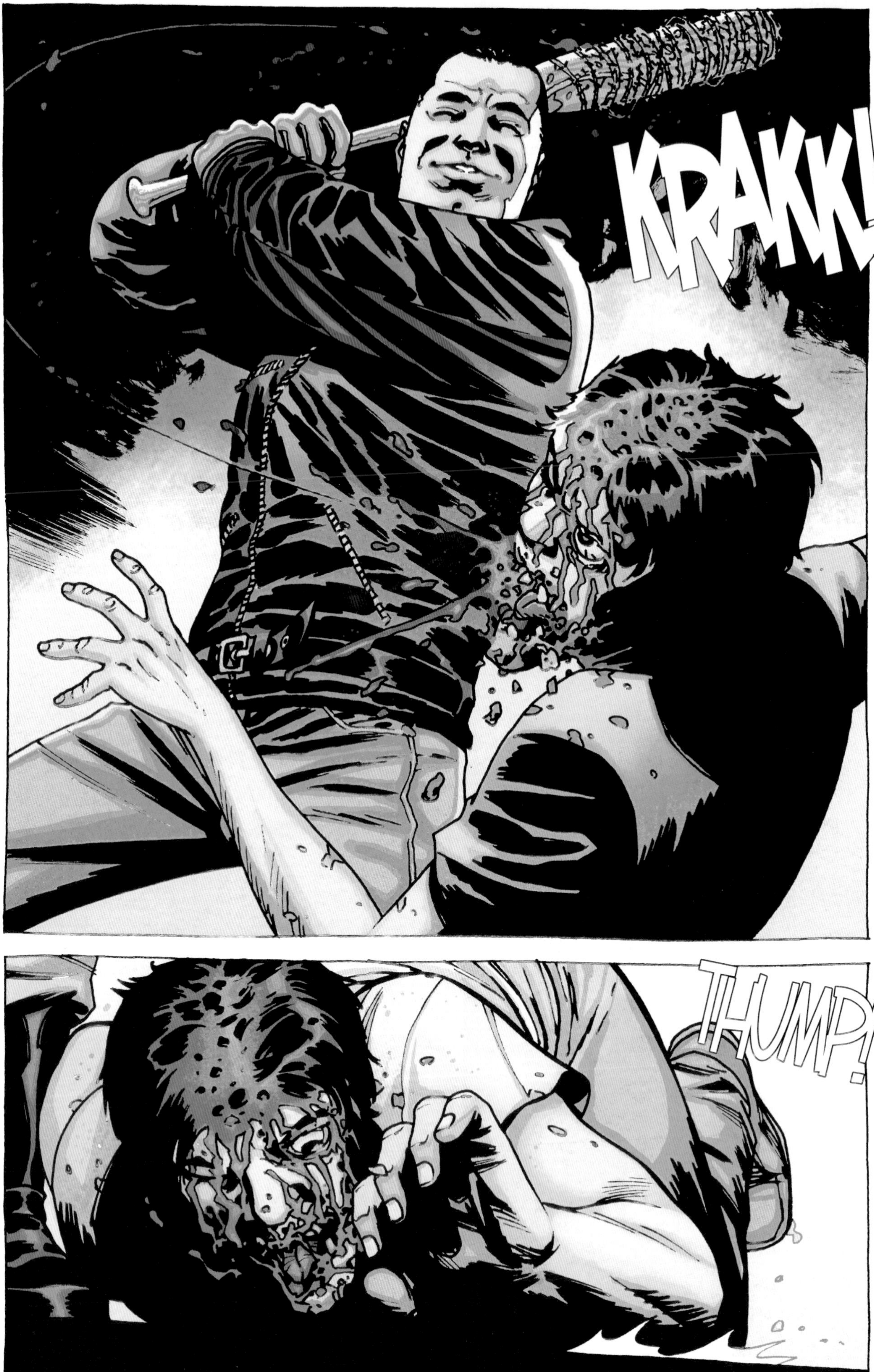
KRAKK!
THUMP!

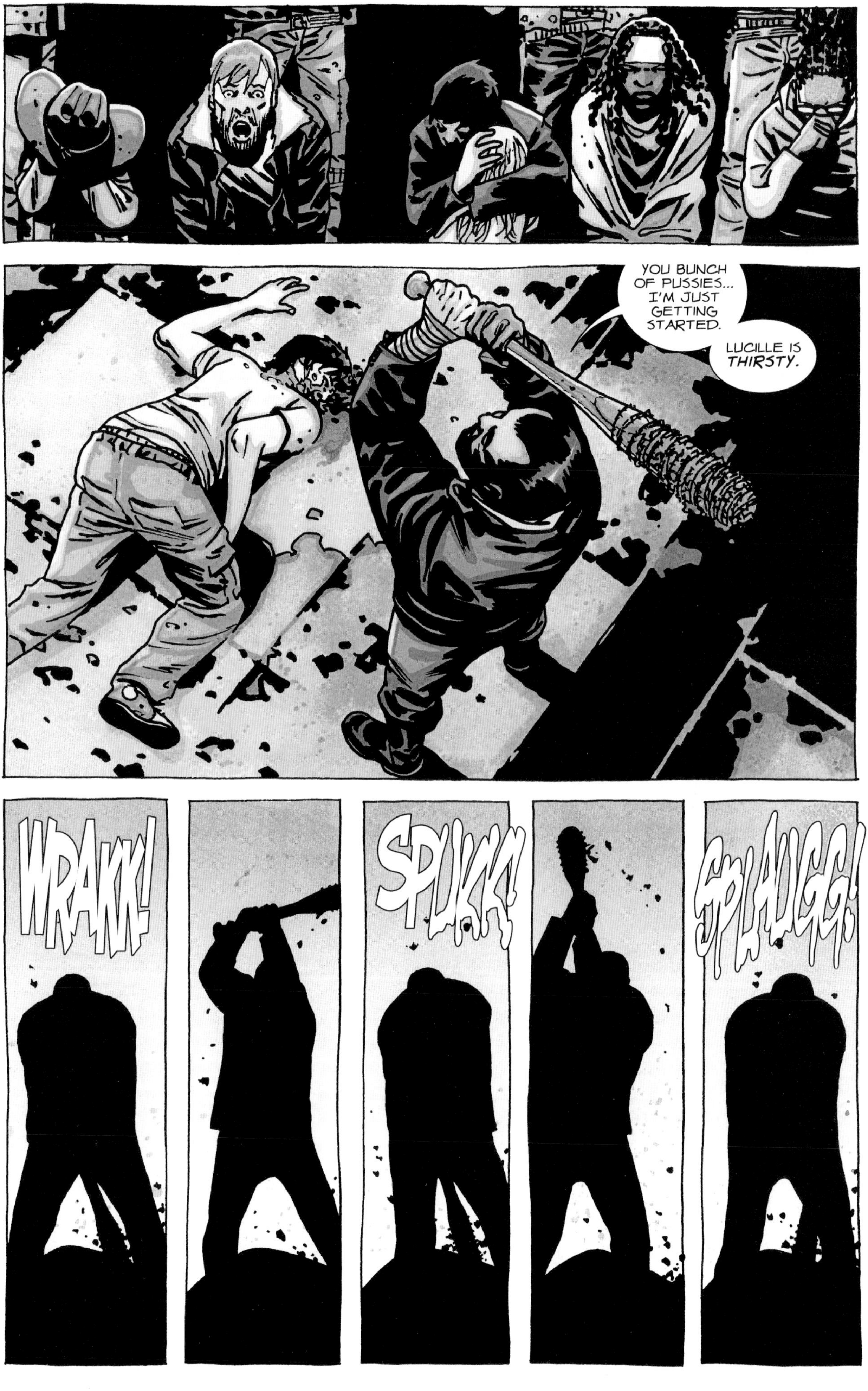
YOU BUNCH OF PUSSIES... I'M JUST GETTING STARTED.
LUCILLE IS *THIRSTY.*
WRAKK!
SPLUKK!
SPLAUGG!

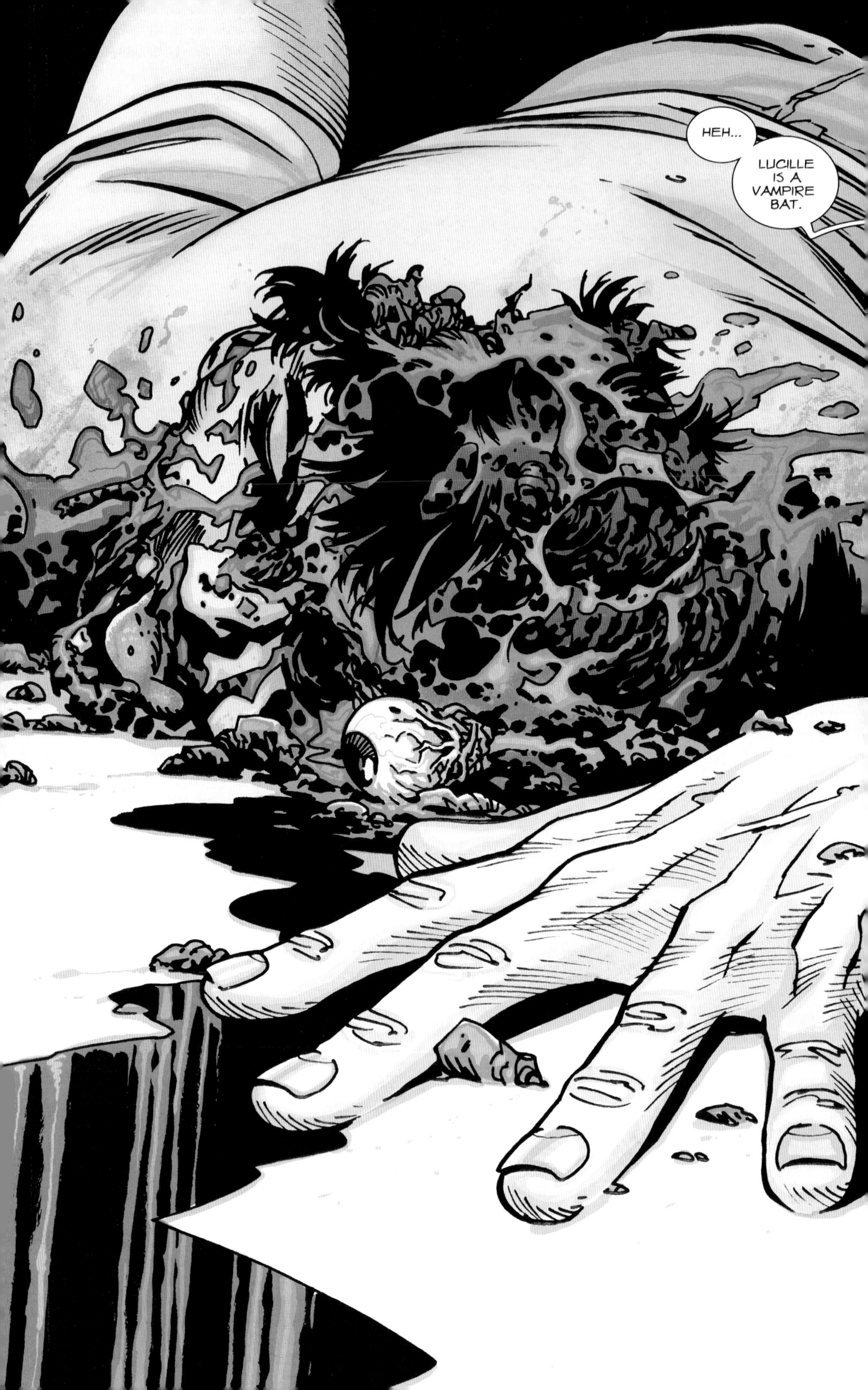
HEH...
LUCILLE IS A VAMPIRE BAT.

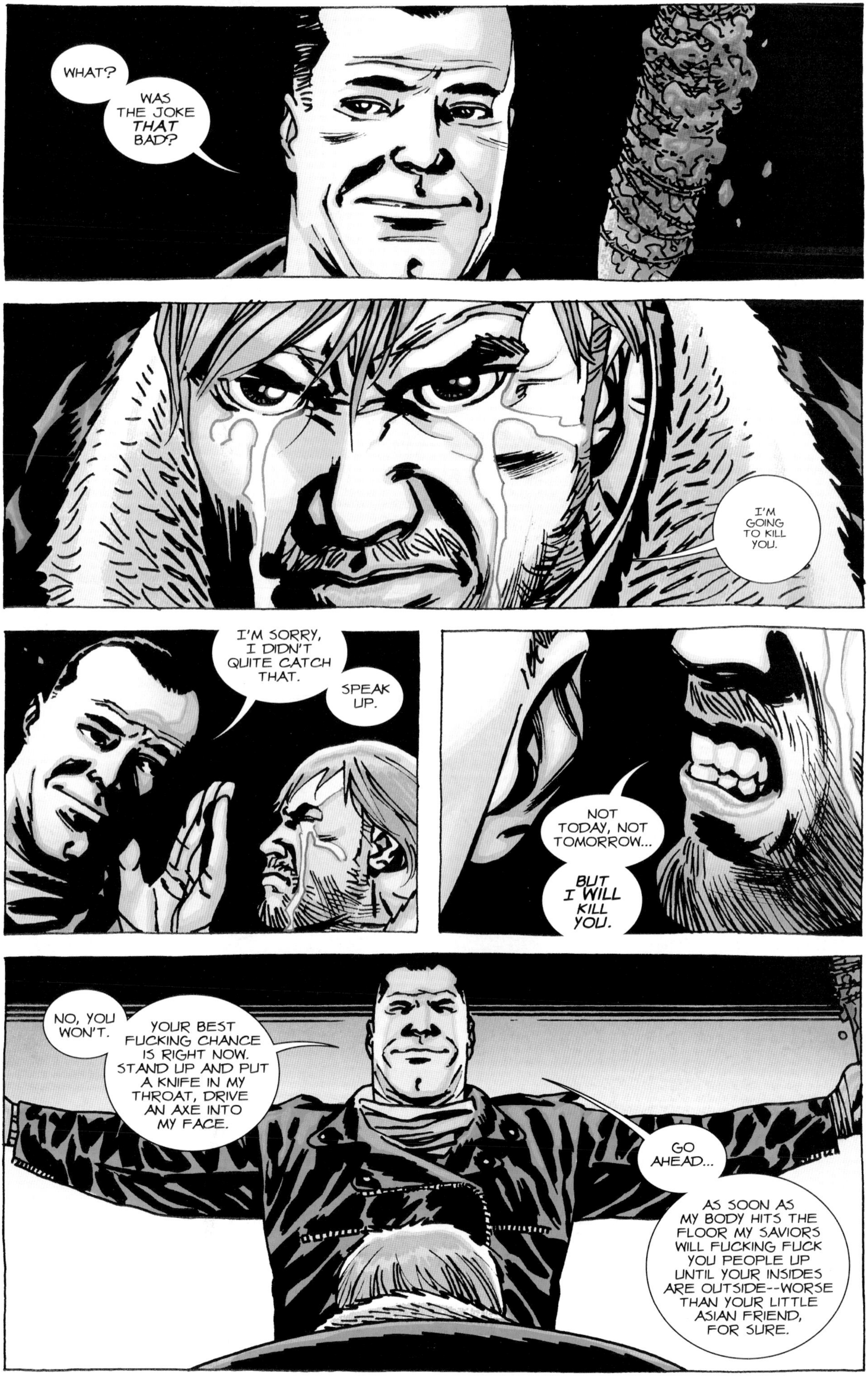
WHAT?
WAS THE JOKE *THAT* BAD?
I'M GOING TO KILL YOU.
I'M SORRY, I DIDN'T QUITE CATCH THAT.
SPEAK UP.
NOT TODAY, NOT TOMORROW...
BUT I WILL KILL YOU.
NO, YOU WON'T.
YOUR BEST FUCKING CHANCE IS RIGHT NOW. STAND UP AND PUT A KNIFE IN MY THROAT, DRIVE AN AXE INTO MY FACE.
GO AHEAD...
AS SOON AS MY BODY HITS THE FLOOR MY SAVIORS WILL FUCKING FUCK YOU PEOPLE UP UNTIL YOUR INSIDES ARE OUTSIDE--WORSE THAN YOUR LITTLE ASIAN FRIEND, FOR SURE.

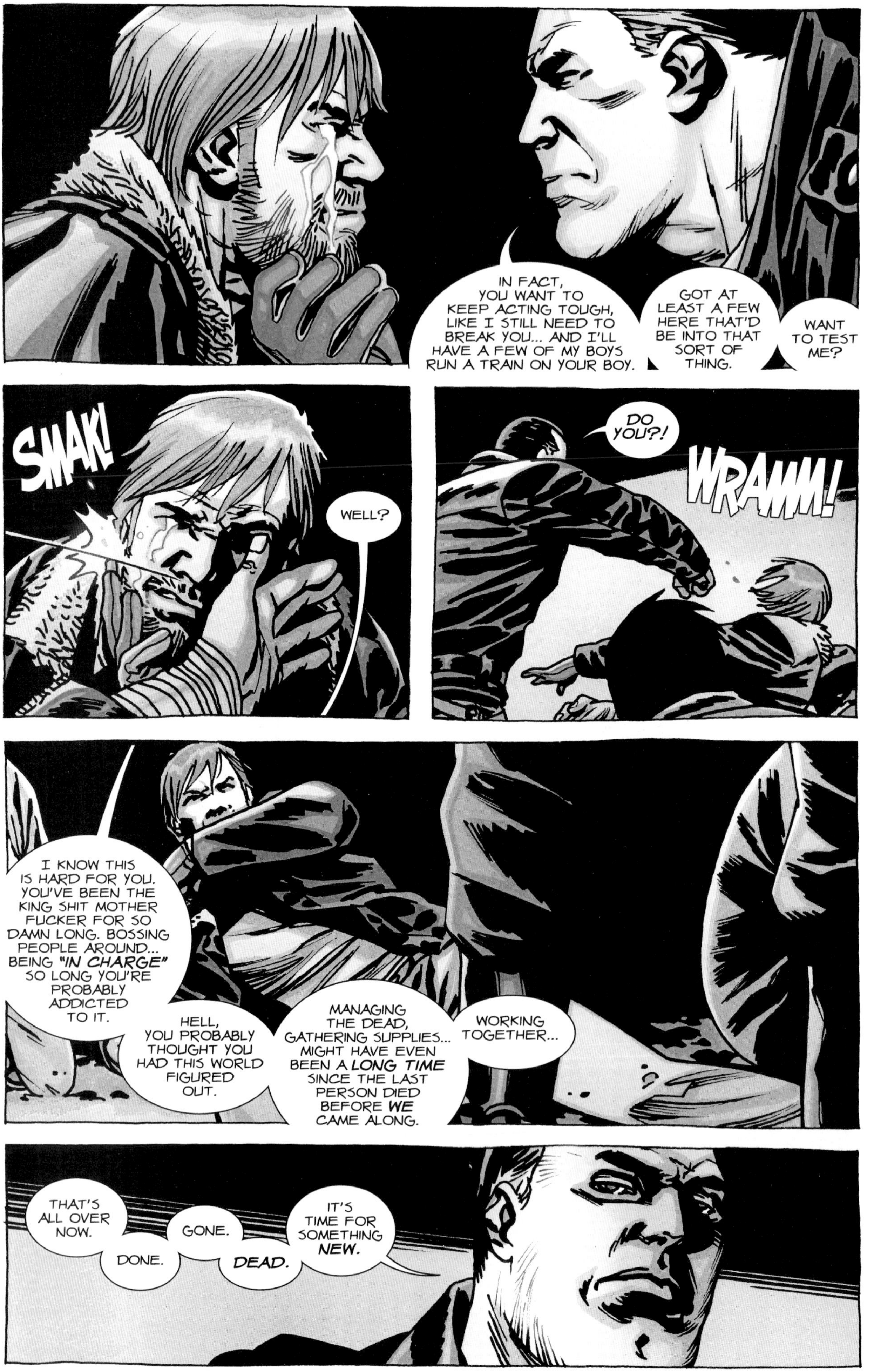
IN FACT, YOU WANT TO KEEP ACTING TOUGH, LIKE I STILL NEED TO BREAK YOU... AND I'LL HAVE A FEW OF MY BOYS RUN A TRAIN ON YOUR BOY.
GOT AT LEAST A FEW HERE THAT'D BE INTO THAT SORT OF THING.
WANT TO TEST ME?
SMAK!
WELL?
DO YOU?!
WRAMM!
I KNOW THIS IS HARD FOR YOU. YOU'VE BEEN THE KING SHIT MOTHER FUCKER FOR SO DAMN LONG. BOSSING PEOPLE AROUND... BEING "IN CHARGE" SO LONG YOU'RE PROBABLY ADDICTED TO IT.
HELL, YOU PROBABLY THOUGHT YOU HAD THIS WORLD FIGURED OUT.
MANAGING THE DEAD, GATHERING SUPPLIES... MIGHT HAVE EVEN BEEN A LONG TIME SINCE THE LAST PERSON DIED BEFORE WE CAME ALONG.
WORKING TOGETHER...
THAT'S ALL OVER NOW.
DONE.
GONE.
DEAD.
IT'S TIME FOR SOMETHING NEW.

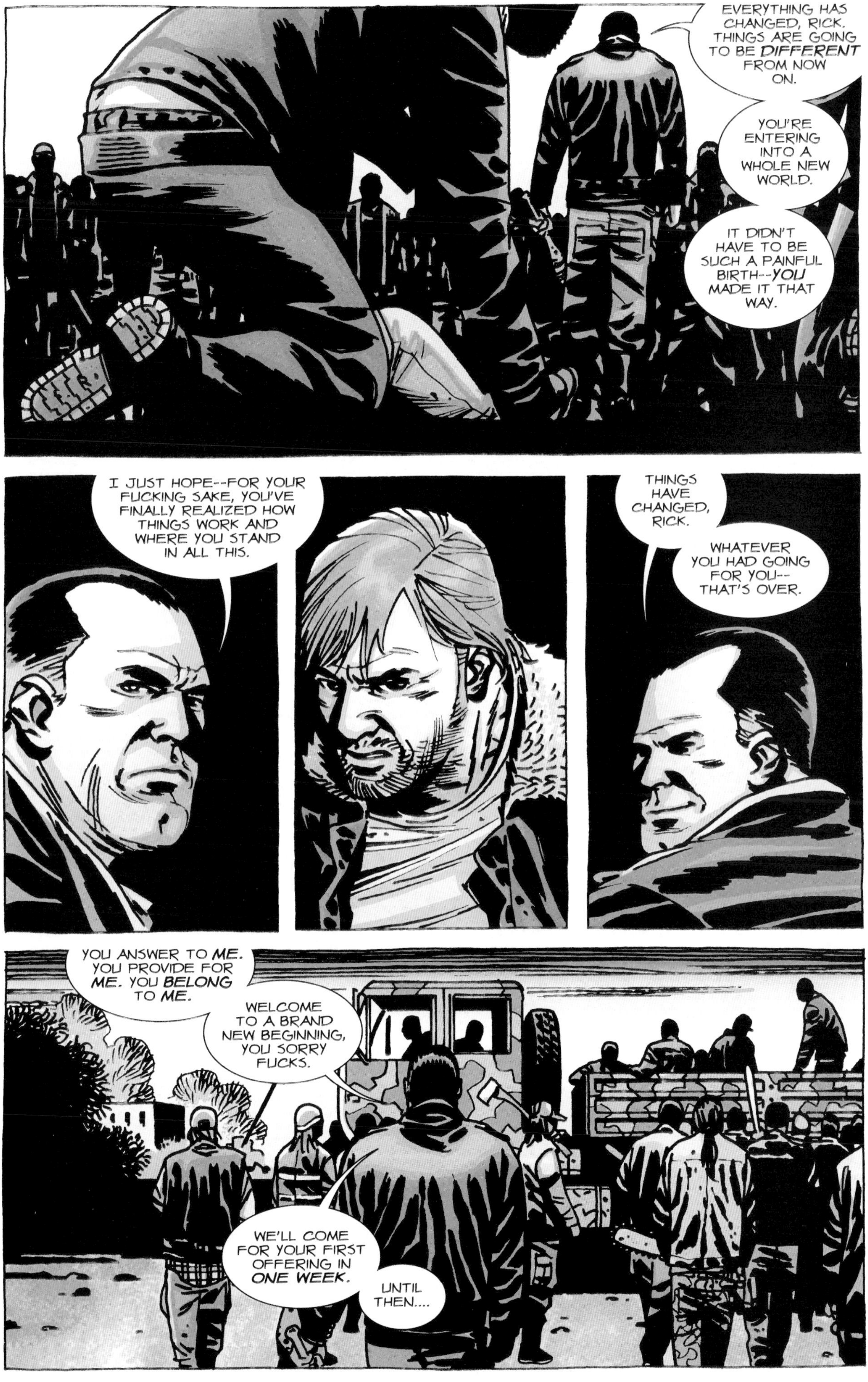
EVERYTHING HAS CHANGED, RICK. THINGS ARE GOING TO BE *DIFFERENT* FROM NOW ON.
YOU'RE ENTERING INTO A WHOLE NEW WORLD.
IT DIDN'T HAVE TO BE SUCH A PAINFUL BIRTH--*YOU* MADE IT THAT WAY.
I JUST HOPE--FOR YOUR FUCKING SAKE, YOU'VE FINALLY REALIZED HOW THINGS WORK AND WHERE YOU STAND IN ALL THIS.
THINGS HAVE CHANGED, RICK.
WHATEVER YOU HAD GOING FOR YOU--THAT'S OVER.
YOU ANSWER TO *ME.* YOU PROVIDE FOR *ME.* YOU *BELONG* TO *ME.*
WELCOME TO A BRAND NEW BEGINNING, YOU SORRY FUCKS.
WE'LL COME FOR YOUR FIRST OFFERING IN *ONE WEEK.*
UNTIL THEN....

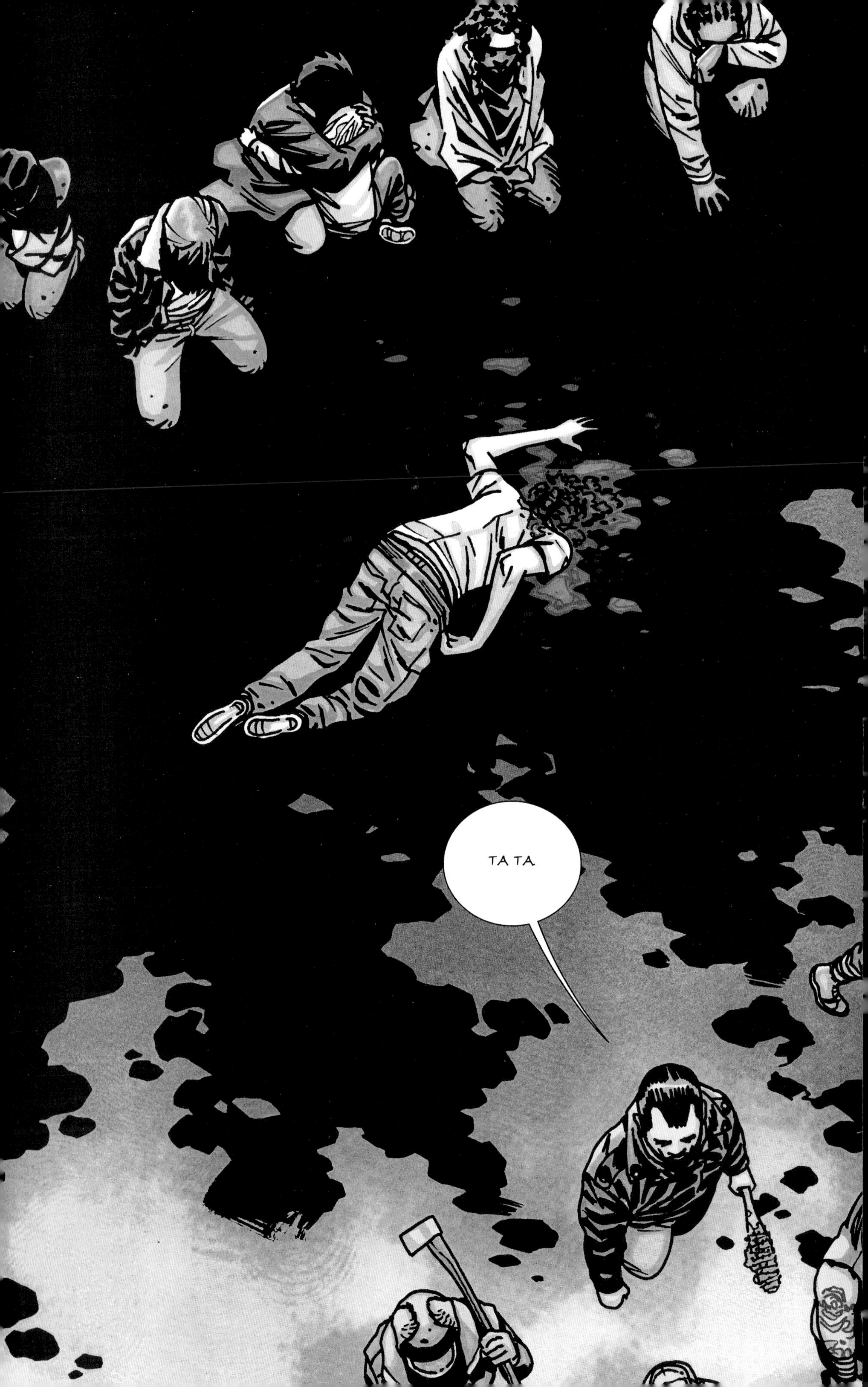
TA TA.

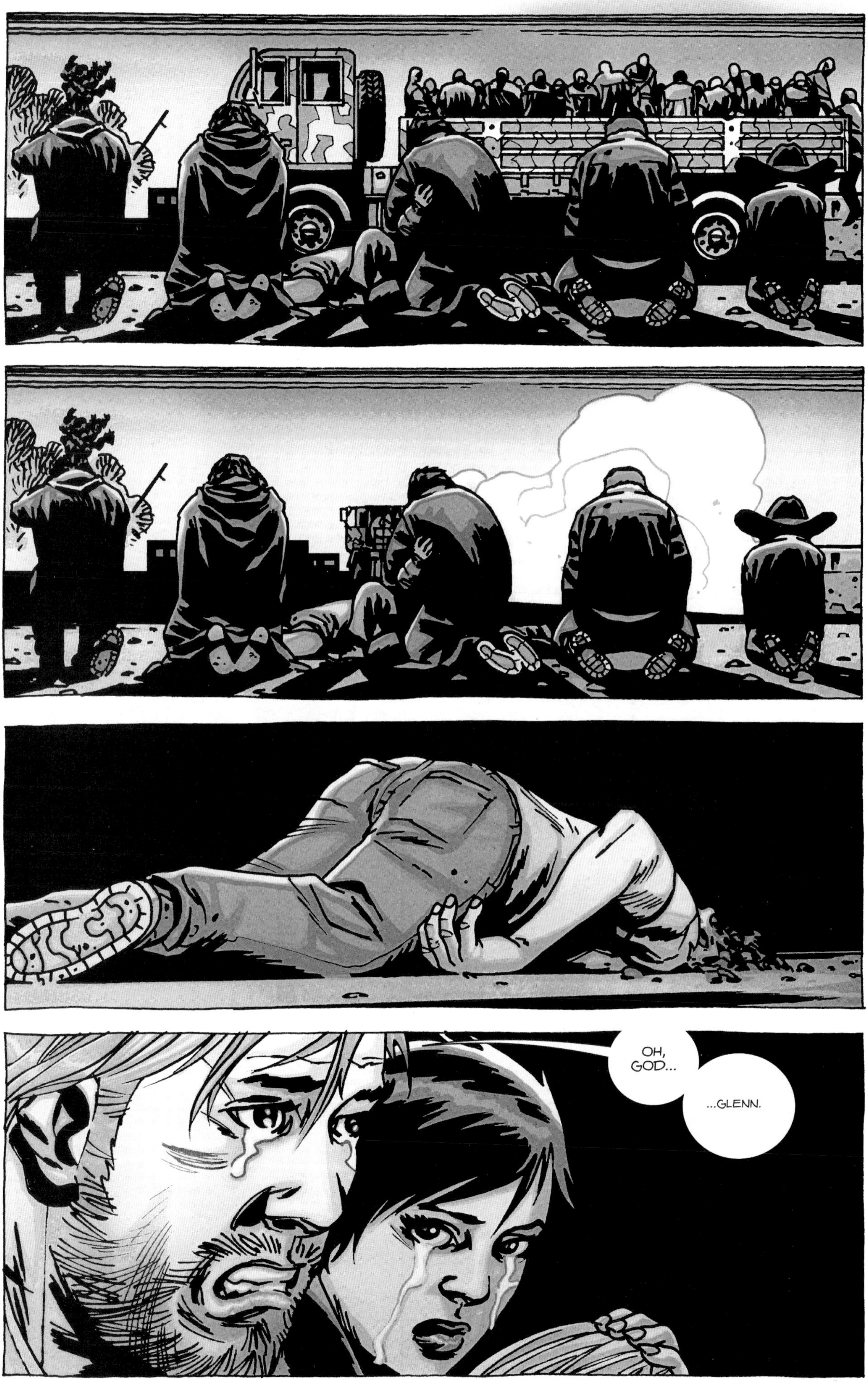
OH, GOD...
...GLENN.

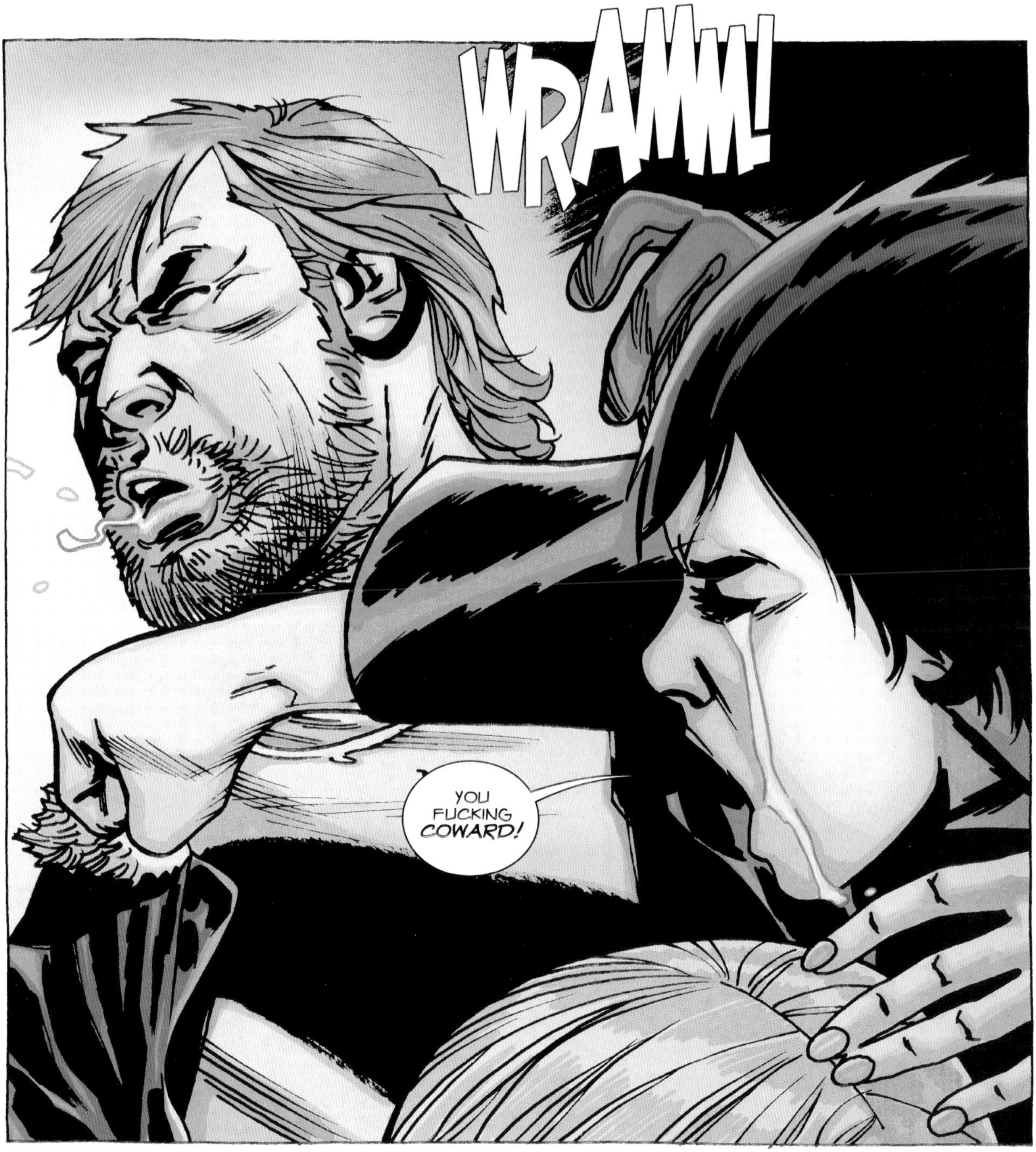
WRAMM!
YOU FUCKING COWARD!

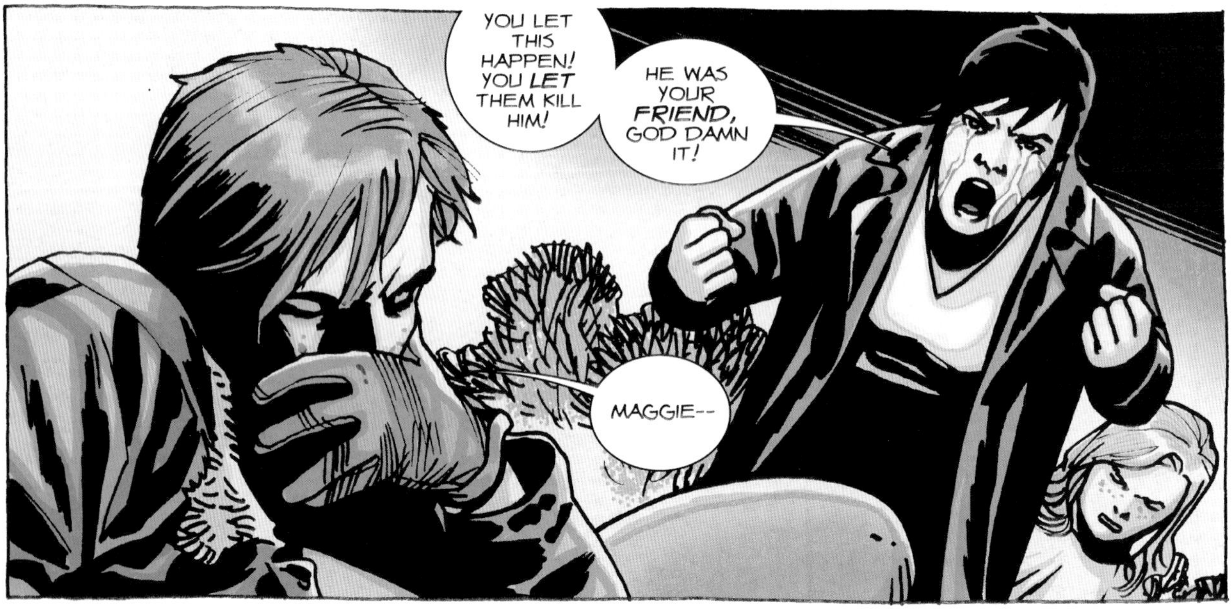
YOU LET THIS HAPPEN! YOU LET THEM KILL HIM!
HE WAS YOUR FRIEND, GOD DAMN IT!
MAGGIE--

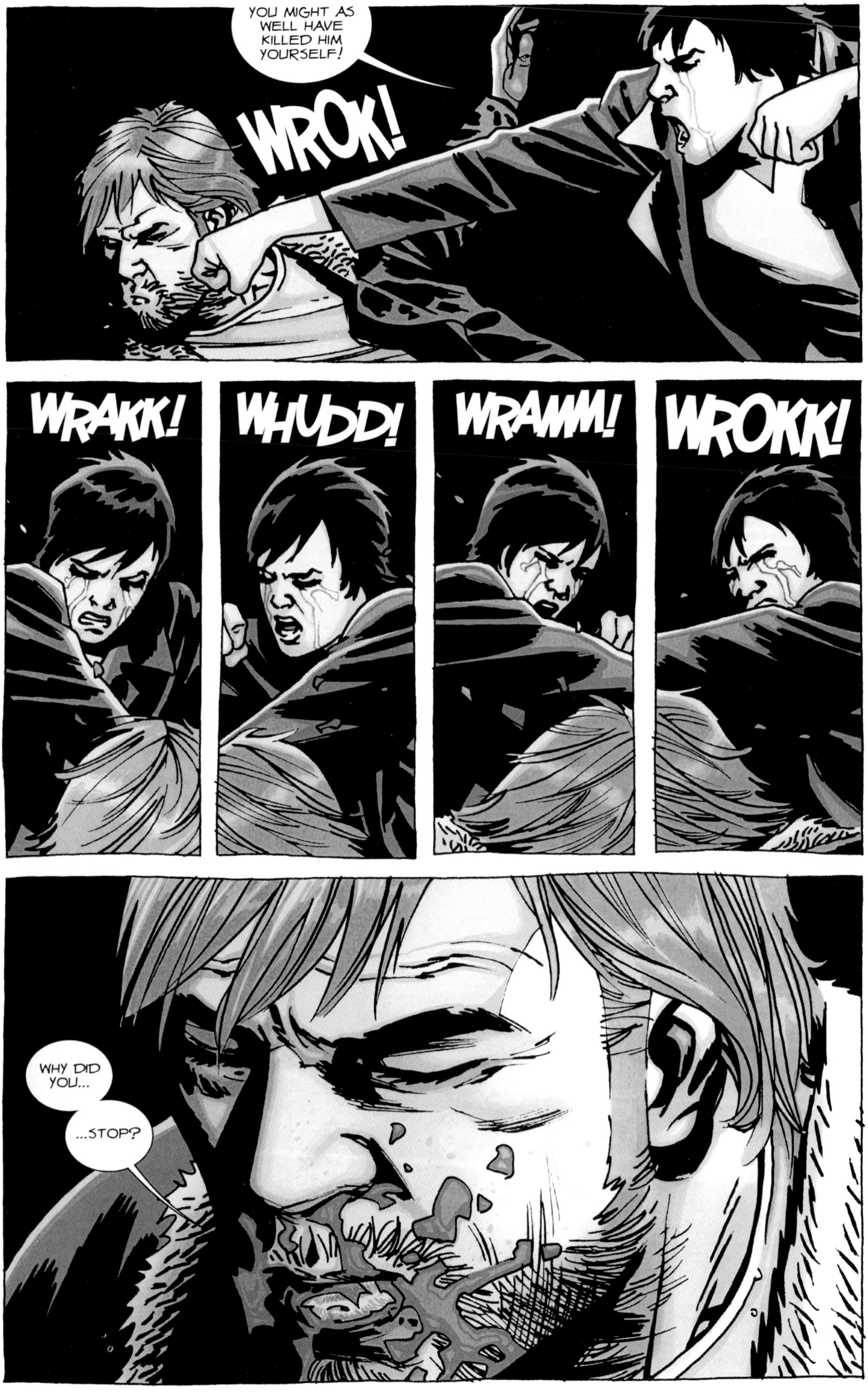
YOU MIGHT AS WELL HAVE KILLED HIM YOURSELF!
WROK!
WRAKK!
WHUDD!
WRAMM!
WROKK!
WHY DID YOU...
...STOP?

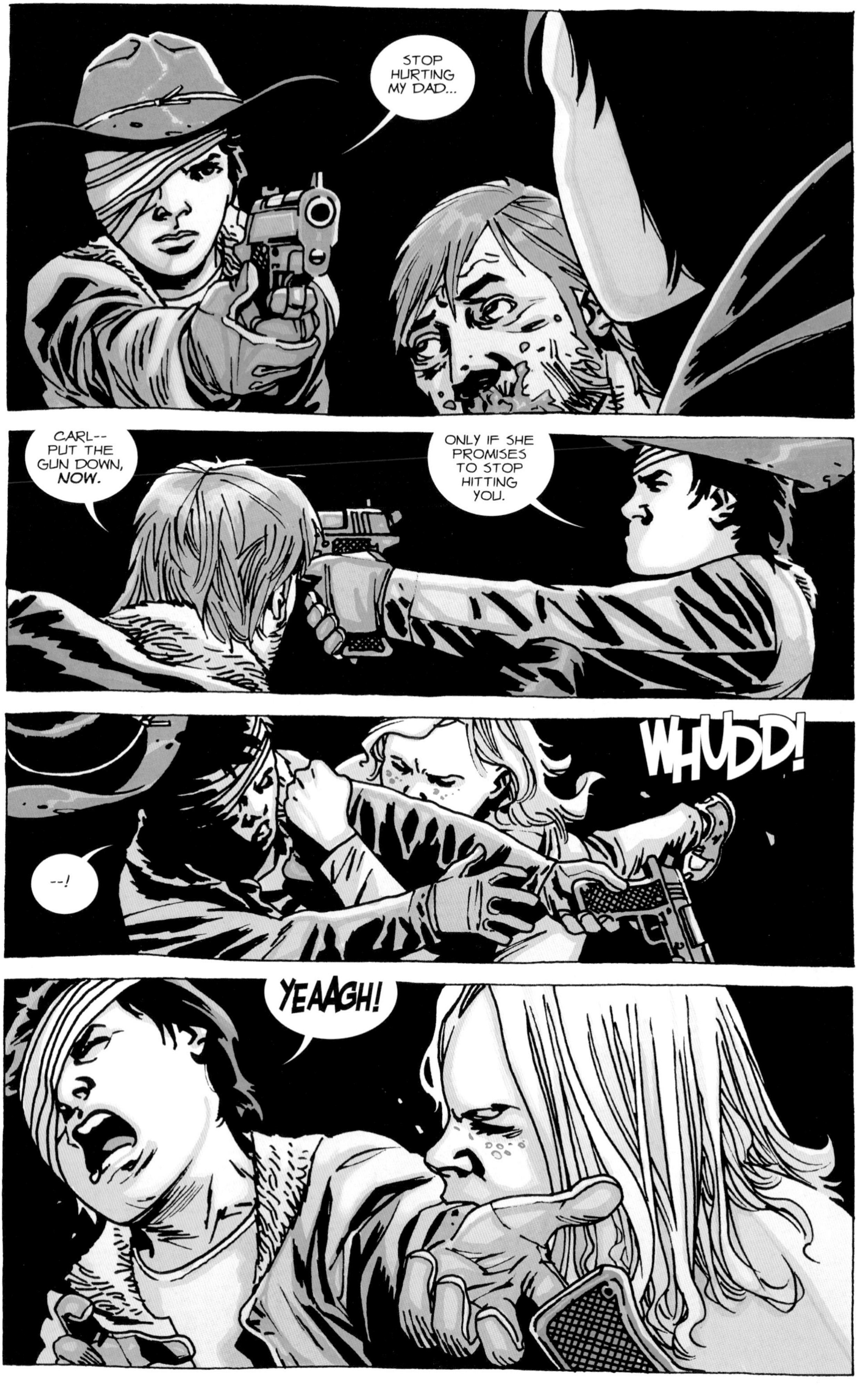
STOP HURTING MY DAD...
CARL-- PUT THE GUN DOWN, **NOW.**
ONLY IF SHE PROMISES TO STOP HITTING YOU.
WHUDD!
--!
YEAAGH!

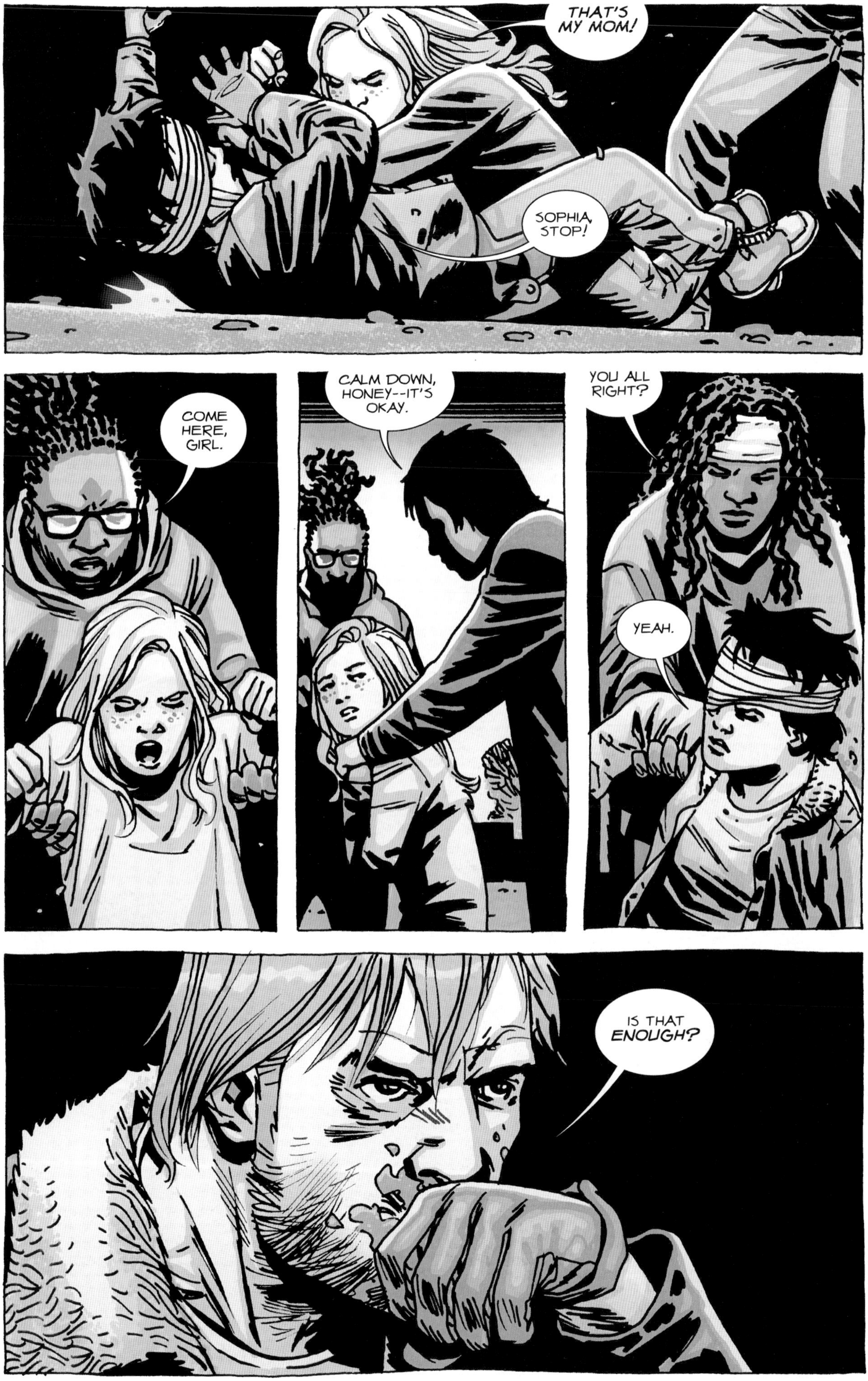
THAT'S MY MOM!
SOPHIA, STOP!
COME HERE, GIRL.
CALM DOWN, HONEY--IT'S OKAY.
YOU ALL RIGHT?
YEAH.
IS THAT ENOUGH?

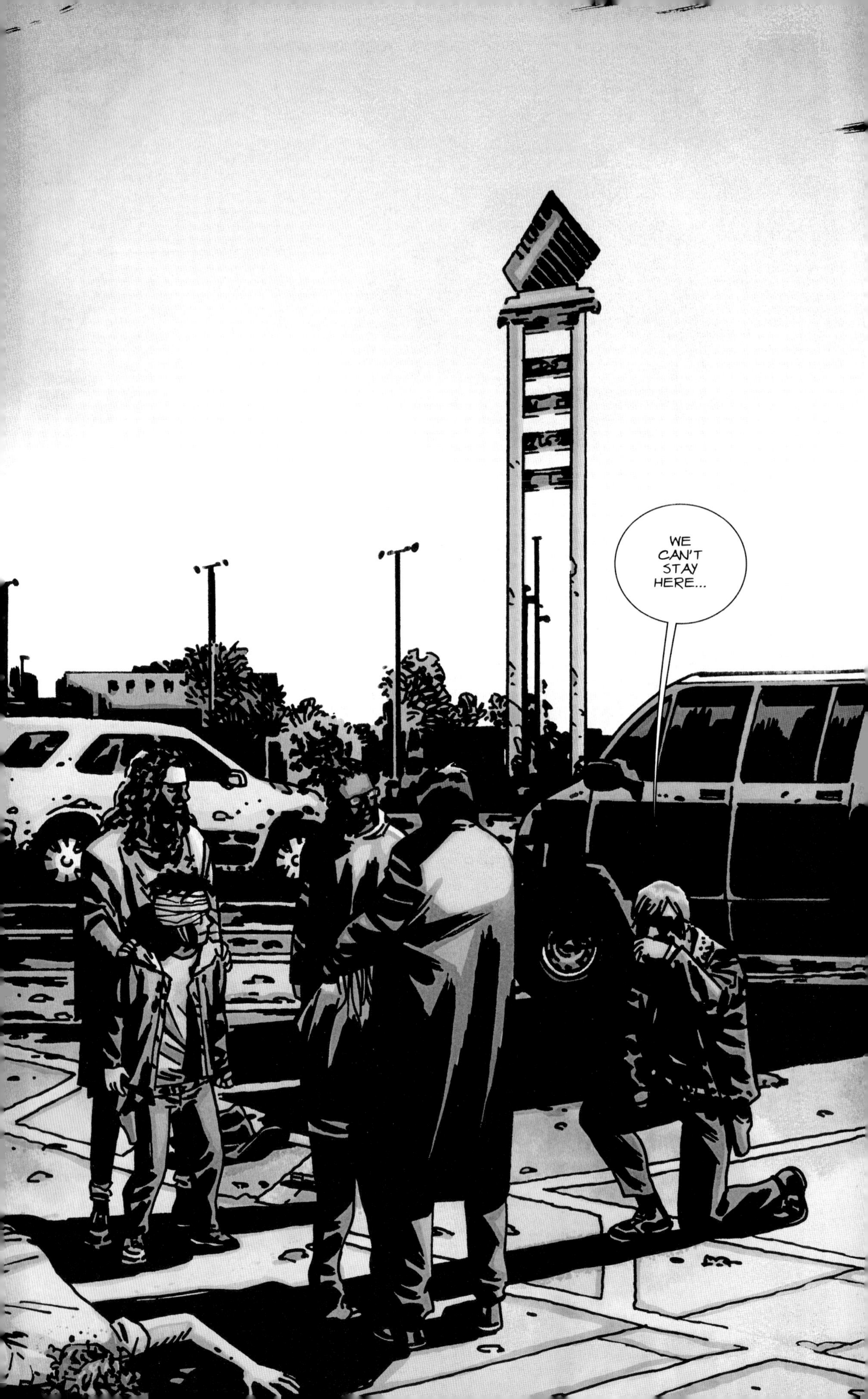
WE CAN'T STAY HERE...

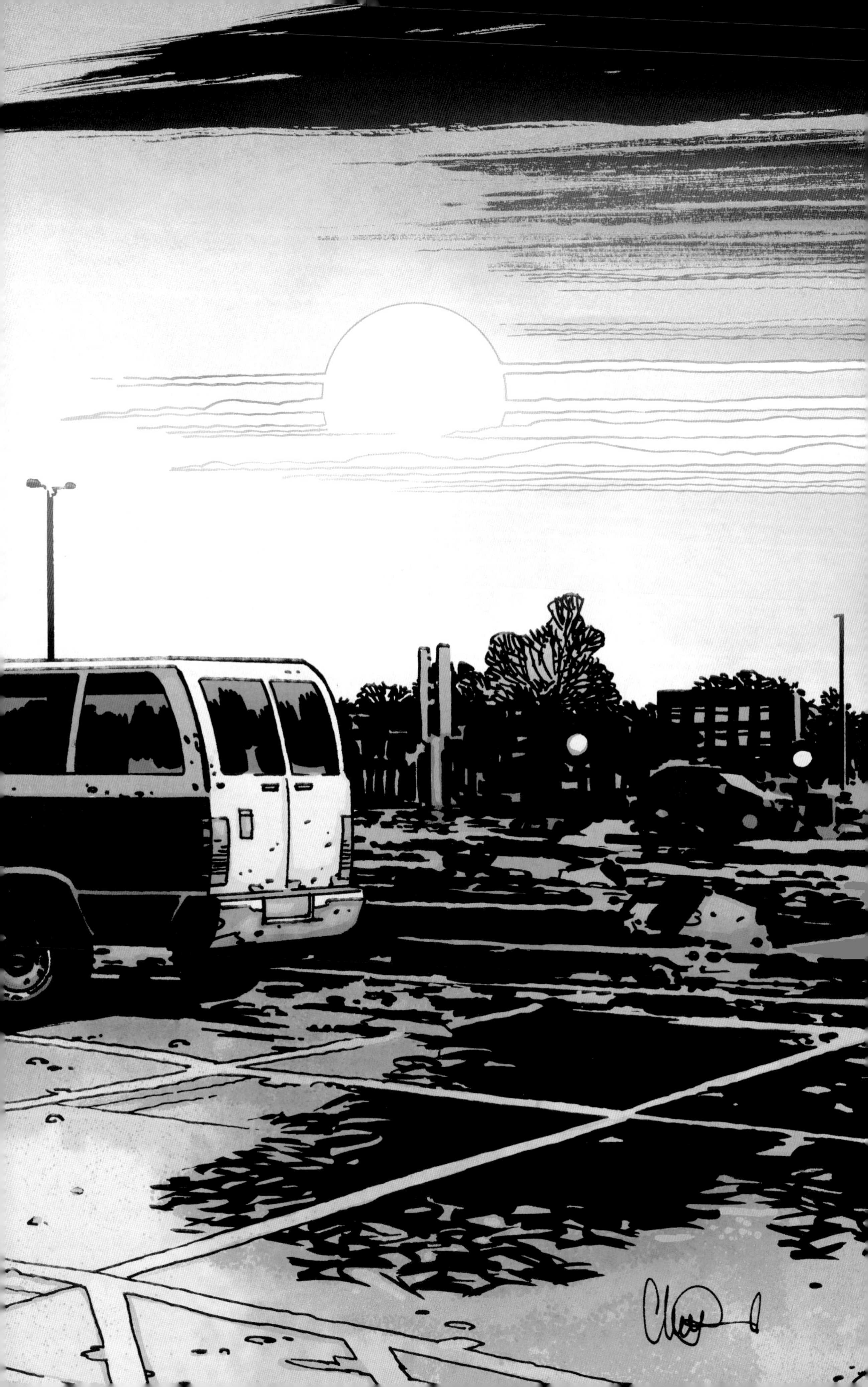

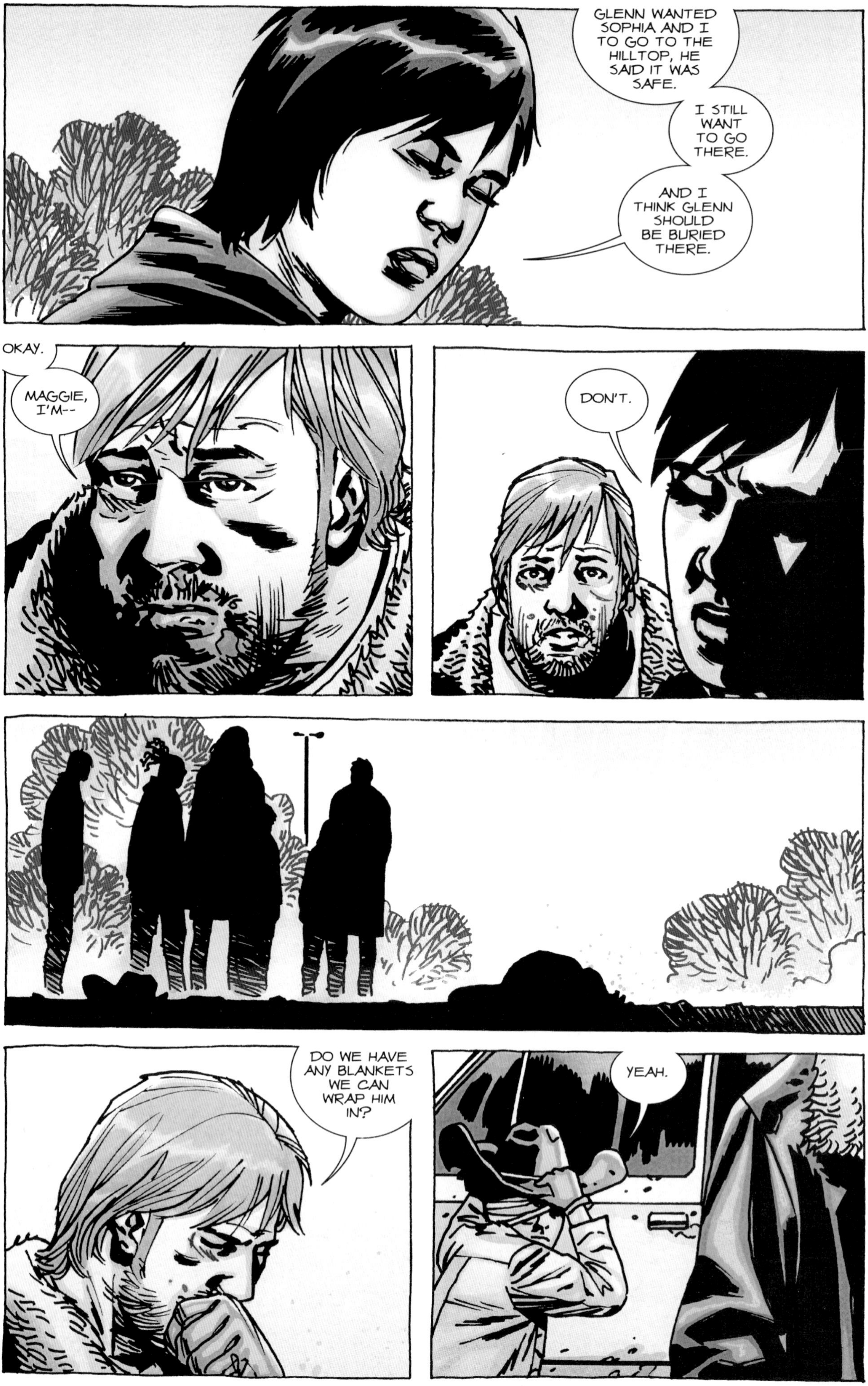
GLENN WANTED SOPHIA AND I TO GO TO THE HILLTOP, HE SAID IT WAS SAFE.
I STILL WANT TO GO THERE.
AND I THINK GLENN SHOULD BE BURIED THERE.
OKAY.
MAGGIE, I'M--
DON'T.
DO WE HAVE ANY BLANKETS WE CAN WRAP HIM IN?
YEAH.

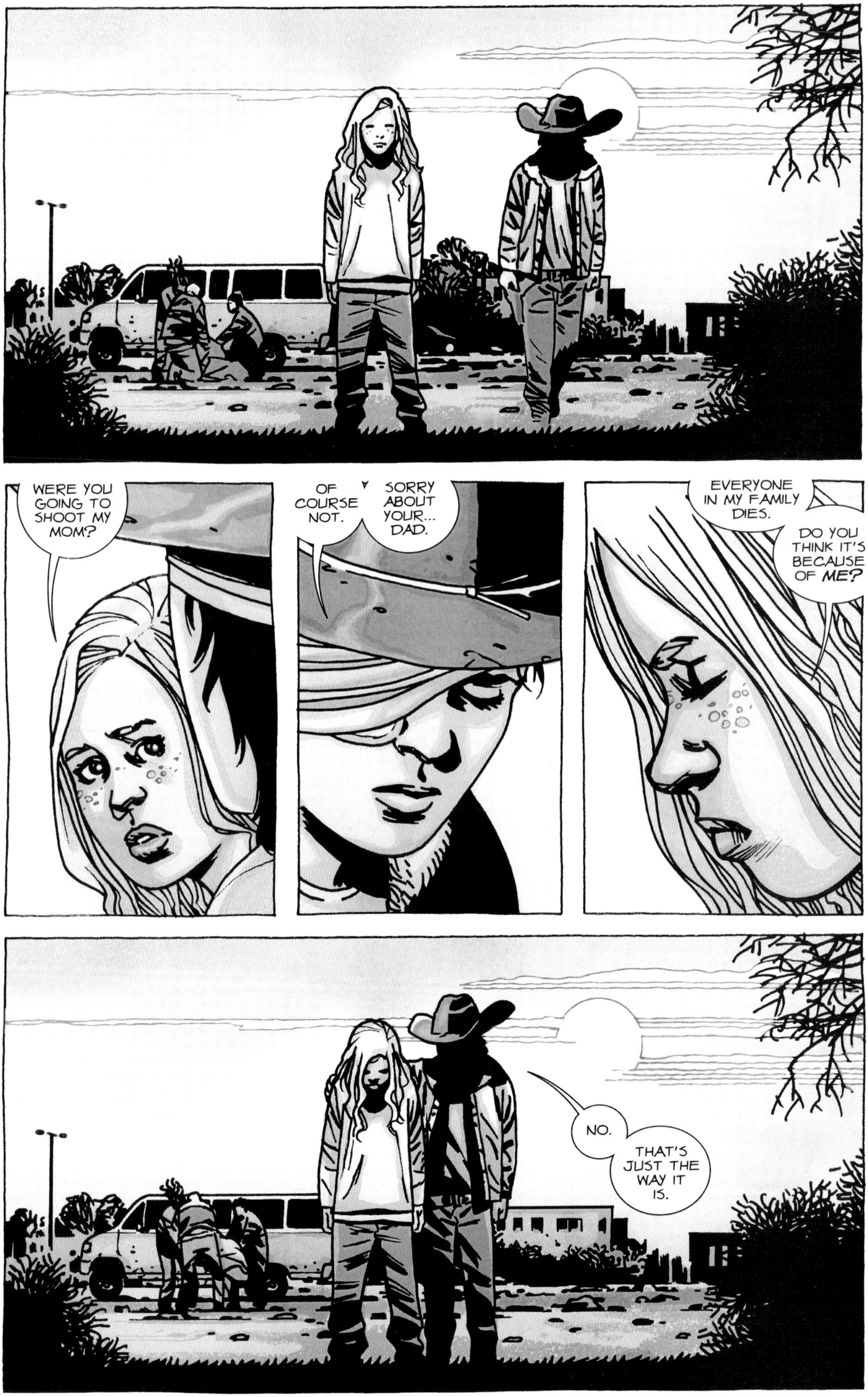
WERE YOU GOING TO SHOOT MY MOM?
OF COURSE NOT.
SORRY ABOUT YOUR... DAD.
EVERYONE IN MY FAMILY DIES.
DO YOU THINK IT'S BECAUSE OF *ME?*
NO.
THAT'S JUST THE WAY IT IS.

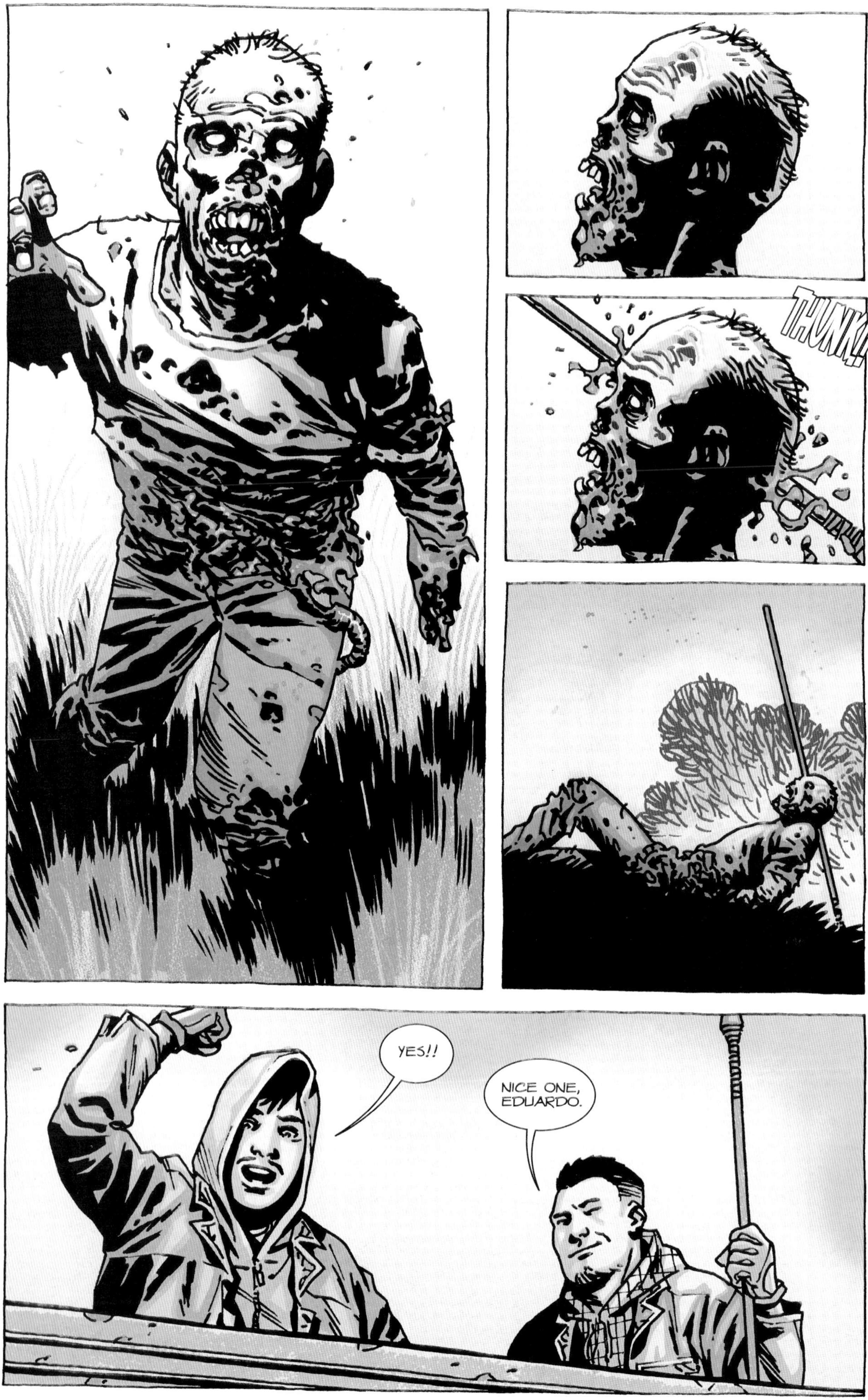
THUNK!!
YES!!
NICE ONE, EDUARDO.

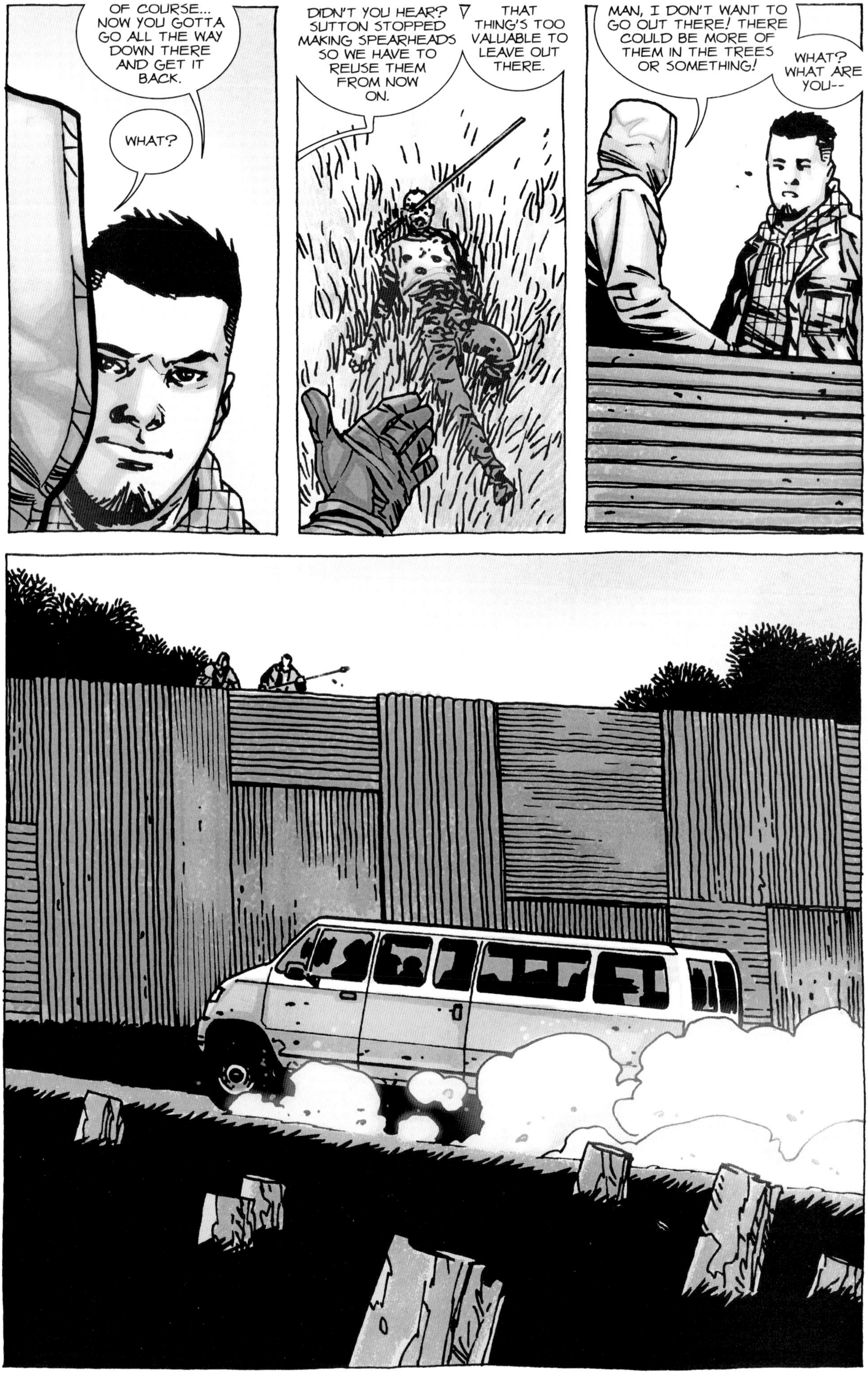

OF COURSE... NOW YOU GOTTA GO ALL THE WAY DOWN THERE AND GET IT BACK.
WHAT?
DIDN'T YOU HEAR? SUTTON STOPPED MAKING SPEARHEADS SO WE HAVE TO REUSE THEM FROM NOW ON.
THAT THING'S TOO VALUABLE TO LEAVE OUT THERE.
MAN, I DON'T WANT TO GO OUT THERE! THERE COULD BE MORE OF THEM IN THE TREES OR SOMETHING!
WHAT? WHAT ARE YOU--

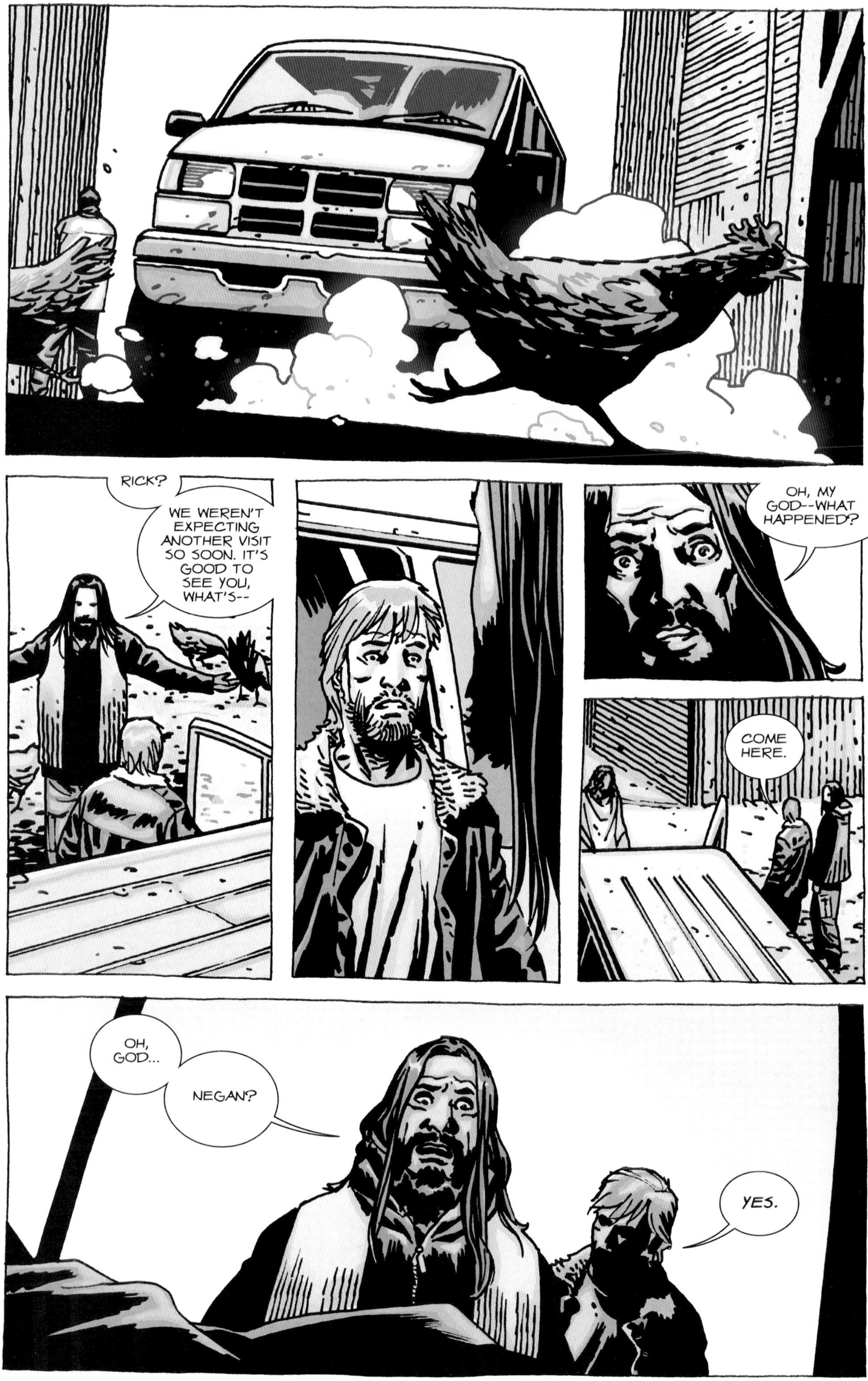
RICK?
WE WEREN'T EXPECTING ANOTHER VISIT SO SOON. IT'S GOOD TO SEE YOU, WHAT'S--
OH, MY GOD--WHAT HAPPENED?
COME HERE.
OH, GOD...
NEGAN?
YES.

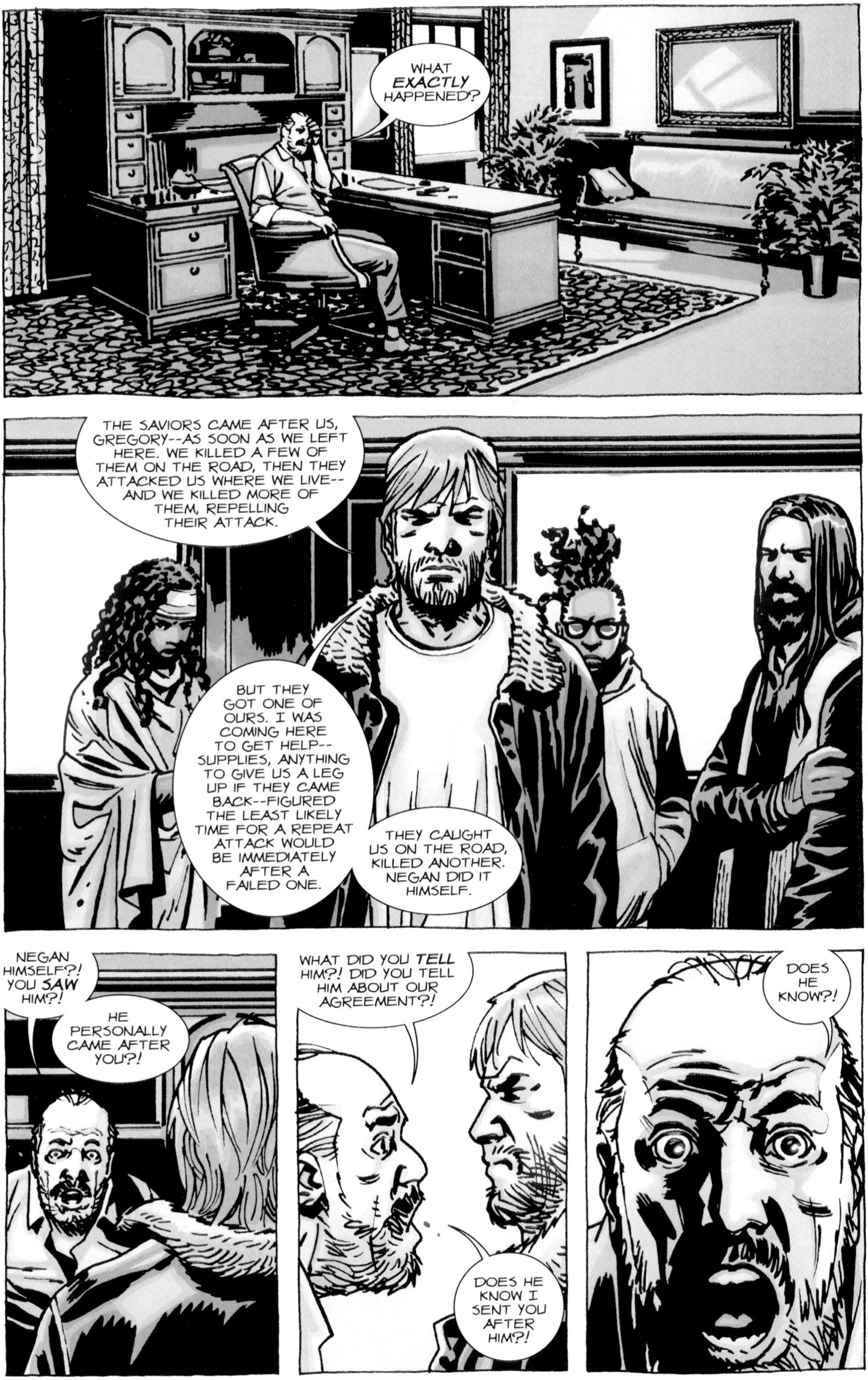

WHAT EXACTLY HAPPENED?
THE SAVIORS CAME AFTER US, GREGORY--AS SOON AS WE LEFT HERE. WE KILLED A FEW OF THEM ON THE ROAD, THEN THEY ATTACKED US WHERE WE LIVE-- AND WE KILLED MORE OF THEM, REPELLING THEIR ATTACK.
BUT THEY GOT ONE OF OURS. I WAS COMING HERE TO GET HELP-- SUPPLIES, ANYTHING TO GIVE US A LEG UP IF THEY CAME BACK--FIGURED THE LEAST LIKELY TIME FOR A REPEAT ATTACK WOULD BE IMMEDIATELY AFTER A FAILED ONE.
THEY CAUGHT US ON THE ROAD, KILLED ANOTHER. NEGAN DID IT HIMSELF.
NEGAN HIMSELF?! YOU SAW HIM?!
HE PERSONALLY CAME AFTER YOU?!
WHAT DID YOU TELL HIM?! DID YOU TELL HIM ABOUT OUR AGREEMENT?!
DOES HE KNOW I SENT YOU AFTER HIM?!
DOES HE KNOW?!

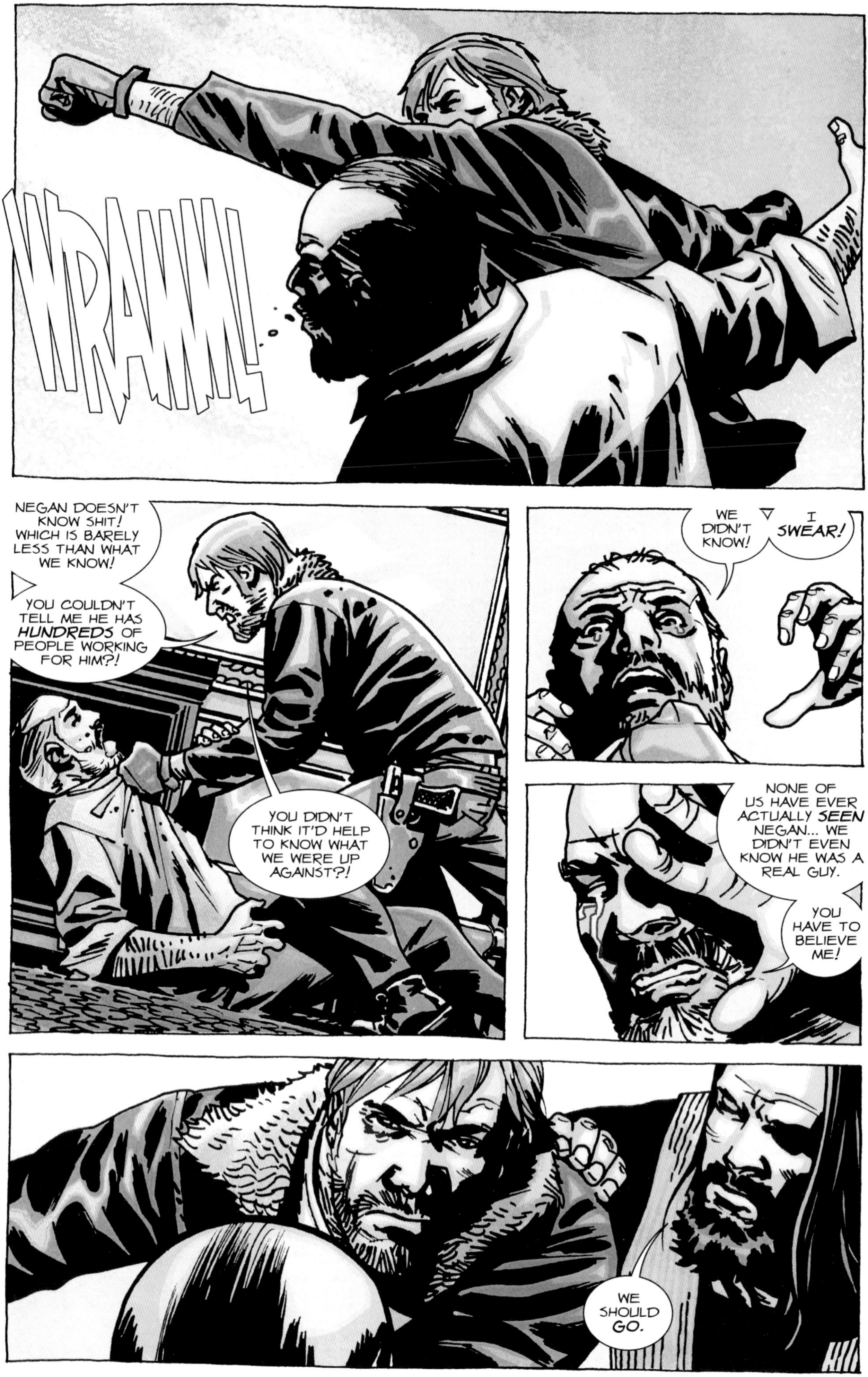
WRAMM!
NEGAN DOESN'T KNOW SHIT! WHICH IS BARELY LESS THAN WHAT WE KNOW!
YOU COULDN'T TELL ME HE HAS HUNDREDS OF PEOPLE WORKING FOR HIM?!
YOU DIDN'T THINK IT'D HELP TO KNOW WHAT WE WERE UP AGAINST?!
WE DIDN'T KNOW!
I SWEAR!
NONE OF US HAVE EVER ACTUALLY SEEN NEGAN... WE DIDN'T EVEN KNOW HE WAS A REAL GUY.
YOU HAVE TO BELIEVE ME!
WE SHOULD GO.

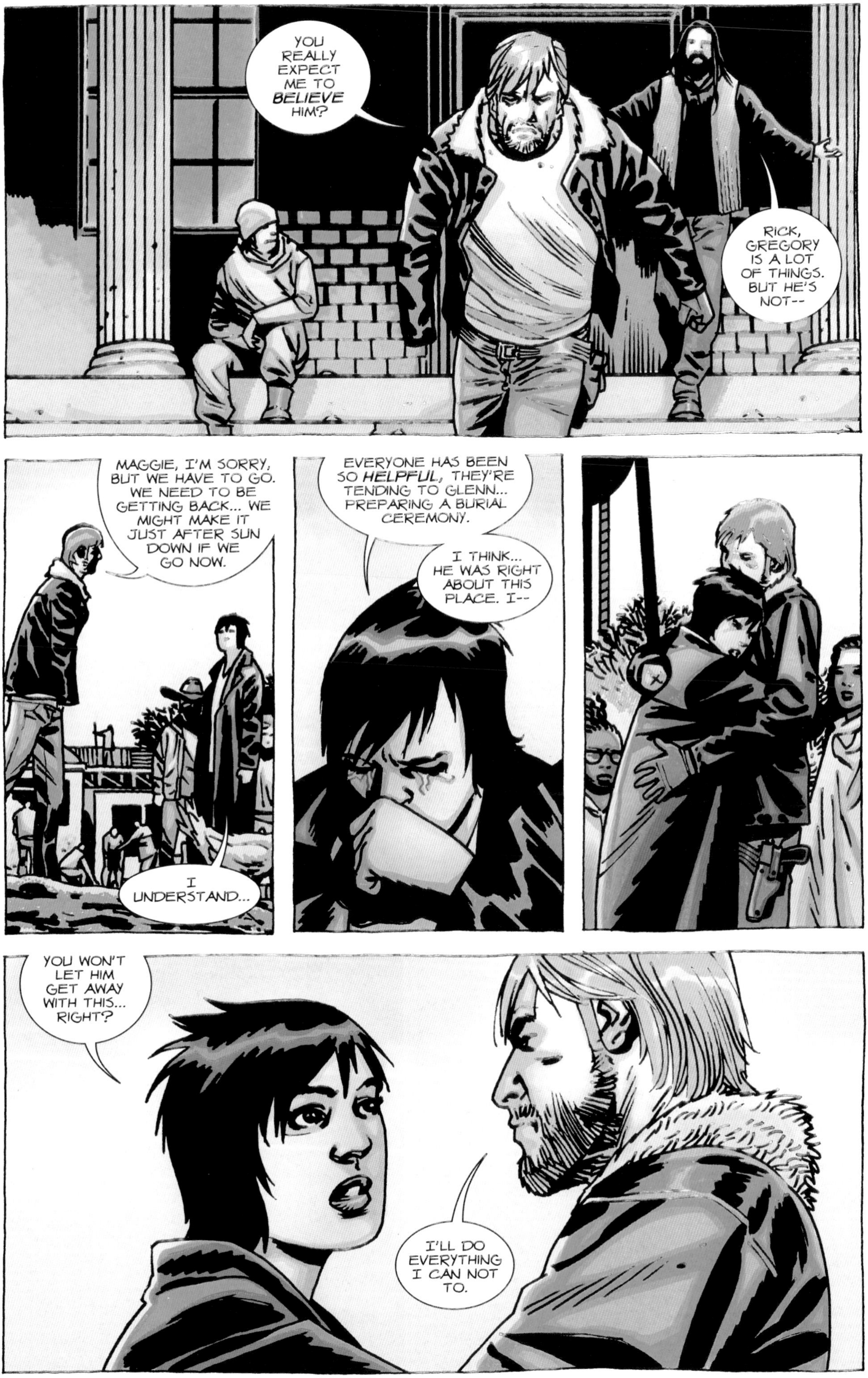
YOU REALLY EXPECT ME TO BELIEVE HIM?
RICK, GREGORY IS A LOT OF THINGS. BUT HE'S NOT--
MAGGIE, I'M SORRY, BUT WE HAVE TO GO. WE NEED TO BE GETTING BACK... WE MIGHT MAKE IT JUST AFTER SUN DOWN IF WE GO NOW.
I UNDERSTAND...
EVERYONE HAS BEEN SO HELPFUL, THEY'RE TENDING TO GLENN... PREPARING A BURIAL CEREMONY.
I THINK... HE WAS RIGHT ABOUT THIS PLACE. I--
YOU WON'T LET HIM GET AWAY WITH THIS... RIGHT?
I'LL DO EVERYTHING I CAN NOT TO.

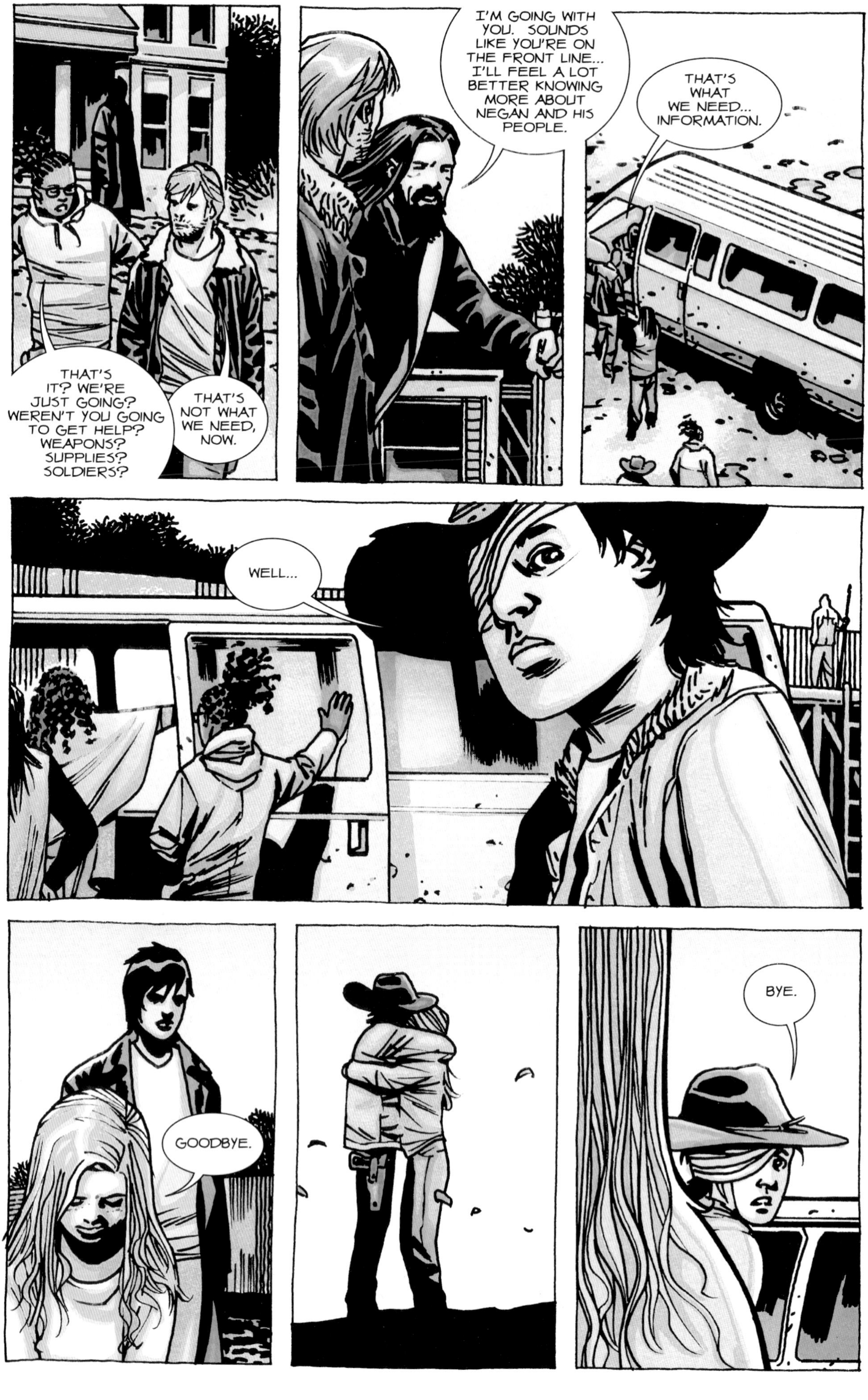
THAT'S IT? WE'RE JUST GOING? WEREN'T YOU GOING TO GET HELP? WEAPONS? SUPPLIES? SOLDIERS?
THAT'S NOT WHAT WE NEED, NOW.
I'M GOING WITH YOU. SOUNDS LIKE YOU'RE ON THE FRONT LINE... I'LL FEEL A LOT BETTER KNOWING MORE ABOUT NEGAN AND HIS PEOPLE.
THAT'S WHAT WE NEED... INFORMATION.
WELL...
GOODBYE.
BYE.

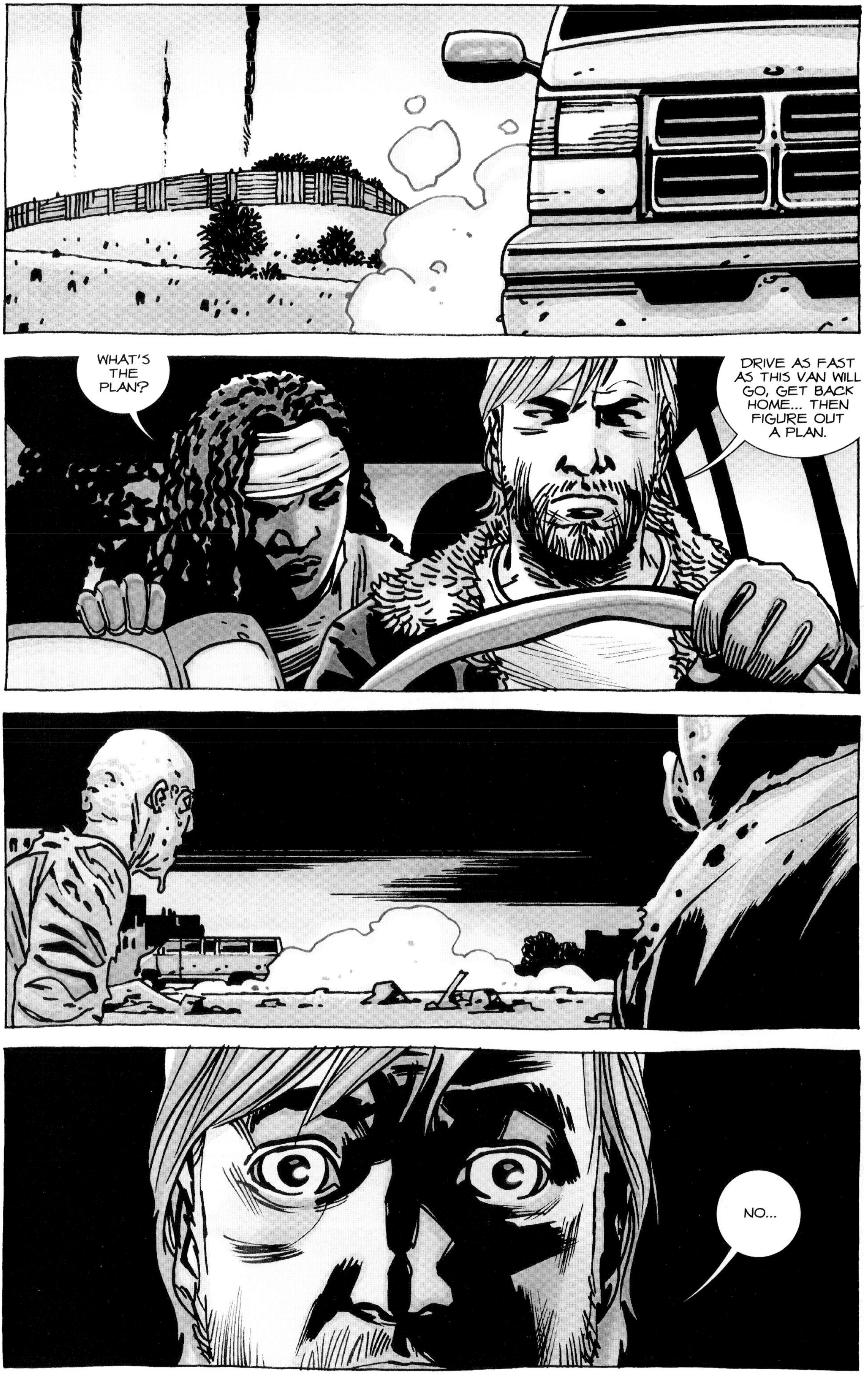
WHAT'S THE PLAN?
DRIVE AS FAST AS THIS VAN WILL GO, GET BACK HOME... THEN FIGURE OUT A PLAN.
NO...

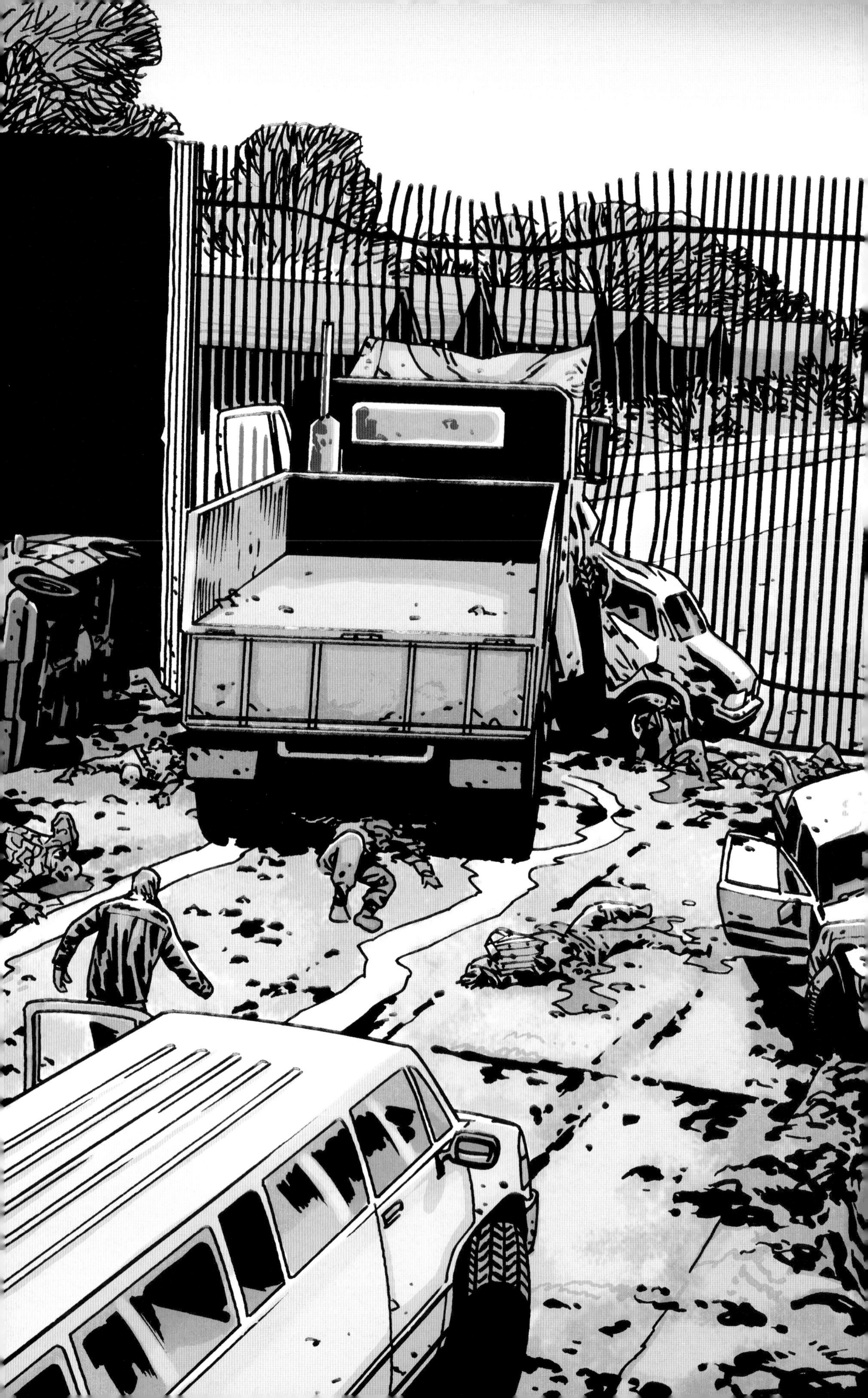

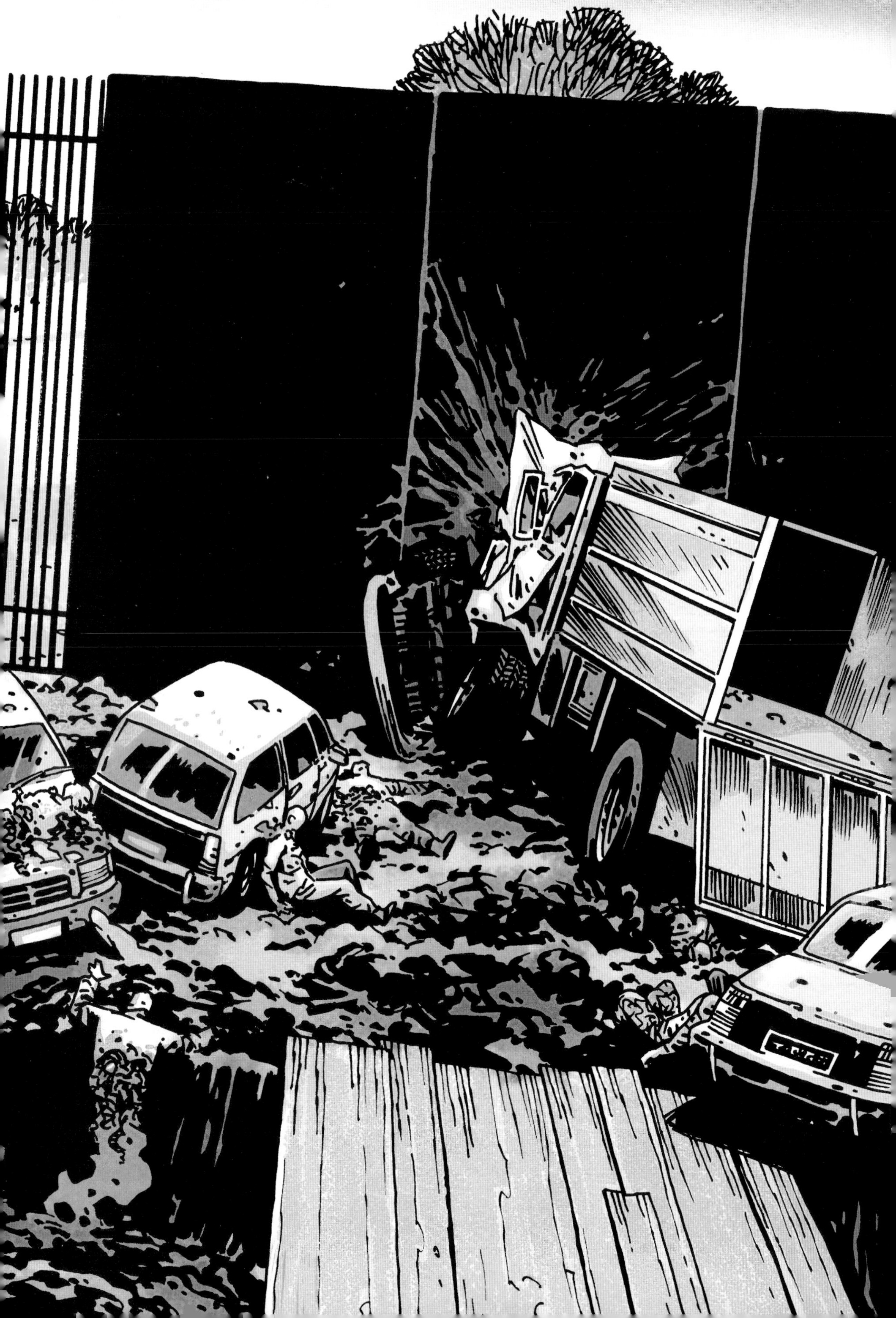

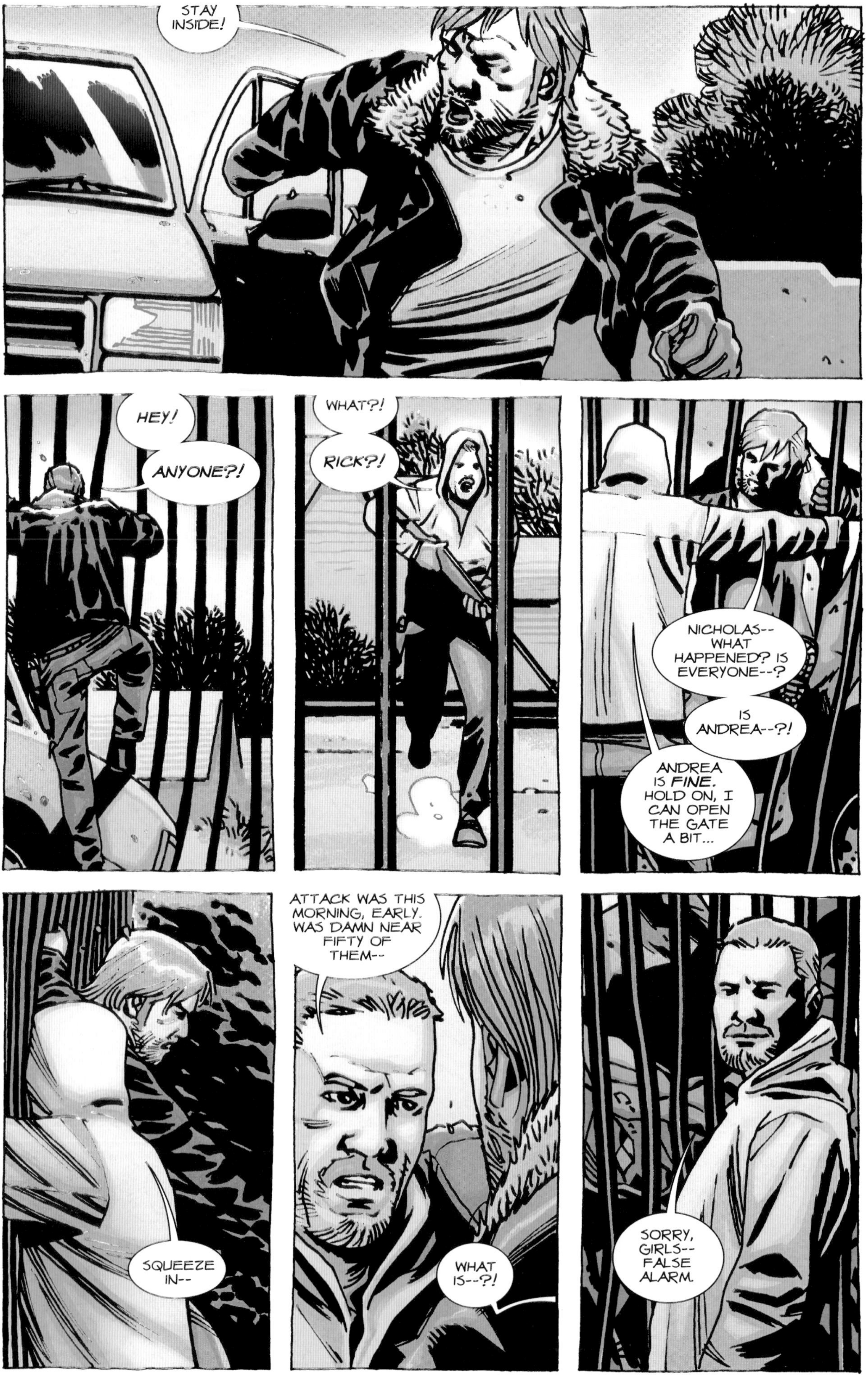
STAY INSIDE!
HEY!
ANYONE?!
WHAT?!
RICK?!
NICHOLAS-- WHAT HAPPENED? IS EVERYONE--?
IS ANDREA--?!
ANDREA IS FINE. HOLD ON, I CAN OPEN THE GATE A BIT...
SQUEEZE IN--
ATTACK WAS THIS MORNING, EARLY. WAS DAMN NEAR FIFTY OF THEM--
WHAT IS--?!
SORRY, GIRLS-- FALSE ALARM.

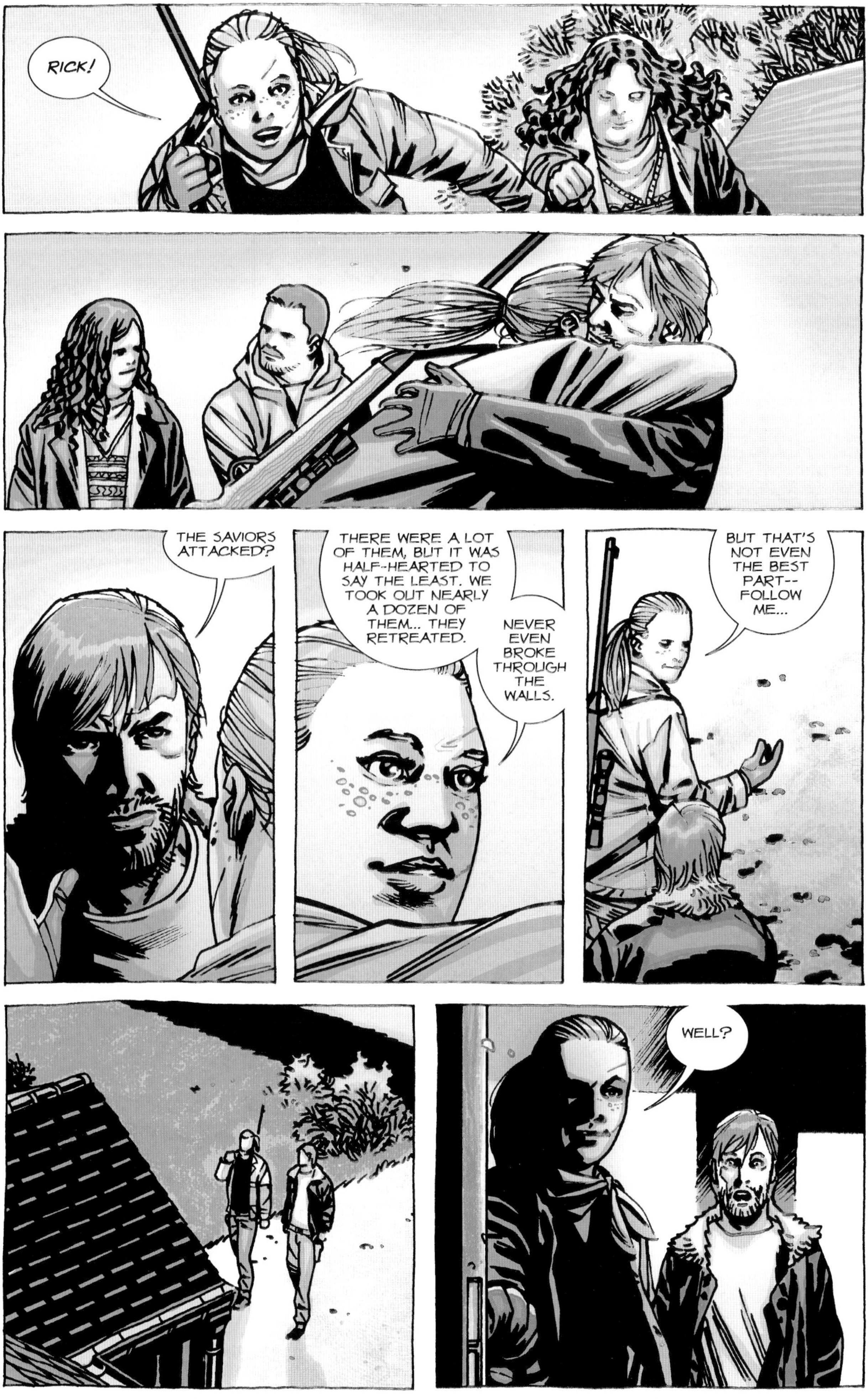
RICK!
THE SAVIORS ATTACKED?
THERE WERE A LOT OF THEM, BUT IT WAS HALF-HEARTED TO SAY THE LEAST. WE TOOK OUT NEARLY A DOZEN OF THEM... THEY RETREATED.
NEVER EVEN BROKE THROUGH THE WALLS.
BUT THAT'S NOT EVEN THE BEST PART-- FOLLOW ME...
WELL?

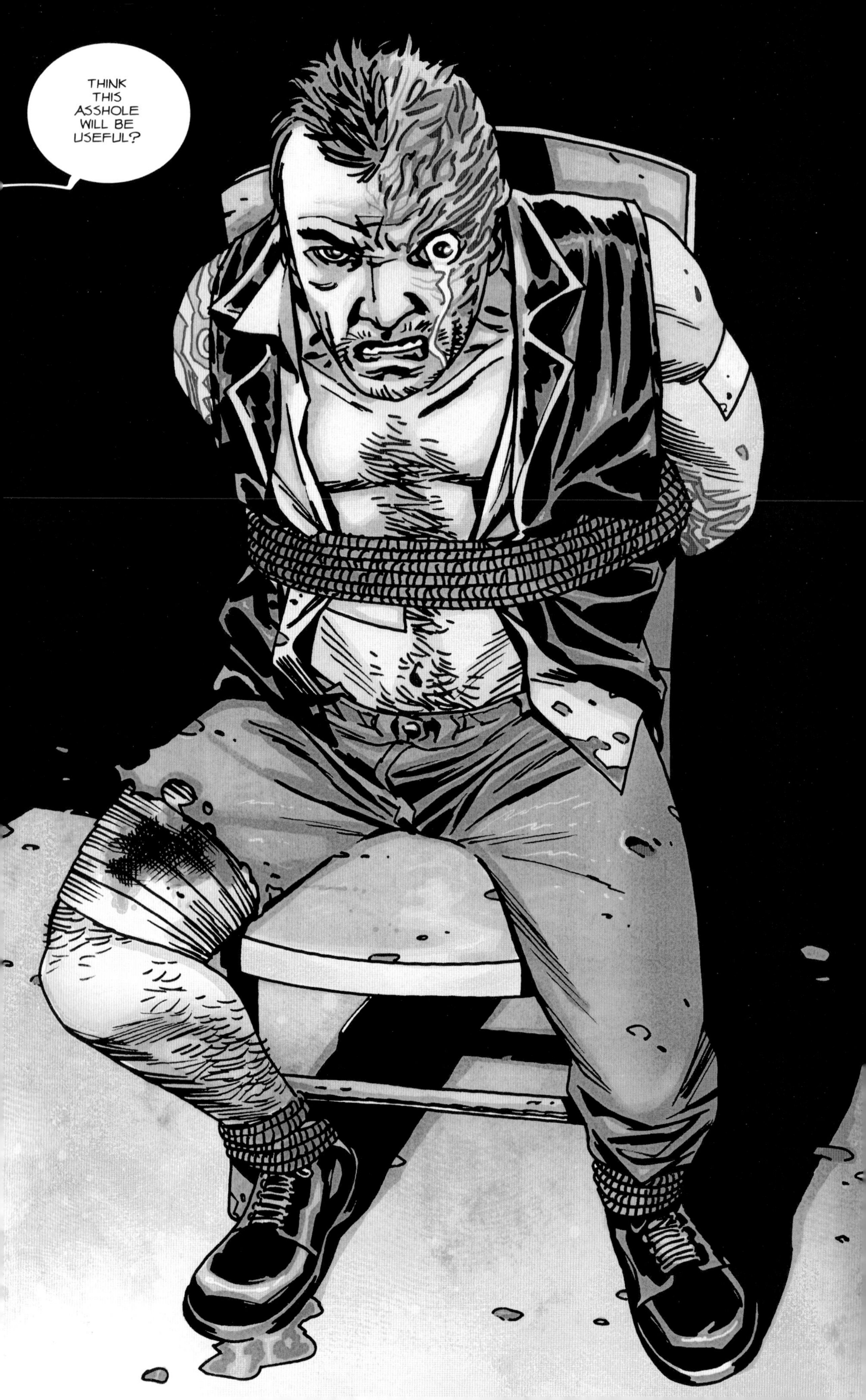
THINK THIS ASSHOLE WILL BE USEFUL?

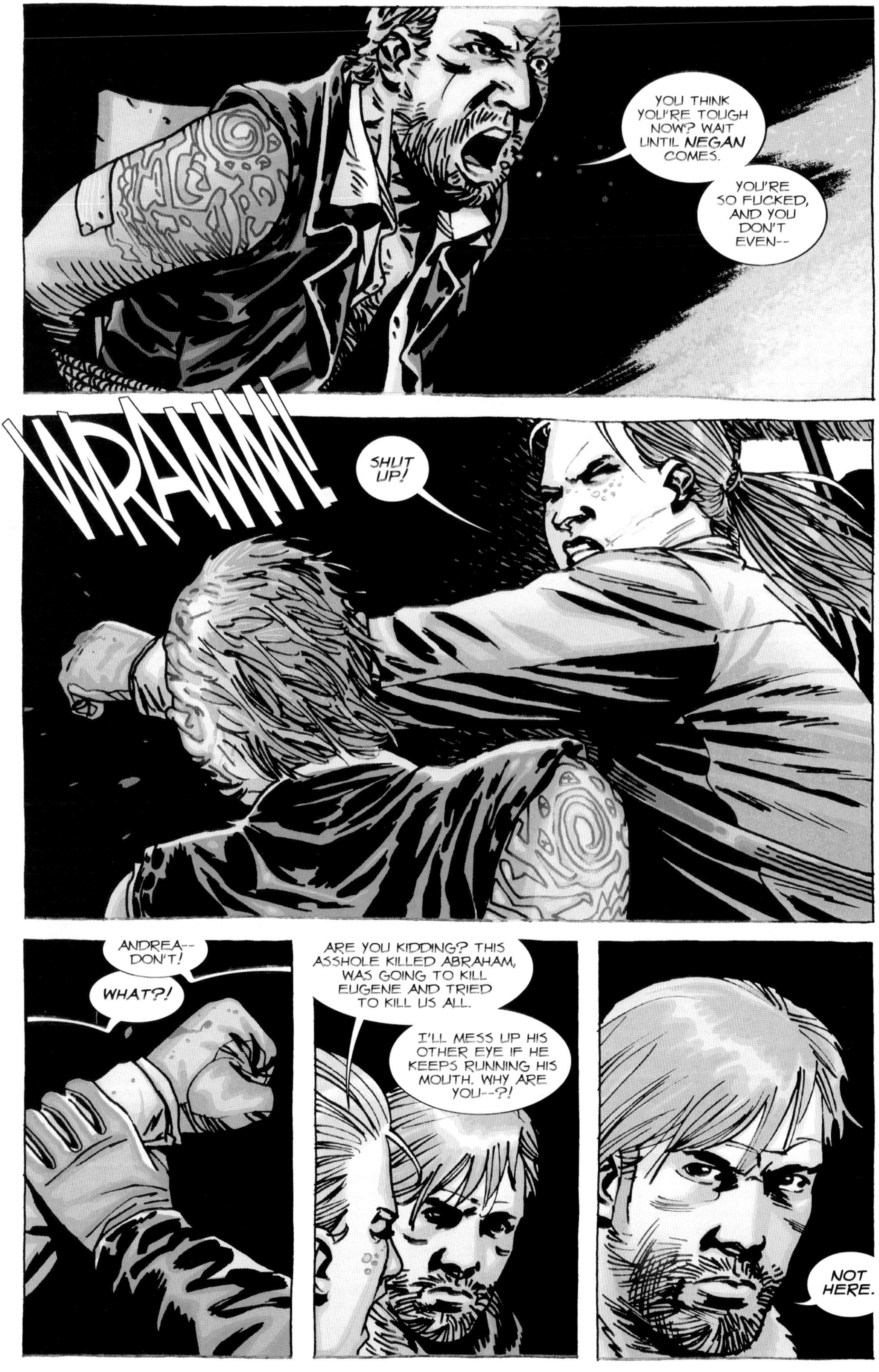
YOU THINK YOU'RE TOUGH NOW? WAIT UNTIL NEGAN COMES.
YOU'RE SO FUCKED, AND YOU DON'T EVEN--
WRAMM!
SHUT UP!
ANDREA-- DON'T!
WHAT?!
ARE YOU KIDDING? THIS ASSHOLE KILLED ABRAHAM, WAS GOING TO KILL EUGENE AND TRIED TO KILL US ALL.
I'LL MESS UP HIS OTHER EYE IF HE KEEPS RUNNING HIS MOUTH. WHY ARE YOU--?!
NOT HERE.

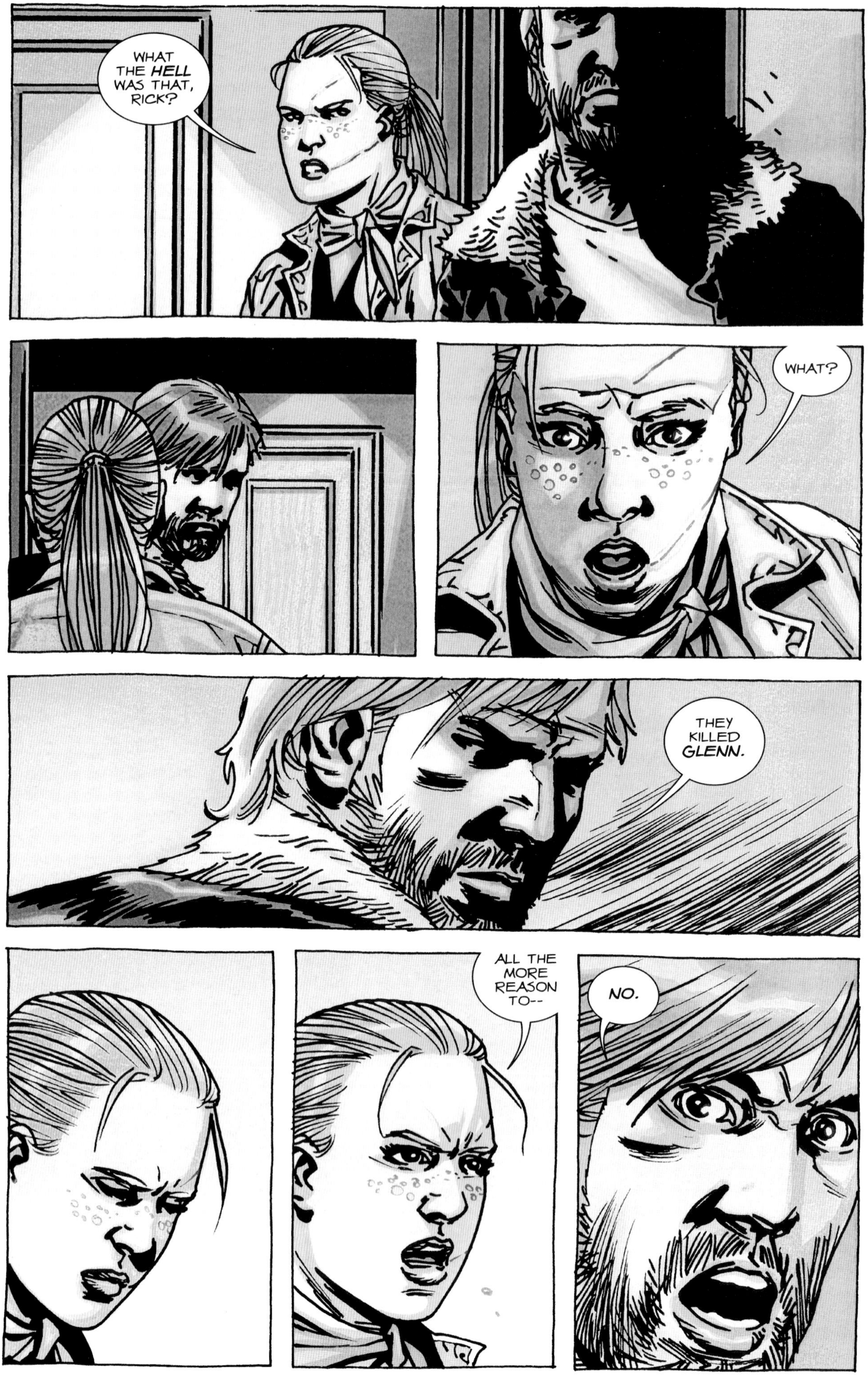
WHAT THE HELL WAS THAT, RICK?
WHAT?
THEY KILLED GLENN.
ALL THE MORE REASON TO--
NO.

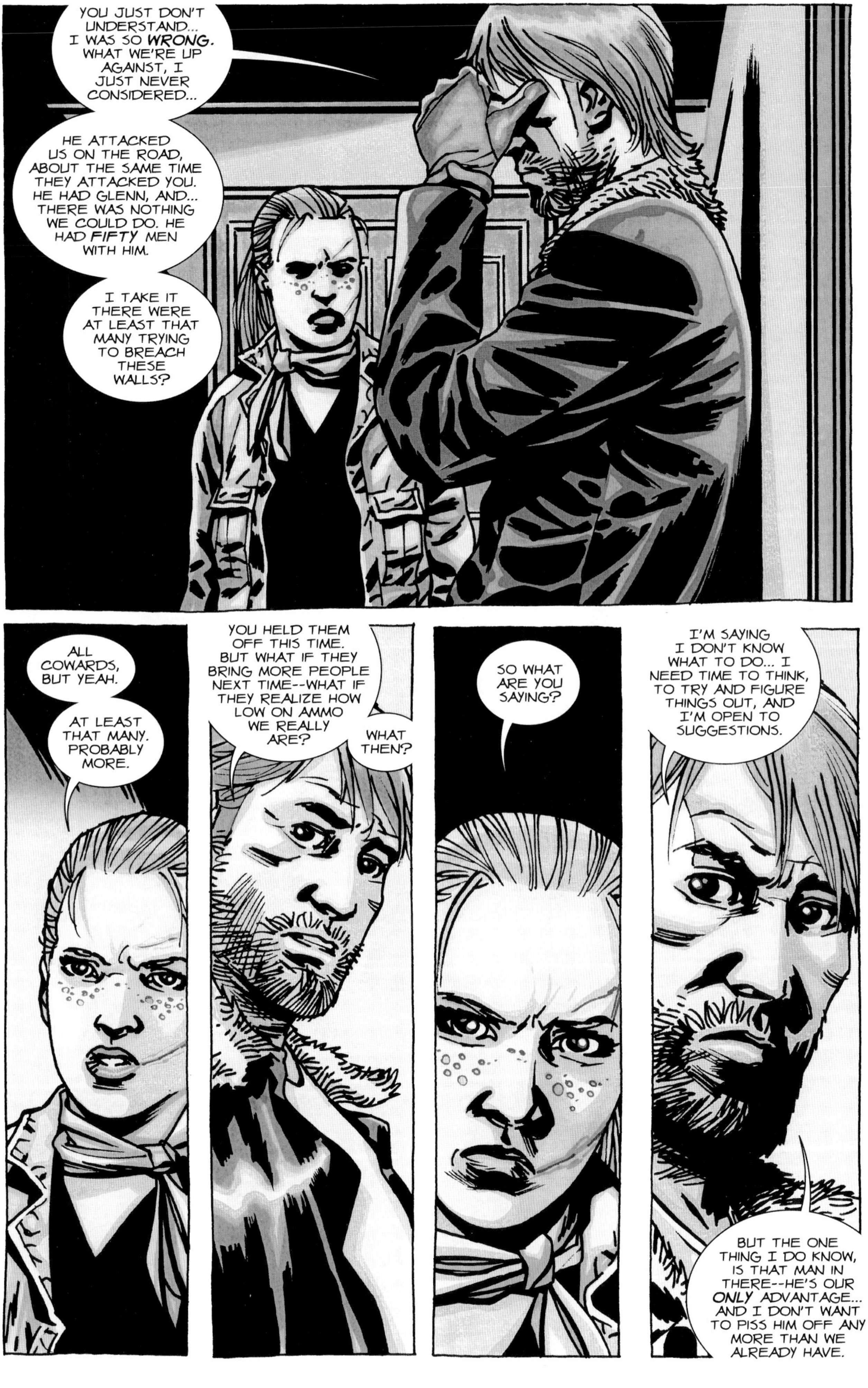
YOU JUST DON'T UNDERSTAND... I WAS SO WRONG. WHAT WE'RE UP AGAINST, I JUST NEVER CONSIDERED...
HE ATTACKED US ON THE ROAD, ABOUT THE SAME TIME THEY ATTACKED YOU. HE HAD GLENN, AND... THERE WAS NOTHING WE COULD DO. HE HAD FIFTY MEN WITH HIM.
I TAKE IT THERE WERE AT LEAST THAT MANY TRYING TO BREACH THESE WALLS?
ALL COWARDS, BUT YEAH.
AT LEAST THAT MANY. PROBABLY MORE.
YOU HELD THEM OFF THIS TIME. BUT WHAT IF THEY BRING MORE PEOPLE NEXT TIME--WHAT IF THEY REALIZE HOW LOW ON AMMO WE REALLY ARE?
WHAT THEN?
SO WHAT ARE YOU SAYING?
I'M SAYING I DON'T KNOW WHAT TO DO... I NEED TIME TO THINK, TO TRY AND FIGURE THINGS OUT, AND I'M OPEN TO SUGGESTIONS.
BUT THE ONE THING I DO KNOW, IS THAT MAN IN THERE--HE'S OUR ONLY ADVANTAGE... AND I DON'T WANT TO PISS HIM OFF ANY MORE THAN WE ALREADY HAVE.

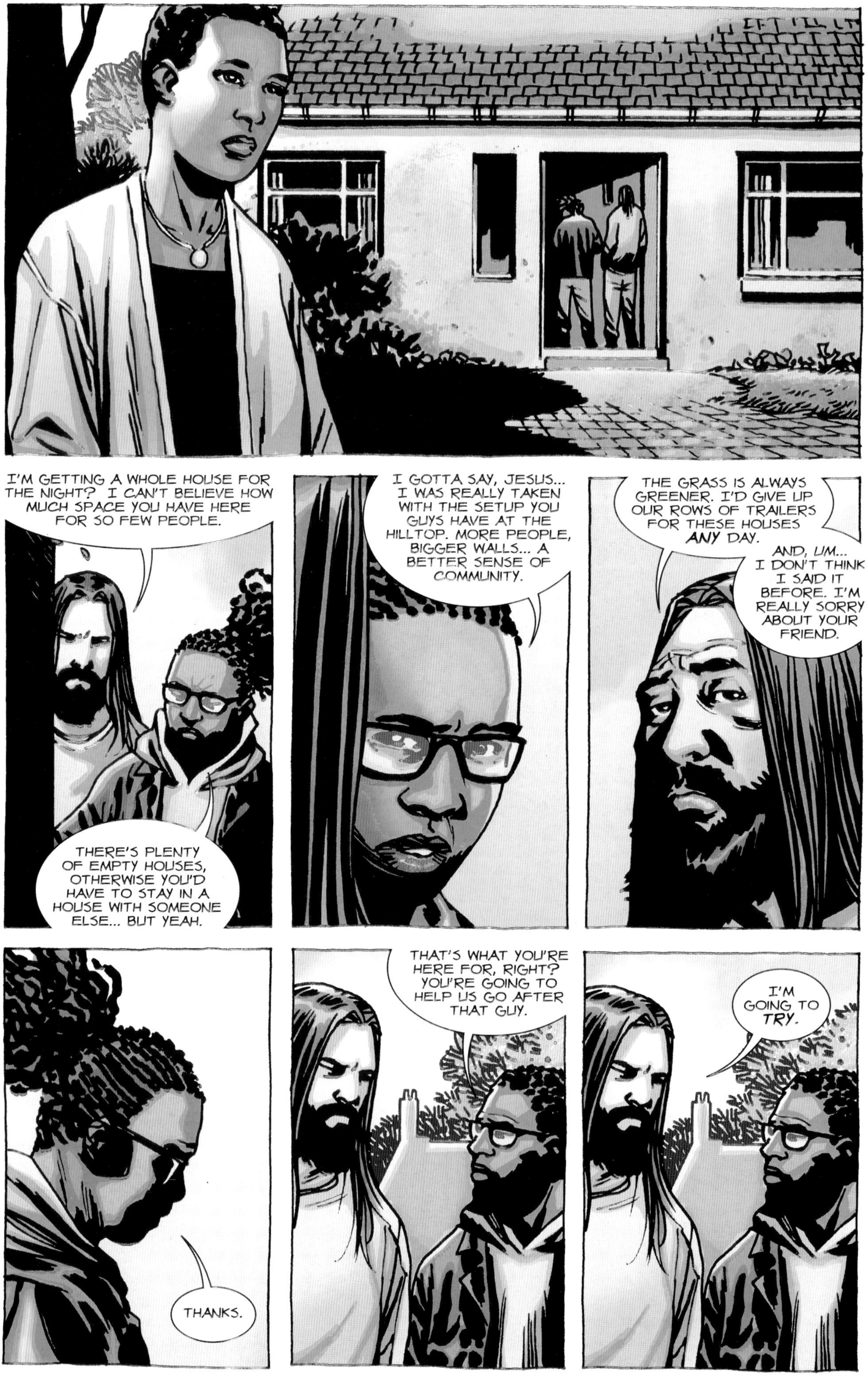
I'M GETTING A WHOLE HOUSE FOR THE NIGHT? I CAN'T BELIEVE HOW MUCH SPACE YOU HAVE HERE FOR SO FEW PEOPLE.
THERE'S PLENTY OF EMPTY HOUSES, OTHERWISE YOU'D HAVE TO STAY IN A HOUSE WITH SOMEONE ELSE... BUT YEAH.
I GOTTA SAY, JESUS... I WAS REALLY TAKEN WITH THE SETUP YOU GUYS HAVE AT THE HILLTOP. MORE PEOPLE, BIGGER WALLS... A BETTER SENSE OF COMMUNITY.
THE GRASS IS ALWAYS GREENER. I'D GIVE UP OUR ROWS OF TRAILERS FOR THESE HOUSES ANY DAY.
AND, UM... I DON'T THINK I SAID IT BEFORE. I'M REALLY SORRY ABOUT YOUR FRIEND.
THANKS.
THAT'S WHAT YOU'RE HERE FOR, RIGHT? YOU'RE GOING TO HELP US GO AFTER THAT GUY.
I'M GOING TO TRY.

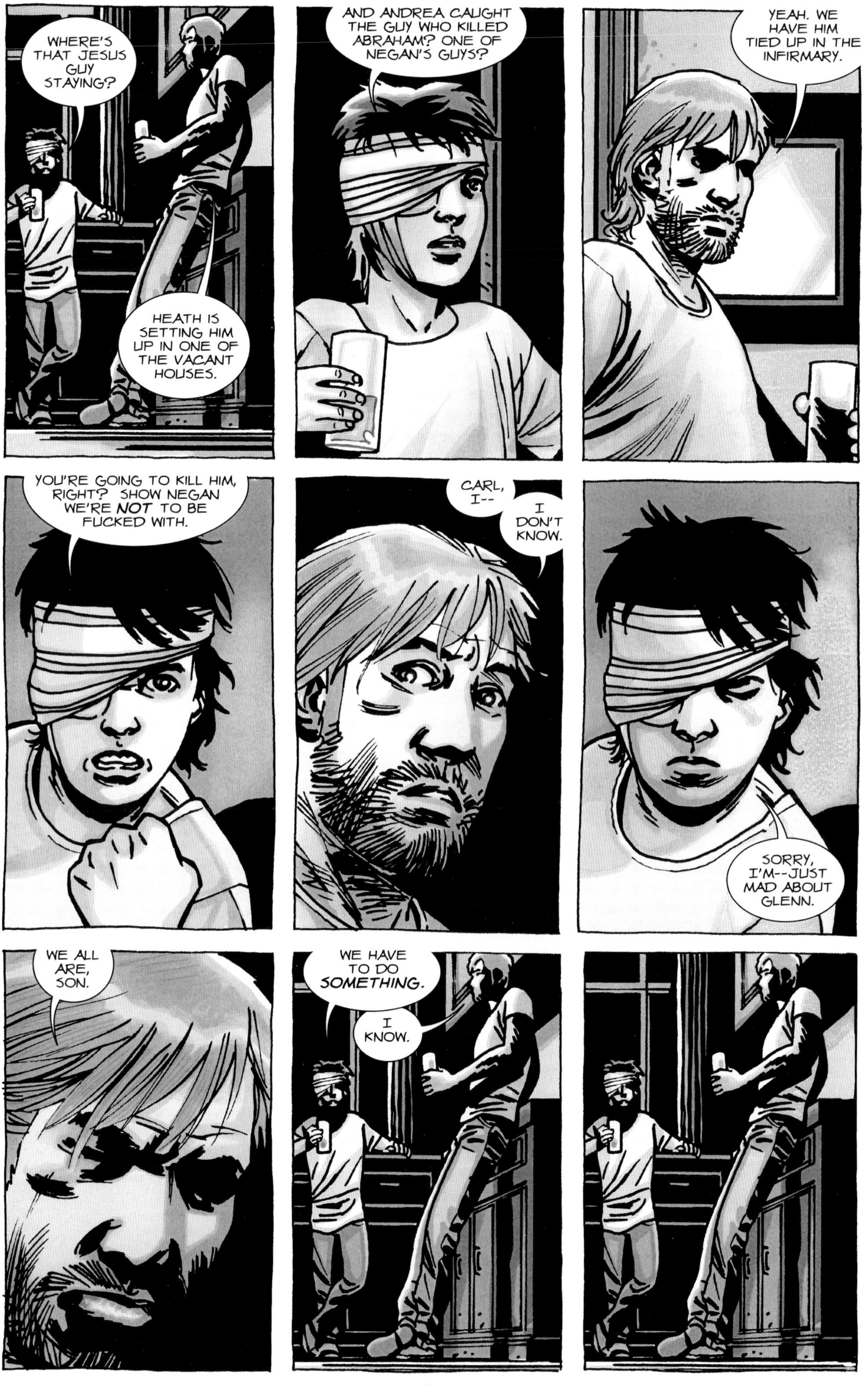
WHERE'S THAT JESUS GUY STAYING?
HEATH IS SETTING HIM UP IN ONE OF THE VACANT HOUSES.
AND ANDREA CAUGHT THE GUY WHO KILLED ABRAHAM? ONE OF NEGAN'S GUYS?
YEAH. WE HAVE HIM TIED UP IN THE INFIRMARY.
YOU'RE GOING TO KILL HIM, RIGHT? SHOW NEGAN WE'RE *NOT* TO BE FUCKED WITH.
CARL, I--
I DON'T KNOW.
SORRY, I'M--JUST MAD ABOUT GLENN.
WE ALL ARE, SON.
WE HAVE TO DO *SOMETHING.*
I KNOW.

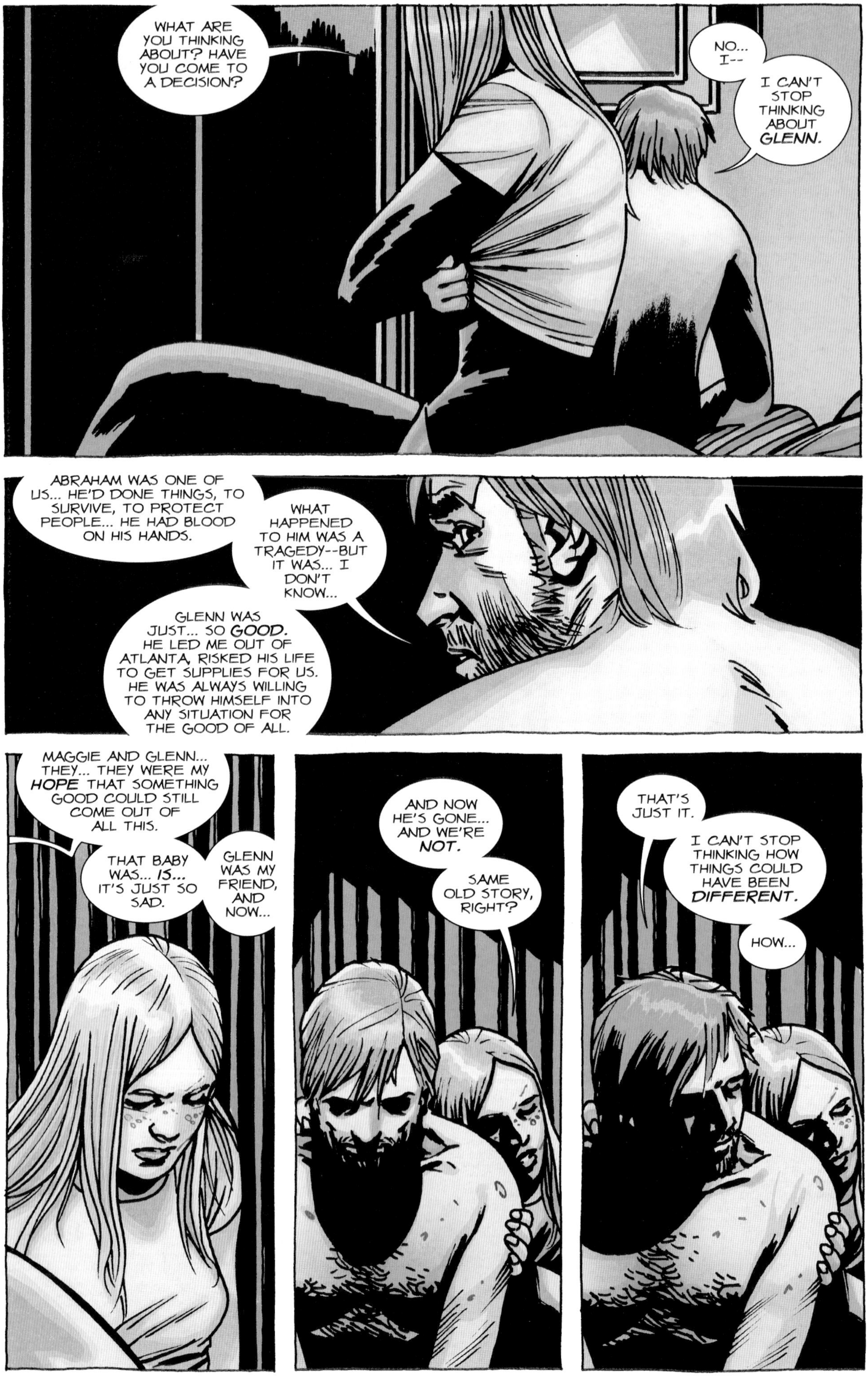
WHAT ARE YOU THINKING ABOUT? HAVE YOU COME TO A DECISION?
NO... I--
I CAN'T STOP THINKING ABOUT *GLENN.*
ABRAHAM WAS ONE OF US... HE'D DONE THINGS, TO SURVIVE, TO PROTECT PEOPLE... HE HAD BLOOD ON HIS HANDS.
WHAT HAPPENED TO HIM WAS A TRAGEDY--BUT IT WAS... I DON'T KNOW...
GLENN WAS JUST... SO *GOOD.* HE LED ME OUT OF ATLANTA, RISKED HIS LIFE TO GET SUPPLIES FOR US. HE WAS ALWAYS WILLING TO THROW HIMSELF INTO ANY SITUATION FOR THE GOOD OF ALL.
MAGGIE AND GLENN... THEY... THEY WERE MY *HOPE* THAT SOMETHING GOOD COULD STILL COME OUT OF ALL THIS.
THAT BABY WAS... *IS...* IT'S JUST SO SAD.
GLENN WAS MY FRIEND, AND NOW...
AND NOW HE'S GONE... AND WE'RE *NOT.*
SAME OLD STORY, RIGHT?
THAT'S JUST IT.
I CAN'T STOP THINKING HOW THINGS COULD HAVE BEEN *DIFFERENT.*
HOW...

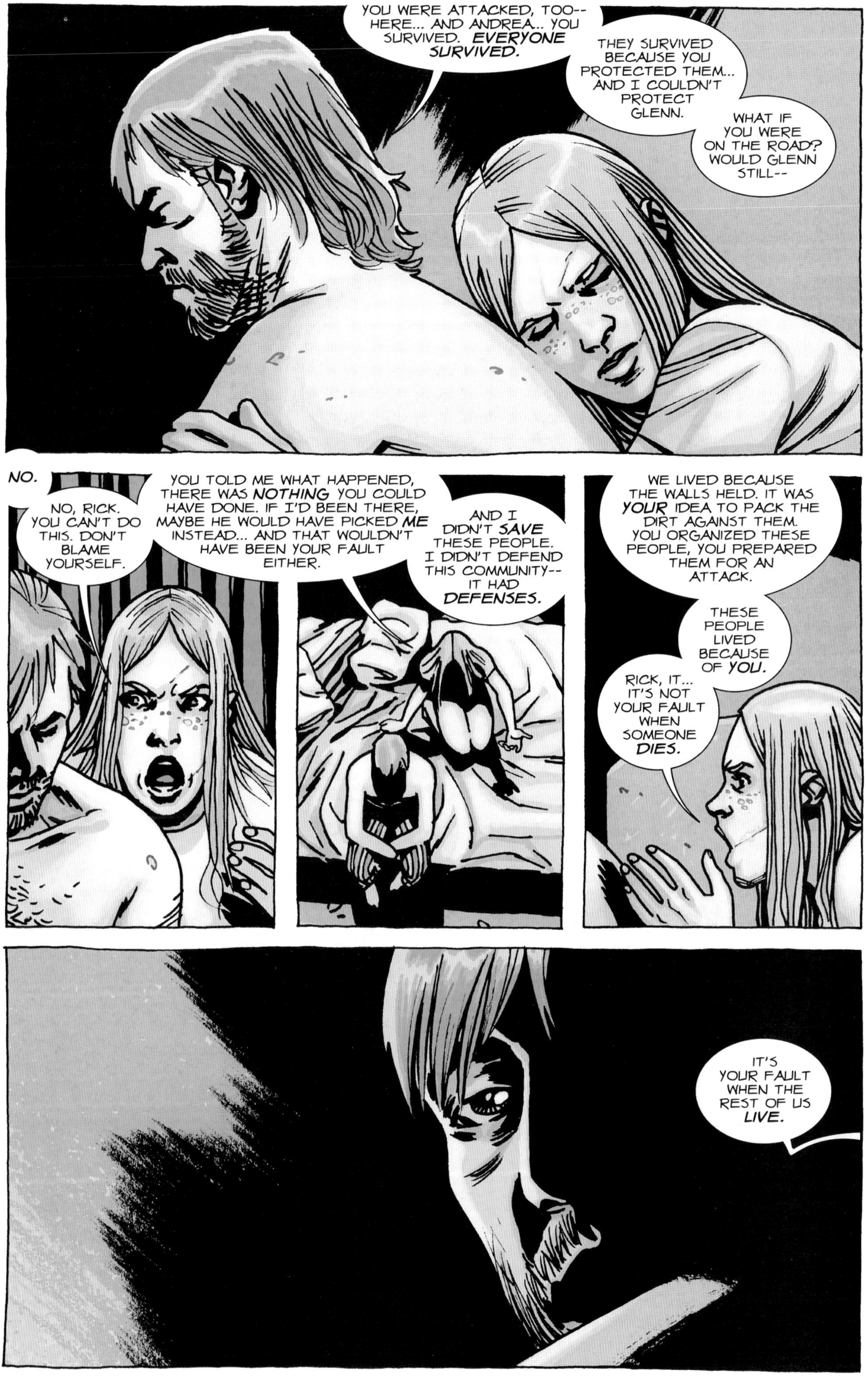

YOU WERE ATTACKED, TOO-- HERE... AND ANDREA... YOU SURVIVED. EVERYONE SURVIVED.
THEY SURVIVED BECAUSE YOU PROTECTED THEM... AND I COULDN'T PROTECT GLENN.
WHAT IF YOU WERE ON THE ROAD? WOULD GLENN STILL--
NO.
NO, RICK. YOU CAN'T DO THIS. DON'T BLAME YOURSELF.
YOU TOLD ME WHAT HAPPENED, THERE WAS NOTHING YOU COULD HAVE DONE. IF I'D BEEN THERE, MAYBE HE WOULD HAVE PICKED ME INSTEAD... AND THAT WOULDN'T HAVE BEEN YOUR FAULT EITHER.
AND I DIDN'T SAVE THESE PEOPLE. I DIDN'T DEFEND THIS COMMUNITY-- IT HAD DEFENSES.
WE LIVED BECAUSE THE WALLS HELD. IT WAS YOUR IDEA TO PACK THE DIRT AGAINST THEM. YOU ORGANIZED THESE PEOPLE, YOU PREPARED THEM FOR AN ATTACK.
THESE PEOPLE LIVED BECAUSE OF YOU.
RICK, IT... IT'S NOT YOUR FAULT WHEN SOMEONE DIES.
IT'S YOUR FAULT WHEN THE REST OF US LIVE.

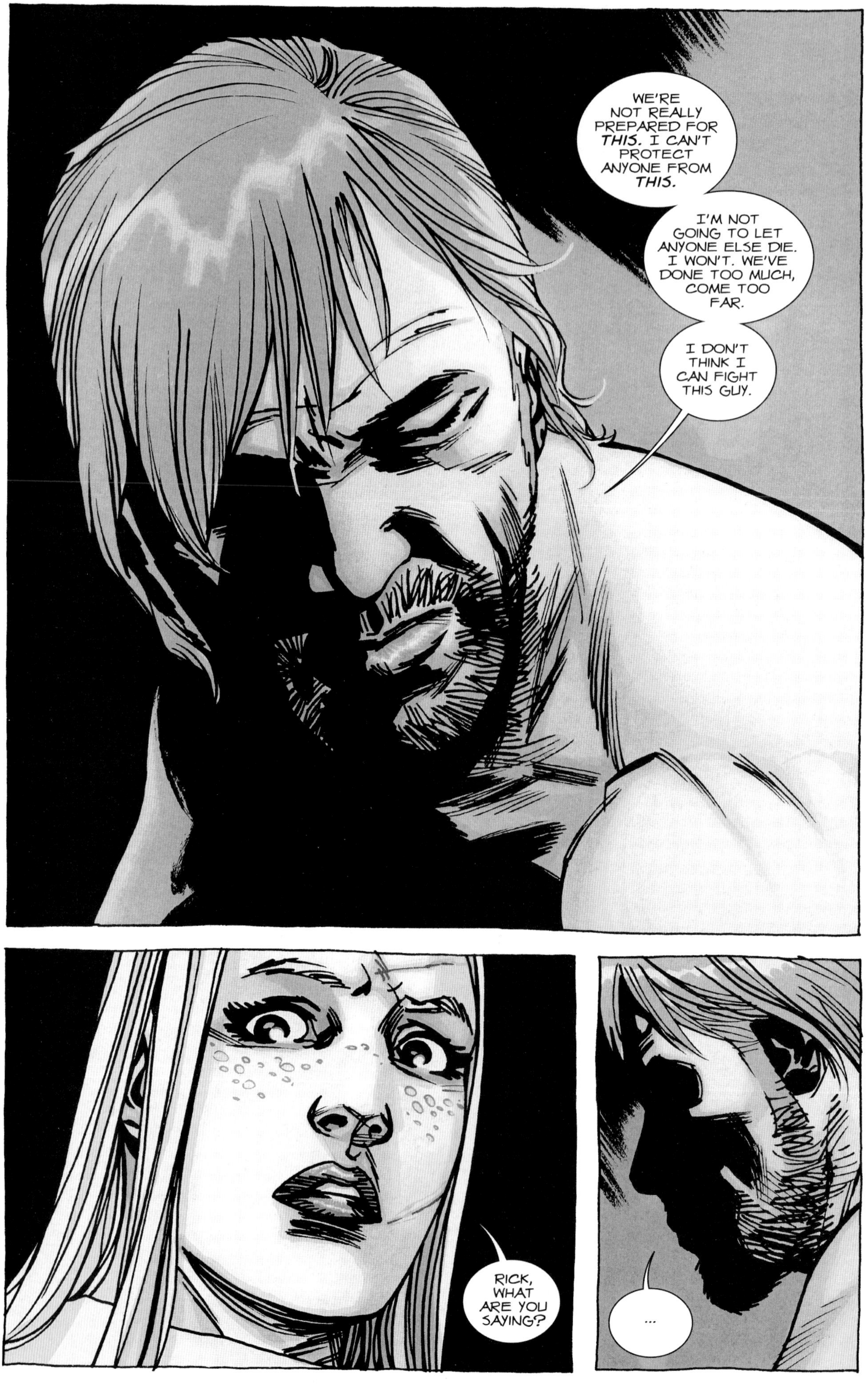
WE'RE NOT REALLY PREPARED FOR *THIS.* I CAN'T PROTECT ANYONE FROM *THIS.*
I'M NOT GOING TO LET ANYONE ELSE DIE. I WON'T. WE'VE DONE TOO MUCH, COME TOO FAR.
I DON'T THINK I CAN FIGHT THIS GUY.
RICK, WHAT ARE YOU SAYING?
...

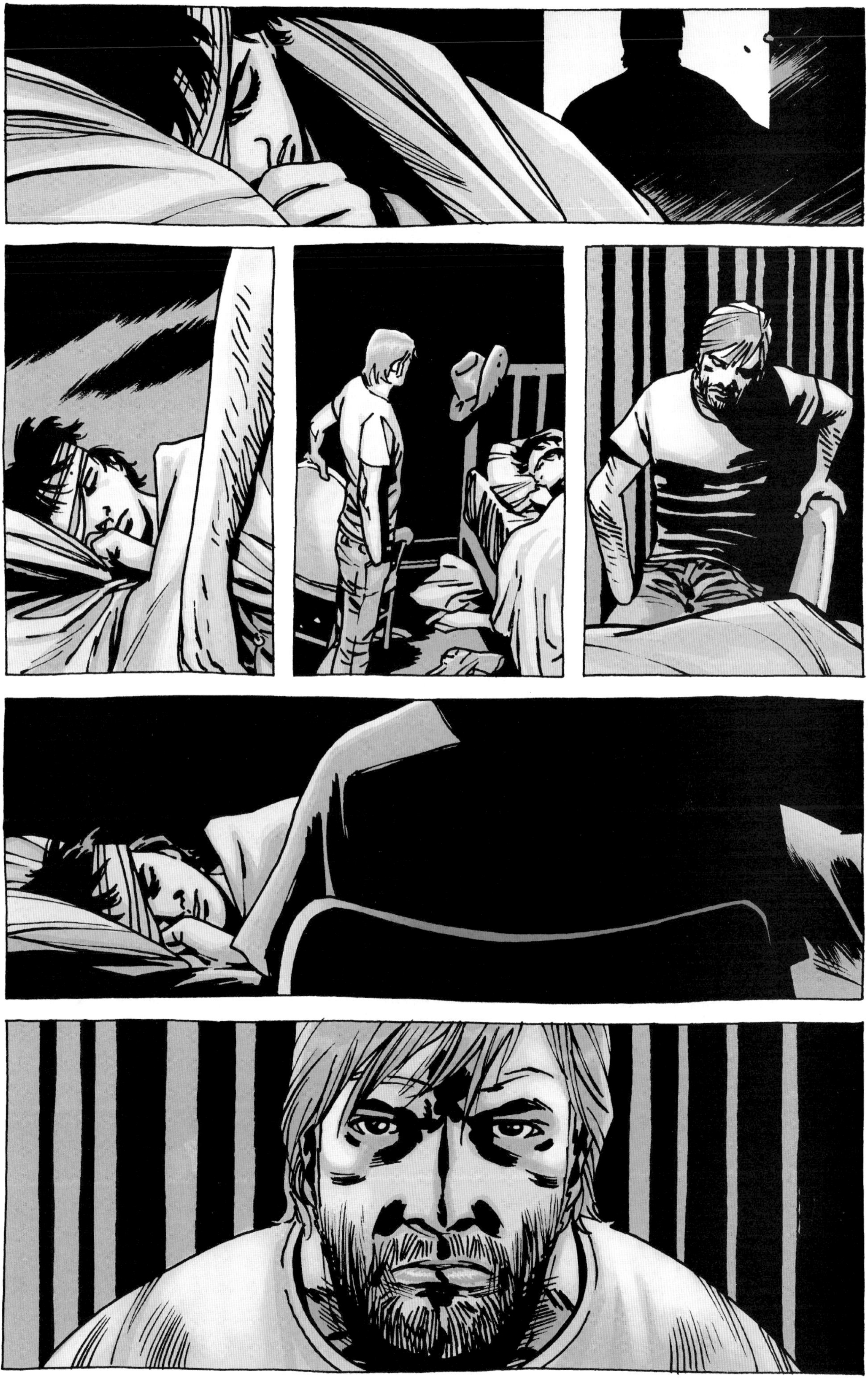

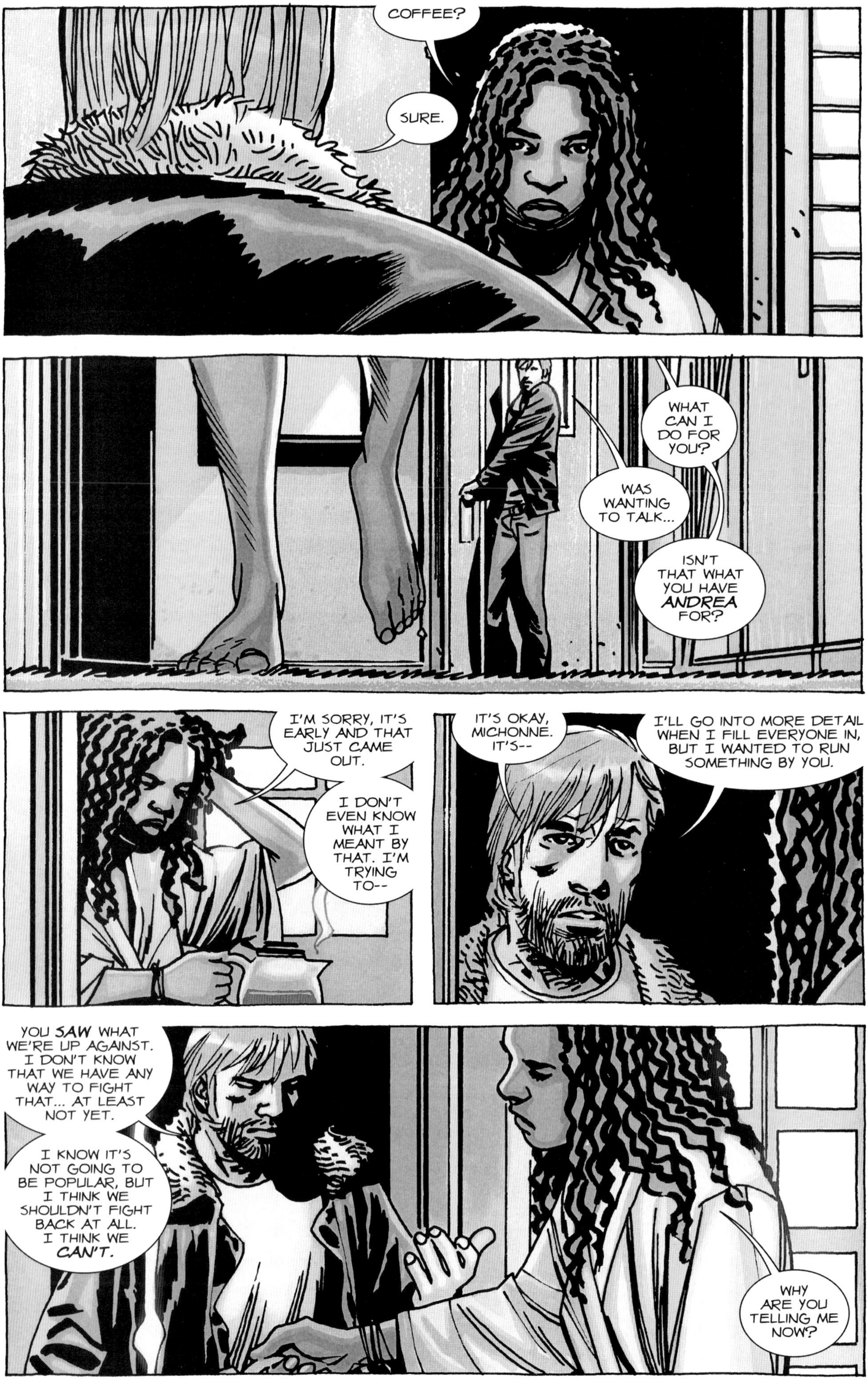
COFFEE?
SURE.
WHAT CAN I DO FOR YOU?
WAS WANTING TO TALK...
ISN'T THAT WHAT YOU HAVE **ANDREA** FOR?
I'M SORRY, IT'S EARLY AND THAT JUST CAME OUT.
I DON'T EVEN KNOW WHAT I MEANT BY THAT. I'M TRYING TO--
IT'S OKAY, MICHONNE. IT'S--
I'LL GO INTO MORE DETAIL WHEN I FILL EVERYONE IN, BUT I WANTED TO RUN SOMETHING BY YOU.
YOU **SAW** WHAT WE'RE UP AGAINST. I DON'T KNOW THAT WE HAVE ANY WAY TO FIGHT THAT... AT LEAST NOT YET.
I KNOW IT'S NOT GOING TO BE POPULAR, BUT I THINK WE SHOULDN'T FIGHT BACK AT ALL. I THINK WE ***CAN'T.***
WHY ARE YOU TELLING ME NOW?

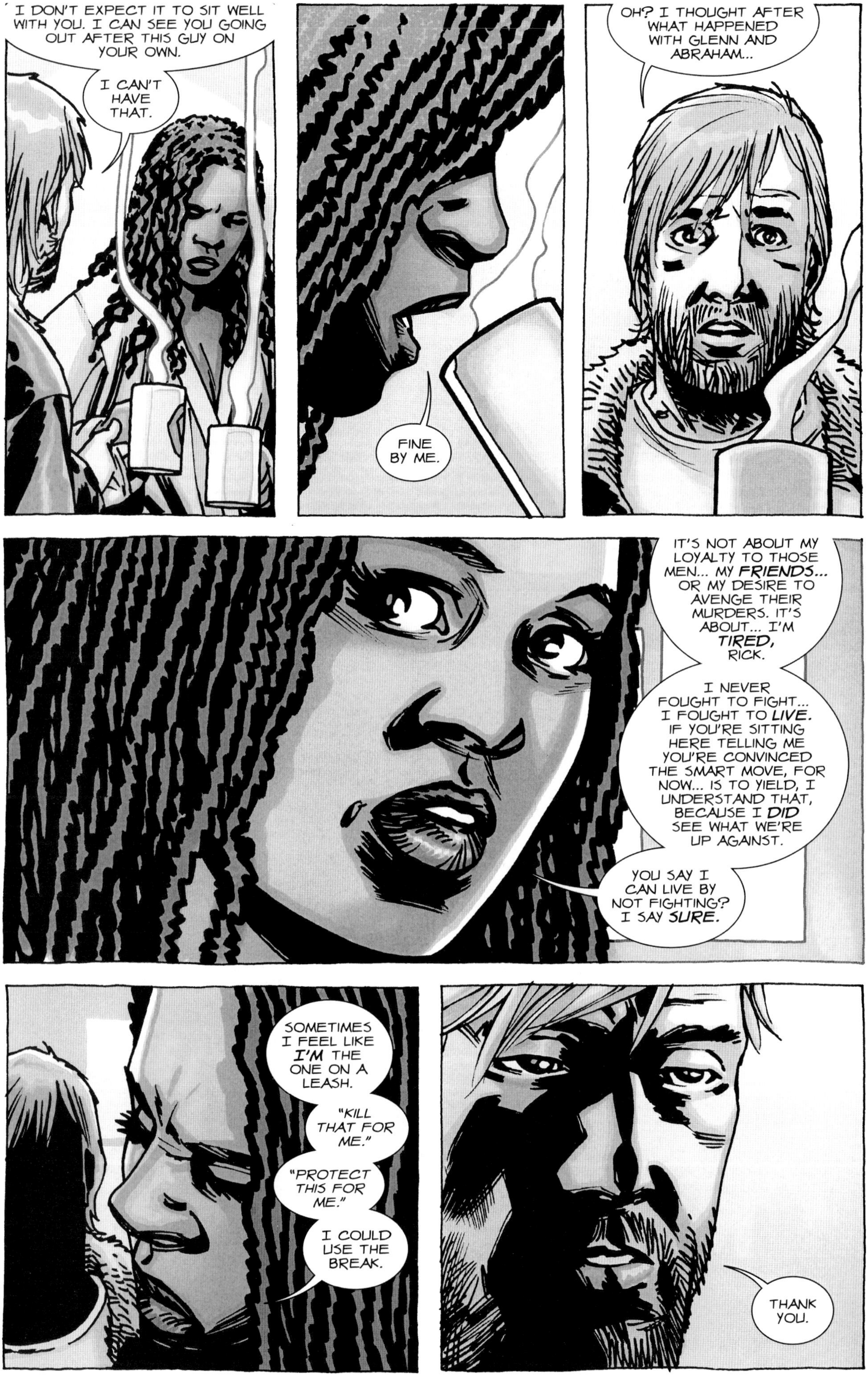
I DON'T EXPECT IT TO SIT WELL WITH YOU. I CAN SEE YOU GOING OUT AFTER THIS GUY ON YOUR OWN.
I CAN'T HAVE THAT.
FINE BY ME.
OH? I THOUGHT AFTER WHAT HAPPENED WITH GLENN AND ABRAHAM...
IT'S NOT ABOUT MY LOYALTY TO THOSE MEN... MY FRIENDS... OR MY DESIRE TO AVENGE THEIR MURDERS. IT'S ABOUT... I'M TIRED, RICK.
I NEVER FOUGHT TO FIGHT... I FOUGHT TO LIVE. IF YOU'RE SITTING HERE TELLING ME YOU'RE CONVINCED THE SMART MOVE, FOR NOW... IS TO YIELD, I UNDERSTAND THAT, BECAUSE I DID SEE WHAT WE'RE UP AGAINST.
YOU SAY I CAN LIVE BY NOT FIGHTING? I SAY SURE.
SOMETIMES I FEEL LIKE I'M THE ONE ON A LEASH.
"KILL THAT FOR ME."
"PROTECT THIS FOR ME."
I COULD USE THE BREAK.
THANK YOU.

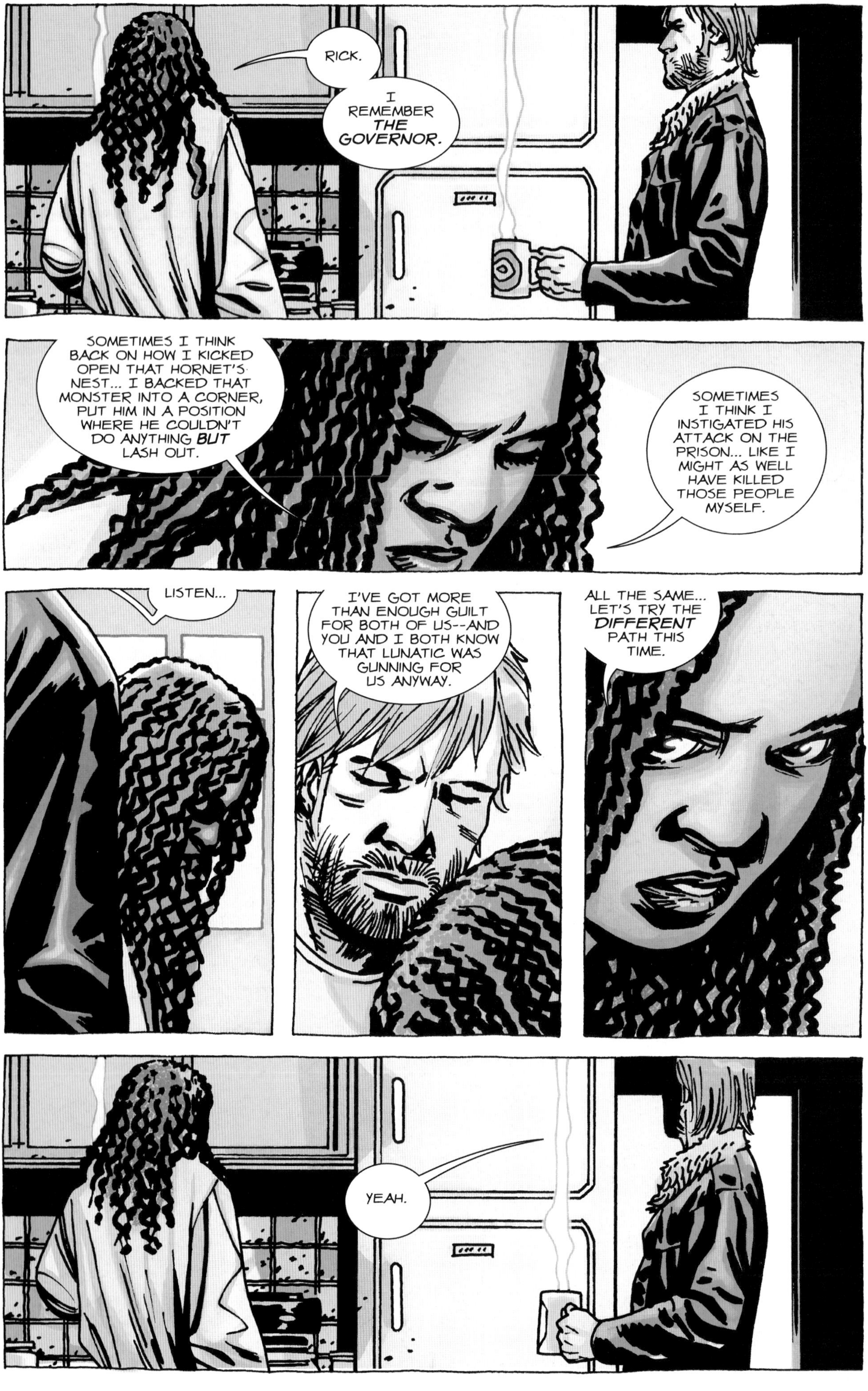
RICK.
I REMEMBER THE GOVERNOR.
SOMETIMES I THINK BACK ON HOW I KICKED OPEN THAT HORNET'S NEST... I BACKED THAT MONSTER INTO A CORNER, PUT HIM IN A POSITION WHERE HE COULDN'T DO ANYTHING BUT LASH OUT.
SOMETIMES I THINK I INSTIGATED HIS ATTACK ON THE PRISON... LIKE I MIGHT AS WELL HAVE KILLED THOSE PEOPLE MYSELF.
LISTEN...
I'VE GOT MORE THAN ENOUGH GUILT FOR BOTH OF US--AND YOU AND I BOTH KNOW THAT LUNATIC WAS GUNNING FOR US ANYWAY.
ALL THE SAME... LET'S TRY THE DIFFERENT PATH THIS TIME.
YEAH.

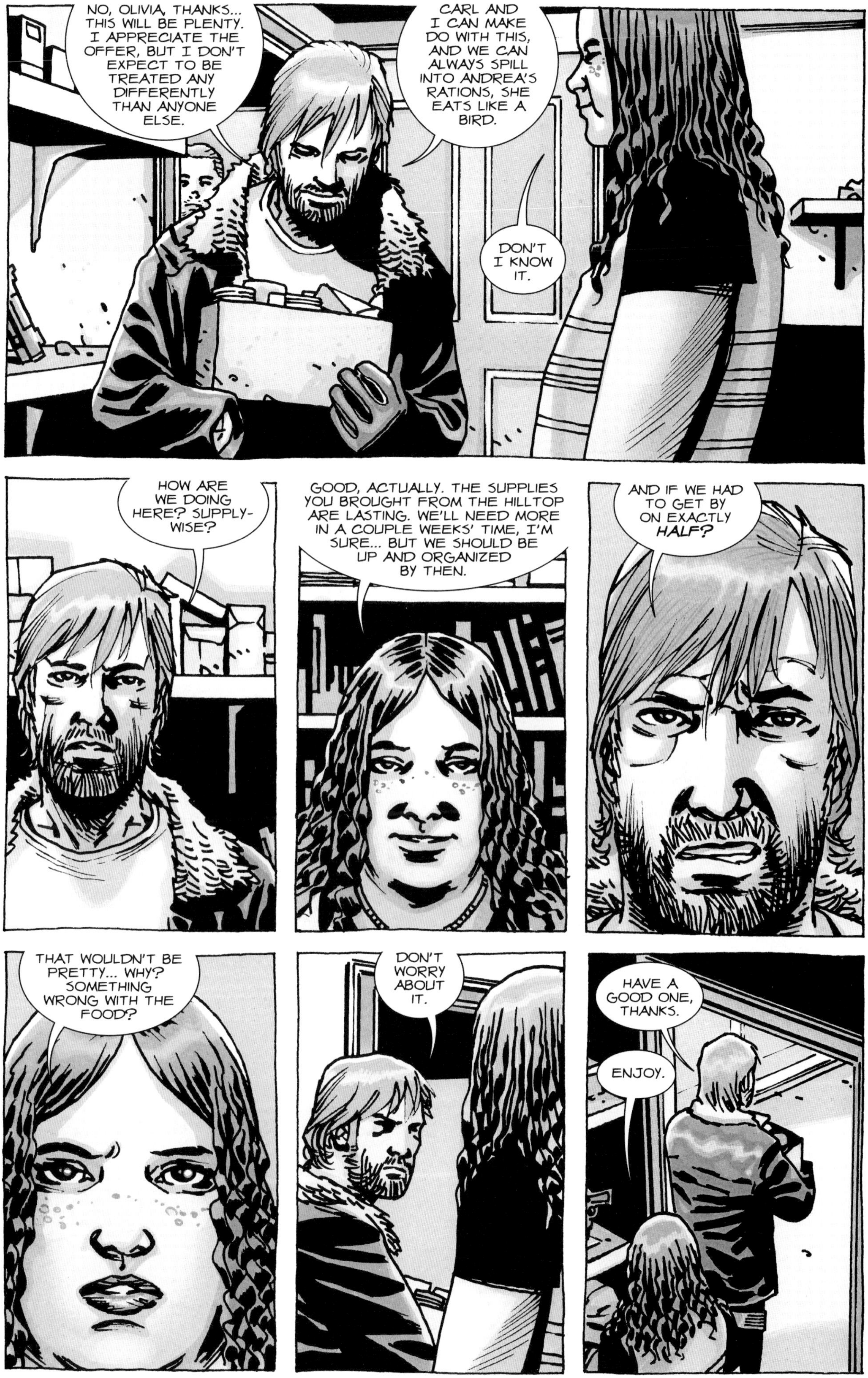
NO, OLIVIA, THANKS... THIS WILL BE PLENTY. I APPRECIATE THE OFFER, BUT I DON'T EXPECT TO BE TREATED ANY DIFFERENTLY THAN ANYONE ELSE.
CARL AND I CAN MAKE DO WITH THIS, AND WE CAN ALWAYS SPILL INTO ANDREA'S RATIONS, SHE EATS LIKE A BIRD.
DON'T I KNOW IT.
HOW ARE WE DOING HERE? SUPPLY-WISE?
GOOD, ACTUALLY. THE SUPPLIES YOU BROUGHT FROM THE HILLTOP ARE LASTING. WE'LL NEED MORE IN A COUPLE WEEKS' TIME, I'M SURE... BUT WE SHOULD BE UP AND ORGANIZED BY THEN.
AND IF WE HAD TO GET BY ON EXACTLY *HALF?*
THAT WOULDN'T BE PRETTY... WHY? SOMETHING WRONG WITH THE FOOD?
DON'T WORRY ABOUT IT.
HAVE A GOOD ONE, THANKS.
ENJOY.

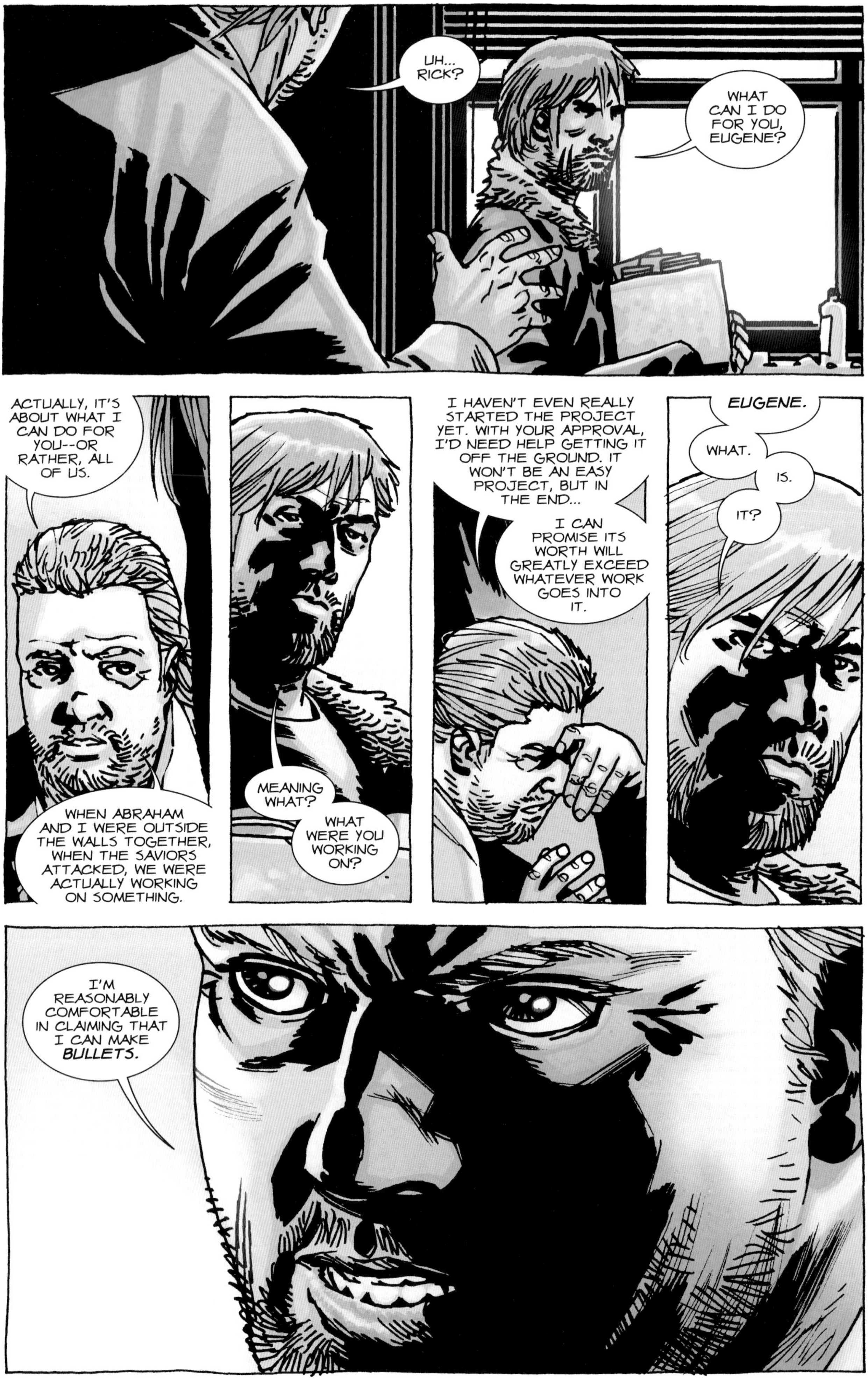
UH... RICK?
WHAT CAN I DO FOR YOU, EUGENE?
ACTUALLY, IT'S ABOUT WHAT I CAN DO FOR YOU--OR RATHER, ALL OF US.
WHEN ABRAHAM AND I WERE OUTSIDE THE WALLS TOGETHER, WHEN THE SAVIORS ATTACKED, WE WERE ACTUALLY WORKING ON SOMETHING.
MEANING WHAT?
WHAT WERE YOU WORKING ON?
I HAVEN'T EVEN REALLY STARTED THE PROJECT YET. WITH YOUR APPROVAL, I'D NEED HELP GETTING IT OFF THE GROUND. IT WON'T BE AN EASY PROJECT, BUT IN THE END...
I CAN PROMISE ITS WORTH WILL GREATLY EXCEED WHATEVER WORK GOES INTO IT.
EUGENE.
WHAT.
IS.
IT?
I'M REASONABLY COMFORTABLE IN CLAIMING THAT I CAN MAKE *BULLETS.*

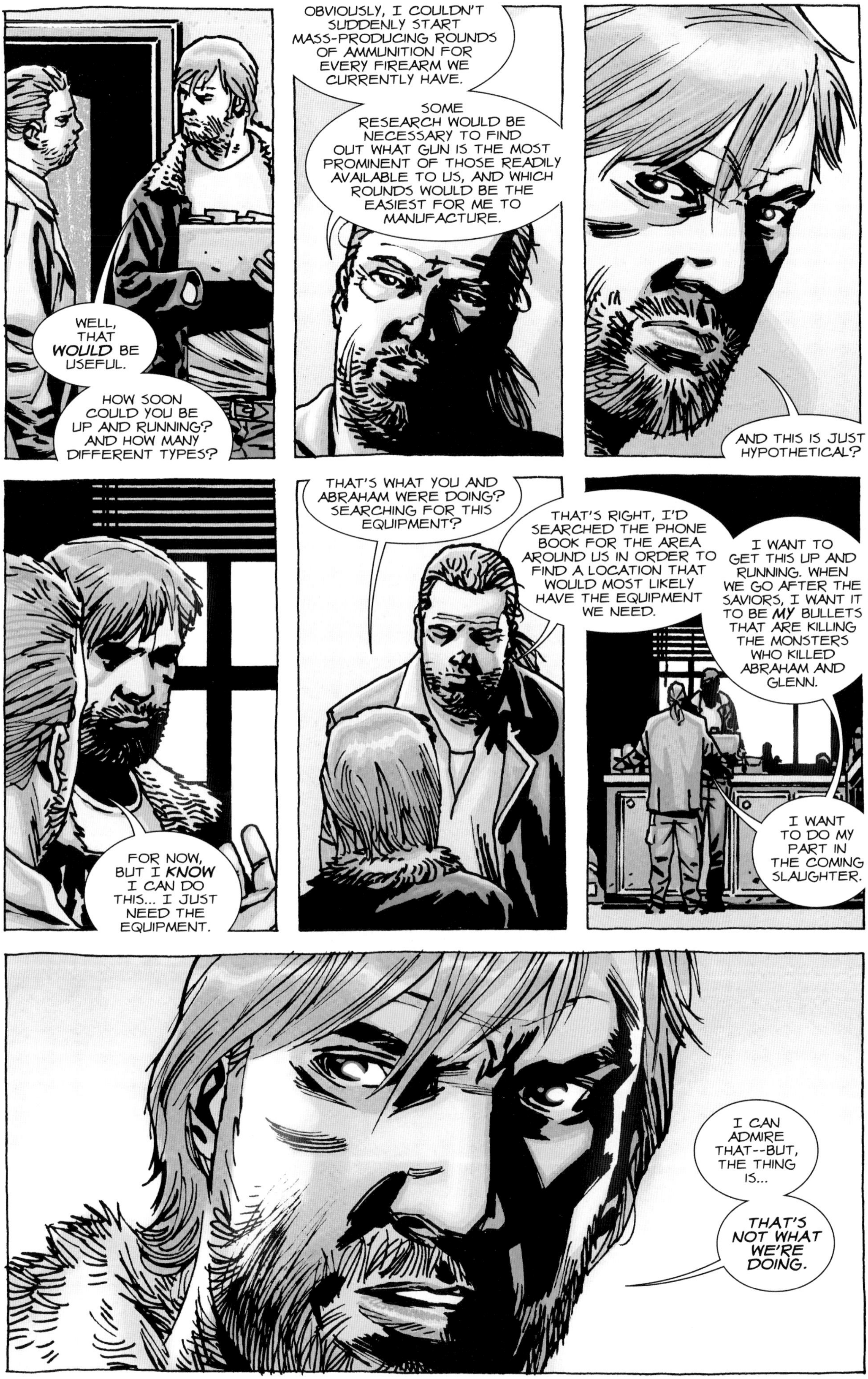
WELL, THAT WOULD BE USEFUL.
HOW SOON COULD YOU BE UP AND RUNNING? AND HOW MANY DIFFERENT TYPES?
OBVIOUSLY, I COULDN'T SUDDENLY START MASS-PRODUCING ROUNDS OF AMMUNITION FOR EVERY FIREARM WE CURRENTLY HAVE.
SOME RESEARCH WOULD BE NECESSARY TO FIND OUT WHAT GUN IS THE MOST PROMINENT OF THOSE READILY AVAILABLE TO US, AND WHICH ROUNDS WOULD BE THE EASIEST FOR ME TO MANUFACTURE.
AND THIS IS JUST HYPOTHETICAL?
FOR NOW, BUT I KNOW I CAN DO THIS... I JUST NEED THE EQUIPMENT.
THAT'S WHAT YOU AND ABRAHAM WERE DOING? SEARCHING FOR THIS EQUIPMENT?
THAT'S RIGHT, I'D SEARCHED THE PHONE BOOK FOR THE AREA AROUND US IN ORDER TO FIND A LOCATION THAT WOULD MOST LIKELY HAVE THE EQUIPMENT WE NEED.
I WANT TO GET THIS UP AND RUNNING. WHEN WE GO AFTER THE SAVIORS, I WANT IT TO BE MY BULLETS THAT ARE KILLING THE MONSTERS WHO KILLED ABRAHAM AND GLENN.
I WANT TO DO MY PART IN THE COMING SLAUGHTER.
I CAN ADMIRE THAT--BUT, THE THING IS...
THAT'S NOT WHAT WE'RE DOING.

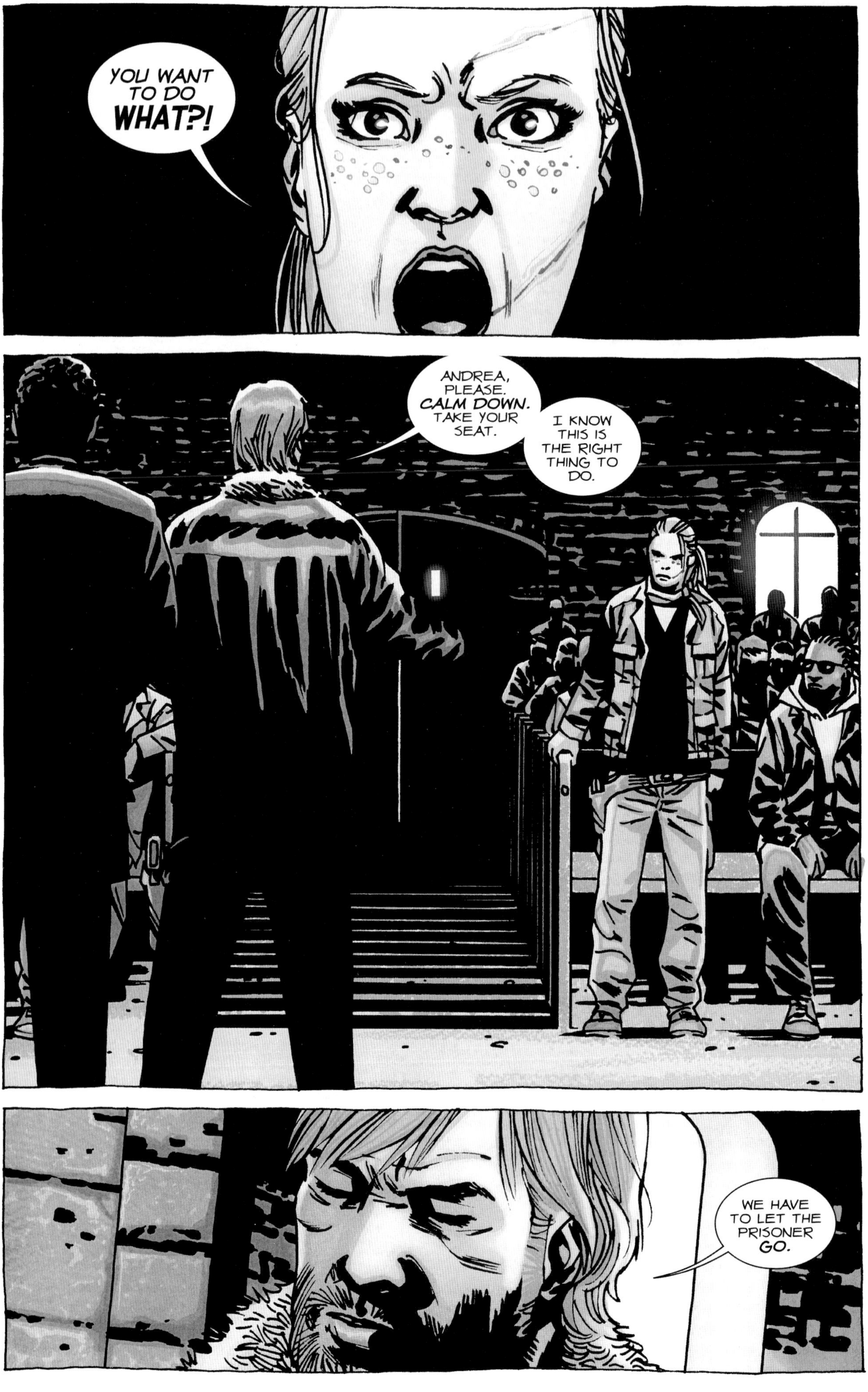
YOU WANT TO DO WHAT?!
ANDREA, PLEASE. CALM DOWN. TAKE YOUR SEAT.
I KNOW THIS IS THE RIGHT THING TO DO.
WE HAVE TO LET THE PRISONER GO.

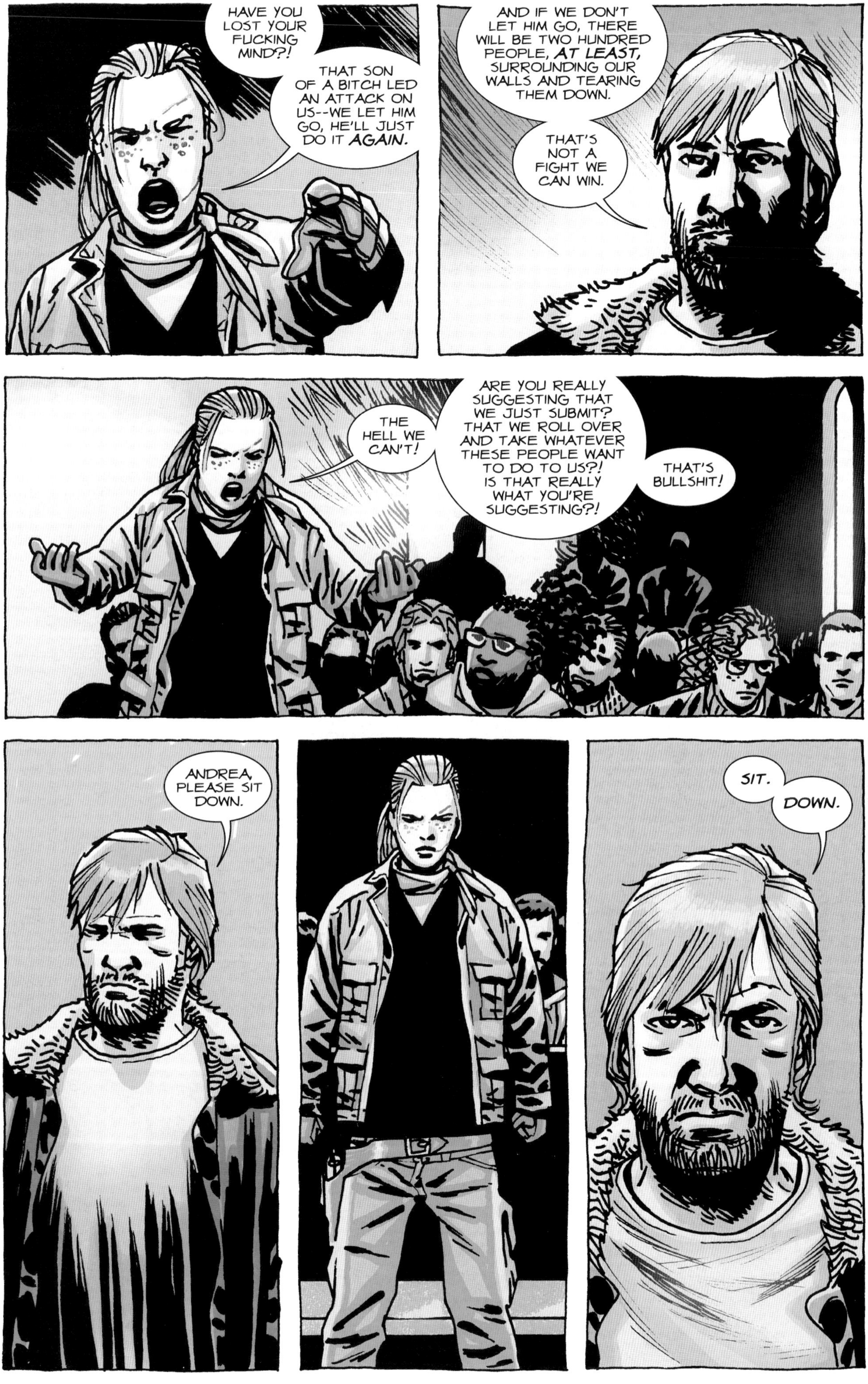
HAVE YOU LOST YOUR FUCKING MIND?!
THAT SON OF A BITCH LED AN ATTACK ON US--WE LET HIM GO, HE'LL JUST DO IT *AGAIN.*
AND IF WE DON'T LET HIM GO, THERE WILL BE TWO HUNDRED PEOPLE, *AT LEAST,* SURROUNDING OUR WALLS AND TEARING THEM DOWN.
THAT'S NOT A FIGHT WE CAN WIN.
THE HELL WE CAN'T!
ARE YOU REALLY SUGGESTING THAT WE JUST SUBMIT? THAT WE ROLL OVER AND TAKE WHATEVER THESE PEOPLE WANT TO DO TO US?! IS THAT REALLY WHAT YOU'RE SUGGESTING?!
THAT'S BULLSHIT!
ANDREA, PLEASE SIT DOWN.
SIT.
DOWN.

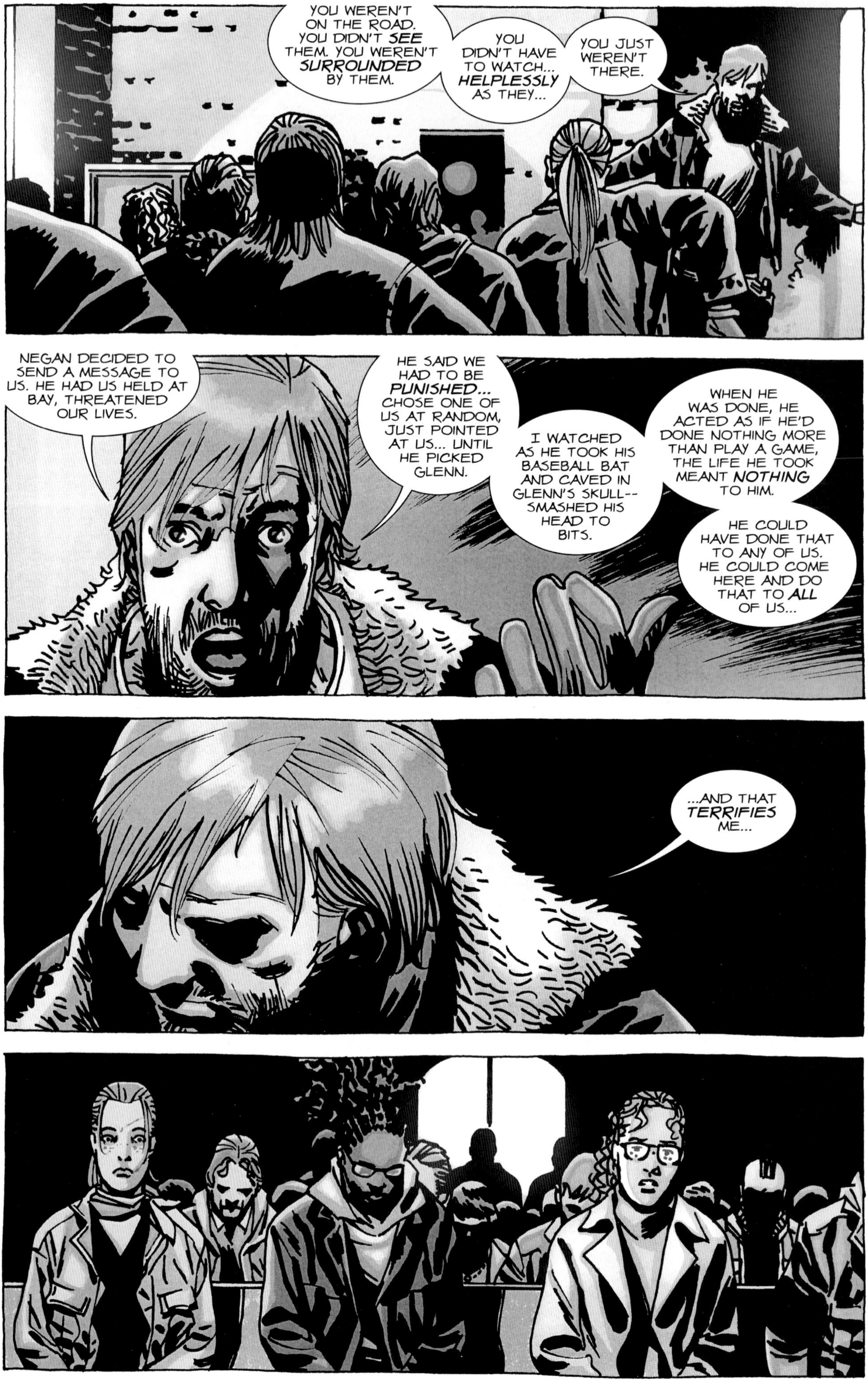
YOU WEREN'T ON THE ROAD. YOU DIDN'T SEE THEM. YOU WEREN'T SURROUNDED BY THEM.
YOU DIDN'T HAVE TO WATCH... HELPLESSLY AS THEY...
YOU JUST WEREN'T THERE.
NEGAN DECIDED TO SEND A MESSAGE TO US. HE HAD US HELD AT BAY, THREATENED OUR LIVES.
HE SAID WE HAD TO BE PUNISHED... CHOSE ONE OF US AT RANDOM, JUST POINTED AT US... UNTIL HE PICKED GLENN.
I WATCHED AS HE TOOK HIS BASEBALL BAT AND CAVED IN GLENN'S SKULL-- SMASHED HIS HEAD TO BITS.
WHEN HE WAS DONE, HE ACTED AS IF HE'D DONE NOTHING MORE THAN PLAY A GAME, THE LIFE HE TOOK MEANT NOTHING TO HIM.
HE COULD HAVE DONE THAT TO ANY OF US. HE COULD COME HERE AND DO THAT TO ALL OF US...
...AND THAT TERRIFIES ME...

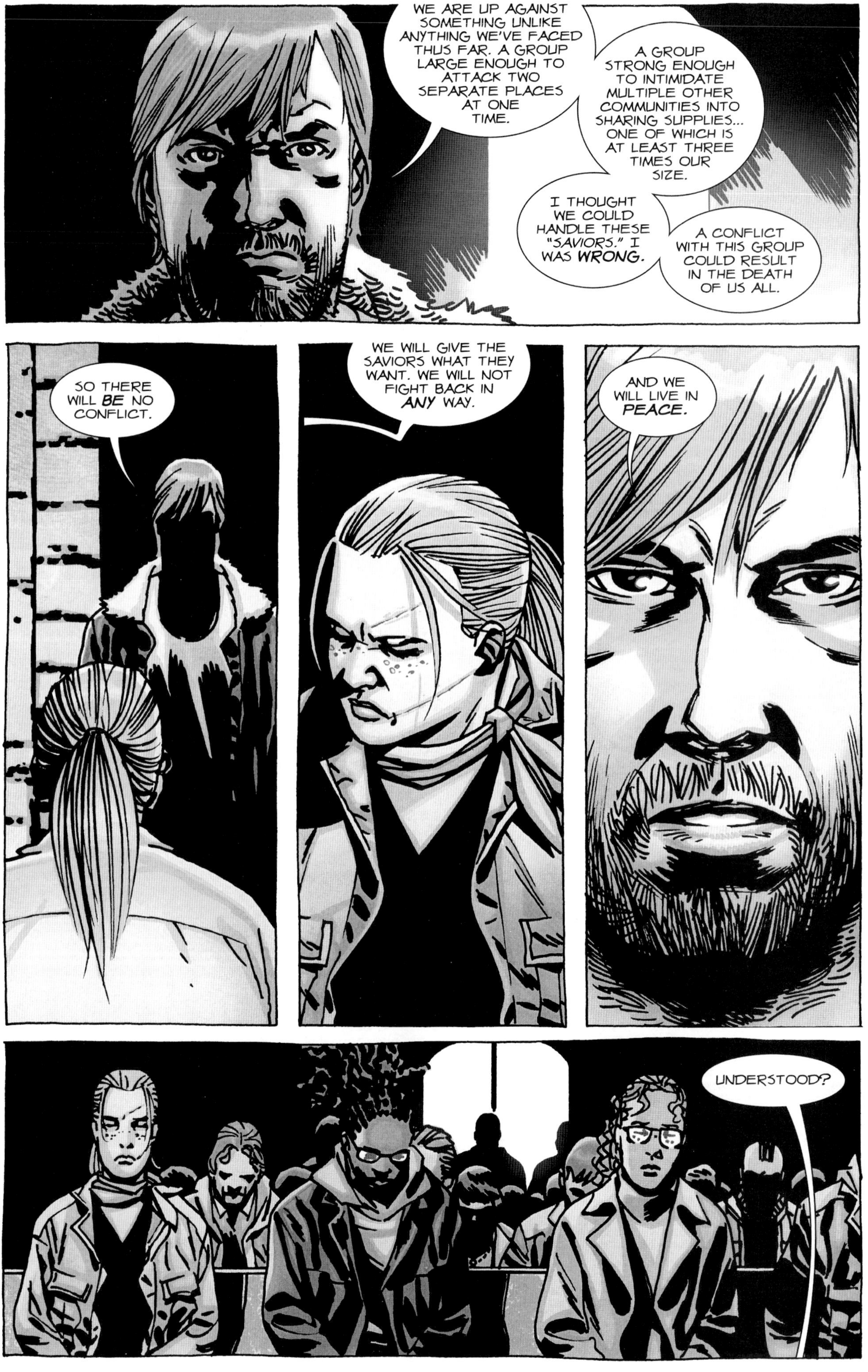
WE ARE UP AGAINST SOMETHING UNLIKE ANYTHING WE'VE FACED THUS FAR. A GROUP LARGE ENOUGH TO ATTACK TWO SEPARATE PLACES AT ONE TIME.
A GROUP STRONG ENOUGH TO INTIMIDATE MULTIPLE OTHER COMMUNITIES INTO SHARING SUPPLIES... ONE OF WHICH IS AT LEAST THREE TIMES OUR SIZE.
I THOUGHT WE COULD HANDLE THESE "SAVIORS." I WAS **WRONG.**
A CONFLICT WITH THIS GROUP COULD RESULT IN THE DEATH OF US ALL.
SO THERE WILL **BE** NO CONFLICT.
WE WILL GIVE THE SAVIORS WHAT THEY WANT. WE WILL NOT FIGHT BACK IN ***ANY*** WAY.
AND WE WILL LIVE IN ***PEACE.***
UNDERSTOOD?

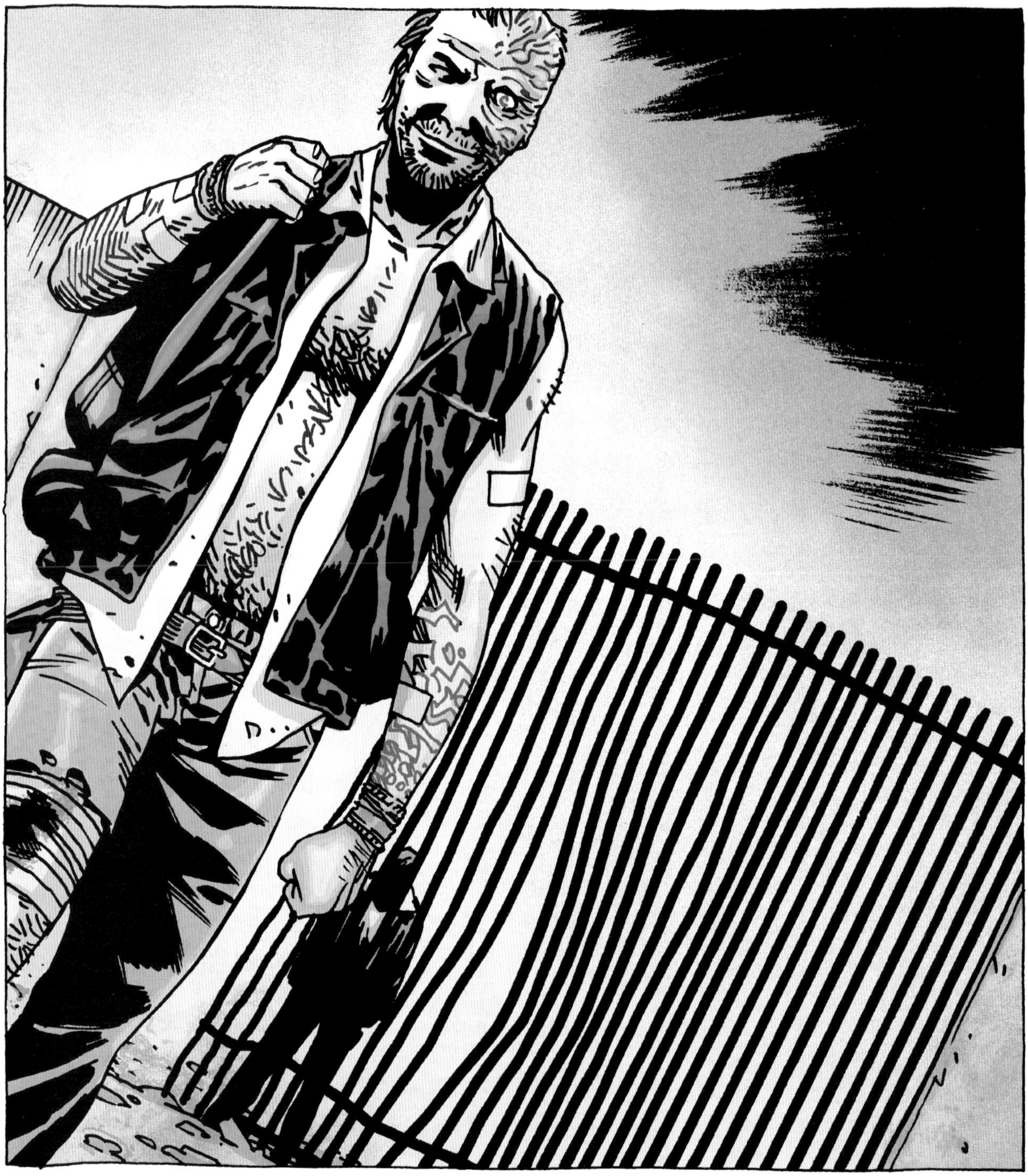
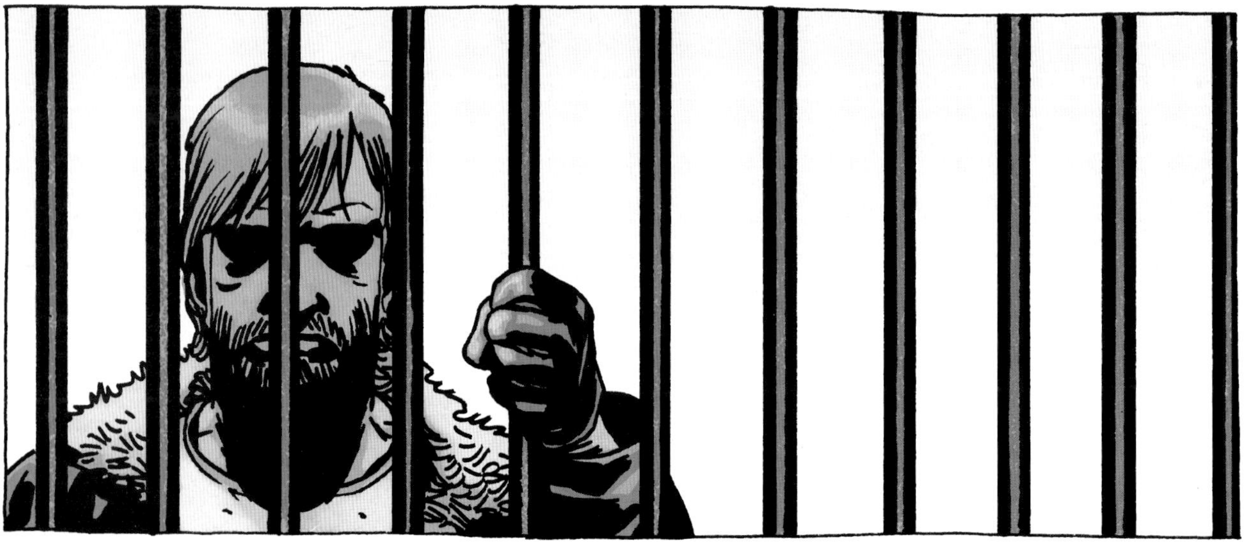

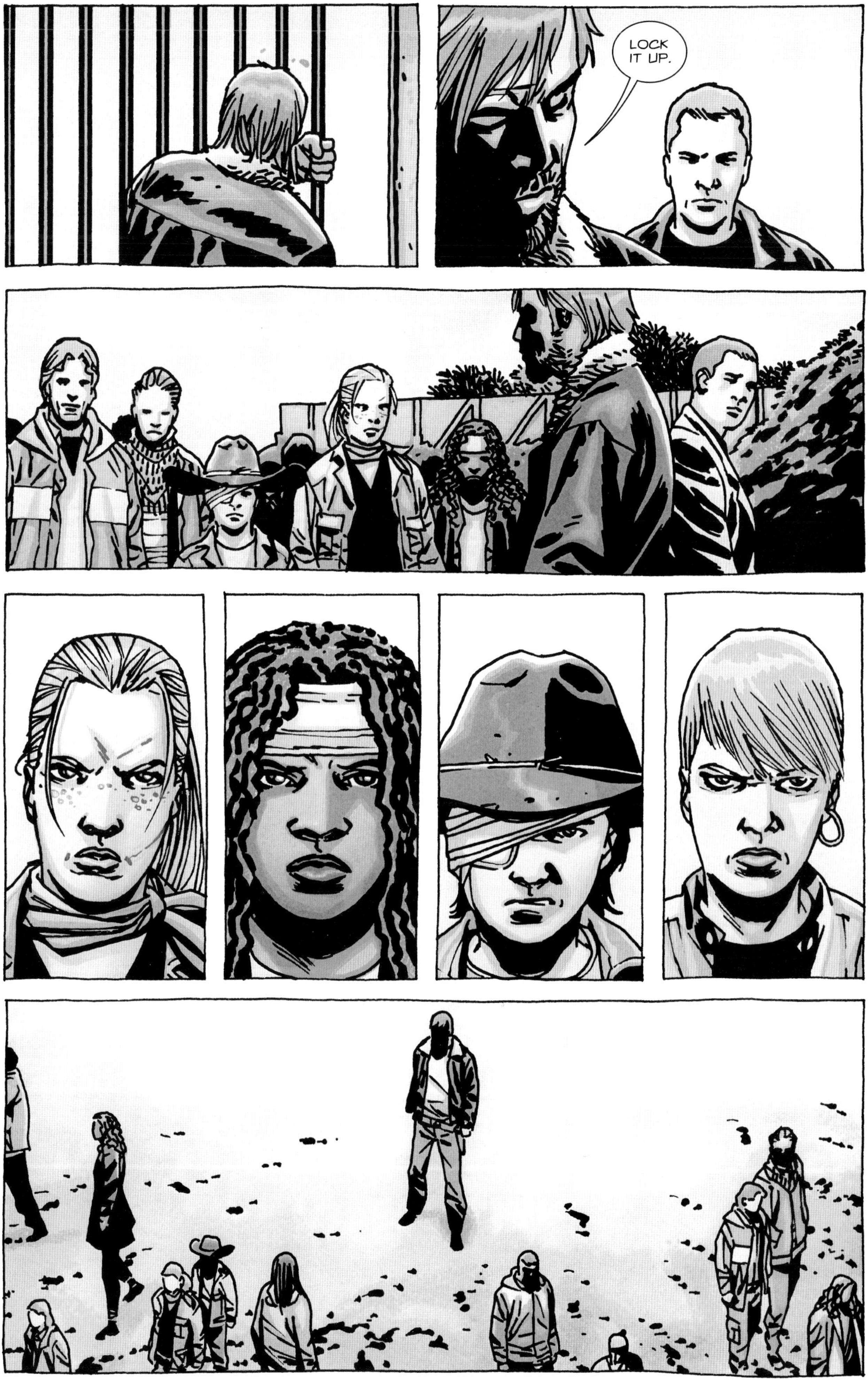
LOCK IT UP.

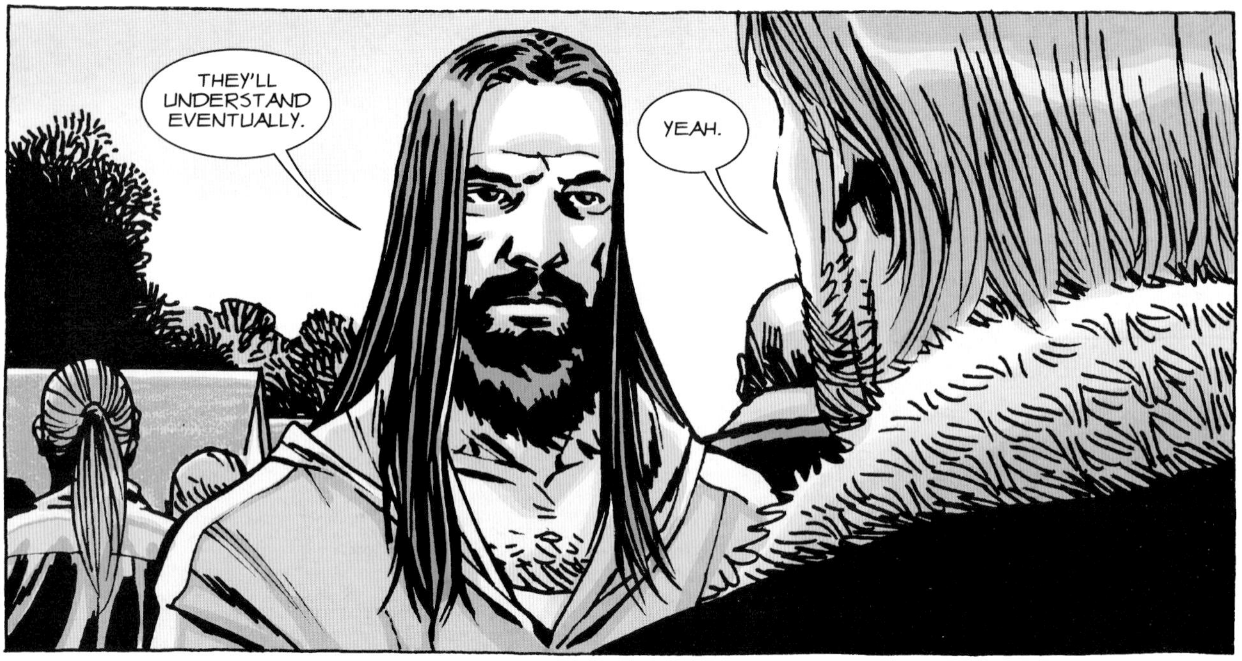
THEY'LL UNDERSTAND EVENTUALLY.
YEAH.

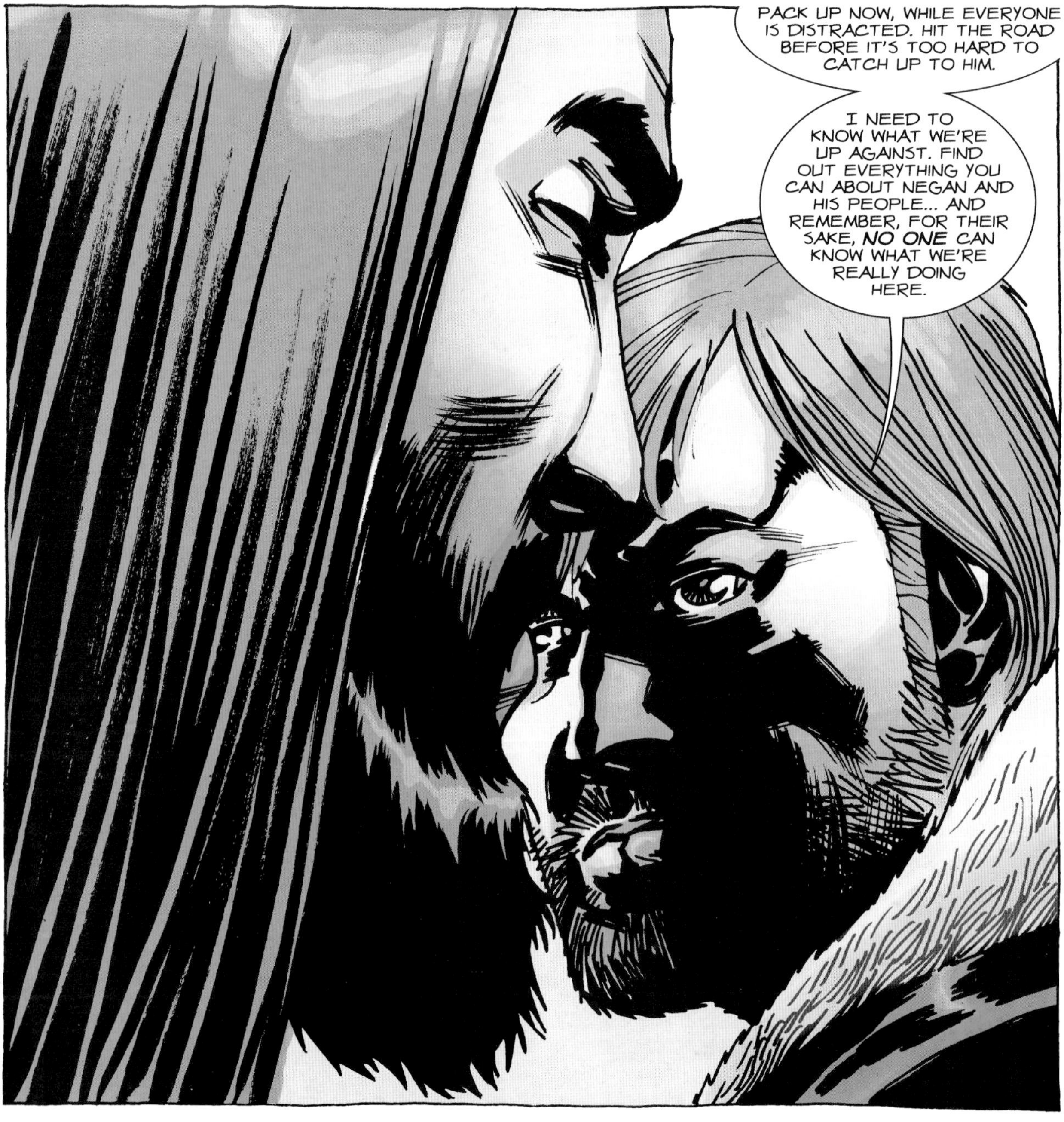
PACK UP NOW, WHILE EVERYONE IS DISTRACTED. HIT THE ROAD BEFORE IT'S TOO HARD TO CATCH UP TO HIM.
I NEED TO KNOW WHAT WE'RE UP AGAINST. FIND OUT EVERYTHING YOU CAN ABOUT NEGAN AND HIS PEOPLE... AND REMEMBER, FOR THEIR SAKE, NO ONE CAN KNOW WHAT WE'RE REALLY DOING HERE.

Chapter Eighteen:
What Comes After

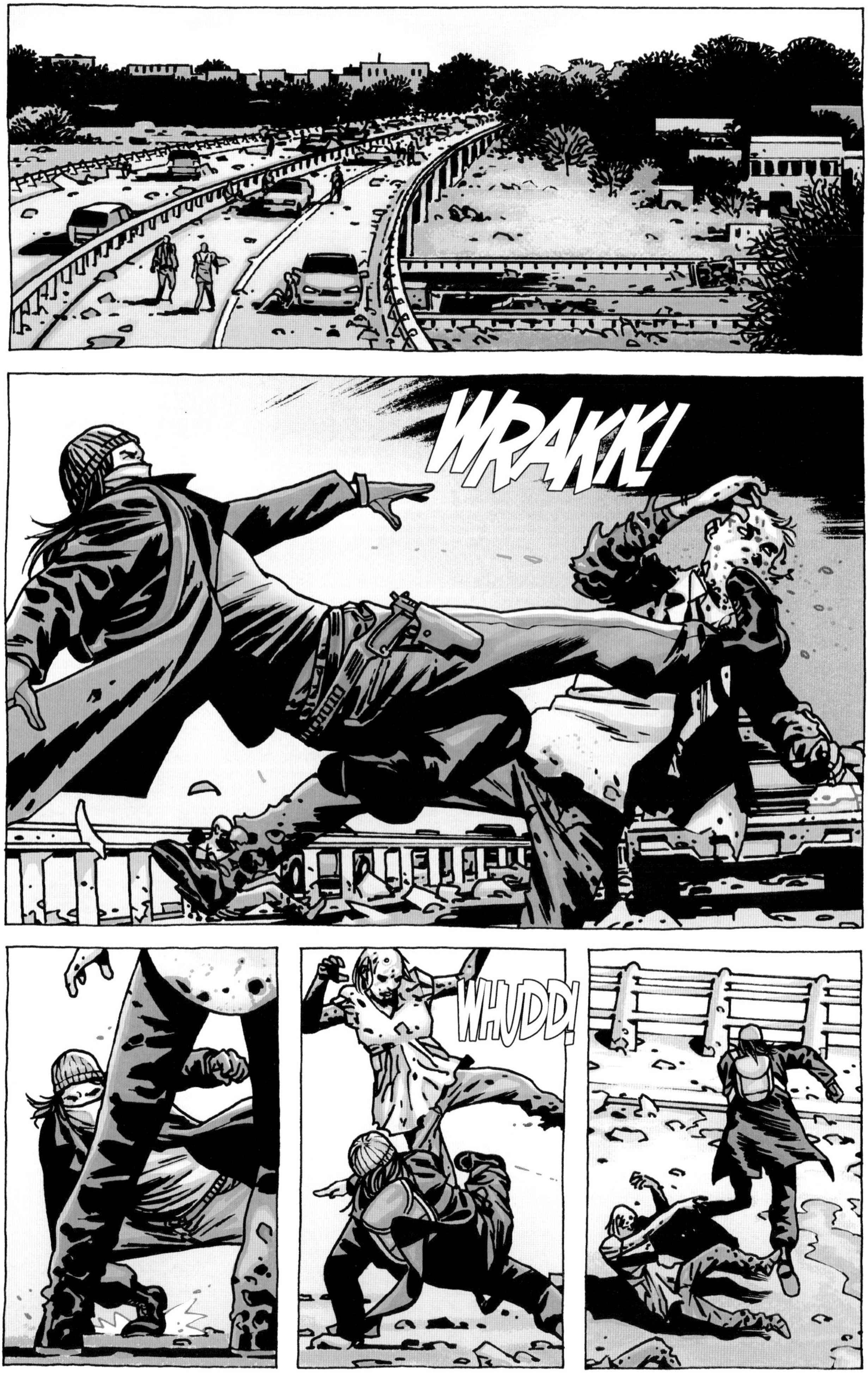
WRAKK!
WHUDD!

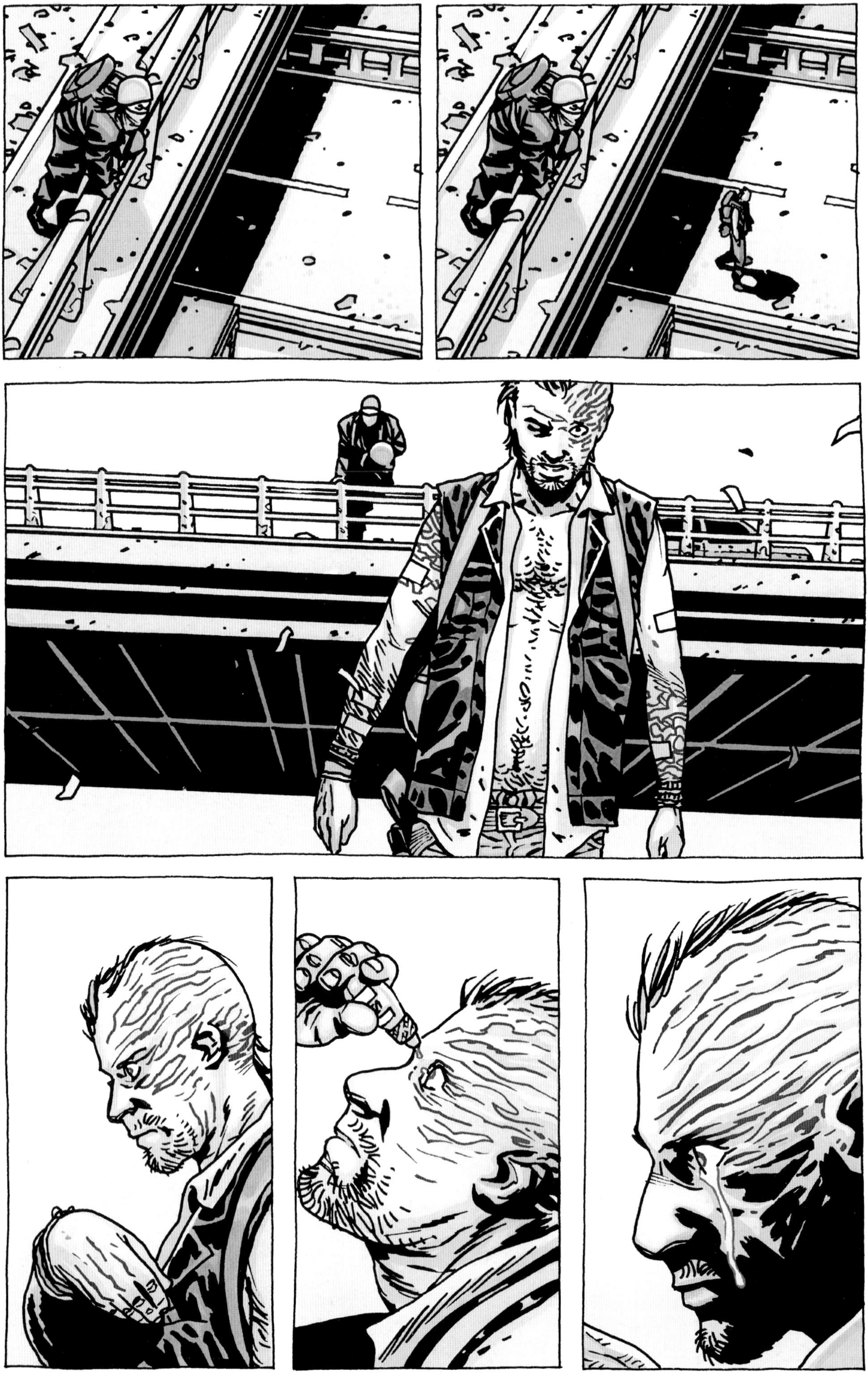

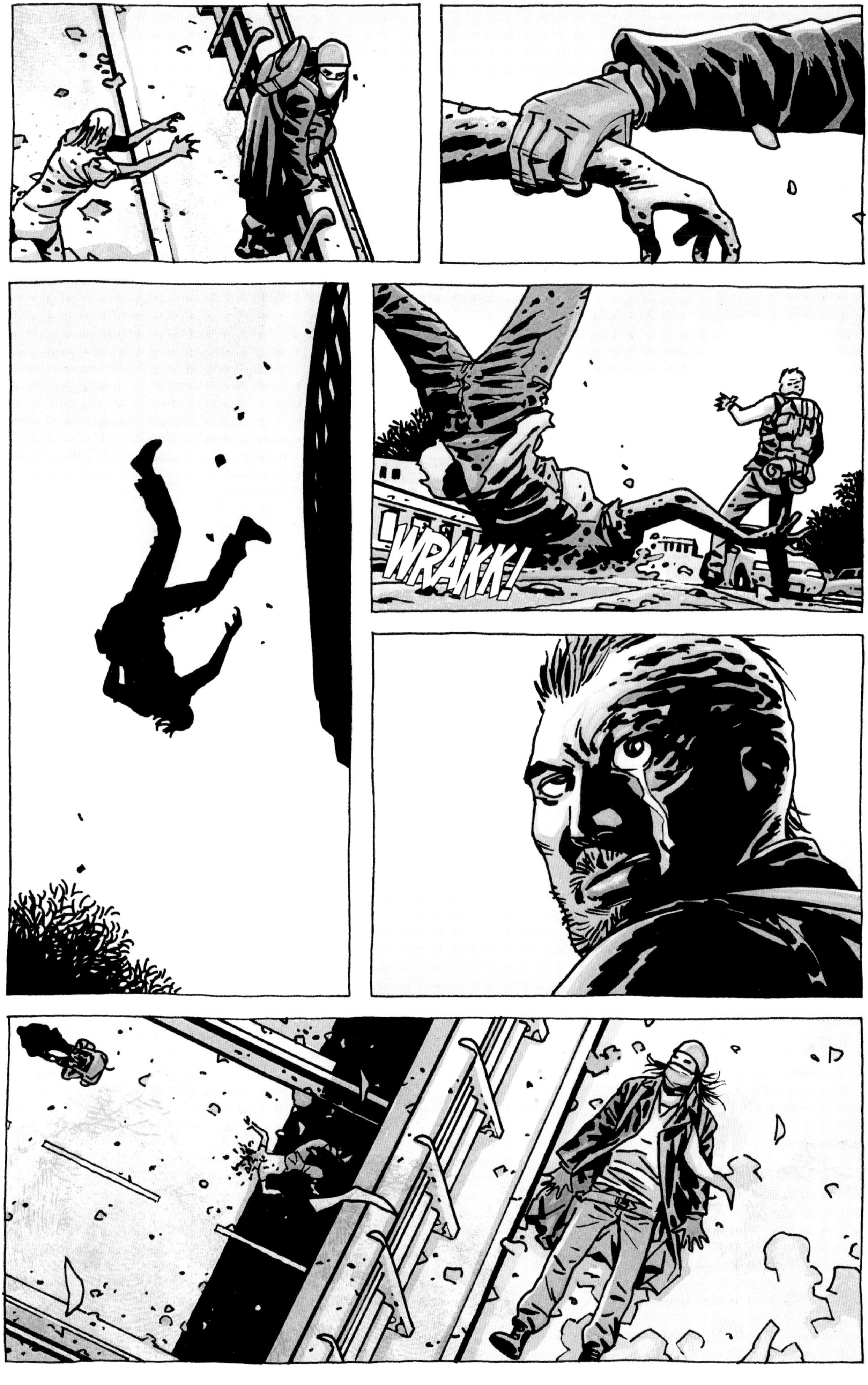
WRAKK!

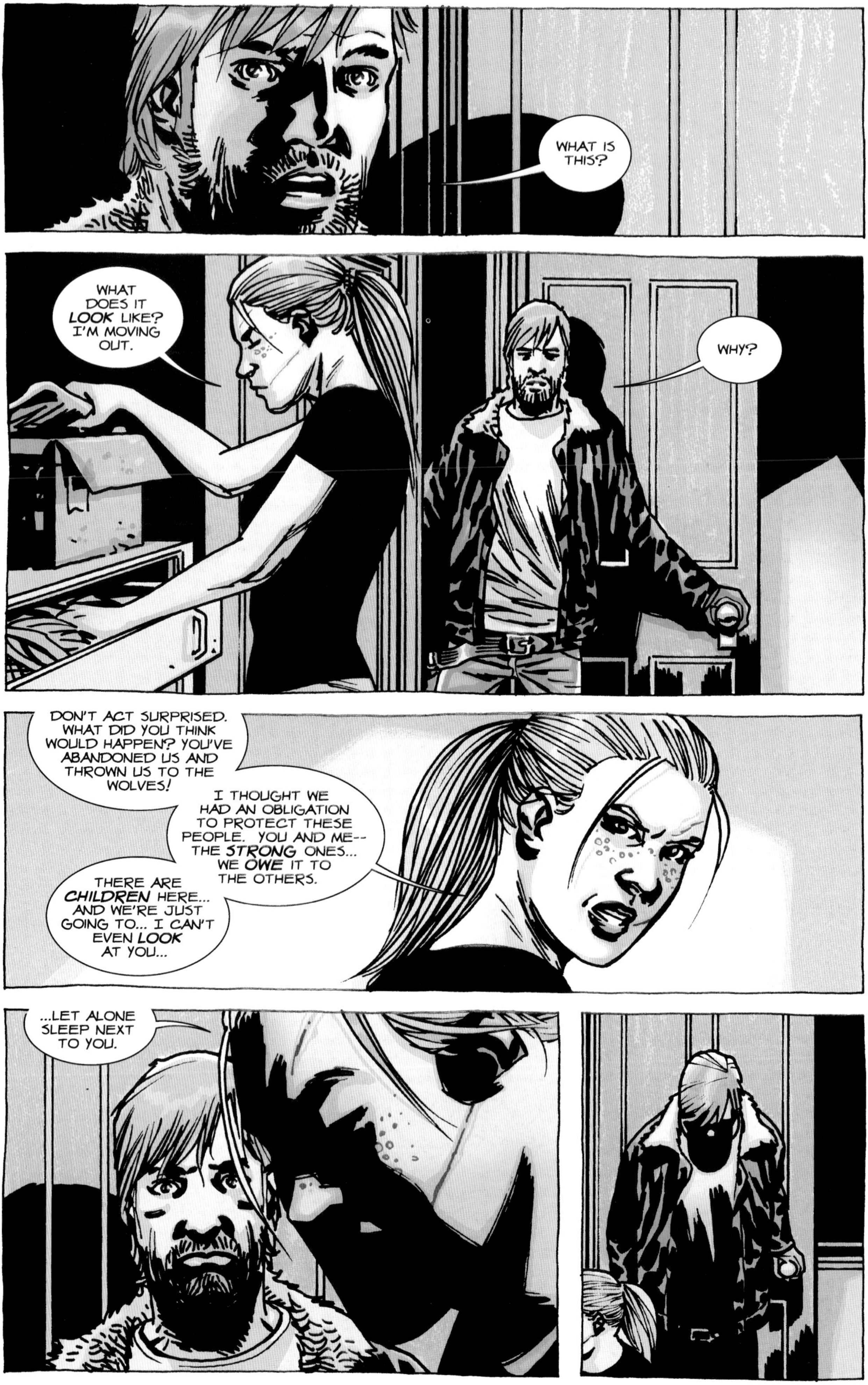
WHAT IS THIS?
WHAT DOES IT LOOK LIKE? I'M MOVING OUT.
WHY?
DON'T ACT SURPRISED. WHAT DID YOU THINK WOULD HAPPEN? YOU'VE ABANDONED US AND THROWN US TO THE WOLVES!
I THOUGHT WE HAD AN OBLIGATION TO PROTECT THESE PEOPLE. YOU AND ME-- THE STRONG ONES... WE OWE IT TO THE OTHERS.
THERE ARE CHILDREN HERE... AND WE'RE JUST GOING TO... I CAN'T EVEN LOOK AT YOU...
...LET ALONE SLEEP NEXT TO YOU.

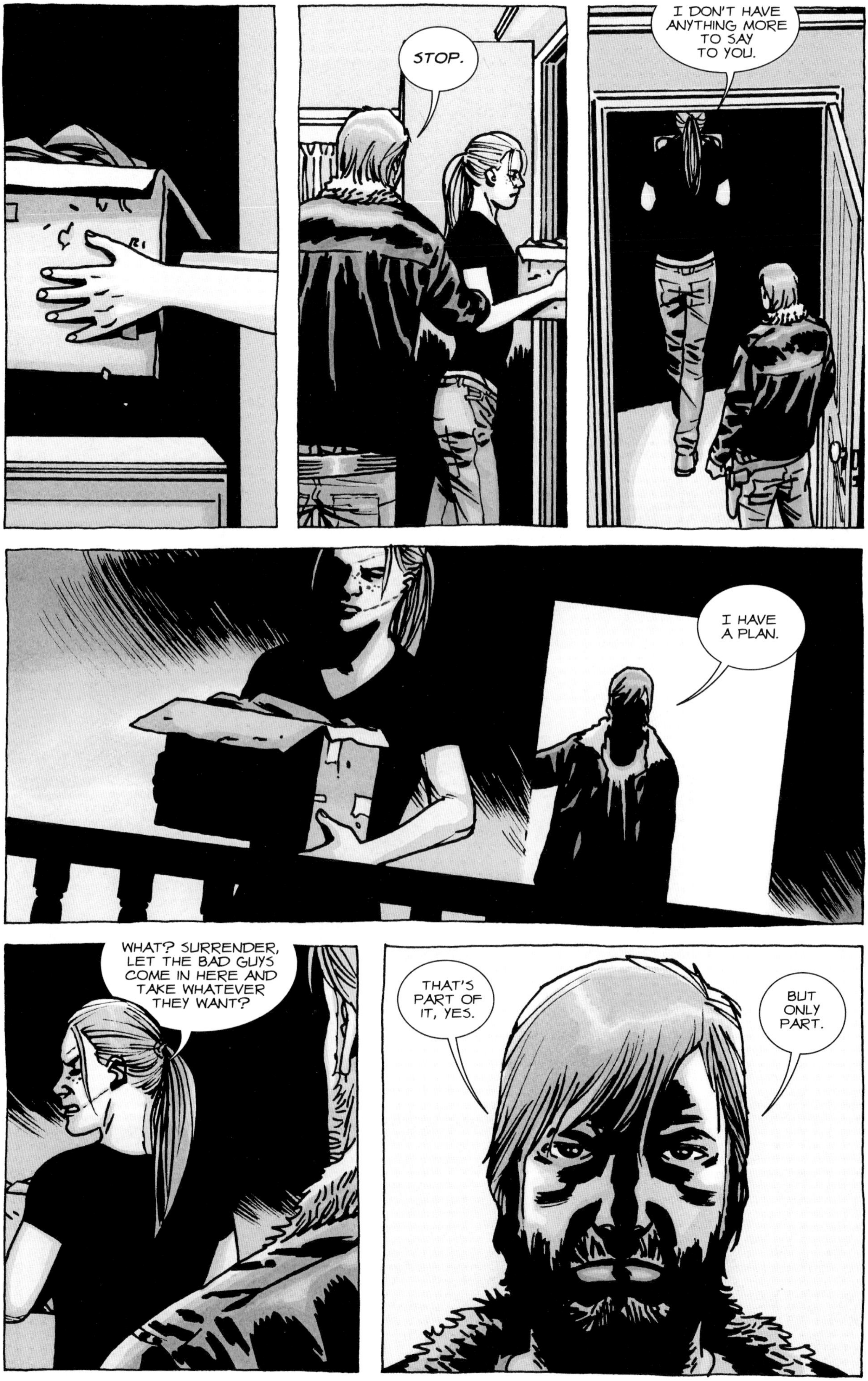
STOP.
I DON'T HAVE ANYTHING MORE TO SAY TO YOU.
I HAVE A PLAN.
WHAT? SURRENDER, LET THE BAD GUYS COME IN HERE AND TAKE WHATEVER THEY WANT?
THAT'S PART OF IT, YES.
BUT ONLY PART.

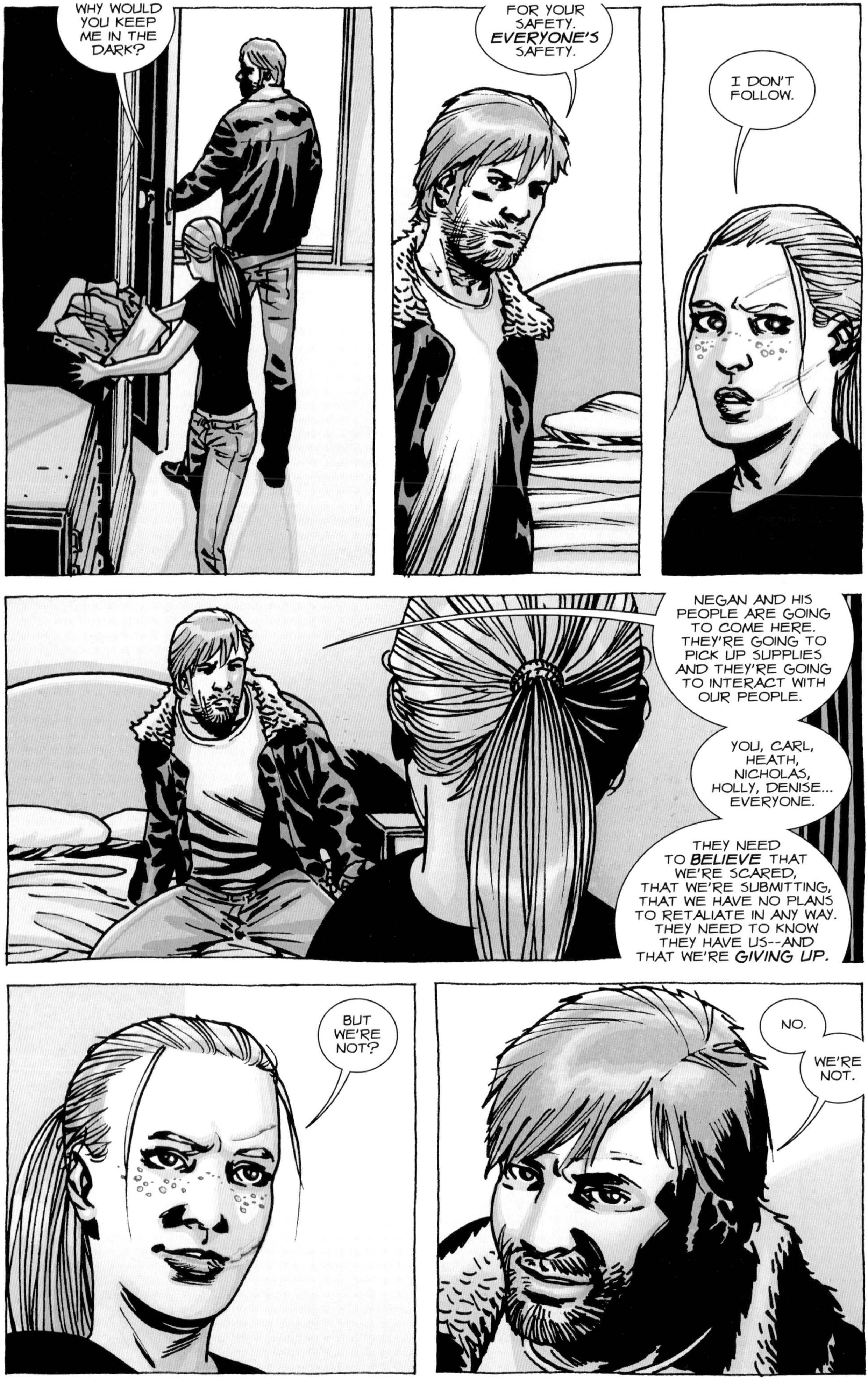
WHY WOULD YOU KEEP ME IN THE DARK?
FOR YOUR SAFETY. EVERYONE'S SAFETY.
I DON'T FOLLOW.
NEGAN AND HIS PEOPLE ARE GOING TO COME HERE. THEY'RE GOING TO PICK UP SUPPLIES AND THEY'RE GOING TO INTERACT WITH OUR PEOPLE.
YOU, CARL, HEATH, NICHOLAS, HOLLY, DENISE... EVERYONE.
THEY NEED TO BELIEVE THAT WE'RE SCARED, THAT WE'RE SUBMITTING, THAT WE HAVE NO PLANS TO RETALIATE IN ANY WAY. THEY NEED TO KNOW THEY HAVE US--AND THAT WE'RE GIVING UP.
BUT WE'RE NOT?
NO.
WE'RE NOT.

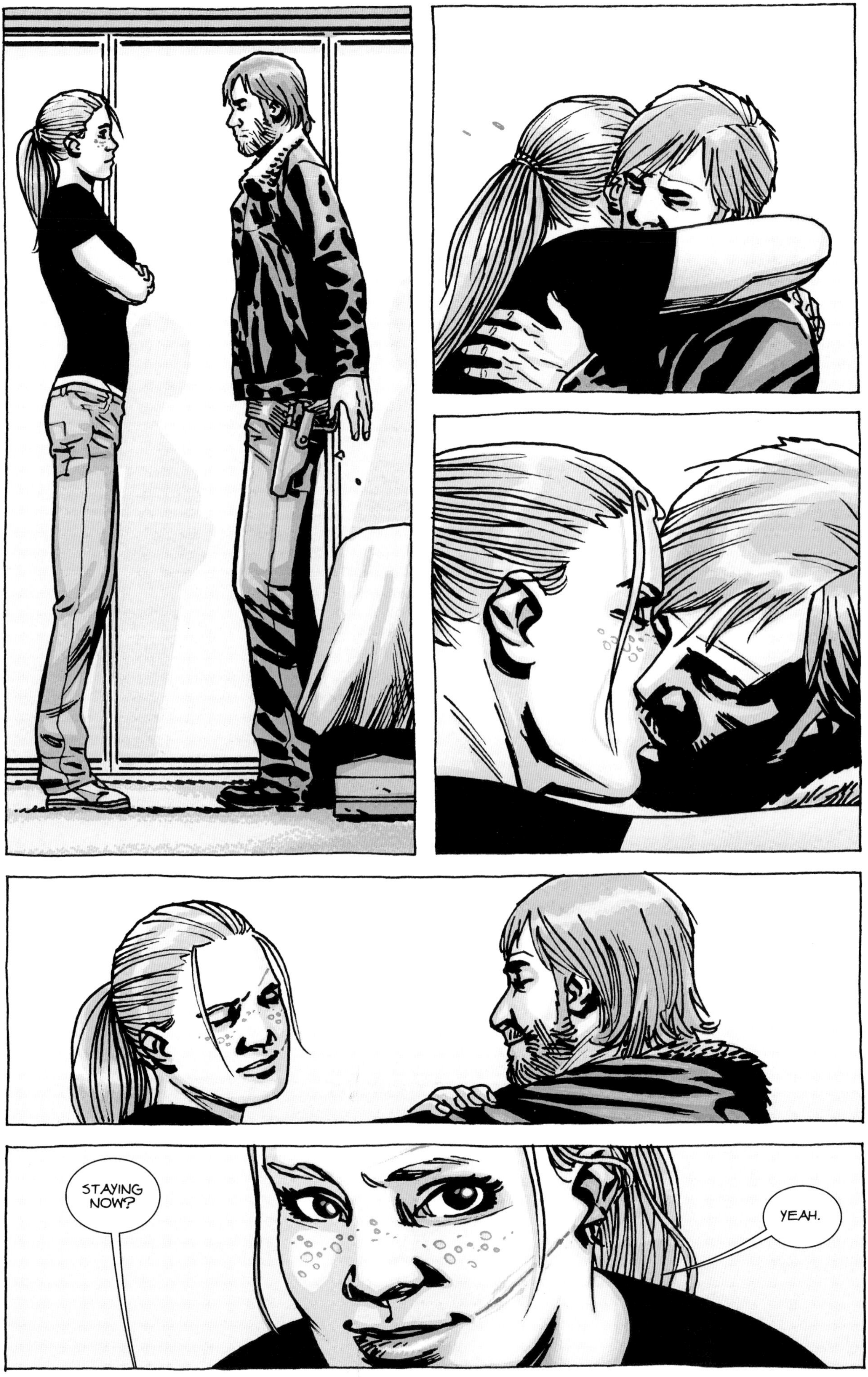
STAYING NOW?
YEAH.

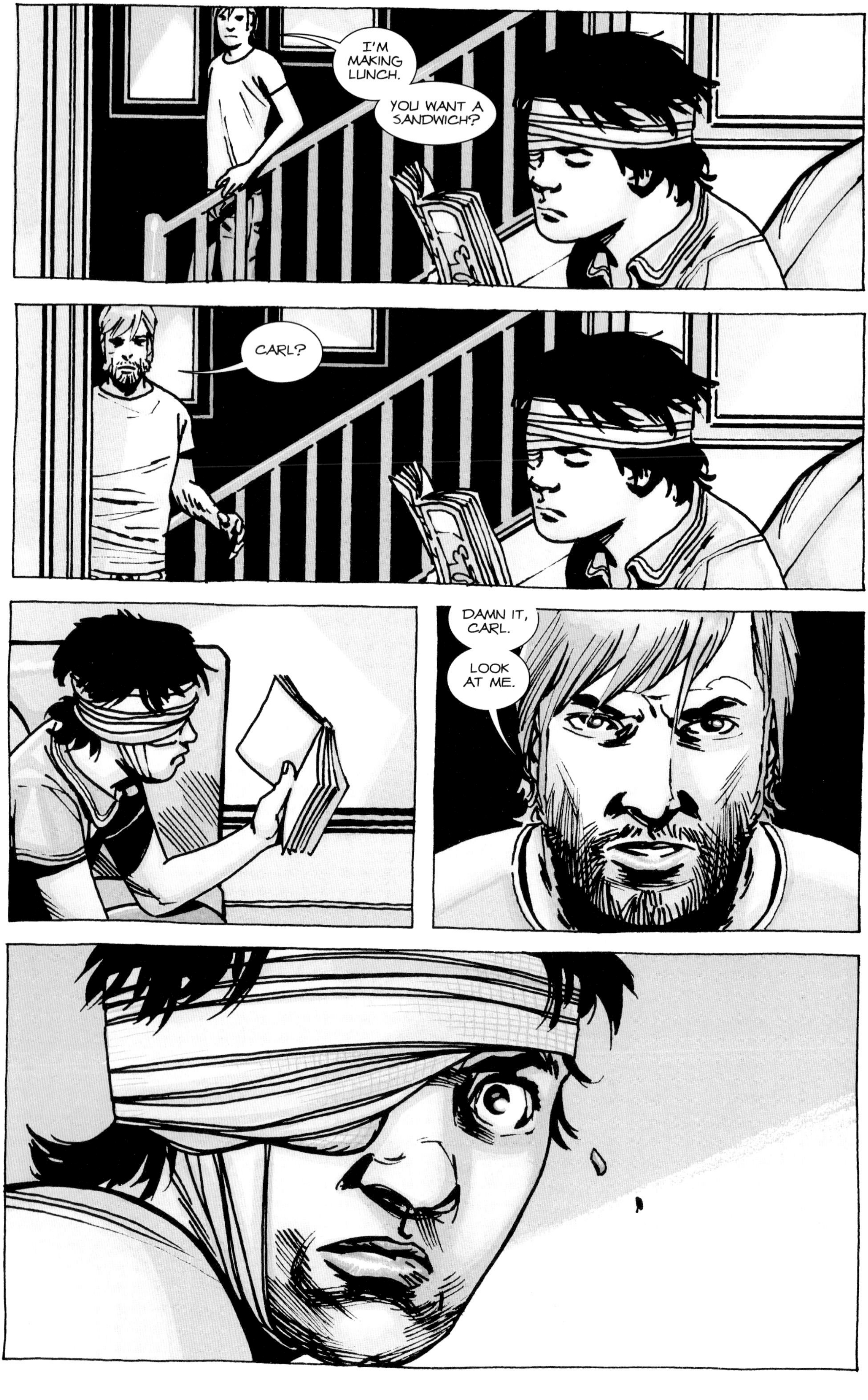
I'M MAKING LUNCH.
YOU WANT A SANDWICH?
CARL?
DAMN IT, CARL.
LOOK AT ME.

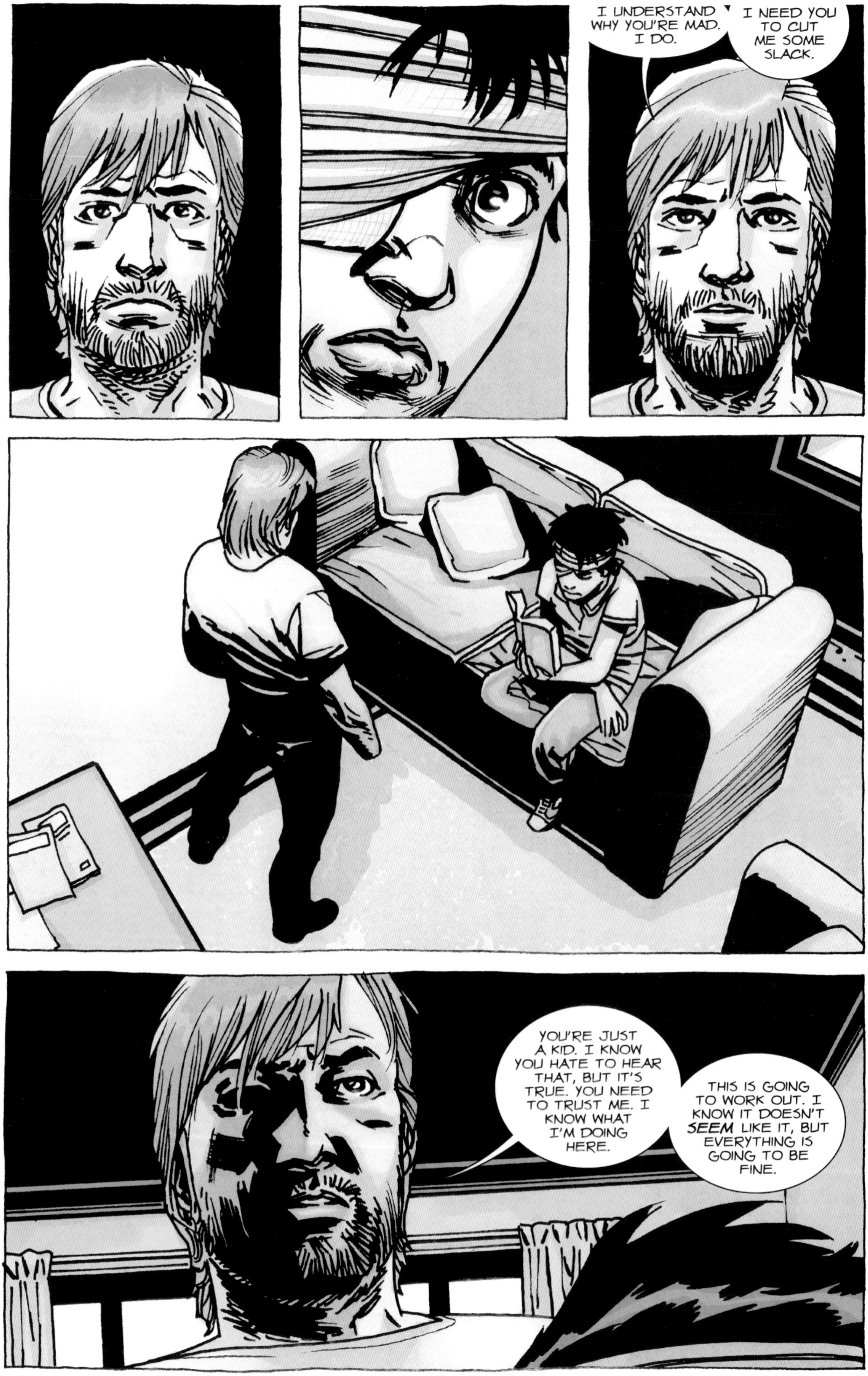
I UNDERSTAND WHY YOU'RE MAD. I DO.
I NEED YOU TO CUT ME SOME SLACK.
YOU'RE JUST A KID. I KNOW YOU HATE TO HEAR THAT, BUT IT'S TRUE. YOU NEED TO TRUST ME. I KNOW WHAT I'M DOING HERE.
THIS IS GOING TO WORK OUT. I KNOW IT DOESN'T *SEEM* LIKE IT, BUT EVERYTHING IS GOING TO BE FINE.

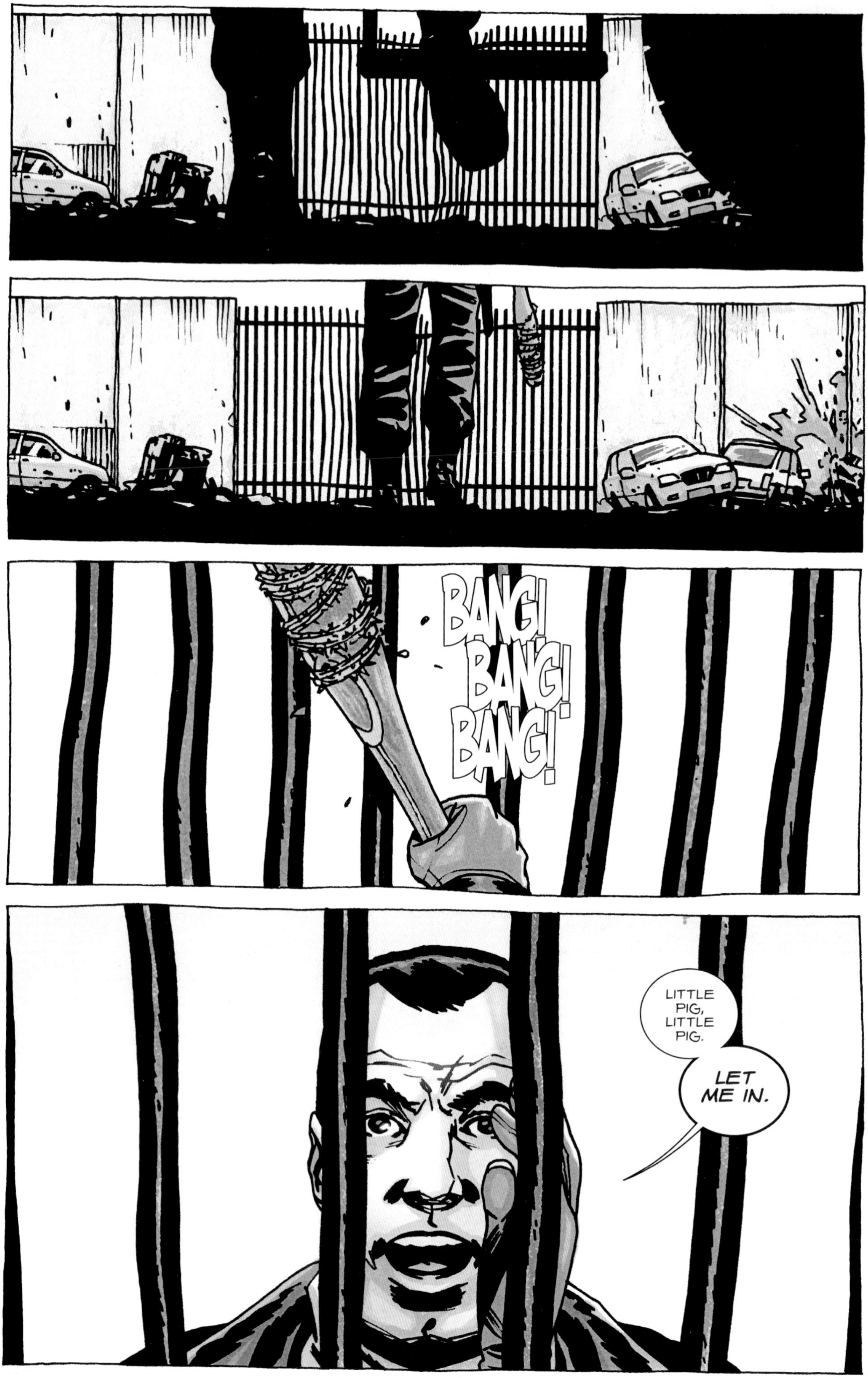
BANG! BANG! BANG!
LITTLE PIG, LITTLE PIG.
LET ME IN.

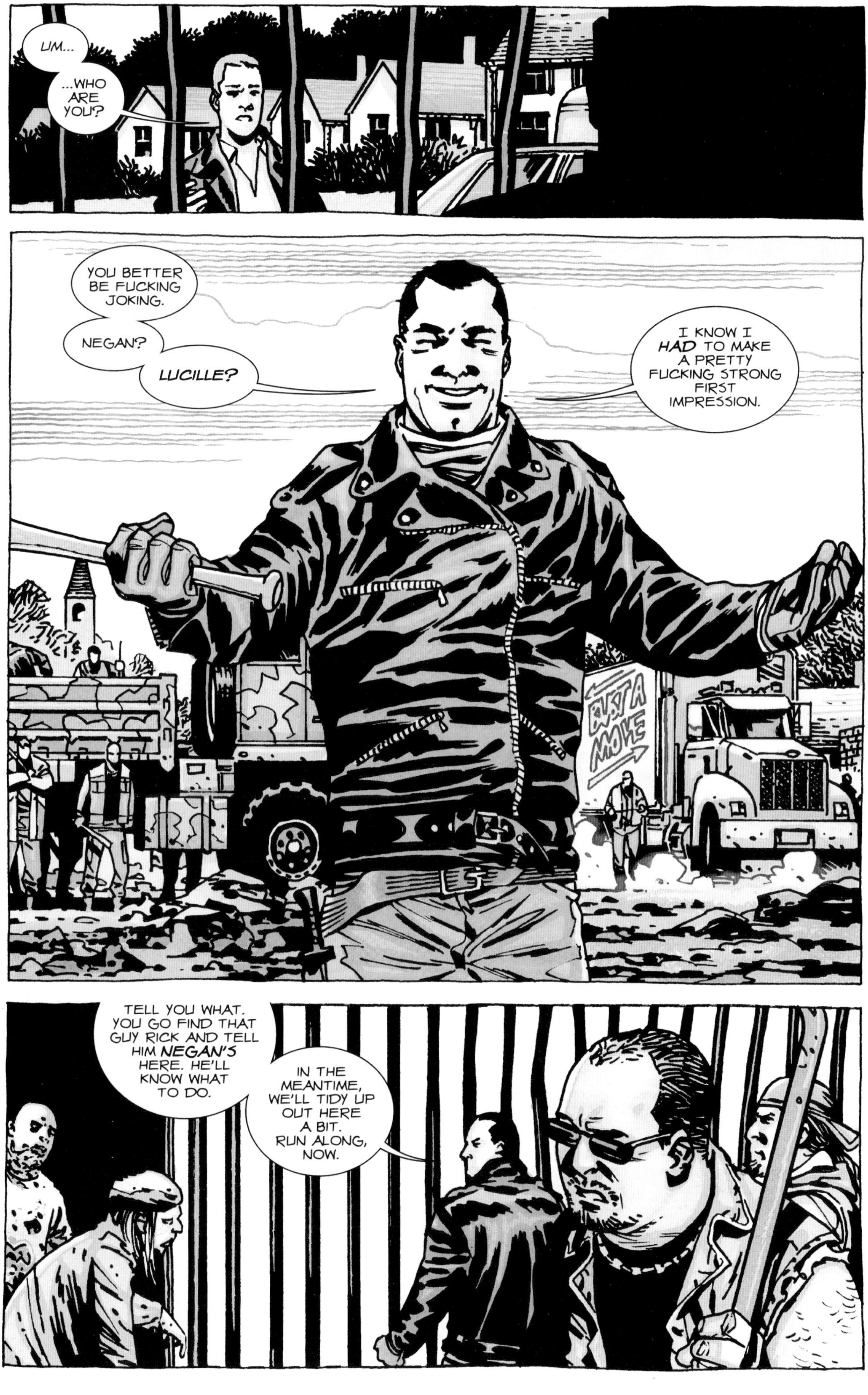
UM...
...WHO ARE YOU?
YOU BETTER BE FUCKING JOKING.
NEGAN?
LUCILLE?
I KNOW I HAD TO MAKE A PRETTY FUCKING STRONG FIRST IMPRESSION.
BUST A MOVE
TELL YOU WHAT. YOU GO FIND THAT GUY RICK AND TELL HIM NEGAN'S HERE. HE'LL KNOW WHAT TO DO.
IN THE MEANTIME, WE'LL TIDY UP OUT HERE A BIT. RUN ALONG, NOW.

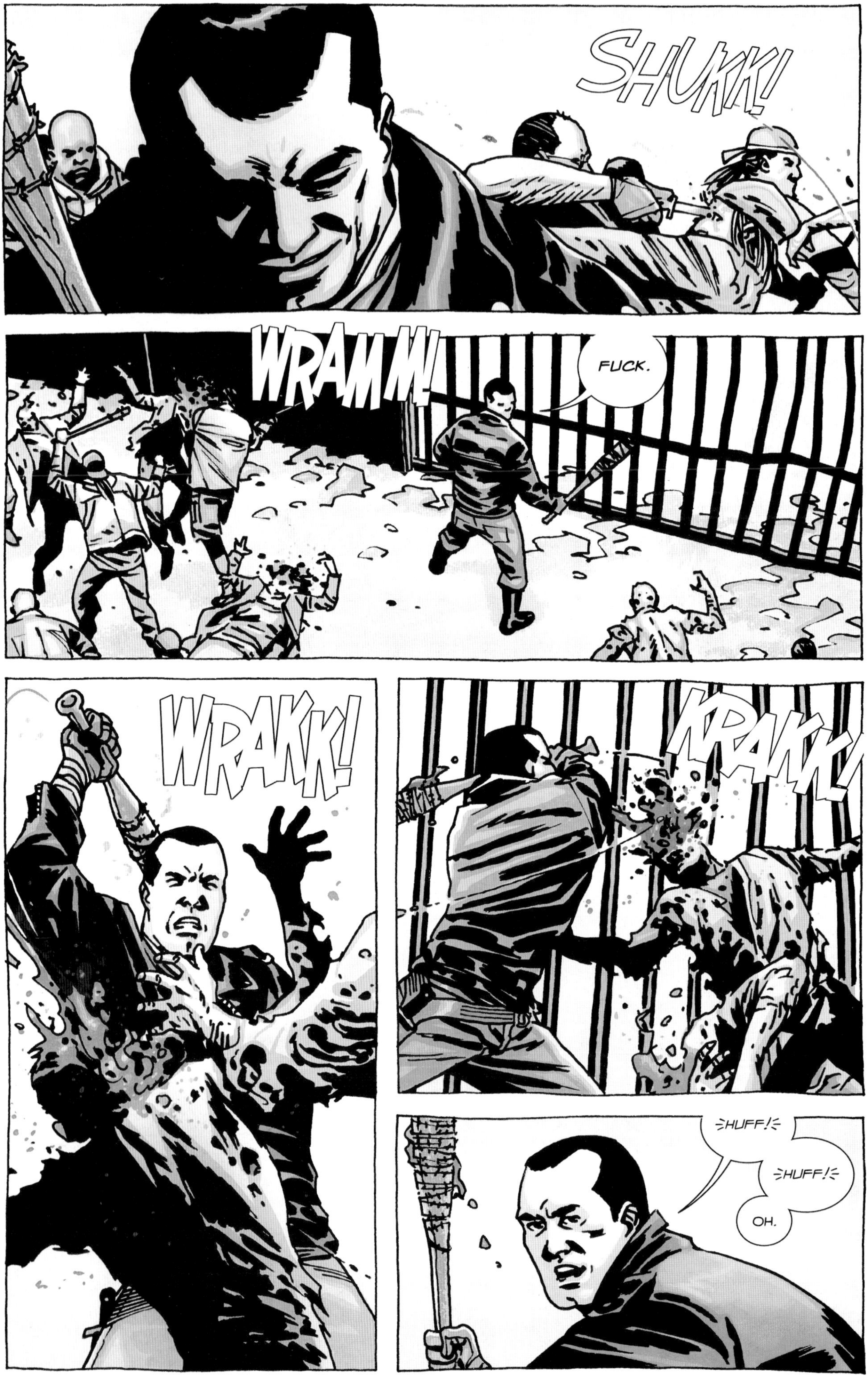
SHUKK!
WRAMM!
FUCK.
WRAKK!
KRAKK!
HUFF!
HUFF!
OH.

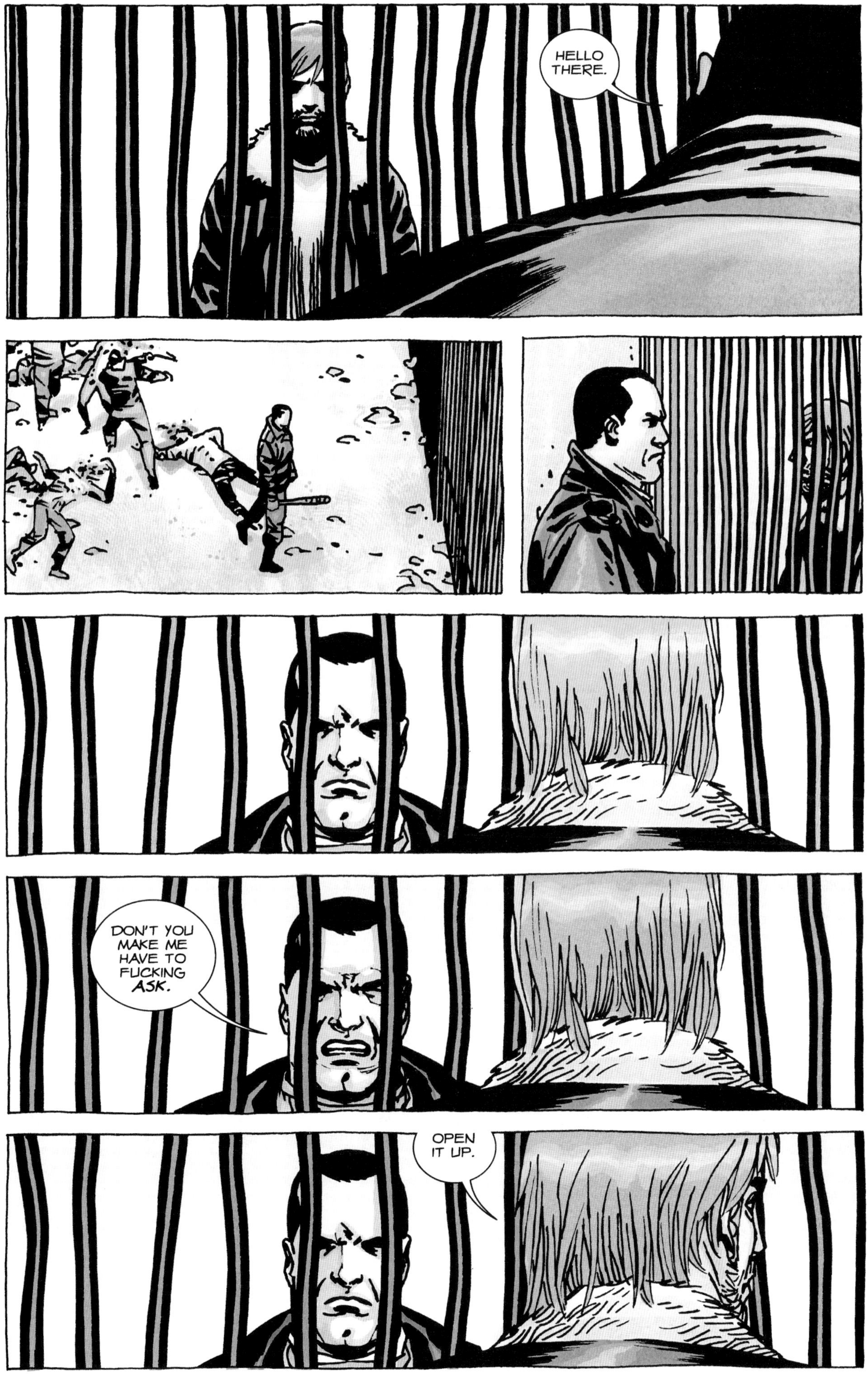
HELLO THERE.
DON'T YOU MAKE ME HAVE TO FUCKING ASK.
OPEN IT UP.

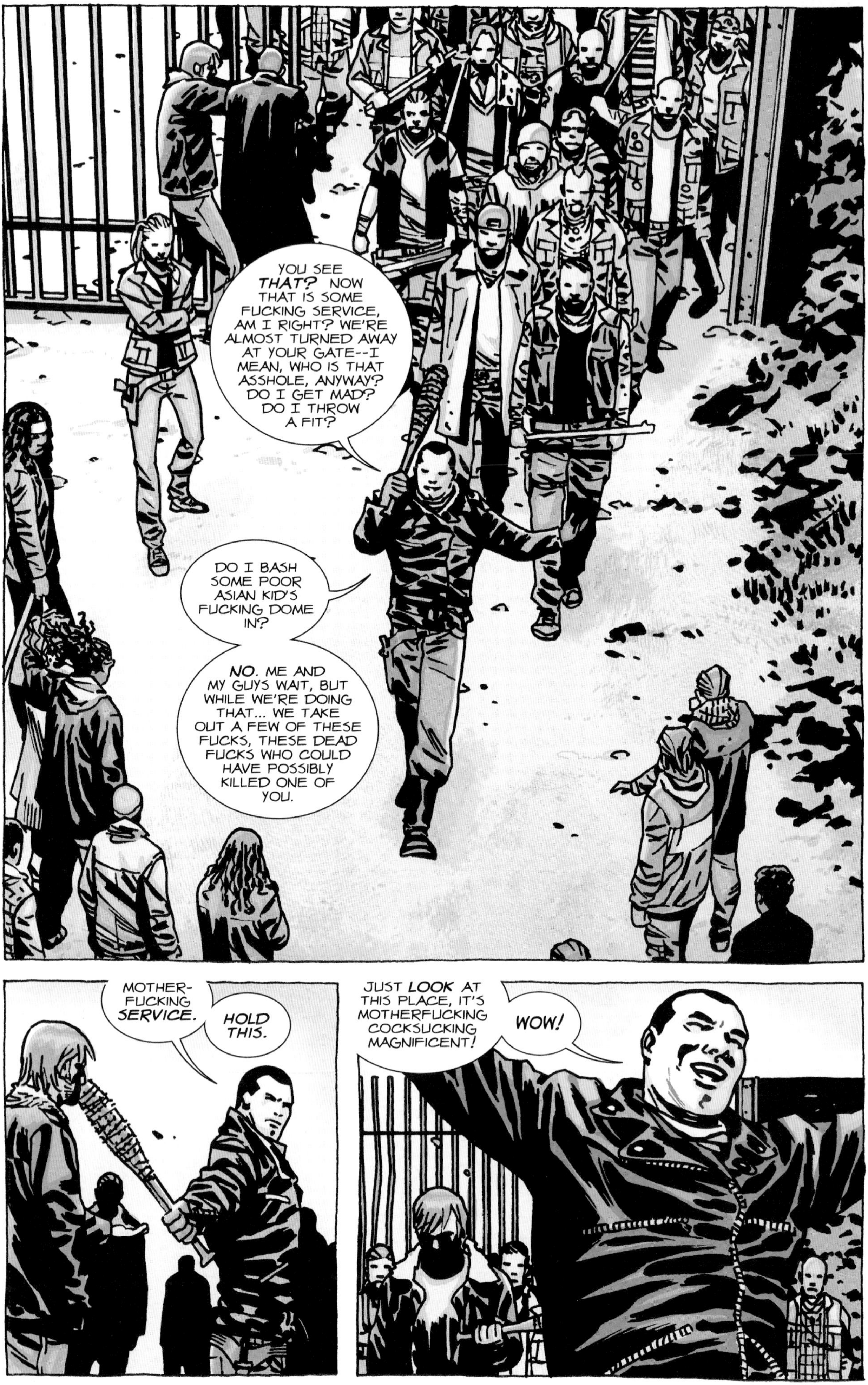
YOU SEE THAT? NOW THAT IS SOME FUCKING SERVICE, AM I RIGHT? WE'RE ALMOST TURNED AWAY AT YOUR GATE--I MEAN, WHO IS THAT ASSHOLE, ANYWAY? DO I GET MAD? DO I THROW A FIT?
DO I BASH SOME POOR ASIAN KID'S FUCKING DOME IN?
NO. ME AND MY GUYS WAIT, BUT WHILE WE'RE DOING THAT... WE TAKE OUT A FEW OF THESE FUCKS, THESE DEAD FUCKS WHO COULD HAVE POSSIBLY KILLED ONE OF YOU.
MOTHER-FUCKING SERVICE.
HOLD THIS.
JUST LOOK AT THIS PLACE, IT'S MOTHERFUCKING COCKSUCKING MAGNIFICENT!
WOW!

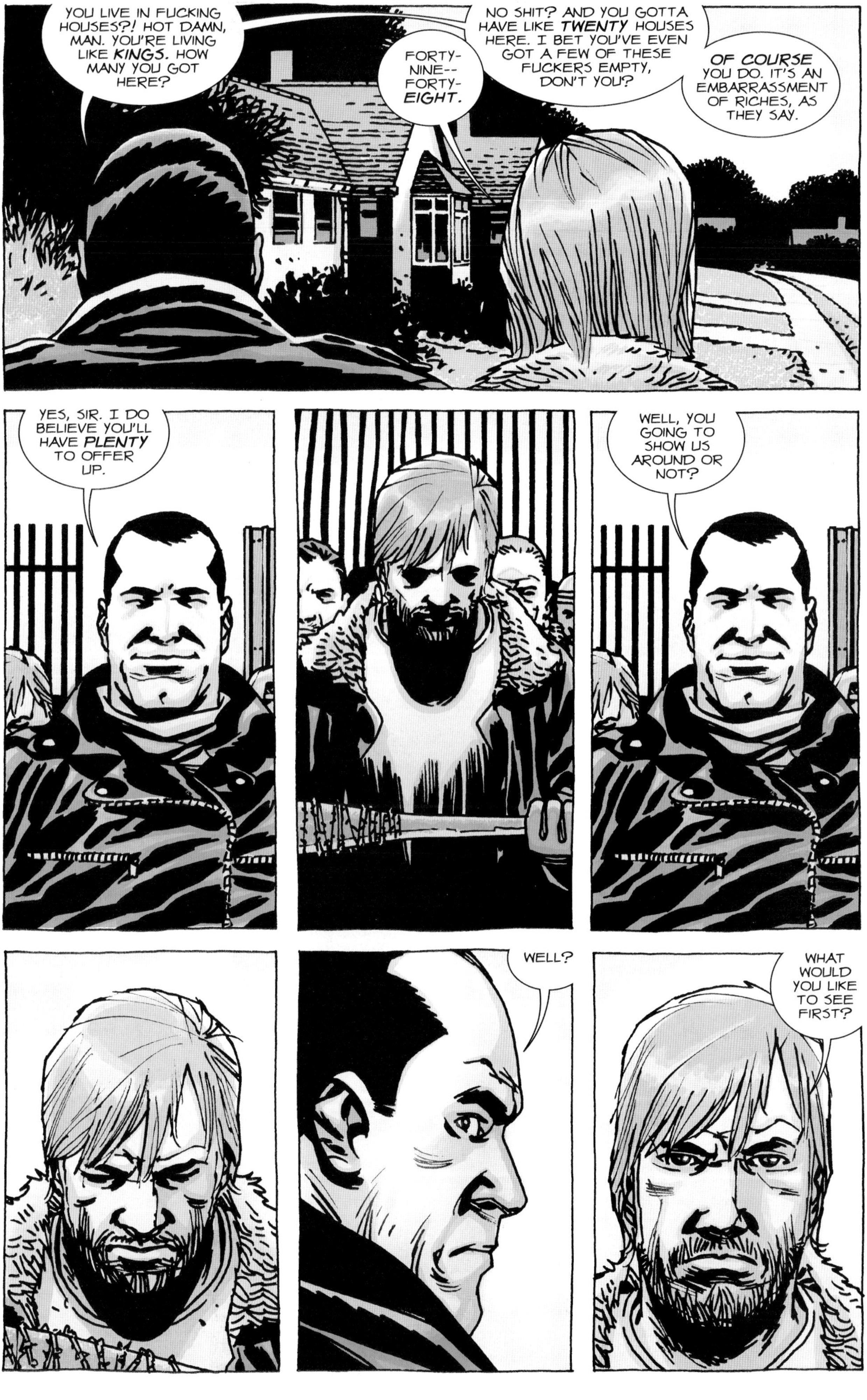
YOU LIVE IN FUCKING HOUSES?! HOT DAMN, MAN. YOU'RE LIVING LIKE KINGS. HOW MANY YOU GOT HERE?
FORTY-NINE--FORTY-EIGHT.
NO SHIT? AND YOU GOTTA HAVE LIKE TWENTY HOUSES HERE. I BET YOU'VE EVEN GOT A FEW OF THESE FUCKERS EMPTY, DON'T YOU?
OF COURSE YOU DO. IT'S AN EMBARRASSMENT OF RICHES, AS THEY SAY.
YES, SIR. I DO BELIEVE YOU'LL HAVE PLENTY TO OFFER UP.
WELL, YOU GOING TO SHOW US AROUND OR NOT?
WELL?
WHAT WOULD YOU LIKE TO SEE FIRST?

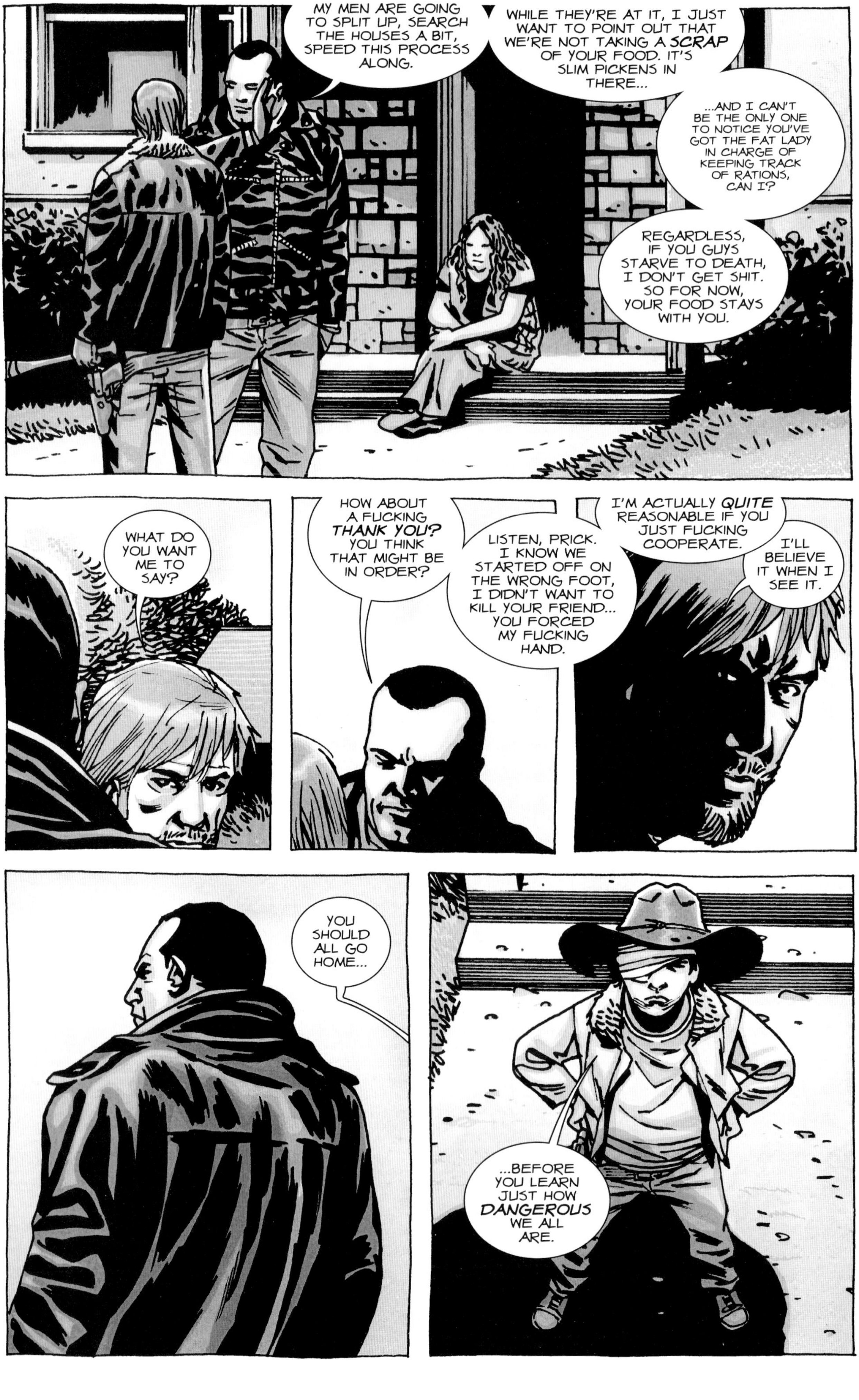
MY MEN ARE GOING TO SPLIT UP, SEARCH THE HOUSES A BIT, SPEED THIS PROCESS ALONG.
WHILE THEY'RE AT IT, I JUST WANT TO POINT OUT THAT WE'RE NOT TAKING A *SCRAP* OF YOUR FOOD. IT'S SLIM PICKENS IN THERE...
...AND I CAN'T BE THE ONLY ONE TO NOTICE YOU'VE GOT THE FAT LADY IN CHARGE OF KEEPING TRACK OF RATIONS, CAN I?
REGARDLESS, IF YOU GUYS STARVE TO DEATH, I DON'T GET SHIT. SO FOR NOW, YOUR FOOD STAYS WITH YOU.
WHAT DO YOU WANT ME TO SAY?
HOW ABOUT A FUCKING *THANK YOU?* YOU THINK THAT MIGHT BE IN ORDER?
LISTEN, PRICK. I KNOW WE STARTED OFF ON THE WRONG FOOT, I DIDN'T WANT TO KILL YOUR FRIEND... YOU FORCED MY FUCKING HAND.
I'M ACTUALLY *QUITE* REASONABLE IF YOU JUST FUCKING COOPERATE.
I'LL BELIEVE IT WHEN I SEE IT.
YOU SHOULD ALL GO HOME...
...BEFORE YOU LEARN JUST HOW *DANGEROUS* WE ALL ARE.

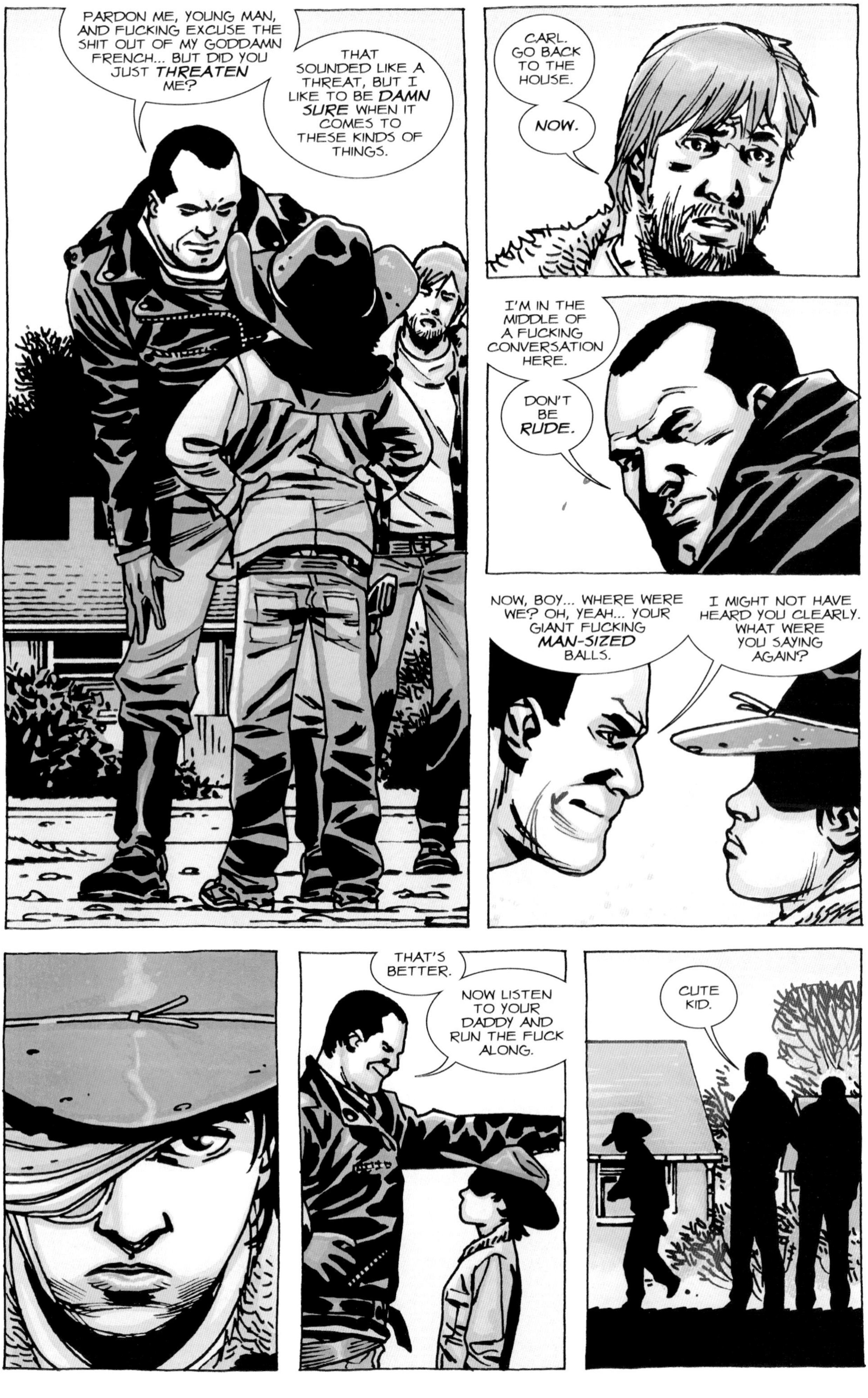
PARDON ME, YOUNG MAN, AND FUCKING EXCUSE THE SHIT OUT OF MY GODDAMN FRENCH... BUT DID YOU JUST THREATEN ME?
THAT SOUNDED LIKE A THREAT, BUT I LIKE TO BE DAMN SURE WHEN IT COMES TO THESE KINDS OF THINGS.
CARL. GO BACK TO THE HOUSE.
NOW.
I'M IN THE MIDDLE OF A FUCKING CONVERSATION HERE.
DON'T BE RUDE.
NOW, BOY... WHERE WERE WE? OH, YEAH... YOUR GIANT FUCKING MAN-SIZED BALLS.
I MIGHT NOT HAVE HEARD YOU CLEARLY. WHAT WERE YOU SAYING AGAIN?
THAT'S BETTER.
NOW LISTEN TO YOUR DADDY AND RUN THE FUCK ALONG.
CUTE KID.

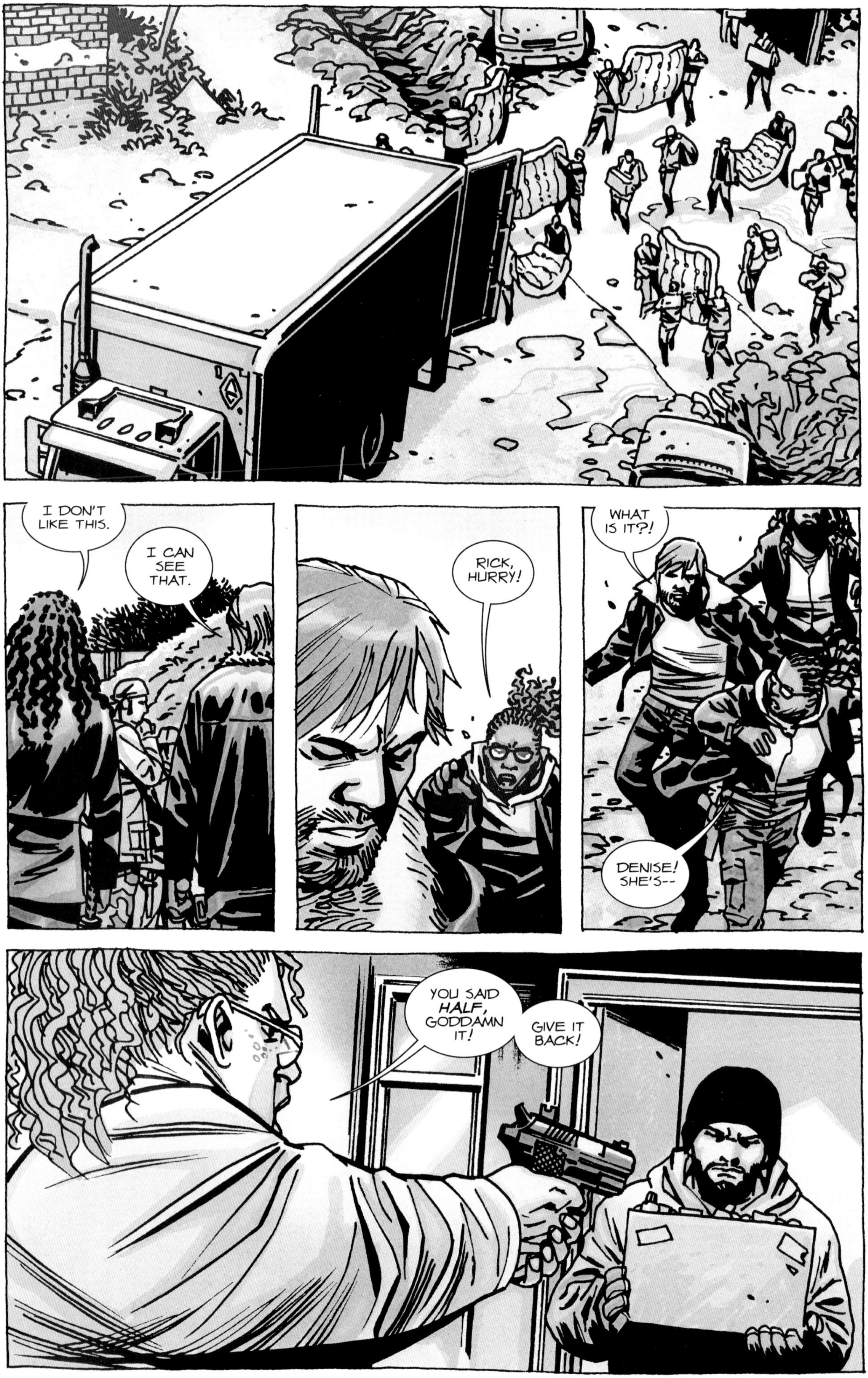
I DON'T LIKE THIS.
I CAN SEE THAT.
RICK, HURRY!
WHAT IS IT?!
DENISE! SHE'S--
YOU SAID *HALF*, GODDAMN IT!
GIVE IT BACK!

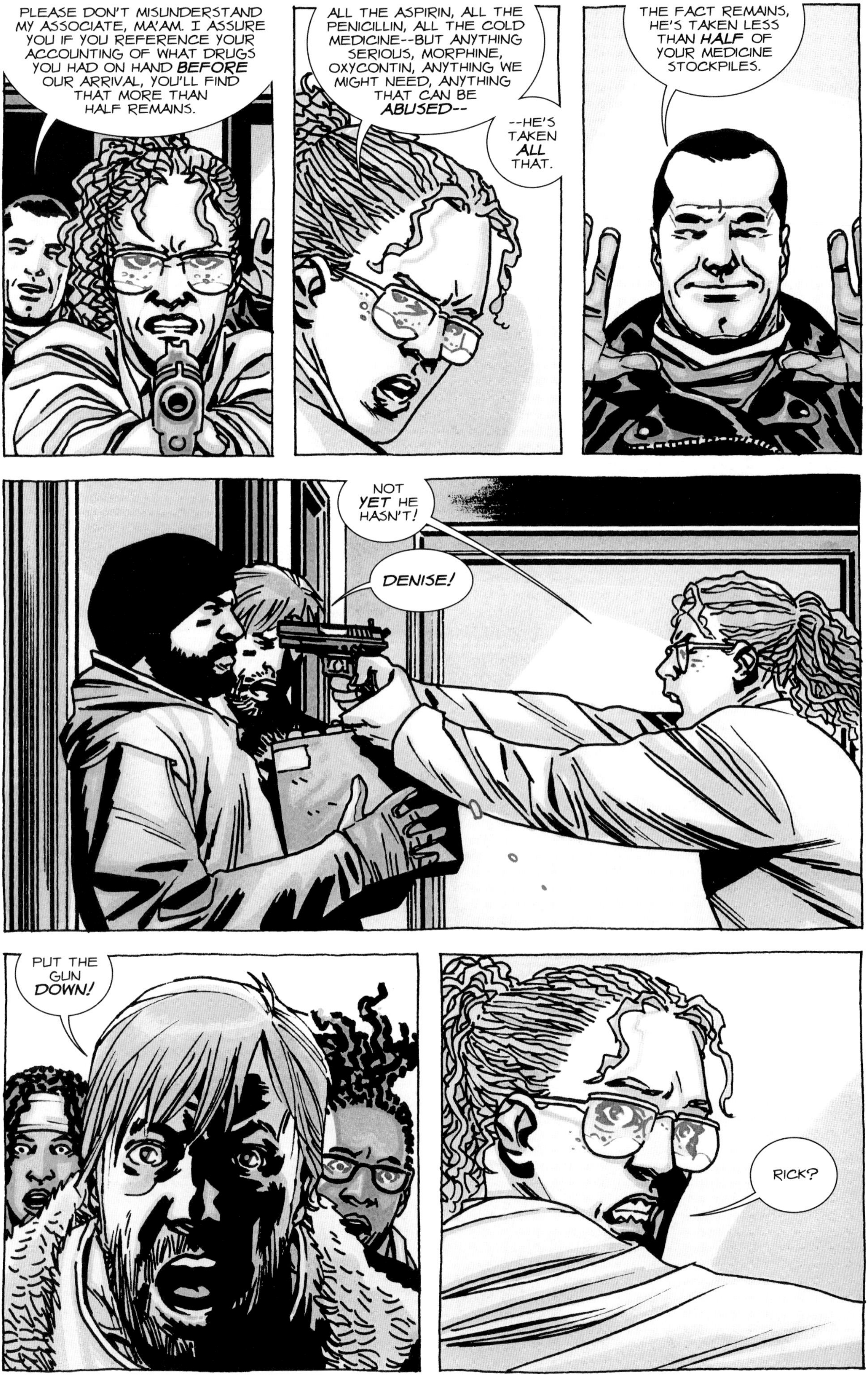
PLEASE DON'T MISUNDERSTAND MY ASSOCIATE, MA'AM. I ASSURE YOU IF YOU REFERENCE YOUR ACCOUNTING OF WHAT DRUGS YOU HAD ON HAND BEFORE OUR ARRIVAL, YOU'LL FIND THAT MORE THAN HALF REMAINS.
ALL THE ASPIRIN, ALL THE PENICILLIN, ALL THE COLD MEDICINE--BUT ANYTHING SERIOUS, MORPHINE, OXYCONTIN, ANYTHING WE MIGHT NEED, ANYTHING THAT CAN BE ABUSED--
--HE'S TAKEN ALL THAT.
THE FACT REMAINS, HE'S TAKEN LESS THAN HALF OF YOUR MEDICINE STOCKPILES.
NOT YET HE HASN'T!
DENISE!
PUT THE GUN DOWN!
RICK?

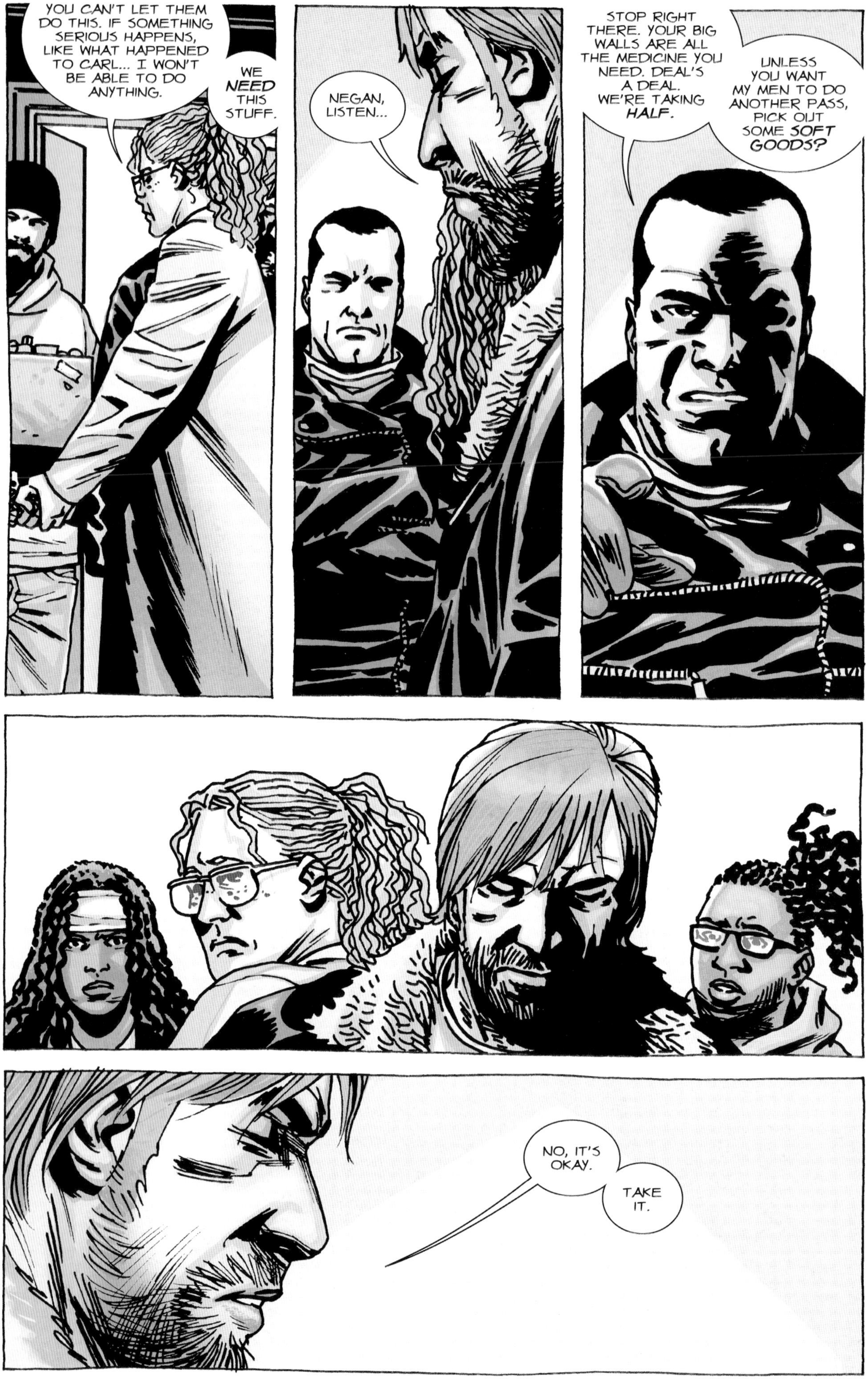
YOU CAN'T LET THEM DO THIS. IF SOMETHING SERIOUS HAPPENS, LIKE WHAT HAPPENED TO CARL... I WON'T BE ABLE TO DO ANYTHING.
WE NEED THIS STUFF.
NEGAN, LISTEN...
STOP RIGHT THERE. YOUR BIG WALLS ARE ALL THE MEDICINE YOU NEED. DEAL'S A DEAL. WE'RE TAKING HALF.
UNLESS YOU WANT MY MEN TO DO ANOTHER PASS, PICK OUT SOME SOFT GOODS?
NO, IT'S OKAY.
TAKE IT.

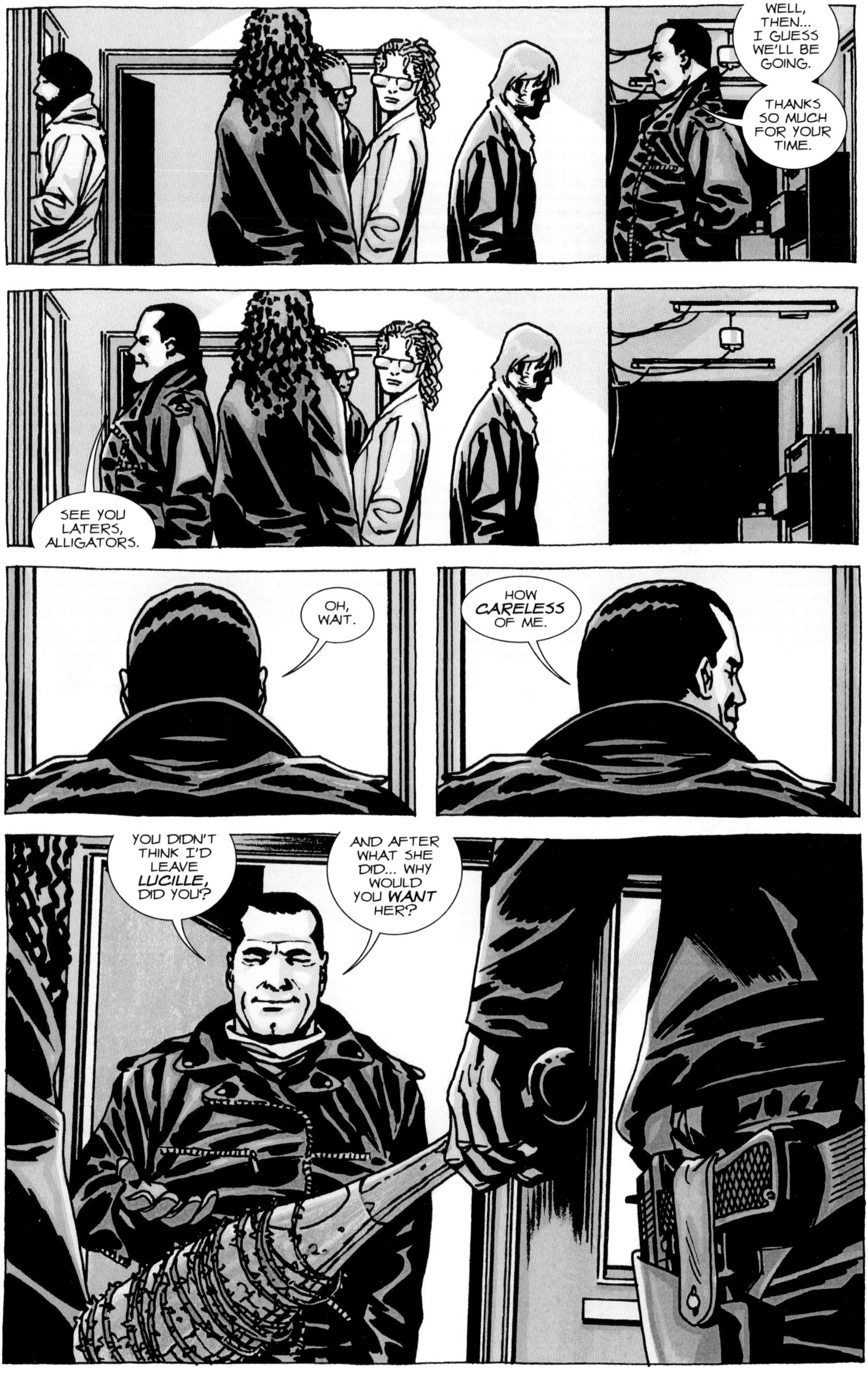
WELL, THEN... I GUESS WE'LL BE GOING.
THANKS SO MUCH FOR YOUR TIME.
SEE YOU LATERS, ALLIGATORS.
OH, WAIT.
HOW CARELESS OF ME.
YOU DIDN'T THINK I'D LEAVE LUCILLE, DID YOU?
AND AFTER WHAT SHE DID... WHY WOULD YOU WANT HER?

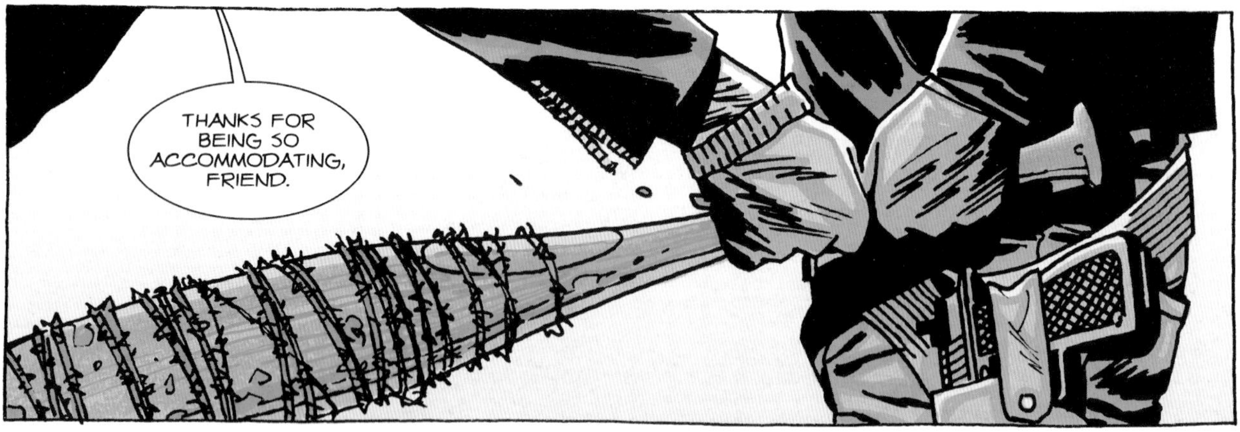
THANKS FOR BEING SO ACCOMMODATING, FRIEND.

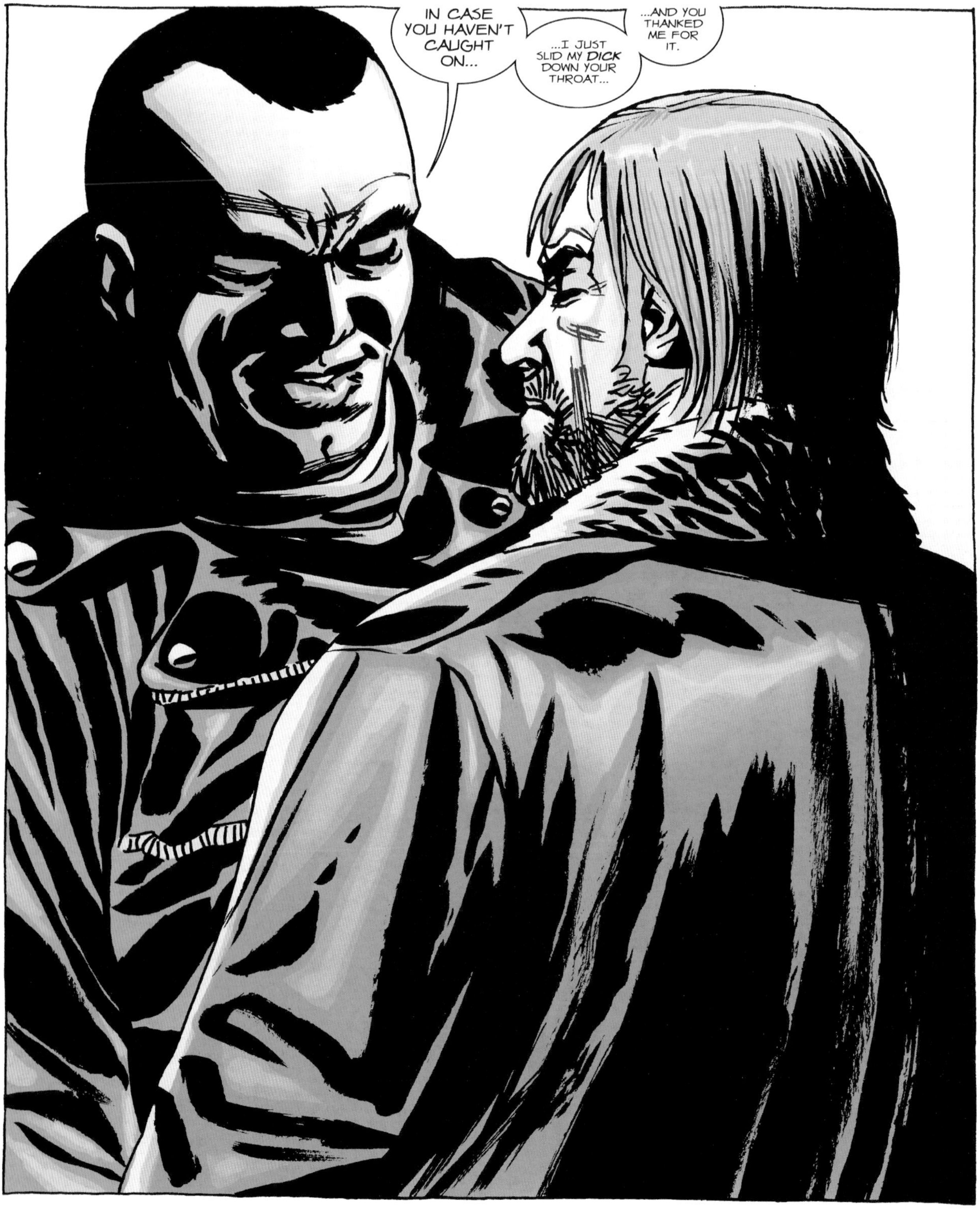
IN CASE YOU HAVEN'T CAUGHT ON...
...I JUST SLID MY DICK DOWN YOUR THROAT...
...AND YOU THANKED ME FOR IT.

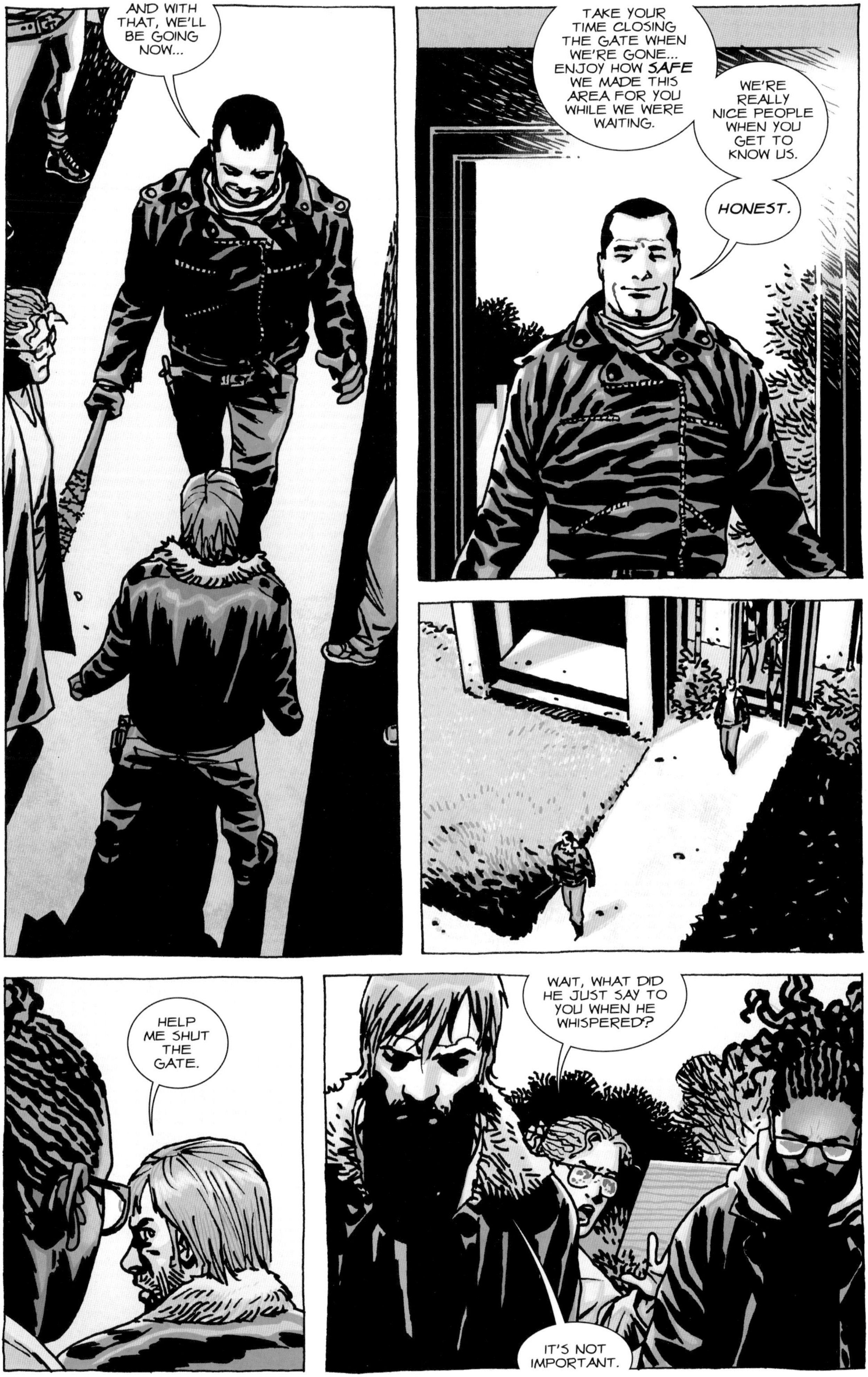
AND WITH THAT, WE'LL BE GOING NOW...
TAKE YOUR TIME CLOSING THE GATE WHEN WE'RE GONE... ENJOY HOW SAFE WE MADE THIS AREA FOR YOU WHILE WE WERE WAITING.
WE'RE REALLY NICE PEOPLE WHEN YOU GET TO KNOW US.
HONEST.
HELP ME SHUT THE GATE.
WAIT, WHAT DID HE JUST SAY TO YOU WHEN HE WHISPERED?
IT'S NOT IMPORTANT.

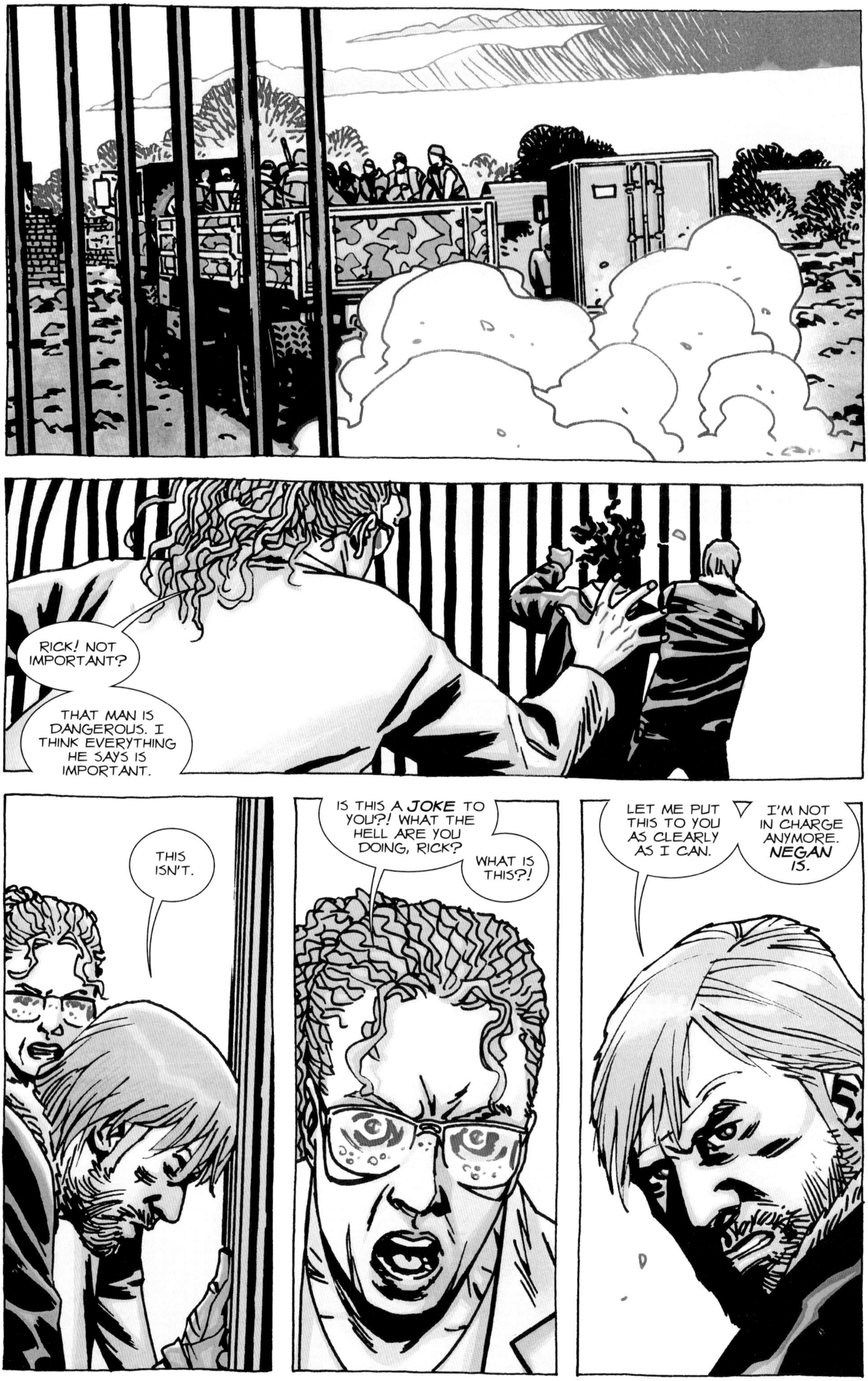
RICK! NOT IMPORTANT?
THAT MAN IS DANGEROUS. I THINK EVERYTHING HE SAYS IS IMPORTANT.
THIS ISN'T.
IS THIS A JOKE TO YOU?! WHAT THE HELL ARE YOU DOING, RICK?
WHAT IS THIS?!
LET ME PUT THIS TO YOU AS CLEARLY AS I CAN.
I'M NOT IN CHARGE ANYMORE. NEGAN IS.

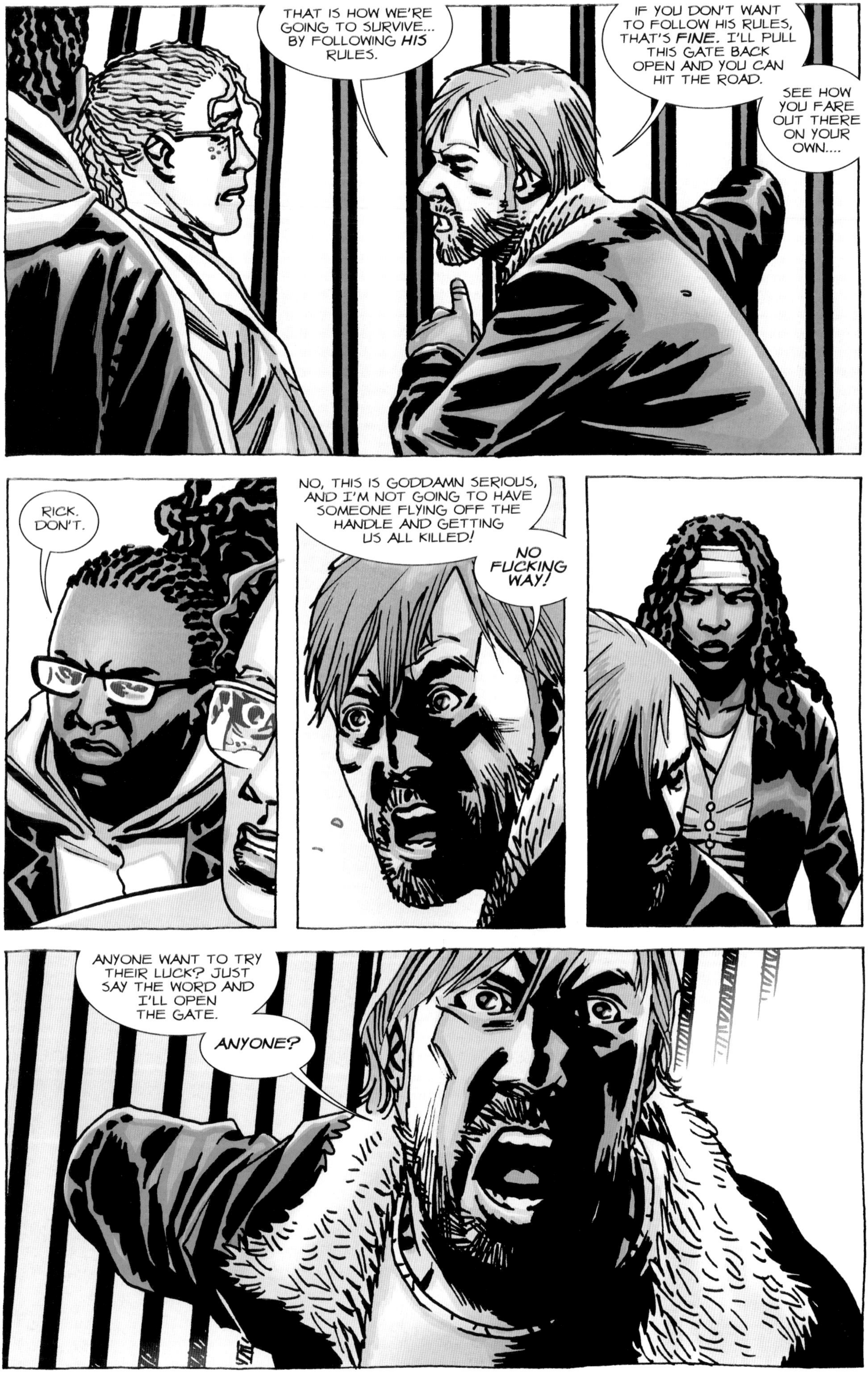
THAT IS HOW WE'RE GOING TO SURVIVE... BY FOLLOWING HIS RULES.
IF YOU DON'T WANT TO FOLLOW HIS RULES, THAT'S FINE. I'LL PULL THIS GATE BACK OPEN AND YOU CAN HIT THE ROAD.
SEE HOW YOU FARE OUT THERE ON YOUR OWN....
RICK. DON'T.
NO, THIS IS GODDAMN SERIOUS, AND I'M NOT GOING TO HAVE SOMEONE FLYING OFF THE HANDLE AND GETTING US ALL KILLED!
NO FUCKING WAY!
ANYONE WANT TO TRY THEIR LUCK? JUST SAY THE WORD AND I'LL OPEN THE GATE.
ANYONE?

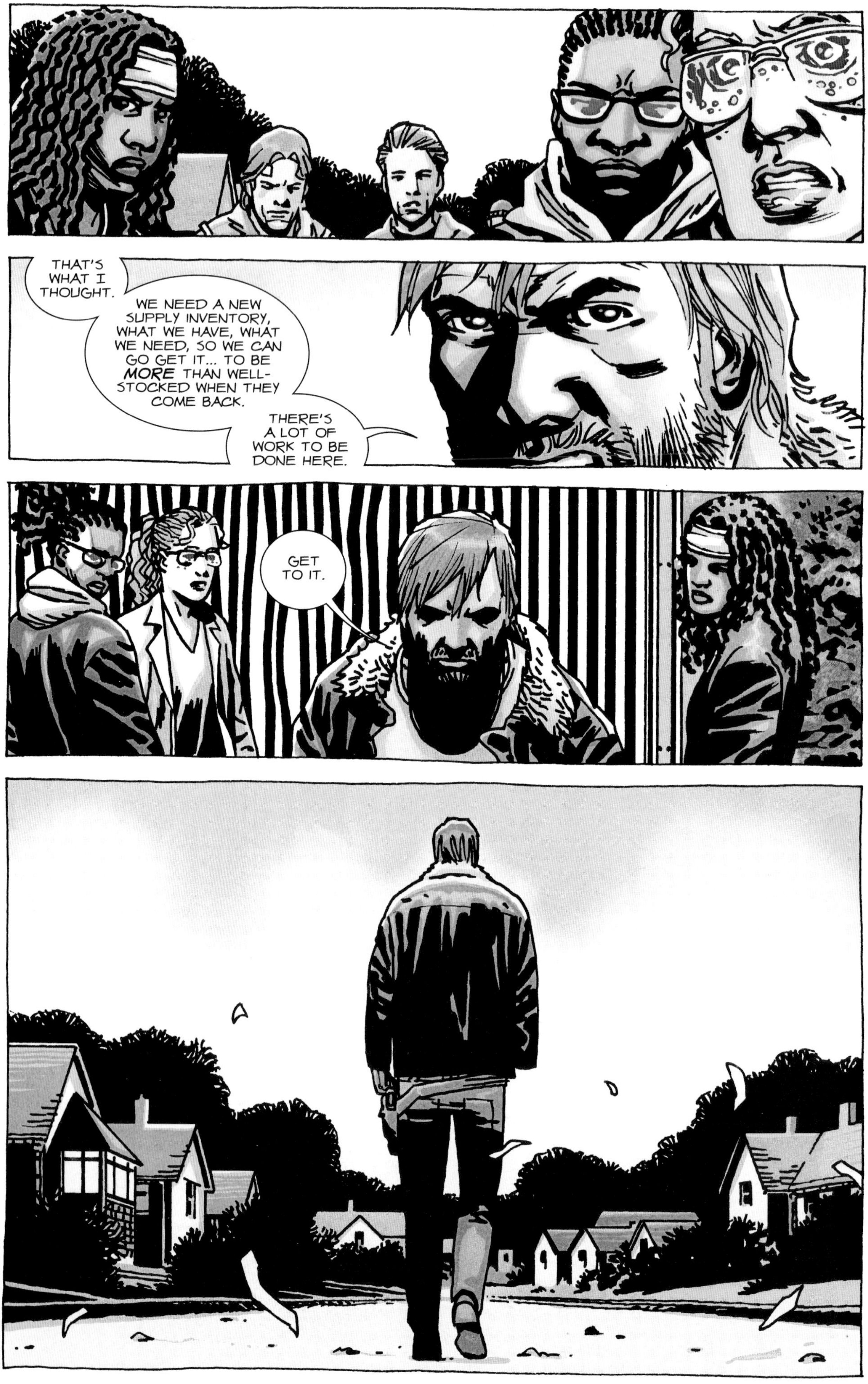
THAT'S WHAT I THOUGHT.
WE NEED A NEW SUPPLY INVENTORY, WHAT WE HAVE, WHAT WE NEED, SO WE CAN GO GET IT... TO BE MORE THAN WELL-STOCKED WHEN THEY COME BACK.
THERE'S A LOT OF WORK TO BE DONE HERE.
GET TO IT.

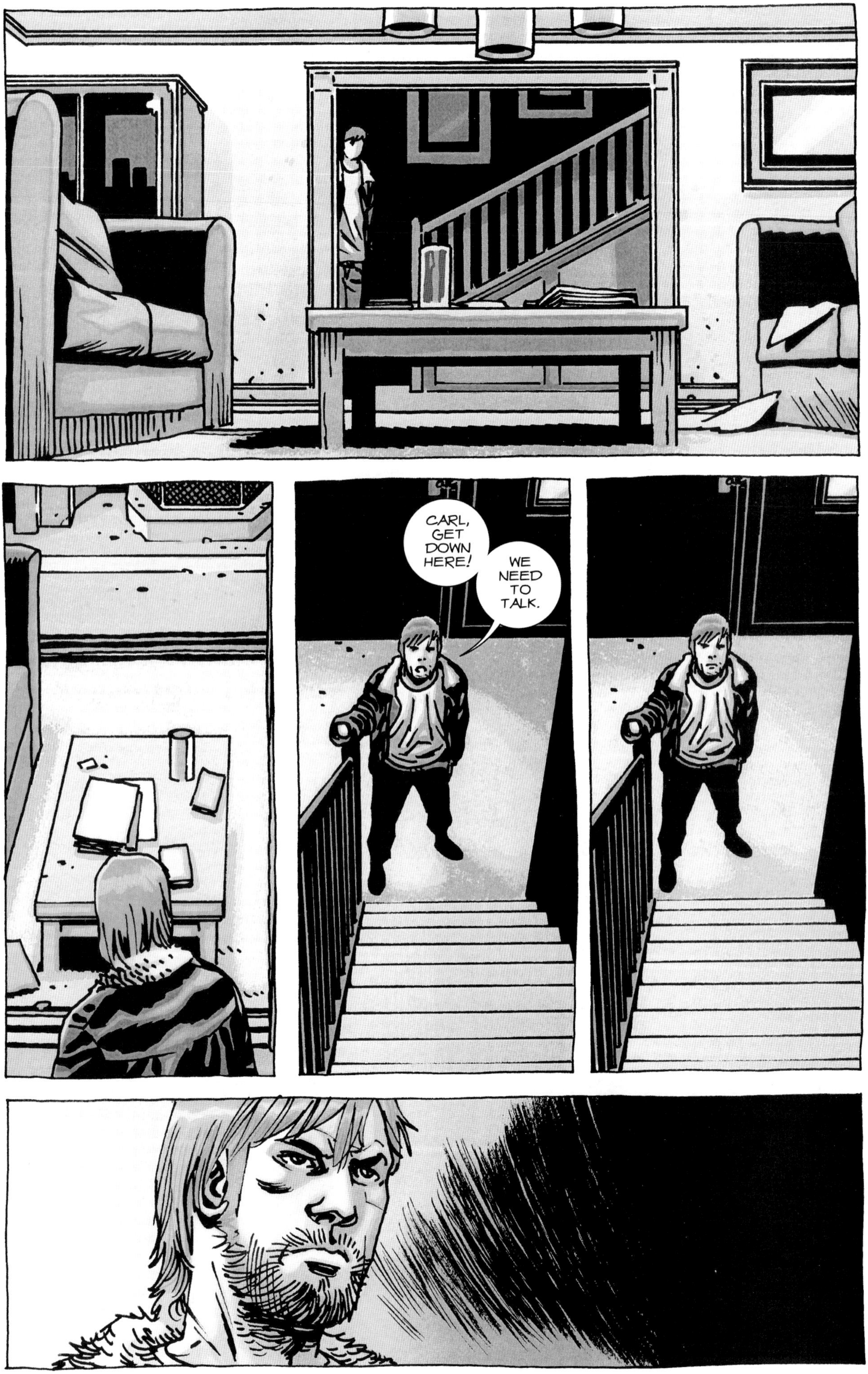
CARL, GET DOWN HERE!
WE NEED TO TALK.

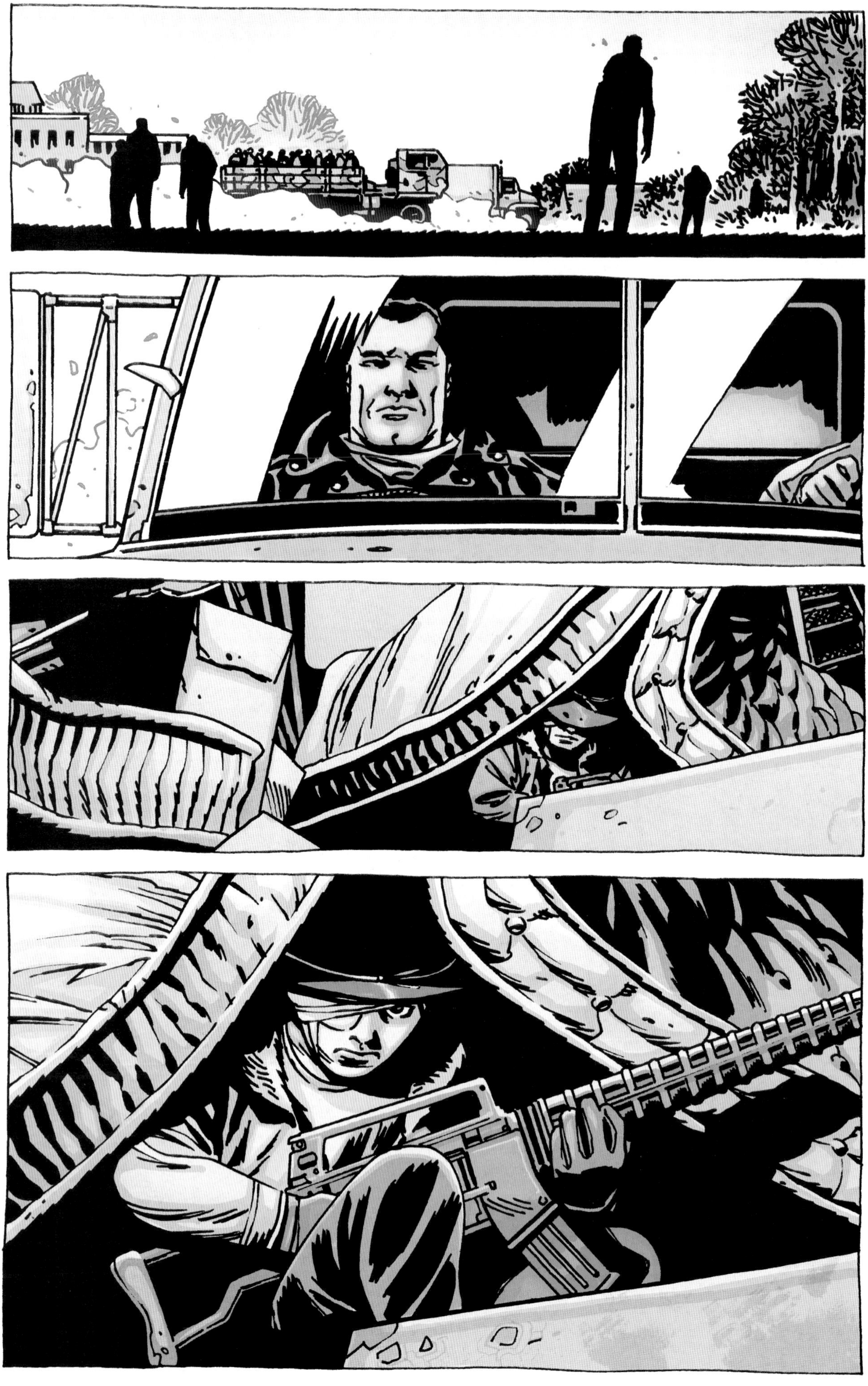

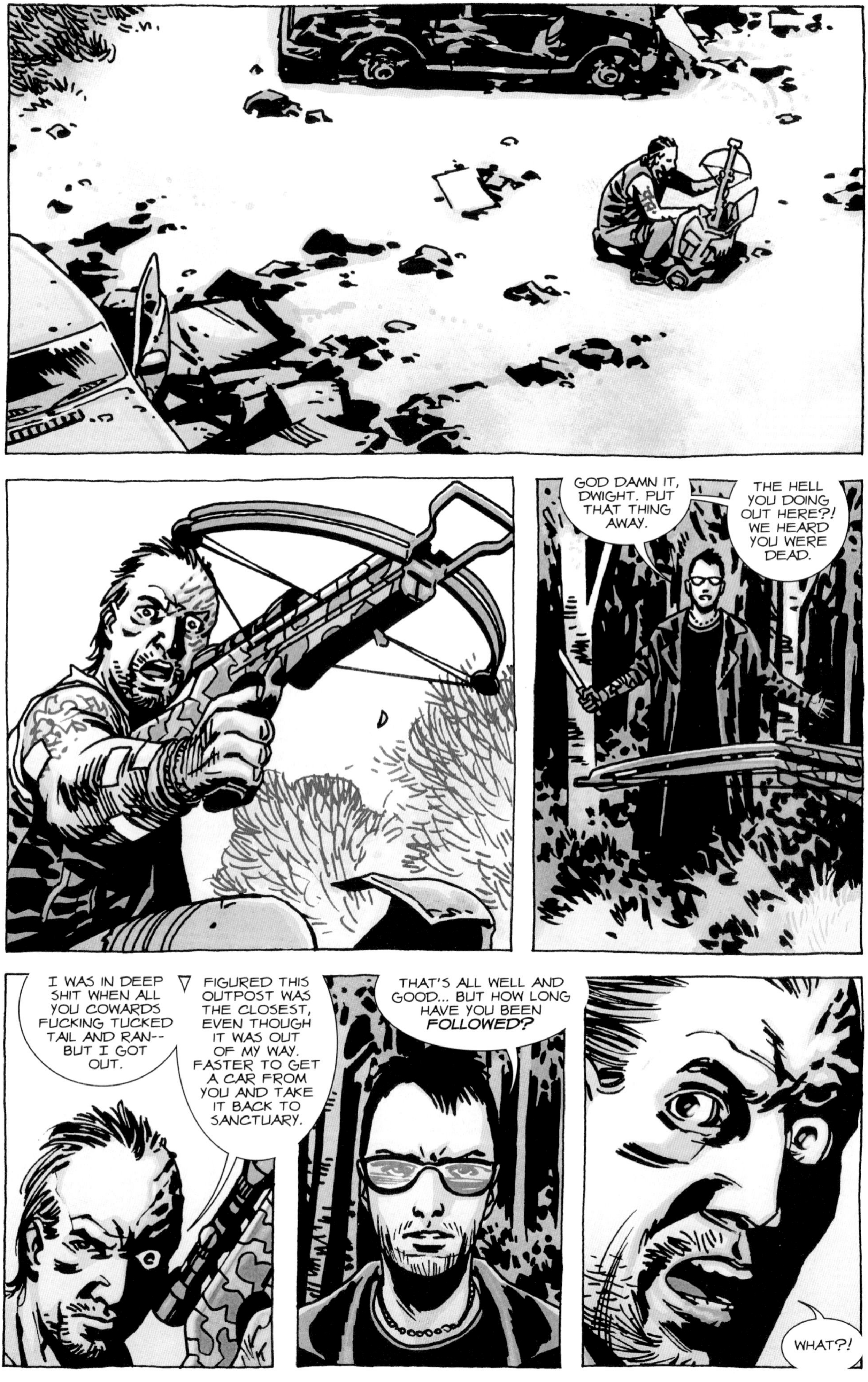
GOD DAMN IT, DWIGHT. PUT THAT THING AWAY.
THE HELL YOU DOING OUT HERE?! WE HEARD YOU WERE DEAD.
I WAS IN DEEP SHIT WHEN ALL YOU COWARDS FUCKING TUCKED TAIL AND RAN-- BUT I GOT OUT.
FIGURED THIS OUTPOST WAS THE CLOSEST, EVEN THOUGH IT WAS OUT OF MY WAY. FASTER TO GET A CAR FROM YOU AND TAKE IT BACK TO SANCTUARY.
THAT'S ALL WELL AND GOOD... BUT HOW LONG HAVE YOU BEEN *FOLLOWED?*
WHAT?!

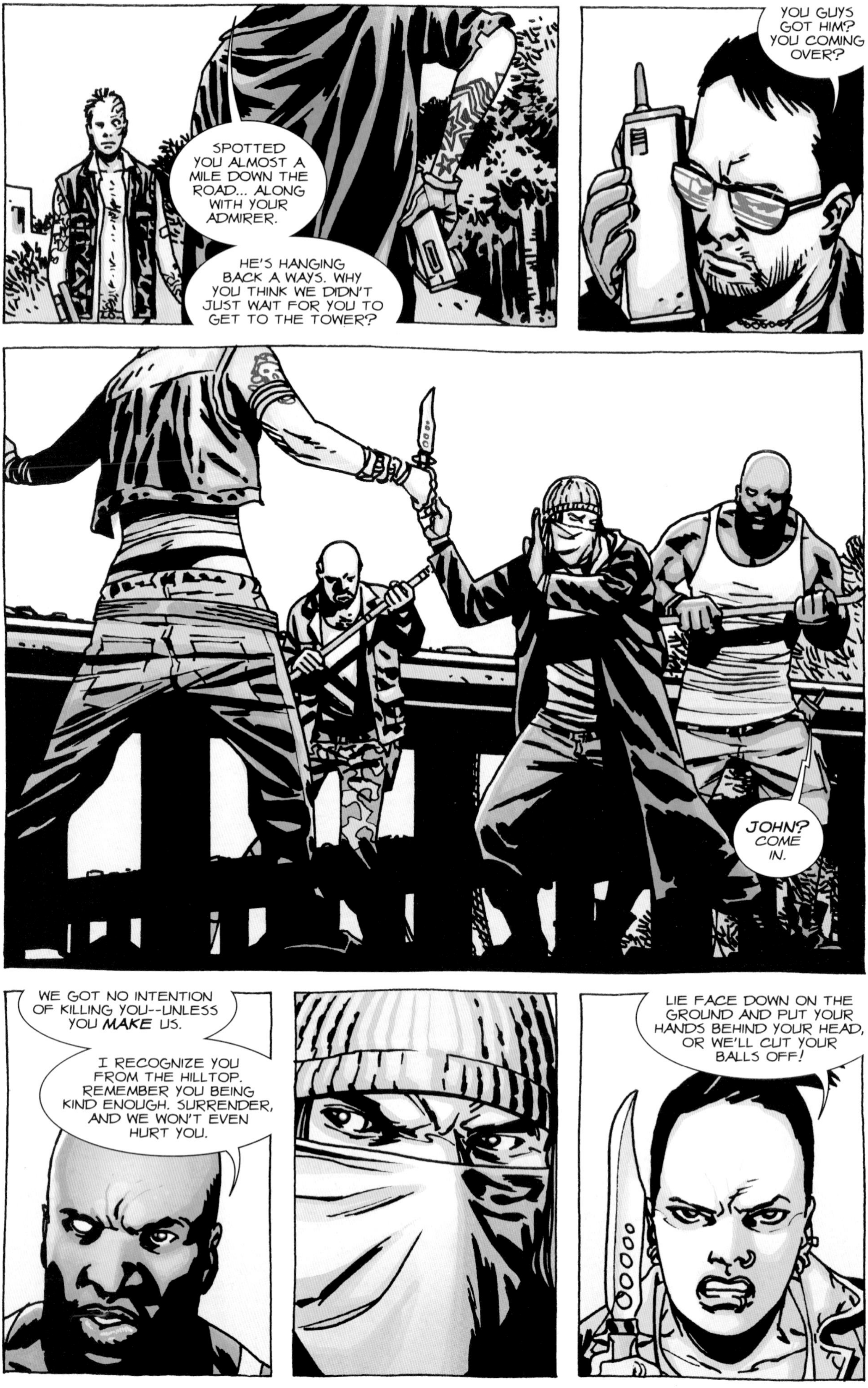
SPOTTED YOU ALMOST A MILE DOWN THE ROAD... ALONG WITH YOUR ADMIRER.
HE'S HANGING BACK A WAYS. WHY YOU THINK WE DIDN'T JUST WAIT FOR YOU TO GET TO THE TOWER?
YOU GUYS GOT HIM? YOU COMING OVER?
JOHN? COME IN.
WE GOT NO INTENTION OF KILLING YOU--UNLESS YOU MAKE US.
I RECOGNIZE YOU FROM THE HILLTOP. REMEMBER YOU BEING KIND ENOUGH. SURRENDER, AND WE WON'T EVEN HURT YOU.
LIE FACE DOWN ON THE GROUND AND PUT YOUR HANDS BEHIND YOUR HEAD, OR WE'LL CUT YOUR BALLS OFF!

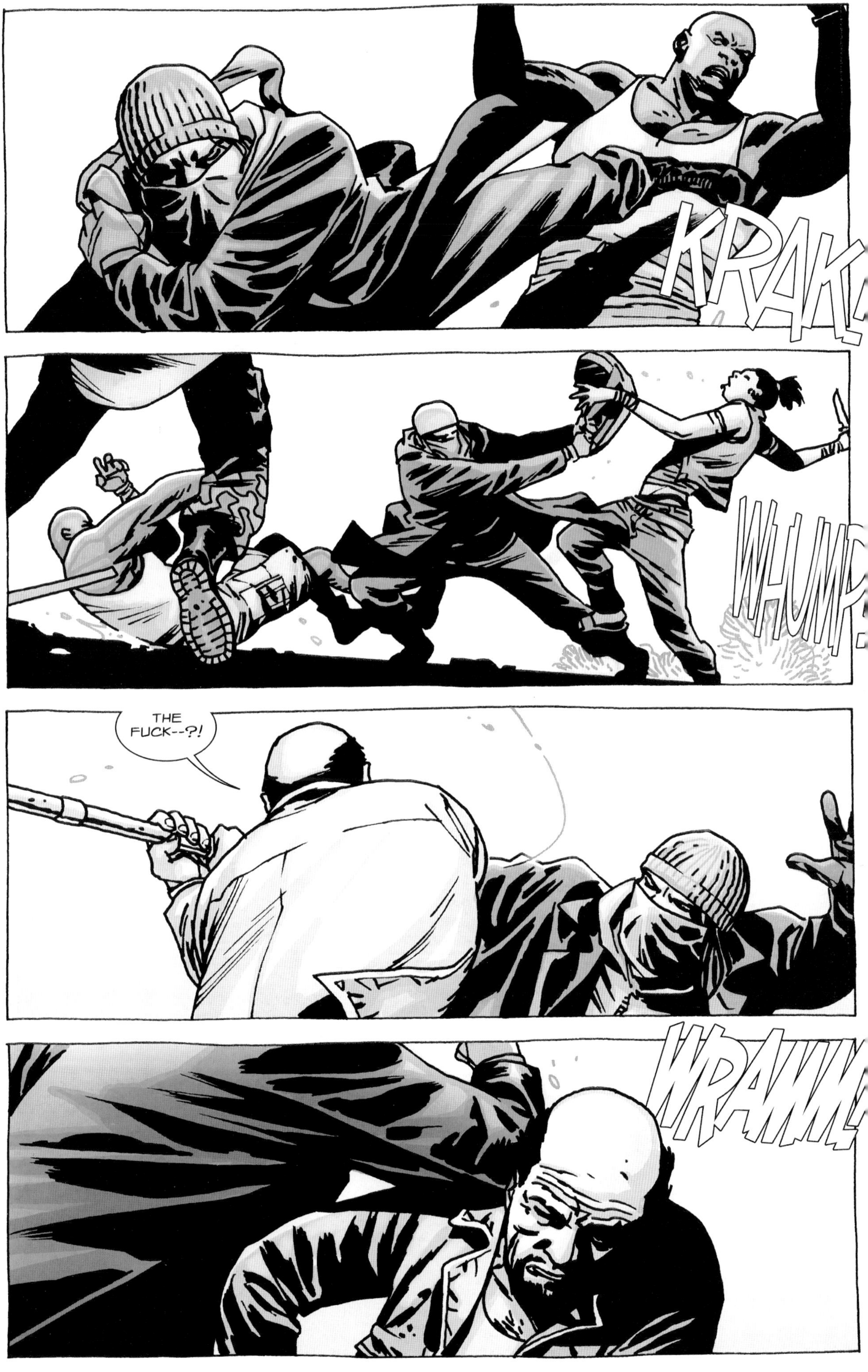
KRAK!
WHUMP!
THE FUCK--?!
WRAMM!

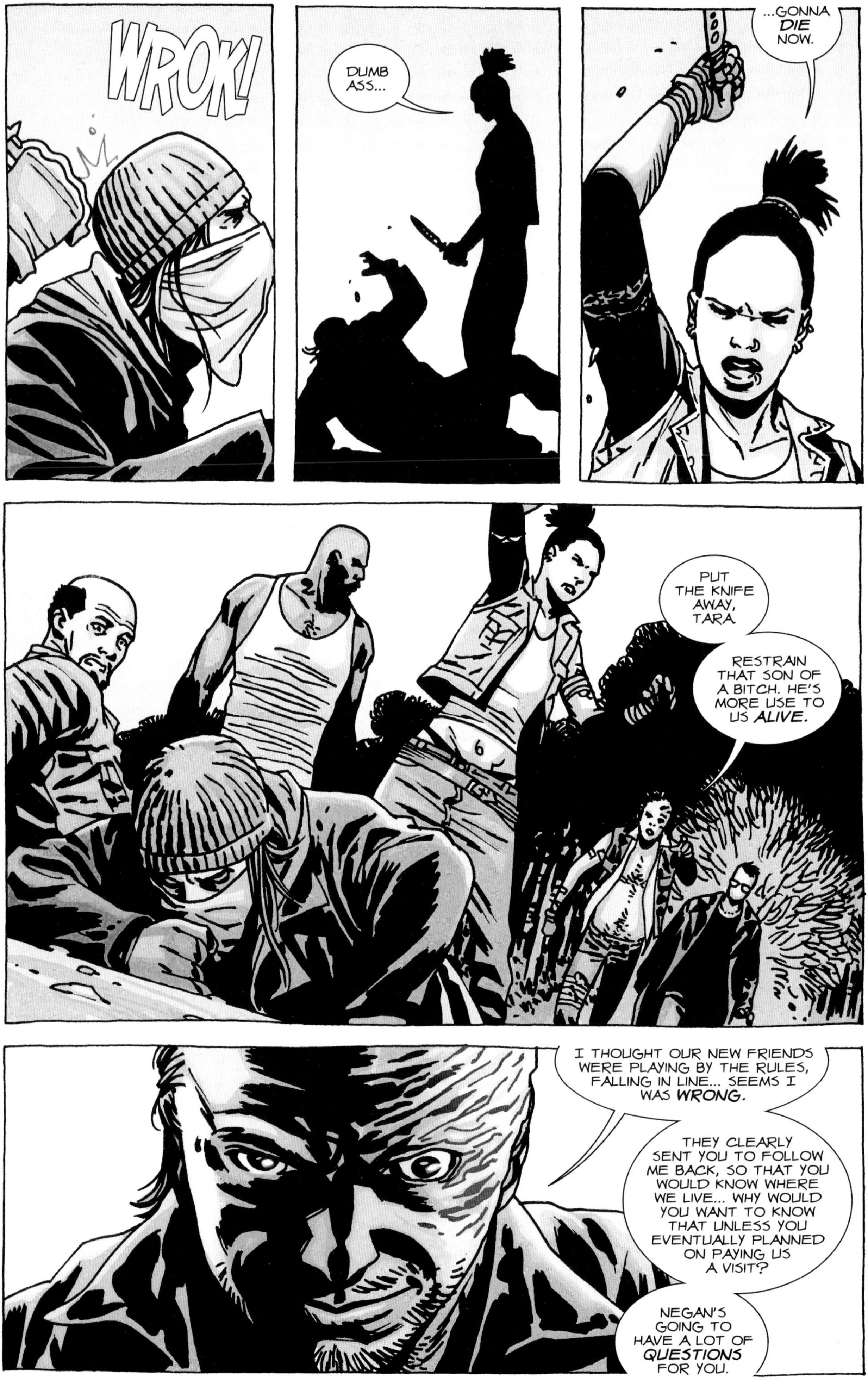
WROK!
DUMB ASS...
...GONNA DIE NOW.
PUT THE KNIFE AWAY, TARA.
RESTRAIN THAT SON OF A BITCH. HE'S MORE USE TO US ALIVE.
I THOUGHT OUR NEW FRIENDS WERE PLAYING BY THE RULES, FALLING IN LINE... SEEMS I WAS WRONG.
THEY CLEARLY SENT YOU TO FOLLOW ME BACK, SO THAT YOU WOULD KNOW WHERE WE LIVE... WHY WOULD YOU WANT TO KNOW THAT UNLESS YOU EVENTUALLY PLANNED ON PAYING US A VISIT?
NEGAN'S GOING TO HAVE A LOT OF QUESTIONS FOR YOU.

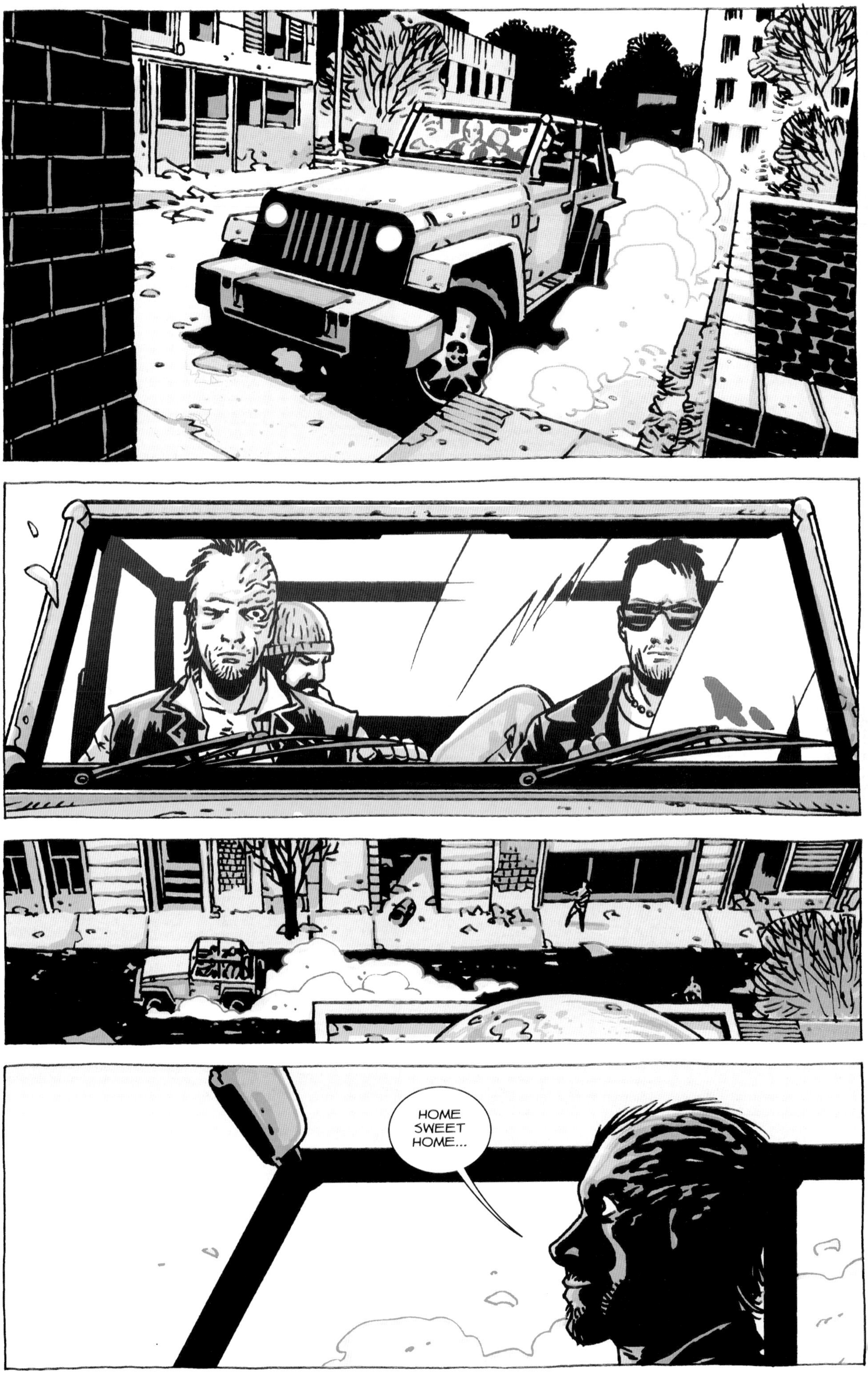
HOME SWEET HOME...

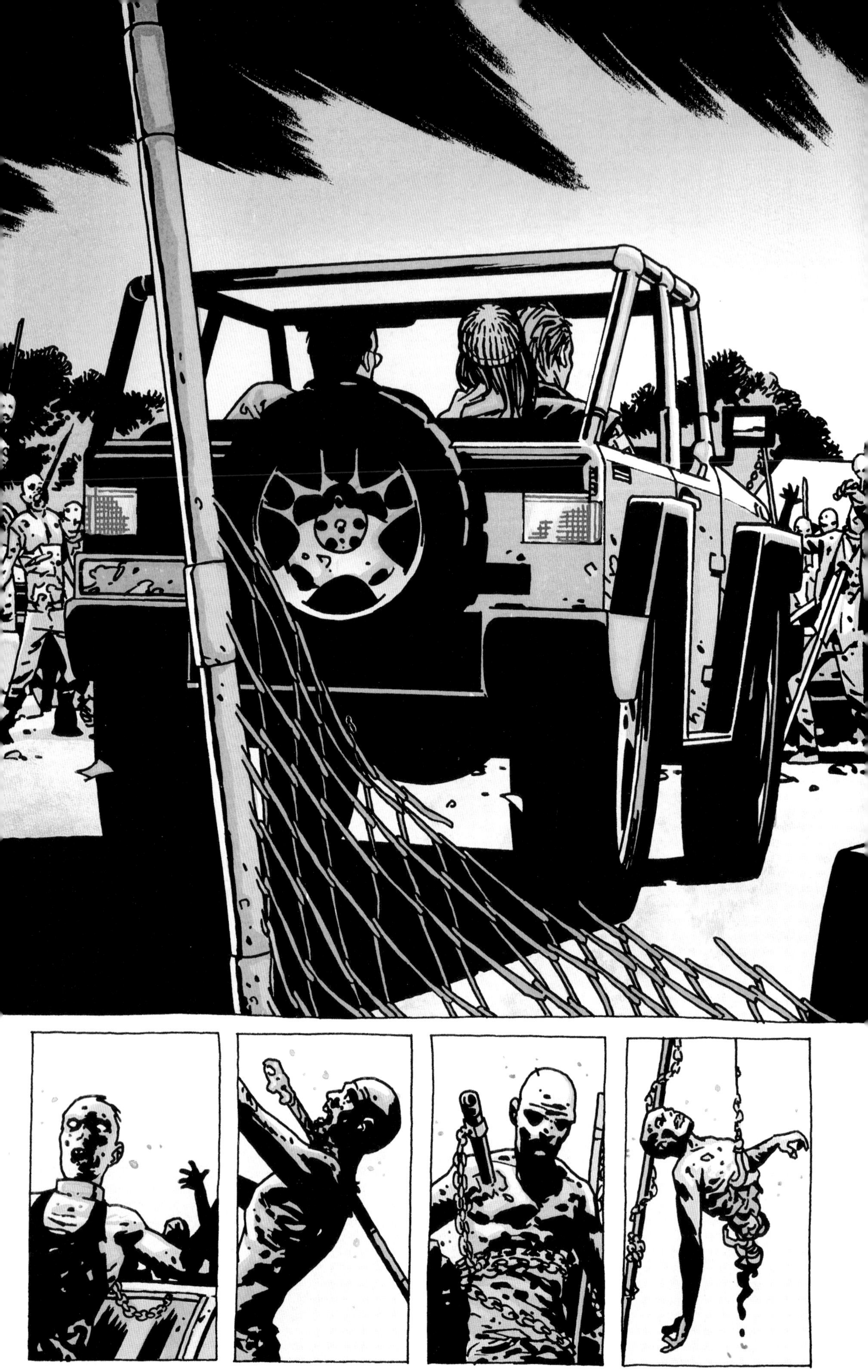

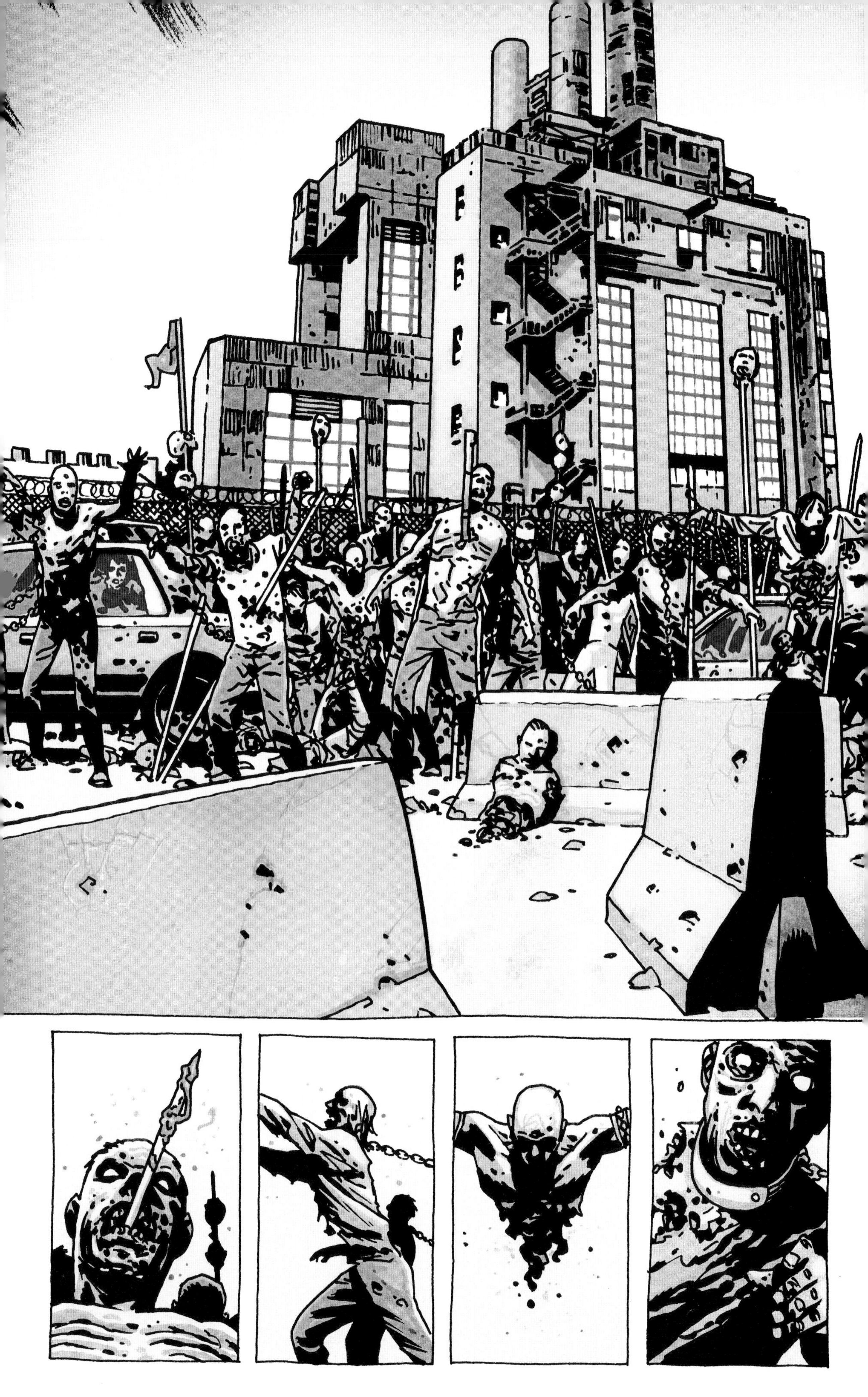

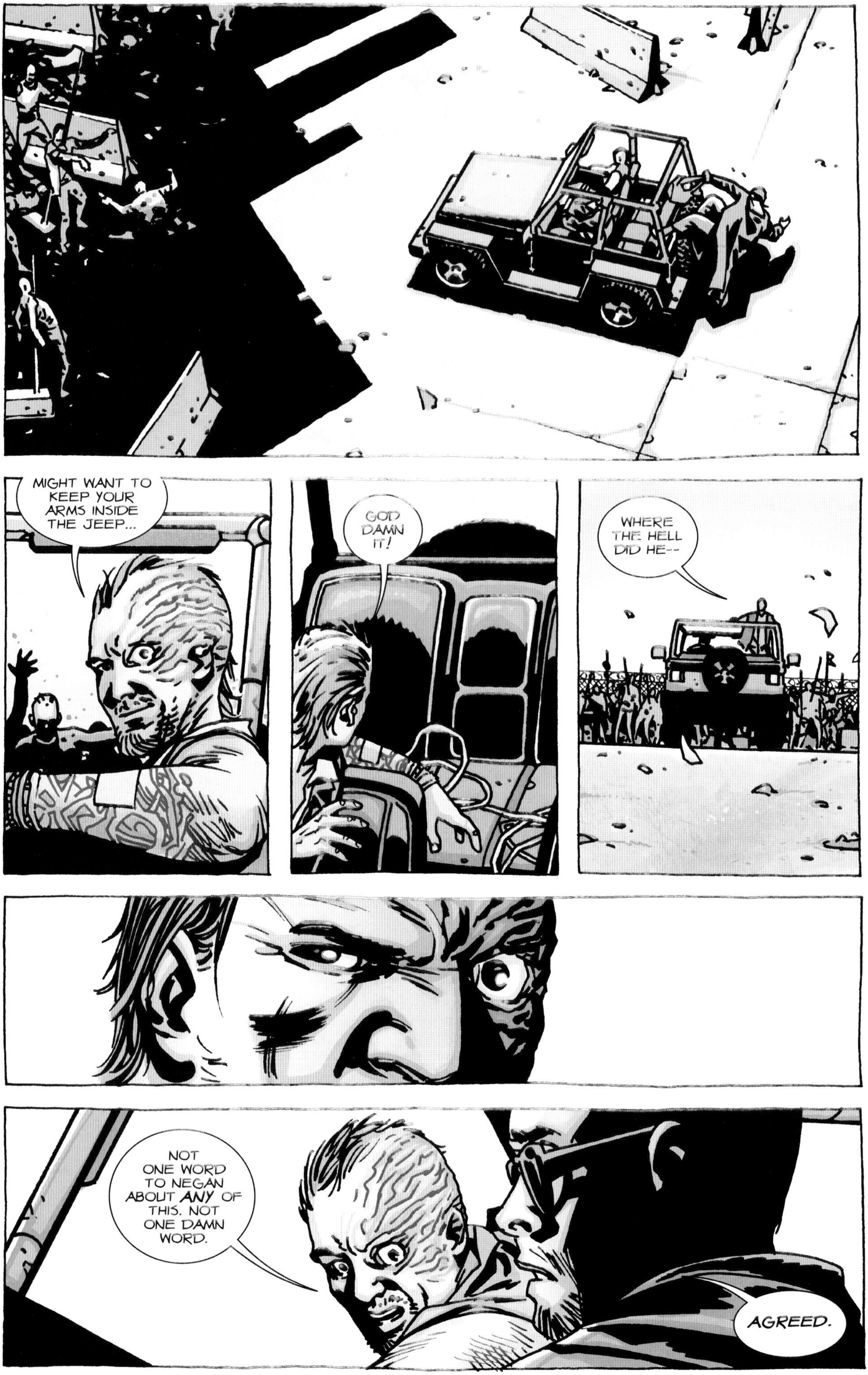
MIGHT WANT TO KEEP YOUR ARMS INSIDE THE JEEP...
GOD DAMN IT!
WHERE THE HELL DID HE--
NOT ONE WORD TO NEGAN ABOUT ANY OF THIS. NOT ONE DAMN WORD.
AGREED.

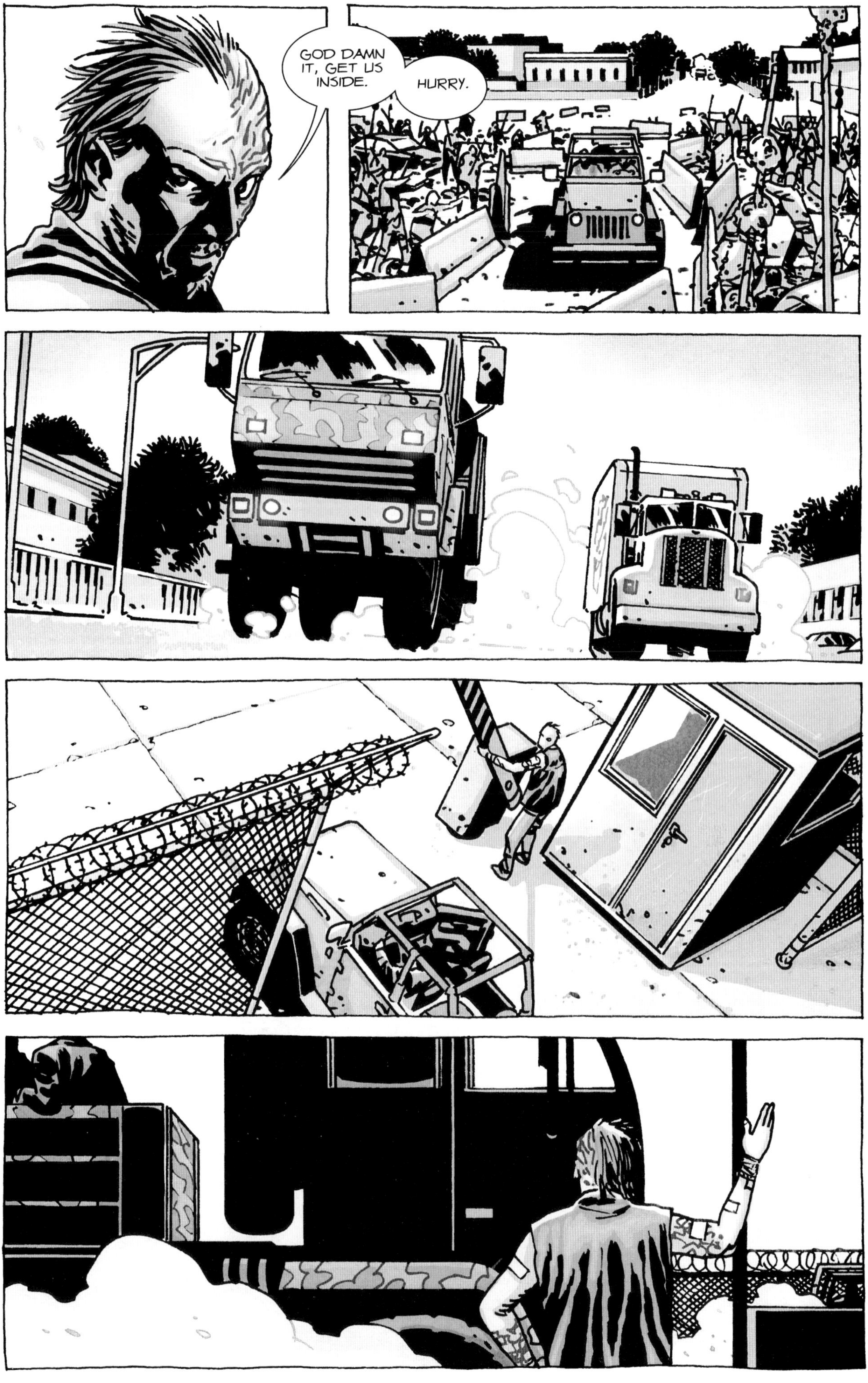
GOD DAMN IT, GET US INSIDE.
HURRY.

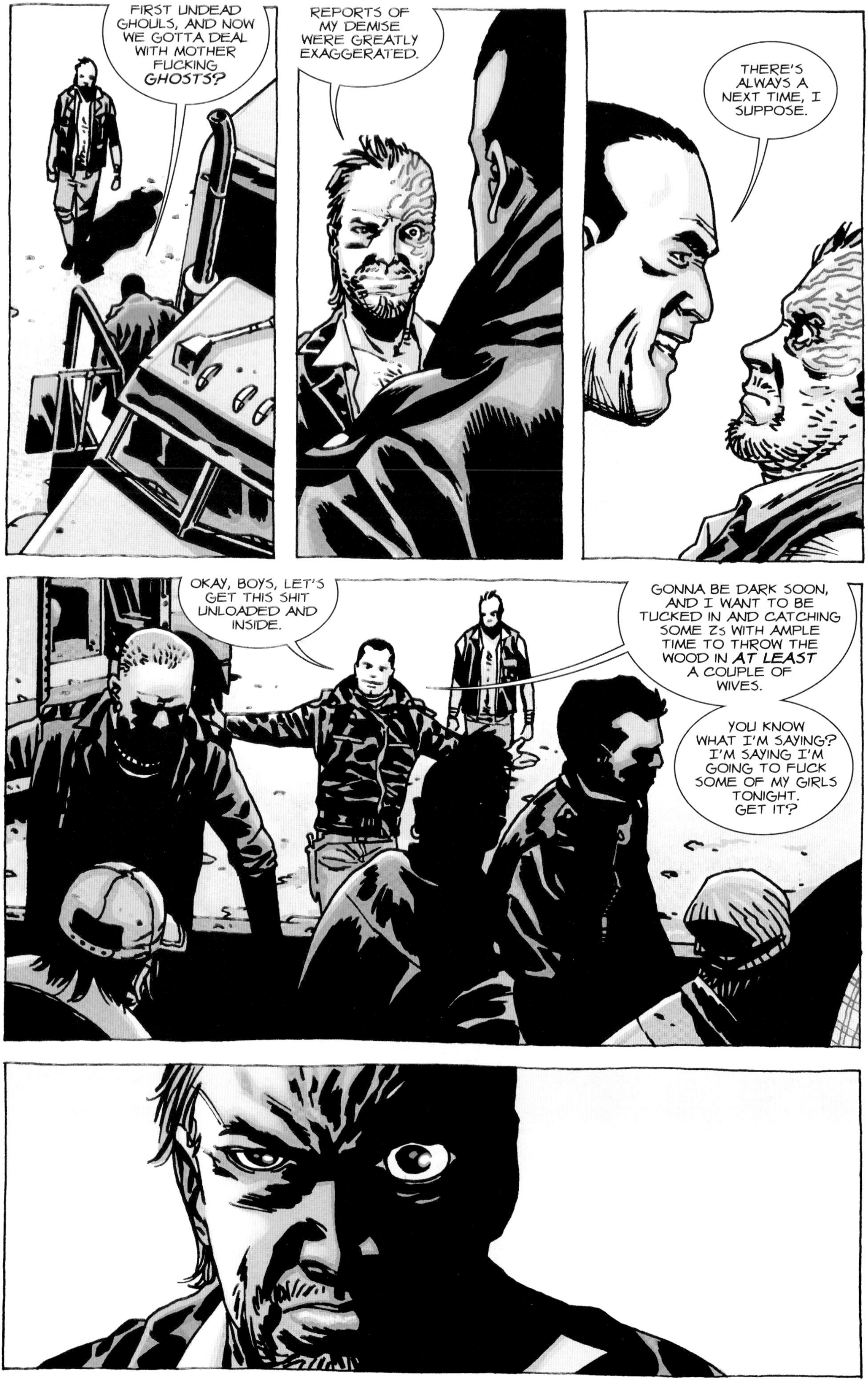
FIRST UNDEAD GHOULS, AND NOW WE GOTTA DEAL WITH MOTHER FUCKING GHOSTS?
REPORTS OF MY DEMISE WERE GREATLY EXAGGERATED.
THERE'S ALWAYS A NEXT TIME, I SUPPOSE.
OKAY, BOYS, LET'S GET THIS SHIT UNLOADED AND INSIDE.
GONNA BE DARK SOON, AND I WANT TO BE TUCKED IN AND CATCHING SOME Zs WITH AMPLE TIME TO THROW THE WOOD IN AT LEAST A COUPLE OF WIVES.
YOU KNOW WHAT I'M SAYING? I'M SAYING I'M GOING TO FUCK SOME OF MY GIRLS TONIGHT. GET IT?

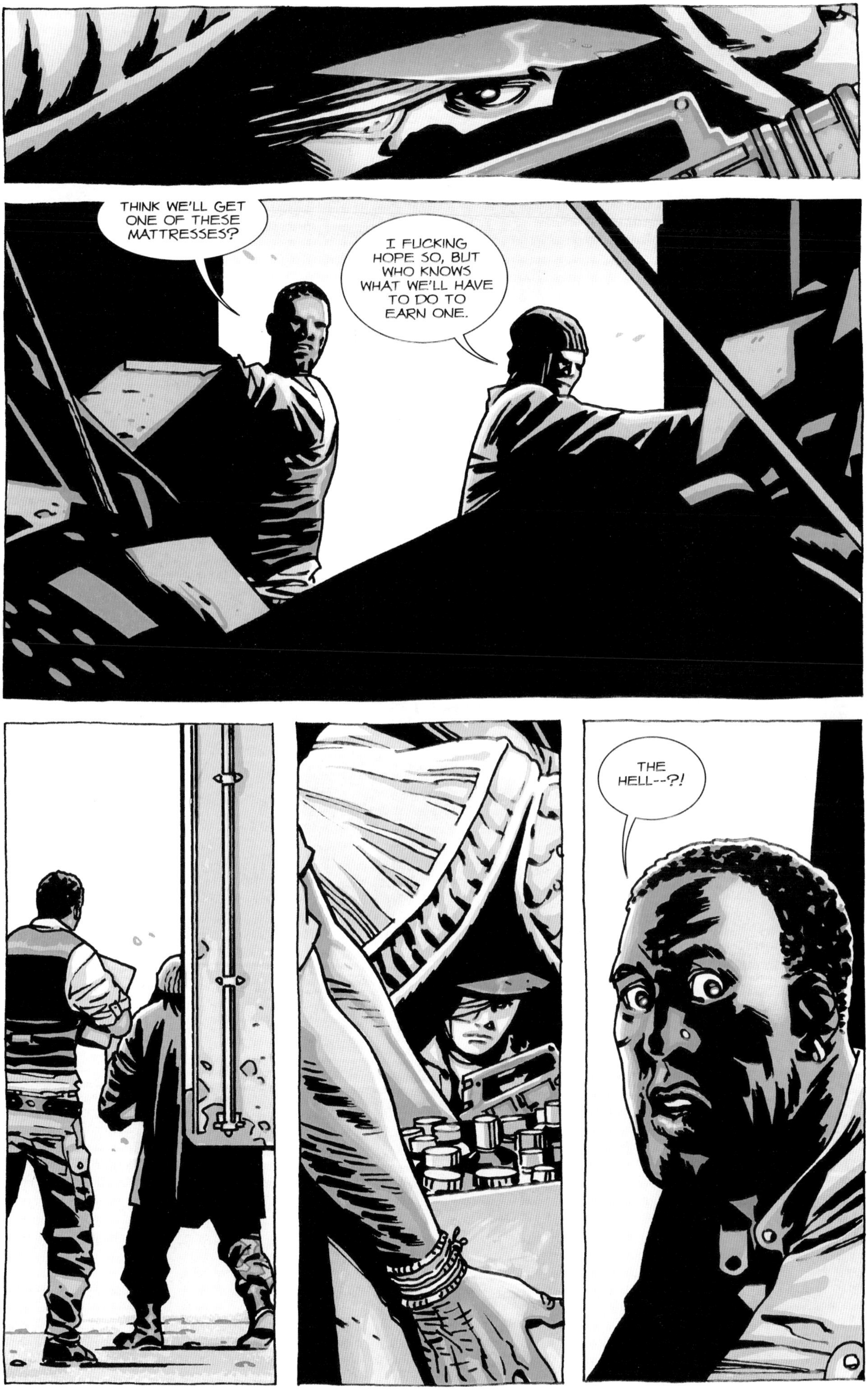
THINK WE'LL GET ONE OF THESE MATTRESSES?
I FUCKING HOPE SO, BUT WHO KNOWS WHAT WE'LL HAVE TO DO TO EARN ONE.
THE HELL--?!

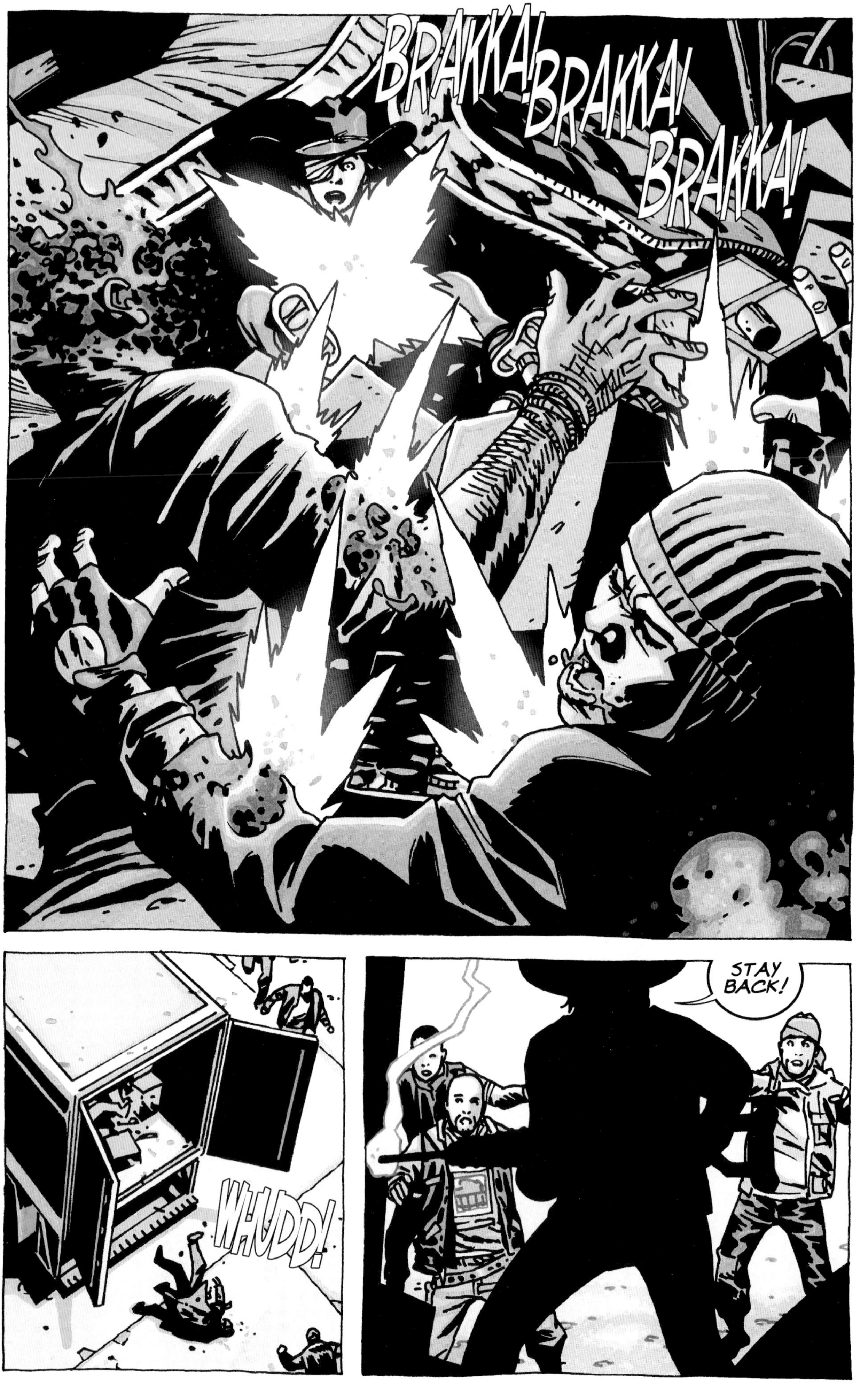
BRAKKA! BRAKKA! BRAKKA!
WHUDD!
STAY BACK!

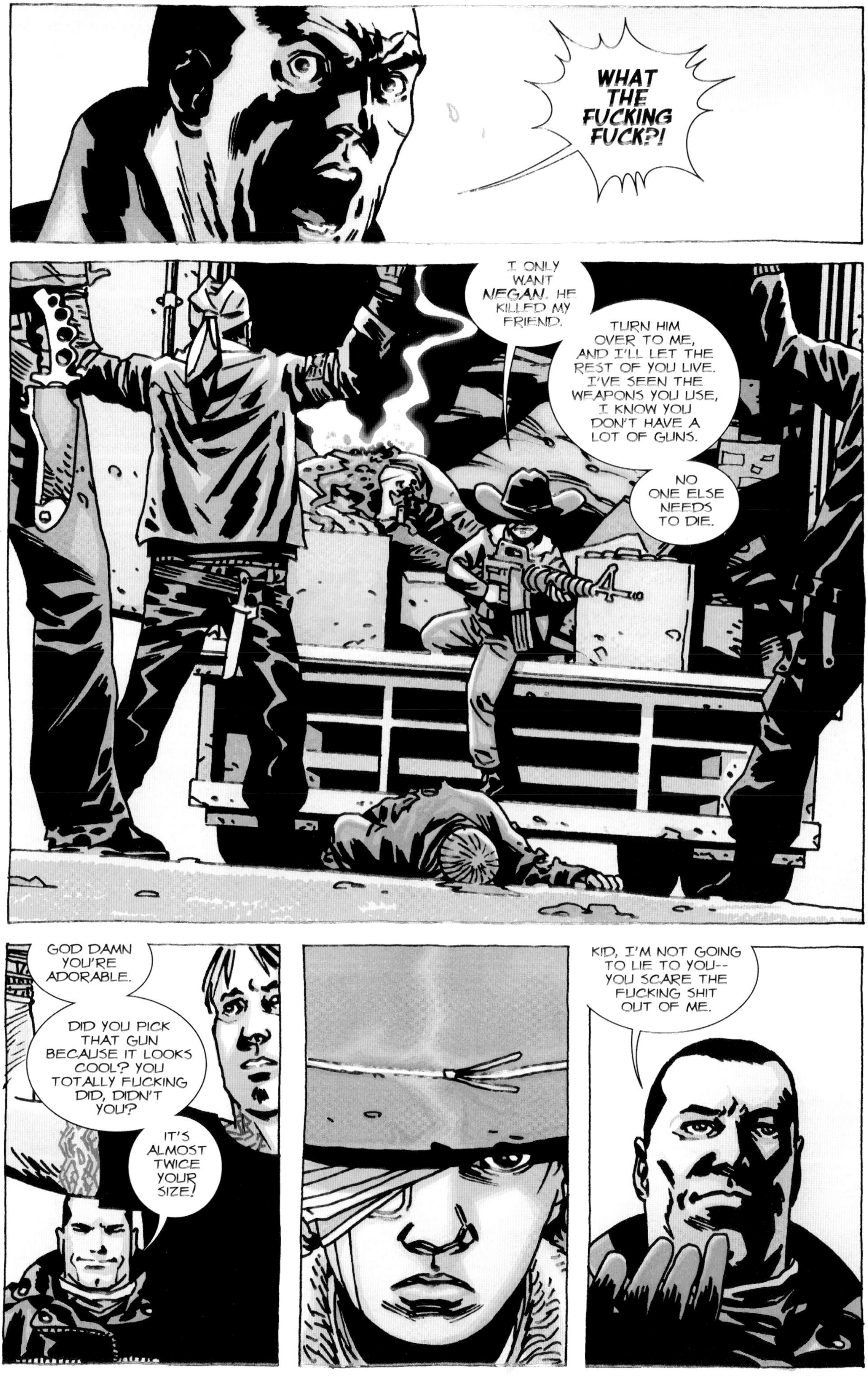
WHAT THE FUCKING FUCK?!
I ONLY WANT NEGAN. HE KILLED MY FRIEND.
TURN HIM OVER TO ME, AND I'LL LET THE REST OF YOU LIVE. I'VE SEEN THE WEAPONS YOU USE, I KNOW YOU DON'T HAVE A LOT OF GUNS.
NO ONE ELSE NEEDS TO DIE.
GOD DAMN YOU'RE ADORABLE.
DID YOU PICK THAT GUN BECAUSE IT LOOKS COOL? YOU TOTALLY FUCKING DID, DIDN'T YOU?
IT'S ALMOST TWICE YOUR SIZE!
KID, I'M NOT GOING TO LIE TO YOU-- YOU SCARE THE FUCKING SHIT OUT OF ME.

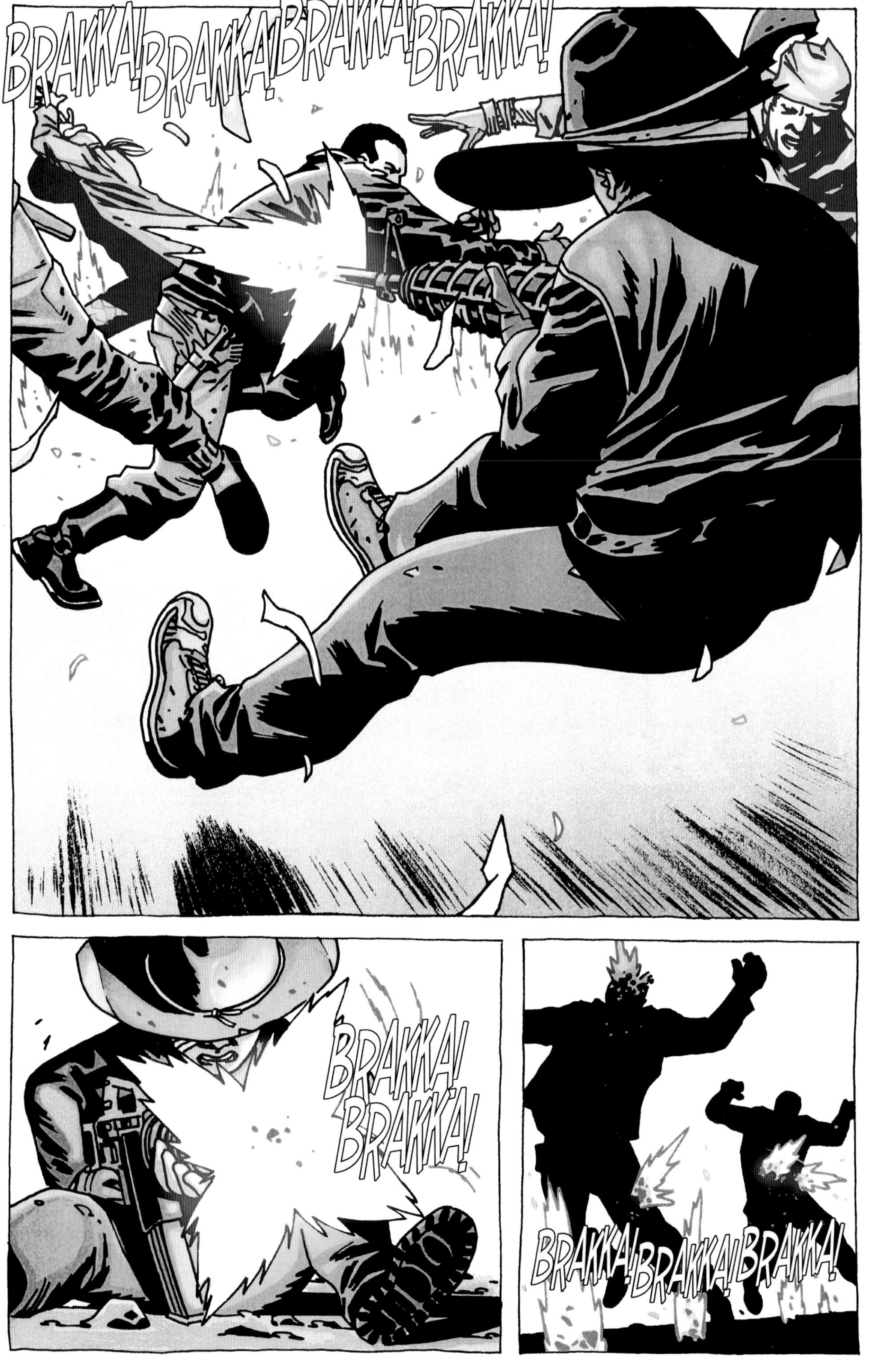
BRAKKA! BRAKKA! BRAKKA! BRAKKA!
BRAKKA! BRAKKA!
BRAKKA! BRAKKA! BRAKKA!

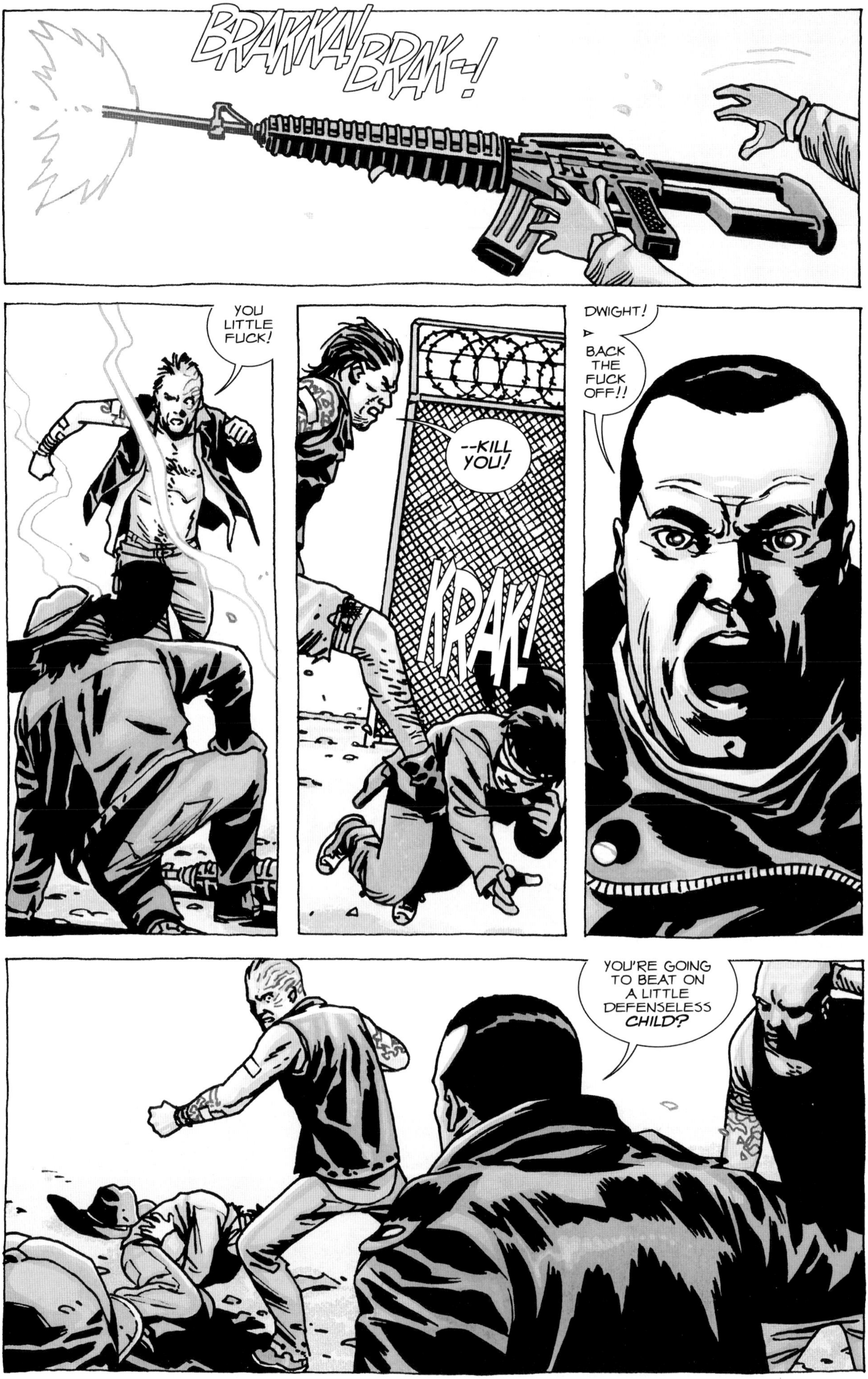
BRAKKA! BRAK--!
YOU LITTLE FUCK!
--KILL YOU!
KRAK!
DWIGHT!
BACK THE FUCK OFF!!
YOU'RE GOING TO BEAT ON A LITTLE DEFENSELESS *CHILD?*

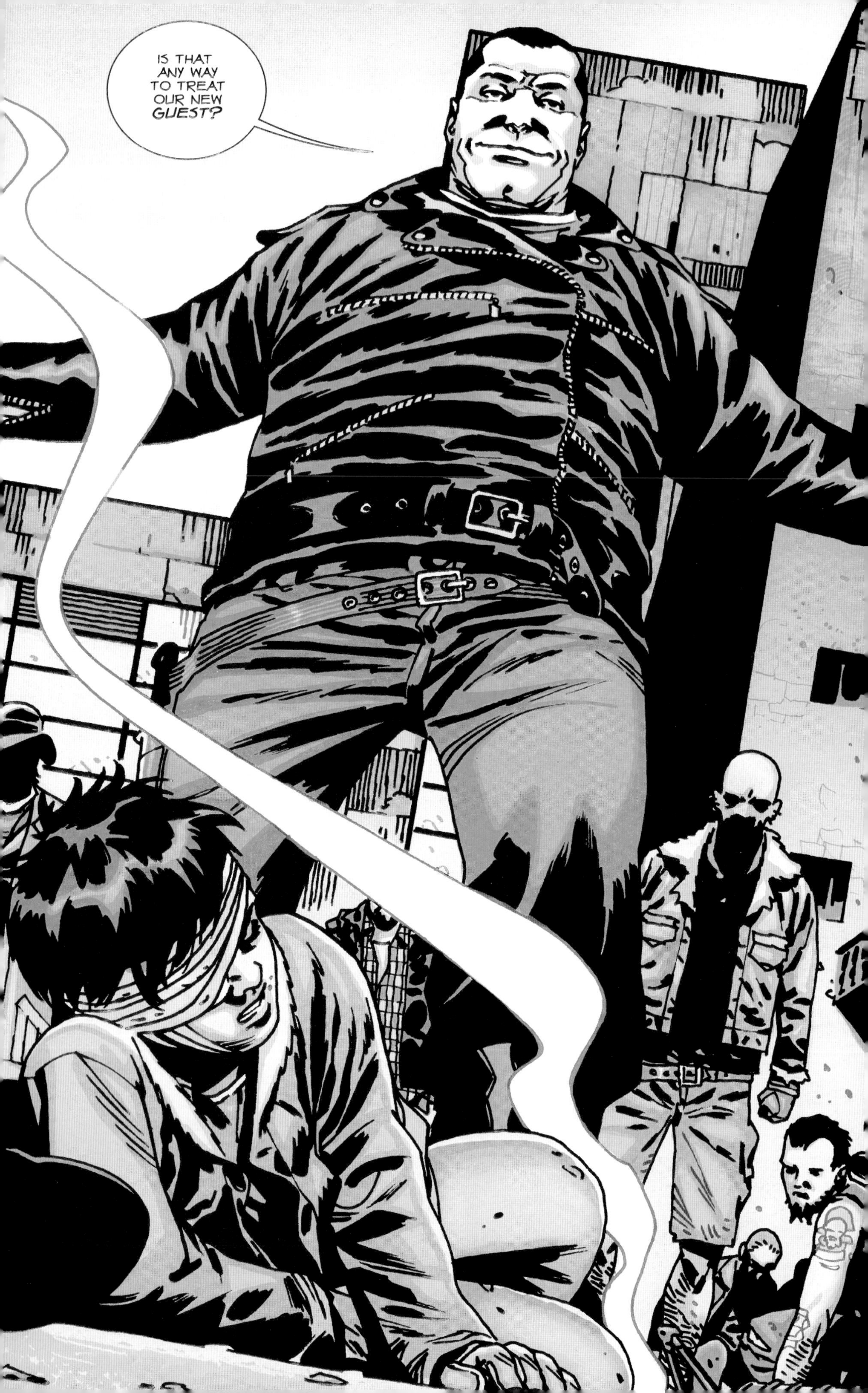
IS THAT ANY WAY TO TREAT OUR NEW GUEST?

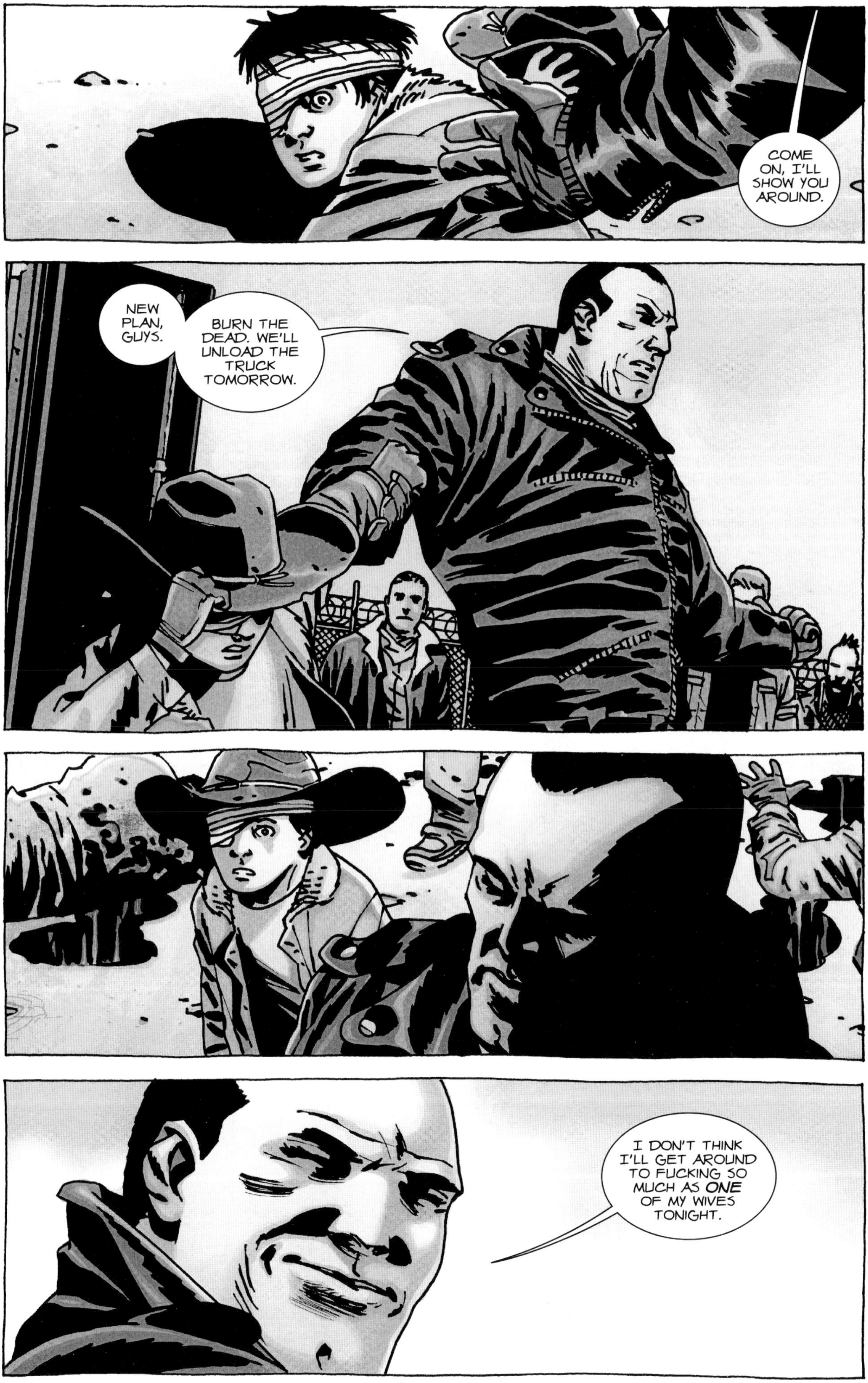
COME ON, I'LL SHOW YOU AROUND.
NEW PLAN, GUYS.
BURN THE DEAD. WE'LL UNLOAD THE TRUCK TOMORROW.
I DON'T THINK I'LL GET AROUND TO FUCKING SO MUCH AS ONE OF MY WIVES TONIGHT.

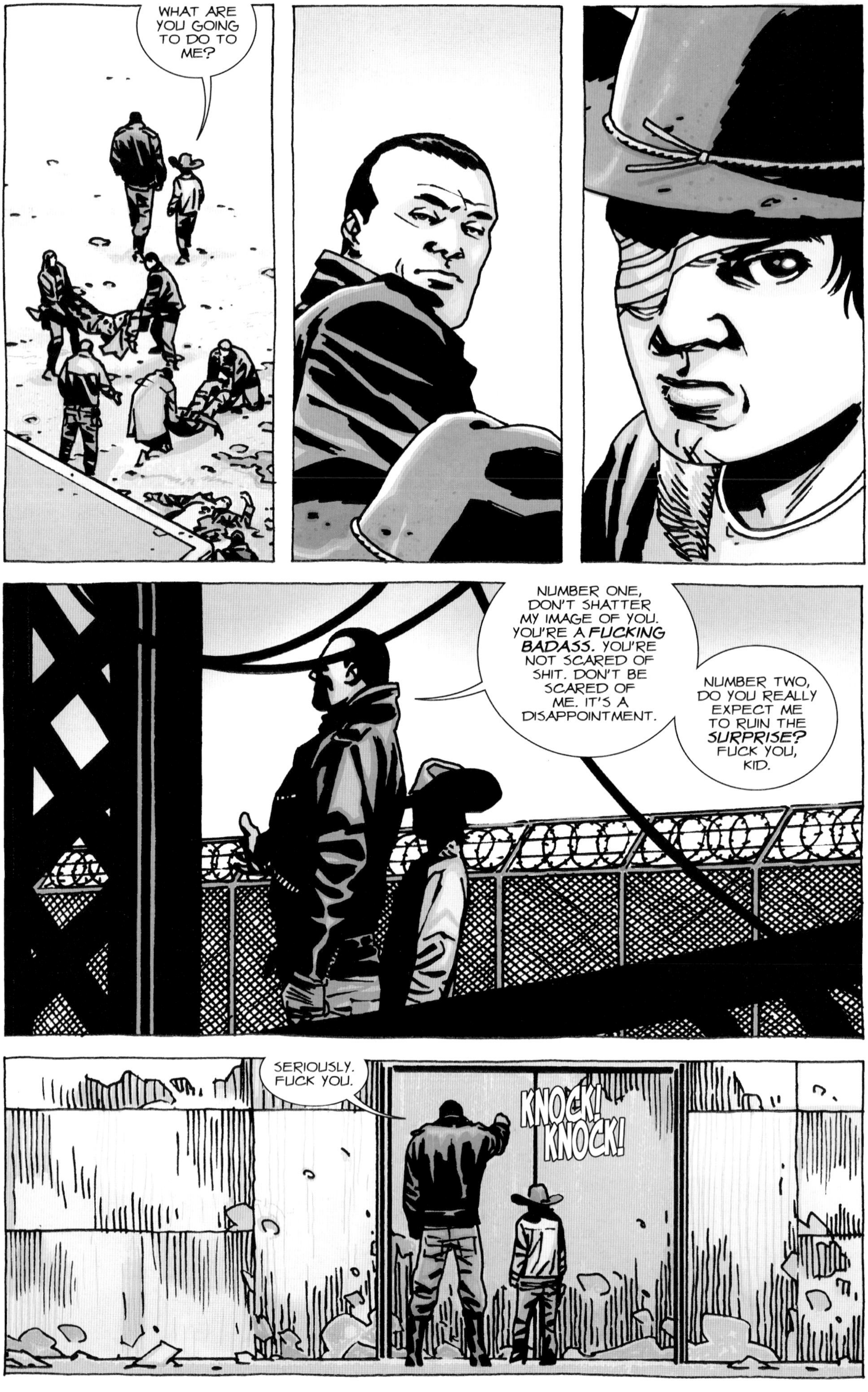
WHAT ARE YOU GOING TO DO TO ME?
NUMBER ONE, DON'T SHATTER MY IMAGE OF YOU. YOU'RE A FUCKING BADASS. YOU'RE NOT SCARED OF SHIT. DON'T BE SCARED OF ME. IT'S A DISAPPOINTMENT.
NUMBER TWO, DO YOU REALLY EXPECT ME TO RUIN THE SURPRISE? FUCK YOU, KID.
SERIOUSLY. FUCK YOU.
KNOCK! KNOCK!

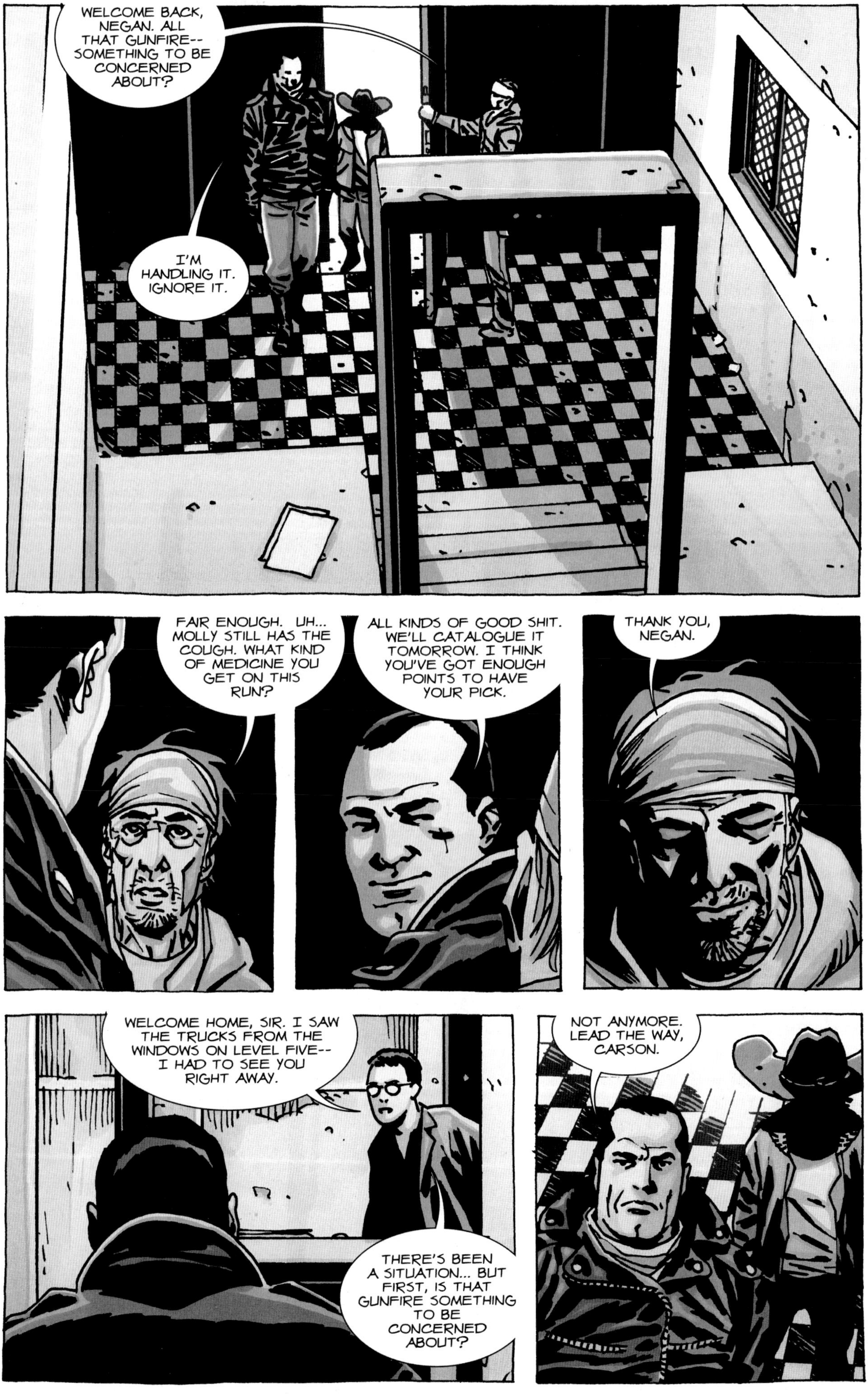
WELCOME BACK, NEGAN. ALL THAT GUNFIRE-- SOMETHING TO BE CONCERNED ABOUT?
I'M HANDLING IT. IGNORE IT.
FAIR ENOUGH. UH... MOLLY STILL HAS THE COUGH. WHAT KIND OF MEDICINE YOU GET ON THIS RUN?
ALL KINDS OF GOOD SHIT. WE'LL CATALOGUE IT TOMORROW. I THINK YOU'VE GOT ENOUGH POINTS TO HAVE YOUR PICK.
THANK YOU, NEGAN.
WELCOME HOME, SIR. I SAW THE TRUCKS FROM THE WINDOWS ON LEVEL FIVE-- I HAD TO SEE YOU RIGHT AWAY.
THERE'S BEEN A SITUATION... BUT FIRST, IS THAT GUNFIRE SOMETHING TO BE CONCERNED ABOUT?
NOT ANYMORE. LEAD THE WAY, CARSON.

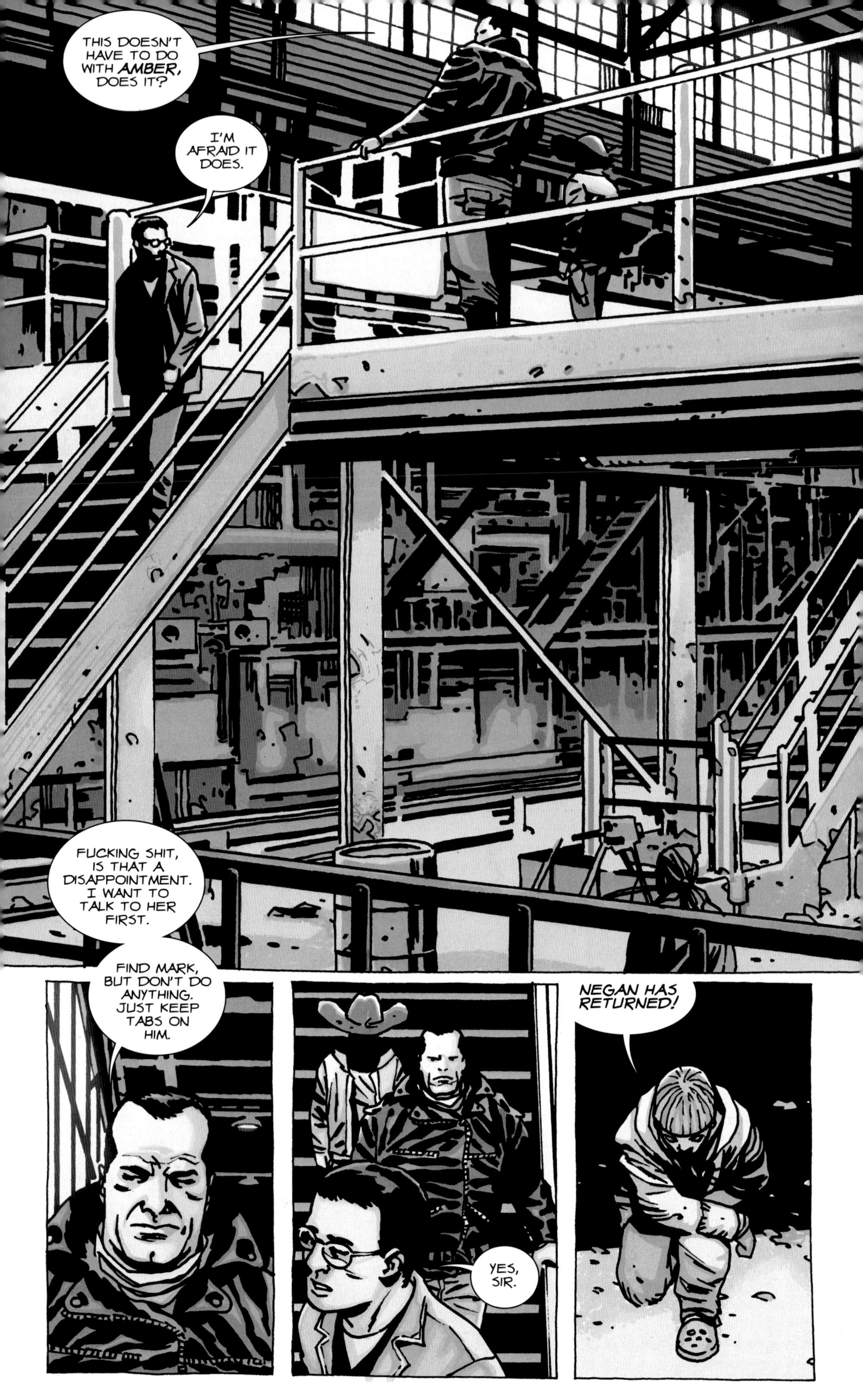
THIS DOESN'T HAVE TO DO WITH AMBER, DOES IT?
I'M AFRAID IT DOES.
FUCKING SHIT, IS THAT A DISAPPOINTMENT. I WANT TO TALK TO HER FIRST.
FIND MARK, BUT DON'T DO ANYTHING. JUST KEEP TABS ON HIM.
YES, SIR.
NEGAN HAS RETURNED!

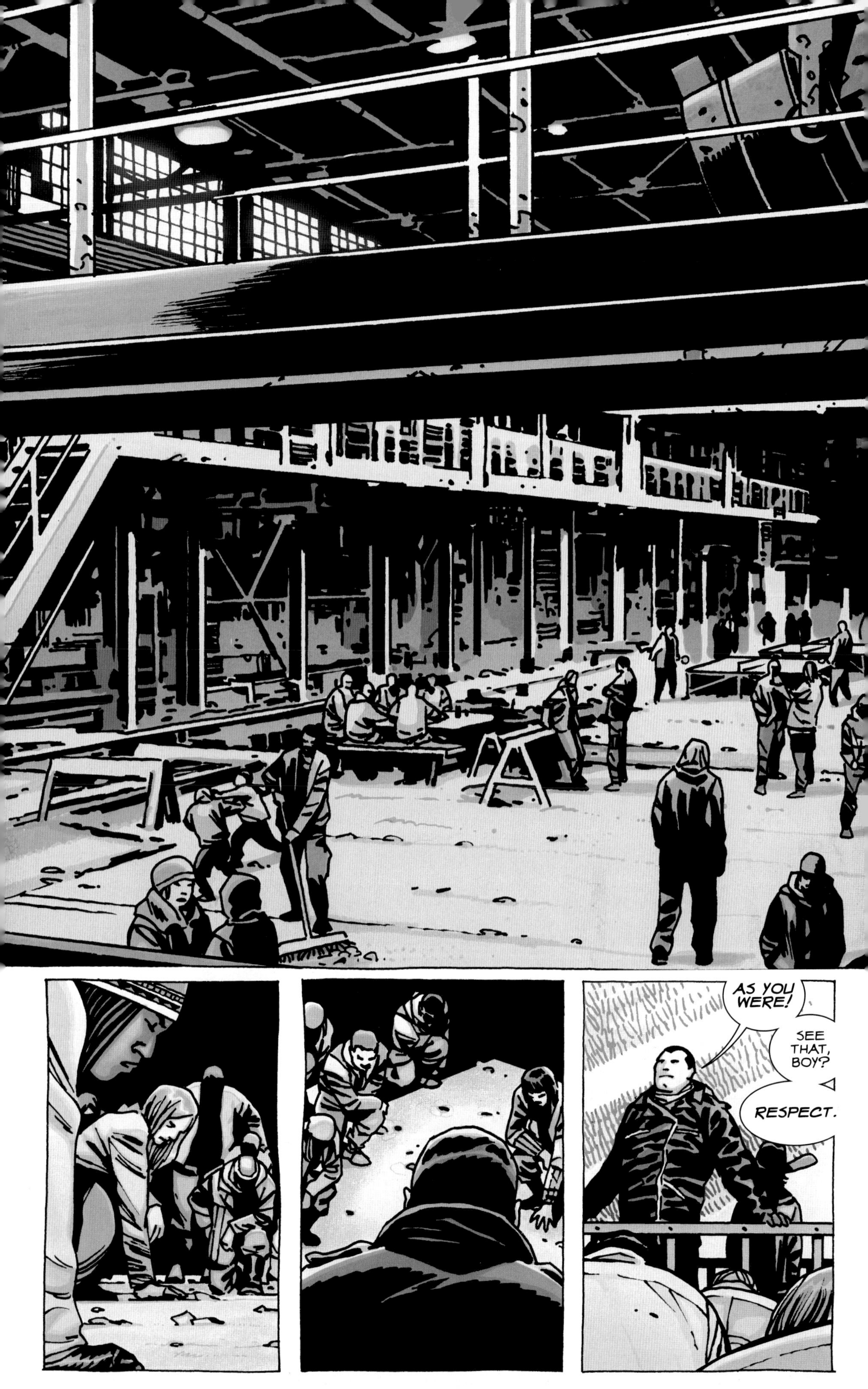
AS YOU WERE!
SEE THAT, BOY?
RESPECT.

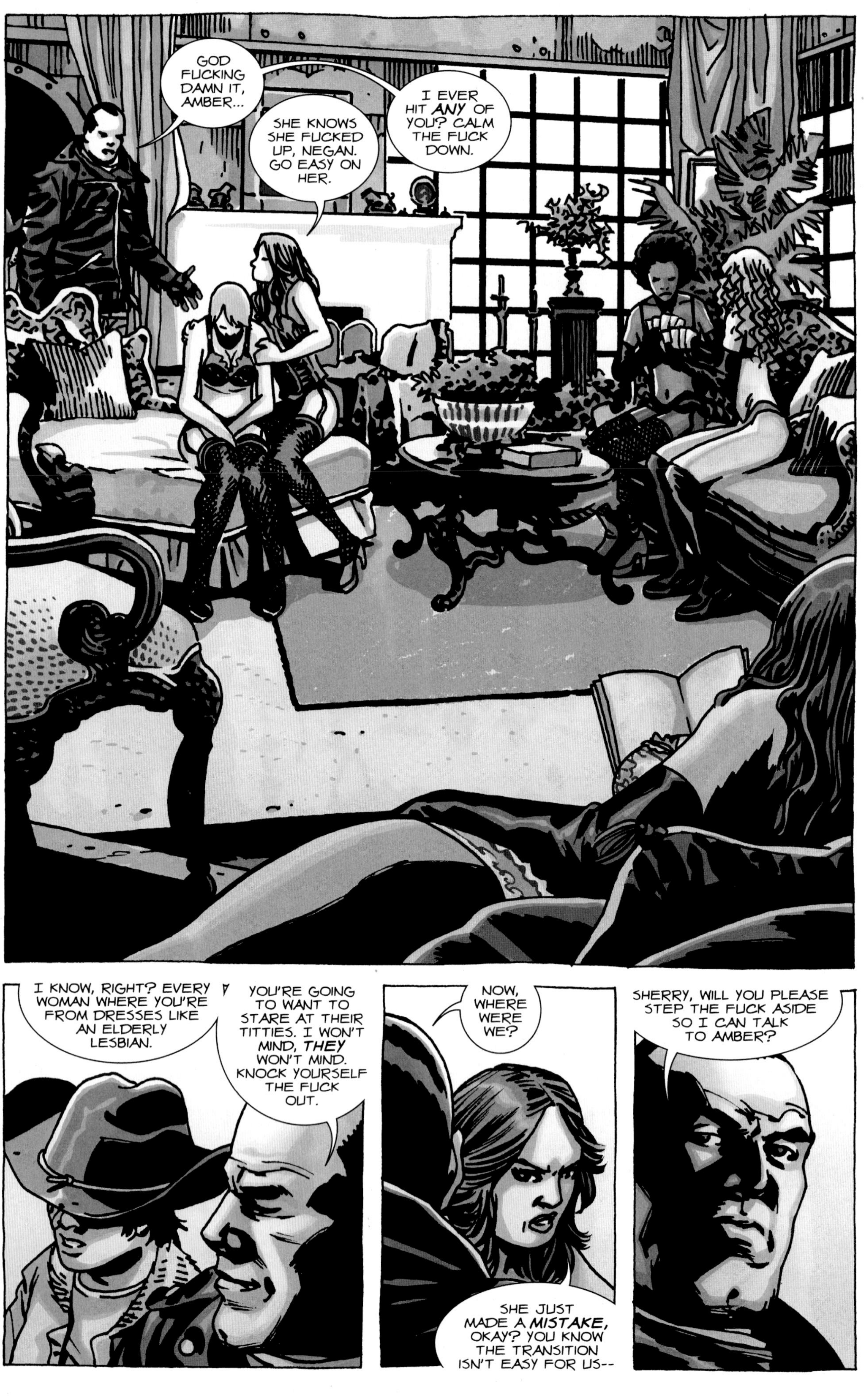
GOD FUCKING DAMN IT, AMBER...
SHE KNOWS SHE FUCKED UP, NEGAN. GO EASY ON HER.
I EVER HIT ANY OF YOU? CALM THE FUCK DOWN.
I KNOW, RIGHT? EVERY WOMAN WHERE YOU'RE FROM DRESSES LIKE AN ELDERLY LESBIAN.
YOU'RE GOING TO WANT TO STARE AT THEIR TITTIES. I WON'T MIND, THEY WON'T MIND. KNOCK YOURSELF THE FUCK OUT.
NOW, WHERE WERE WE?
SHE JUST MADE A MISTAKE, OKAY? YOU KNOW THE TRANSITION ISN'T EASY FOR US--
SHERRY, WILL YOU PLEASE STEP THE FUCK ASIDE SO I CAN TALK TO AMBER?

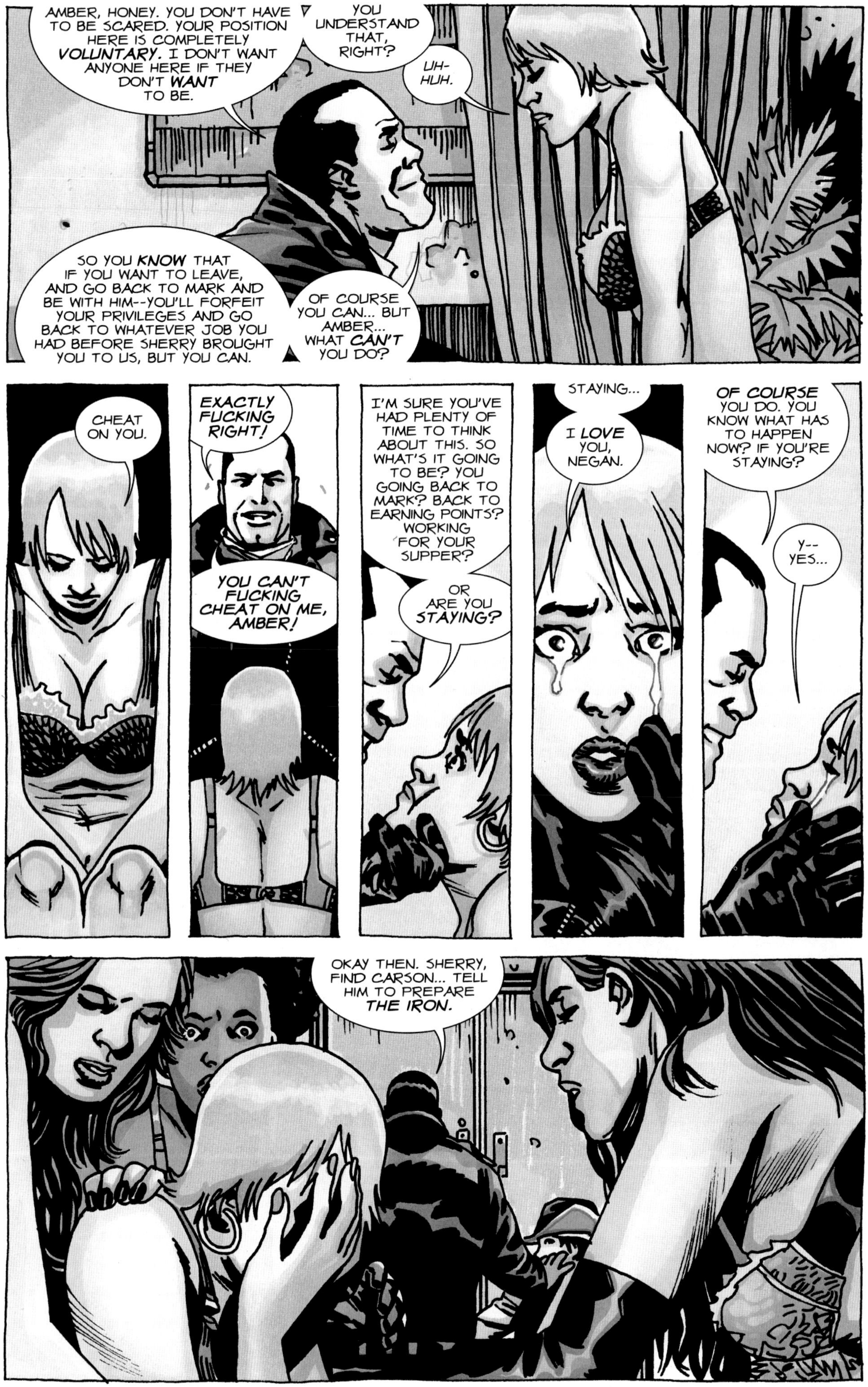
AMBER, HONEY. YOU DON'T HAVE TO BE SCARED. YOUR POSITION HERE IS COMPLETELY VOLUNTARY. I DON'T WANT ANYONE HERE IF THEY DON'T WANT TO BE.
YOU UNDERSTAND THAT, RIGHT?
UH-HUH.
SO YOU KNOW THAT IF YOU WANT TO LEAVE, AND GO BACK TO MARK AND BE WITH HIM--YOU'LL FORFEIT YOUR PRIVILEGES AND GO BACK TO WHATEVER JOB YOU HAD BEFORE SHERRY BROUGHT YOU TO US, BUT YOU CAN.
OF COURSE YOU CAN... BUT AMBER... WHAT CAN'T YOU DO?
CHEAT ON YOU.
EXACTLY FUCKING RIGHT!
YOU CAN'T FUCKING CHEAT ON ME, AMBER!
I'M SURE YOU'VE HAD PLENTY OF TIME TO THINK ABOUT THIS. SO WHAT'S IT GOING TO BE? YOU GOING BACK TO MARK? BACK TO EARNING POINTS? WORKING FOR YOUR SUPPER?
OR ARE YOU STAYING?
STAYING...
I LOVE YOU, NEGAN.
OF COURSE YOU DO. YOU KNOW WHAT HAS TO HAPPEN NOW? IF YOU'RE STAYING?
Y-- YES...
OKAY THEN. SHERRY, FIND CARSON... TELL HIM TO PREPARE THE IRON.

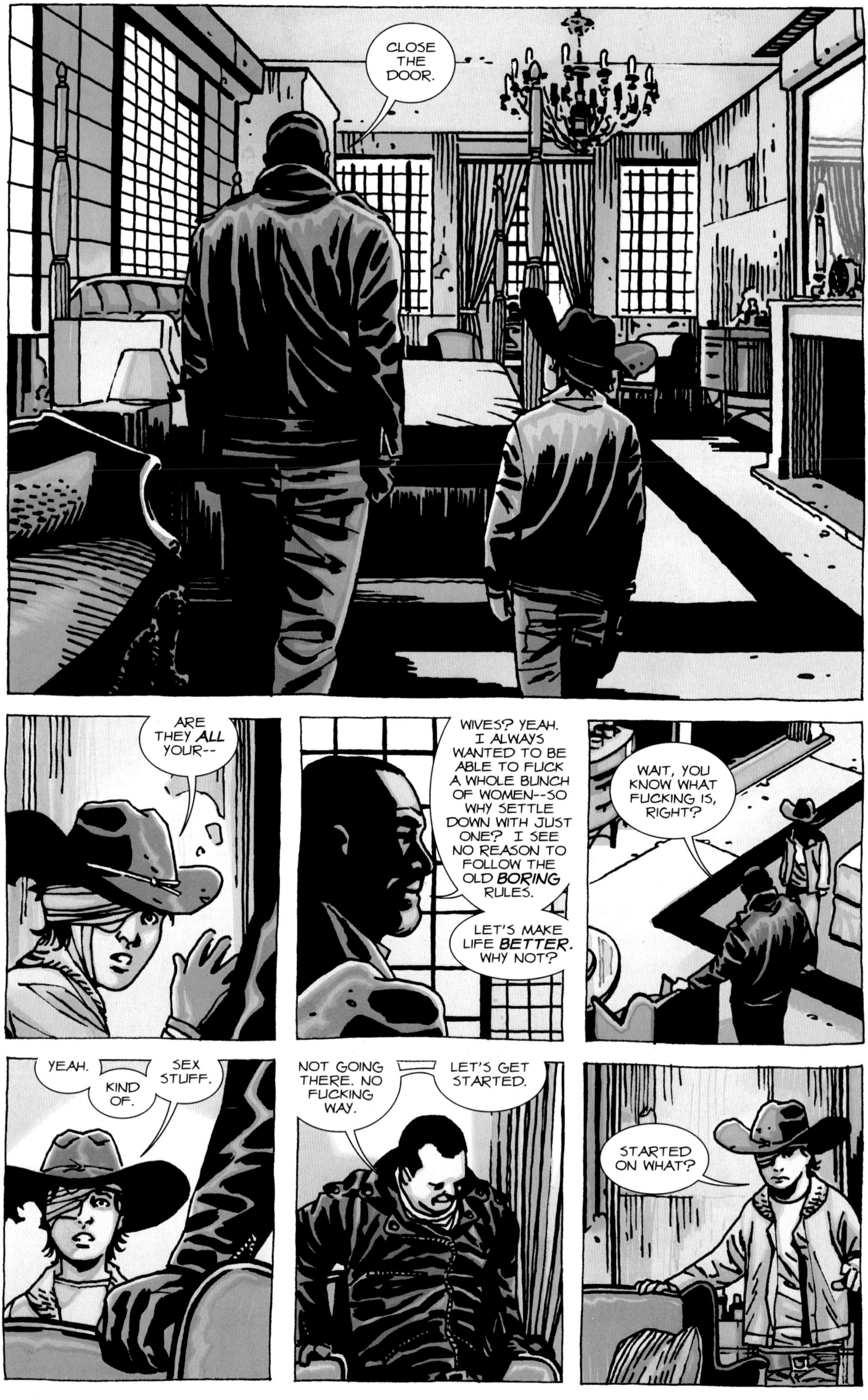
CLOSE THE DOOR.
ARE THEY ALL YOUR--
WIVES? YEAH. I ALWAYS WANTED TO BE ABLE TO FUCK A WHOLE BUNCH OF WOMEN--SO WHY SETTLE DOWN WITH JUST ONE? I SEE NO REASON TO FOLLOW THE OLD BORING RULES.
LET'S MAKE LIFE BETTER. WHY NOT?
WAIT, YOU KNOW WHAT FUCKING IS, RIGHT?
YEAH.
KIND OF.
SEX STUFF.
NOT GOING THERE. NO FUCKING WAY.
LET'S GET STARTED.
STARTED ON WHAT?

I'D LIKE TO GET TO KNOW YOU A LITTLE BETTER, CARL.

FIRST, I WANT TO TELL YOU HOW MOTHERFUCKING **SMART** YOU ARE, JUST IN CASE YOU DON'T ALREADY KNOW. YOU'RE WHAT, **TWELVE?** WHO CARES?

I'D EXPECT A KID YOUR AGE TO BE RUNNING AWAY, TRYING TO GET OUT--HAVING MY PEOPLE CHASE YOU ALL OVER THIS MILL. BUT YOU STAYED RIGHT WITH ME. I BARELY EVEN HAD TO LOOK AT YOU.

BECAUSE YOU **KNEW** THAT IF YOU FUCKED SOMETHING ELSE UP, I'D CHASE YOU DOWN AND BREAK YOUR LITTLE KID NECK. RIGHT?

I--

DOESN'T MATTER.

YOU KILLED LIKE FIVE OR SIX OF MY MEN JUST NOW--SO MANY I DIDN'T EVEN GET A GOOD FUCKING COUNT.

THIS CAN'T GO UNPUNISHED, SO--

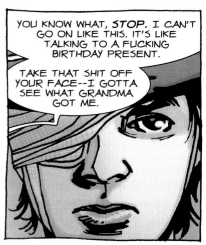

YOU KNOW WHAT, **STOP.** I CAN'T GO ON LIKE THIS. IT'S LIKE TALKING TO A FUCKING BIRTHDAY PRESENT.

TAKE THAT SHIT OFF YOUR FACE--I GOTTA SEE WHAT GRANDMA GOT ME.

NO.

SIX MEN. PUNISHMENT.

REALLY WANT TO PISS ME OFF?

THAT'S BETTER.

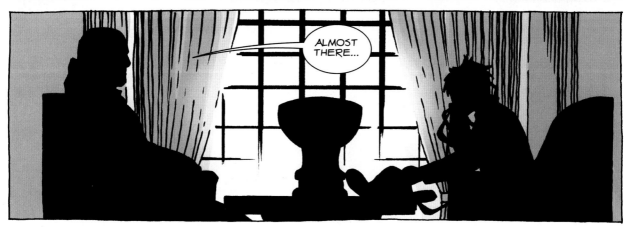

ALMOST THERE...

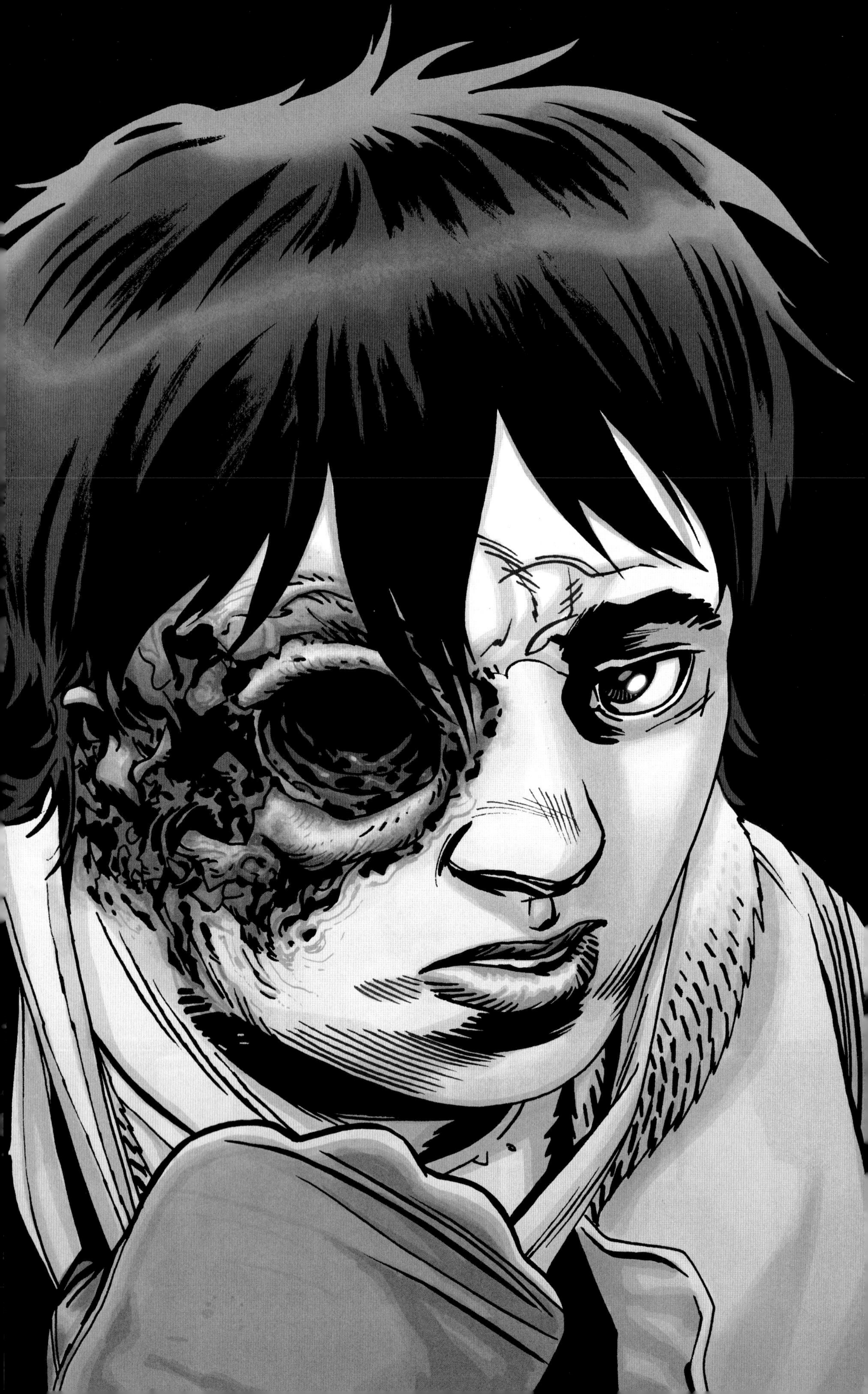

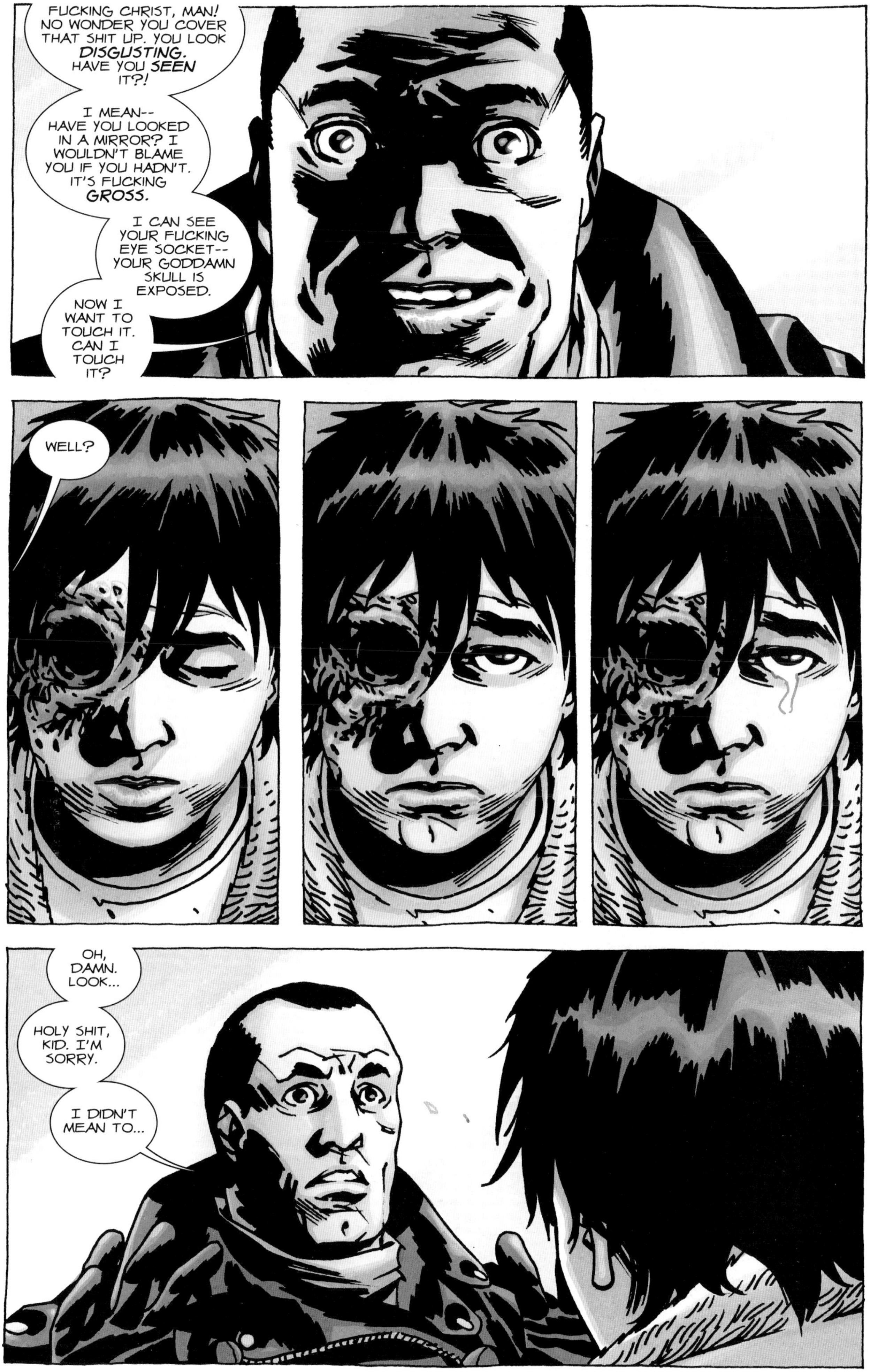
FUCKING CHRIST, MAN! NO WONDER YOU COVER THAT SHIT UP. YOU LOOK **DISGUSTING.** HAVE YOU **SEEN** IT?!
I MEAN-- HAVE YOU LOOKED IN A MIRROR? I WOULDN'T BLAME YOU IF YOU HADN'T. IT'S FUCKING **GROSS.**
I CAN SEE YOUR FUCKING EYE SOCKET-- YOUR GODDAMN SKULL IS EXPOSED.
NOW I WANT TO TOUCH IT. CAN I TOUCH IT?
WELL?
OH, DAMN. LOOK...
HOLY SHIT, KID. I'M SORRY.
I DIDN'T MEAN TO...

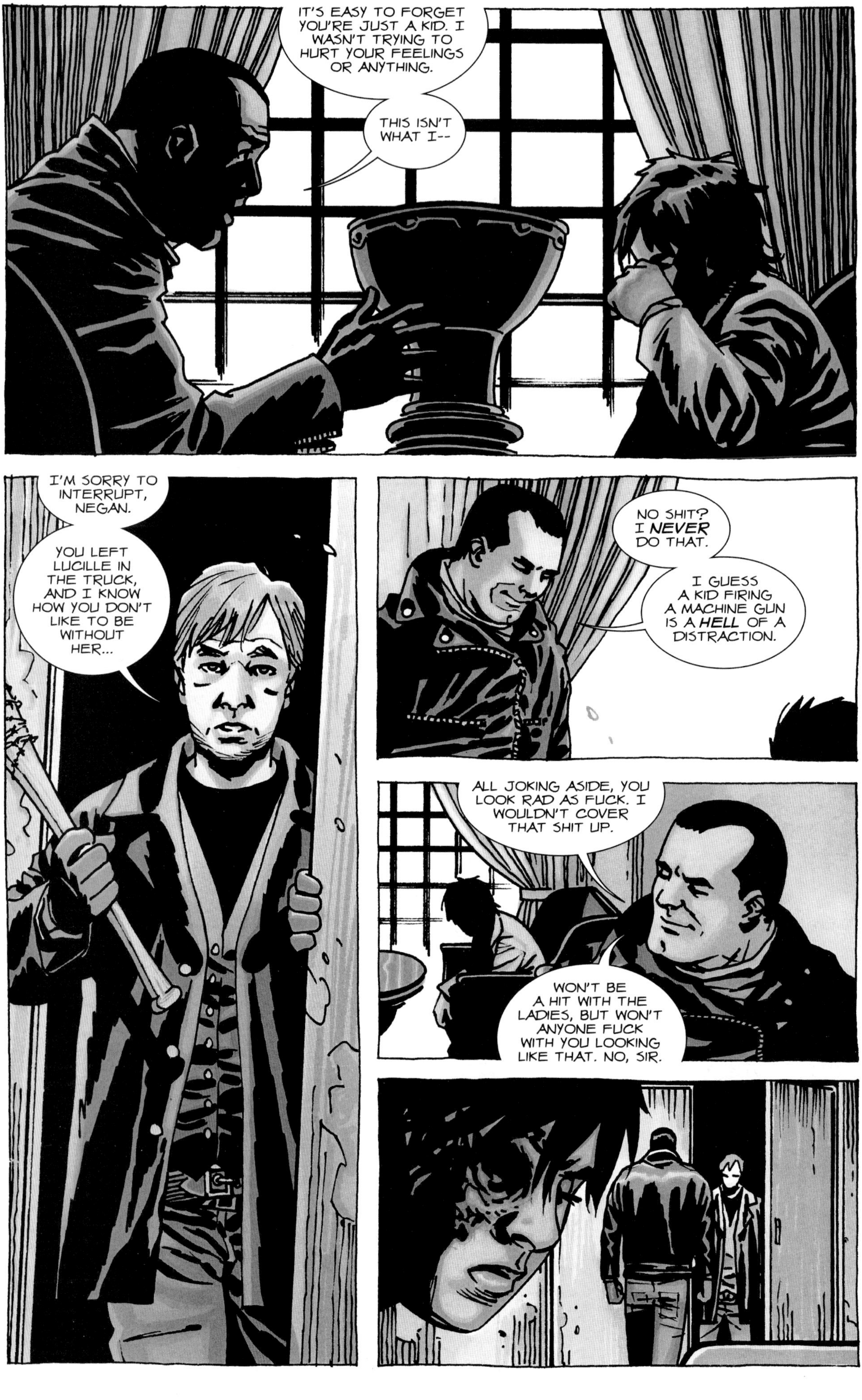
IT'S EASY TO FORGET YOU'RE JUST A KID. I WASN'T TRYING TO HURT YOUR FEELINGS OR ANYTHING.
THIS ISN'T WHAT I--
I'M SORRY TO INTERRUPT, NEGAN.
YOU LEFT LUCILLE IN THE TRUCK, AND I KNOW HOW YOU DON'T LIKE TO BE WITHOUT HER...
NO SHIT? I NEVER DO THAT.
I GUESS A KID FIRING A MACHINE GUN IS A HELL OF A DISTRACTION.
ALL JOKING ASIDE, YOU LOOK RAD AS FUCK. I WOULDN'T COVER THAT SHIT UP.
WON'T BE A HIT WITH THE LADIES, BUT WON'T ANYONE FUCK WITH YOU LOOKING LIKE THAT. NO, SIR.

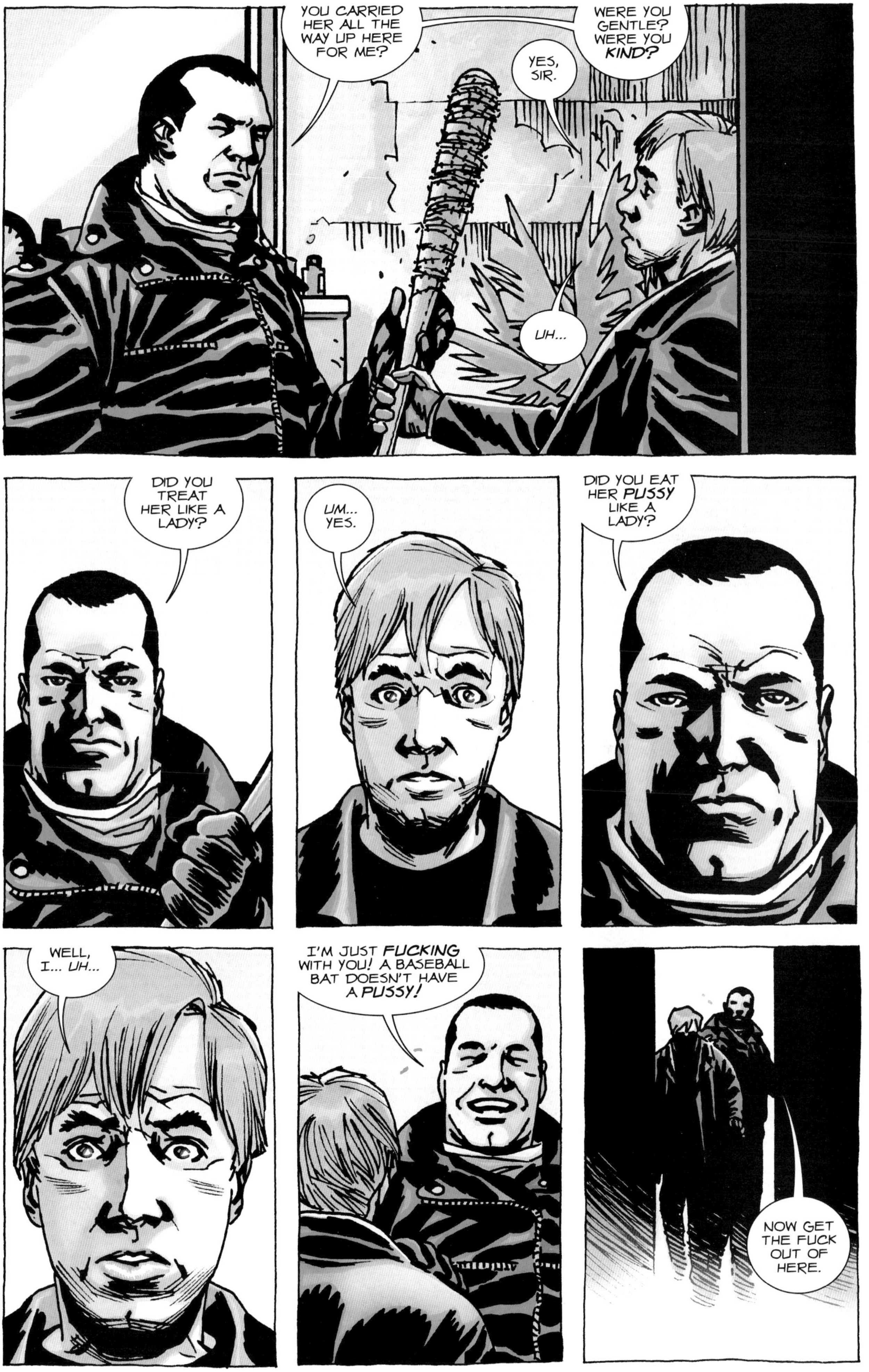
YOU CARRIED HER ALL THE WAY UP HERE FOR ME?
YES, SIR.
WERE YOU GENTLE? WERE YOU KIND?
UH...
DID YOU TREAT HER LIKE A LADY?
UM... YES.
DID YOU EAT HER PUSSY LIKE A LADY?
WELL, I... UH...
I'M JUST FUCKING WITH YOU! A BASEBALL BAT DOESN'T HAVE A PUSSY!
NOW GET THE FUCK OUT OF HERE.

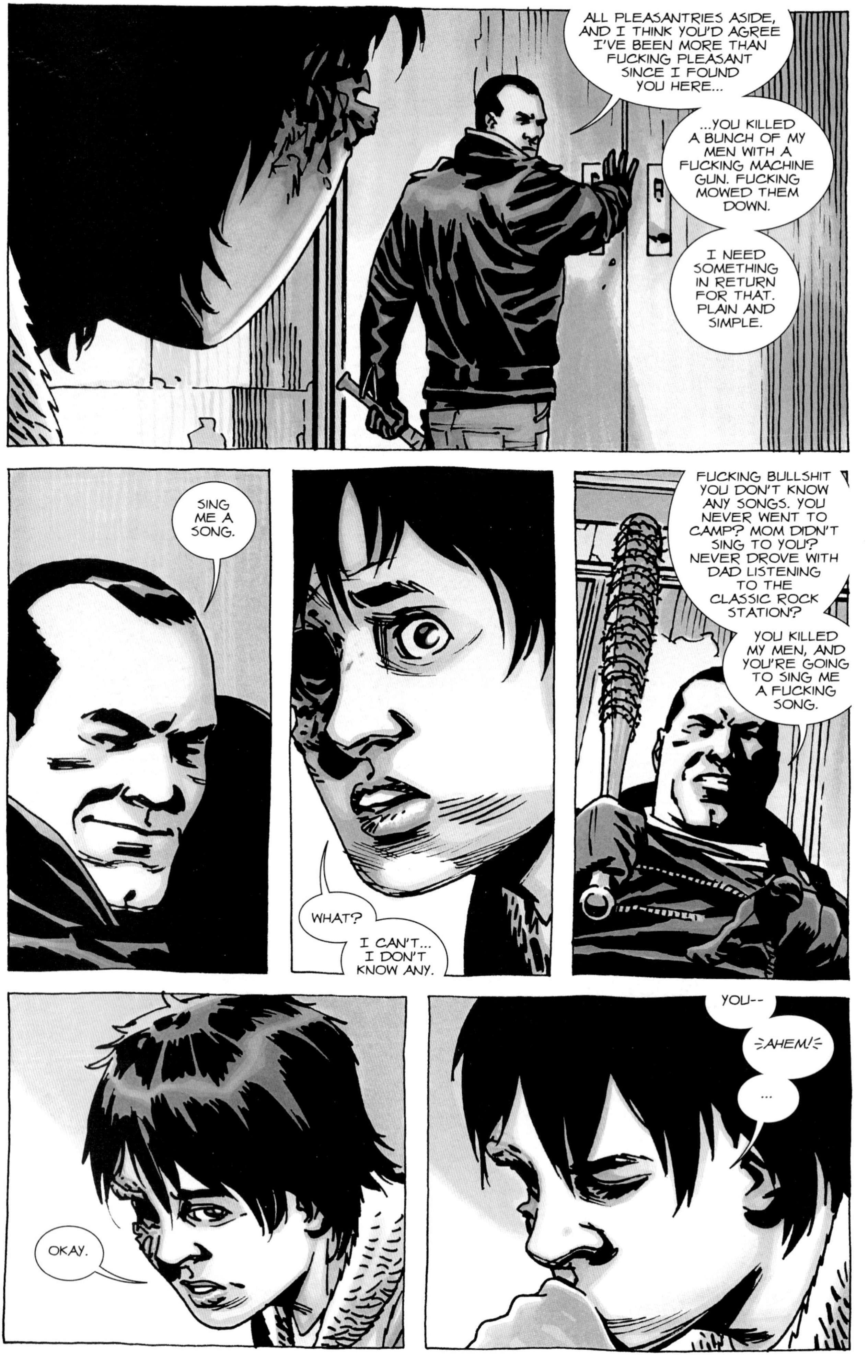
ALL PLEASANTRIES ASIDE, AND I THINK YOU'D AGREE I'VE BEEN MORE THAN FUCKING PLEASANT SINCE I FOUND YOU HERE...
...YOU KILLED A BUNCH OF MY MEN WITH A FUCKING MACHINE GUN. FUCKING MOWED THEM DOWN.
I NEED SOMETHING IN RETURN FOR THAT. PLAIN AND SIMPLE.
SING ME A SONG.
WHAT?
I CAN'T... I DON'T KNOW ANY.
FUCKING BULLSHIT YOU DON'T KNOW ANY SONGS. YOU NEVER WENT TO CAMP? MOM DIDN'T SING TO YOU? NEVER DROVE WITH DAD LISTENING TO THE CLASSIC ROCK STATION?
YOU KILLED MY MEN, AND YOU'RE GOING TO SING ME A FUCKING SONG.
OKAY.
YOU--
AHEM!
...

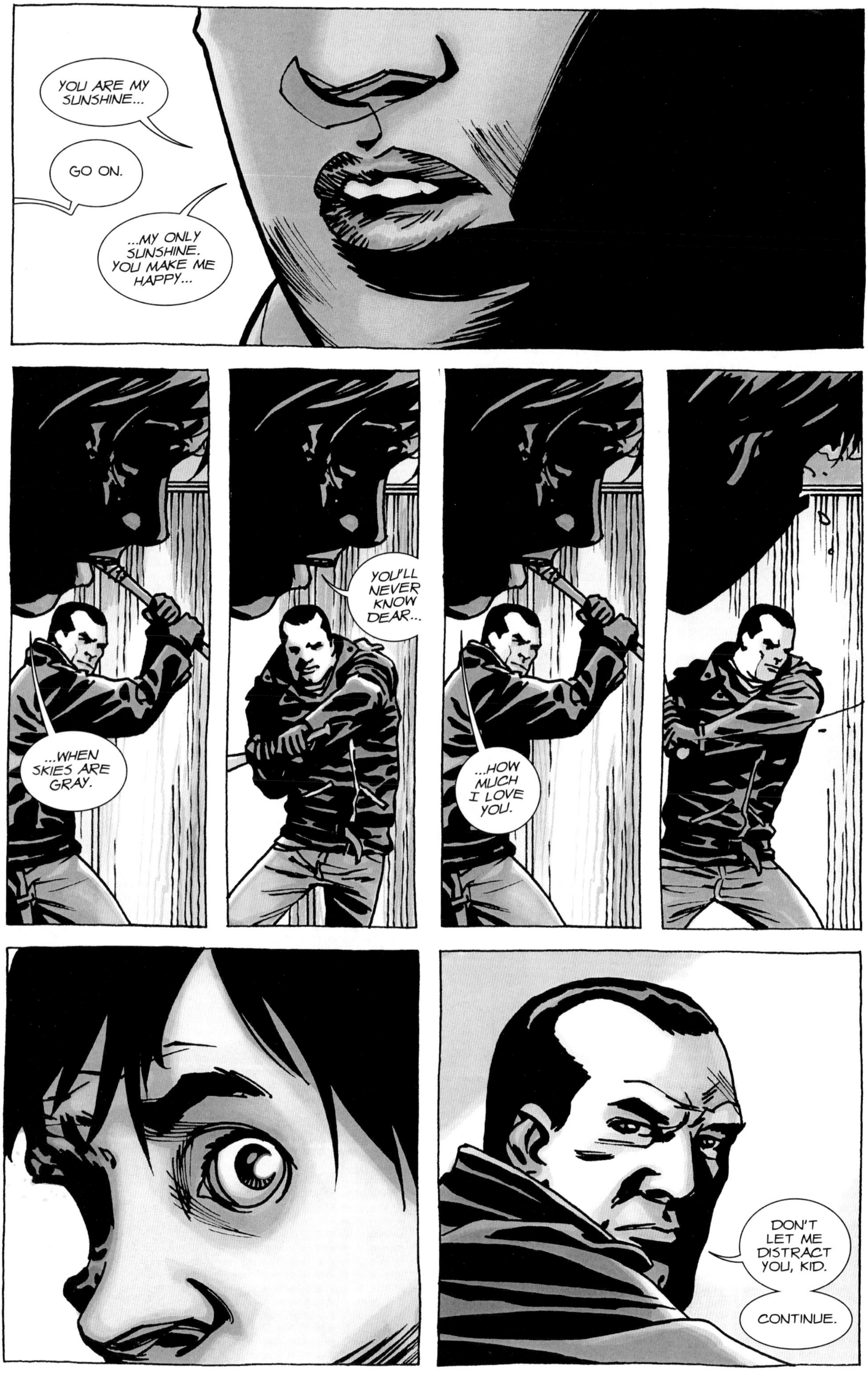
YOU ARE MY SUNSHINE...
GO ON.
...MY ONLY SUNSHINE. YOU MAKE ME HAPPY...
...WHEN SKIES ARE GRAY.
YOU'LL NEVER KNOW DEAR...
...HOW MUCH I LOVE YOU.
DON'T LET ME DISTRACT YOU, KID.
CONTINUE.

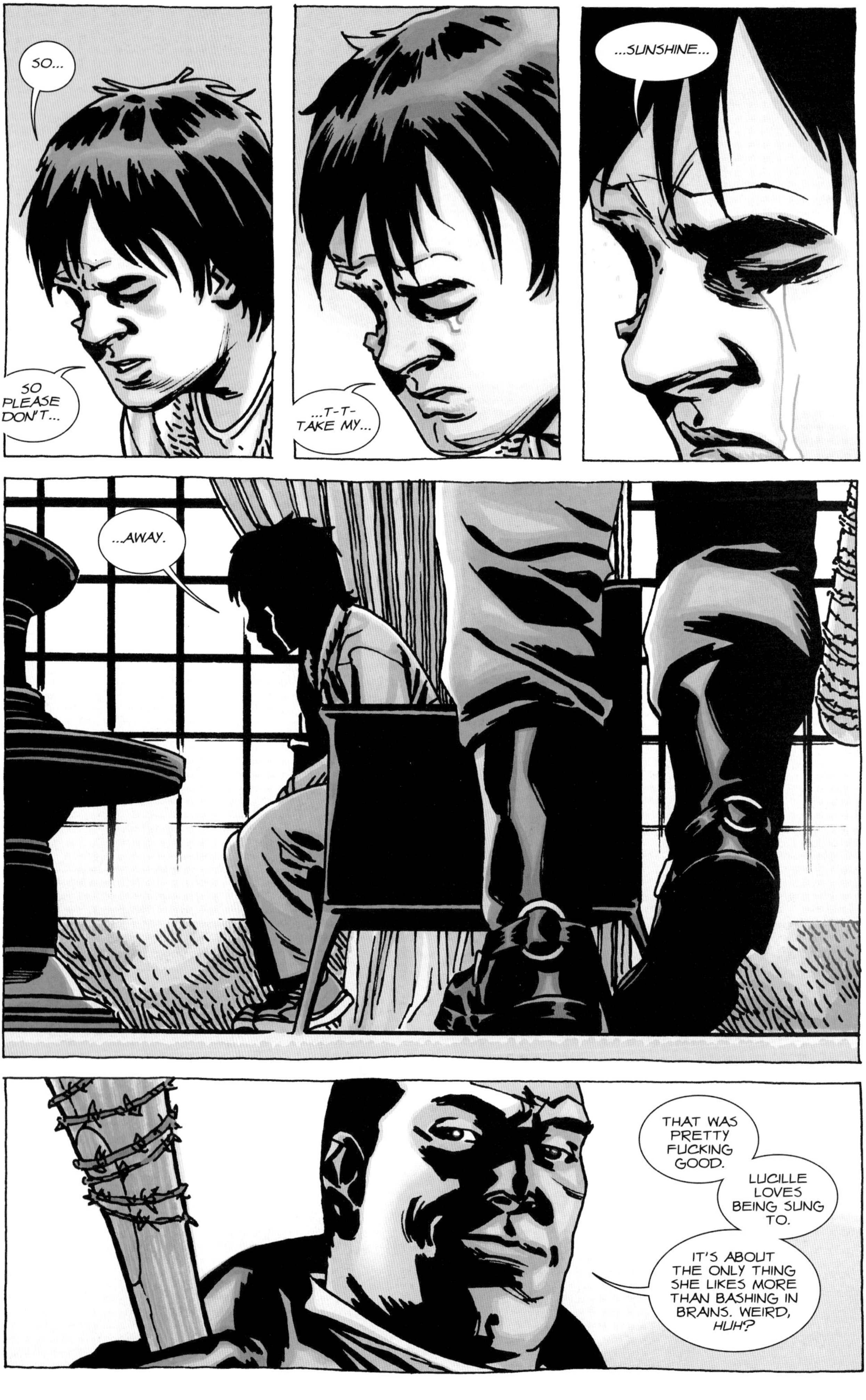
SO...
SO PLEASE DON'T...
...T-T- TAKE MY...
...SUNSHINE...
...AWAY.
THAT WAS PRETTY FUCKING GOOD.
LUCILLE LOVES BEING SUNG TO.
IT'S ABOUT THE ONLY THING SHE LIKES MORE THAN BASHING IN BRAINS. WEIRD, HUH?

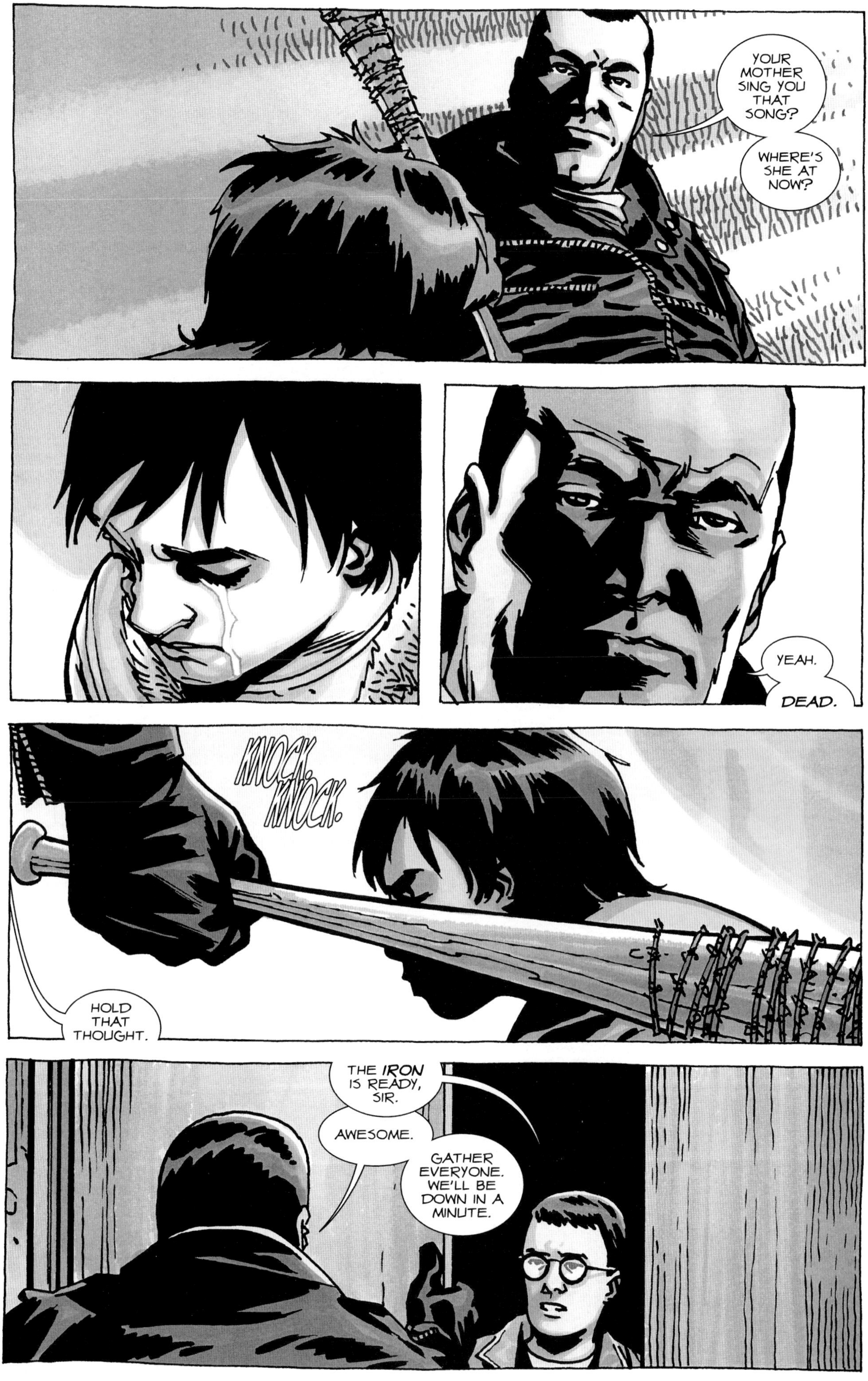
YOUR MOTHER SING YOU THAT SONG?
WHERE'S SHE AT NOW?
YEAH.
DEAD.
KNOCK. KNOCK.
HOLD THAT THOUGHT.
THE IRON IS READY, SIR.
AWESOME.
GATHER EVERYONE. WE'LL BE DOWN IN A MINUTE.

WE'RE ALL HERE, NEGAN. WE'RE READY TO BEGIN.

AIN'T THAT GRAND.

HOLD THIS FOR ME.

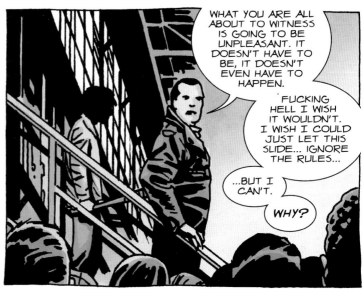

WHAT YOU ARE ALL ABOUT TO WITNESS IS GOING TO BE UNPLEASANT. IT DOESN'T HAVE TO BE, IT DOESN'T EVEN HAVE TO HAPPEN.

FUCKING HELL I WISH IT WOULDN'T. I WISH I COULD JUST LET THIS SLIDE... IGNORE THE RULES...

...BUT I CAN'T.

WHY?

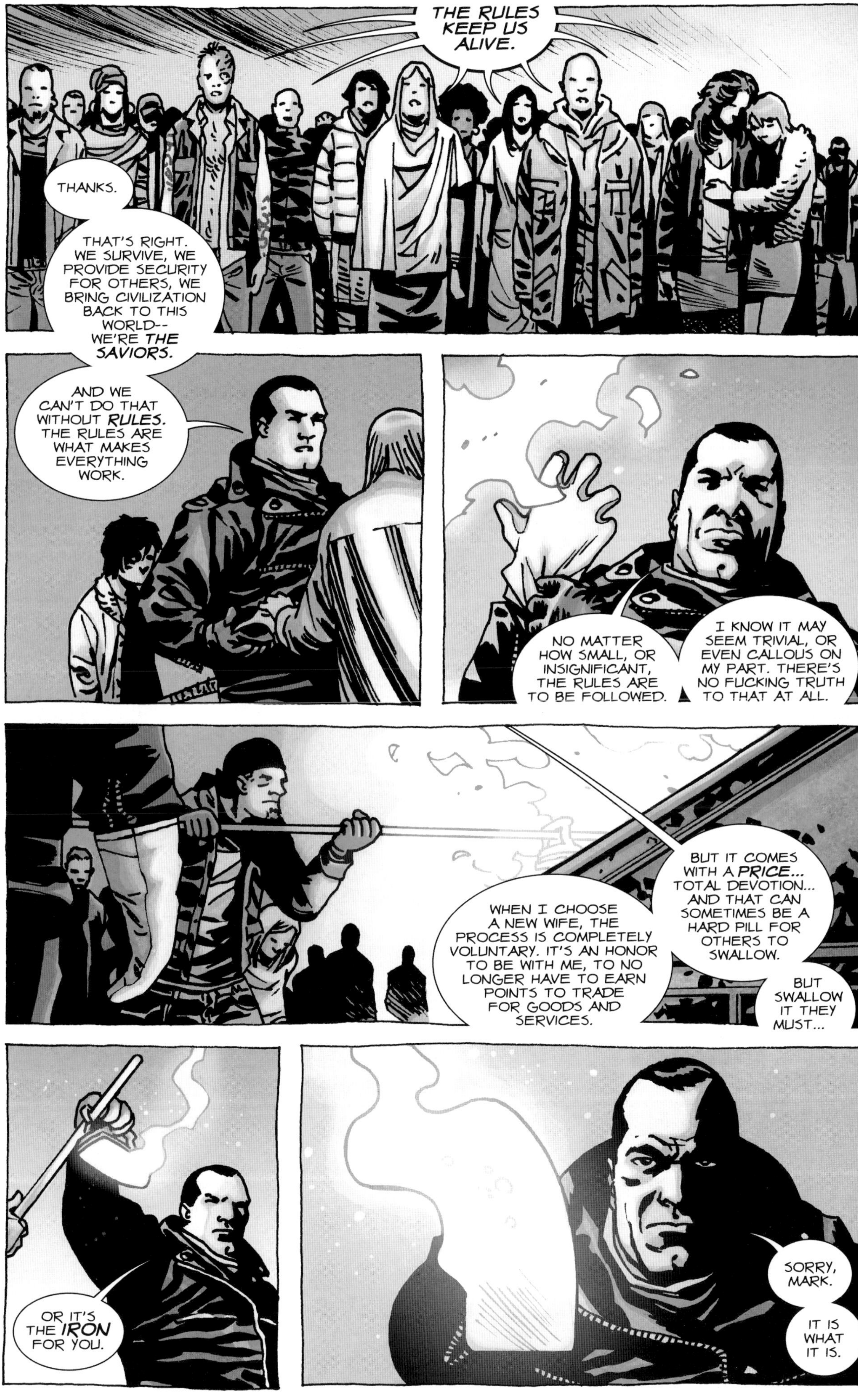
THE RULES KEEP US ALIVE.
THANKS.
THAT'S RIGHT. WE SURVIVE, WE PROVIDE SECURITY FOR OTHERS, WE BRING CIVILIZATION BACK TO THIS WORLD-- WE'RE *THE SAVIORS.*
AND WE CAN'T DO THAT WITHOUT *RULES.* THE RULES ARE WHAT MAKES EVERYTHING WORK.
NO MATTER HOW SMALL, OR INSIGNIFICANT, THE RULES ARE TO BE FOLLOWED.
I KNOW IT MAY SEEM TRIVIAL, OR EVEN CALLOUS ON MY PART. THERE'S NO FUCKING TRUTH TO THAT AT ALL.
WHEN I CHOOSE A NEW WIFE, THE PROCESS IS COMPLETELY VOLUNTARY. IT'S AN HONOR TO BE WITH ME, TO NO LONGER HAVE TO EARN POINTS TO TRADE FOR GOODS AND SERVICES.
BUT IT COMES WITH A *PRICE...* TOTAL DEVOTION... AND THAT CAN SOMETIMES BE A HARD PILL FOR OTHERS TO SWALLOW.
BUT SWALLOW IT THEY MUST...
OR IT'S THE *IRON* FOR YOU.
SORRY, MARK.
IT IS WHAT IT IS.

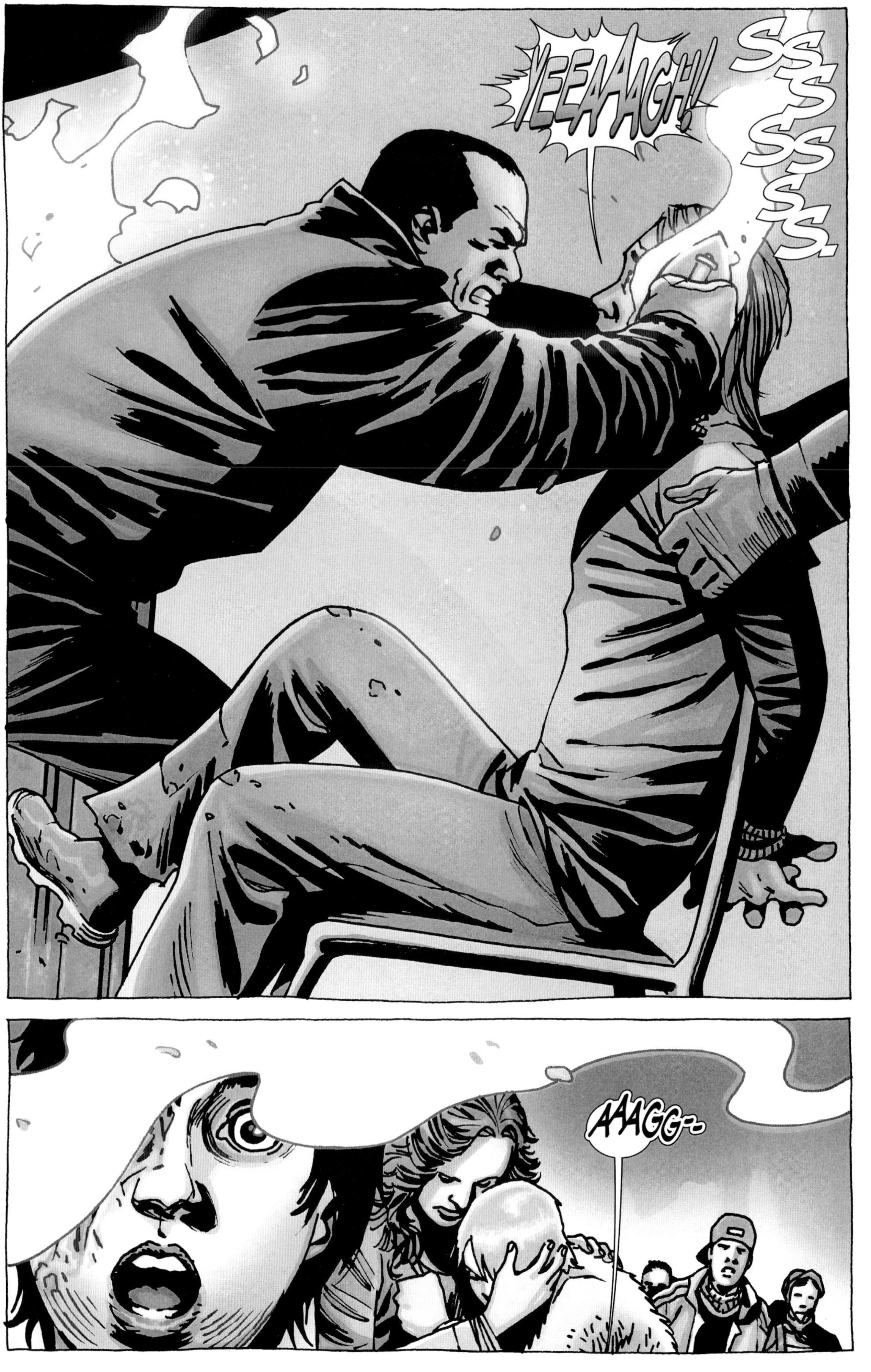

YEEAAAGH!!
SSSSSSS
AAAGG--

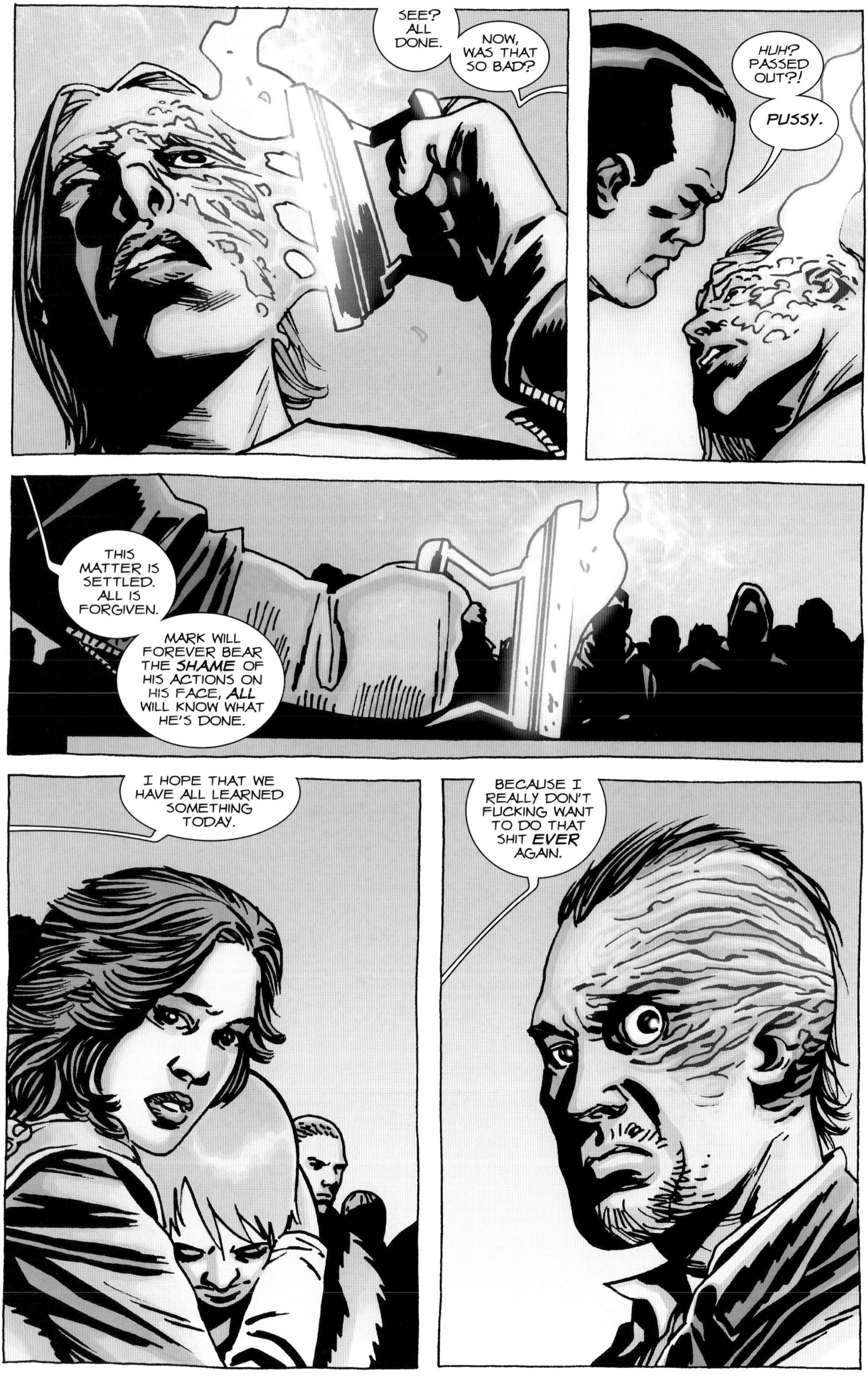
SEE? ALL DONE.
NOW, WAS THAT SO BAD?
HUH? PASSED OUT?!
PUSSY.
THIS MATTER IS SETTLED. ALL IS FORGIVEN.
MARK WILL FOREVER BEAR THE SHAME OF HIS ACTIONS ON HIS FACE, ALL WILL KNOW WHAT HE'S DONE.
I HOPE THAT WE HAVE ALL LEARNED SOMETHING TODAY.
BECAUSE I REALLY DON'T FUCKING WANT TO DO THAT SHIT EVER AGAIN.

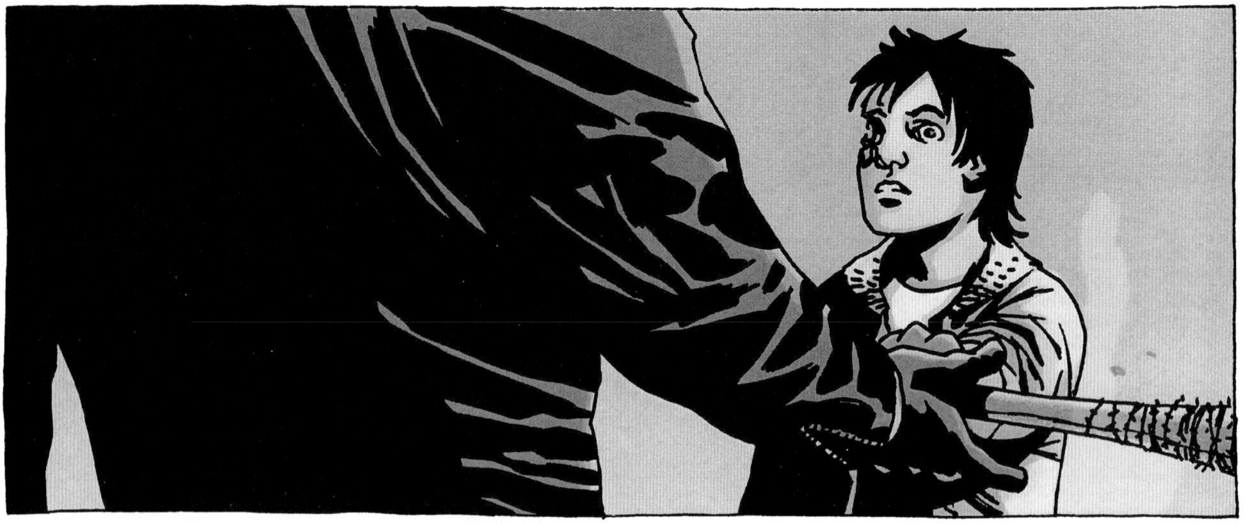

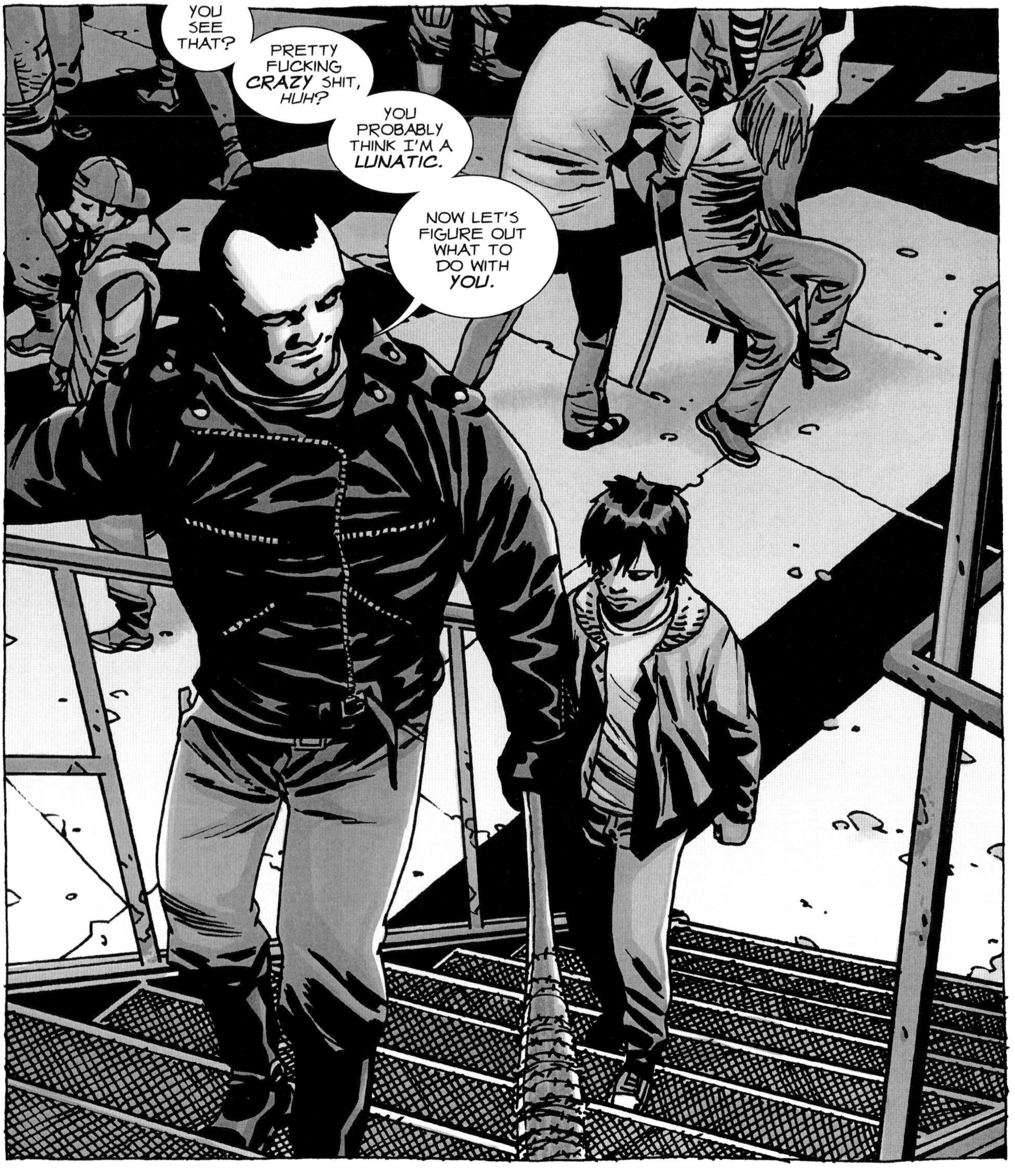
YOU SEE THAT?
PRETTY FUCKING CRAZY SHIT, HUH?
YOU PROBABLY THINK I'M A LUNATIC.
NOW LET'S FIGURE OUT WHAT TO DO WITH YOU.

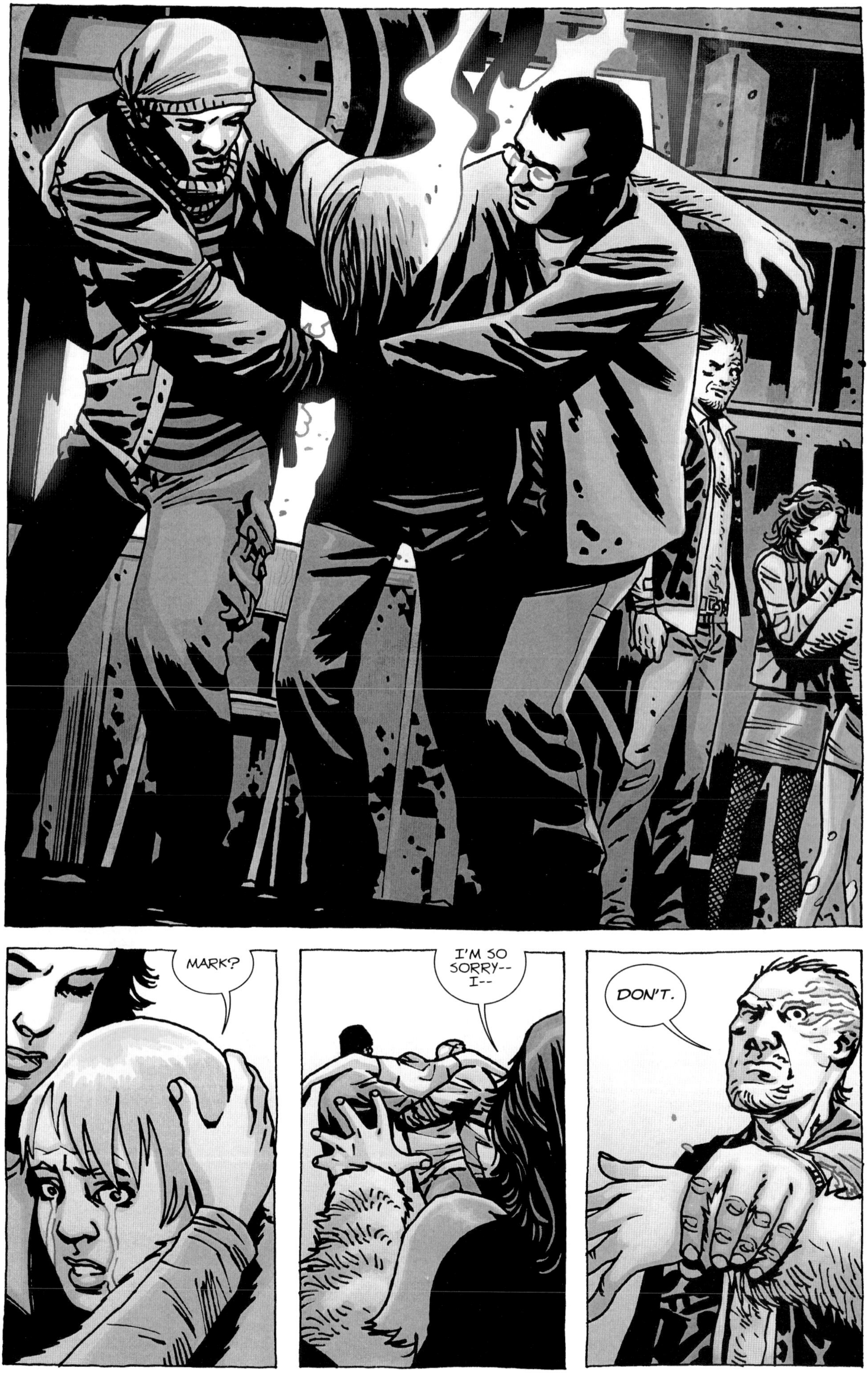
MARK?
I'M SO SORRY-- I--
DON'T.

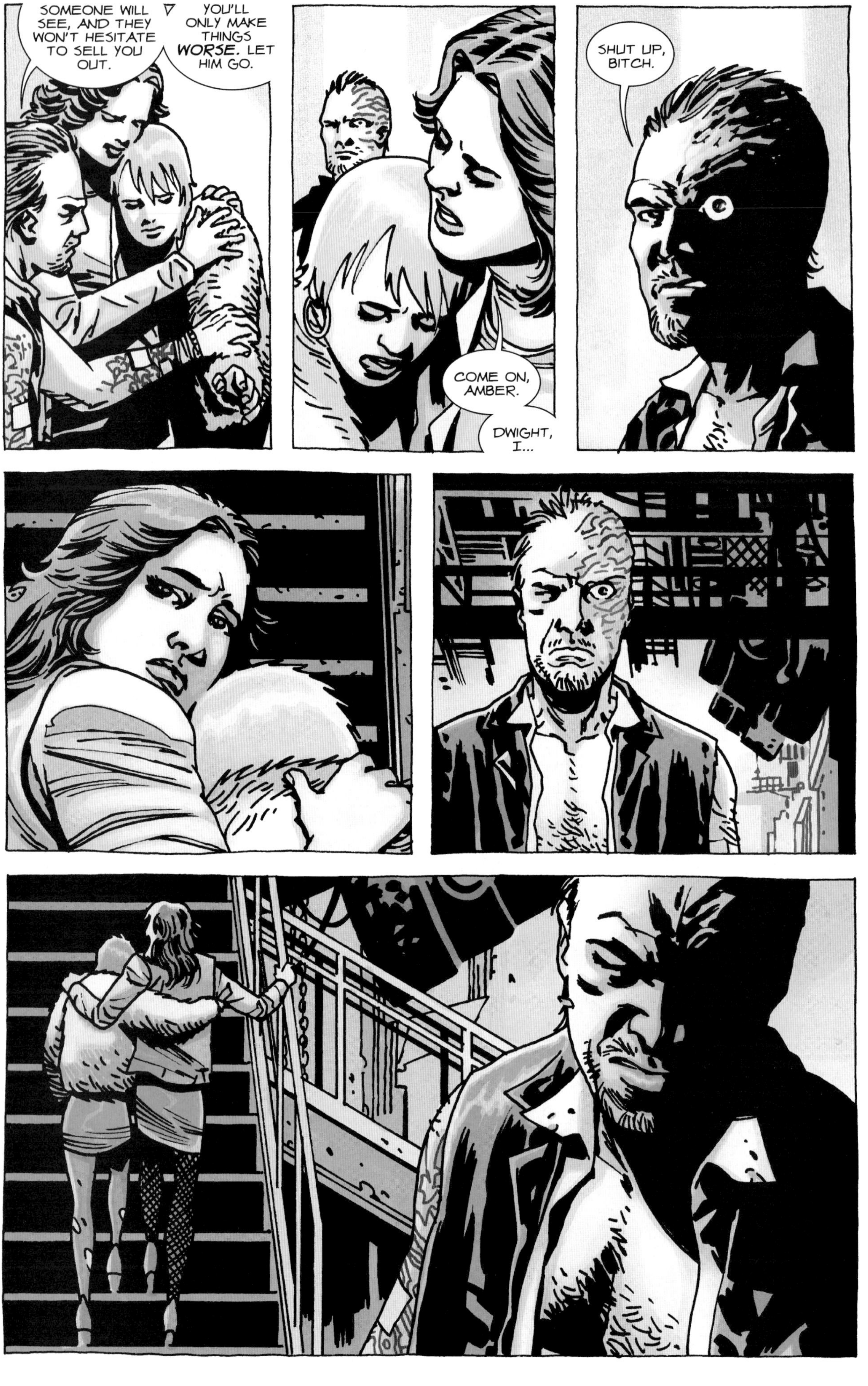
SOMEONE WILL SEE, AND THEY WON'T HESITATE TO SELL YOU OUT.
YOU'LL ONLY MAKE THINGS WORSE. LET HIM GO.
COME ON, AMBER.
DWIGHT, I...
SHUT UP, BITCH.

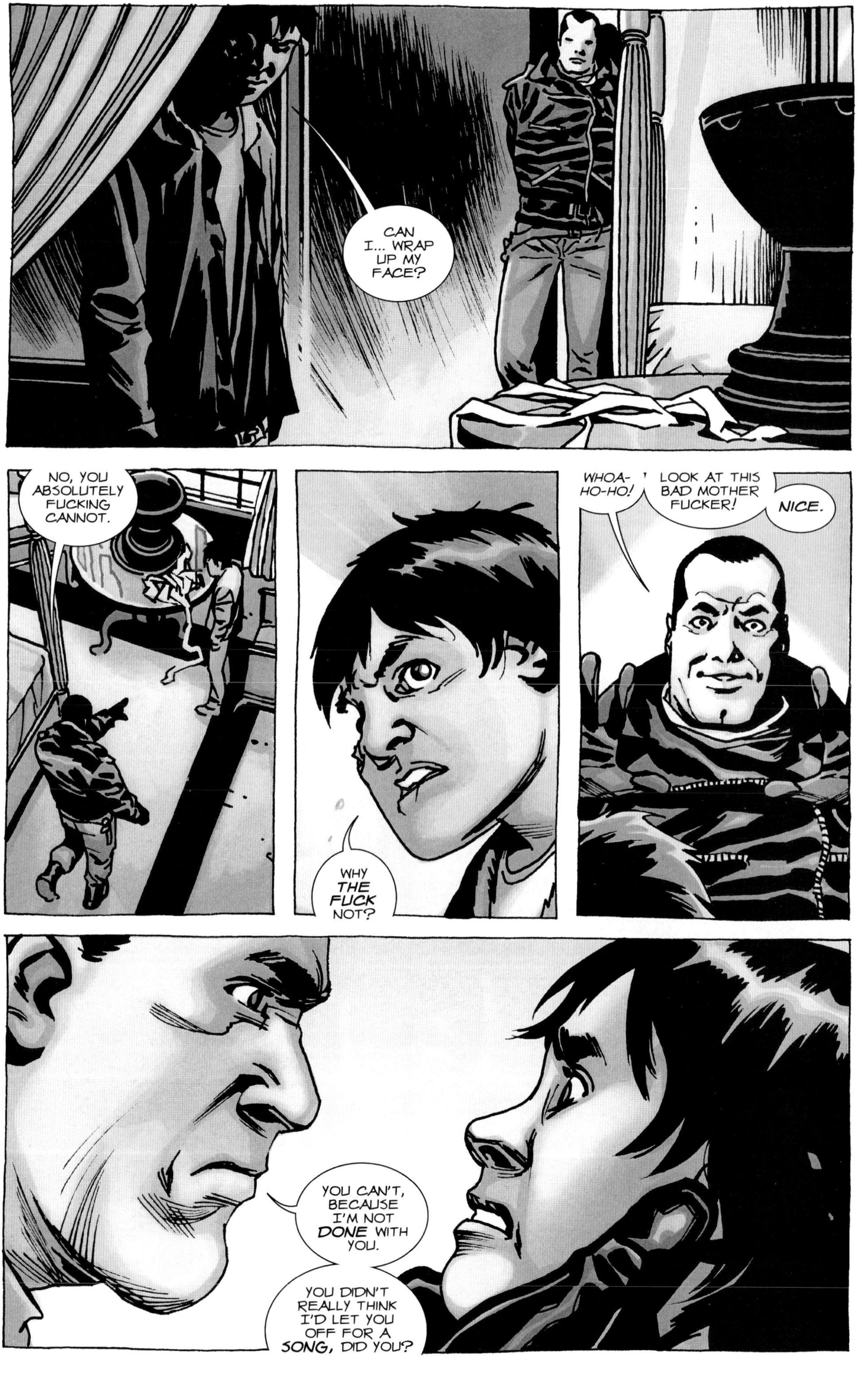
CAN I... WRAP UP MY FACE?
NO, YOU ABSOLUTELY FUCKING CANNOT.
WHY *THE FUCK* NOT?
WHOA-HO-HO!
LOOK AT THIS BAD MOTHER FUCKER!
NICE.
YOU CAN'T, BECAUSE I'M NOT *DONE* WITH YOU.
YOU DIDN'T REALLY THINK I'D LET YOU OFF FOR A *SONG*, DID YOU?

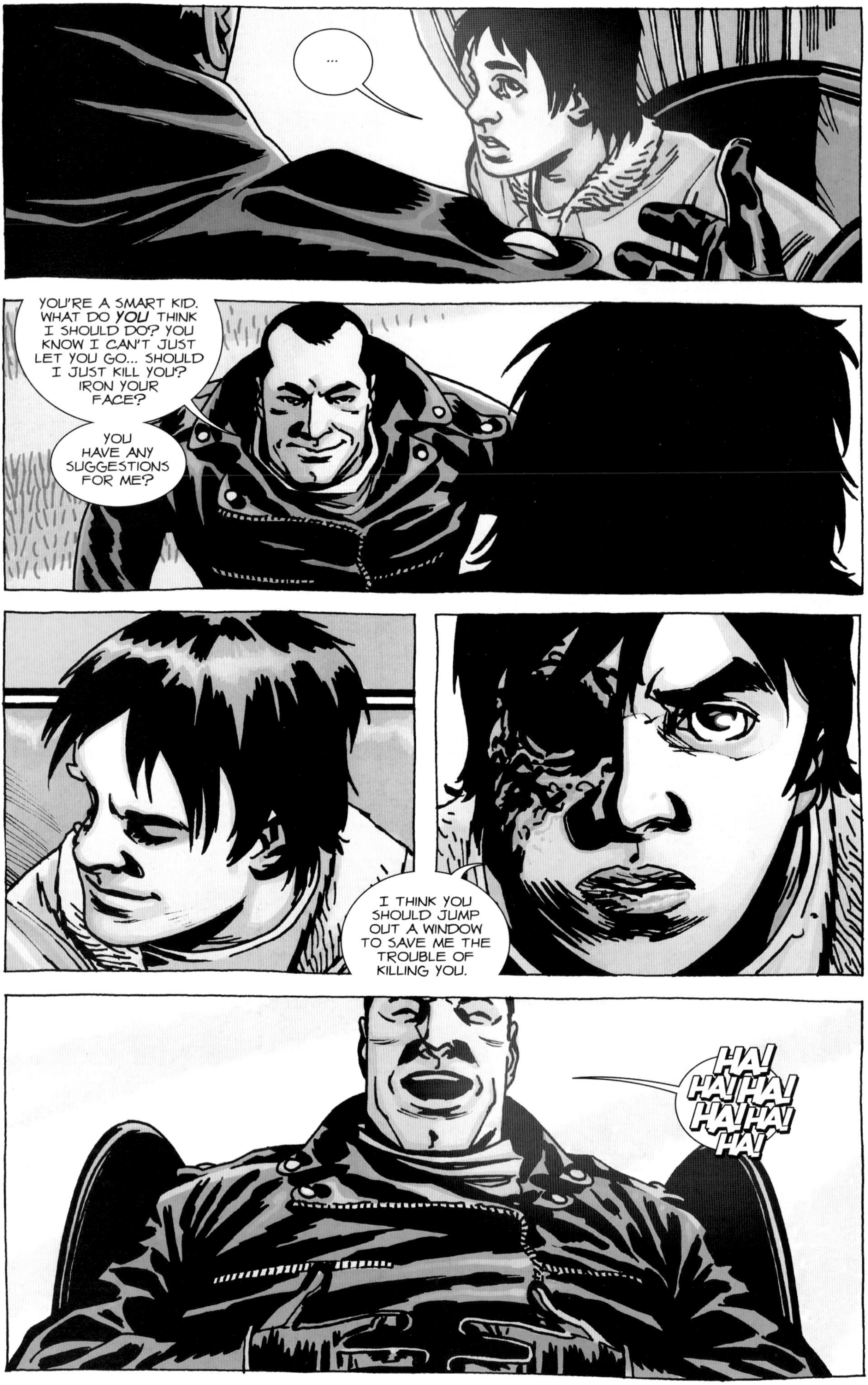
...
YOU'RE A SMART KID. WHAT DO YOU THINK I SHOULD DO? YOU KNOW I CAN'T JUST LET YOU GO... SHOULD I JUST KILL YOU? IRON YOUR FACE?
YOU HAVE ANY SUGGESTIONS FOR ME?
I THINK YOU SHOULD JUMP OUT A WINDOW TO SAVE ME THE TROUBLE OF KILLING YOU.
HA! HA! HA! HA! HA! HA!

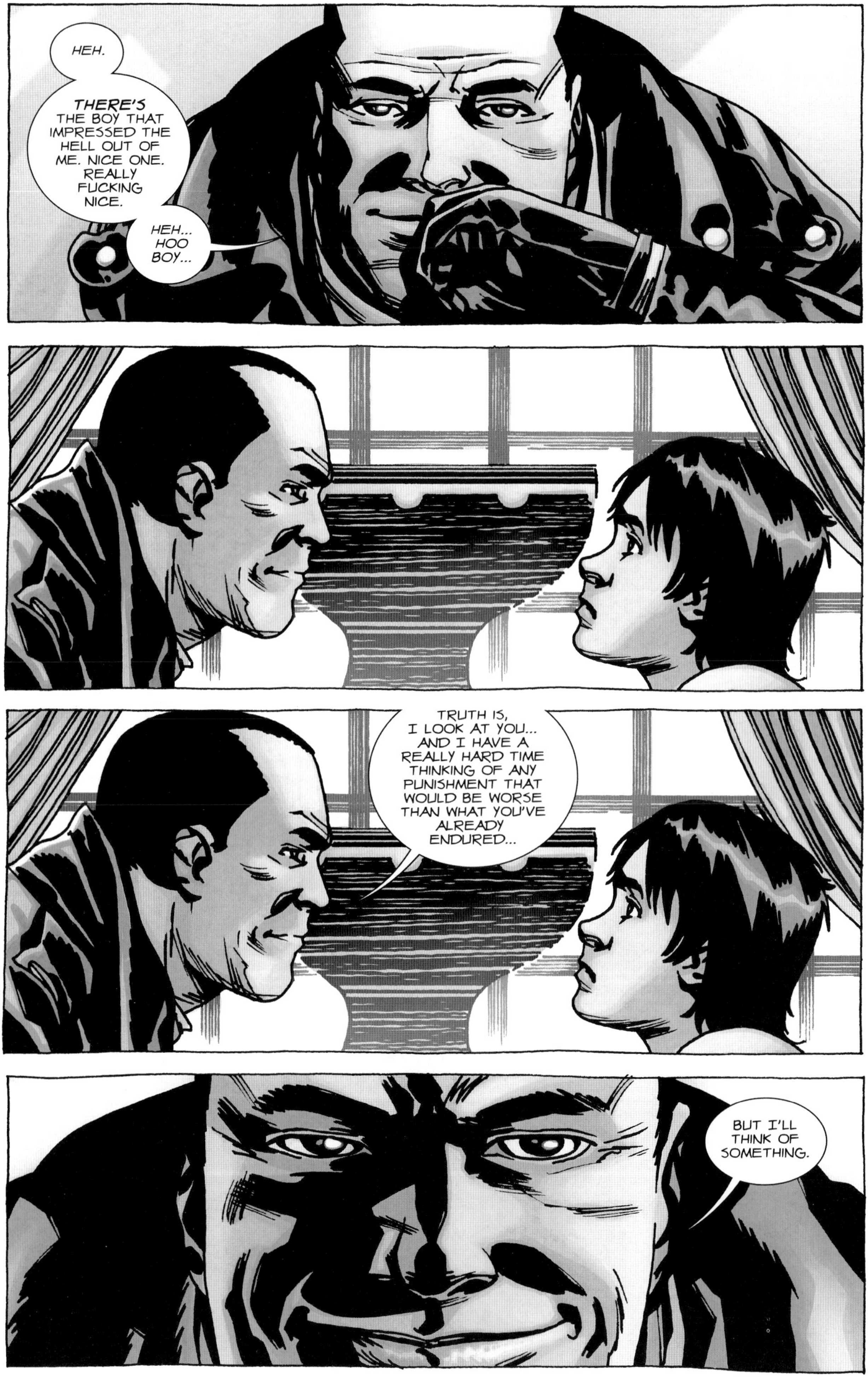
HEH.
THERE'S THE BOY THAT IMPRESSED THE HELL OUT OF ME. NICE ONE. REALLY FUCKING NICE.
HEH... HOO BOY...
TRUTH IS, I LOOK AT YOU... AND I HAVE A REALLY HARD TIME THINKING OF ANY PUNISHMENT THAT WOULD BE WORSE THAN WHAT YOU'VE ALREADY ENDURED...
BUT I'LL THINK OF SOMETHING.

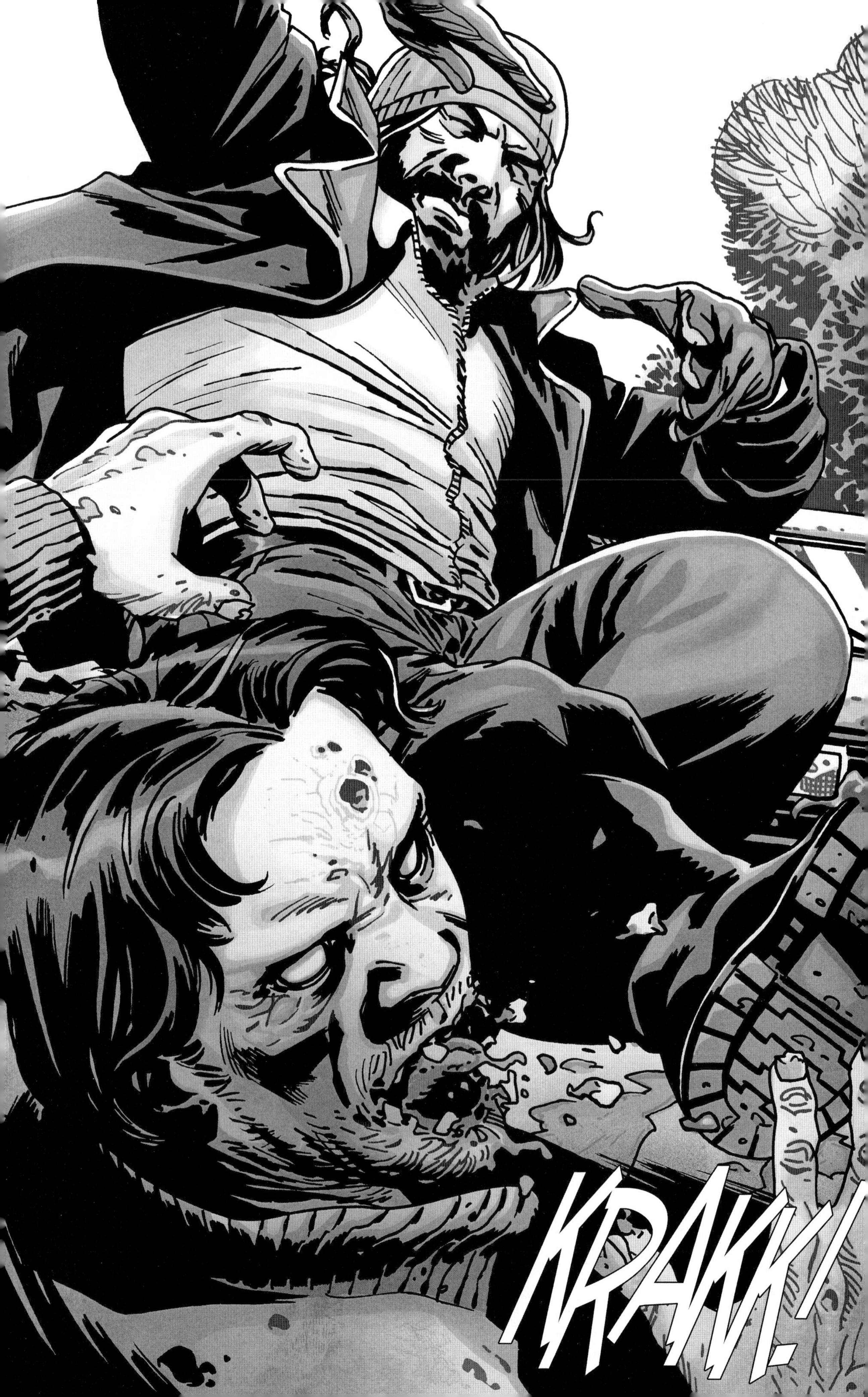
KRAKK!

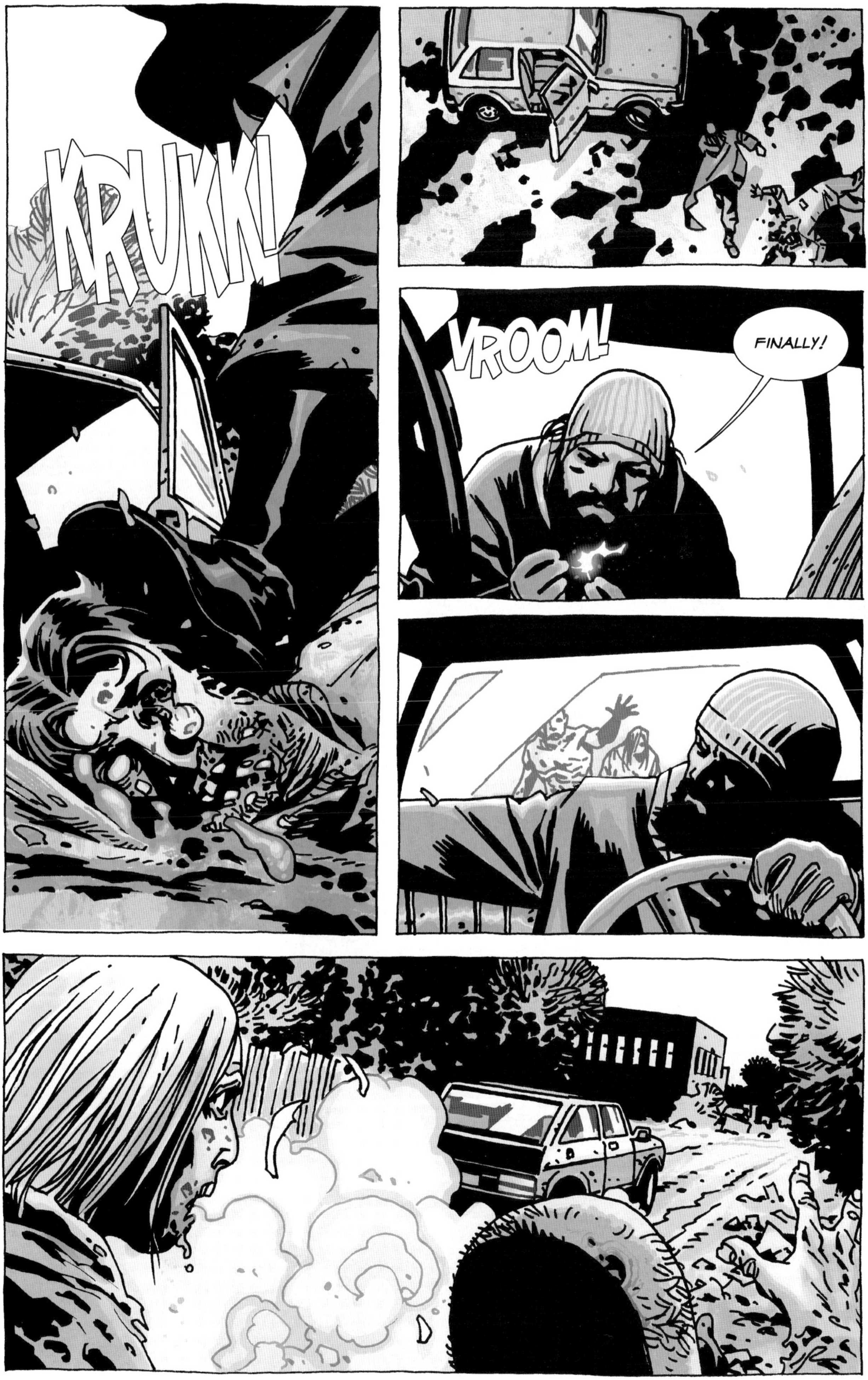
KRUKK!
VROOM!
FINALLY!

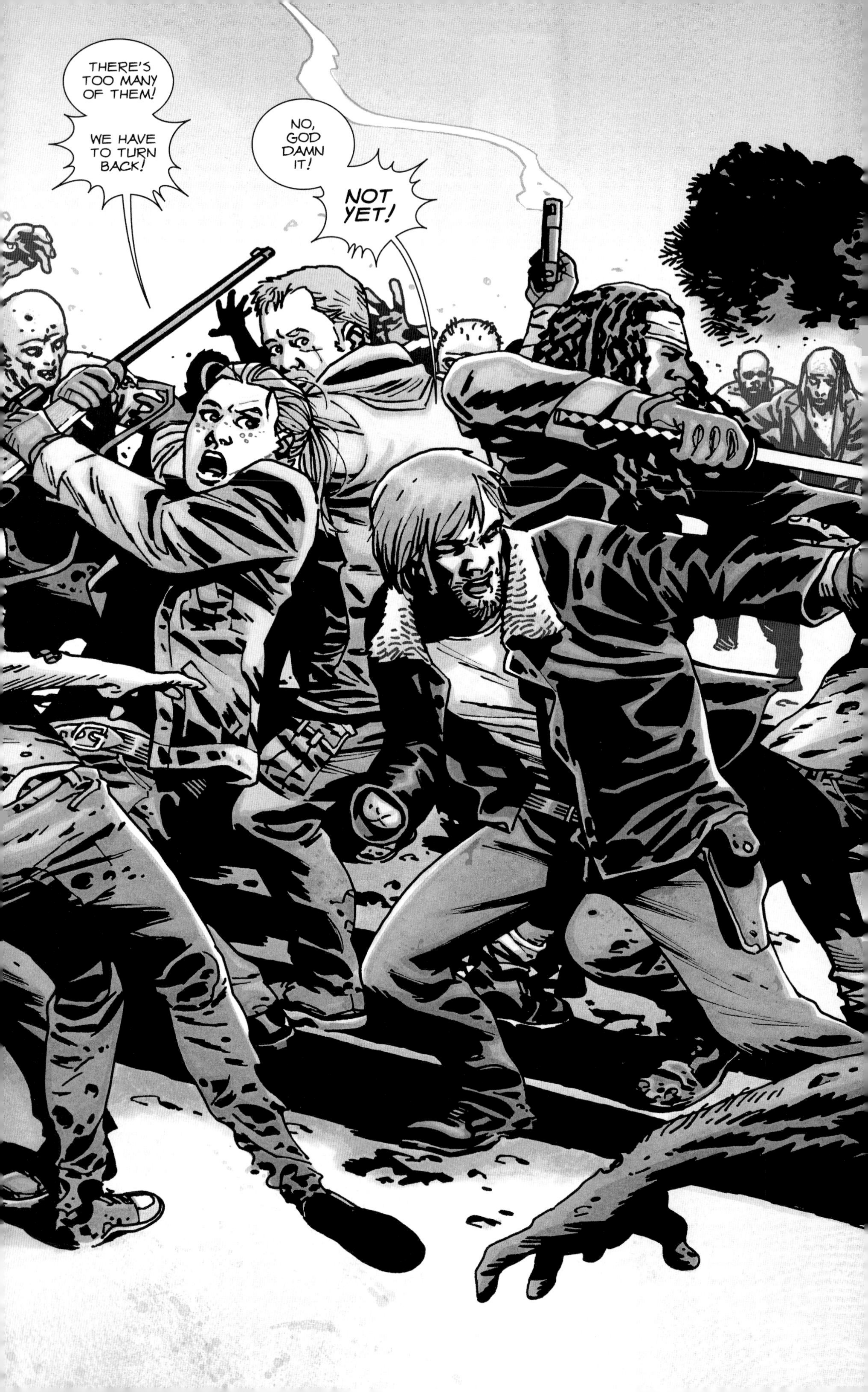
THERE'S TOO MANY OF THEM!
WE HAVE TO TURN BACK!
NO, GOD DAMN IT!
NOT YET!

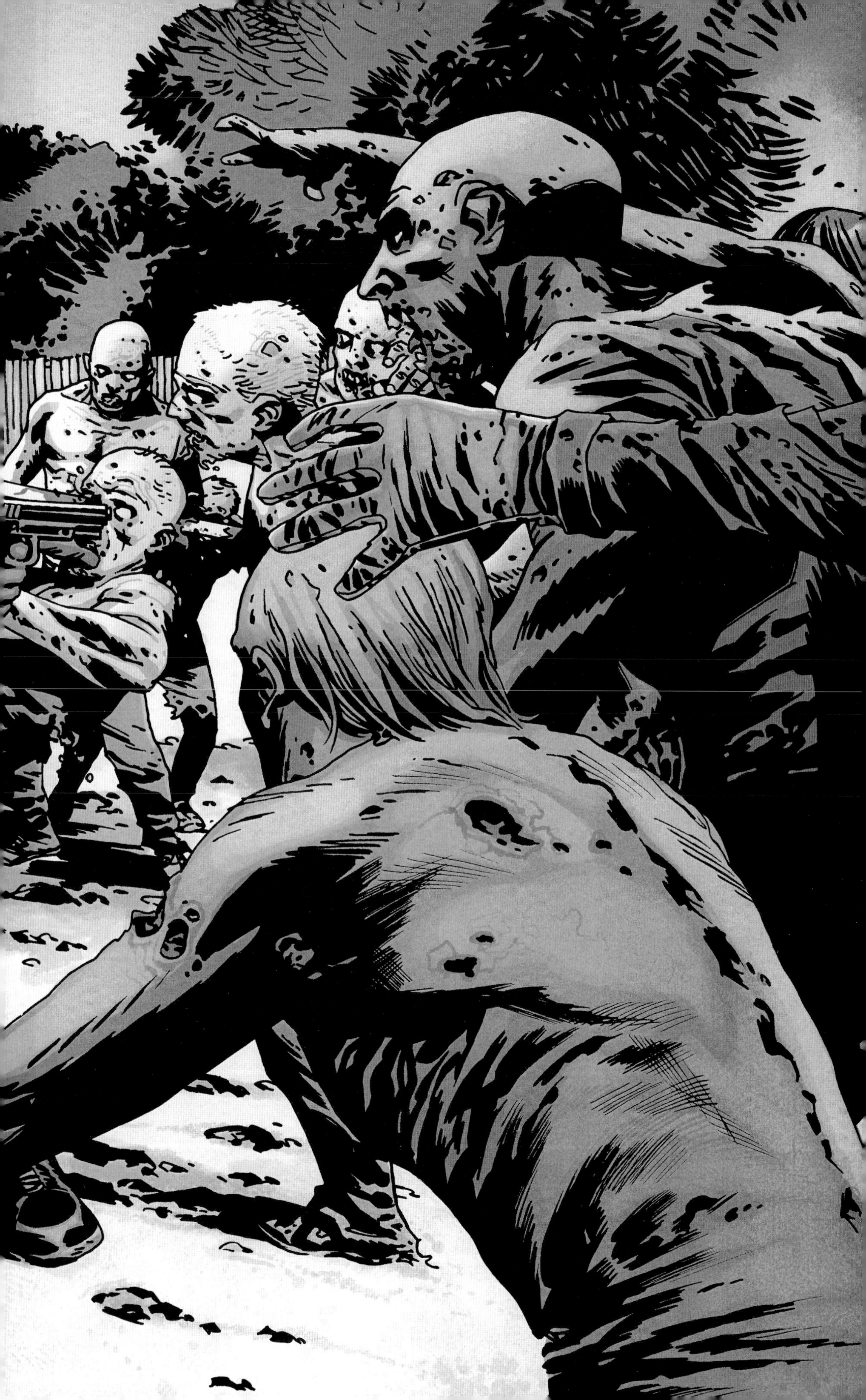

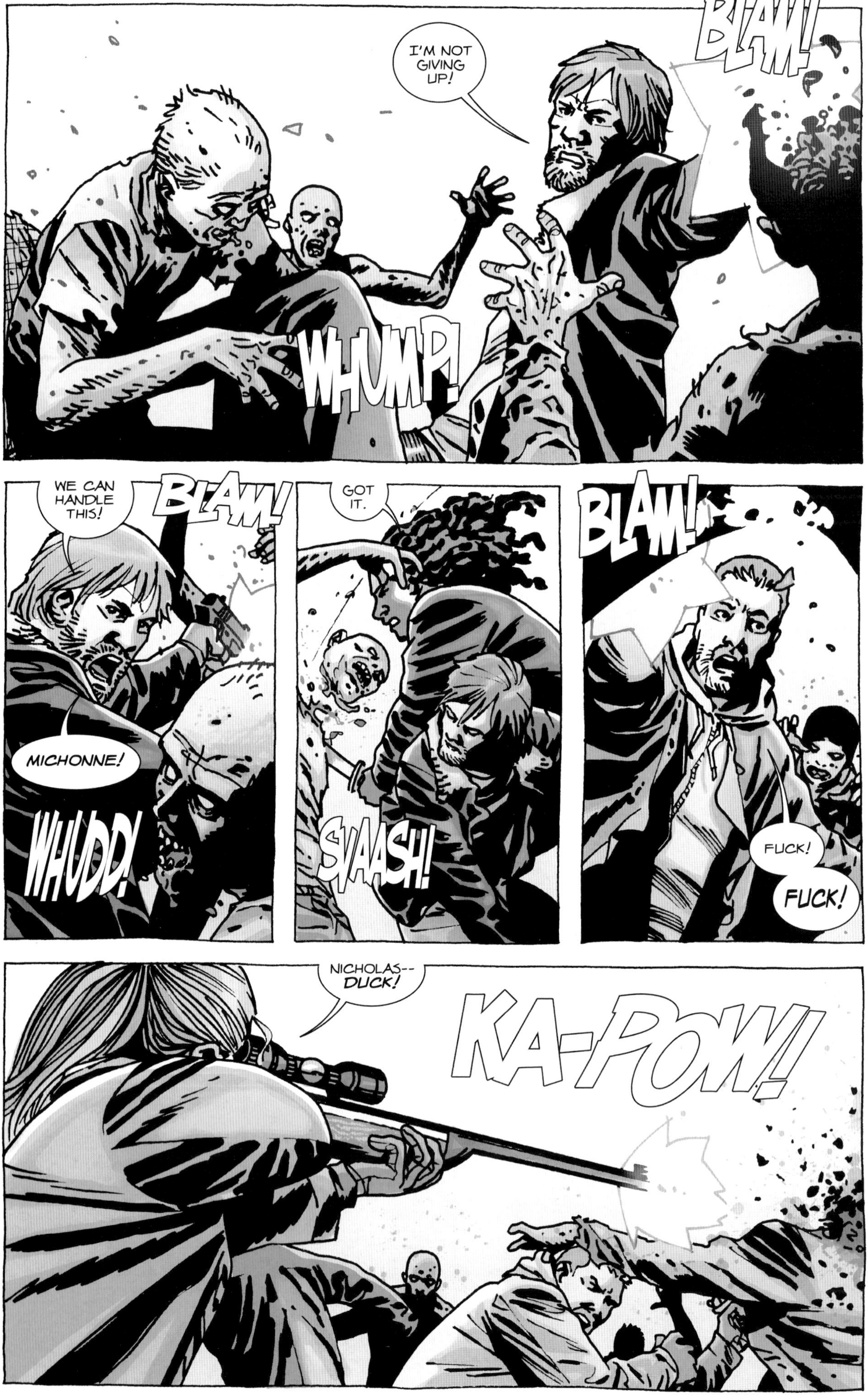
BLAM!
I'M NOT GIVING UP!
WHUMP!
WE CAN HANDLE THIS!
BLAM!
MICHONNE!
WHUDD!
GOT IT.
SWAASH!
BLAM!
FUCK!
FUCK!
NICHOLAS-- DUCK!
KA-POW!

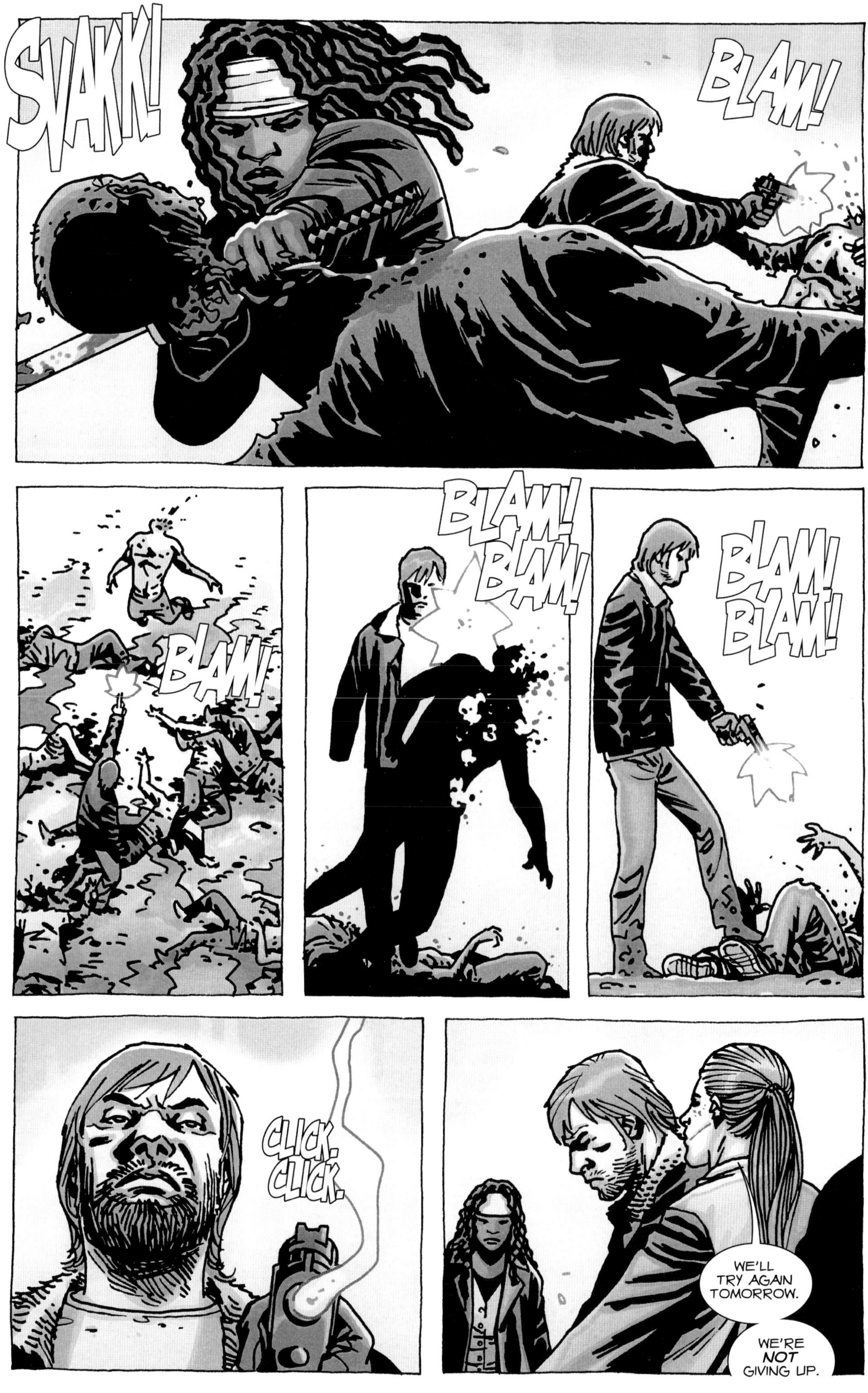

SVAKK!
BLAM!
BLAM!
BLAM!
BLAM!
BLAM!
BLAM!
CLICK.
CLICK.
WE'LL TRY AGAIN TOMORROW.
WE'RE NOT GIVING UP.

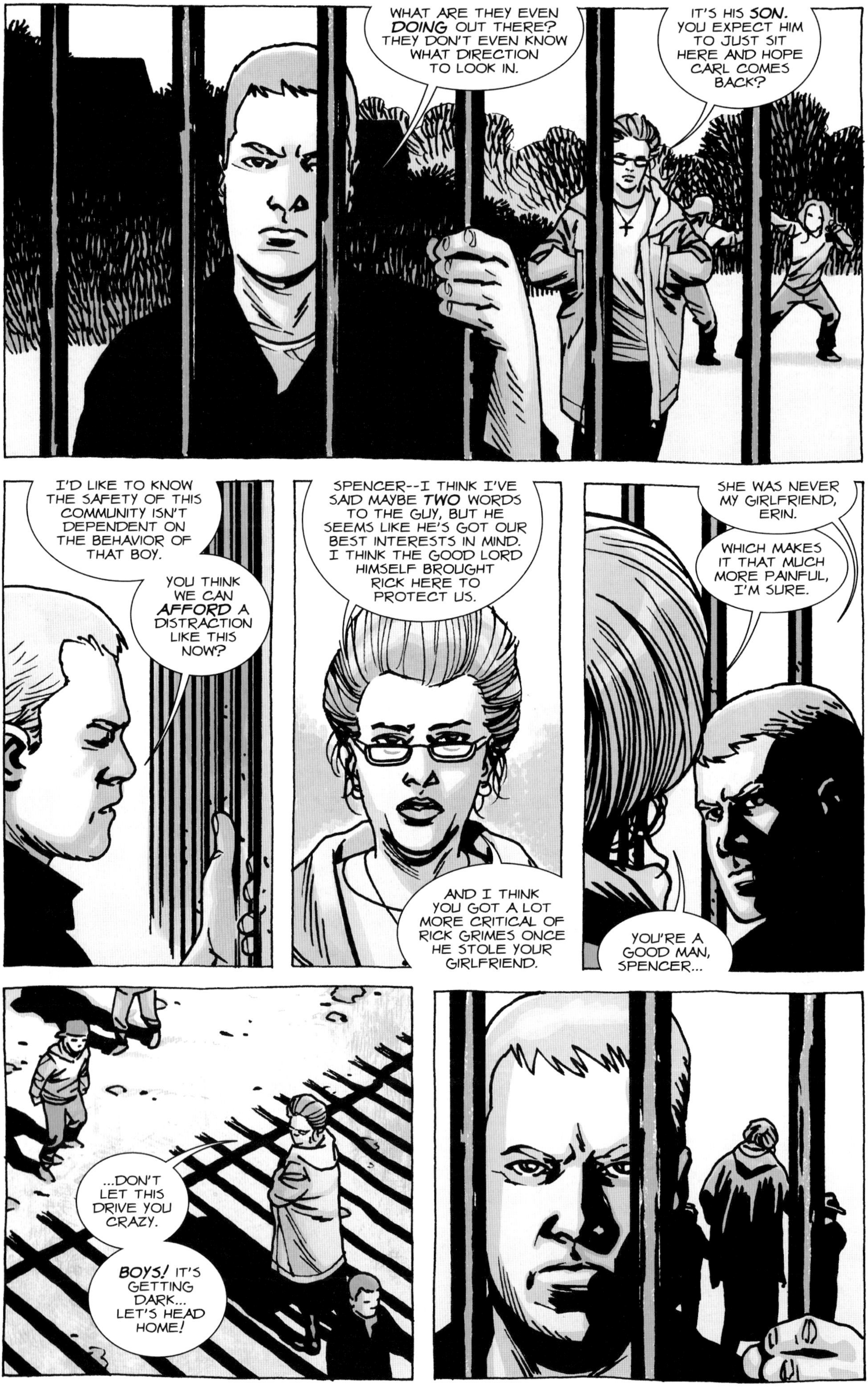

WHAT ARE THEY EVEN DOING OUT THERE? THEY DON'T EVEN KNOW WHAT DIRECTION TO LOOK IN.
IT'S HIS SON. YOU EXPECT HIM TO JUST SIT HERE AND HOPE CARL COMES BACK?
I'D LIKE TO KNOW THE SAFETY OF THIS COMMUNITY ISN'T DEPENDENT ON THE BEHAVIOR OF THAT BOY.
YOU THINK WE CAN AFFORD A DISTRACTION LIKE THIS NOW?
SPENCER--I THINK I'VE SAID MAYBE TWO WORDS TO THE GUY, BUT HE SEEMS LIKE HE'S GOT OUR BEST INTERESTS IN MIND. I THINK THE GOOD LORD HIMSELF BROUGHT RICK HERE TO PROTECT US.
AND I THINK YOU GOT A LOT MORE CRITICAL OF RICK GRIMES ONCE HE STOLE YOUR GIRLFRIEND.
SHE WAS NEVER MY GIRLFRIEND, ERIN.
WHICH MAKES IT THAT MUCH MORE PAINFUL, I'M SURE.
YOU'RE A GOOD MAN, SPENCER...
...DON'T LET THIS DRIVE YOU CRAZY.
BOYS! IT'S GETTING DARK... LET'S HEAD HOME!

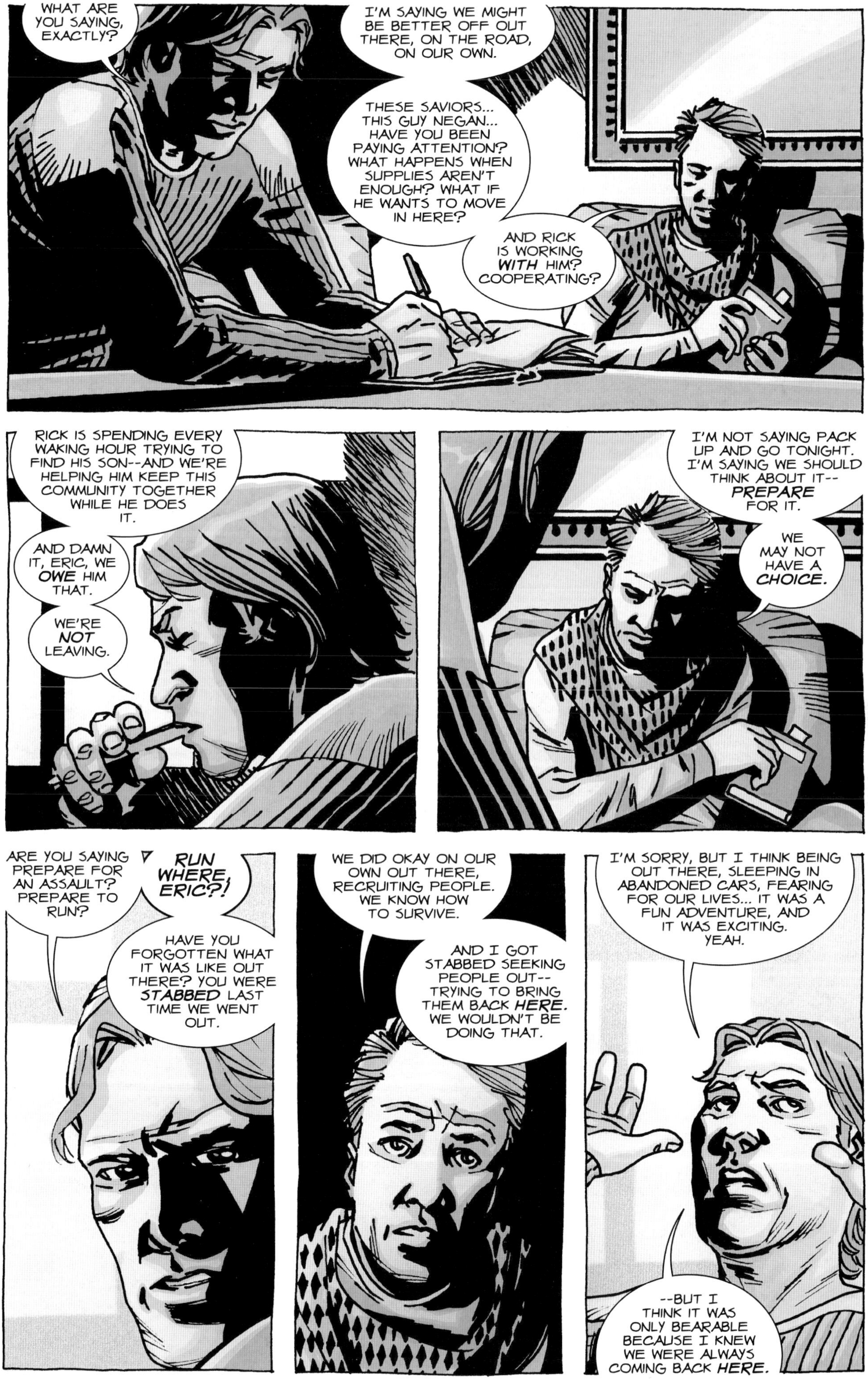
WHAT ARE YOU SAYING, EXACTLY?
I'M SAYING WE MIGHT BE BETTER OFF OUT THERE, ON THE ROAD, ON OUR OWN.
THESE SAVIORS... THIS GUY NEGAN... HAVE YOU BEEN PAYING ATTENTION? WHAT HAPPENS WHEN SUPPLIES AREN'T ENOUGH? WHAT IF HE WANTS TO MOVE IN HERE?
AND RICK IS WORKING *WITH* HIM? COOPERATING?
RICK IS SPENDING EVERY WAKING HOUR TRYING TO FIND HIS SON--AND WE'RE HELPING HIM KEEP THIS COMMUNITY TOGETHER WHILE HE DOES IT.
AND DAMN IT, ERIC, WE *OWE* HIM THAT.
WE'RE *NOT* LEAVING.
I'M NOT SAYING PACK UP AND GO TONIGHT. I'M SAYING WE SHOULD THINK ABOUT IT-- *PREPARE* FOR IT.
WE MAY NOT HAVE A *CHOICE.*
ARE YOU SAYING PREPARE FOR AN ASSAULT? PREPARE TO RUN?
RUN WHERE, ERIC?!
HAVE YOU FORGOTTEN WHAT IT WAS LIKE OUT THERE? YOU WERE *STABBED* LAST TIME WE WENT OUT.
WE DID OKAY ON OUR OWN OUT THERE, RECRUITING PEOPLE. WE KNOW HOW TO SURVIVE.
AND I GOT STABBED SEEKING PEOPLE OUT-- TRYING TO BRING THEM BACK *HERE.* WE WOULDN'T BE DOING THAT.
I'M SORRY, BUT I THINK BEING OUT THERE, SLEEPING IN ABANDONED CARS, FEARING FOR OUR LIVES... IT WAS A FUN ADVENTURE, AND IT WAS EXCITING. YEAH.
--BUT I THINK IT WAS ONLY BEARABLE BECAUSE I KNEW WE WERE ALWAYS COMING BACK *HERE.*

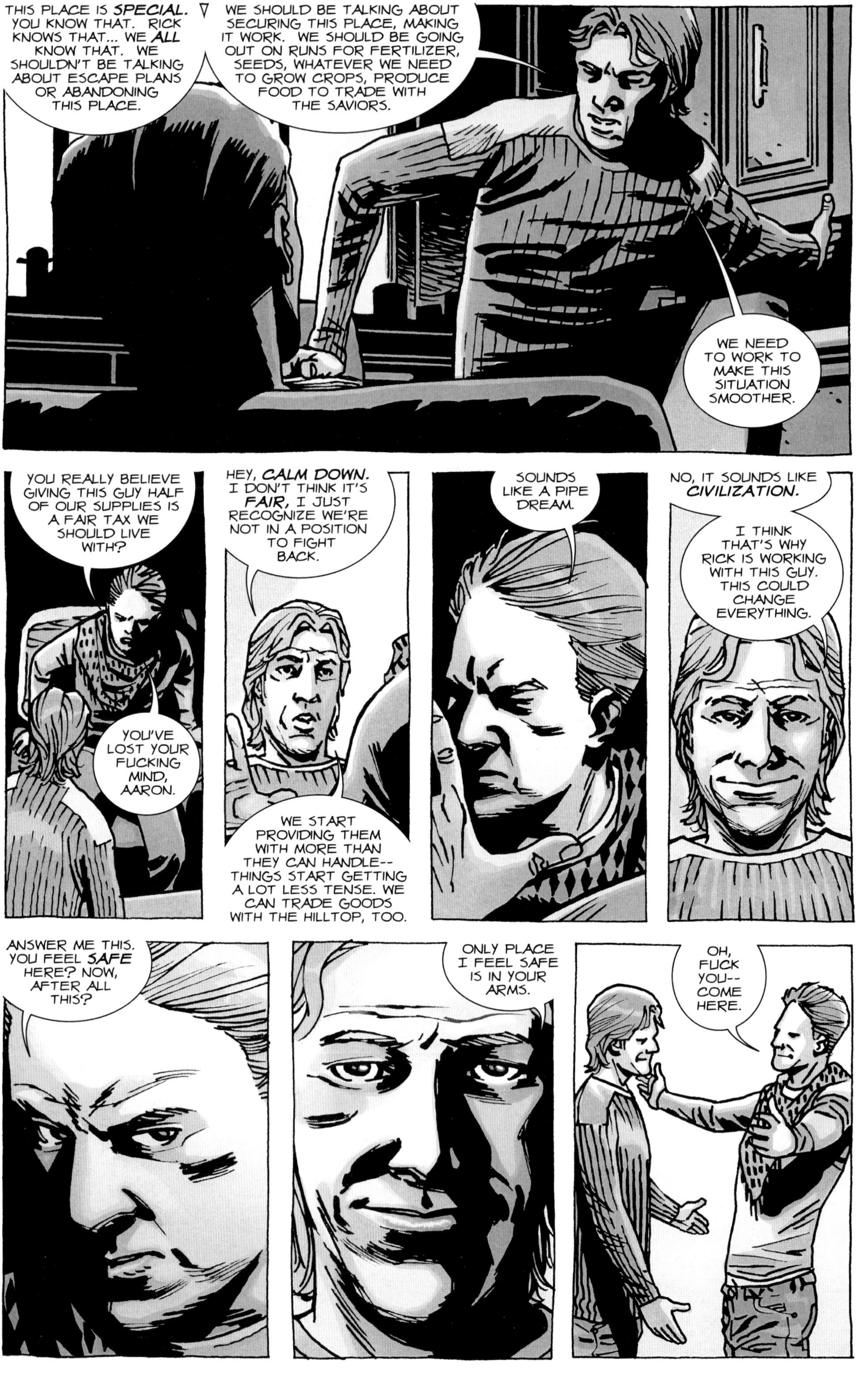
THIS PLACE IS SPECIAL. YOU KNOW THAT. RICK KNOWS THAT... WE ALL KNOW THAT. WE SHOULDN'T BE TALKING ABOUT ESCAPE PLANS OR ABANDONING THIS PLACE.
WE SHOULD BE TALKING ABOUT SECURING THIS PLACE, MAKING IT WORK. WE SHOULD BE GOING OUT ON RUNS FOR FERTILIZER, SEEDS, WHATEVER WE NEED TO GROW CROPS, PRODUCE FOOD TO TRADE WITH THE SAVIORS.
WE NEED TO WORK TO MAKE THIS SITUATION SMOOTHER.
YOU REALLY BELIEVE GIVING THIS GUY HALF OF OUR SUPPLIES IS A FAIR TAX WE SHOULD LIVE WITH?
YOU'VE LOST YOUR FUCKING MIND, AARON.
HEY, CALM DOWN. I DON'T THINK IT'S FAIR, I JUST RECOGNIZE WE'RE NOT IN A POSITION TO FIGHT BACK.
WE START PROVIDING THEM WITH MORE THAN THEY CAN HANDLE-- THINGS START GETTING A LOT LESS TENSE. WE CAN TRADE GOODS WITH THE HILLTOP, TOO.
SOUNDS LIKE A PIPE DREAM.
NO, IT SOUNDS LIKE CIVILIZATION.
I THINK THAT'S WHY RICK IS WORKING WITH THIS GUY. THIS COULD CHANGE EVERYTHING.
ANSWER ME THIS. YOU FEEL SAFE HERE? NOW, AFTER ALL THIS?
ONLY PLACE I FEEL SAFE IS IN YOUR ARMS.
OH, FUCK YOU-- COME HERE.

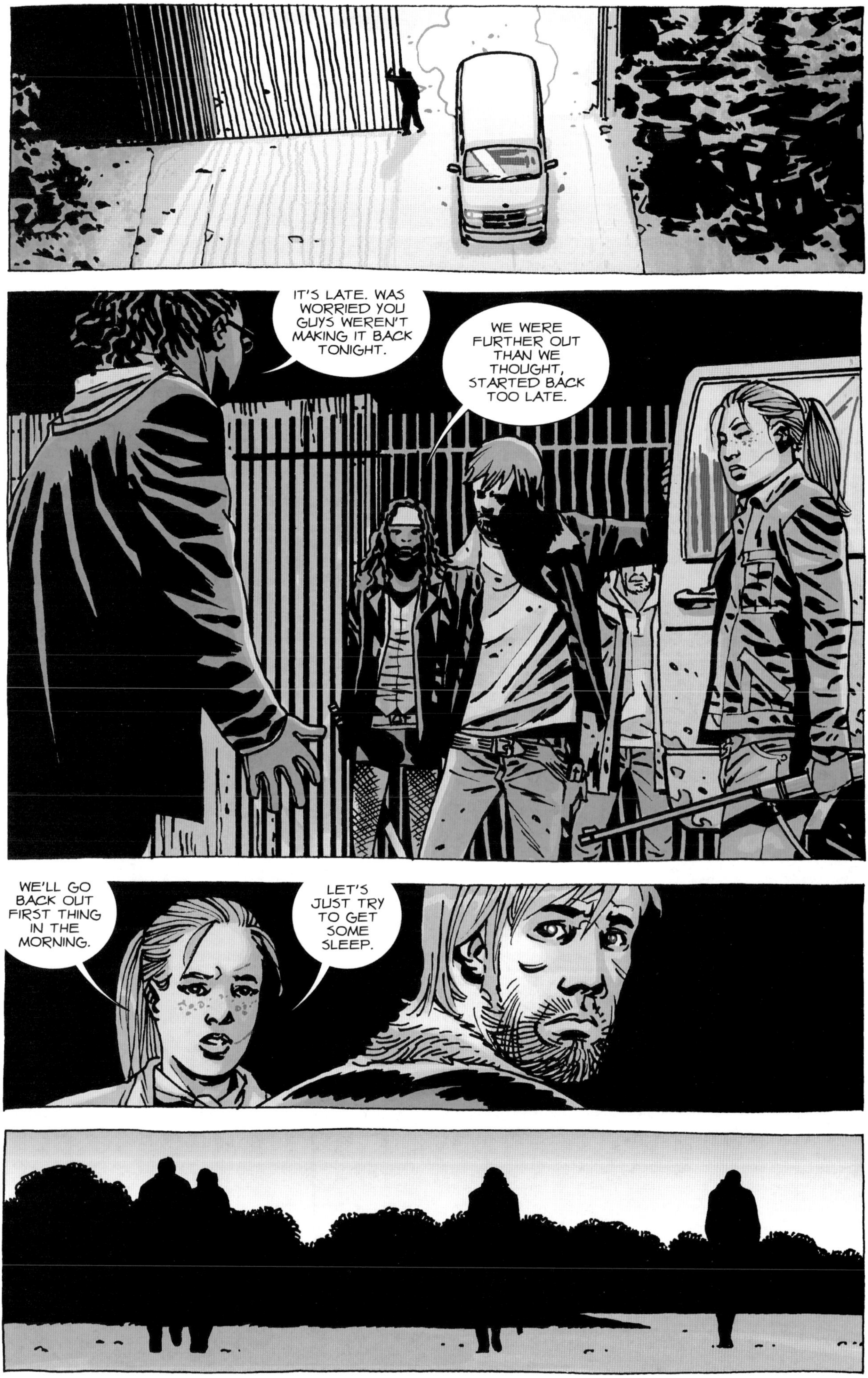
IT'S LATE. WAS WORRIED YOU GUYS WEREN'T MAKING IT BACK TONIGHT.
WE WERE FURTHER OUT THAN WE THOUGHT, STARTED BACK TOO LATE.
WE'LL GO BACK OUT FIRST THING IN THE MORNING.
LET'S JUST TRY TO GET SOME SLEEP.

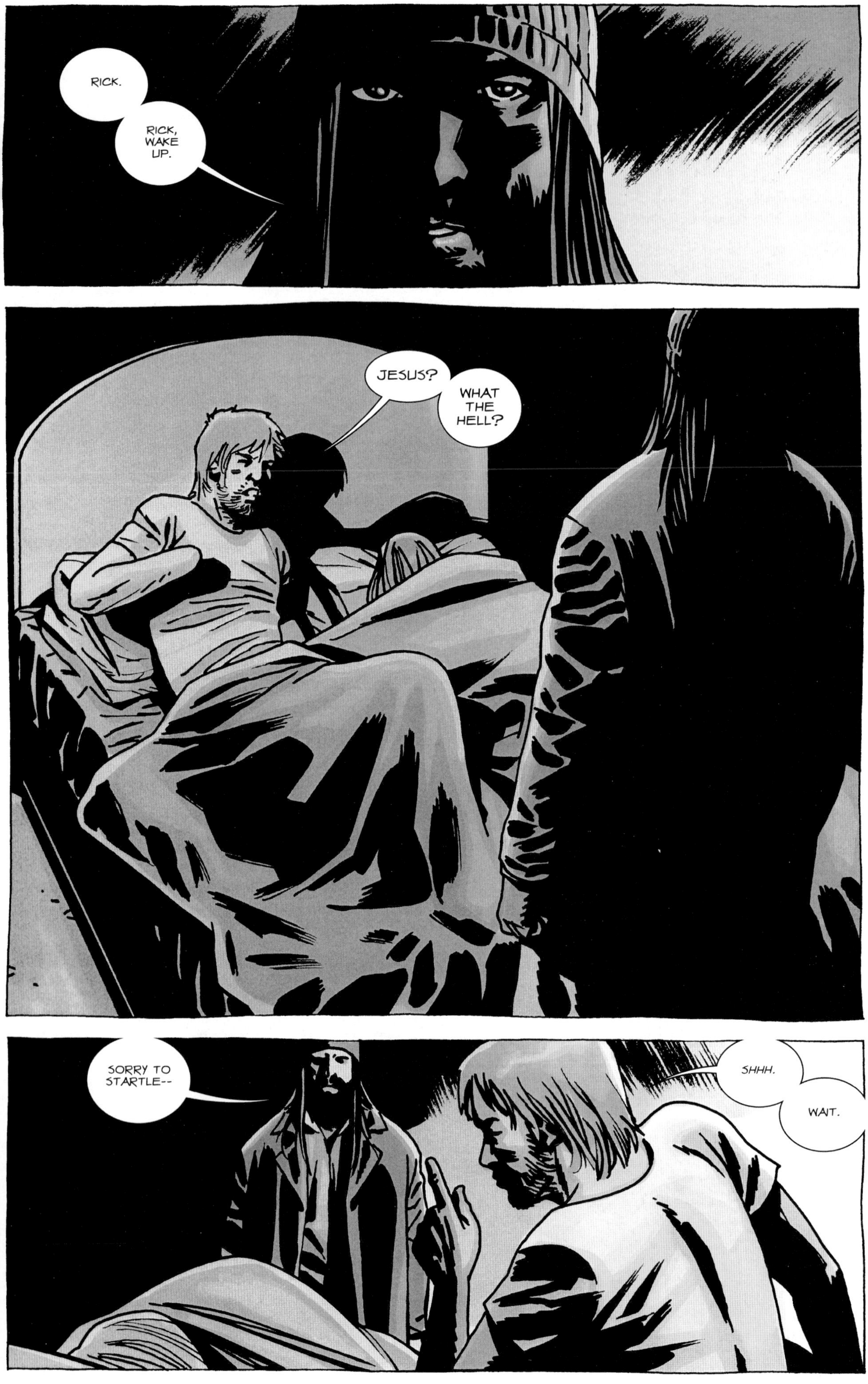
RICK.
RICK, WAKE UP.
JESUS?
WHAT THE HELL?
SORRY TO STARTLE--
SHHH.
WAIT.

DIDN'T WANT TO WAKE YOU BUT I THOUGHT THIS NEWS WAS WORTH--

WRAMM!

HOW DID YOU GET IN HERE?!

HEATH LET ME IN THE GATE... AND YOU DIDN'T LOCK YOUR FRONT DOOR. I *KNOCKED* IF IT MAKES YOU FEEL ANY BETTER.

RICK... I FOUND *NEGAN*... I KNOW WHERE HE *LIVES.*

DID YOU SEE *CARL?*

NO. WHERE? IS HE IN HIS ROOM?

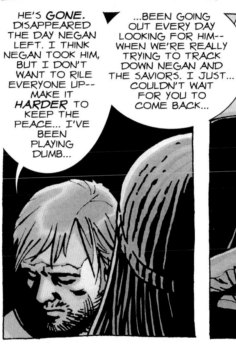

HE'S *GONE.* DISAPPEARED THE DAY NEGAN LEFT. I THINK NEGAN TOOK HIM, BUT I DON'T WANT TO RILE EVERYONE UP-- MAKE IT *HARDER* TO KEEP THE PEACE... I'VE BEEN PLAYING DUMB...

...BEEN GOING OUT EVERY DAY LOOKING FOR HIM-- WHEN WE'RE REALLY TRYING TO TRACK DOWN NEGAN AND THE SAVIORS. I JUST... COULDN'T WAIT FOR YOU TO COME BACK...

SAW HIS CARAVAN ENTER-- THEY'VE GOT A WALL, CAN'T REALLY SEE INSIDE. AS I WAS STARTING BACK ON MY WAY HERE--I HEARD AUTOMATIC WEAPON FIRE... DON'T KNOW WHAT THAT WAS ABOUT.

ABRAHAM'S MACHINE GUN IS MISSING.

I CAN TAKE YOU THERE IN THE MORNING.

I CAN'T WAIT THAT LONG.

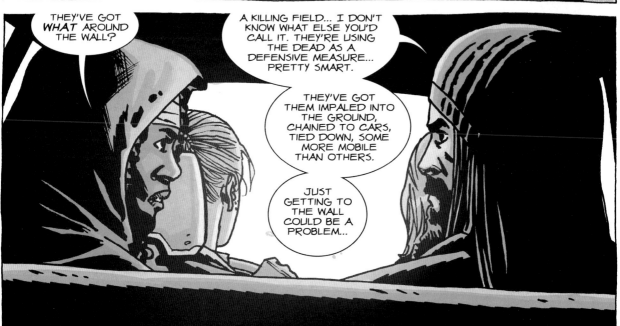

THEY'VE GOT *WHAT* AROUND THE WALL?

A KILLING FIELD... I DON'T KNOW WHAT ELSE YOU'D CALL IT. THEY'RE USING THE DEAD AS A DEFENSIVE MEASURE... PRETTY SMART.

THEY'VE GOT THEM IMPALED INTO THE GROUND, CHAINED TO CARS, TIED DOWN, SOME MORE MOBILE THAN OTHERS.

JUST GETTING TO THE WALL COULD BE A PROBLEM...

I KNOW A WAY.

ROAMERS WON'T EVEN NOTICE US.

AND ONCE WE'RE INSIDE--HOW DO WE FIND HIM? YOU SAID THIS PLACE HAS HOW MANY FLOORS?

I DON'T KNOW... A BUNCH. TEN? IT'S A HUGE PLACE.

THAT DOESN'T SOUND PROMISING.

THERE A PLACE NEARBY WHERE I COULD SET UP, WATCH THEM THROUGH MY SCOPE? IT'D BE BEST TO KNOW WHAT WE'RE RUNNING INTO-- MAYBE I'D SEE CARL.

SOME TALL TREES NEARBY--DON'T KNOW HOW CLEAR A VIEW YOU COULD GET WITHOUT RISK OF BEING SPOTTED.

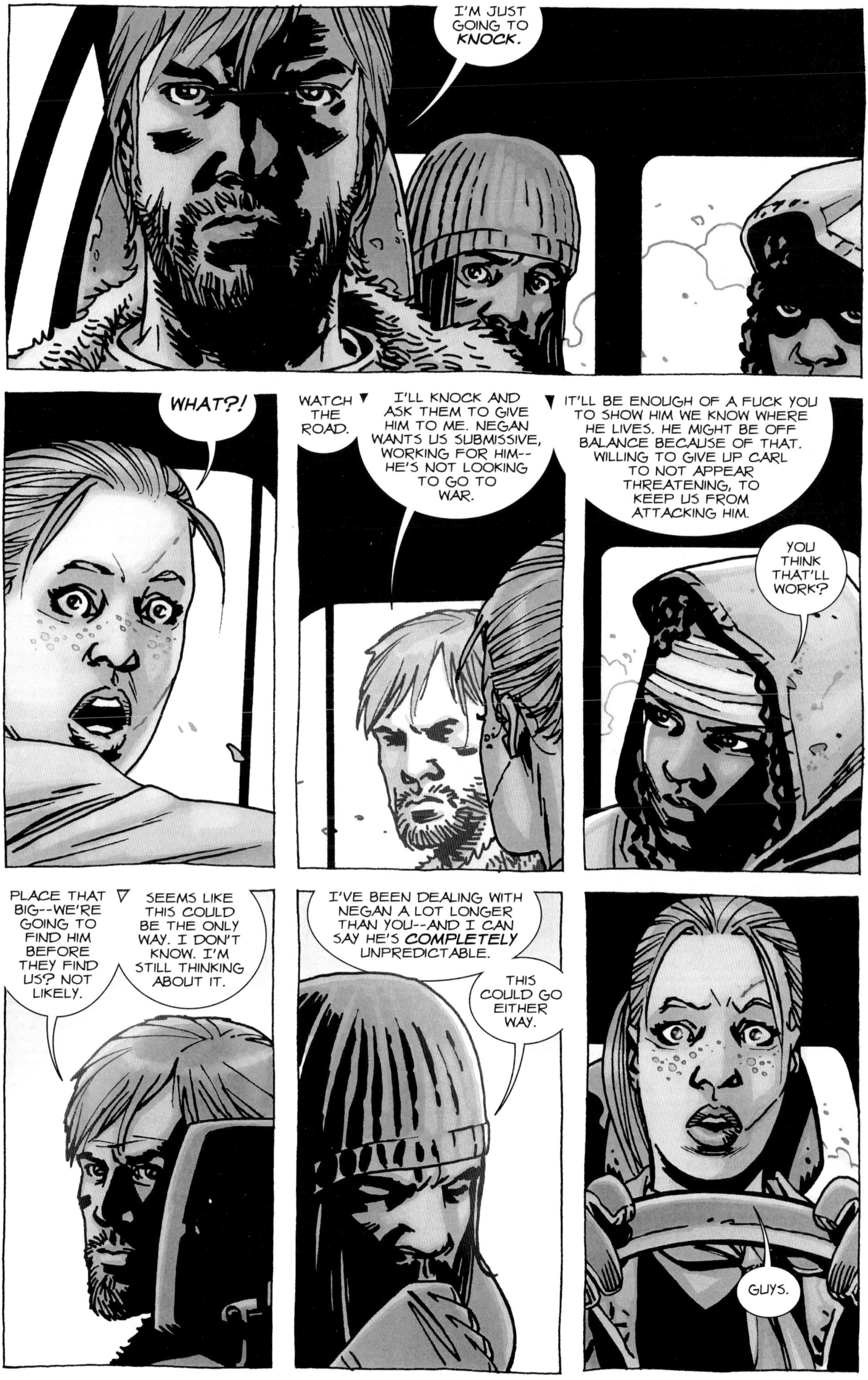
I'M JUST GOING TO *KNOCK.*
WHAT?!
WATCH THE ROAD.
I'LL KNOCK AND ASK THEM TO GIVE HIM TO ME. NEGAN WANTS US SUBMISSIVE, WORKING FOR HIM-- HE'S NOT LOOKING TO GO TO WAR.
IT'LL BE ENOUGH OF A FUCK YOU TO SHOW HIM WE KNOW WHERE HE LIVES. HE MIGHT BE OFF BALANCE BECAUSE OF THAT. WILLING TO GIVE UP CARL TO NOT APPEAR THREATENING, TO KEEP US FROM ATTACKING HIM.
YOU THINK THAT'LL WORK?
PLACE THAT BIG--WE'RE GOING TO FIND HIM BEFORE THEY FIND US? NOT LIKELY.
SEEMS LIKE THIS COULD BE THE ONLY WAY. I DON'T KNOW. I'M STILL THINKING ABOUT IT.
I'VE BEEN DEALING WITH NEGAN A LOT LONGER THAN YOU--AND I CAN SAY HE'S *COMPLETELY* UNPREDICTABLE.
THIS COULD GO EITHER WAY.
GUYS.

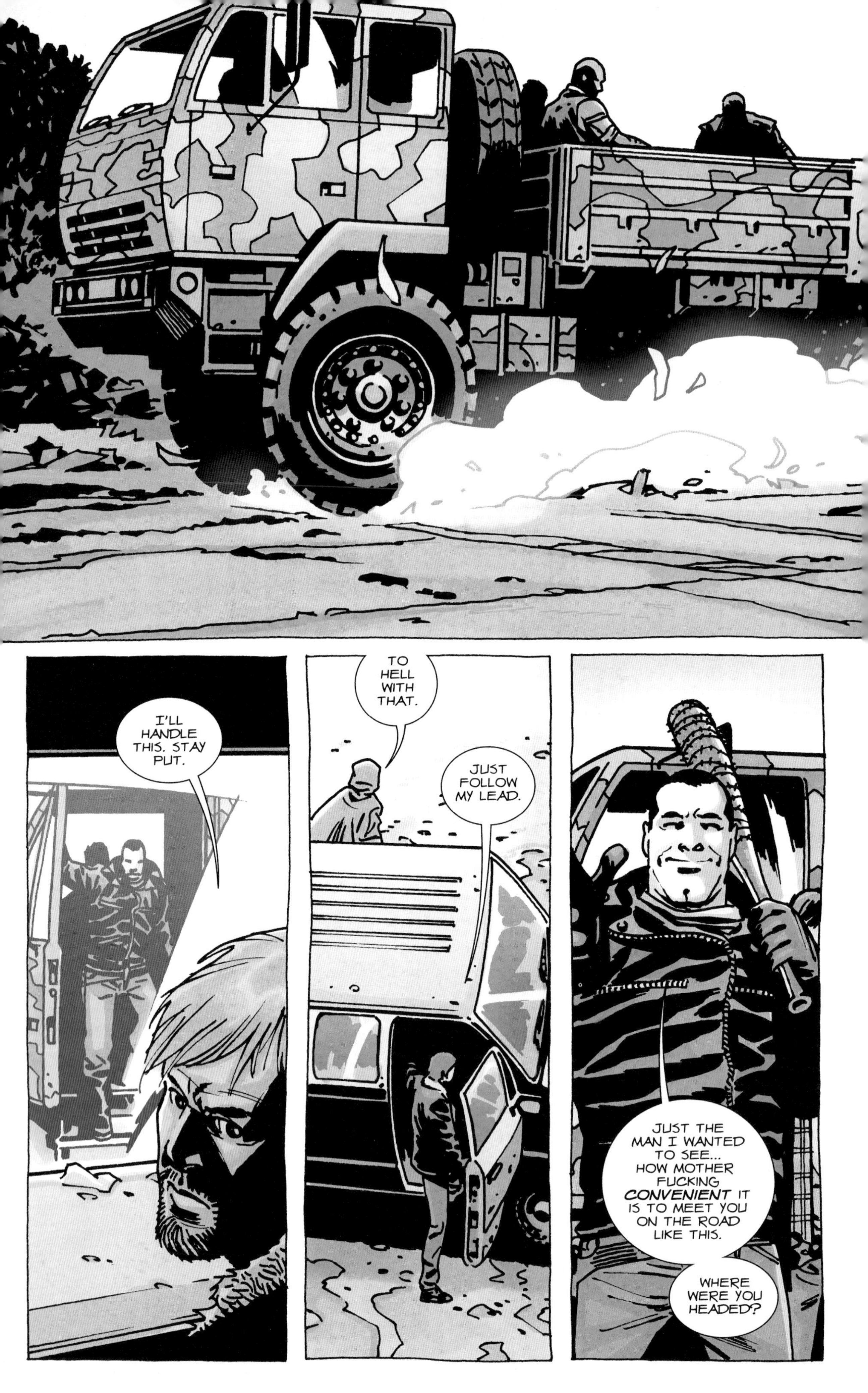
I'LL HANDLE THIS. STAY PUT.
TO HELL WITH THAT.
JUST FOLLOW MY LEAD.
JUST THE MAN I WANTED TO SEE... HOW MOTHER FUCKING *CONVENIENT* IT IS TO MEET YOU ON THE ROAD LIKE THIS.
WHERE WERE YOU HEADED?

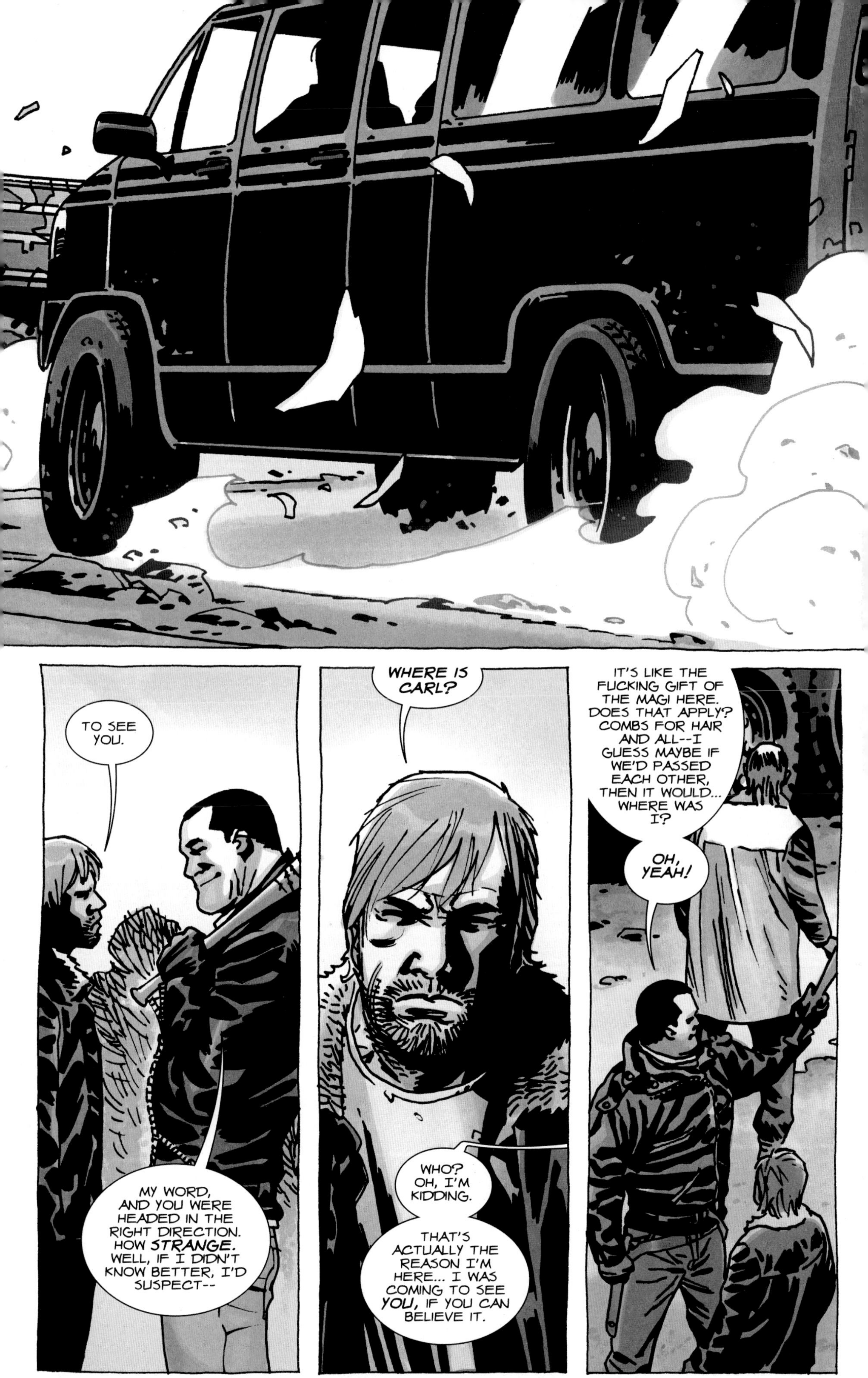
TO SEE YOU.
MY WORD, AND YOU WERE HEADED IN THE RIGHT DIRECTION. HOW STRANGE. WELL, IF I DIDN'T KNOW BETTER, I'D SUSPECT--
WHERE IS CARL?
WHO? OH, I'M KIDDING.
THAT'S ACTUALLY THE REASON I'M HERE... I WAS COMING TO SEE YOU, IF YOU CAN BELIEVE IT.
IT'S LIKE THE FUCKING GIFT OF THE MAGI HERE. DOES THAT APPLY? COMBS FOR HAIR AND ALL--I GUESS MAYBE IF WE'D PASSED EACH OTHER, THEN IT WOULD... WHERE WAS I?
OH, YEAH!

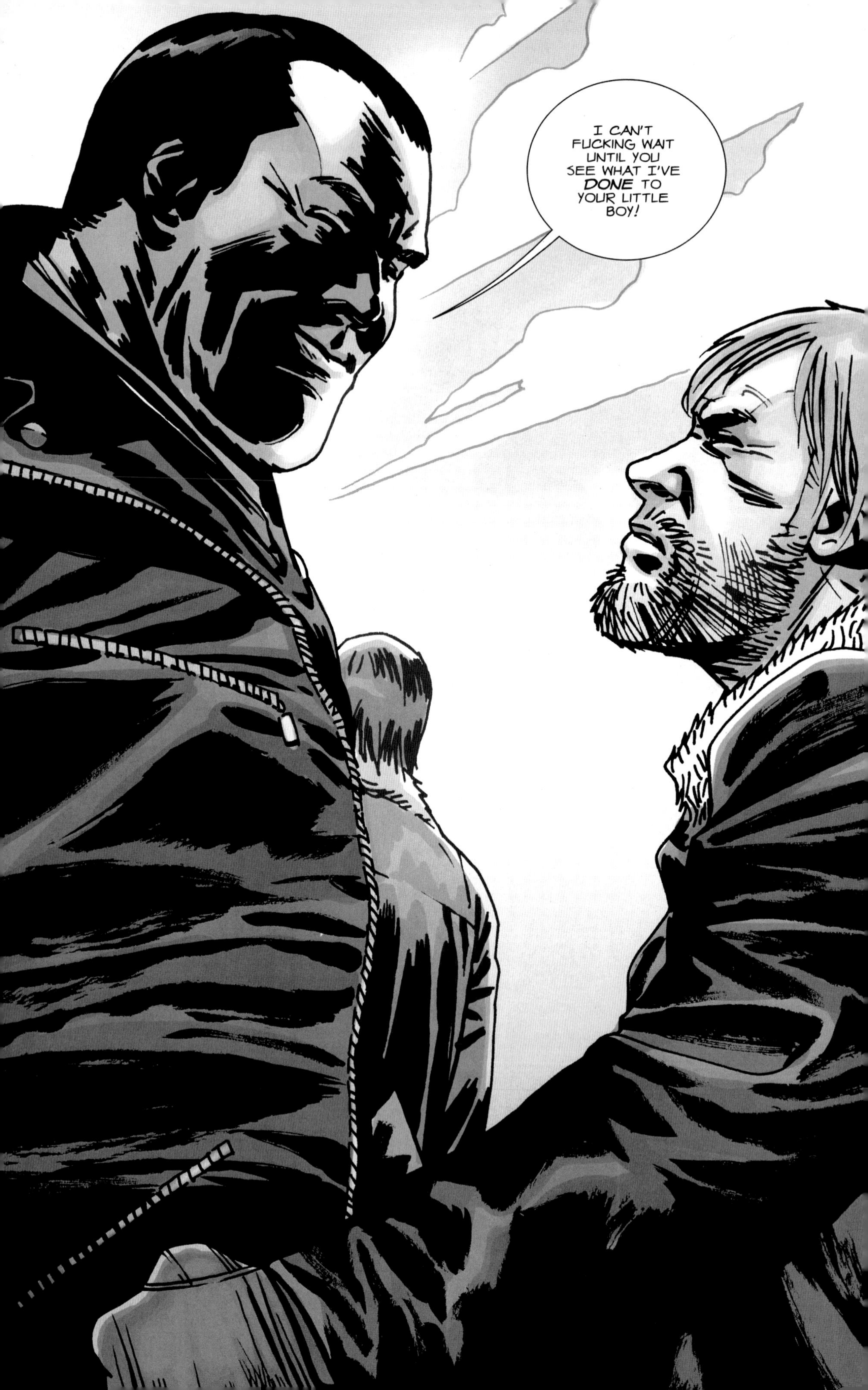
I CAN'T FUCKING WAIT UNTIL YOU SEE WHAT I'VE *DONE* TO YOUR LITTLE BOY!

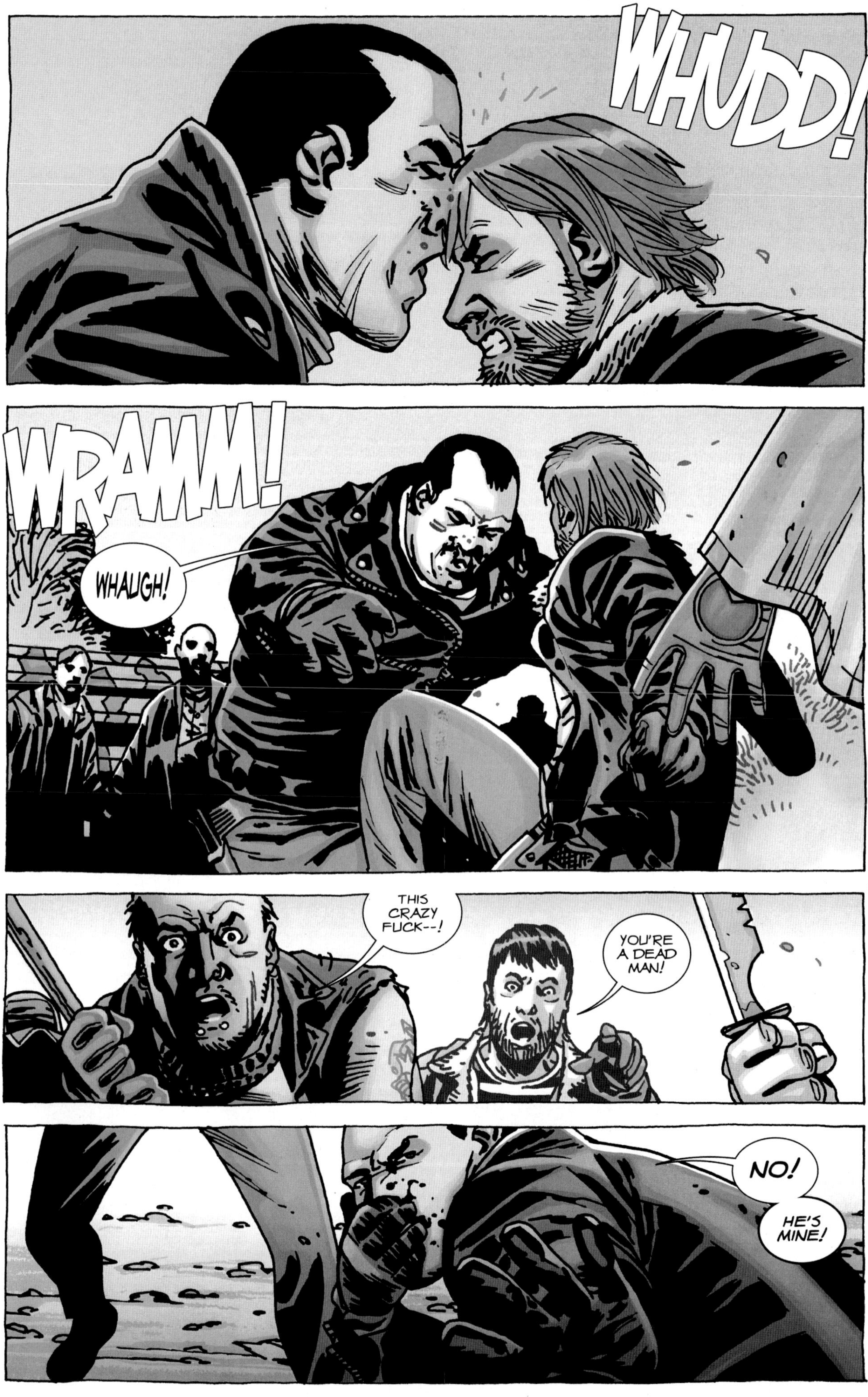
WHUDD!
WRAMM!
WHAUGH!
THIS CRAZY FUCK--!
YOU'RE A DEAD MAN!
NO!
HE'S MINE!

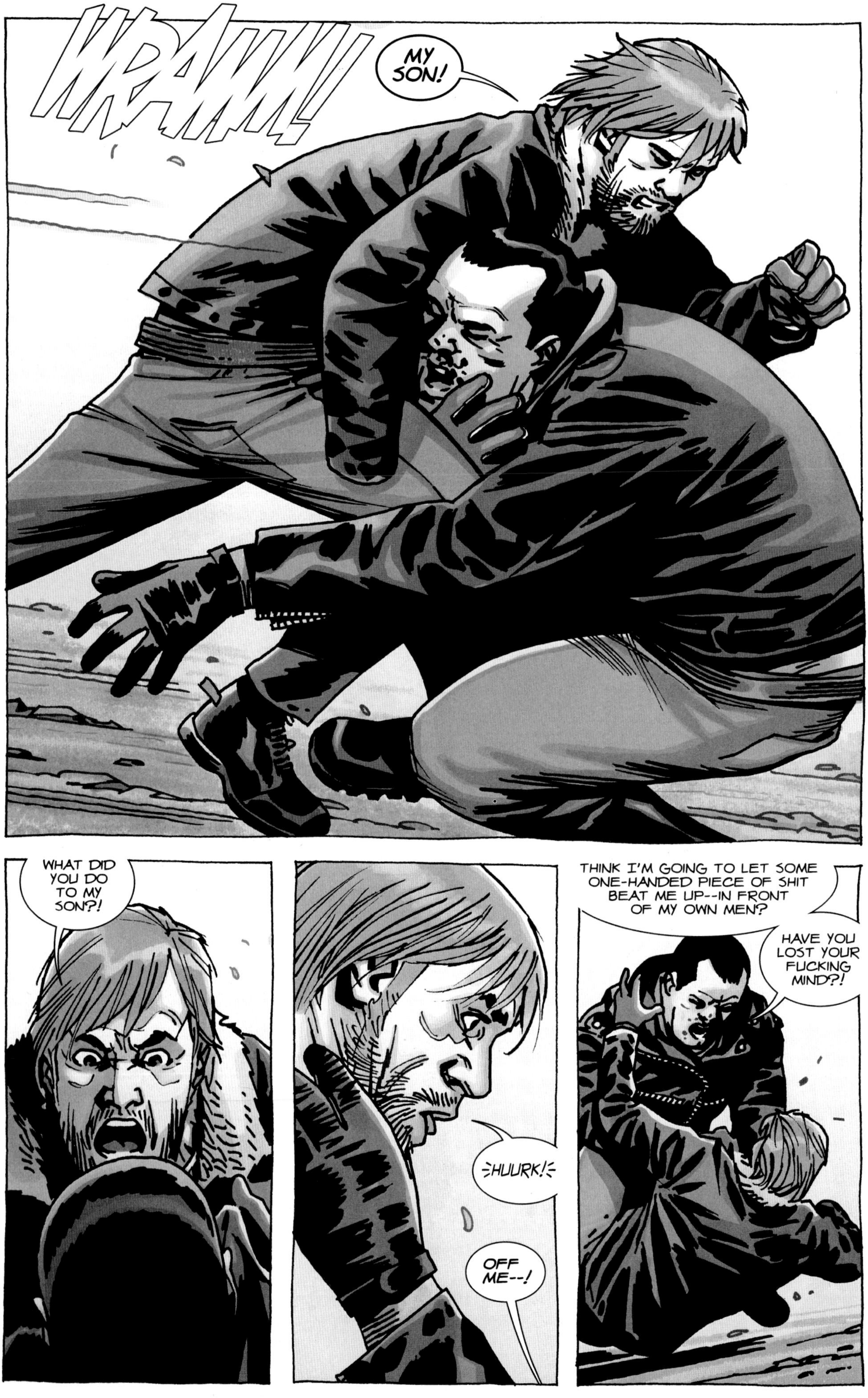
WRAMM!
MY SON!
WHAT DID YOU DO TO MY SON?!
HUURK!
OFF ME--!
THINK I'M GOING TO LET SOME ONE-HANDED PIECE OF SHIT BEAT ME UP--IN FRONT OF MY OWN MEN?
HAVE YOU LOST YOUR FUCKING MIND?!

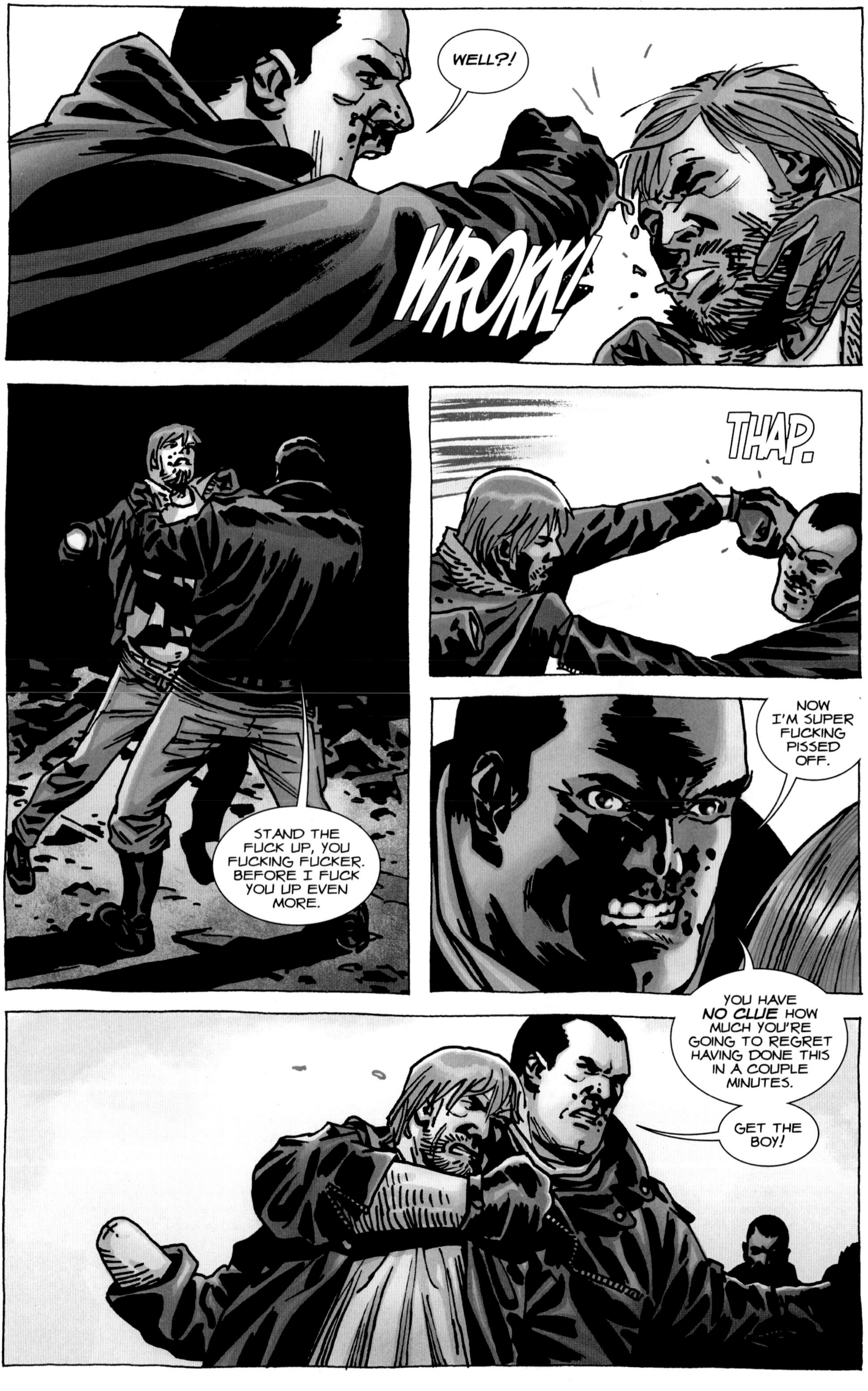
WELL?!
WROKK!
STAND THE FUCK UP, YOU FUCKING FUCKER. BEFORE I FUCK YOU UP EVEN MORE.
THAP.
NOW I'M SUPER FUCKING PISSED OFF.
YOU HAVE NO CLUE HOW MUCH YOU'RE GOING TO REGRET HAVING DONE THIS IN A COUPLE MINUTES.
GET THE BOY!

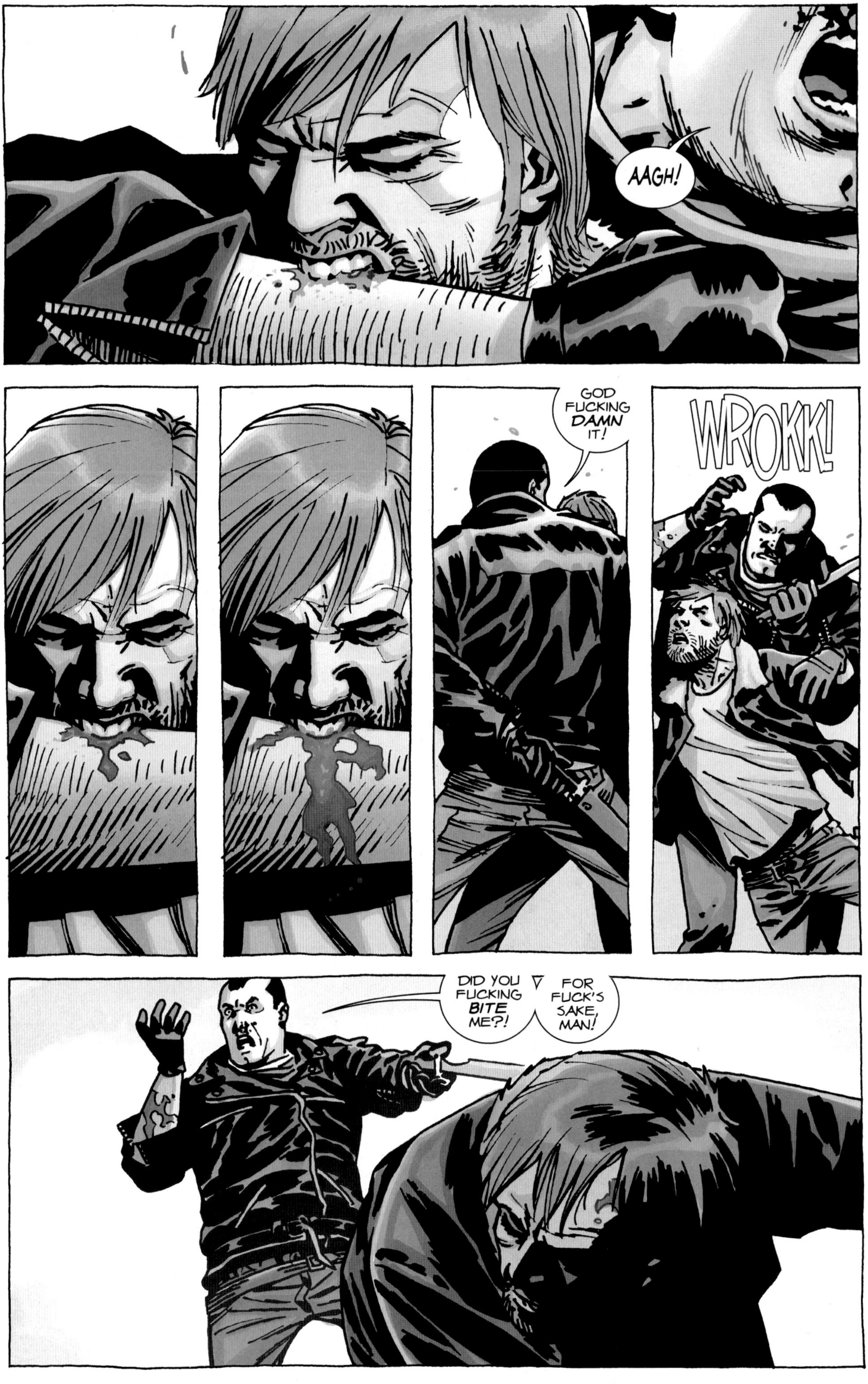
AAGH!
GOD FUCKING DAMN IT!
WROKK!
DID YOU FUCKING BITE ME?!
FOR FUCK'S SAKE, MAN!

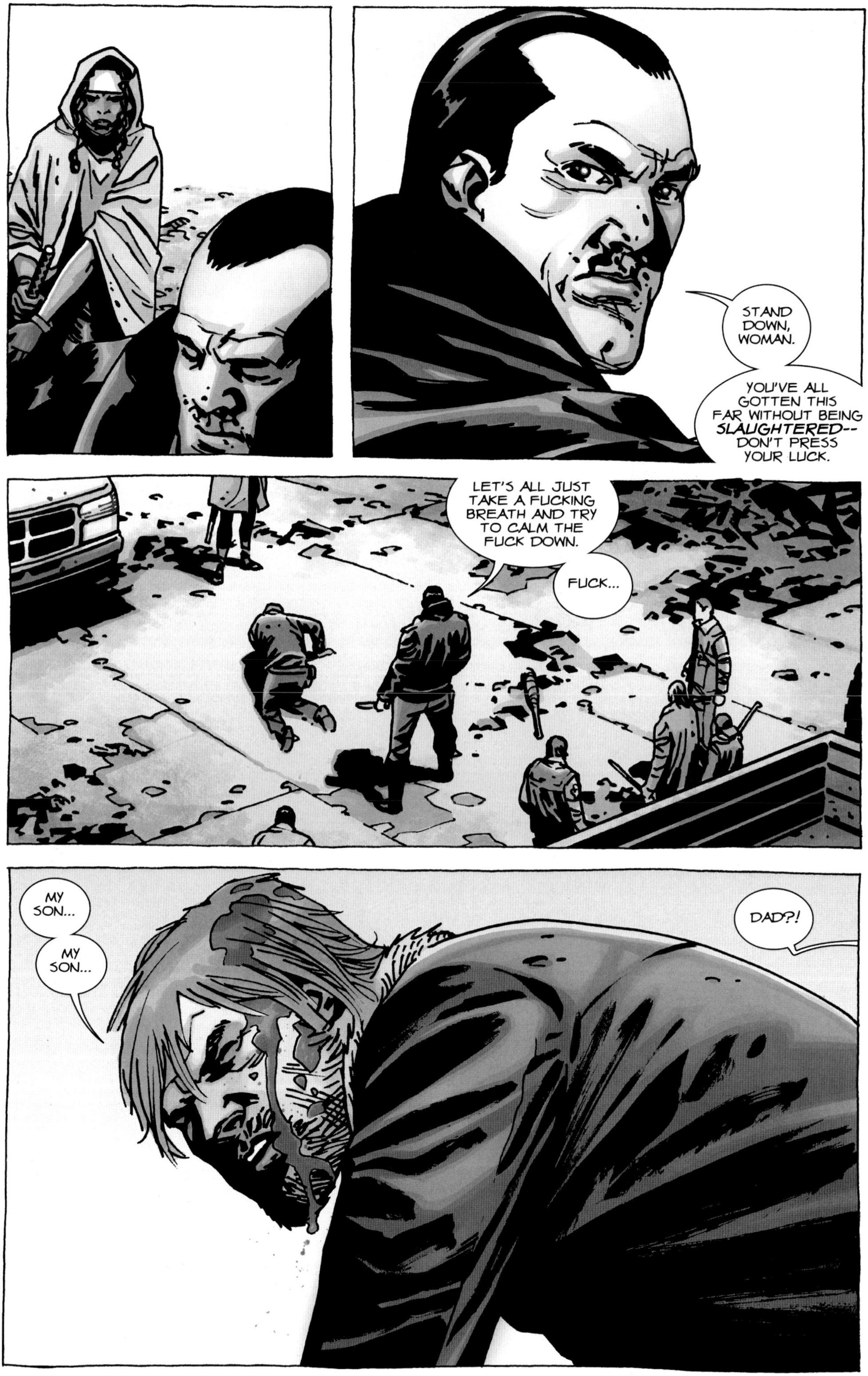
STAND DOWN, WOMAN.
YOU'VE ALL GOTTEN THIS FAR WITHOUT BEING SLAUGHTERED-- DON'T PRESS YOUR LUCK.
LET'S ALL JUST TAKE A FUCKING BREATH AND TRY TO CALM THE FUCK DOWN.
FUCK...
MY SON...
MY SON...
DAD?!

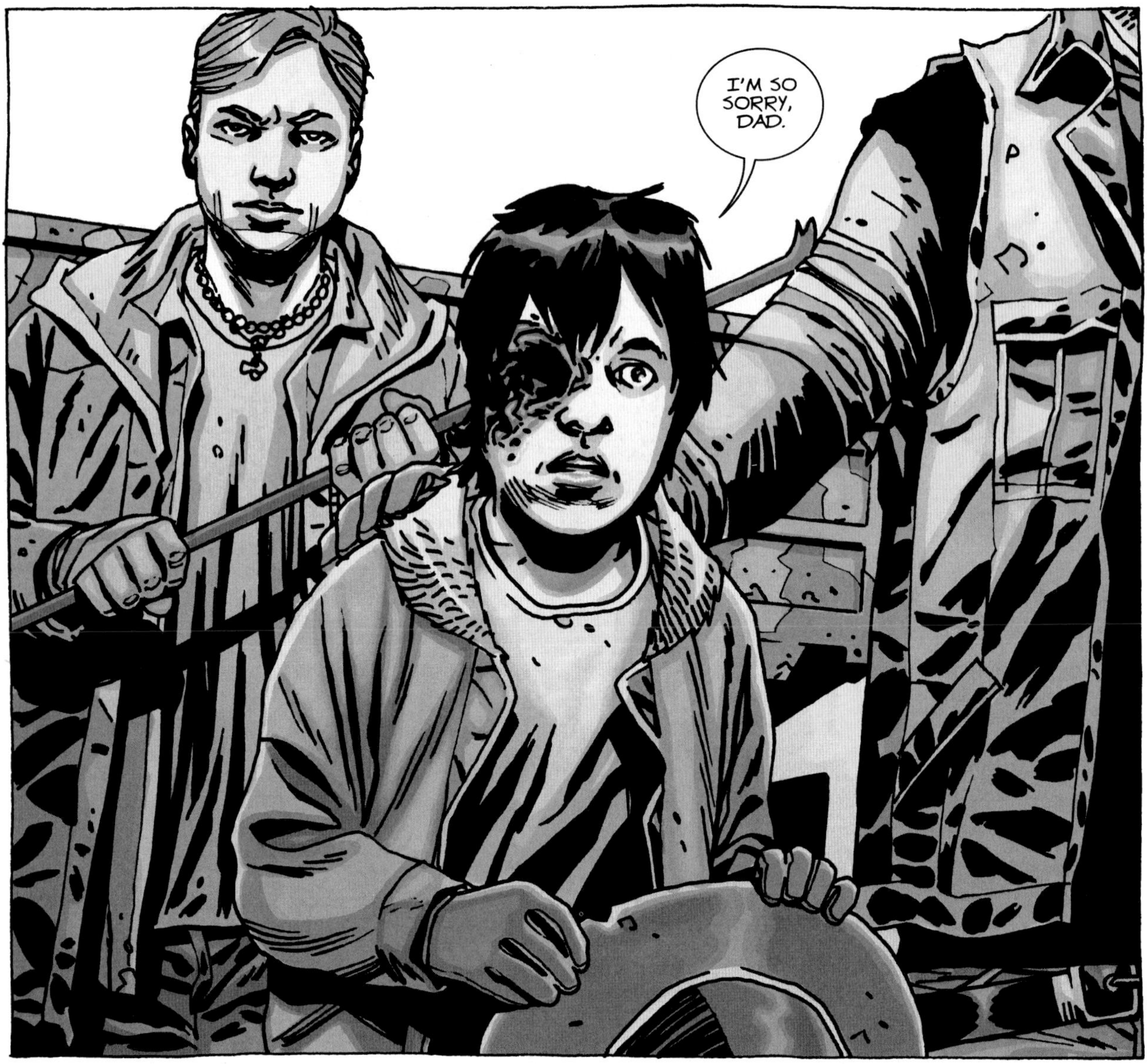
I'M SO SORRY, DAD.

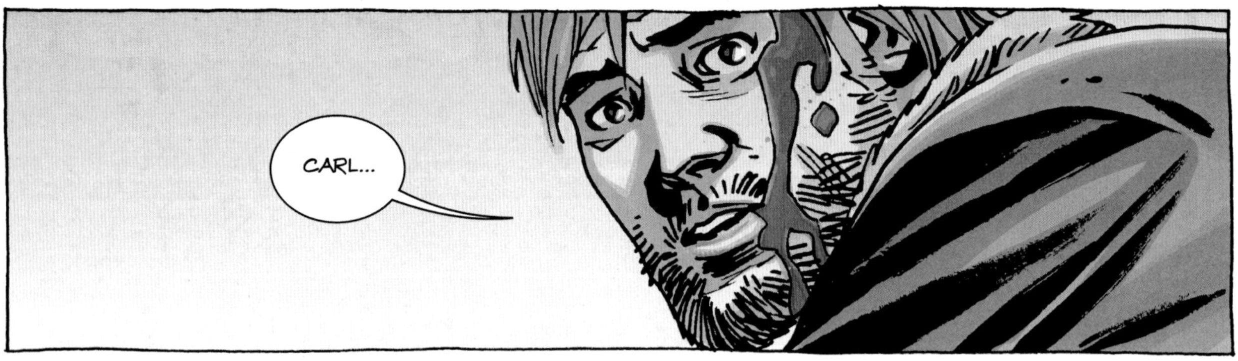
CARL...

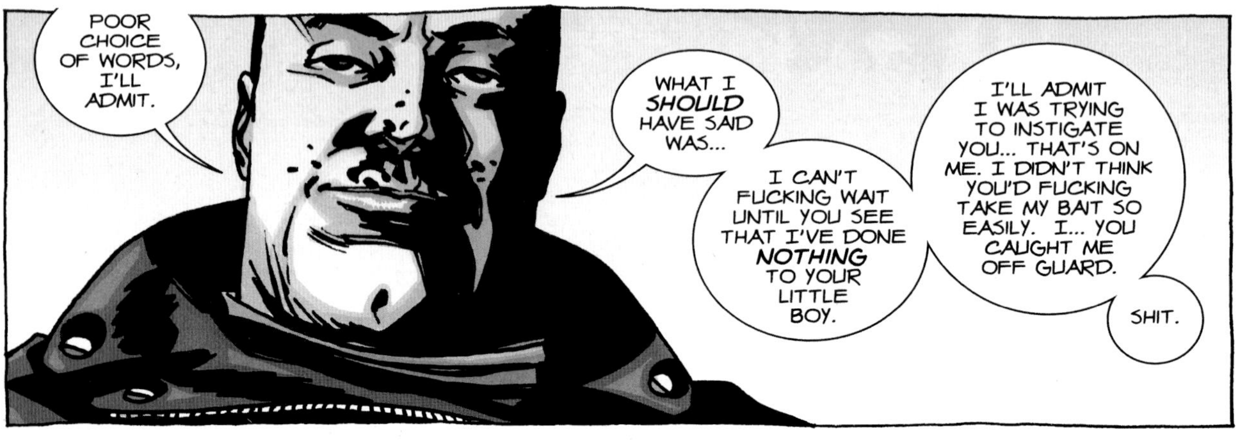
POOR CHOICE OF WORDS, I'LL ADMIT.
WHAT I *SHOULD* HAVE SAID WAS...
I CAN'T FUCKING WAIT UNTIL YOU SEE THAT I'VE DONE *NOTHING* TO YOUR LITTLE BOY.
I'LL ADMIT I WAS TRYING TO INSTIGATE YOU... THAT'S ON ME. I DIDN'T THINK YOU'D FUCKING TAKE MY BAIT SO EASILY. I... YOU CAUGHT ME OFF GUARD.
SHIT.

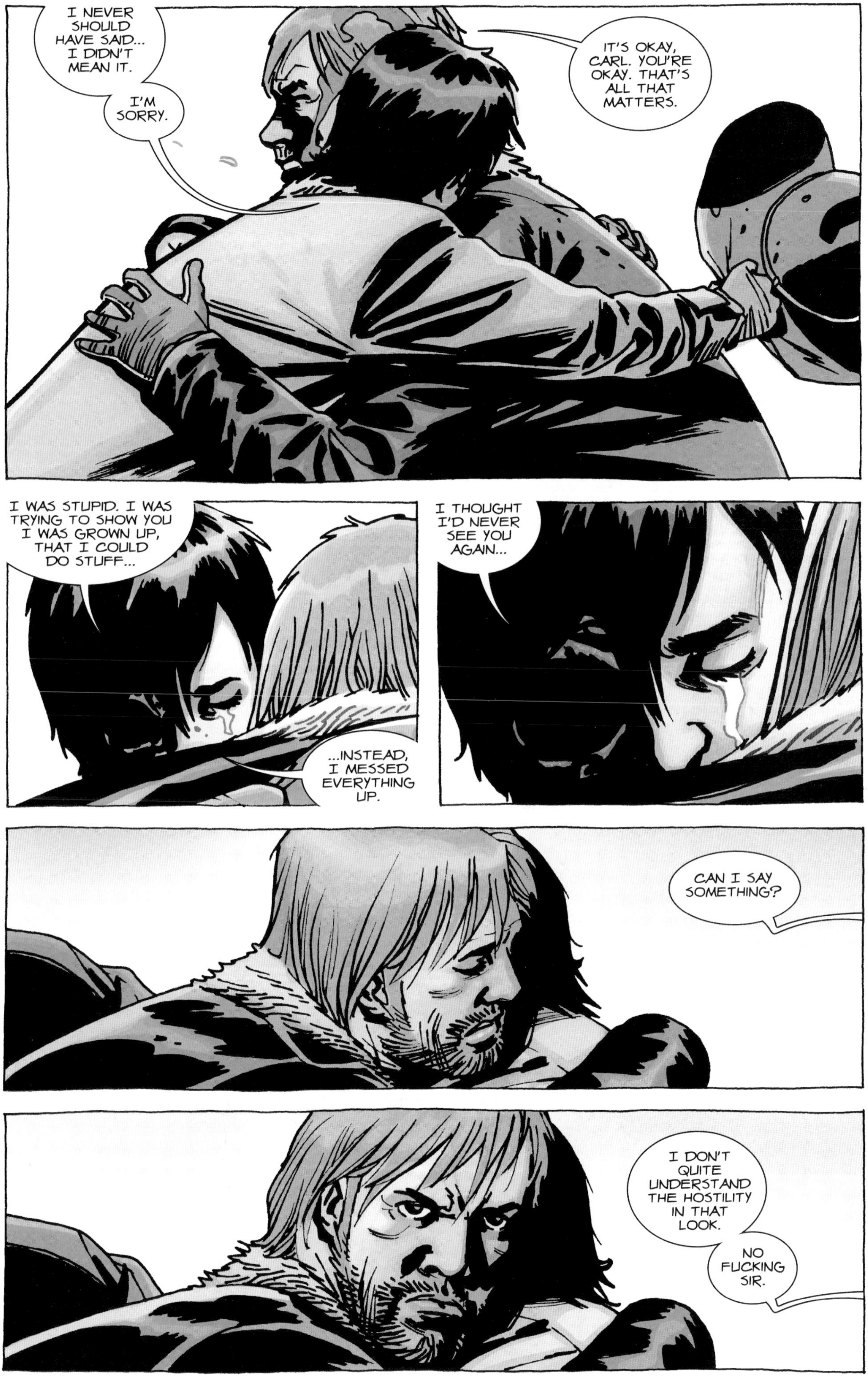
I NEVER SHOULD HAVE SAID... I DIDN'T MEAN IT.
I'M SORRY.
IT'S OKAY, CARL. YOU'RE OKAY. THAT'S ALL THAT MATTERS.
I WAS STUPID. I WAS TRYING TO SHOW YOU I WAS GROWN UP, THAT I COULD DO STUFF...
...INSTEAD, I MESSED EVERYTHING UP.
I THOUGHT I'D NEVER SEE YOU AGAIN...
CAN I SAY SOMETHING?
I DON'T QUITE UNDERSTAND THE HOSTILITY IN THAT LOOK.
NO FUCKING SIR.

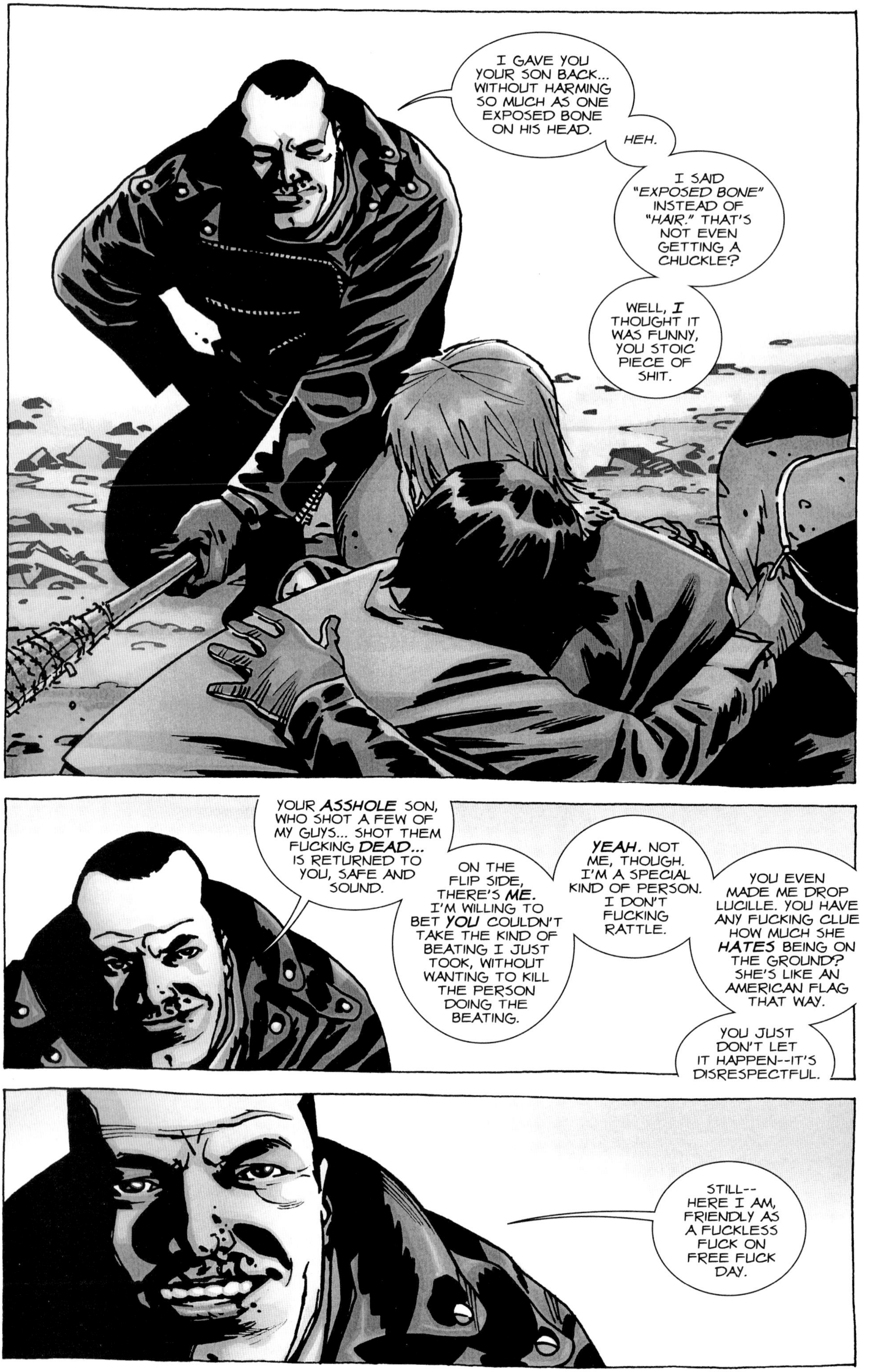
I GAVE YOU YOUR SON BACK... WITHOUT HARMING SO MUCH AS ONE EXPOSED BONE ON HIS HEAD.
HEH.
I SAID "EXPOSED BONE" INSTEAD OF "HAIR." THAT'S NOT EVEN GETTING A CHUCKLE?
WELL, I THOUGHT IT WAS FUNNY, YOU STOIC PIECE OF SHIT.
YOUR ASSHOLE SON, WHO SHOT A FEW OF MY GUYS... SHOT THEM FUCKING DEAD... IS RETURNED TO YOU, SAFE AND SOUND.
ON THE FLIP SIDE, THERE'S ME. I'M WILLING TO BET YOU COULDN'T TAKE THE KIND OF BEATING I JUST TOOK, WITHOUT WANTING TO KILL THE PERSON DOING THE BEATING.
YEAH. NOT ME, THOUGH. I'M A SPECIAL KIND OF PERSON. I DON'T FUCKING RATTLE.
YOU EVEN MADE ME DROP LUCILLE. YOU HAVE ANY FUCKING CLUE HOW MUCH SHE HATES BEING ON THE GROUND? SHE'S LIKE AN AMERICAN FLAG THAT WAY.
YOU JUST DON'T LET IT HAPPEN--IT'S DISRESPECTFUL.
STILL-- HERE I AM, FRIENDLY AS A FUCKLESS FUCK ON FREE FUCK DAY.

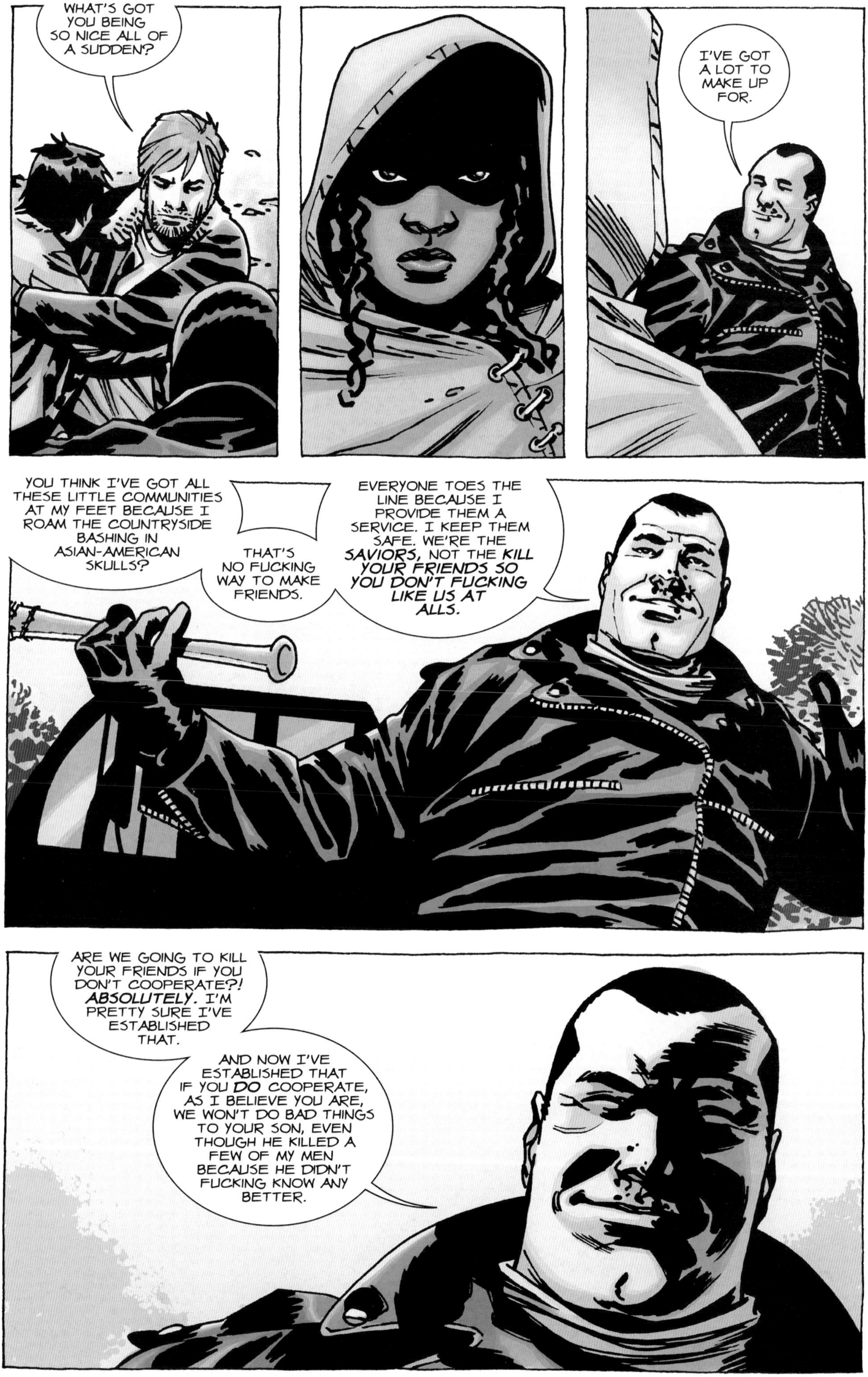
WHAT'S GOT YOU BEING SO NICE ALL OF A SUDDEN?
I'VE GOT A LOT TO MAKE UP FOR.
YOU THINK I'VE GOT ALL THESE LITTLE COMMUNITIES AT MY FEET BECAUSE I ROAM THE COUNTRYSIDE BASHING IN ASIAN-AMERICAN SKULLS?
THAT'S NO FUCKING WAY TO MAKE FRIENDS.
EVERYONE TOES THE LINE BECAUSE I PROVIDE THEM A SERVICE. I KEEP THEM SAFE. WE'RE THE *SAVIORS,* NOT THE *KILL YOUR FRIENDS SO YOU DON'T FUCKING LIKE US AT ALLS.*
ARE WE GOING TO KILL YOUR FRIENDS IF YOU DON'T COOPERATE?! *ABSOLUTELY.* I'M PRETTY SURE I'VE ESTABLISHED THAT.
AND NOW I'VE ESTABLISHED THAT IF YOU *DO* COOPERATE, AS I BELIEVE YOU ARE, WE WON'T DO BAD THINGS TO YOUR SON, EVEN THOUGH HE KILLED A FEW OF MY MEN BECAUSE HE DIDN'T FUCKING KNOW ANY BETTER.

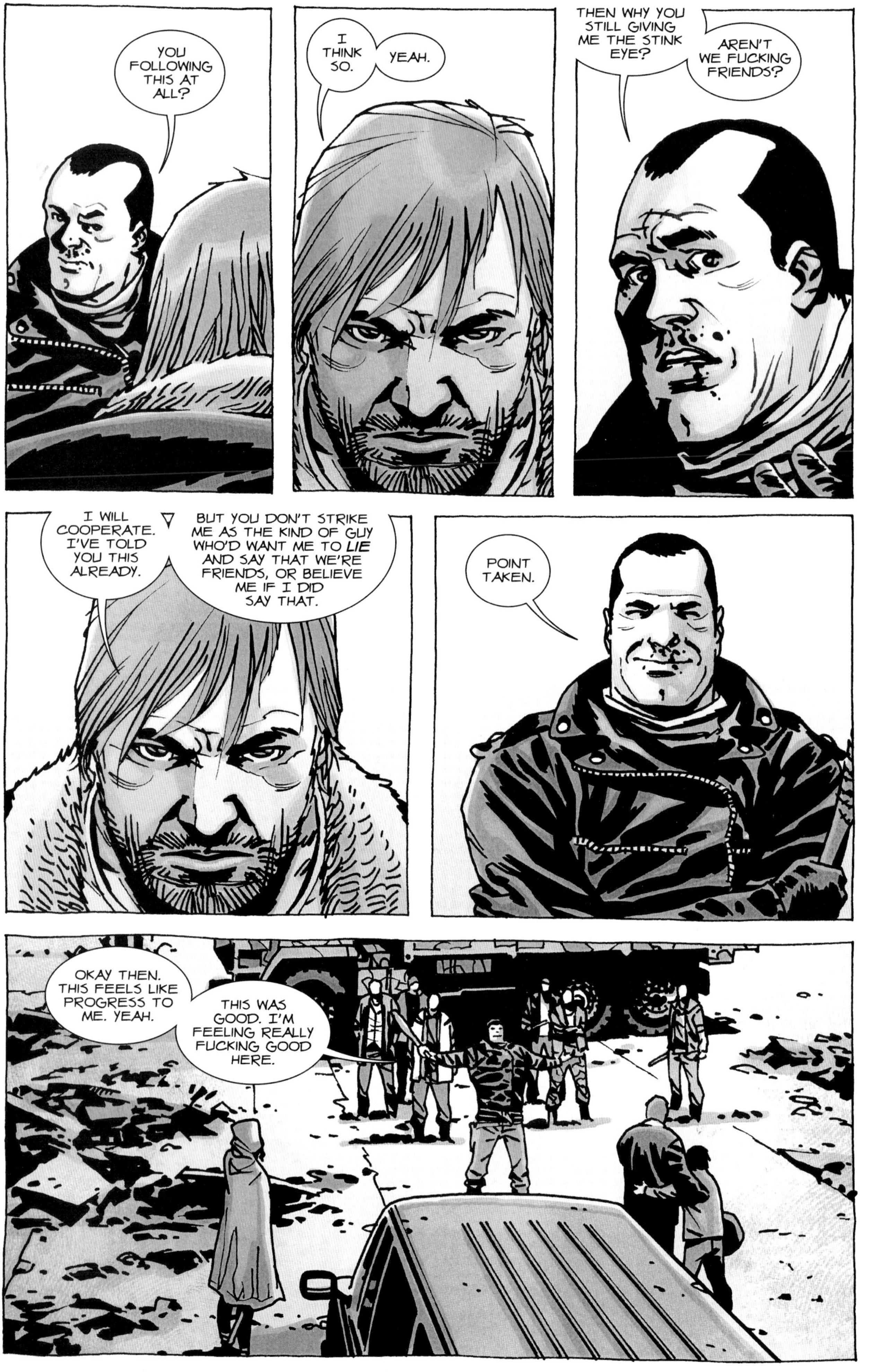
YOU FOLLOWING THIS AT ALL?
I THINK SO.
YEAH.
THEN WHY YOU STILL GIVING ME THE STINK EYE?
AREN'T WE FUCKING FRIENDS?
I WILL COOPERATE. I'VE TOLD YOU THIS ALREADY.
BUT YOU DON'T STRIKE ME AS THE KIND OF GUY WHO'D WANT ME TO LIE AND SAY THAT WE'RE FRIENDS, OR BELIEVE ME IF I DID SAY THAT.
POINT TAKEN.
OKAY THEN. THIS FEELS LIKE PROGRESS TO ME. YEAH.
THIS WAS GOOD. I'M FEELING REALLY FUCKING GOOD HERE.

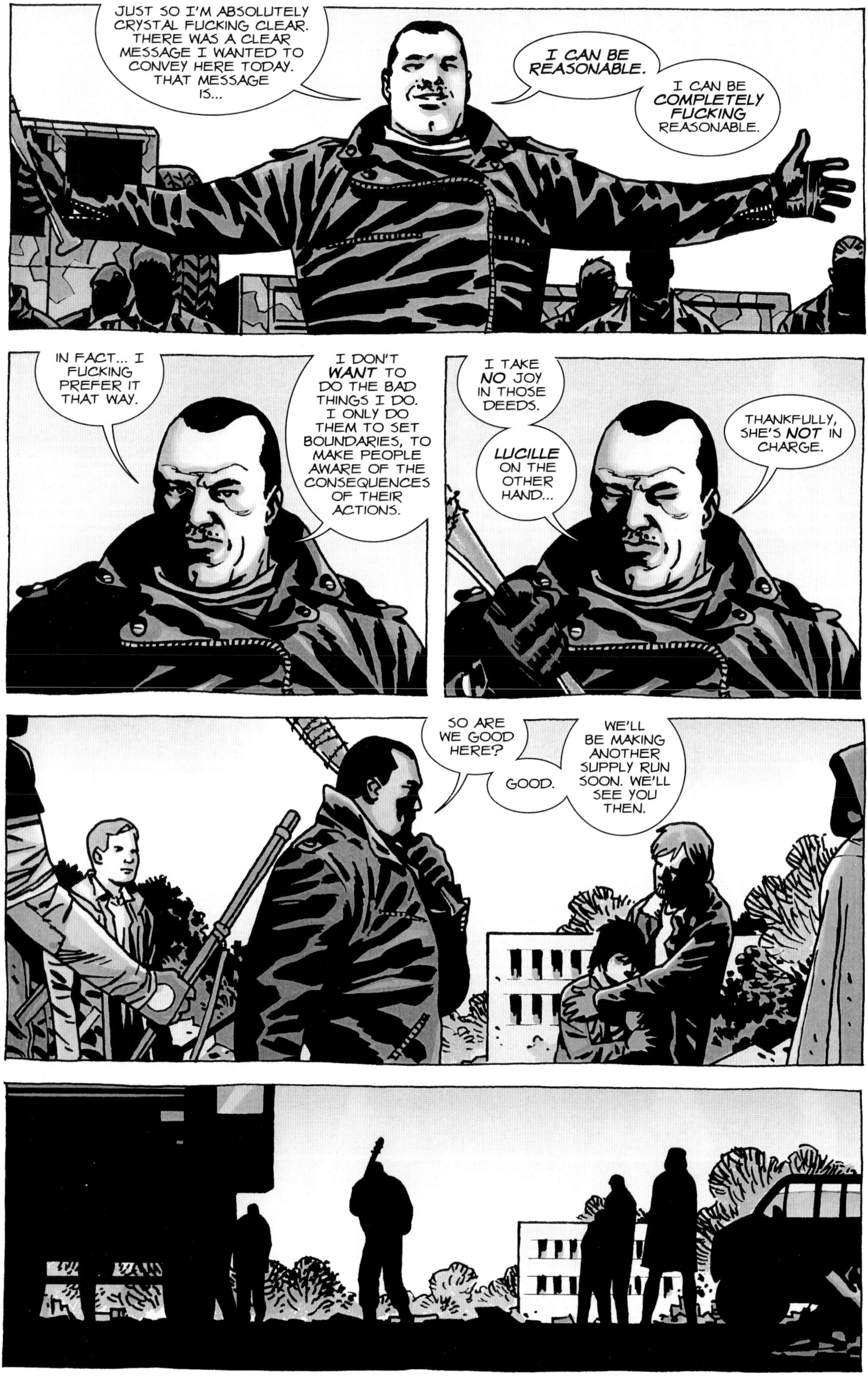
JUST SO I'M ABSOLUTELY CRYSTAL FUCKING CLEAR. THERE WAS A CLEAR MESSAGE I WANTED TO CONVEY HERE TODAY. THAT MESSAGE IS...
I CAN BE REASONABLE.
I CAN BE COMPLETELY FUCKING REASONABLE.
IN FACT... I FUCKING PREFER IT THAT WAY.
I DON'T WANT TO DO THE BAD THINGS I DO. I ONLY DO THEM TO SET BOUNDARIES, TO MAKE PEOPLE AWARE OF THE CONSEQUENCES OF THEIR ACTIONS.
I TAKE NO JOY IN THOSE DEEDS.
LUCILLE ON THE OTHER HAND...
THANKFULLY, SHE'S NOT IN CHARGE.
SO ARE WE GOOD HERE?
GOOD.
WE'LL BE MAKING ANOTHER SUPPLY RUN SOON. WE'LL SEE YOU THEN.

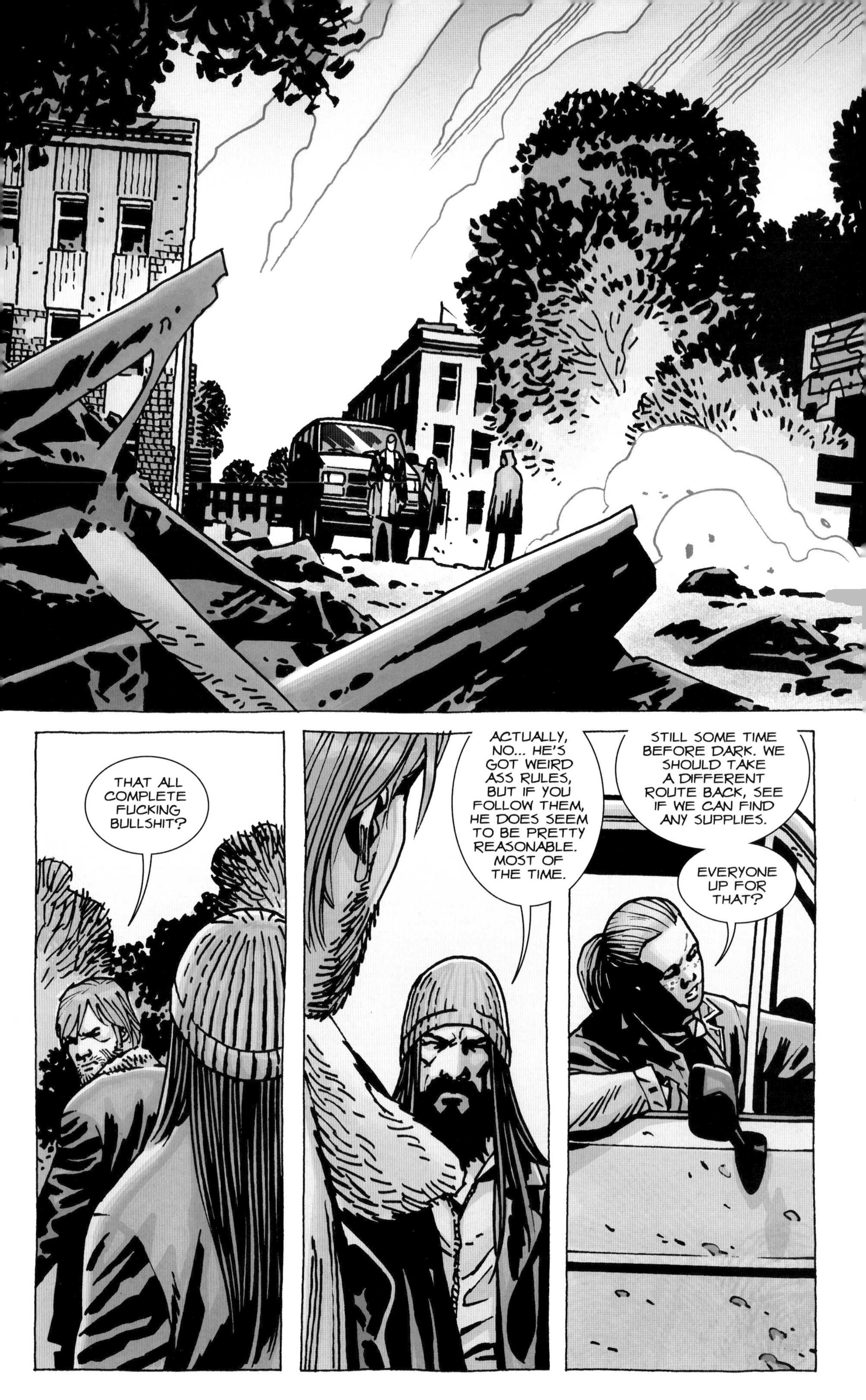
THAT ALL COMPLETE FUCKING BULLSHIT?
ACTUALLY, NO... HE'S GOT WEIRD ASS RULES, BUT IF YOU FOLLOW THEM, HE DOES SEEM TO BE PRETTY REASONABLE. MOST OF THE TIME.
STILL SOME TIME BEFORE DARK. WE SHOULD TAKE A DIFFERENT ROUTE BACK, SEE IF WE CAN FIND ANY SUPPLIES.
EVERYONE UP FOR THAT?

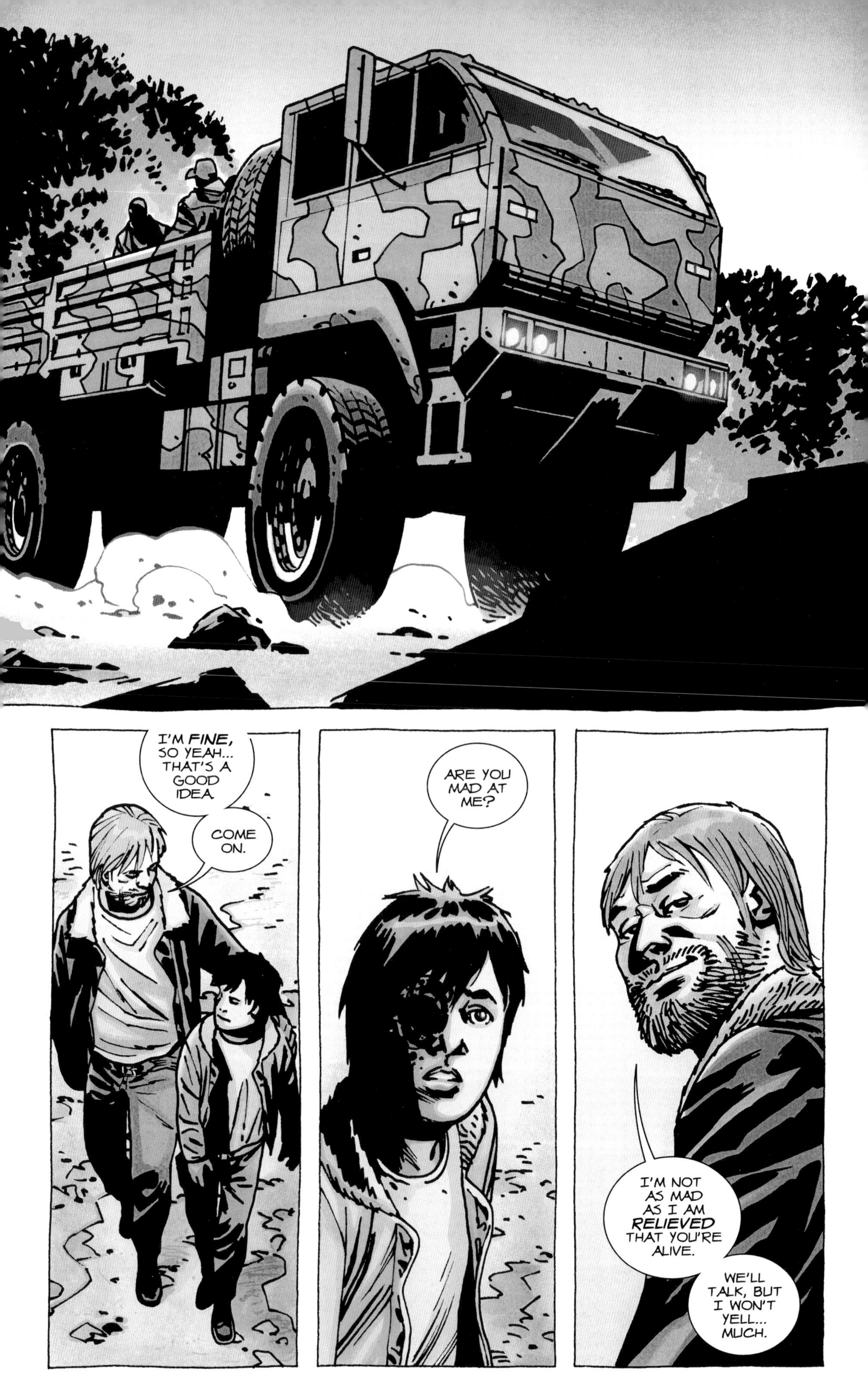
I'M FINE, SO YEAH... THAT'S A GOOD IDEA.
COME ON.
ARE YOU MAD AT ME?
I'M NOT AS MAD AS I AM RELIEVED THAT YOU'RE ALIVE.
WE'LL TALK, BUT I WON'T YELL... MUCH.

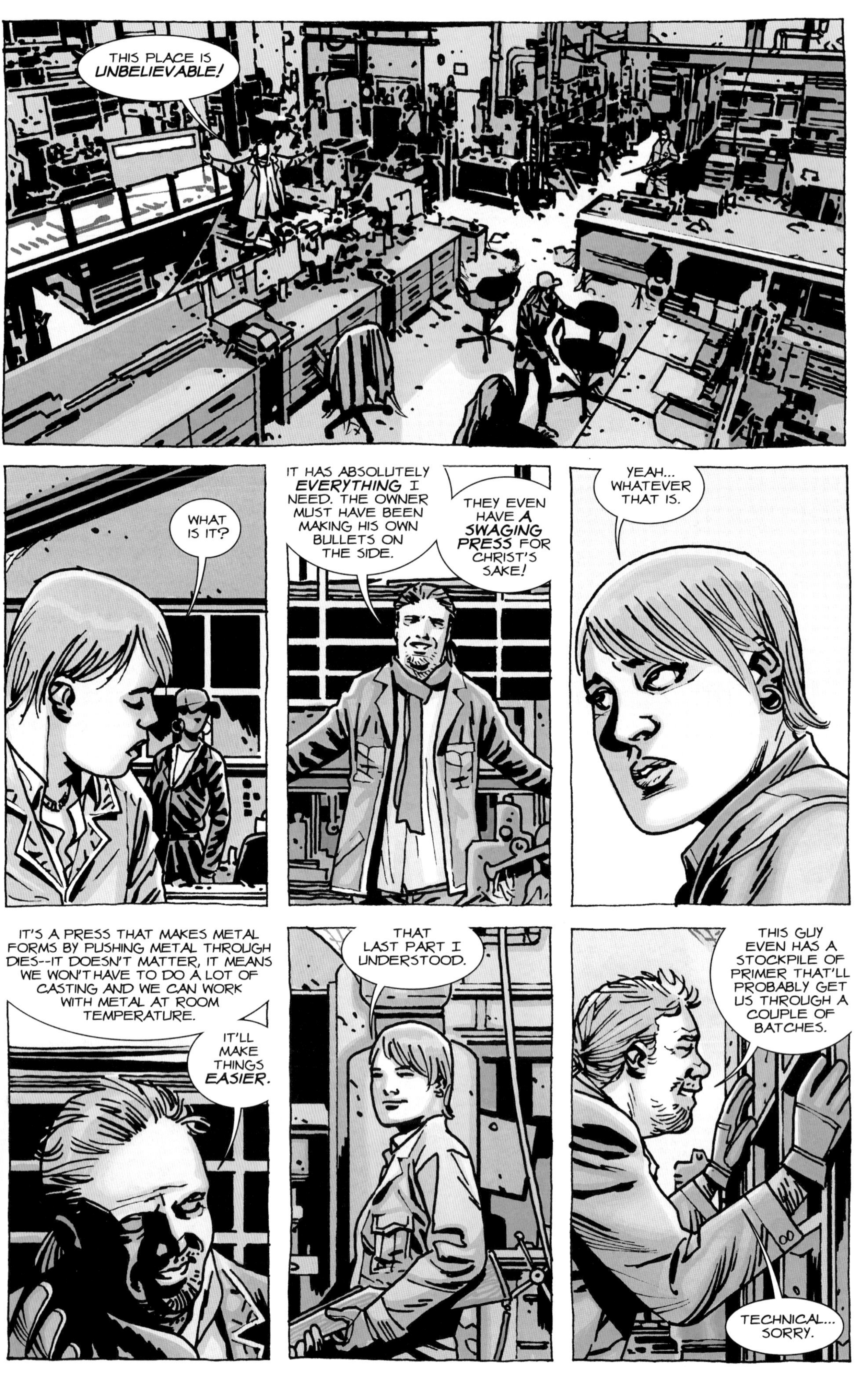
THIS PLACE IS UNBELIEVABLE!
WHAT IS IT?
IT HAS ABSOLUTELY EVERYTHING I NEED. THE OWNER MUST HAVE BEEN MAKING HIS OWN BULLETS ON THE SIDE.
THEY EVEN HAVE A SWAGING PRESS FOR CHRIST'S SAKE!
YEAH... WHATEVER THAT IS.
IT'S A PRESS THAT MAKES METAL FORMS BY PUSHING METAL THROUGH DIES--IT DOESN'T MATTER, IT MEANS WE WON'T HAVE TO DO A LOT OF CASTING AND WE CAN WORK WITH METAL AT ROOM TEMPERATURE.
IT'LL MAKE THINGS EASIER.
THAT LAST PART I UNDERSTOOD.
THIS GUY EVEN HAS A STOCKPILE OF PRIMER THAT'LL PROBABLY GET US THROUGH A COUPLE OF BATCHES.
TECHNICAL... SORRY.

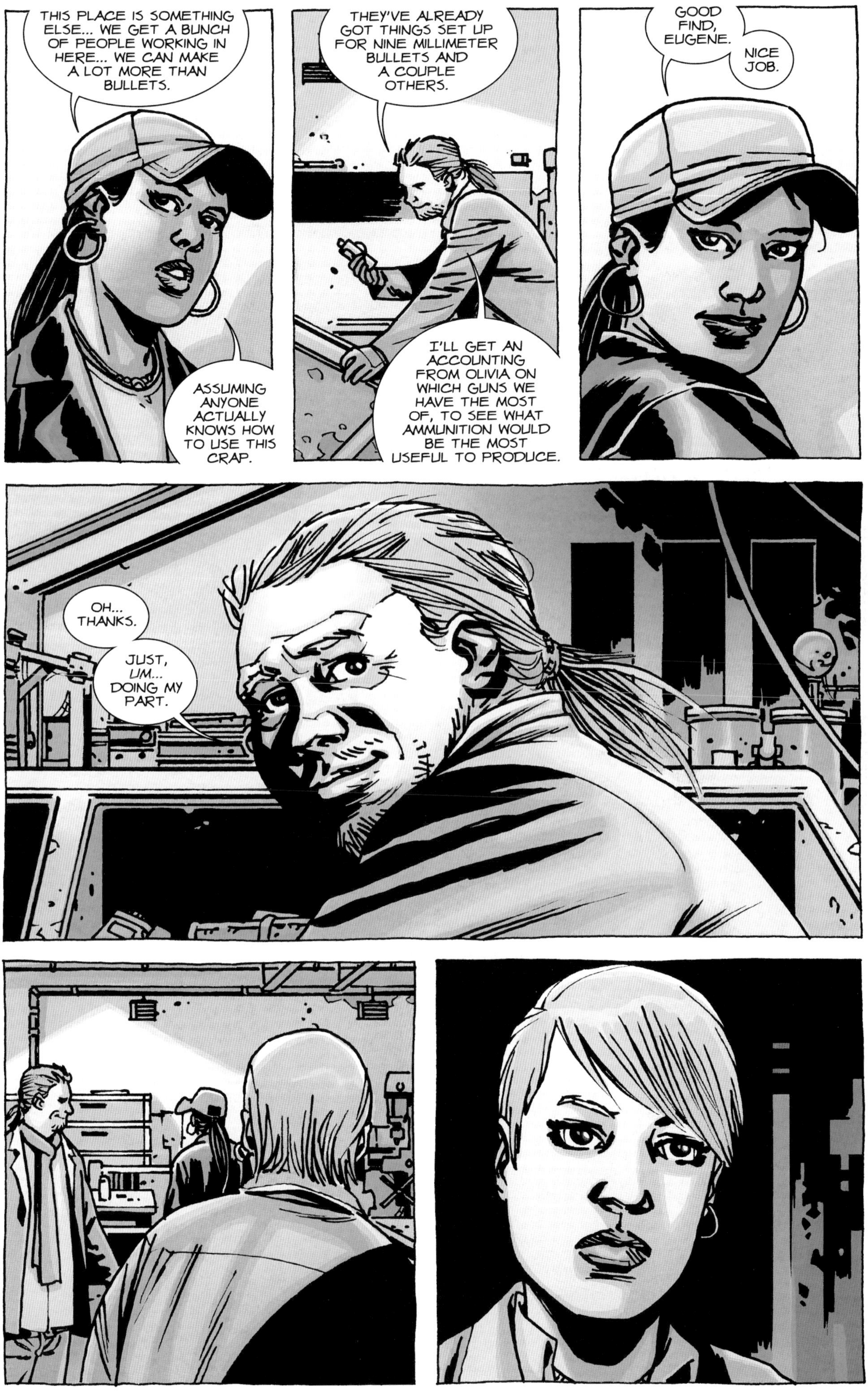
THIS PLACE IS SOMETHING ELSE... WE GET A BUNCH OF PEOPLE WORKING IN HERE... WE CAN MAKE A LOT MORE THAN BULLETS.
ASSUMING ANYONE ACTUALLY KNOWS HOW TO USE THIS CRAP.
THEY'VE ALREADY GOT THINGS SET UP FOR NINE MILLIMETER BULLETS AND A COUPLE OTHERS.
I'LL GET AN ACCOUNTING FROM OLIVIA ON WHICH GUNS WE HAVE THE MOST OF, TO SEE WHAT AMMUNITION WOULD BE THE MOST USEFUL TO PRODUCE.
GOOD FIND, EUGENE.
NICE JOB.
OH... THANKS.
JUST, UM... DOING MY PART.

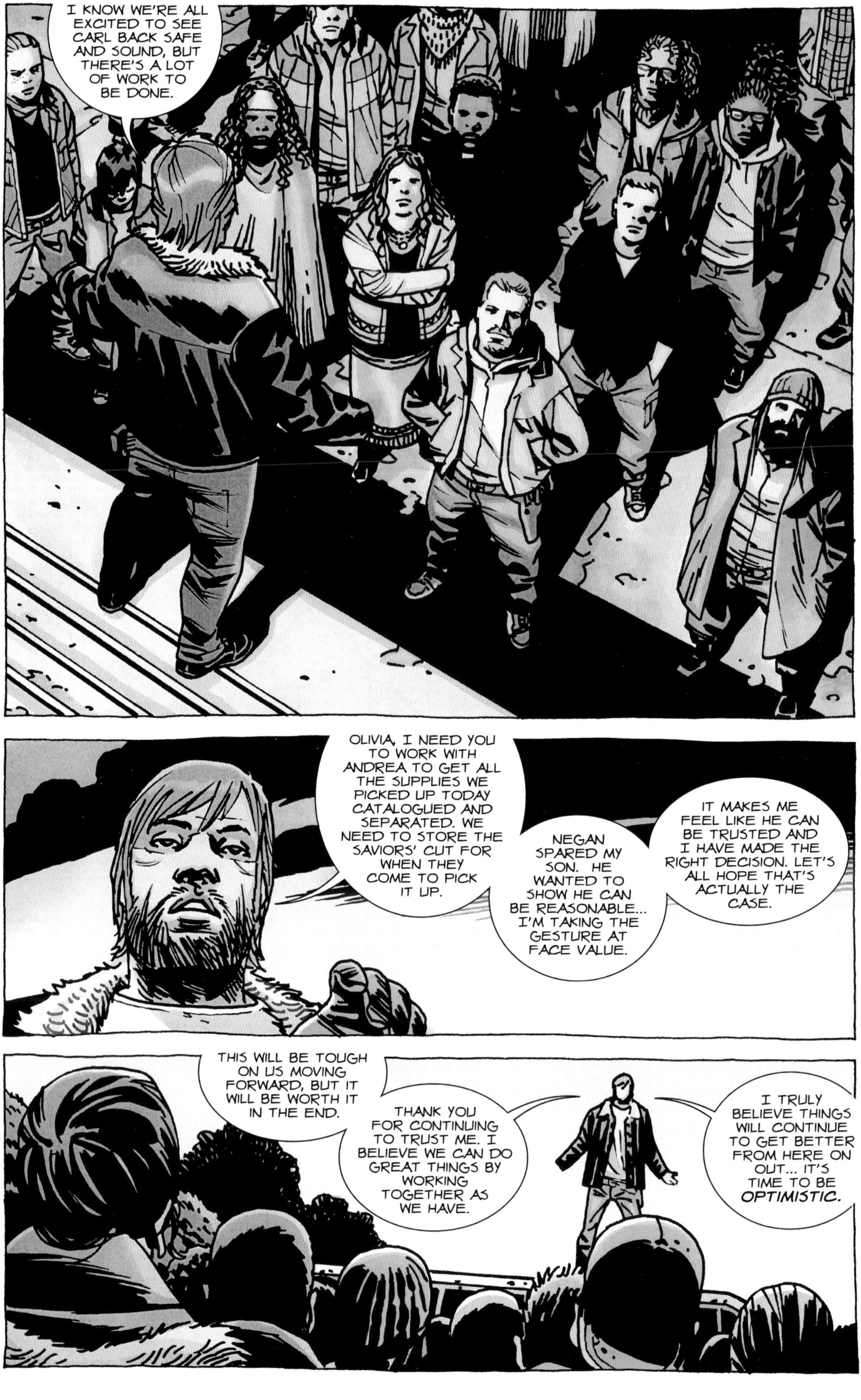
I KNOW WE'RE ALL EXCITED TO SEE CARL BACK SAFE AND SOUND, BUT THERE'S A LOT OF WORK TO BE DONE.
OLIVIA, I NEED YOU TO WORK WITH ANDREA TO GET ALL THE SUPPLIES WE PICKED UP TODAY CATALOGUED AND SEPARATED. WE NEED TO STORE THE SAVIORS' CUT FOR WHEN THEY COME TO PICK IT UP.
NEGAN SPARED MY SON. HE WANTED TO SHOW HE CAN BE REASONABLE... I'M TAKING THE GESTURE AT FACE VALUE.
IT MAKES ME FEEL LIKE HE CAN BE TRUSTED AND I HAVE MADE THE RIGHT DECISION. LET'S ALL HOPE THAT'S ACTUALLY THE CASE.
THIS WILL BE TOUGH ON US MOVING FORWARD, BUT IT WILL BE WORTH IT IN THE END.
THANK YOU FOR CONTINUING TO TRUST ME. I BELIEVE WE CAN DO GREAT THINGS BY WORKING TOGETHER AS WE HAVE.
I TRULY BELIEVE THINGS WILL CONTINUE TO GET BETTER FROM HERE ON OUT... IT'S TIME TO BE *OPTIMISTIC.*

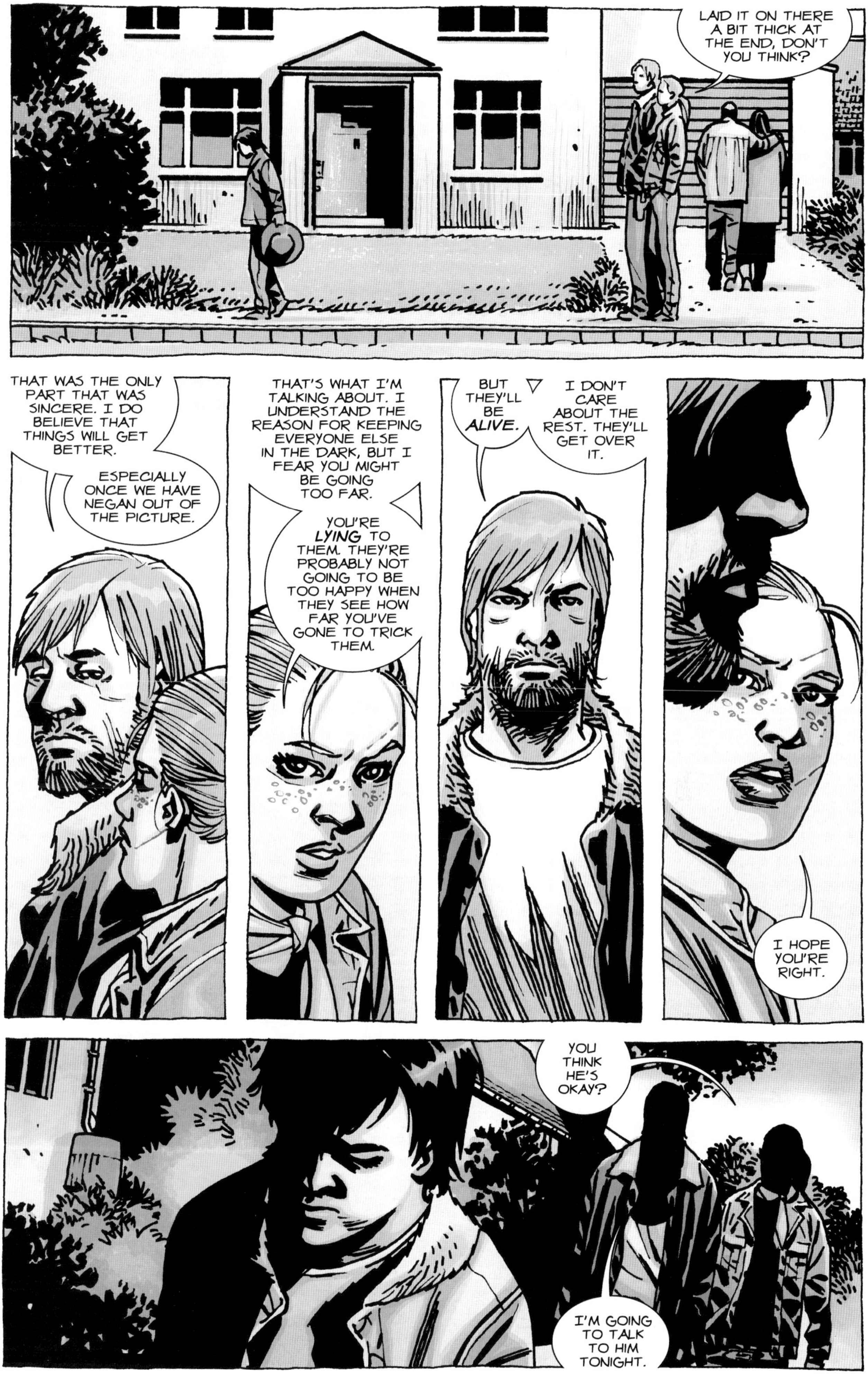
LAID IT ON THERE A BIT THICK AT THE END, DON'T YOU THINK?
THAT WAS THE ONLY PART THAT WAS SINCERE. I DO BELIEVE THAT THINGS WILL GET BETTER.
ESPECIALLY ONCE WE HAVE NEGAN OUT OF THE PICTURE.
THAT'S WHAT I'M TALKING ABOUT. I UNDERSTAND THE REASON FOR KEEPING EVERYONE ELSE IN THE DARK, BUT I FEAR YOU MIGHT BE GOING TOO FAR.
YOU'RE LYING TO THEM. THEY'RE PROBABLY NOT GOING TO BE TOO HAPPY WHEN THEY SEE HOW FAR YOU'VE GONE TO TRICK THEM.
BUT THEY'LL BE ALIVE.
I DON'T CARE ABOUT THE REST. THEY'LL GET OVER IT.
I HOPE YOU'RE RIGHT.
YOU THINK HE'S OKAY?
I'M GOING TO TALK TO HIM TONIGHT.

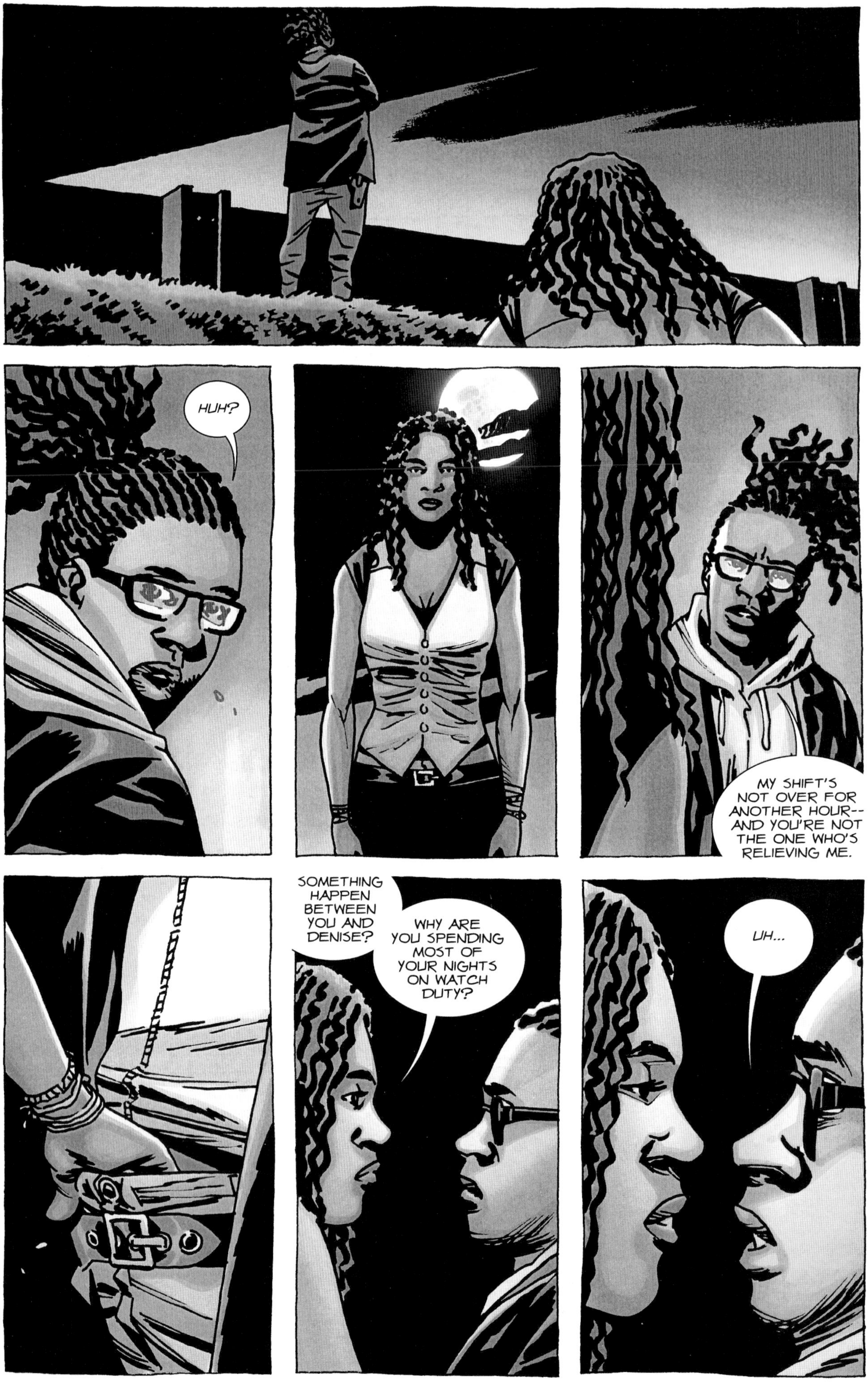
HUH?
MY SHIFT'S NOT OVER FOR ANOTHER HOUR-- AND YOU'RE NOT THE ONE WHO'S RELIEVING ME.
SOMETHING HAPPEN BETWEEN YOU AND DENISE?
WHY ARE YOU SPENDING MOST OF YOUR NIGHTS ON WATCH DUTY?
UH...

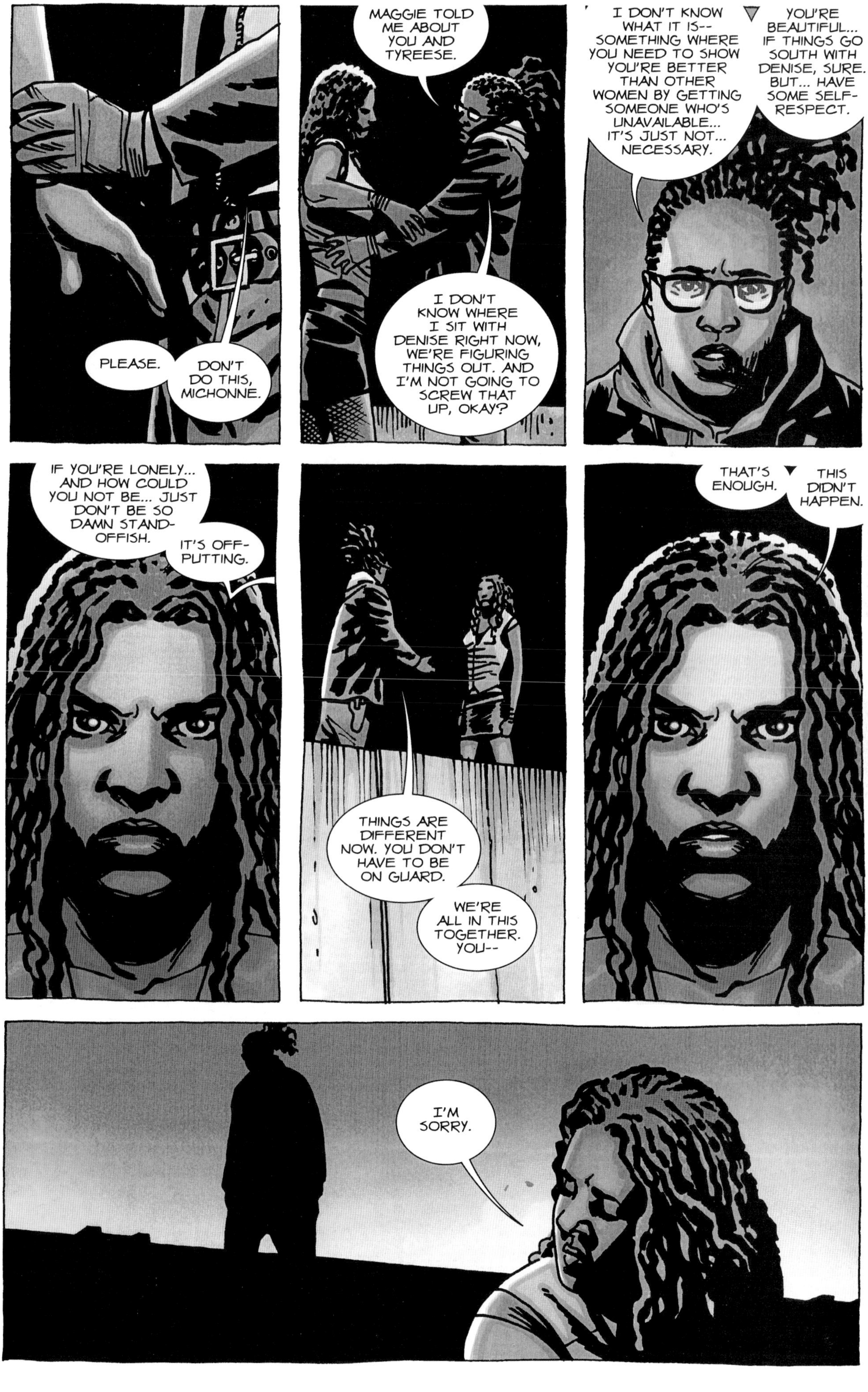
PLEASE.
DON'T DO THIS, MICHONNE.
MAGGIE TOLD ME ABOUT YOU AND TYREESE.
I DON'T KNOW WHERE I SIT WITH DENISE RIGHT NOW, WE'RE FIGURING THINGS OUT. AND I'M NOT GOING TO SCREW THAT UP, OKAY?
I DON'T KNOW WHAT IT IS-- SOMETHING WHERE YOU NEED TO SHOW YOU'RE BETTER THAN OTHER WOMEN BY GETTING SOMEONE WHO'S UNAVAILABLE... IT'S JUST NOT... NECESSARY.
YOU'RE BEAUTIFUL... IF THINGS GO SOUTH WITH DENISE, SURE. BUT... HAVE SOME SELF-RESPECT.
IF YOU'RE LONELY... AND HOW COULD YOU NOT BE... JUST DON'T BE SO DAMN STAND-OFFISH.
IT'S OFF-PUTTING.
THINGS ARE DIFFERENT NOW. YOU DON'T HAVE TO BE ON GUARD.
WE'RE ALL IN THIS TOGETHER. YOU--
THAT'S ENOUGH.
THIS DIDN'T HAPPEN.
I'M SORRY.

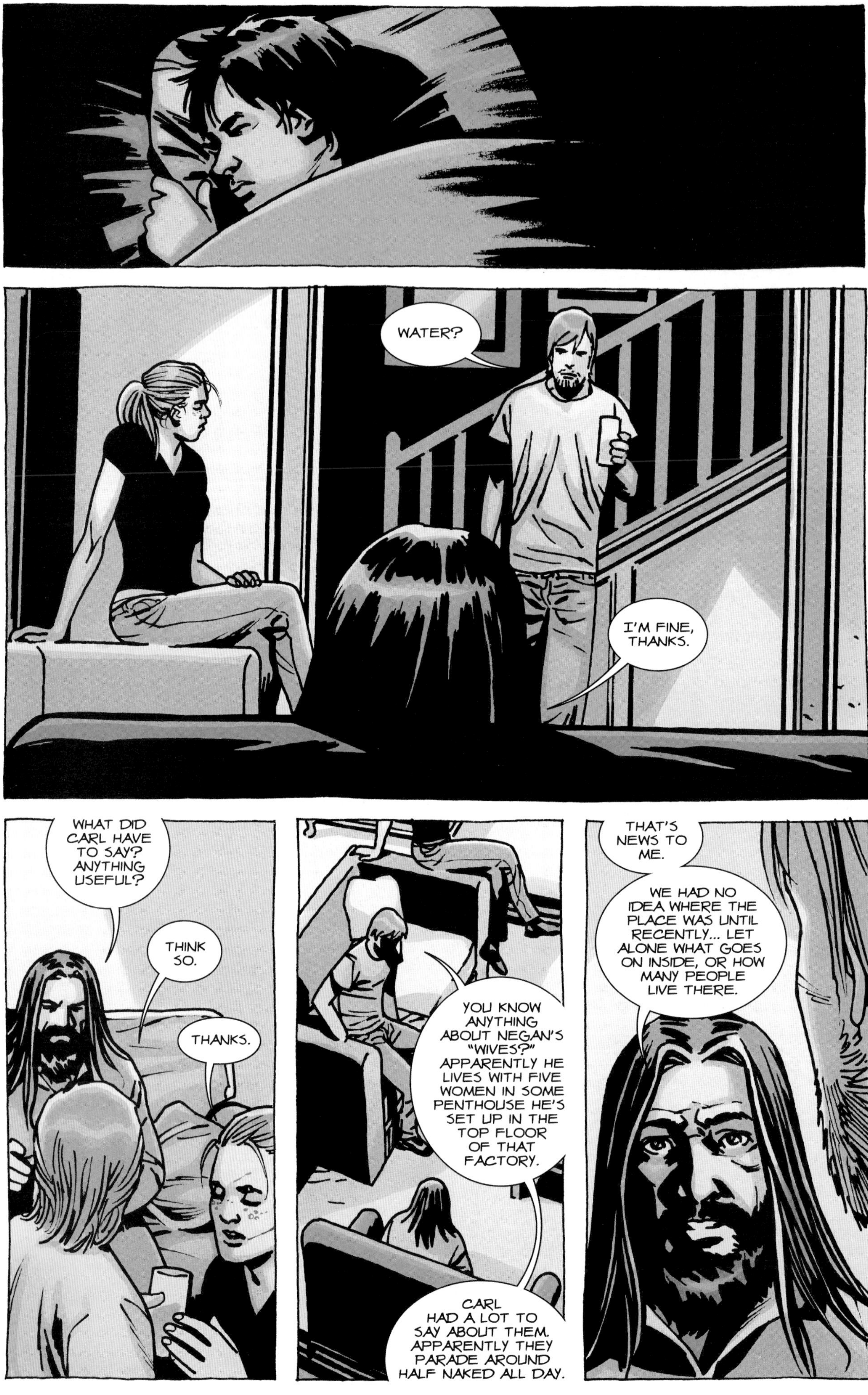
WATER?
I'M FINE, THANKS.
WHAT DID CARL HAVE TO SAY? ANYTHING USEFUL?
THINK SO.
THANKS.
YOU KNOW ANYTHING ABOUT NEGAN'S "WIVES?" APPARENTLY HE LIVES WITH FIVE WOMEN IN SOME PENTHOUSE HE'S SET UP IN THE TOP FLOOR OF THAT FACTORY.
CARL HAD A LOT TO SAY ABOUT THEM. APPARENTLY THEY PARADE AROUND HALF NAKED ALL DAY.
THAT'S NEWS TO ME.
WE HAD NO IDEA WHERE THE PLACE WAS UNTIL RECENTLY... LET ALONE WHAT GOES ON INSIDE, OR HOW MANY PEOPLE LIVE THERE.

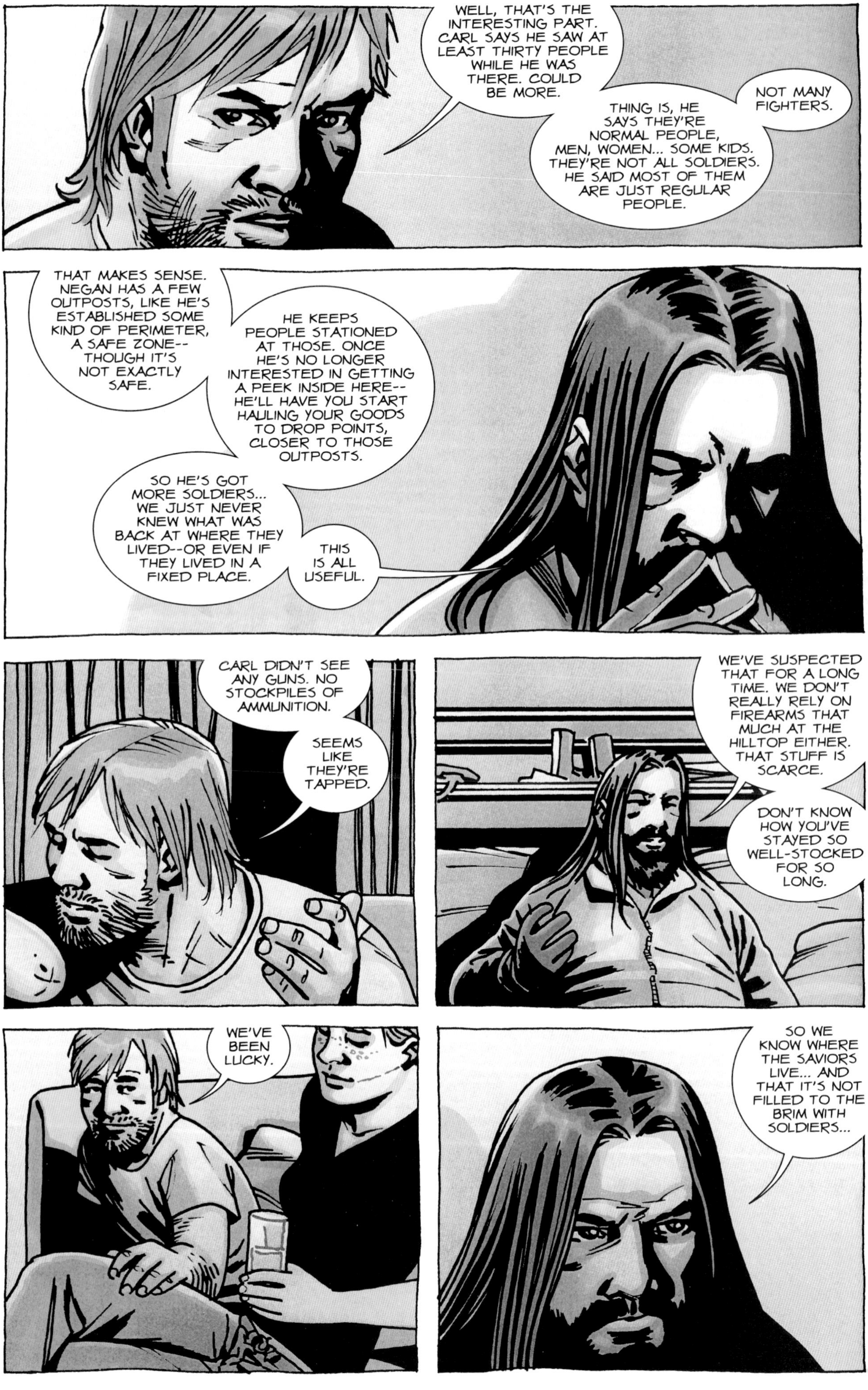
WELL, THAT'S THE INTERESTING PART. CARL SAYS HE SAW AT LEAST THIRTY PEOPLE WHILE HE WAS THERE. COULD BE MORE.
THING IS, HE SAYS THEY'RE NORMAL PEOPLE, MEN, WOMEN... SOME KIDS. THEY'RE NOT ALL SOLDIERS. HE SAID MOST OF THEM ARE JUST REGULAR PEOPLE.
NOT MANY FIGHTERS.
THAT MAKES SENSE. NEGAN HAS A FEW OUTPOSTS, LIKE HE'S ESTABLISHED SOME KIND OF PERIMETER, A SAFE ZONE-- THOUGH IT'S NOT EXACTLY SAFE.
HE KEEPS PEOPLE STATIONED AT THOSE. ONCE HE'S NO LONGER INTERESTED IN GETTING A PEEK INSIDE HERE-- HE'LL HAVE YOU START HAULING YOUR GOODS TO DROP POINTS, CLOSER TO THOSE OUTPOSTS.
SO HE'S GOT MORE SOLDIERS... WE JUST NEVER KNEW WHAT WAS BACK AT WHERE THEY LIVED--OR EVEN IF THEY LIVED IN A FIXED PLACE.
THIS IS ALL USEFUL.
CARL DIDN'T SEE ANY GUNS. NO STOCKPILES OF AMMUNITION.
SEEMS LIKE THEY'RE TAPPED.
WE'VE SUSPECTED THAT FOR A LONG TIME. WE DON'T REALLY RELY ON FIREARMS THAT MUCH AT THE HILLTOP EITHER. THAT STUFF IS SCARCE.
DON'T KNOW HOW YOU'VE STAYED SO WELL-STOCKED FOR SO LONG.
WE'VE BEEN LUCKY.
SO WE KNOW WHERE THE SAVIORS LIVE... AND THAT IT'S NOT FILLED TO THE BRIM WITH SOLDIERS...

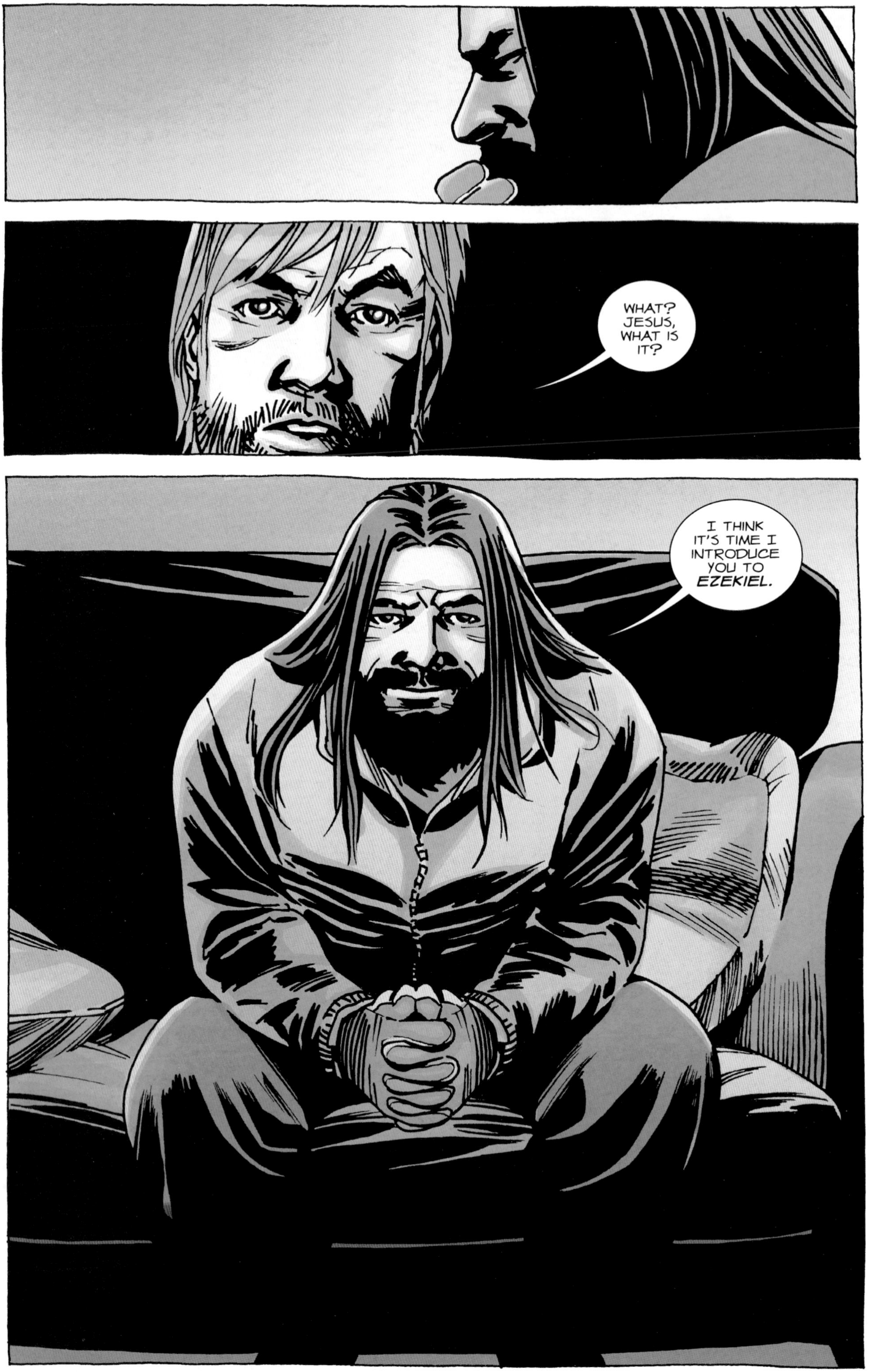
WHAT? JESUS, WHAT IS IT?
I THINK IT'S TIME I INTRODUCE YOU TO *EZEKIEL.*

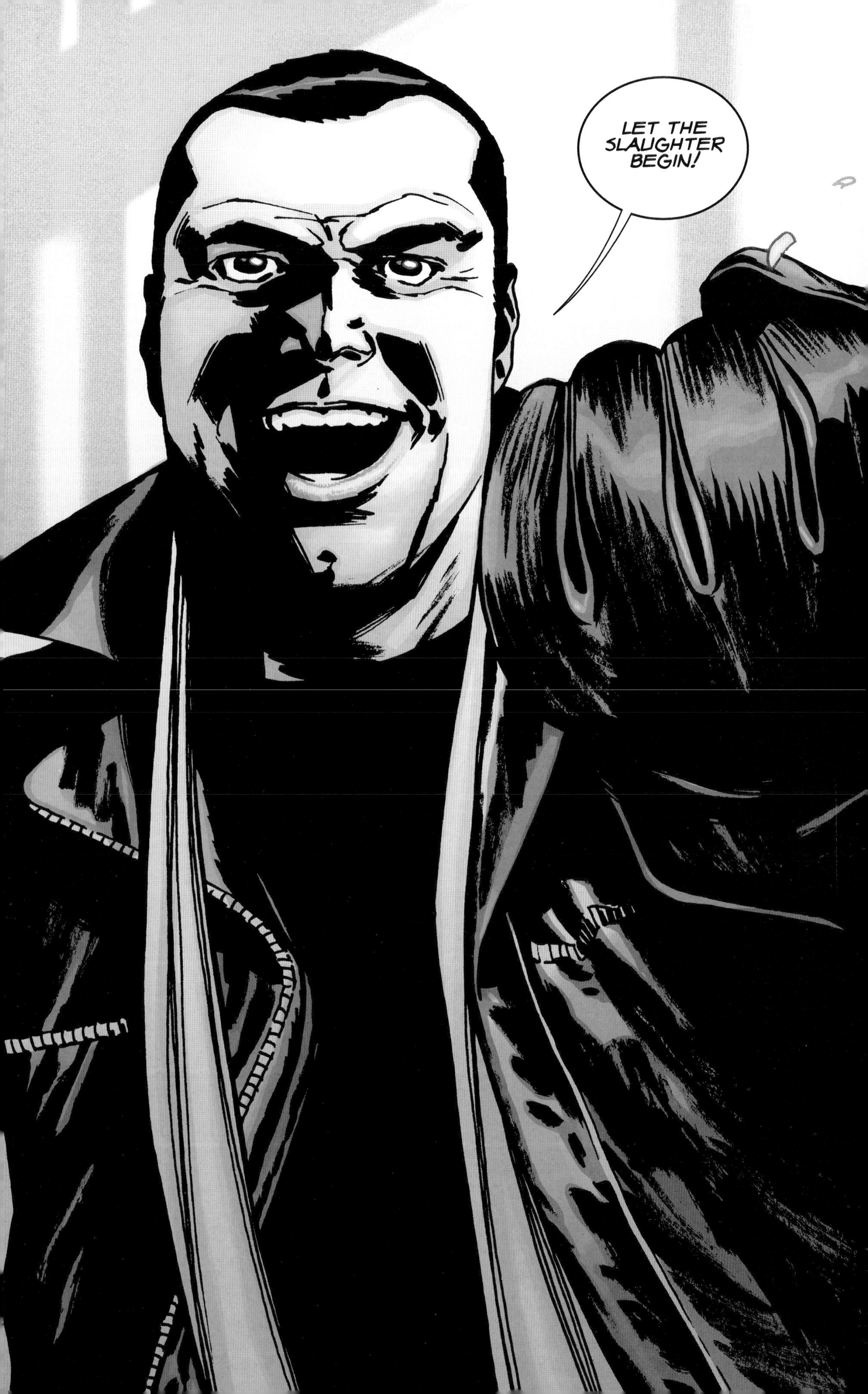
LET THE SLAUGHTER BEGIN!

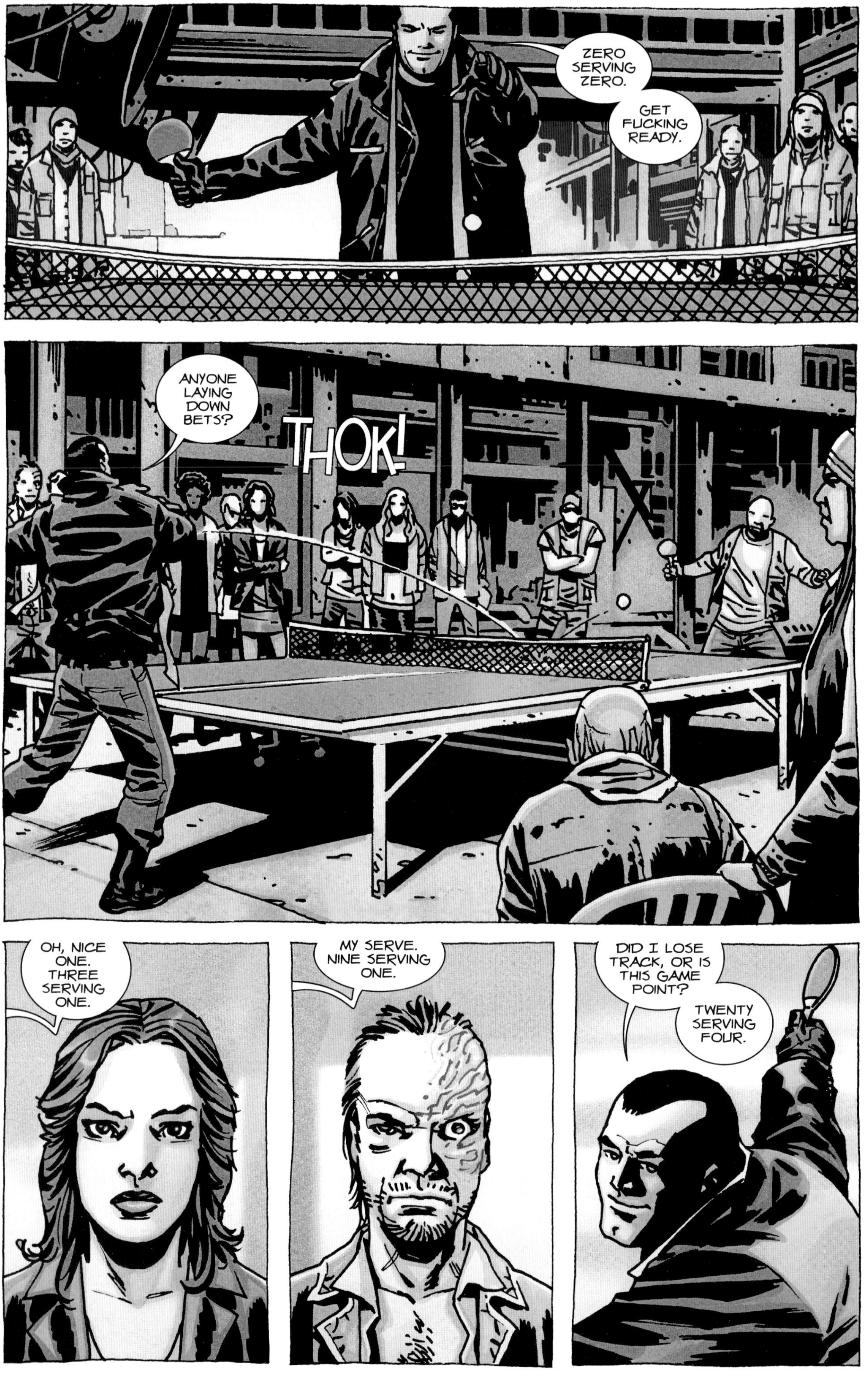
ZERO SERVING ZERO.
GET FUCKING READY.
ANYONE LAYING DOWN BETS?
THOK!
OH, NICE ONE. THREE SERVING ONE.
MY SERVE. NINE SERVING ONE.
DID I LOSE TRACK, OR IS THIS GAME POINT?
TWENTY SERVING FOUR.

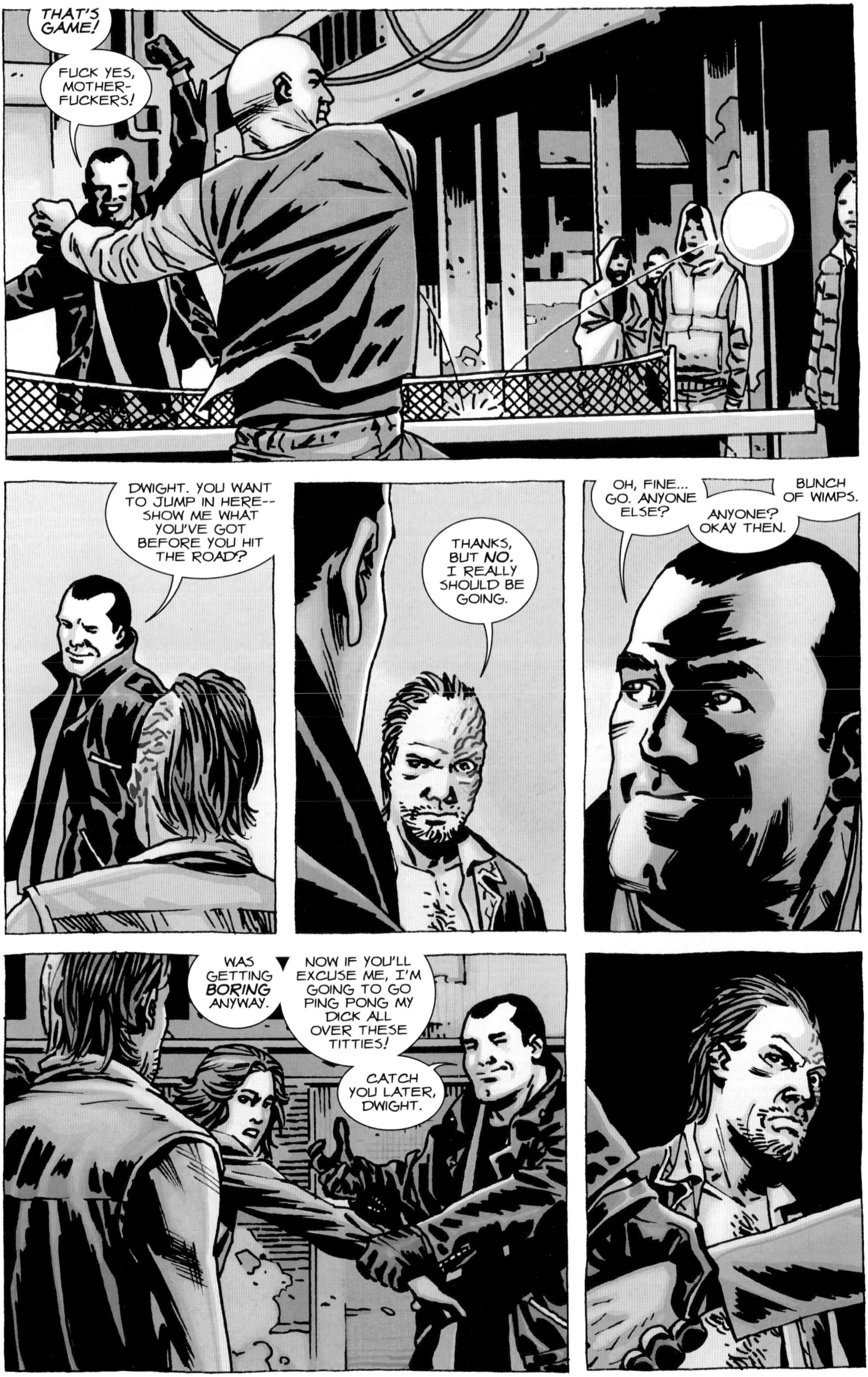
THAT'S GAME!
FUCK YES, MOTHER-FUCKERS!
DWIGHT. YOU WANT TO JUMP IN HERE--SHOW ME WHAT YOU'VE GOT BEFORE YOU HIT THE ROAD?
THANKS, BUT NO. I REALLY SHOULD BE GOING.
OH, FINE... GO. ANYONE ELSE?
ANYONE? OKAY THEN.
BUNCH OF WIMPS.
WAS GETTING BORING ANYWAY.
NOW IF YOU'LL EXCUSE ME, I'M GOING TO GO PING PONG MY DICK ALL OVER THESE TITTIES!
CATCH YOU LATER, DWIGHT.

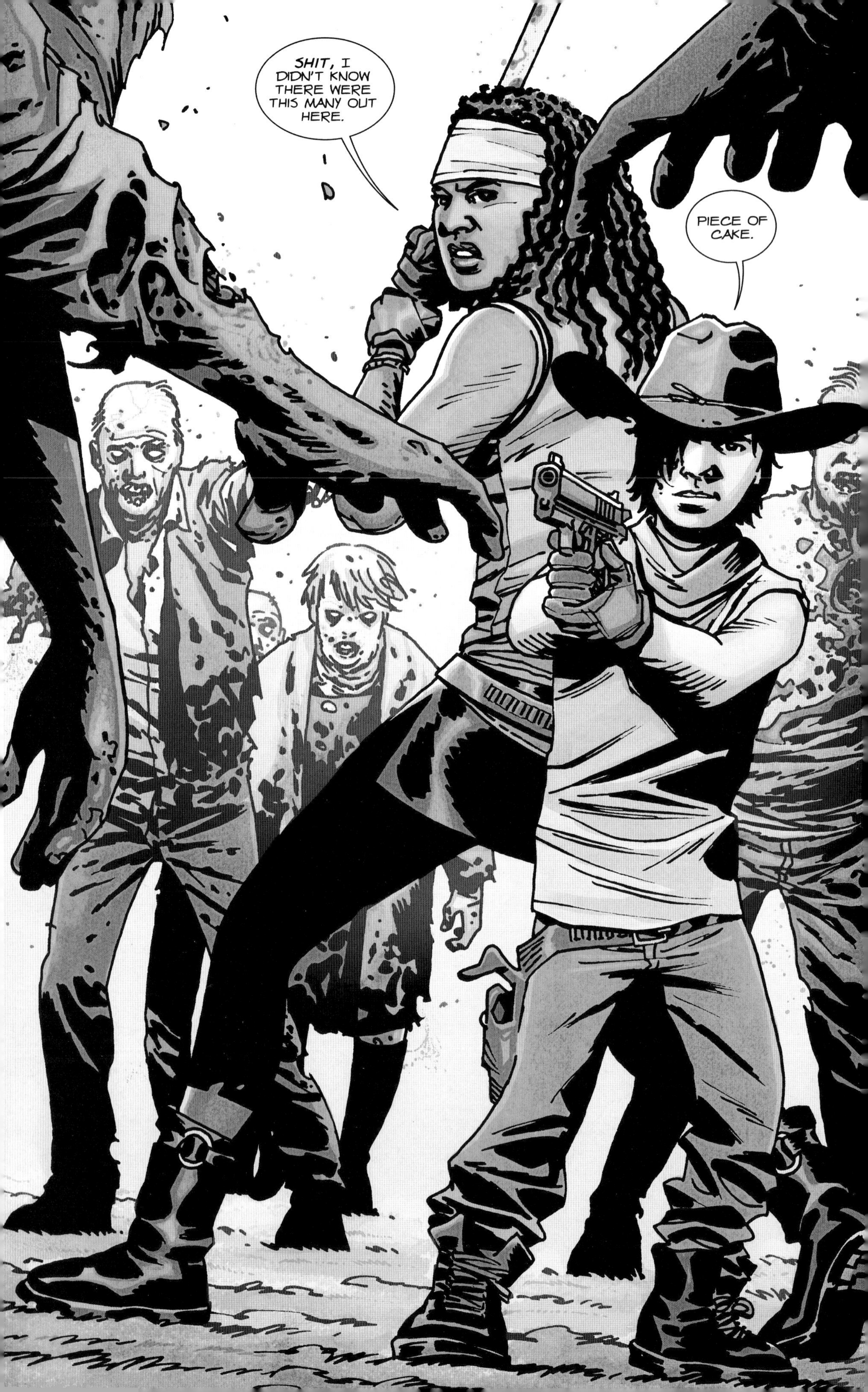
SHIT, I DIDN'T KNOW THERE WERE THIS MANY OUT HERE.
PIECE OF CAKE.

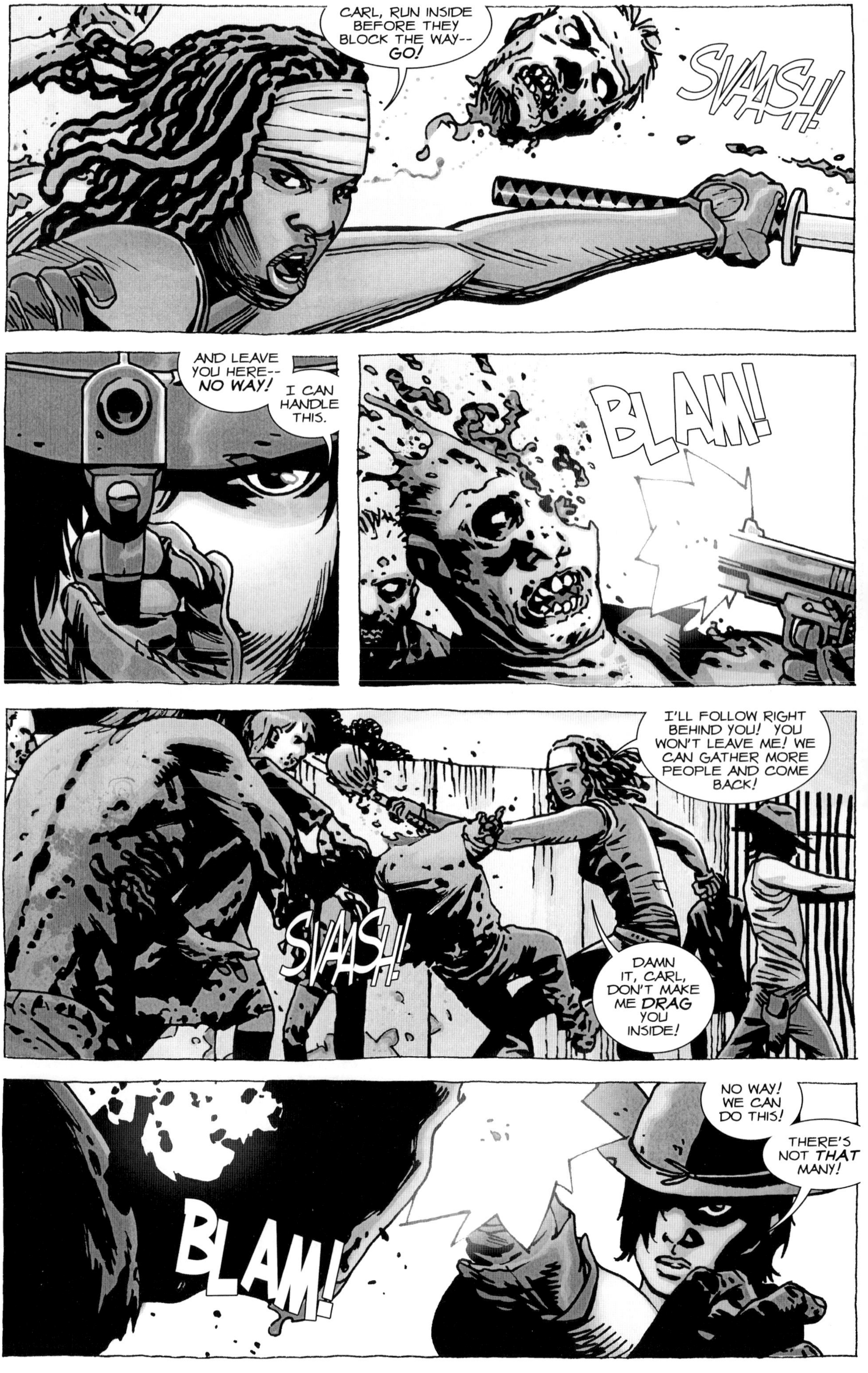
CARL, RUN INSIDE BEFORE THEY BLOCK THE WAY-- GO!
SVAASH!
AND LEAVE YOU HERE-- NO WAY!
I CAN HANDLE THIS.
BLAM!
I'LL FOLLOW RIGHT BEHIND YOU! YOU WON'T LEAVE ME! WE CAN GATHER MORE PEOPLE AND COME BACK!
SVAASH!
DAMN IT, CARL, DON'T MAKE ME DRAG YOU INSIDE!
BLAM!
NO WAY! WE CAN DO THIS!
THERE'S NOT THAT MANY!

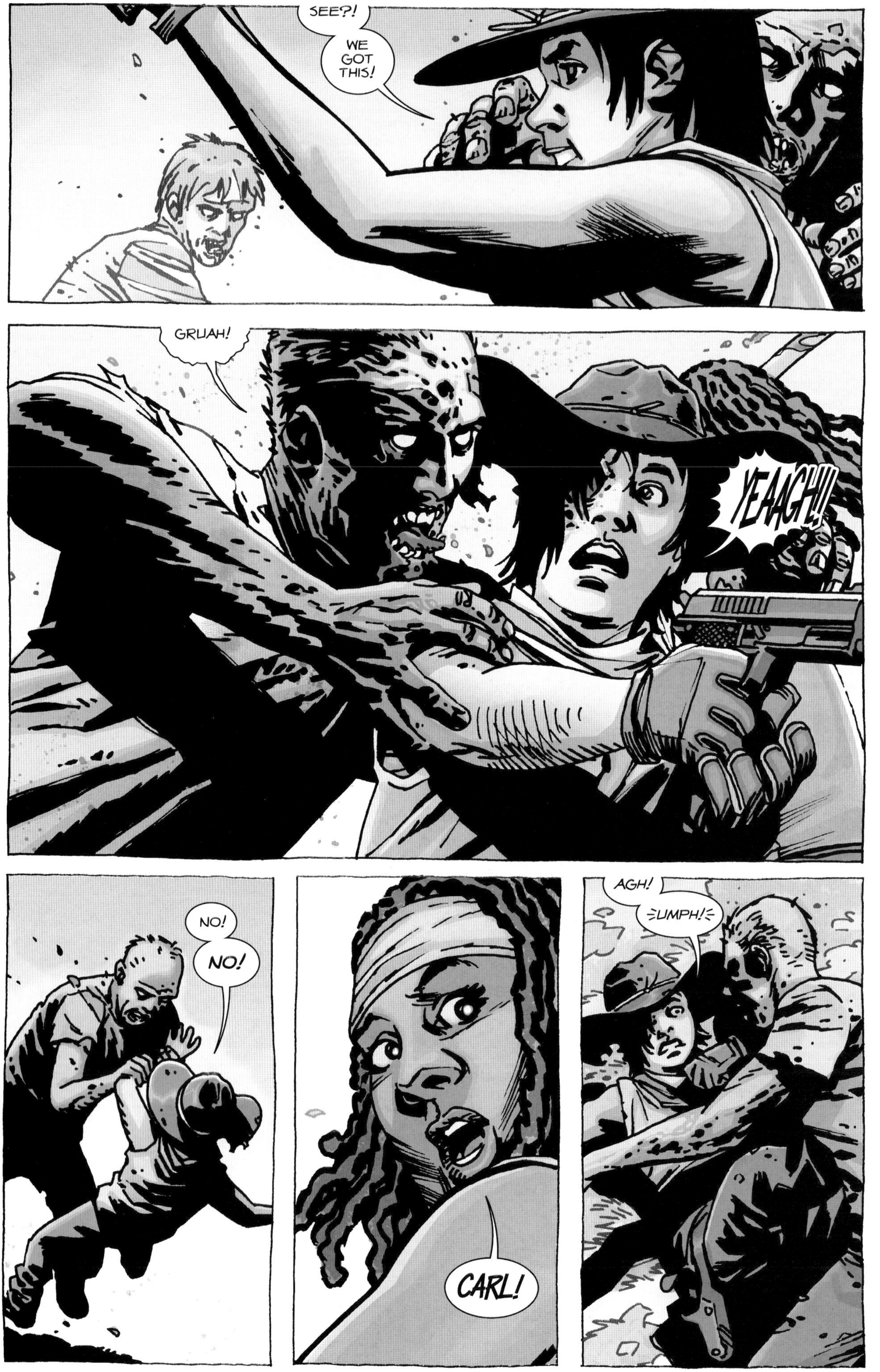
SEE?!
WE GOT THIS!
GRUAH!
YEAAGH!!
NO!
NO!
CARL!
AGH!
UMPH!

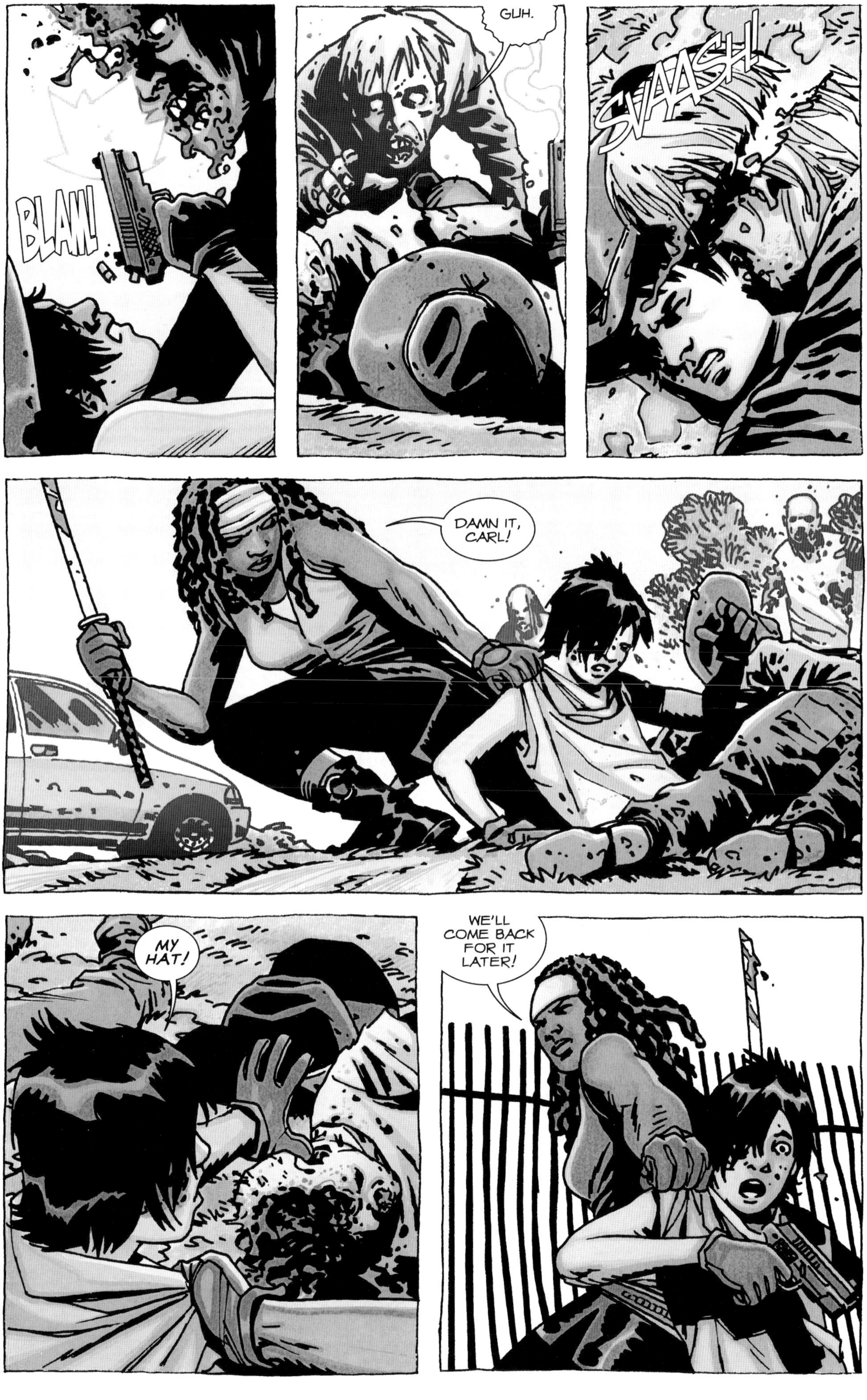
BLAM!
GUH.
SVAASH!
DAMN IT, CARL!
MY HAT!
WE'LL COME BACK FOR IT LATER!

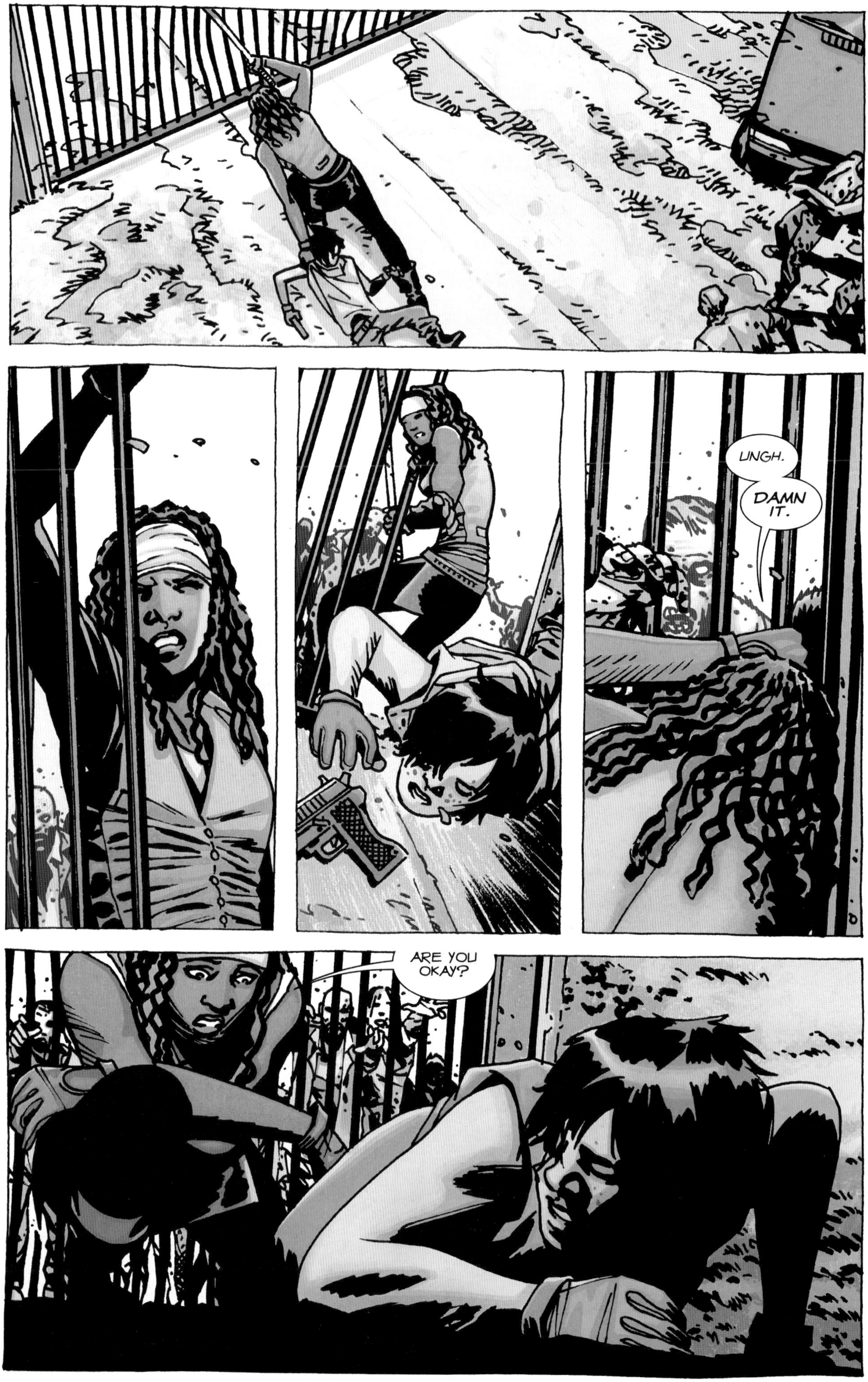

UNGH.
DAMN IT.
ARE YOU OKAY?

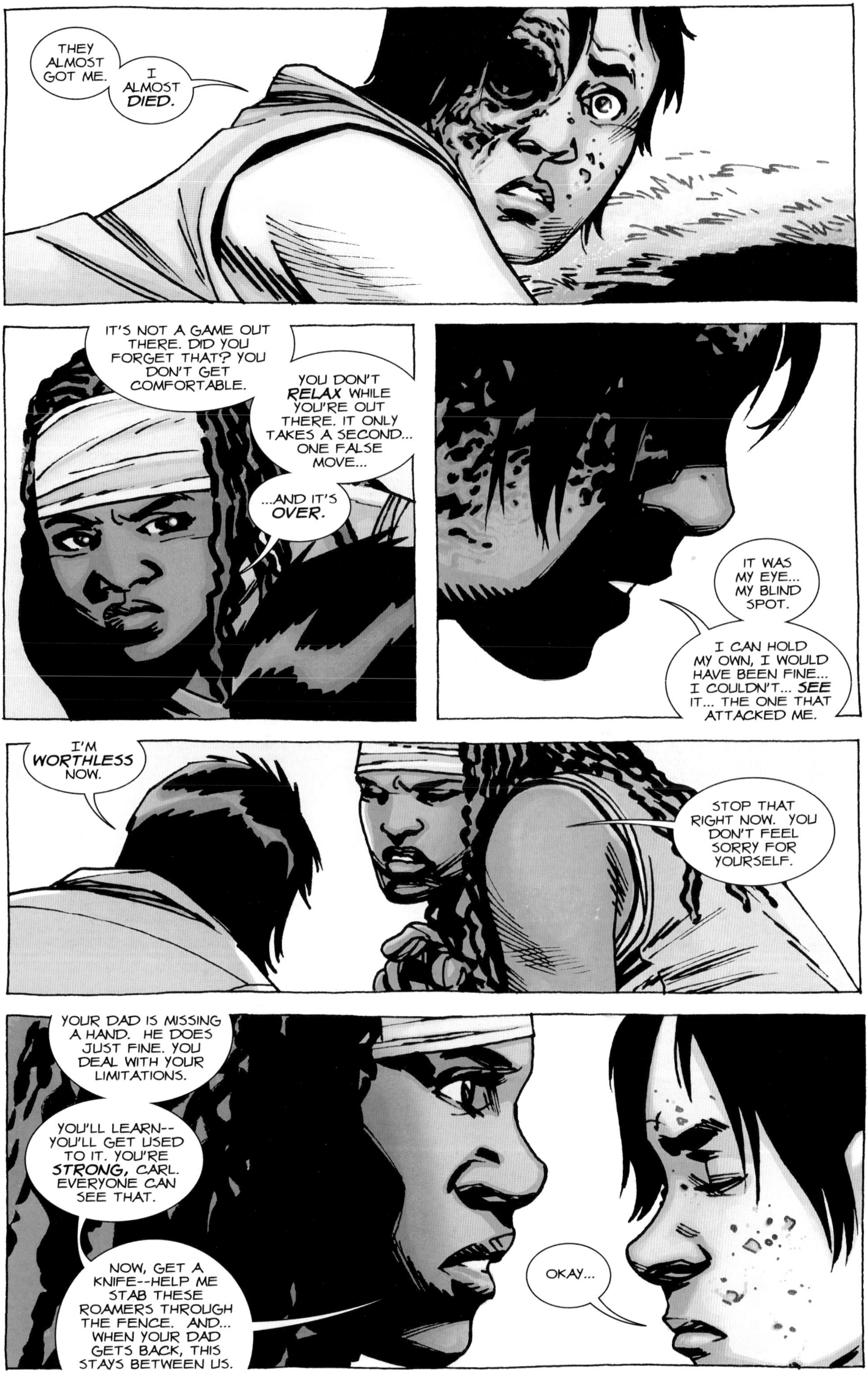
THEY ALMOST GOT ME.
I ALMOST *DIED.*
IT'S NOT A GAME OUT THERE. DID YOU FORGET THAT? YOU DON'T GET COMFORTABLE.
YOU DON'T *RELAX* WHILE YOU'RE OUT THERE. IT ONLY TAKES A SECOND... ONE FALSE MOVE...
...AND IT'S *OVER.*
IT WAS MY EYE... MY BLIND SPOT.
I CAN HOLD MY OWN, I WOULD HAVE BEEN FINE... I COULDN'T... *SEE* IT... THE ONE THAT ATTACKED ME.
I'M *WORTHLESS* NOW.
STOP THAT RIGHT NOW. YOU DON'T FEEL SORRY FOR YOURSELF.
YOUR DAD IS MISSING A HAND. HE DOES JUST FINE. YOU DEAL WITH YOUR LIMITATIONS.
YOU'LL LEARN-- YOU'LL GET USED TO IT. YOU'RE *STRONG,* CARL. EVERYONE CAN SEE THAT.
NOW, GET A KNIFE--HELP ME STAB THESE ROAMERS THROUGH THE FENCE. AND... WHEN YOUR DAD GETS BACK, THIS STAYS BETWEEN US.
OKAY...

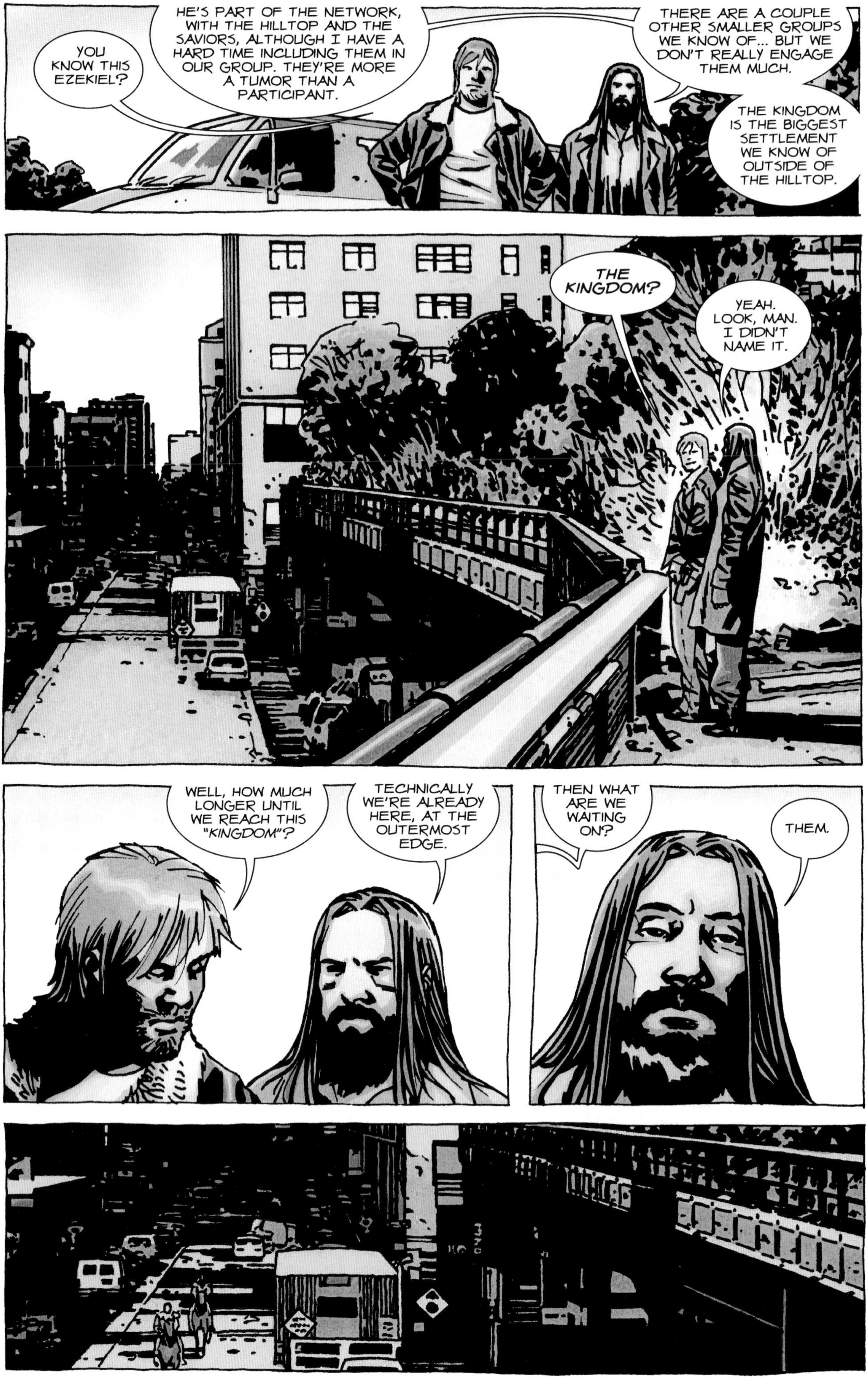
YOU KNOW THIS EZEKIEL?
HE'S PART OF THE NETWORK, WITH THE HILLTOP AND THE SAVIORS, ALTHOUGH I HAVE A HARD TIME INCLUDING THEM IN OUR GROUP. THEY'RE MORE A TUMOR THAN A PARTICIPANT.
THERE ARE A COUPLE OTHER SMALLER GROUPS WE KNOW OF... BUT WE DON'T REALLY ENGAGE THEM MUCH.
THE KINGDOM IS THE BIGGEST SETTLEMENT WE KNOW OF OUTSIDE OF THE HILLTOP.
THE KINGDOM?
YEAH. LOOK, MAN. I DIDN'T NAME IT.
WELL, HOW MUCH LONGER UNTIL WE REACH THIS "KINGDOM"?
TECHNICALLY WE'RE ALREADY HERE, AT THE OUTERMOST EDGE.
THEN WHAT ARE WE WAITING ON?
THEM.

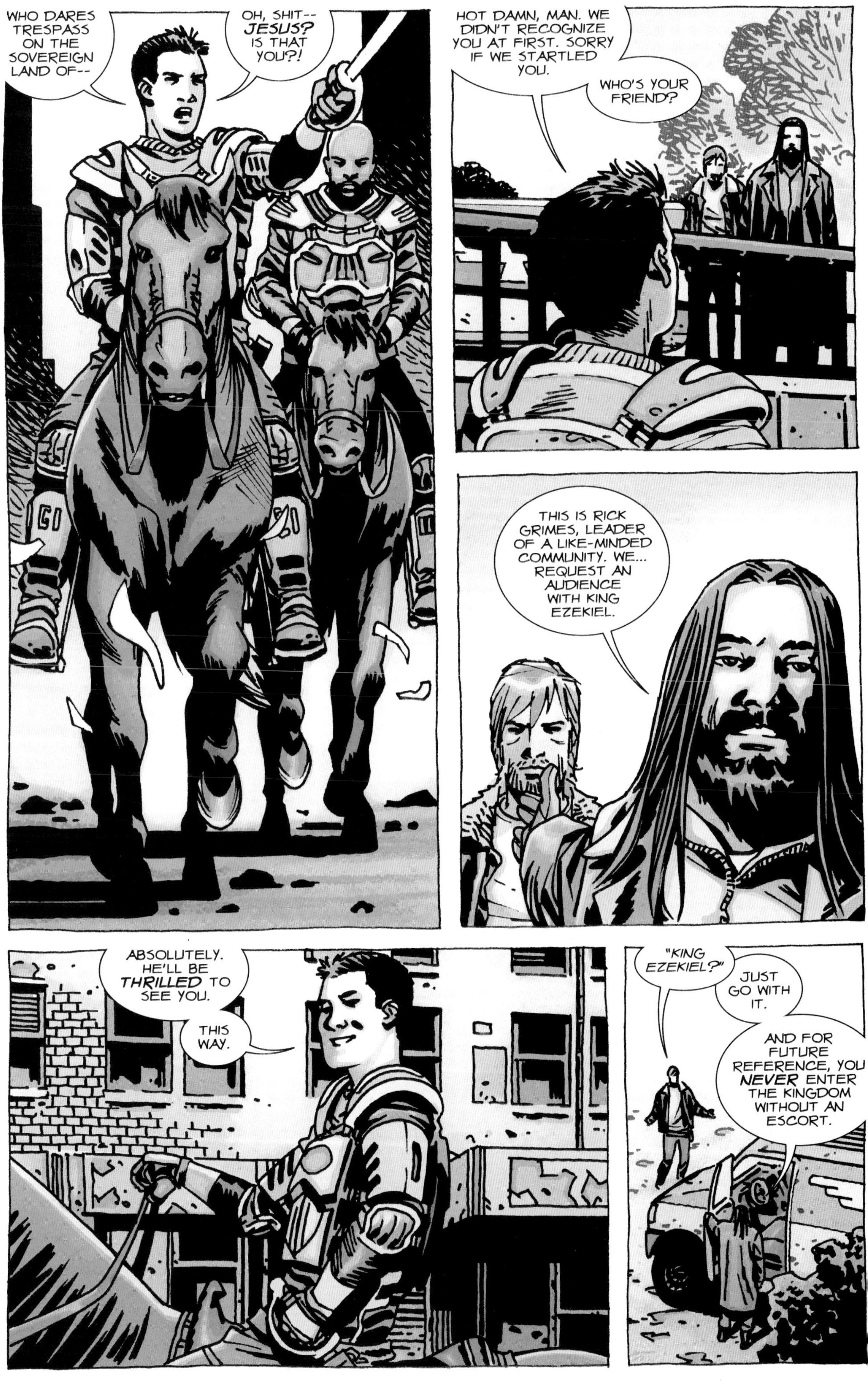
WHO DARES TRESPASS ON THE SOVEREIGN LAND OF--
OH, SHIT-- JESUS? IS THAT YOU?!
HOT DAMN, MAN. WE DIDN'T RECOGNIZE YOU AT FIRST. SORRY IF WE STARTLED YOU.
WHO'S YOUR FRIEND?
THIS IS RICK GRIMES, LEADER OF A LIKE-MINDED COMMUNITY. WE... REQUEST AN AUDIENCE WITH KING EZEKIEL.
ABSOLUTELY. HE'LL BE THRILLED TO SEE YOU.
THIS WAY.
"KING EZEKIEL?"
JUST GO WITH IT.
AND FOR FUTURE REFERENCE, YOU NEVER ENTER THE KINGDOM WITHOUT AN ESCORT.

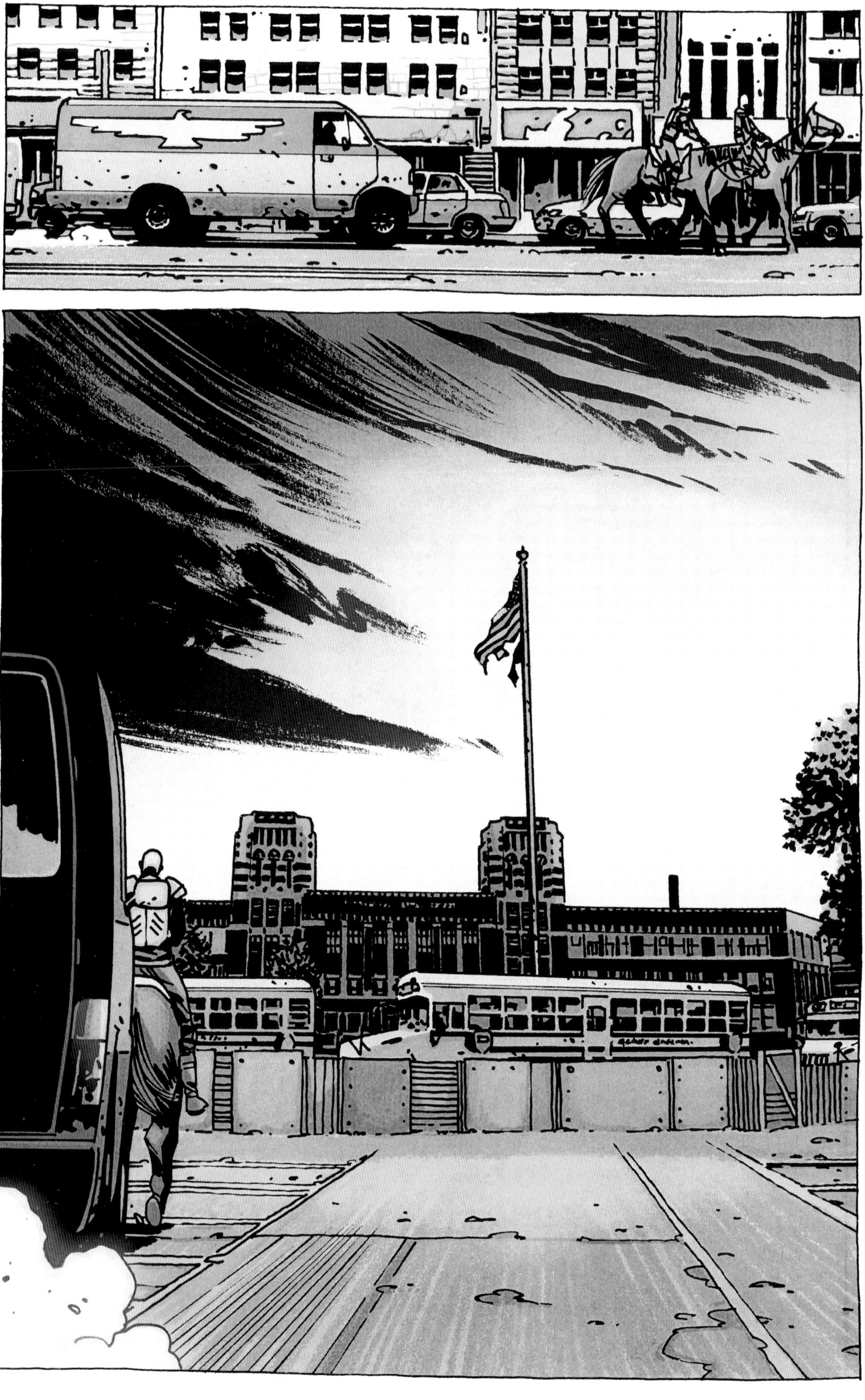

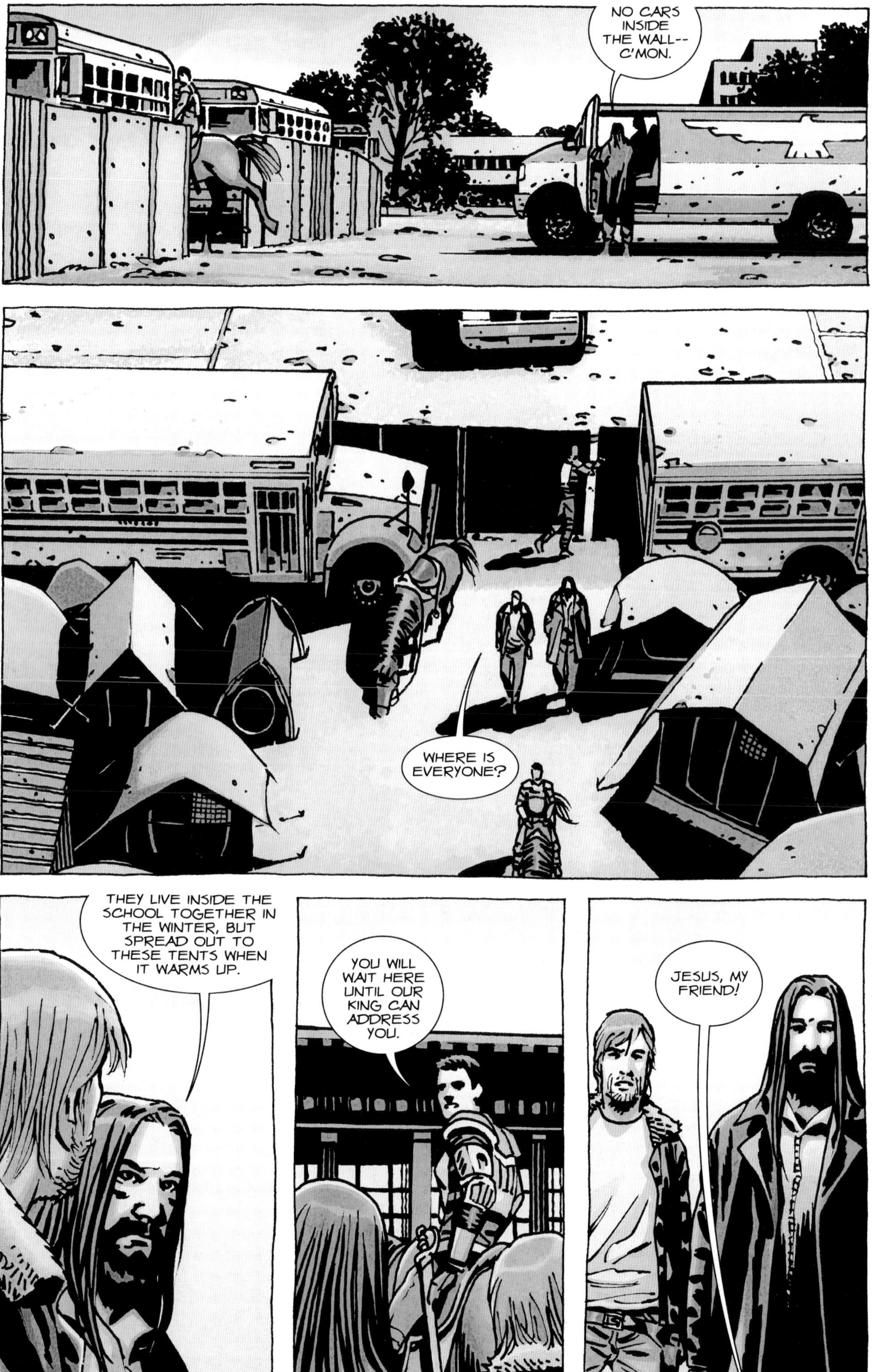
NO CARS INSIDE THE WALL-- C'MON.
WHERE IS EVERYONE?
THEY LIVE INSIDE THE SCHOOL TOGETHER IN THE WINTER, BUT SPREAD OUT TO THESE TENTS WHEN IT WARMS UP.
YOU WILL WAIT HERE UNTIL OUR KING CAN ADDRESS YOU.
JESUS, MY FRIEND!

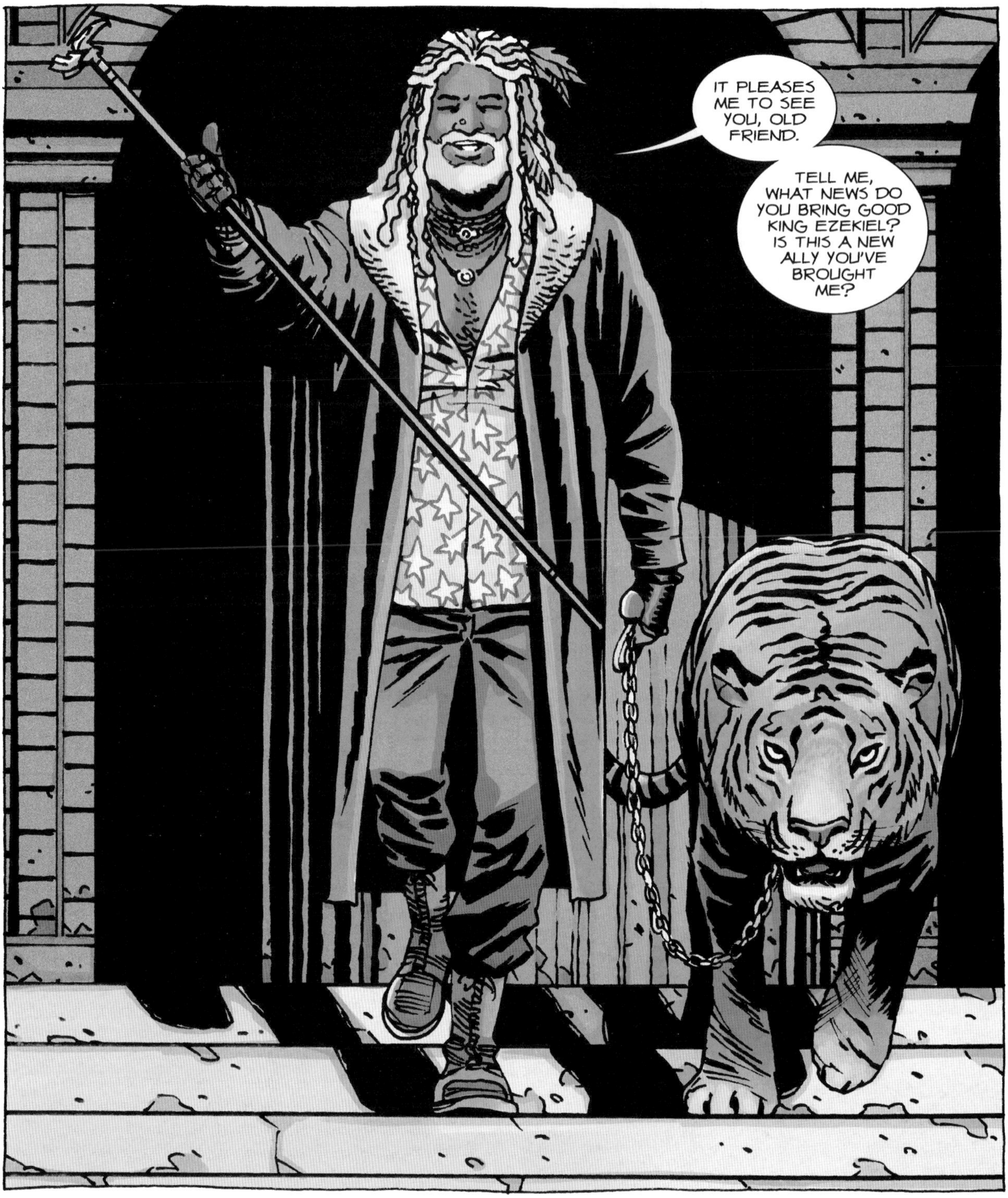
IT PLEASES ME TO SEE YOU, OLD FRIEND.
TELL ME, WHAT NEWS DO YOU BRING GOOD KING EZEKIEL? IS THIS A NEW ALLY YOU'VE BROUGHT ME?

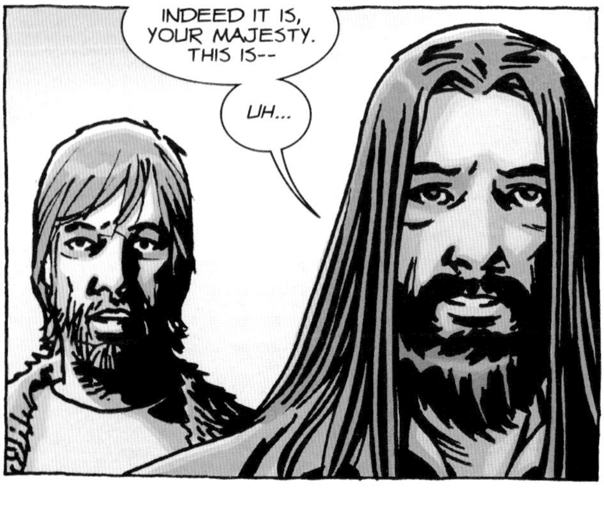
INDEED IT IS, YOUR MAJESTY. THIS IS--
UH...

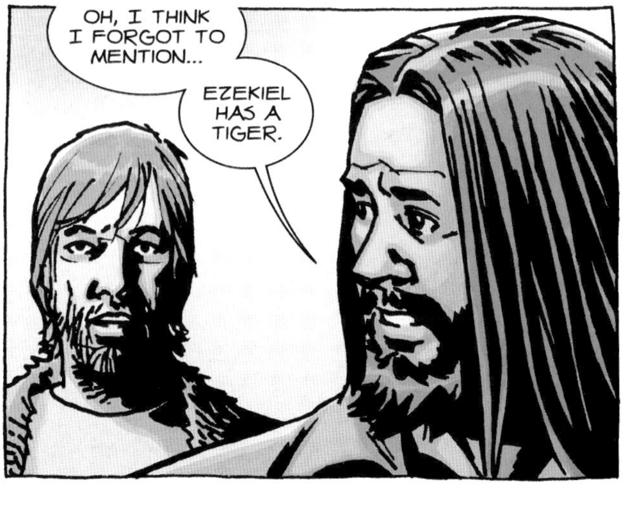
OH, I THINK I FORGOT TO MENTION...
EZEKIEL HAS A TIGER.

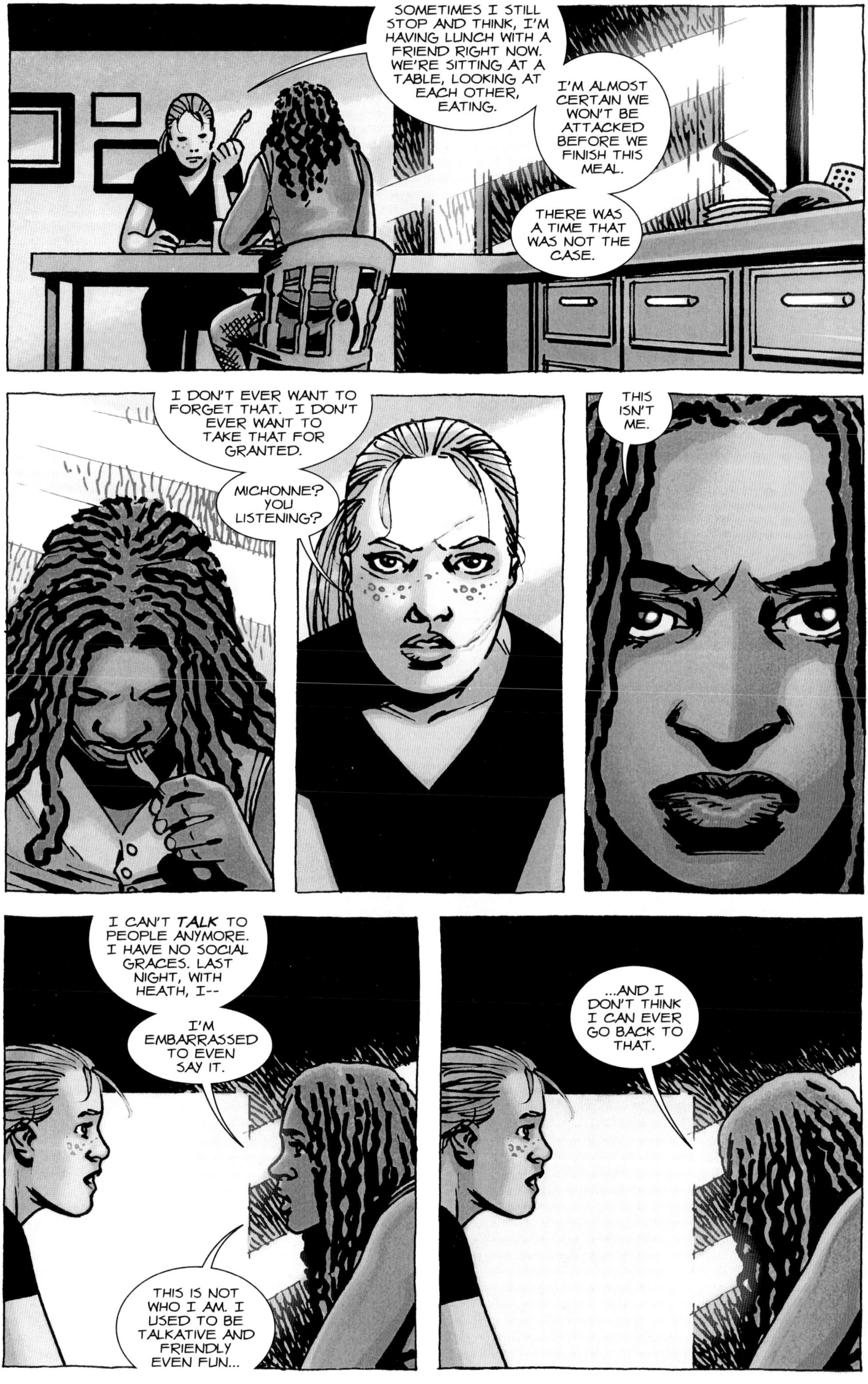
SOMETIMES I STILL STOP AND THINK, I'M HAVING LUNCH WITH A FRIEND RIGHT NOW. WE'RE SITTING AT A TABLE, LOOKING AT EACH OTHER, EATING.
I'M ALMOST CERTAIN WE WON'T BE ATTACKED BEFORE WE FINISH THIS MEAL.
THERE WAS A TIME THAT WAS NOT THE CASE.
I DON'T EVER WANT TO FORGET THAT. I DON'T EVER WANT TO TAKE THAT FOR GRANTED.
MICHONNE? YOU LISTENING?
THIS ISN'T ME.
I CAN'T *TALK* TO PEOPLE ANYMORE. I HAVE NO SOCIAL GRACES. LAST NIGHT, WITH HEATH, I--
I'M EMBARRASSED TO EVEN SAY IT.
THIS IS NOT WHO I AM. I USED TO BE TALKATIVE AND FRIENDLY EVEN FUN...
...AND I DON'T THINK I CAN EVER GO BACK TO THAT.

GOOD AFTERNOON, SPENCER. WHAT CAN I DO FOR YOU?

NOTHING, UH... FATHER GABRIEL... I WAS WONDERING IF I COULD JUST HAVE A MINUTE ON THE ALTAR...

OF COURSE. GO RIGHT AHEAD.

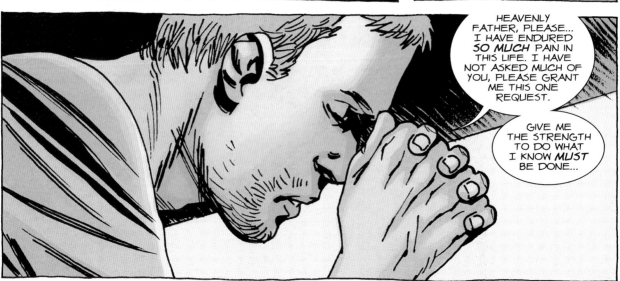

HEAVENLY FATHER, PLEASE... I HAVE ENDURED SO MUCH PAIN IN THIS LIFE. I HAVE NOT ASKED MUCH OF YOU, PLEASE GRANT ME THIS ONE REQUEST.

GIVE ME THE STRENGTH TO DO WHAT I KNOW MUST BE DONE...

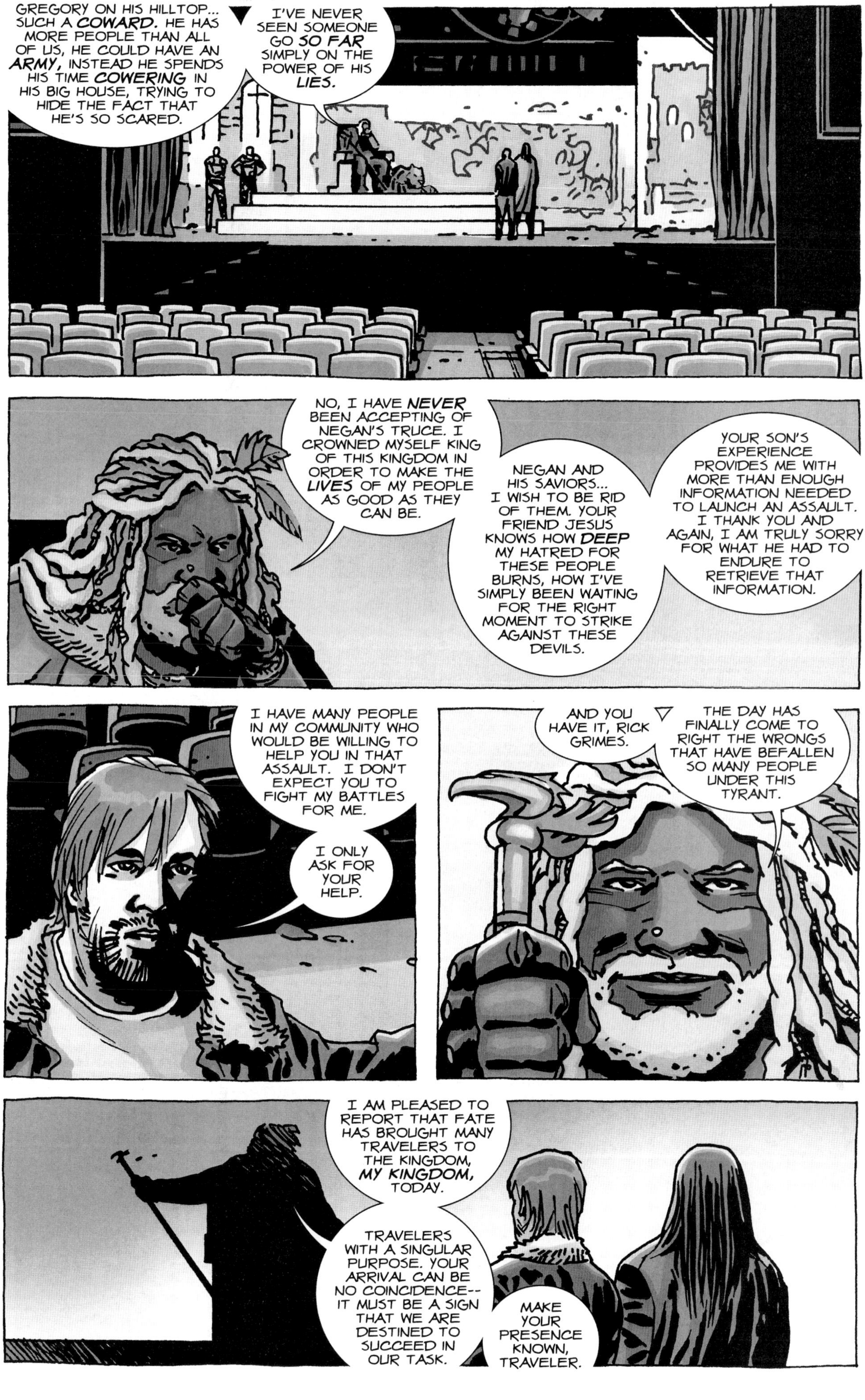
GREGORY ON HIS HILLTOP... SUCH A COWARD. HE HAS MORE PEOPLE THAN ALL OF US, HE COULD HAVE AN ARMY, INSTEAD HE SPENDS HIS TIME COWERING IN HIS BIG HOUSE, TRYING TO HIDE THE FACT THAT HE'S SO SCARED.
I'VE NEVER SEEN SOMEONE GO SO FAR SIMPLY ON THE POWER OF HIS LIES.
NO, I HAVE NEVER BEEN ACCEPTING OF NEGAN'S TRUCE. I CROWNED MYSELF KING OF THIS KINGDOM IN ORDER TO MAKE THE LIVES OF MY PEOPLE AS GOOD AS THEY CAN BE.
NEGAN AND HIS SAVIORS... I WISH TO BE RID OF THEM. YOUR FRIEND JESUS KNOWS HOW DEEP MY HATRED FOR THESE PEOPLE BURNS, HOW I'VE SIMPLY BEEN WAITING FOR THE RIGHT MOMENT TO STRIKE AGAINST THESE DEVILS.
YOUR SON'S EXPERIENCE PROVIDES ME WITH MORE THAN ENOUGH INFORMATION NEEDED TO LAUNCH AN ASSAULT. I THANK YOU AND AGAIN, I AM TRULY SORRY FOR WHAT HE HAD TO ENDURE TO RETRIEVE THAT INFORMATION.
I HAVE MANY PEOPLE IN MY COMMUNITY WHO WOULD BE WILLING TO HELP YOU IN THAT ASSAULT. I DON'T EXPECT YOU TO FIGHT MY BATTLES FOR ME.
I ONLY ASK FOR YOUR HELP.
AND YOU HAVE IT, RICK GRIMES.
THE DAY HAS FINALLY COME TO RIGHT THE WRONGS THAT HAVE BEFALLEN SO MANY PEOPLE UNDER THIS TYRANT.
I AM PLEASED TO REPORT THAT FATE HAS BROUGHT MANY TRAVELERS TO THE KINGDOM, MY KINGDOM, TODAY.
TRAVELERS WITH A SINGULAR PURPOSE. YOUR ARRIVAL CAN BE NO COINCIDENCE-- IT MUST BE A SIGN THAT WE ARE DESTINED TO SUCCEED IN OUR TASK.
MAKE YOUR PRESENCE KNOWN, TRAVELER.

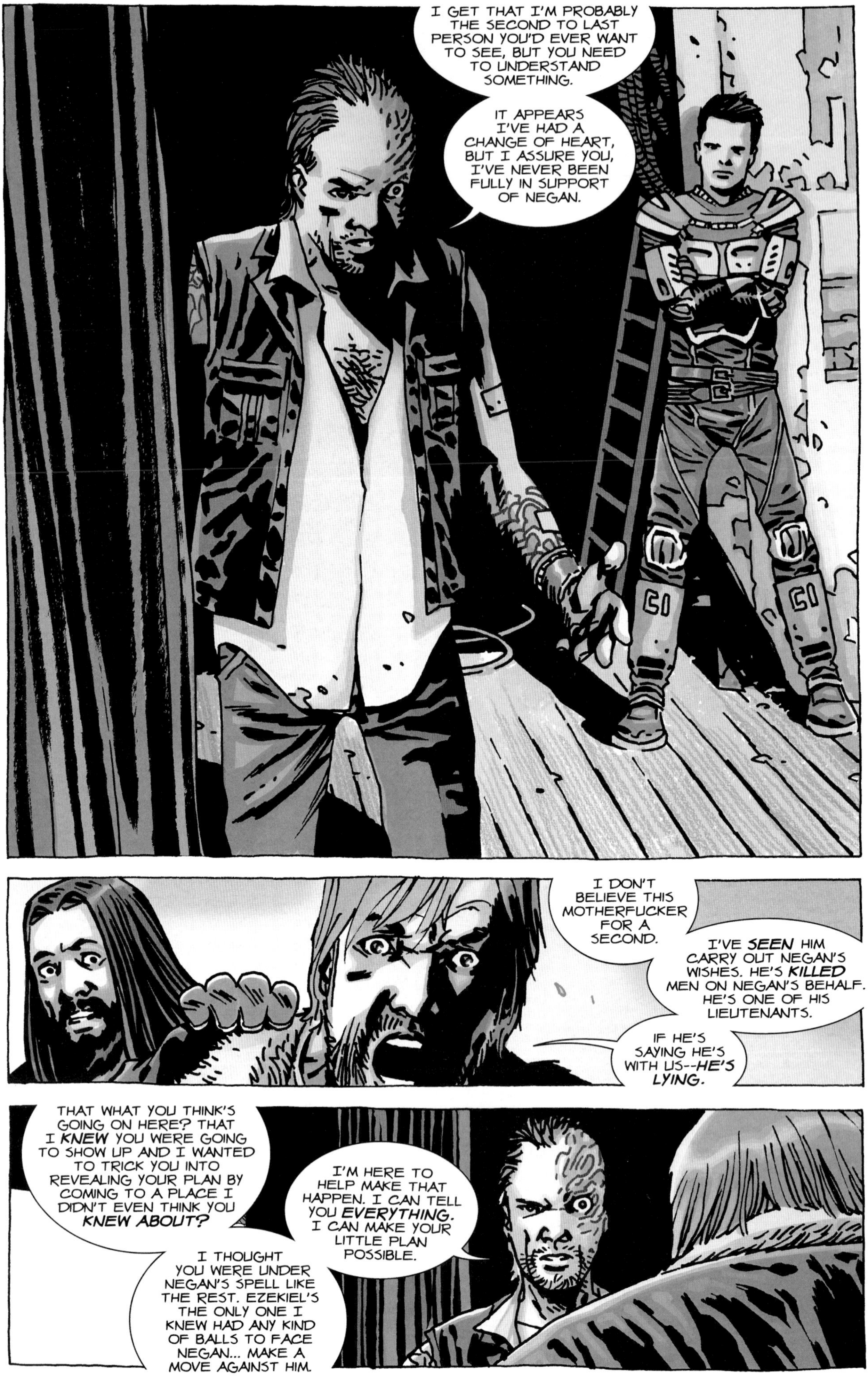
I GET THAT I'M PROBABLY THE SECOND TO LAST PERSON YOU'D EVER WANT TO SEE, BUT YOU NEED TO UNDERSTAND SOMETHING.
IT APPEARS I'VE HAD A CHANGE OF HEART, BUT I ASSURE YOU, I'VE NEVER BEEN FULLY IN SUPPORT OF NEGAN.
I DON'T BELIEVE THIS MOTHERFUCKER FOR A SECOND.
I'VE SEEN HIM CARRY OUT NEGAN'S WISHES. HE'S KILLED MEN ON NEGAN'S BEHALF. HE'S ONE OF HIS LIEUTENANTS.
IF HE'S SAYING HE'S WITH US--HE'S LYING.
THAT WHAT YOU THINK'S GOING ON HERE? THAT I KNEW YOU WERE GOING TO SHOW UP AND I WANTED TO TRICK YOU INTO REVEALING YOUR PLAN BY COMING TO A PLACE I DIDN'T EVEN THINK YOU KNEW ABOUT?
I THOUGHT YOU WERE UNDER NEGAN'S SPELL LIKE THE REST. EZEKIEL'S THE ONLY ONE I KNEW HAD ANY KIND OF BALLS TO FACE NEGAN... MAKE A MOVE AGAINST HIM.
I'M HERE TO HELP MAKE THAT HAPPEN. I CAN TELL YOU EVERYTHING. I CAN MAKE YOUR LITTLE PLAN POSSIBLE.

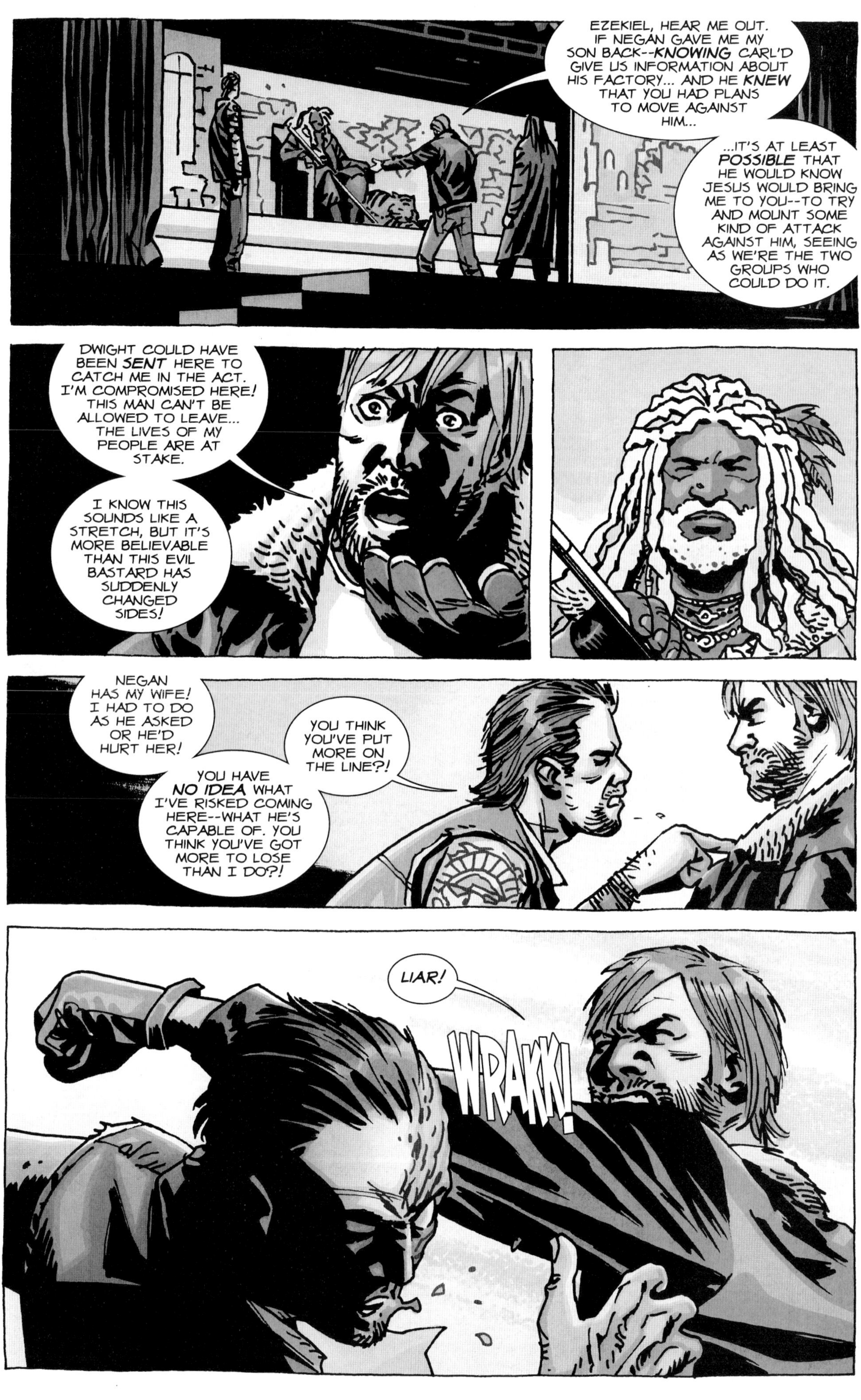
EZEKIEL, HEAR ME OUT. IF NEGAN GAVE ME MY SON BACK--KNOWING CARL'D GIVE US INFORMATION ABOUT HIS FACTORY... AND HE KNEW THAT YOU HAD PLANS TO MOVE AGAINST HIM...
...IT'S AT LEAST POSSIBLE THAT HE WOULD KNOW JESUS WOULD BRING ME TO YOU--TO TRY AND MOUNT SOME KIND OF ATTACK AGAINST HIM, SEEING AS WE'RE THE TWO GROUPS WHO COULD DO IT.
DWIGHT COULD HAVE BEEN SENT HERE TO CATCH ME IN THE ACT. I'M COMPROMISED HERE! THIS MAN CAN'T BE ALLOWED TO LEAVE... THE LIVES OF MY PEOPLE ARE AT STAKE.
I KNOW THIS SOUNDS LIKE A STRETCH, BUT IT'S MORE BELIEVABLE THAN THIS EVIL BASTARD HAS SUDDENLY CHANGED SIDES!
NEGAN HAS MY WIFE! I HAD TO DO AS HE ASKED OR HE'D HURT HER!
YOU THINK YOU'VE PUT MORE ON THE LINE?!
YOU HAVE NO IDEA WHAT I'VE RISKED COMING HERE--WHAT HE'S CAPABLE OF. YOU THINK YOU'VE GOT MORE TO LOSE THAN I DO?!
LIAR!
WRAKK!

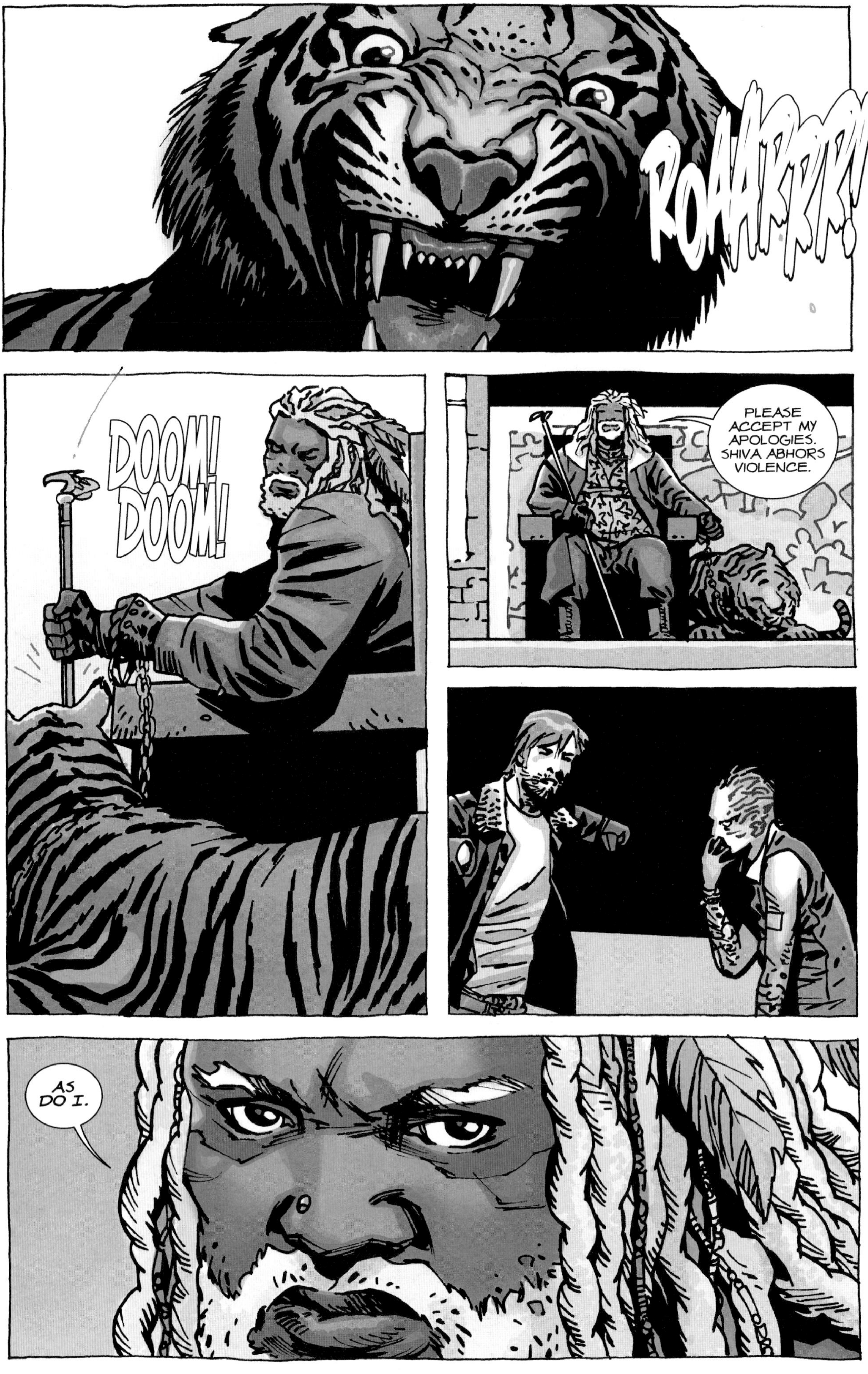
ROAARRR!
DOOM! DOOM!
PLEASE ACCEPT MY APOLOGIES. SHIVA ABHORS VIOLENCE.
AS DO I.

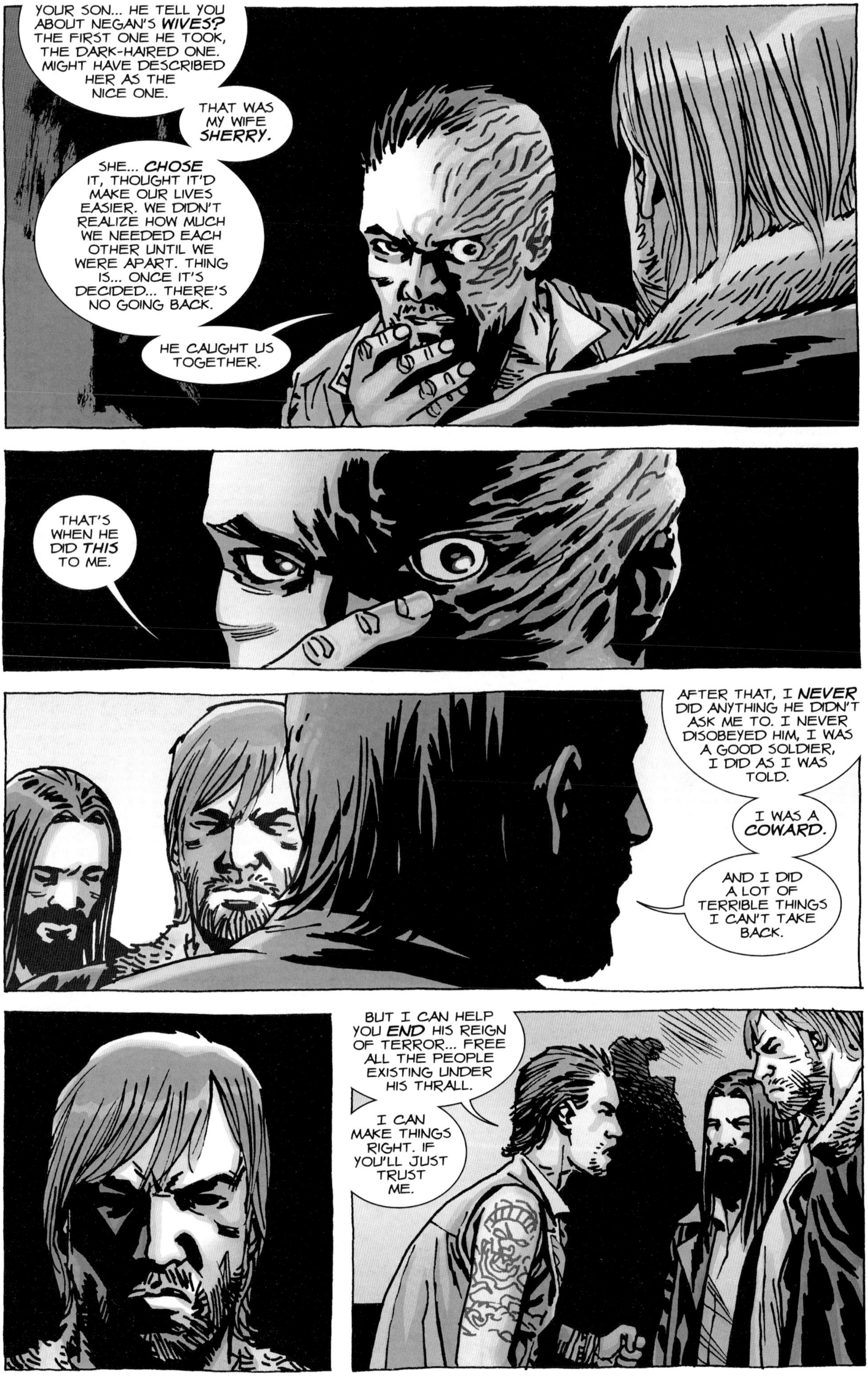
YOUR SON... HE TELL YOU ABOUT NEGAN'S WIVES? THE FIRST ONE HE TOOK, THE DARK-HAIRED ONE. MIGHT HAVE DESCRIBED HER AS THE NICE ONE.
THAT WAS MY WIFE SHERRY.
SHE... CHOSE IT, THOUGHT IT'D MAKE OUR LIVES EASIER. WE DIDN'T REALIZE HOW MUCH WE NEEDED EACH OTHER UNTIL WE WERE APART. THING IS... ONCE IT'S DECIDED... THERE'S NO GOING BACK.
HE CAUGHT US TOGETHER.
THAT'S WHEN HE DID THIS TO ME.
AFTER THAT, I NEVER DID ANYTHING HE DIDN'T ASK ME TO. I NEVER DISOBEYED HIM, I WAS A GOOD SOLDIER, I DID AS I WAS TOLD.
I WAS A COWARD.
AND I DID A LOT OF TERRIBLE THINGS I CAN'T TAKE BACK.
BUT I CAN HELP YOU END HIS REIGN OF TERROR... FREE ALL THE PEOPLE EXISTING UNDER HIS THRALL.
I CAN MAKE THINGS RIGHT. IF YOU'LL JUST TRUST ME.

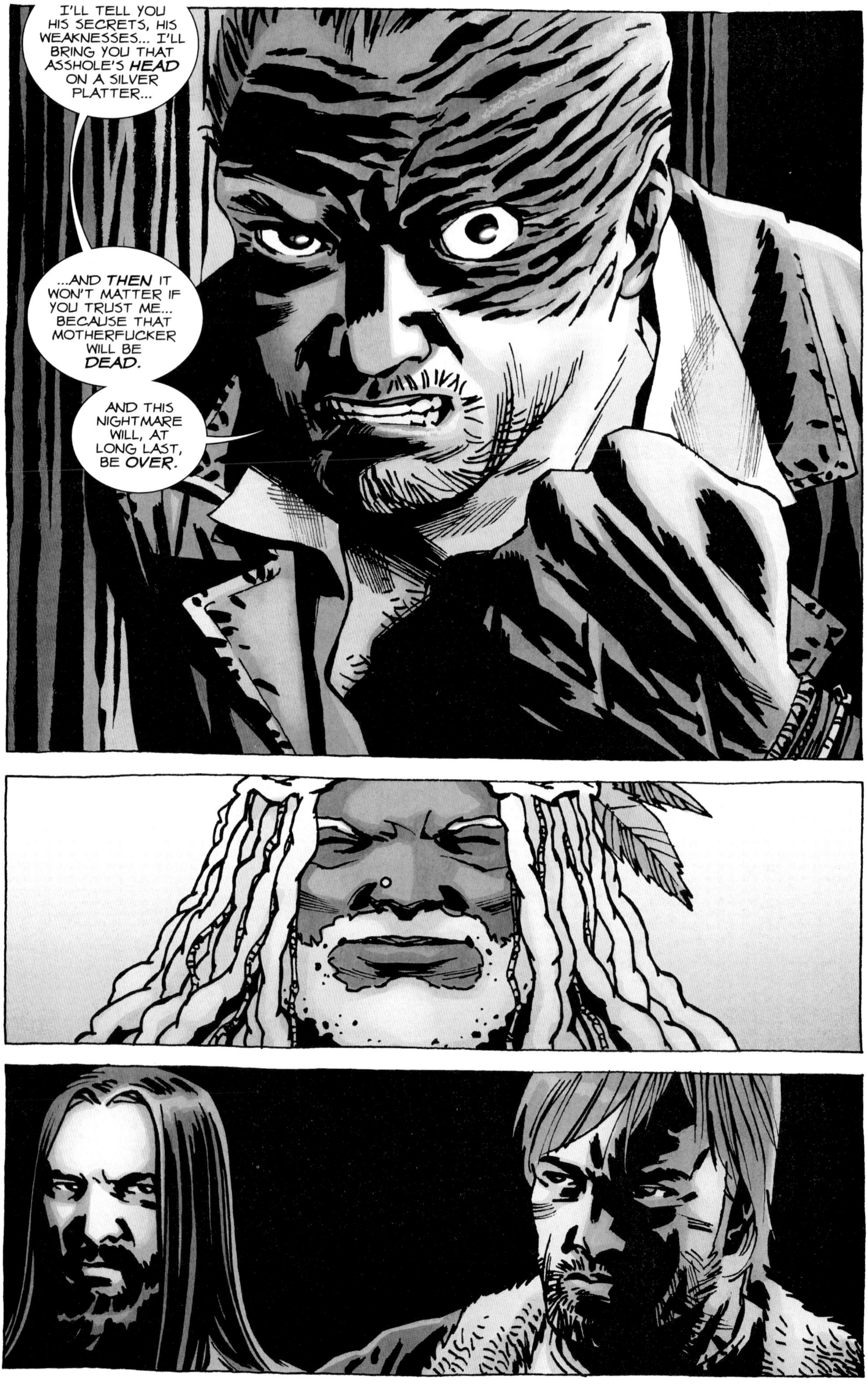
I'LL TELL YOU HIS SECRETS, HIS WEAKNESSES... I'LL BRING YOU THAT ASSHOLE'S **HEAD** ON A SILVER PLATTER...
...AND **THEN** IT WON'T MATTER IF YOU TRUST ME... BECAUSE THAT MOTHERFUCKER WILL BE **DEAD.**
AND THIS NIGHTMARE WILL, AT LONG LAST, BE **OVER.**

to be continued...

Sketchbook

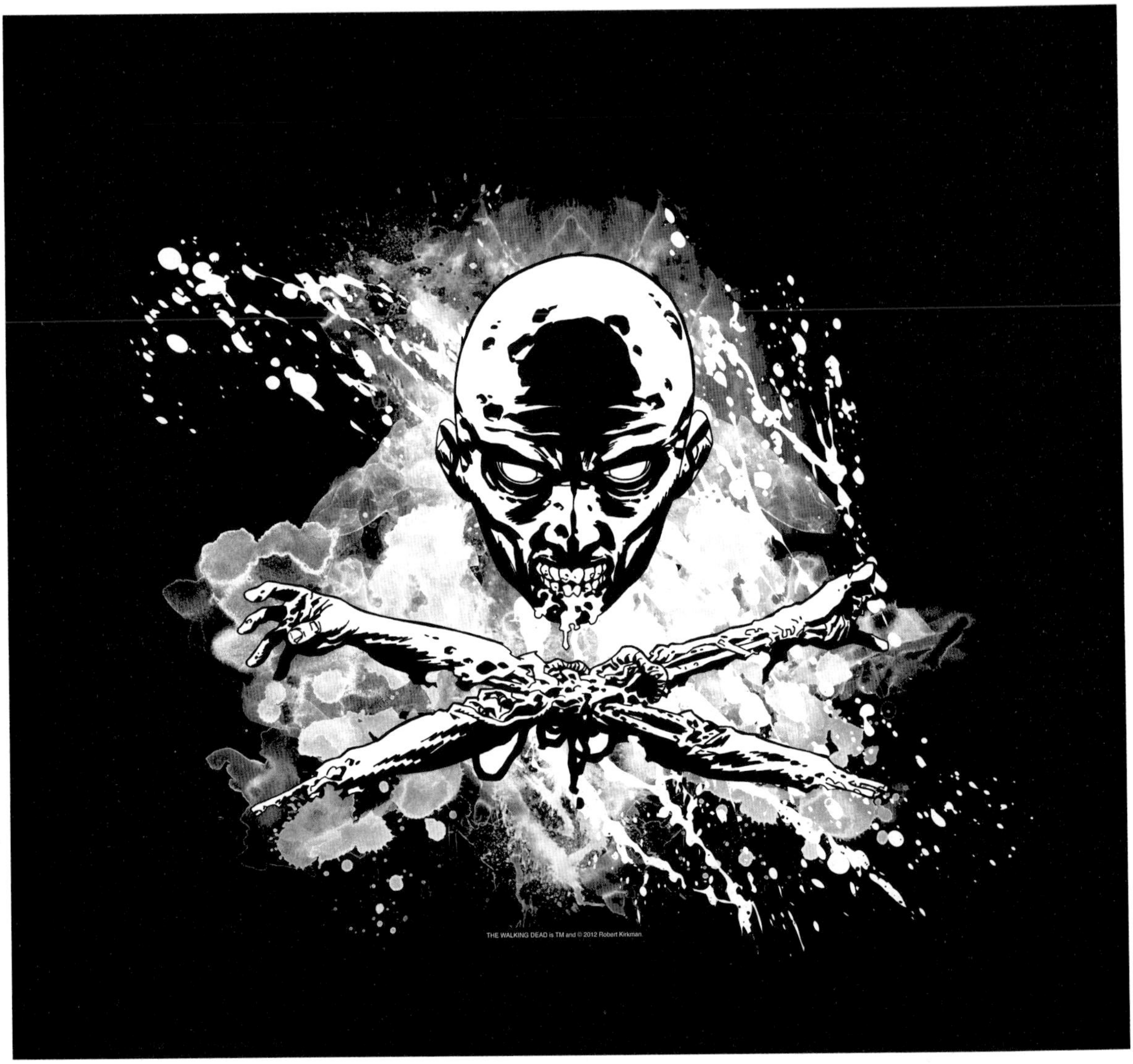
THE WALKING DEAD is TM and © 2012 Robert Kirkman

Get ready to feast your eyes on some fantastic Walking Dead goodness from everyone's favorite Charlie Adlard! On this page you'll see a pretty sweet original t-shirt design that Charlie did. You can find all kinds of cool shirts like this one for sale at thewalkingdead.com if you are so inclined. Otherwise, I recommend youtube.com for some pretty funny videos. I recommend a search for "Louis C.K."

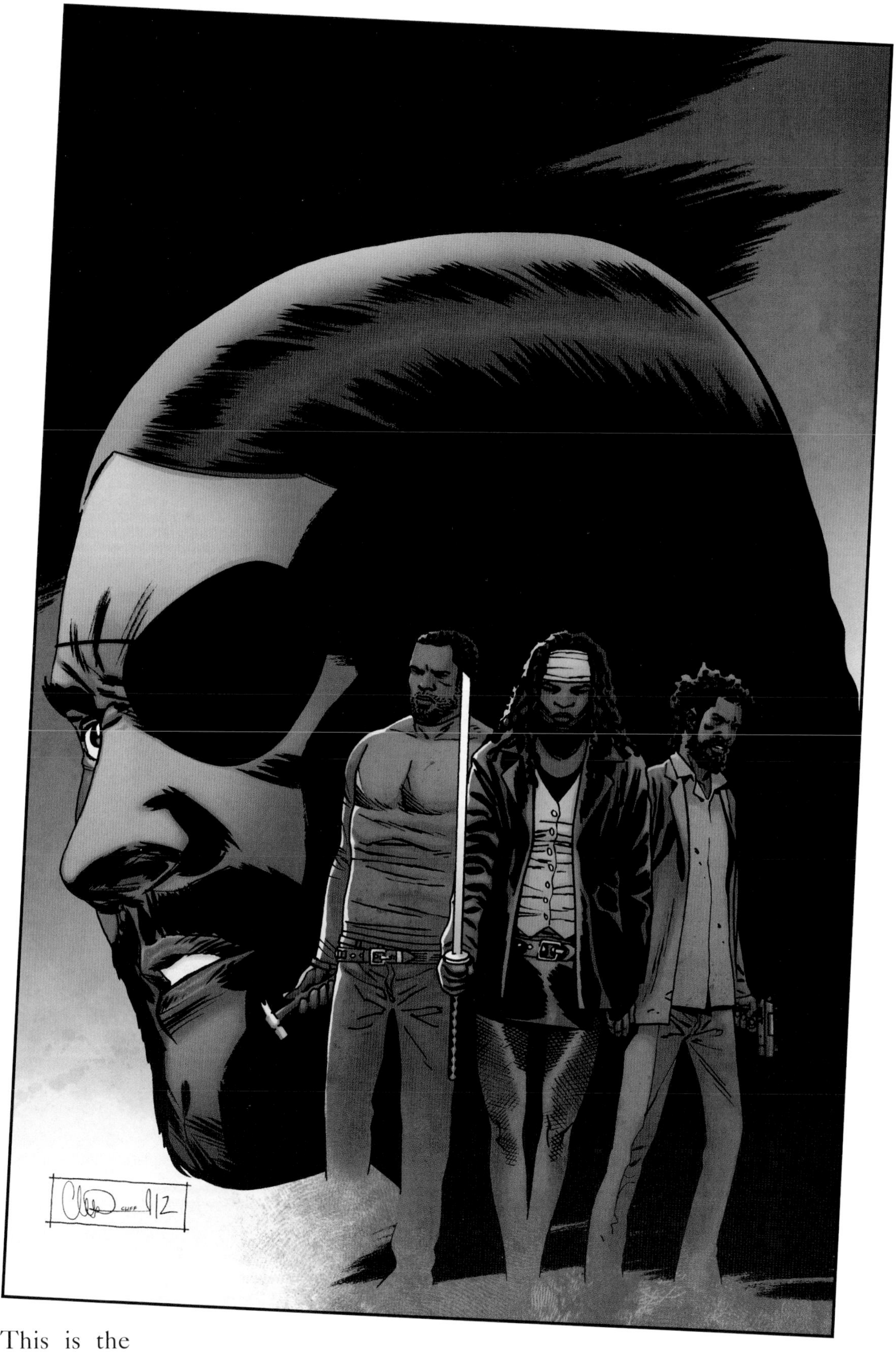

This is the cover to the Free Comic Book Day Special that was given away completely for free on Free Comic Book Day to anyone who wanted something free and was in a comic shop on Free Comic Book Day (see what I did there?). The issue collected the four short stories we've done that have appeared in various magazines and special books throughout the years that starred The Governor, Michonne, Tyreese and Morgan. They're swell.

This Michonne art was the cover for the convention exclusive Compendium 2 hardcover, which collected the Compendium 2 paperback (cover below), which collected issues 49-96 in hardcover form. I really love the playing card style covers Charlie does for the compendiums. Seeing our cast as zombies is always a treat.

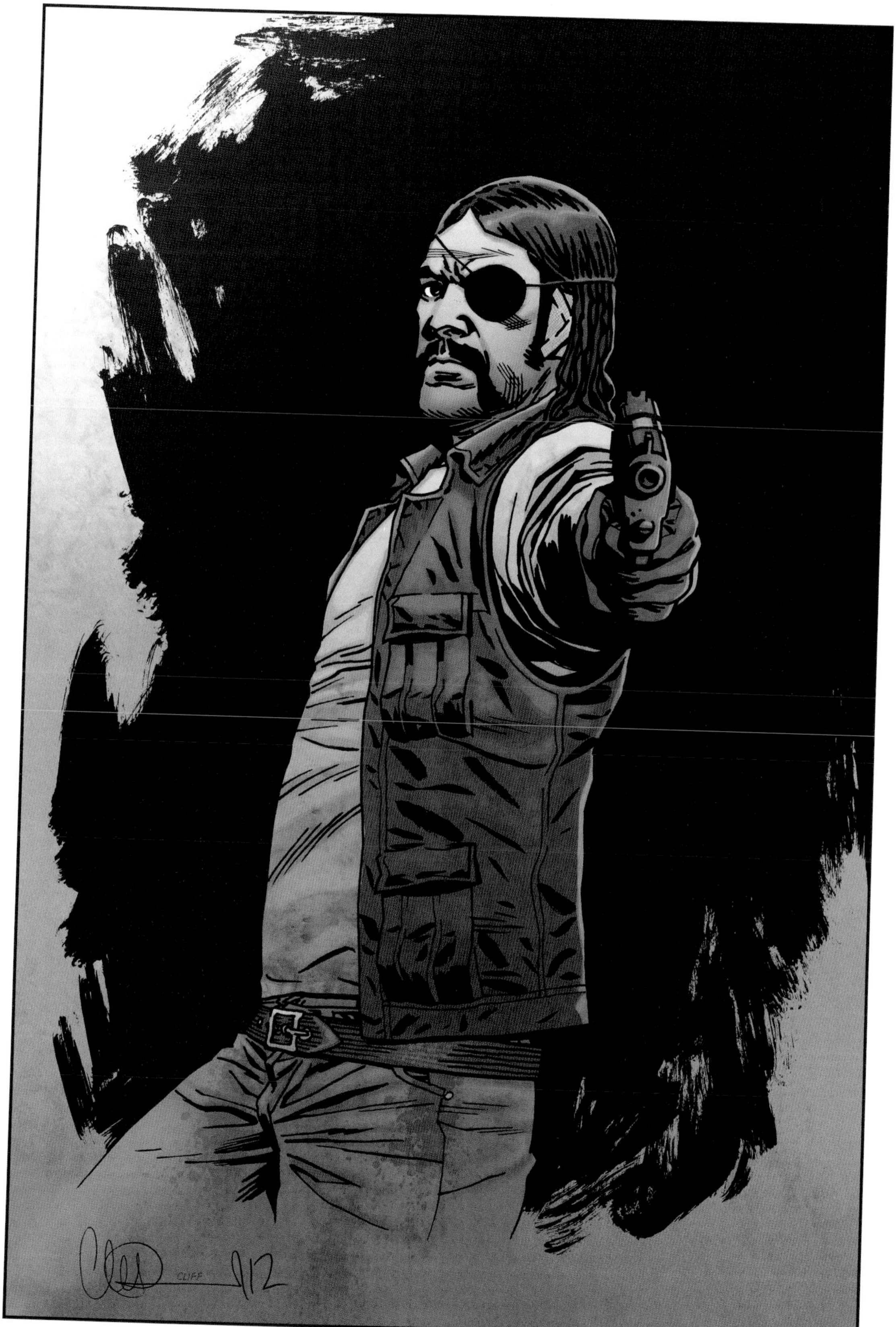

This is the cover for THE GOVERNOR SPECIAL... which collected The Governor's first appearance in issue 27 as well as The Governor story that appeared in a CBLDF charity comic that Image Comics published.

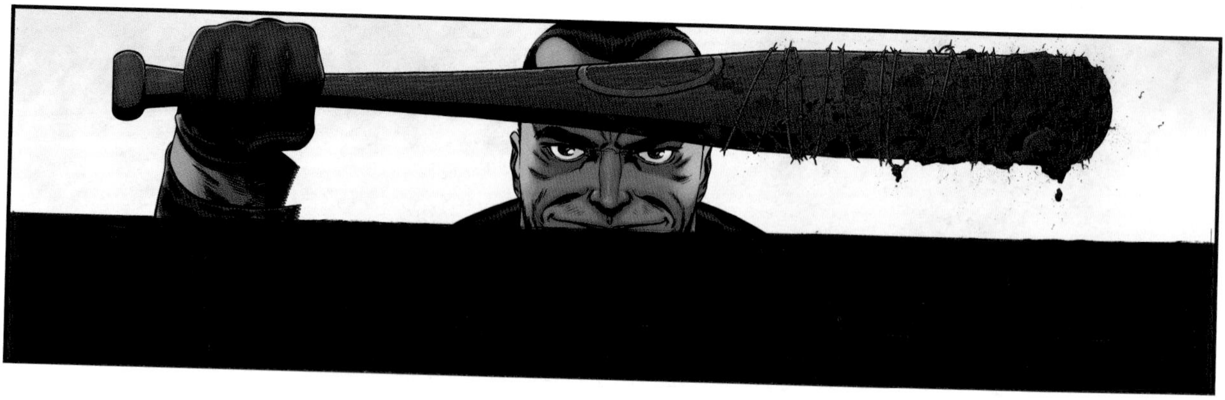

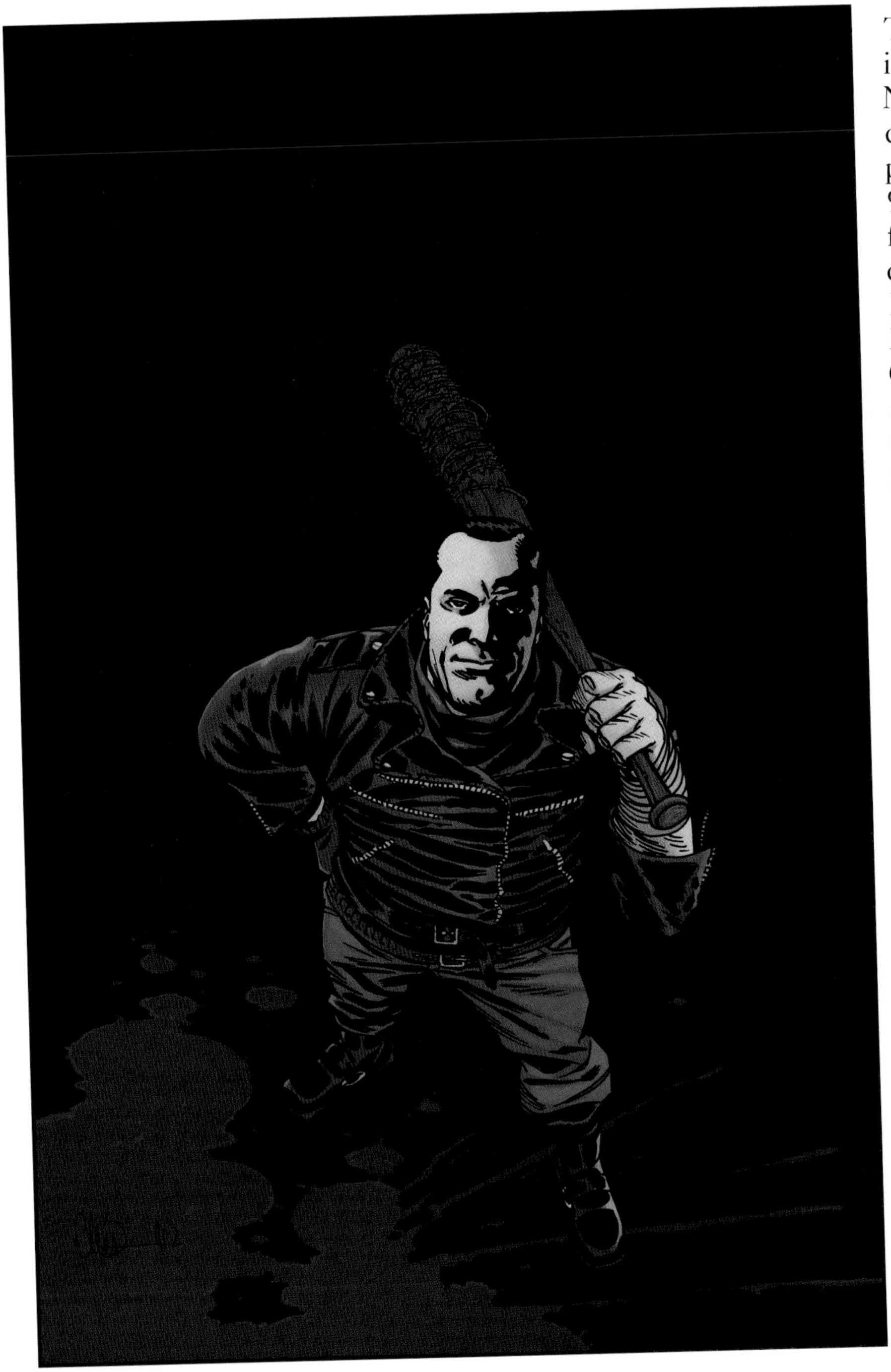

That SWEET wide image you see of Negan is the variant covers of the additional printings of issues 97-102. As a comics fan, I'm a real nut for connecting covers. I'm really happy with how this turned out. Charlie and Cliff did a really great job. One thing that bugs me though, issue 100 printed a little warmer in tone than the other covers, so if you get all the covers framed (like I did) issue 100 doesn't match up so well. Bummer.

This other Negan image is the 2nd printing cover for issue 100. I love Negan. I'm sorry if you guys all hate him... he's just too much fun to write!

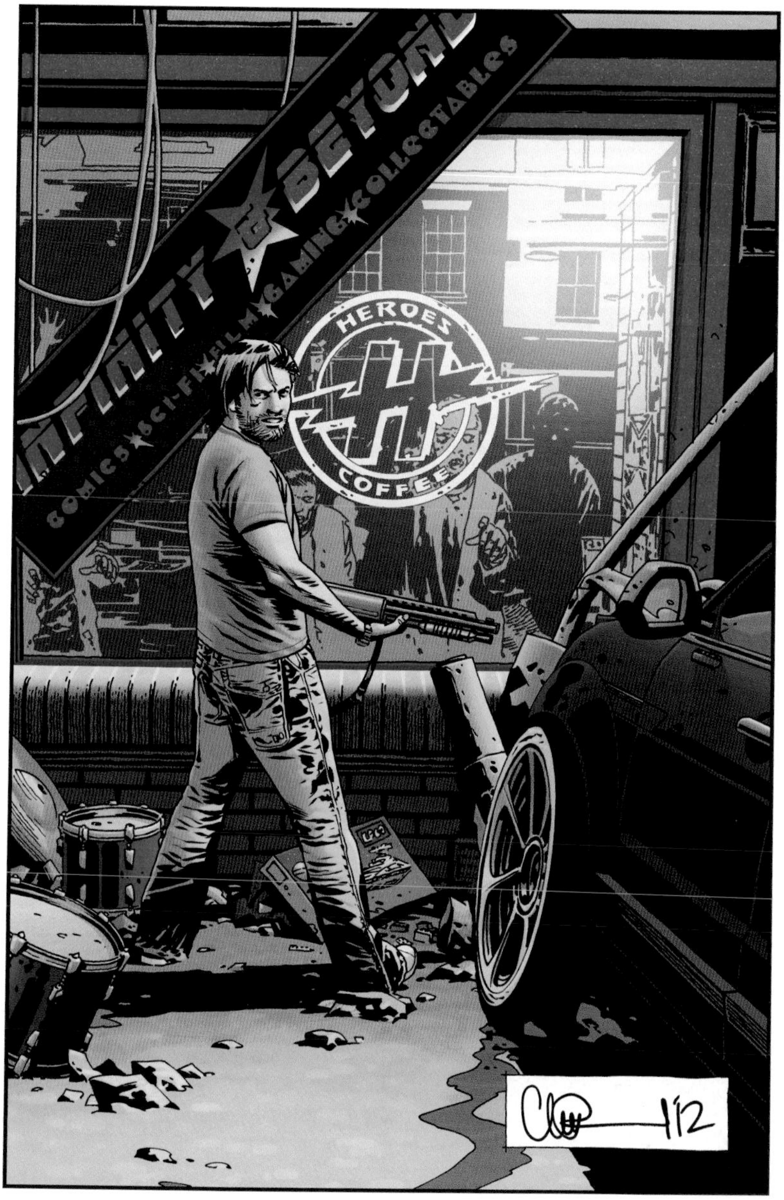
INFINITY ★ BEYOND
COMICS ★ SCI-FI ★ FILM ★ GAMING ★ COLLECTABLES
HEROES
COFFEE

A retailer variant Charlie did for Infinity & Beyond where my favorite narcissist drew himself on a cover to celebrate his 100th issue (issue 106). And below it... our sweet Comic-Con booth banner, colored by none other than Dave Stewart!!

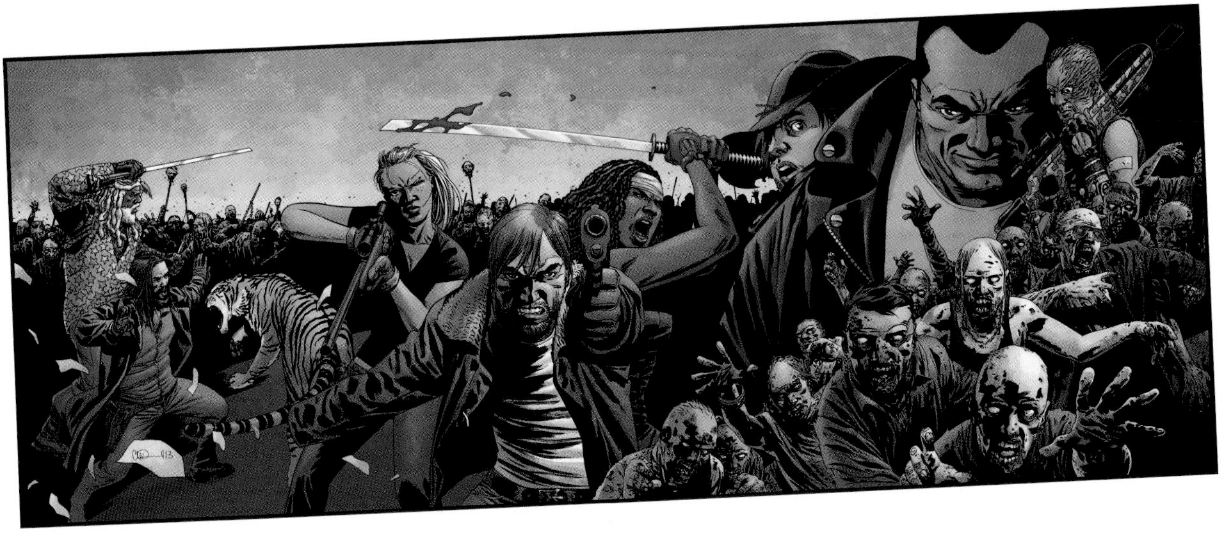

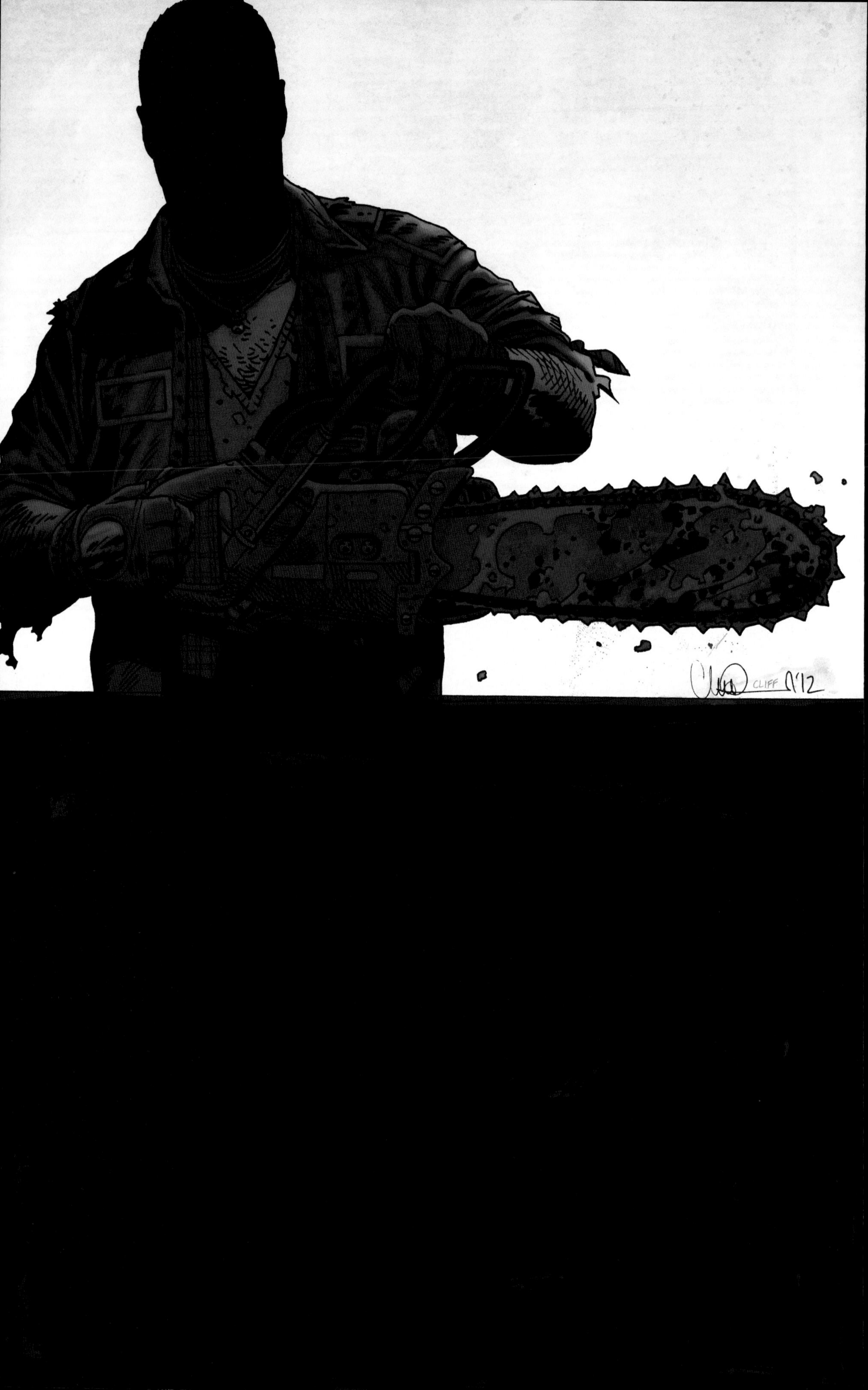
CLIFF

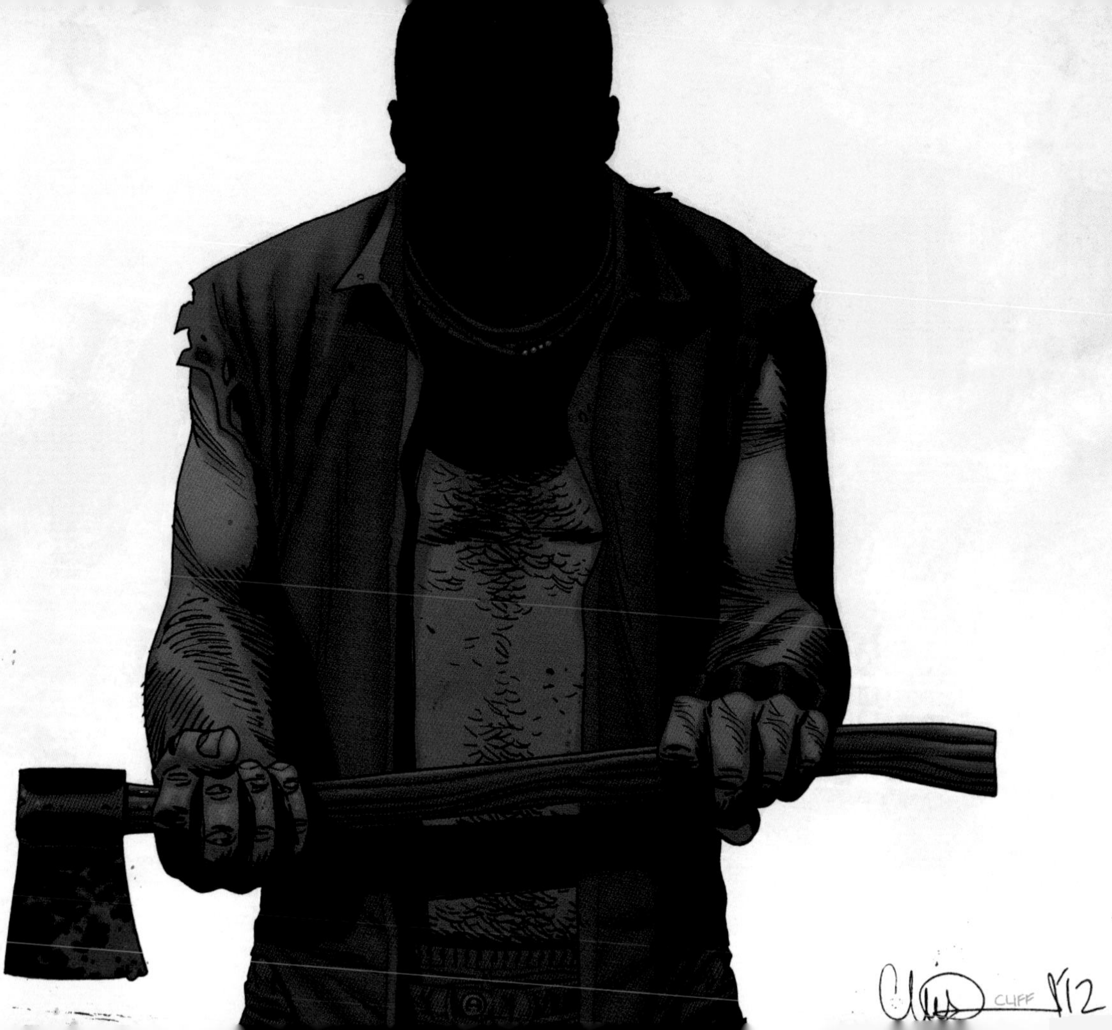
CLIFF

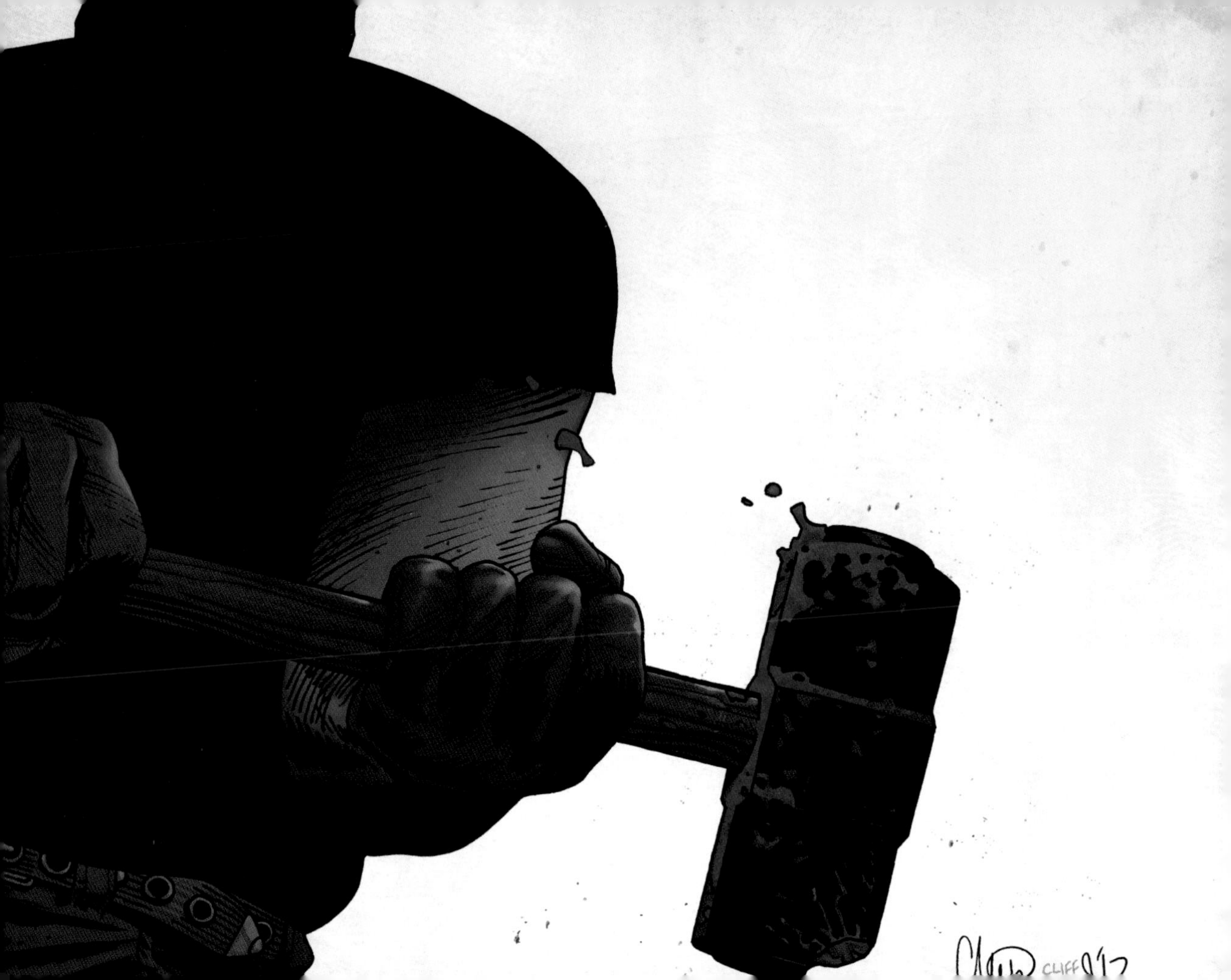
CLIFF

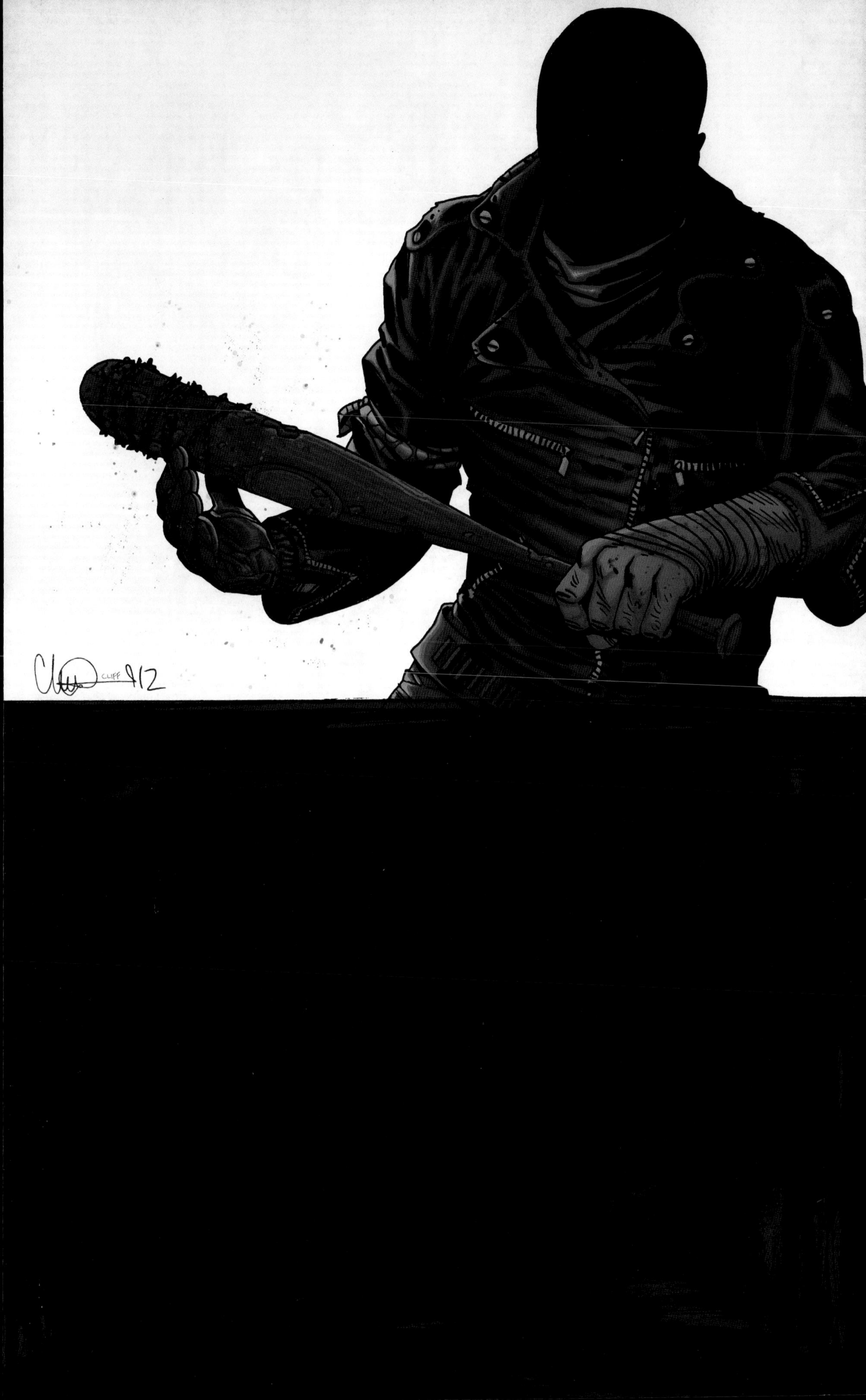
CLIFF

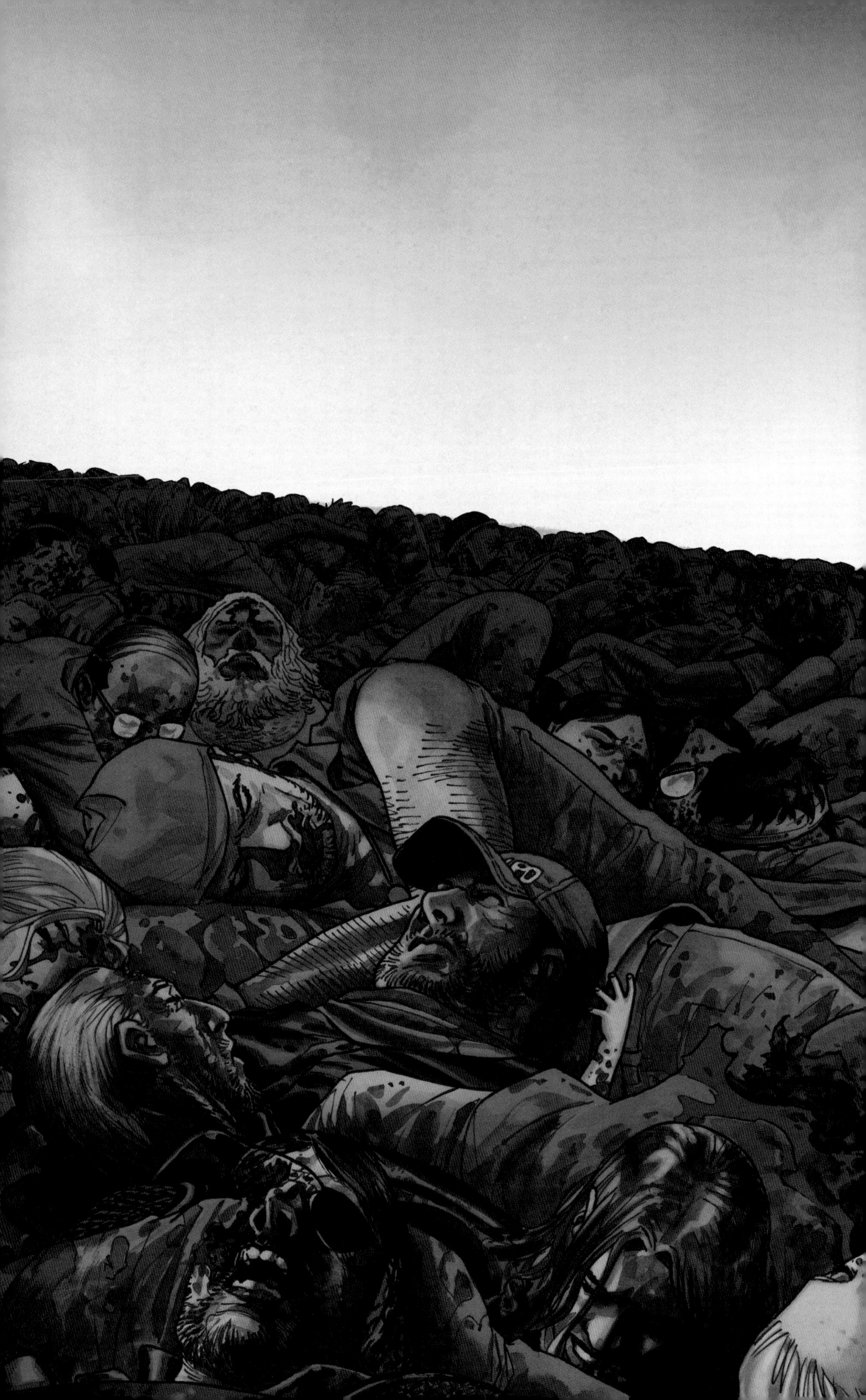

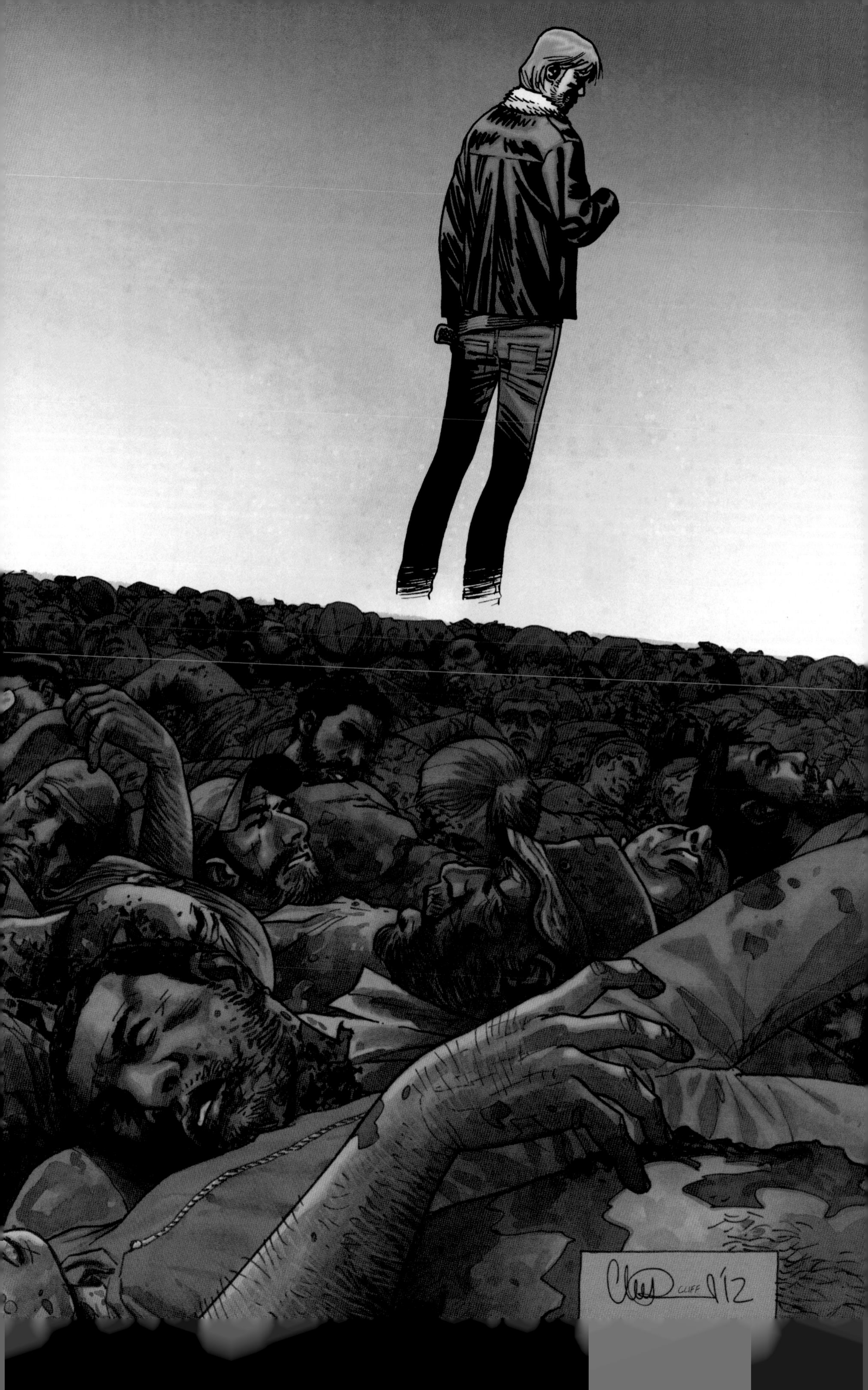

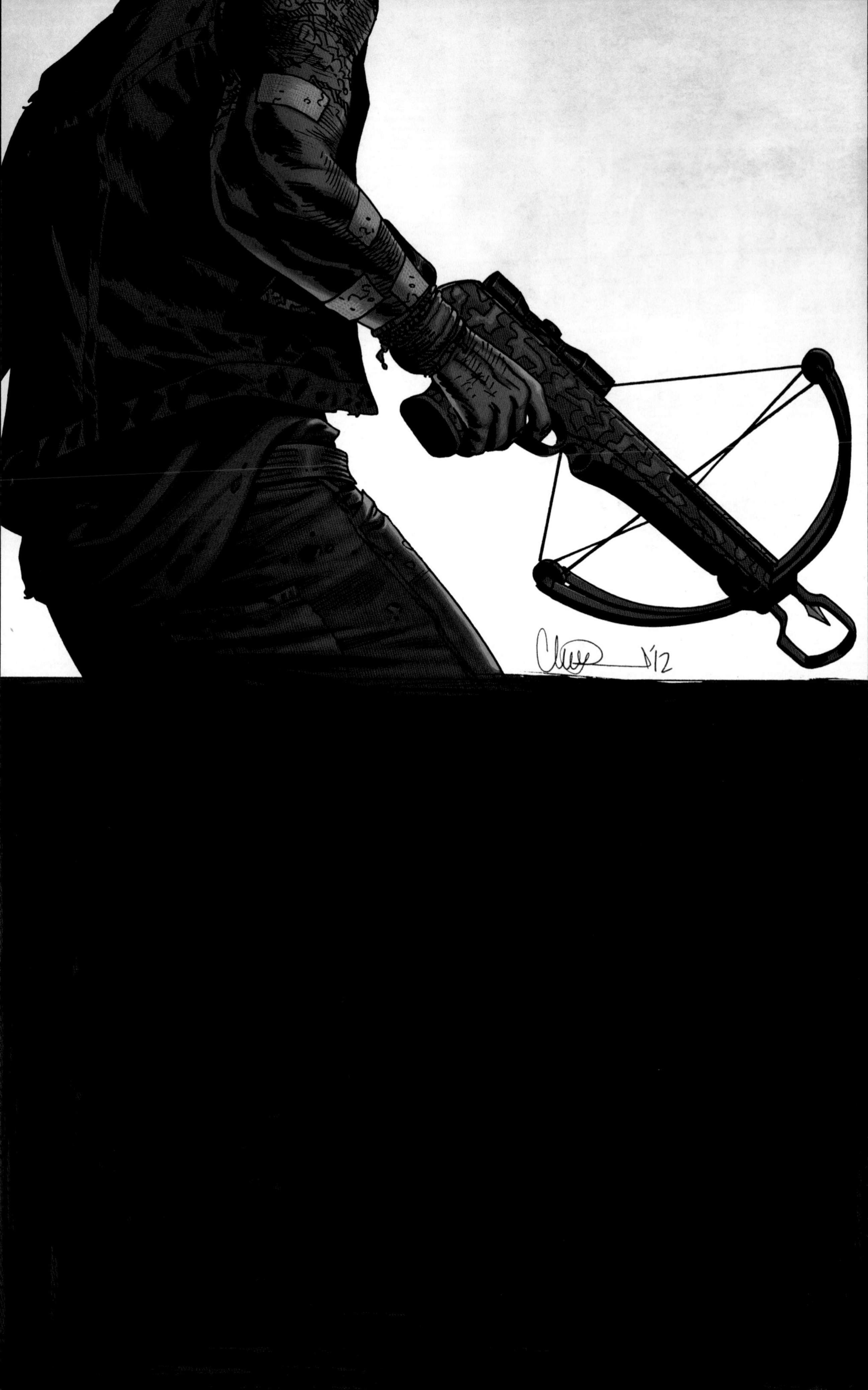

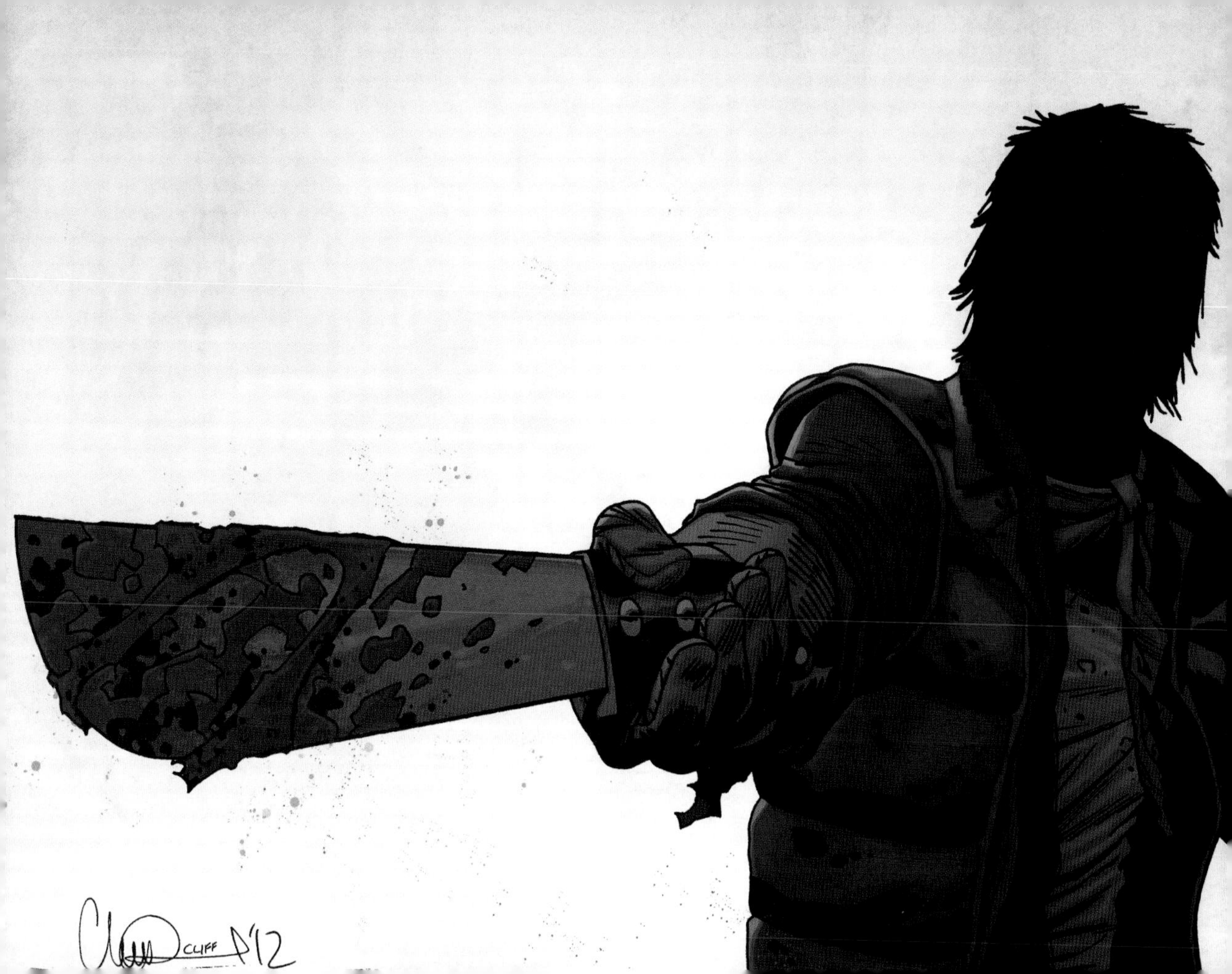

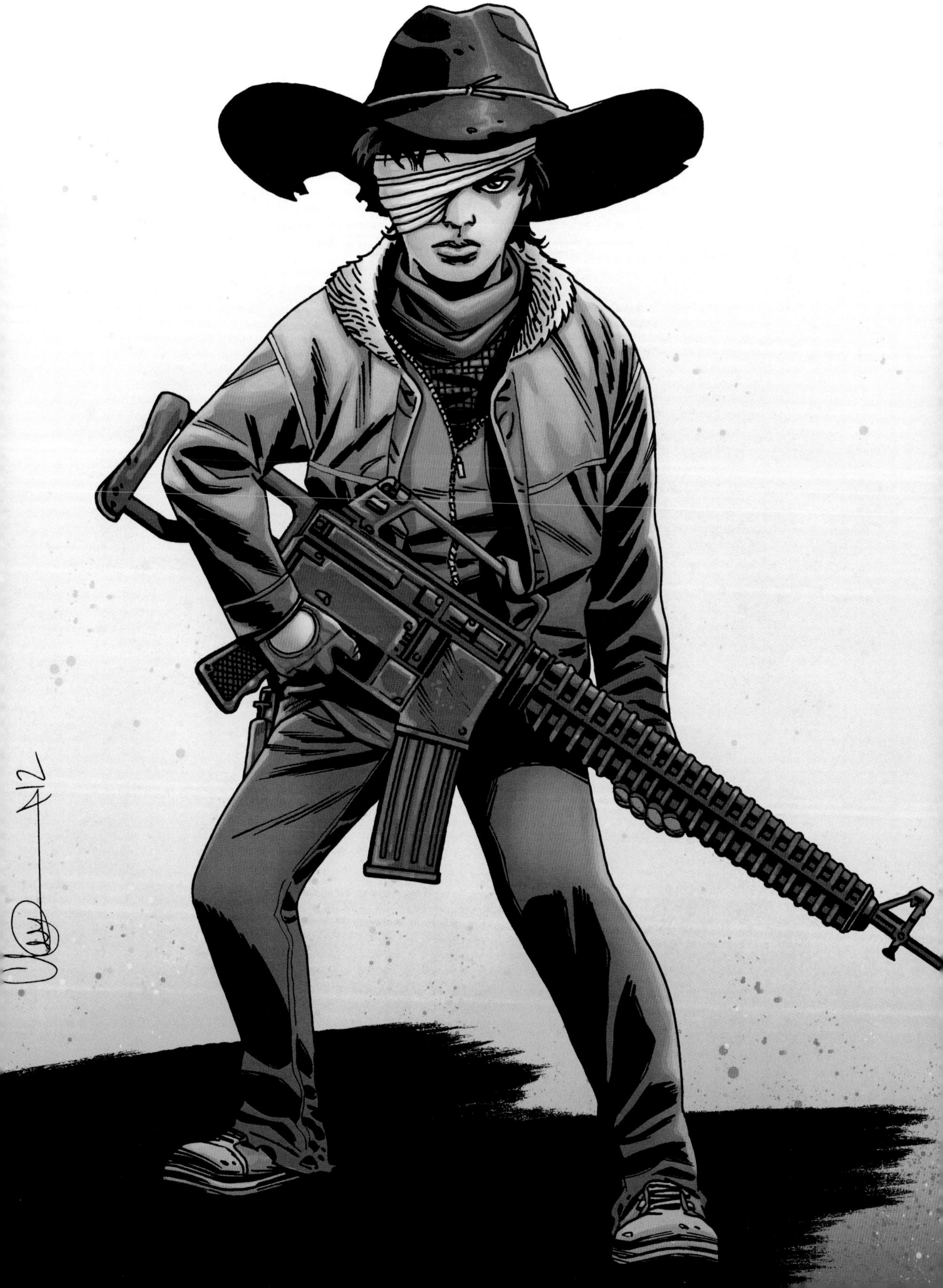

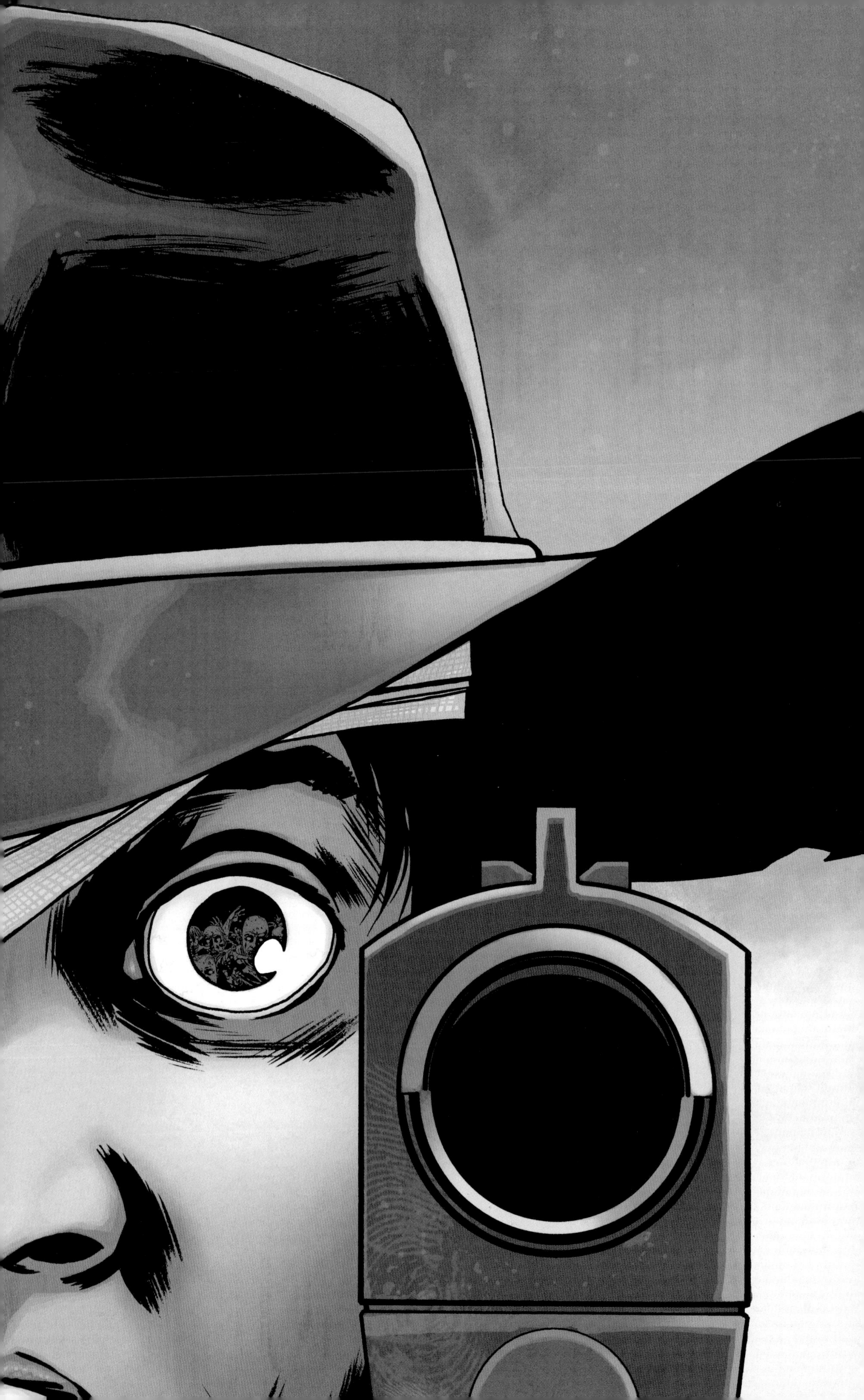

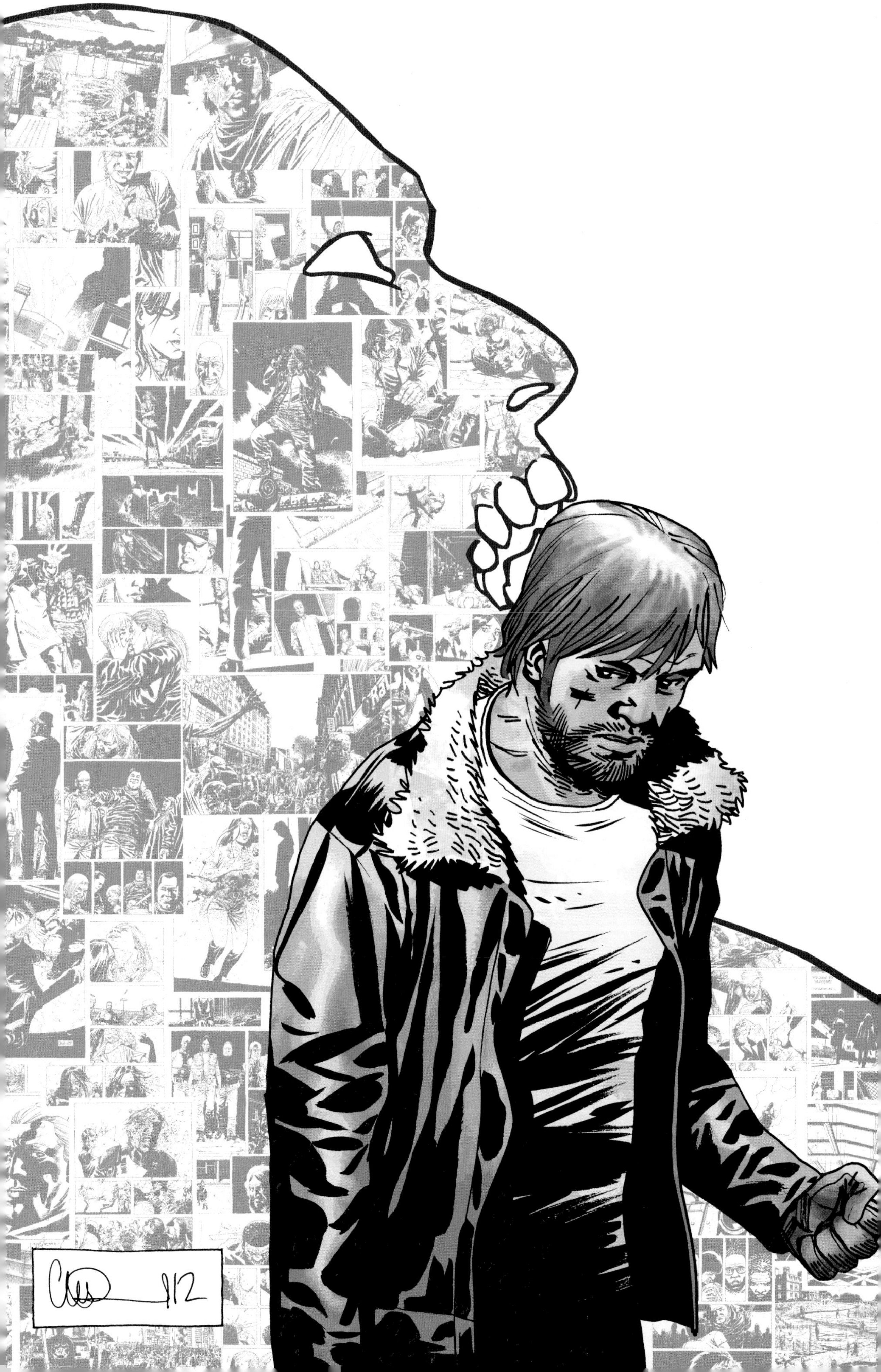

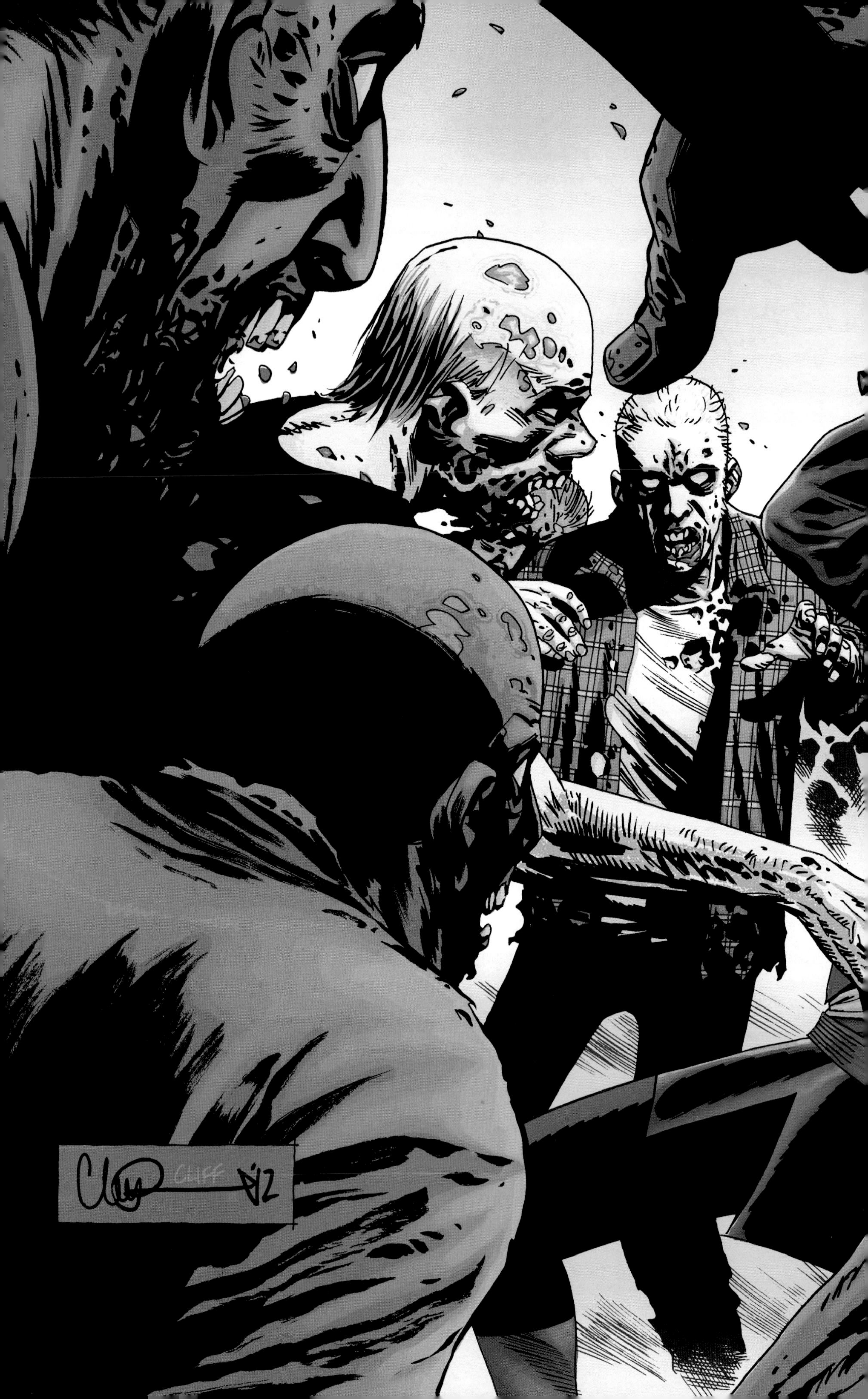
CLIFF

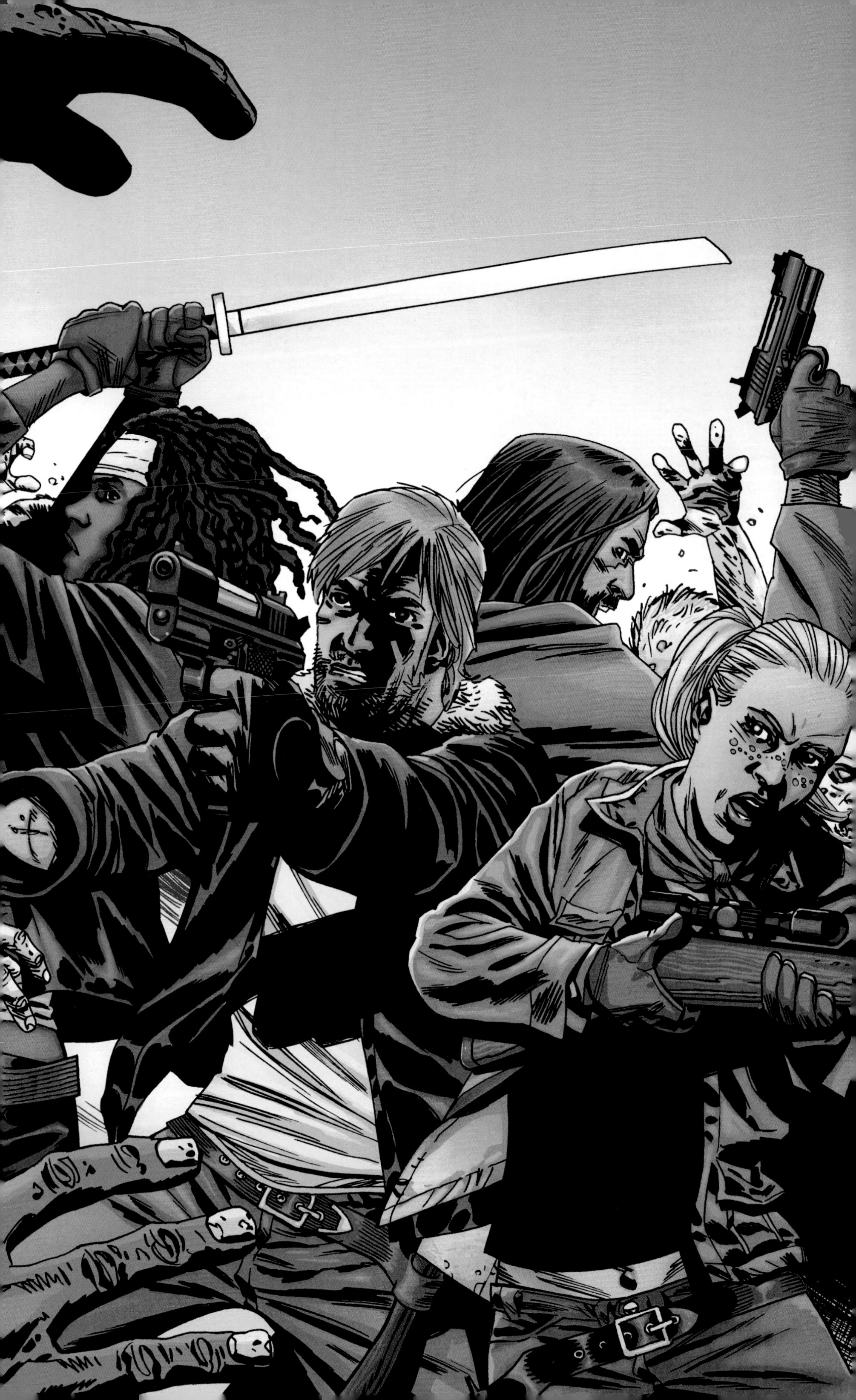

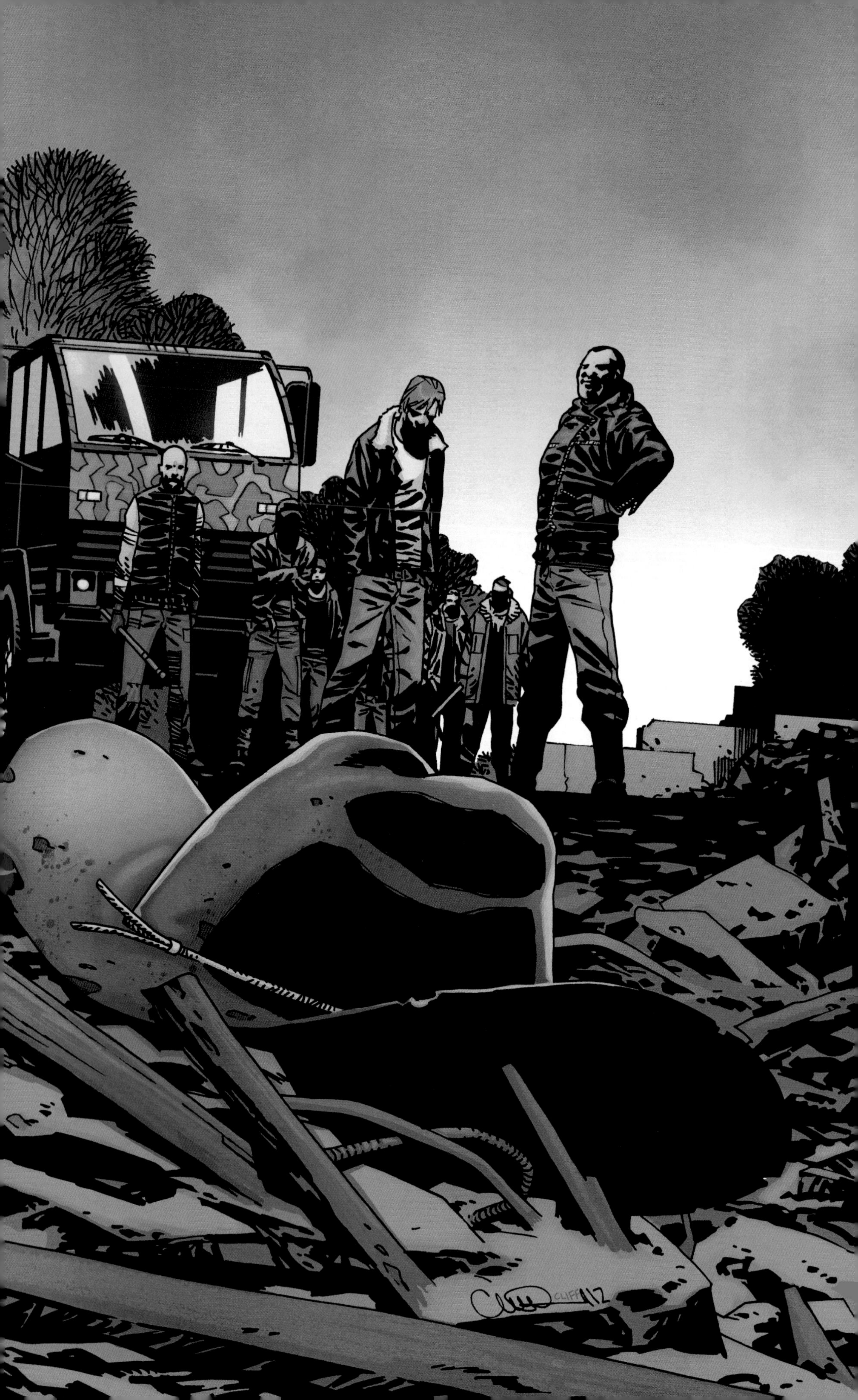

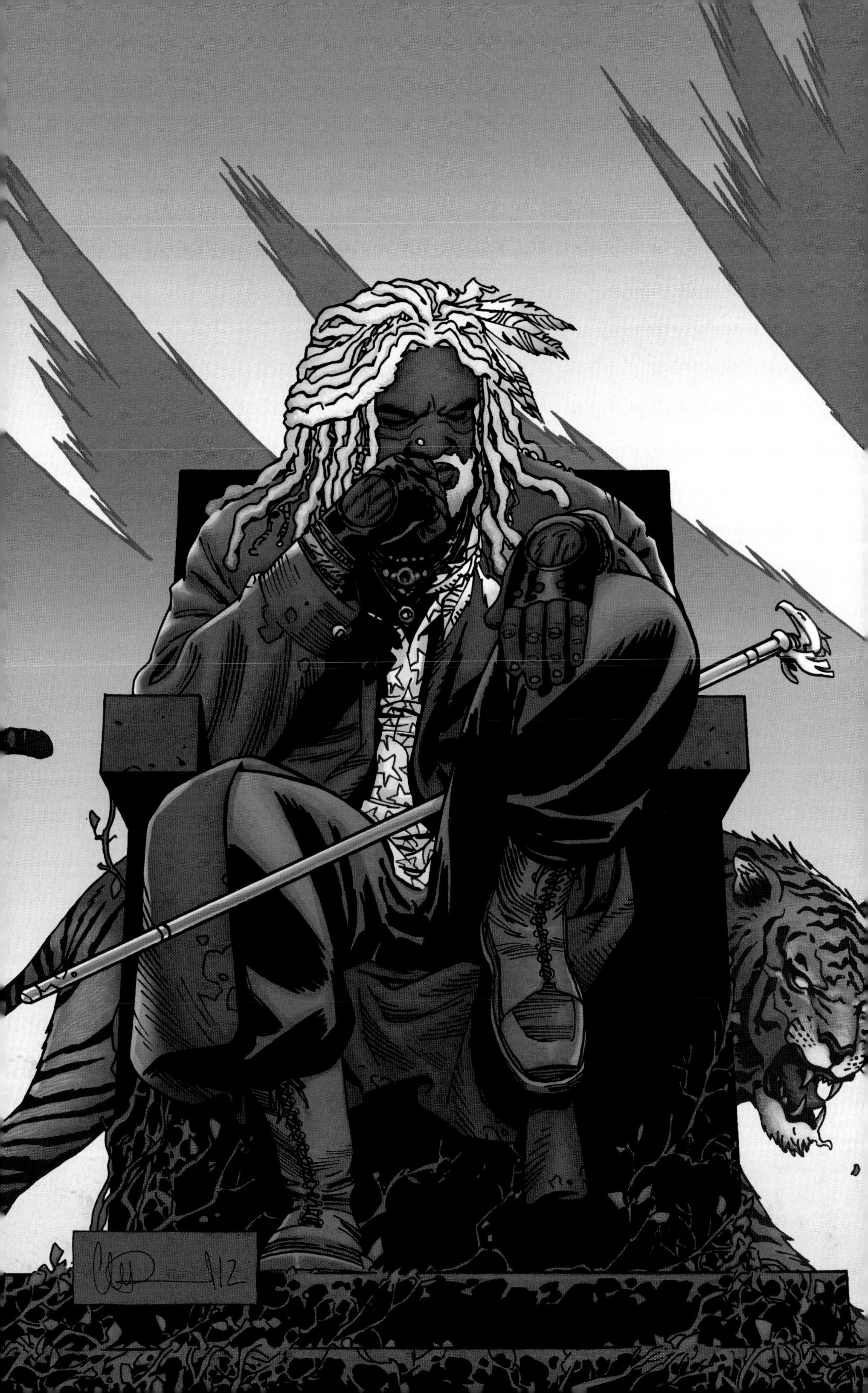

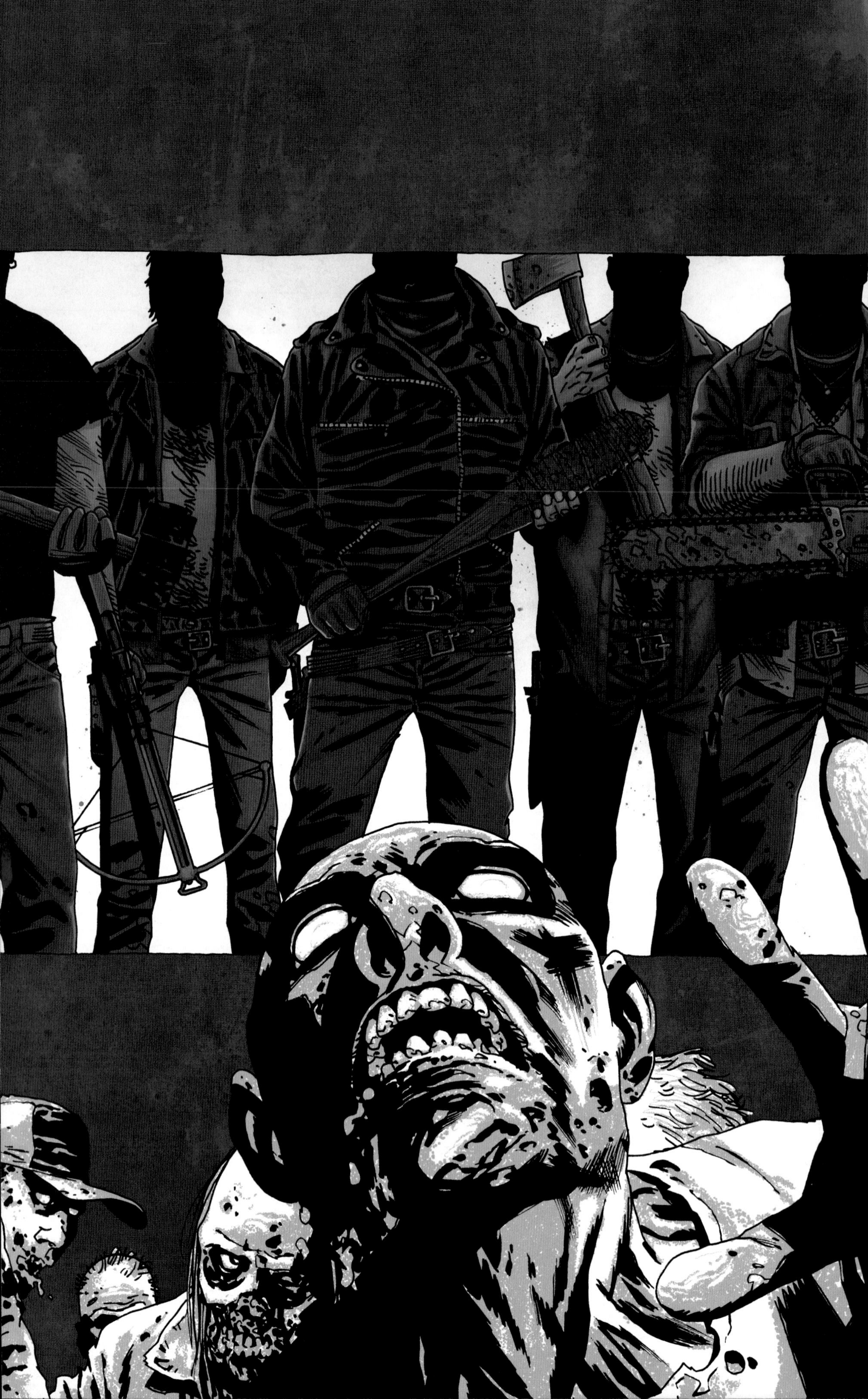

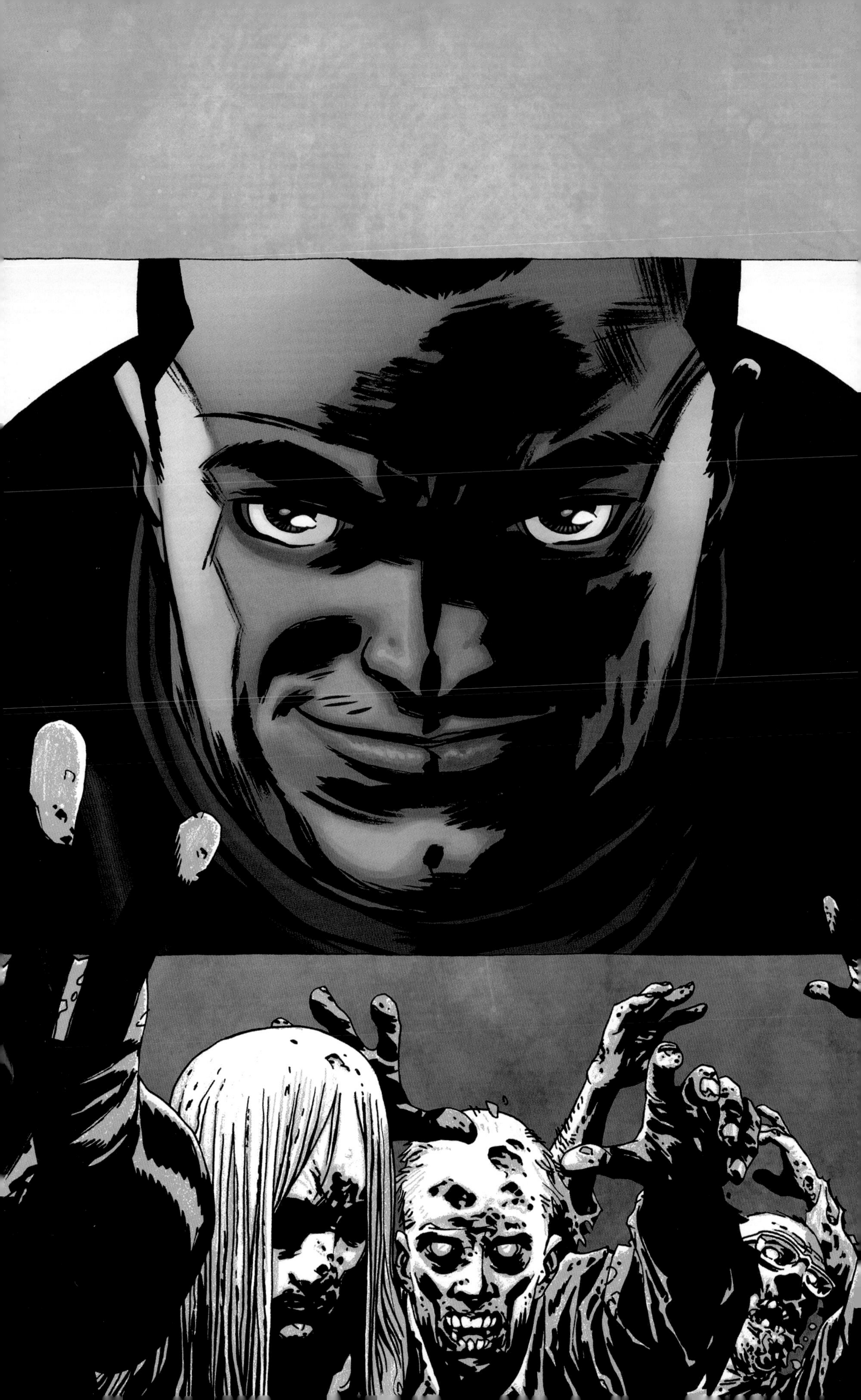

FOR MORE OF THE WALKING DEAD

TRADEPAPERBACKS

ROBERT KIRKMAN TONY MOORE
THE WALKING DEAD
VOLUME 1
DAYS GONE BYE

VOL. 1: DAYS GONE BYE TP
ISBN: 978-1-58240-672-5
$14.99

VOL. 2: MILES BEHIND US TP
ISBN: 978-1-58240-775-3
$14.99

VOL. 3: SAFETY BEHIND BARS TP
ISBN: 978-1-58240-805-7
$14.99

VOL. 4: THE HEART'S DESIRE TP
ISBN: 978-1-58240-530-8
$14.99

VOL. 5: THE BEST DEFENSE TP
ISBN: 978-1-58240-612-1
$14.99

VOL. 6: THIS SORROWFUL LIFE TP
ISBN: 978-1-58240-684-8
$14.99

VOL. 7: THE CALM BEFORE TP
ISBN: 978-1-58240-828-6
$14.99

VOL. 8: MADE TO SUFFER TP
ISBN: 978-1-58240-883-5
$14.99

VOL. 9: HERE WE REMAIN TP
ISBN: 978-1-60706-022-2
$14.99

VOL. 10: WHAT WE BECOME TP
ISBN: 978-1-60706-075-8
$14.99

VOL. 11: FEAR THE HUNTERS TP
ISBN: 978-1-60706-181-6
$14.99

VOL. 12: LIFE AMONG THEM TP
ISBN: 978-1-60706-254-7
$14.99

VOL. 13: TOO FAR GONE TP
ISBN: 978-1-60706-329-2
$14.99

VOL. 14: NO WAY OUT TP
ISBN: 978-1-60706-392-6
$14.99

VOL. 15: WE FIND OURSELVES TP
ISBN: 978-1-60706-440-4
$14.99

VOL. 16: A LARGER WORLD TP
ISBN: 978-1-60706-559-3
$14.99

VOL. 17: SOMETHING TO FEAR TP
ISBN: 978-1-60706-615-6
$14.99

VOL. 18: WHAT COMES AFTER TP
ISBN: 978-1-60706-687-3
$14.99

HARDCOVERS

THE WALKING DEAD
BOOK ONE
a continuing story of survival horror.

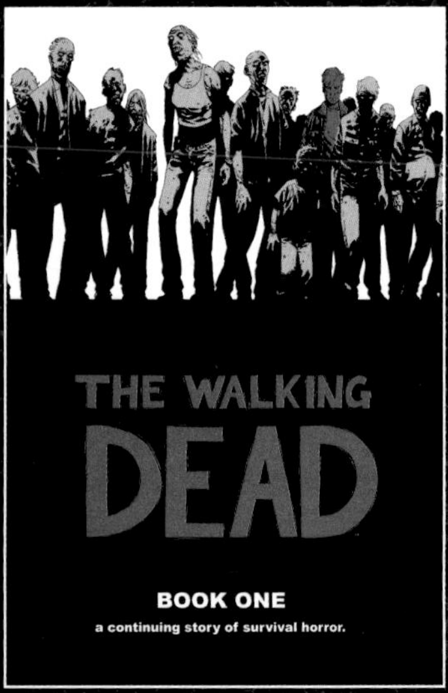

BOOK ONE HC
ISBN: 978-1-58240-619-0
$34.99

BOOK TWO HC
ISBN: 978-1-58240-698-5
$34.99

BOOK THREE HC
ISBN: 978-1-58240-825-5
$34.99

BOOK FOUR HC
ISBN: 978-1-60706-000-0
$34.99

BOOK FIVE HC
ISBN: 978-1-60706-171-7
$34.99

BOOK SIX HC
ISBN: 978-1-60706-327-8
$34.99

BOOK SEVEN HC
ISBN: 978-1-60706-439-8
$34.99

BOOK EIGHT HC
ISBN: 978-1-60706-593-7
$34.99

BOOK NINE HC
ISBN: 978-1-60706-798-6
$34.99

COMPENDIUMS

The ultimate edition of The New York Times bestseller!
THE WALKING DEAD
COMPENDIUM ONE
Robert Kirkman • Charlie Adlard • Tony Moore • Cliff Rathburn

COMPENDIUM TP, VOL. 1
ISBN: 978-1-60706-076-5
$59.99

COMPENDIUM TP, VOL. 2
ISBN: 978-1-60706-596-8
$59.99

SPECIALTY BOOKS

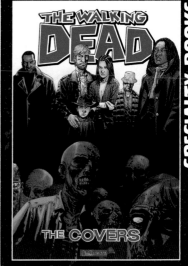

THE WALKING DEAD
THE COVERS

THE WALKING DEAD: THE COVERS, VOL. 1 HC
ISBN: 978-1-60706-002-4
$24.99

THE WALKING DEAD SURVIVORS' GUIDE
ISBN: 978-1-60706-458-9
$12.99

OMNIBUS

THE WALKING DEAD

OMNIBUS, VOL. 1
ISBN: 978-1-60706-503-6
$100.00

OMNIBUS, VOL. 2
ISBN: 978-1-60706-515-9
$100.00

OMNIBUS, VOL. 3
ISBN: 978-1-60706-330-8
$100.00

OMNIBUS, VOL. 4
ISBN: 978-1-60706-616-3
$100.00